The Girl in the White Coat on the Delta Eagle

The Girl in the White Coat on the Delta Eagle

by *Gary Youree*

W·W·NORTON & COMPANY

NEW YORK·LONDON

Library of Congress Cataloging in Publication Data

Youree, Gary.
    The girl in the white coat on the Delta Eagle.

    I. Title.
PZ4.Y87Gi [PS3575.093]   823   79-13087
ISBN 0-393-01278-6

1 2 3 4 5 6 7 8 9 0

The Girl in the White Coat on the Delta Eagle

"It is not good that man should be alone."

— GOD

"Whatsoever a man soweth, that shall he also reap."

— JESUS

"Whatsoever a man rip, that shall he also sew."

— THE MYSTERIOUS STRANGER

1

DR. KOCHBAUM'S office will end up smaller than it first seemed. It will commence to shrink right in this paragraph. In the penultimate chapter it will be blatantly exposed, like new wine in old skins, like old movie sets demystified by new movies on old films. But it intimated infinity the first time I entered it. Dr. Kochbaum's office. It seemed as remotely together as a galaxy yet as neat as a molecule. Well, it had taste. It was *taste*ful; a tastefully appointed model universe too tasty, actually, for the *best* of taste. Hear me, a cordwood cutter then, taste on my mind. What I'm getting at is one looks for flaws when one sees none. One goes one-eyed at the intimation of perfection—one gets suspicious . . . suspicious, hell: one *knows* one is being conned, one thinks. A major flaw was in order in Dr. Kochbaum's furnishings—or, a devilishly random fling of minor flaws. Like interstellar gas. The place was a cube universe, a box. The box was leathery, walnutty, woolly (naturally) and it was indirectly lit (and Kochbaum said: *Let there be indirect light* . . .). It was dim in there, "soft" some would say. The light of day was veiled away behind cloud-colored drapes. Like Dr. Einstein's universe, Dr. K's was finite but unbounded, and curved back in on itself (and without a quantum leap in it either; no dice). Maybe I should say "squared" back in on itself, it being a box, but no matter, for as soon as my pupils had dilated for the gloom I perceived a noticeable shrink, and my first real question there was directed to myself: "Why am I here?"

I had passed some churches coming here. Each wagged its spire at me.

I punched out one short ring of the bell and looked up, pocketing my hands. I turned right oblique, staring straight ahead, then spun on, completing a 180 with eyes downcast. On I turned, on and on, full circle to face the door again, eyeballs glazed meanly now out of focus. When the door opened I had been allowed to wait out a proper interval—about the span an out-of-shape man can hold his breath. I was in excellent physical condition. Dr. Kochbaum said my name with a question mark to which I responded in kind, and further amenities omitted, I was ushered to a heather-green stuffed leather couch.

This was more abrupt than I had anticipated. No desk work first. Like some of those driving schools, put you in heavy traffic the first day. It was a big couch, so big that my mouth crept into a sly smile. It was twice the width of my conception of a doctor of psychology's couch. I had to firm up my smile, to contain a tasteless quip ("Couch for shrinking two, huh?").

You see, I had resolved to try sincerely to take this crap seriously. I was about to lose a woman I thought I ought to love. She was about to lose me. I was sure that she loved me, or ought to. We were about to lose. Losing gets old. The older you get, the harder finding gets. When nothing else has worked, you hire a Ute to do a conjure dance, you go to Lourdes, kiss the Blarney Stone.

"Won't you sit, Mr. Hanks?"

I had that falling feeling sitting on the couch. It sank, sank and sank, sank beneath my weight. I plunged into it as I had emerged from my mom—a breech, but let's not make too much of a mushy couch not much denser than a heavy fog. I realized, falling into it, that I'd found the necessary flaw in this perfect box. It was I.

I could have laughed out loud. I could have cried.

I spied Dr. Kochbaum receding into the gloom, leaving me sunk in her deep-green couch. I was alone. Images commenced to form; familiar images: select reruns of the world out there were beaming into the closed circuit in my head. The images focused in sharp relief with now and then a zoom-in: a newsreel of past ecstasies and agonies plus some meaningful areas of gray: the levity and gravity of it all. Dr. Kochbaum returned with an upholstered armchair in tow, dragging it with a soft husssssssssh across deep pile horizon-to-horizon carpeting; with a deft pirouette on a hind leg the chair came to rest. It fooshed when the doctor sat in it, knee to knee with me. I heard music from somewhere within the walls. There was a funny smell. I was in a cleverly crafted satellite of inner space. It was engineered to beam back into me, edited to be sure, the real world after all. I was merely whelmed.

Dr. Kochbaum flipped open a small looseleaf notebook and poised a needlepointed pencil over it. In a voice that neither boomed down from Olympus nor was that *still small voice* of I Kings 19:12: "Why have you come to me, Mr. Hanks?"

I didn't know what to say, but I knew that whatever I said would be construed as significant. Knowing better, I said, "Didn't Tamara tell you?" then grinned to cover it, knowing full well that the grin's the skull's permanent expression. There's no way to escape analysis while under it.

"But let's hear your version, Mr. Hanks. Why are you here?"

I looked down at my feet, clasping and unclasping my fingers, hoping to give the appearance of introspecting for the truthfulest answer to *why are you here?* If human motivations are onions, we have already disposed of the outer skin, implicit in *Didn't Tamara tell you?* The silence lengthens, deepens, while I examine the next layer, peel it away . . . while Dr. K waits patiently, and why not? Doctors of psychology charge for their patience. The fee's the same for fifty minutes of silence as it is for fifty minutes of your life's fuckups wailed at them at a hundred and eighty-six hysterical wpm. I peel away another layer, and another (consider these peeled layers the leaves of this book), realizing that I really am introspecting for the truthfulest answer. Abruptly I opt to go for the pristine heart of the onion, the primordial tear:

"I don't know why I'm here."

"Then guess, Mr. Hanks."

"Tamara and I made a deal, and to tell the truth I don't believe you can help us. You're not God."

Dr. Kochbaum made a note, then looking back at me, proclaimed, "Nor do I aspire to godhood, Mr. Hanks—nor to be one's representative. Unlike deity, I do not require faith in me as a prerequisite for conversation. Why don't you tell me a few things about yourself, and place in escrow the question of whether you're going to find help here? Tell me about this deal you made with Tamara."

"I agreed to keep this appointment with you if she'd try prayer."

"Prayer?"

"Prayer."

"Prayer," muttered Dr. Kochbaum, making a note.

"Don't think much of prayer, do you?" I said. "Well, it's at least as effective as this . . . ," patting the couch, " . . . even when it's for rain. And it's free, prayer is, monetarily speaking."

"Fully as free as talk, at least," said Dr. Kochbaum, closing her little notebook. "Well, Mr. Hanks, do you feel that the presence of your warm body here, rather than in a movie, satisfies your end of this deal with Tamara?"

I gave a one-shouldered shrug and said, "Uh-huh, considering that she has about as much faith in prayer as I do in you. That's part of our problem, I guess."

Nodding, the doctor reopened her notebook and with the needlepointed pencil made a note. She was sitting unslumped in the upholstered armchair, her legs crossed, elbows on the chair arms, notebook in her lap. Noting the close fit of her pants, I looked away. Let her deny it until the cock crows himself hoarse, but she was if not a god(ess) at least a high priestess in her temple, this little universe, this thing of cultic gravity in static orbit around her. Dr. A. K. Kochbaum, Ph.D., high priestess in the Profession, the cult. Sacrosanct. I smiled to recollect a hick named Ossie Lee Somebody who claimed to have pulled up a nun's habit at a bus stop once when he was a kid, and swore there was nothing underneath. Ossie Lee was the first Catholic I ever knew, and one of the worst. When the day comes that mysteries are being solved, I'll have Ossie Lee admit that he saw legs, just plain old legs. Then, the truth established, I'll grant Ossie Lee his license to declaim, in epic hexameter, "I saw a sweet old nun with untooled leather hymen." I wondered what Dr. Kochbaum had inside her smart Lord & Taylor pants suit. A text on abnormal psych—the stacks? The funny smell which had waned now waxed.

"If you do see part of your problem, Mr. Hanks, you're on your way to a grasp of the whole—tail of the elephant."

"Just follow the tail up to the whole elephant, huh?"

She nodded.

"Right on up the elephant's ass, huh?"

"Right to the heart of the matter, Mr. Hanks. I think, though, that we can dispense with the analogy."

"Heart of the matter, then. The problem is this: It's us. I am Tamara's problem, and she's mine."

Silence.

"In what way do you feel that you are Tamara's problem?"

"Wouldn't that be Tamara's problem?"

"Would not the way you are Tamara's problem be your problem?"

Another silence sealed the truth of that.

"You have been married, have you not, Mr. Hanks?"

"No. Well, I mean, this old childhood sweetheart and I stood in a wedding ceremony, held hands and lied 'I do.' We didn't. Of course you will see some connection between defunct wedding and defuncting shackup, but run it on further back before asking me to discuss it. Back to my birth, and further, through my forebears and on back, the apes, the fish, primordial gas, none of which I want to discuss. Some things cannot be resolved. I'm resigned to that."

"What, then, do you want to talk about, Mr. Hanks?"

Glancing back at the tight fit of her pants, I said, "Frankly, nothing."

"Then why don't you leave?"

"Because I promised Tamara I'd stick out the full fifty minutes."

Dr. Kochbaum uncrossed her legs and had herself a quick stretch. I looked away again. She sighed, I coughed.

"Okay, we can talk about something, I guess. Warm bodies being silent get too loud anyway. Guess some good could come of it. A man can get some good out of talking to a tree. I know. I've rapped on a lot of trees."

Slumped now in her chair, the notebook closed again, Dr. Kochbaum said, "Tamara mentioned that you were in the cordwood business?"

"Firewood," nodding.

"And *cord* is . . . "

"Generally conceived as two stacks of two-foot-long splits of wood placed side by side so as to measure four by four by eight feet. But a cord can be got no matter how you stack it long as the volume is one hundred and twenty-eight cubic feet, air spaces included. Air spaces are important in the cordwood business. A cord of air dry hickory would weigh eight thousand and sixty-four pounds without air spaces. You can forget green hickory."

"Is peddling firewood lucrative, Mr. Hanks?"

"It feeds the wolf at the door."

"Do you find it satisfying?"

"Oh, I like the woods, keep in shape, perform a useful service helping other folks keep warm. Thoreau said that he who cuts his own wood is twice warmed by it. Times I've delivered a cord to a comely customer, got invited in, to be thrice warmed by it. How I make my living isn't on my list of complaints, ma'am."

"Then you are satisfied to identify yourself as a cordwood cutter?"

I had never concerned myself much with how I identified myself, and thus went kind of blank.

"Upward mobility, Mr. Hanks—or does the concept pass completely over you?"

"Up—— oh, yes. That's passed completely over me, upward mobility has. Like a kite. Like a box kite parted from its string and child. Gone with the wind. The way I feed the wolf at the door is not the first irrelevancy to surface on my cerebral cortex when asked to identify myself."

"Then correctly identify yourself, Mr. Hanks."

"Bud Hanks."

"But who is Bud Hanks?"

"Oh, many whos. Once he was a poet."

"Of course. What kind of poetry?"

"Hard to say."

"Love poetry?"

"Love poetry? Love poetry . . . um, maybe—but not in the romantic sense of love that festers behind those reductionist shibboleths you've subscribed to and memorized to be you *qua* Dr. Kochbaum, Sister."

Dr. Kochbaum's mask cracked into what surprised me as a smile. She said, "I'm not a behaviorist, Mr. Hanks. Now you mentioned prayer as your escape. Do you write religious verse?"

My mask cracked into what she was to have been surprised by as a smile; if it was a smile and it surprised her, her mask did not reflect the fact. I said, "I didn't say prayer was my 'escape'. Obviously there are no escapes, or neither of us would be here. I didn't mention 'religion' either, and I don't like the word. If you believe that the Word became flesh, you don't split existence into the 'religious' and the 'secular'. Everything is essentially . . . "

"Mr. Hanks, I don't think that your preaching to me will be of much benefit to you, but if you wish to go on preaching, I shall be happy to listen, at my regular fee of fifty dollars an hour."

"*Fifty* dollars an *hour!*" I gasped.

"A bargain. But welcome back to *terra firma*. What do you get for a cord of wood? Perhaps we can barter."

"My city price is a hundred and fifty bucks a cord, split, delivered and stacked. Twenty bucks a shirttail full. And I'll stoke your fireplace on the house."

Dr. Kochbaum nodded and made a note. "Tamara said that you had quite a few affairs before she met you."

"So? I didn't miss many meals either, before I met her. My appetites are normal."

"Yet you have never been in love?"

"I eat to live, not vice versa."

"Then all your previous affairs, including your marriage, simply petered out through loss of appetite, like this thing with Tamara?"

"If life was as simple as most women think it is, we'd still be in the Garden."

"You think that most women think life is simple, Mr. Hanks?"

"They think it would be if only men would see it the way they do."

"You seem to think that you know a lot about women, Mr. Hanks."

I did not set myself up by trying to answer that. Dr. Kochbaum tapped her pencil on the chair arm until the point broke, then she went on, "Tamara tells me that women—her words —'fall all over you,' Mr. Hanks. Just what is this fatal attraction? You aren't rich, nor ambitious. You're not exactly handsome, and I suspect you would have to be scratched for talent. Are you bright?"

"It's my feet," I said, augmenting an honest smile to grin proportions. "I have big feet. Tamara once told me that I exude peace and strength and have big feet. Mostly she fell for my feet, which is about all I've got left far as she's concerned, and they're about to walk."

"Big feet?" frowned Dr. Kochbaum.

"Thirteens."

She shifted in her chair, alternating the cross of her legs, casting a furtive glance at my feet. She nibbled reflectively on her pencil eraser, and said, "They look narrow."

"Thirteen B. Long and narrow. Big feet mean a big wang, according to Tamara. She had a few affairs, too, and claims to know."

"Wang?" said Dr. Kochbaum. "Whose euphemism is *wang?* Tamara's?"

"Nome. *Cock* is Tamara's euphemism. Wang just popped off the side of my head, perchance I was in polite company."

Taking the pencil from her mouth, Dr. Kochbaum said, "Do you feel that women are attracted to a big euphemism, Mr. Hanks?"

"I would say that the exuding of peace and strength is fully as important to your average woman—especially to those who say it's not the size but how you use your euphemism."

Dr. Kochbaum nodded thoughtfully, getting my eye before she administered: "Tell me about your potency problem, Mr. Hanks."

"Potency problem?" I spluttered.

Silence.

"You mean *sexual* potency?"

"Come now, Mr. Hanks. You know what I mean."

I let my eyes ride roughshod over her, even her eyes, then I glanced down at my feet. Potency problem? Did Dr. Kochbaum think I was impotent? Sexually dysfunctioned—whatever the new euphemism is? Funny how it makes a man bristle to have a woman accuse him of impotence, how the accusation carries the infection: were I to attempt to prove now to her that I was potent, I'd likely not be up to the challenge, and that made me feel impotent.

"Well," I said, at length, "if omnipotence is your standard, we're all . . . "

"Mr. Hanks, my clientele is almost exclusively sexually dysfunctioning men. Can't get it up or can't keep it up. Non- and premature ejaculators. I enjoy a high rate of success with clients who cooperate. I'm here to help you, not judge you. But I must have your full cooperation."

"Hell, woman, I function adequately when aroused. What the hell? I mean . . . " I went, limply.

Silence.

What is this noise? I stared at Dr. Kochbaum, at her clinical gaze. There she sat, awaiting my anguished tale. A hole for me to pour my "impotence" in. I looked away, going out of focus. I could see how people get started unloading in a hole like this, this black hole in the inner universe, and never stop—can't stop; wretchedly retching fifty or a hundred minutes a week, week in week out, down this bottomless psychic urpbag, lost in chronic therapy, nausea ad nauseam . . . who was it, Ossie Lee? asked me what gets larger the more you take away from it? A hole. I looked back at Dr. Kochbaum's professional expression. It was not exactly an uncaring countenance; it was not even without warmth. It was the visage of a mass an hour priest at a busy big city cathedral. I stared on at it, harder, until I saw through her mask—or fancied that I did.

A little girl was playing back there, behind Dr. Kochbaum's mask, and my heart went out to her. I tried to slough off my mask so that the Bud Hanks behind it could wink a message to that little girl, and win a wink, but before we could steal that sweet we lost our nerve, leaving two faceless Cheshire cats to remask each other. Oh how I would have loved to reach into Dr. Kochbaum and grab that little girl and run with her . . . love lies inchoate in all of us, Lady—I'll run off with you in a minute if you just give a hint that we can let love loose, and then bridle it: that's my problem. Not impotency when forced to intercourse with an old mask.

Tamara. I first saw her coming down the library steps as I was going up. I turned and followed her, something I had never done before, follow a strange woman, but one look at her had smitten me mightily with—there's but one word for it: LUST. I remember reflecting, as she passed by one of the stone lions, that it did not pounce on her. There is a saying in New York that when a virgin passes by one of the stone lions in front of the library, it will pounce on her. I caught up with her at the corner of Fifth and Forty-second and pounced, "Excuse me." She glanced back, startled, stumbling, dropped the load of books she had checked out. They scattered in the gutter, trendy, occultish, pop-psych straws in the winds of a dis-eased century. I stooped and helped her pick them up. As we picked them up she stared at my feet, and when we arose from the gutter she fetched me a quick, moist thankyou kiss on the port side of my lips. Our eyes remained fastened behind the kiss. She had great almond eyes with long lashes that whisked me in and swept me down, down, toward the feathered end of time's arrow—way down yonder to the rich alluvial soil of Mesopotamia, cradle of religion, law, and order, and I said, "More," and she dropped the books again, casting another glance at my feet, and locked her long arms around my neck. We kissed.

The air grew turbulent with our kiss there on Fifth and Forty-second. It was a wet kiss, a long one, hot and viscous. A sloppy kiss. A swamp. When we slithered out of it, the lady said, "Um. Where can we go?" We went to my place. I thought she was Egyptian, and called her Nefertiti. Turns out she was Jewish, a look-alike of—and kin to, she would claim—Barbra Streisand. That was just over a year ago. Now I sit before Tamara's high priestess, charged with the crime of impotence, because we no longer copulate, because I just can't seem to make it with the soul around the hole. Tamara.

"To acknowledge the existence of a problem is the first step in solving it," the doctor seemed to be saying, and I seem to have said that the problem might be original sin, for I recall her quipping, "We could use a good original sin." Of course she would say something like that—how boring it must be in her cultus, hearing the same old sins confessed and bragged about, day in, day out.

"Fear of impotence is a principle cause of it, Mr. Hanks."

"All we have to fear is fuck itself, and their inversion, Dr. Kochbaum."

She arose and receded into the farthermost corner of her office and sat behind a small desk that grew there. A tiny lamp came on, casting baroque shadows on her face.

"Have you made this prayer-for-therapy deal with other women?"

"Never had to before. Tamara is the first woman who absolutely refused to pray with me. Said it would be too embarrassing. She's supposed to be praying these fifty minutes that I'm here."

Dr. Kochbaum put her hands behind her head and leaned back. She had nice big teats. They looked like mountains in the moonlight of her lamp. I wondered what the library lions would do with her. She said, "Apparently, the efficacy of prayer has not manifested itself in a binding relationship between you and a woman—assuming that such is the object of your prayers."

"It helps us split as lovers but stick as friends, which is no small thing," I said. "Prayer doesn't change things. It changes people."

"How has prayer changed you, Mr. Hanks?"

"Hard to say."

She brought her arms down, tapped her watch, and said, "That will be all for today. Come back next week, same time, and bring those poems that you and Tamara had the fight over. I should like to read them. And for my fee bring me half a cord of nicely seasoned hardwood. Don't make the sticks too long, because my fireplace is narrow."

2

TAMARA was curled in the rocker by the phone. She had on her green terrycloth shorty robe which left exposed a great smoothly sinewy tangle of olive-hued limbs. Tamara had wonderful legs and a fine hard ass. Feathered, her arms would have made good wings. She was a dancer, or had been. She hadn't danced much since moving in with me. She had been in some ballets, and did a stint on the plyboard go-go stage, but Modern Interpretive—I believe she called it—was her real love. Her big slanty eyes cut up at me from the phone in her tangle of limbs, batted once in recognition, then cut back. She was doing more listening than talking on the phone, and when she did talk it was in the husky mumble she always used on that medium, unintelligible to me. I grunted and went into my den.

I sat in my swivel, took a carpenter's rule from the desk, and measured the distance of two corners of my private box of poetry fragments from the edge of the desk. The box had been moved. Tamara had been prying again. I decided not to make another issue of it, to try and be reasonable, be fair, to share. I decided to buy a padlock and keep my box locked in a desk drawer. Tamara opened the door.

"Hey man, how'd it go at Dr. K's?"

"No surprises. How'd it go here?"

"Jaliker?" Tamara pursued, framed there in my den doorway, in that green terrycloth shorty robe she had once looked so fetching in, that exotic anachronism who almost brought me to climax with one long kiss the day we met on Fifth and

Forty-second . . . what was missing now? She still looked the same. Who was missing it? Our eyes met and mine misted over, misting for the myth. I tried to frame a simple answer for her simple question, simply ambiguous—*jaliker?*—and decided to ignore it.

"Tamara, you've been into my box again," I muttered, thinking, oh Tamara, don't you see what's happening, what's happened? That first wild rush we felt the day we met, that fizz that nature hypes us with, without discrimination, to keep the species propagated, has petered out.

> It takes hard work to keep love blooming,
>   its roots deepening,
> once that first flower has withered,
>   its petals fallen,

but did I say that? Who spouts like that outside of old and heavy movies?

"Hey man, you knew I'd do it, or whydju leave it out? Don't give me any shit."

"I gave you a sheathe of poems to read and you haven't touched them. They're still on the back of the toilet."

"Those in the box are better, the ones you didn't give me. I want what you haven't given me, man."

She moved in on me saying that, so that I caught the wind of the end of it. She stood so close I got the scent of her. It was not unlike the strange smell in Dr. Kochbaum's office, but then the latter may have still lingered in my nostrils, enough to confuse the issue. The sash of Tamara's robe was on a level with my eyes. The hem of her robe flared but a short ways below the sash, her great long smoothly muscled legs curving down in odd perspective into her flat dancer's feet with the painted, always red-painted toenails. Tamara made me nervous when things weren't going right. I couldn't put my finger on the reason: it was like there was a whole side of her I didn't know. The inside. I picked up my box of poetry fragments and balanced it on my head.

"Here. They are just fragments of poetry. I consider them personal because they are but short bursts from my inmost innards, and are incomplete, as I am not yet finished . . ." I paused to jot that down." . . . Take and read them every one if you can't resist them, but keep them in order. They aren't dated."

"Shove them up your ass," said Tamara.

Nodding the box off my head and catching it, I said, "That's the spirit," and tossed the box carelessly on my desk, and pulled the sash on Tamara's robe. A brief glimpse of her long, brown-nippled jugs, her wide hips with a gap between the thighs, that deepblack diamond-shaped bush being quickly and indignantly re-veiled, caused me to blurt: "Want to make love?"

"Not with you, man," she snapped, exiting.

For the first time in a month I wanted her body. I reached the living room as the bedroom door slammed shut behind her. "Tamara, will you marry me?" I whispered, just loud enough to scare myself, to turn me on. In a minute I would go in and get in bed with her, sweettalk her some, and we'd screw; she had got me terribly aroused. Something had. I went back into my den and closed the door; commenced to pray in the swivel —or to think about praying. I was wondering if Tamara had kept her end of the deal when she called through the door.

"Hey man, you gonna see Dr. K again?"

"No."

"Whacha doing in there, masturbating?"

"Trying to pray. Did you pray today like you promised?"

Silence. A draining kind of silence. Once, in another kind of silence, Tamara and I had come close to *in* love, whatever that is. It was soon after she had moved in with me, and I had confessed that when she first told me her name, which was a couple days after we had met, I thought she had said "tomorrow," which is how Tamara is pronounced. I had thought she was playing a game, so the next day I reminded her that she had promised to tell me her name today, and she said *Tamara*, spelling it, and I had been too embarrassed to admit my mistake. We had laughed and fallen silent then, gazing into each other's eyes, and *it* had almost happened. Recalling that warm silence now in this cold silence I felt like screaming. Screaming something like: "LET'S GET MARRIED!" We had joked some about getting married, neither of us—at least not I—admitting truth in jest. Mean to say, you don't marry somebody you pick up off the street, do you? Do you? No? Why not? Why not marry Tamara tomorrow, down at City Hall? Or in a little church somewhere, around some corner? Yes, in a little church. Wedding. Marriage. It would make us happy, bringing the state, the church, some inlaws, into this dying love affair; would quicken it, commit us to some commitment.

"Hey man, I kept my promise all right, and no more prayer for me."

Hey man. Will you take this man, *hey man*, to be your lawful wedded husband? *Man!* How come Tamara hardly ever calls my name? Always *man, hey man*. Where did she get that shit? From her last ex-lover, that's who, a black man with huge feet. I met him once. He was a poet, too. Tamara introduced us at a poetry reading. He called her *hey man*, too.

"Whaja get scared of, woman?"

"Nothing. Just got scared. Sudden terror pounced up in me out of nowhere. *Oooey!* Got worse and worse . . . if I hadn't popped a downer I'd be right off the wall now. I've said my last *amen*, man."

She needed me. How had she managed before we met? And I want children. Getting old, want some babies. Why *not* get married?

"Hell, woman, all you had was a little ol' anxiety attack. It's a good sign. Means you were getting through. Darkness before the dawn thing. Nothing to be afraid of."

"*Nothing?* Well *nothing* scares me shitless, man."

"Well, woman, if nothing scares you then nothing scares you, so how come you got scared?"

"I got scared of what scared me, man."

"But it was nothing. Anxiety is fear of nothing."

"Well being scared is *something*, man. The fucking *scare* scared me. Bite down on that."

"Well, keep on praying, woman, and you'll see the dawn peek through nothing. Just keep . . . "

"Not me, man. No more. I'm not going bananas praying to nothing."

"Don't be thick, woman. How can you pray to nothing?"

"Cause there's nothing to pray to."

I might have said, "Except your fear, since you're afraid of nothing," but no, I got up and looked out the window, seeing nothing, for it had gotten dark. "Be not unequally yoked together with unbelievers," I remember Paul telling the Corinthians ("mismated" in the revised version). I stood there looking out at the dark, wondering if one really *looks* at darkness. Only in hell, I guessed, in the gospel according to John Milton. I looked at my hands. My hands are almost as big as my feet, and weren't as rough as you would expect a woodcutter's hands to be. I wore heavy leather gloves when working, kid gloves when playing, making love. I prayed barehanded. I was a hypocrite, of course. *"Follow me and I'll make you a mender of nets."*

"Tamara, are you still out there?"

"Yeah, man. I don't know why."

I could see her in the darkness outside my den window. The robe, the long fine legs, the almost too low tittybulges. Our copulations came to mind. How well we meshed, how fluidly, how rhythmically we pumped, how pneumatically, how marvelously in sync we got right from the beginning. Always came together. Once, just over the crest of climax, I opened my eyes and saw that her eyes were tightly closed, her head aside, and realized that she too was somewhere else. But oh that woman and I were great in bed together. We jerked each other off in perfect harmony. A team of mules in parallel ruts, pulling that one wagon with a vengeance, with blinders on. *Scudda hoo, scudda hump!* Almost aloud I said, "Tamara, we were so good together, makes me feel so good thinking about it, that I must love you?"

"Bu-ud?" through my den door.

My name, at last. And most tenderly—but wasn't it a whine? I think she whined my name. So rare the times she said it and then she had to whine it. And I hate a whining woman worse than a howling wind, when I have to be in it unprotected. I went *"What?"* like a shot.

"Did you ball her?"

Ball her? Ball who? Ball Dr. K? Sex Therapist? Was that expected of me, a ball? Is that why her couch was wide enough for pre- and post-coital embracing? A ballfield, a court. For balling. I was supposed to rebound potently to you, balls and all, behind a bounce on Kochbaum's couch? Hell, woman, we don't need Dr. K for that. All we need is *you*. And *me*, of course. The two of us. Rolled in a ball. Ball. Odd euphemism for that pneumatic act required by nature in our production; demanded by most of us, far beyond the call of nature, in the fucking of the rest of us. Enough to make you bawl. What is this ball, a game? How many games revolve around a ball? What is our national pastime? What the fuck *is* this dance? Is it merely frivolous, worldly, this ball? Come to think, it's not so odd a euphemism at all; it's most appropriate, no matter which kinky way it bounces, huh oddball?

"Ball who?" I said.

"Forget it, man."

"Forgotten, woman."

"You want to break up, is that it, man?"

"Suit yourself, woman."

"Just tell me one thing first, okay?"

"I'm shrugging."

"Who was that girl in a white coat you fell in love with?"

"Girl in a white coat I fell in love with?"

" 'A girl in a white coat on the Delta Eagle sped by in the lonesome night and I loved her at once and forever. Delta Eagle tore a thing from in me out and down the tracks,' " that woman misquoted from a fragment from my private box of them, prosaically, by heart, by rote, and I resented it.

Out there in the dark somewhere, beyond or in my windowpane, I saw her, the girl in the white coat, and my heart was out there with her, in the dark. I turned from the window and faced the door that stood between me and Tamara. I tried to see her through the door, but couldn't see her face . . . I saw her bush, her big black wiry bush that no longer burned for me. She was a good woman. I had to love her. I was getting old. I wanted some babies. I need to hold a little hand born of me and womankind and hear that sweet magic "Daddy!" wring meaning from this dada world I'm growing old in.

I said, "That's just part of an old poem, Tamara."

"You tore both ends off the page."

"So? Maybe so."

"So you must have written more about her and tore out the middle."

"Maybe I just tore off the ends, I don't remember."

Silence. I tap a knuckle on the windowpane to cadence it. *Call my name again, Tamara, but don't whine it—or don't call it—just come in and say 'hey man, why don't you marry me?'* . . . I wished I was in Dixie. Away, away.

"Hey man, listen, I love ya, yaknow."

"I love you too, woman."

"Then I don't understand. If we love each other, why can't we make it?"

Silence.

"That *girl,* right? In the white coat, whoever she is or was. It's *her.* You told me you'd never been in love, but you're in love with her, right?"

I tightened, drew in, short-reined, holding on . . . white-knuckled . . .

                                                —then
suddenly I'm bifurcated, split.
I mean *sundered:* heart and mind wild-horsed
apart at that forking road: ripped.
I turned and fell into my swivel, what
was left of me. It was simple now,
to say what I had to say. It was simply
—to coin a phrase—
let the chips fall where they may. Why plan,
rehearse the words, the lines, until they sound
that way? When one has but to wait until
the pressure spouts the message like Old Faithless
      just about to pop . . .

"It's just a piece of an old poem, Tamara, I never met her,
she never knew I existed, you call that *in* love?"

"I don't know what to call it, man. I don't know what to call
you. All I know is you've got only one love poem in that
private box of yours, and it was about *her,* that girl you saw
on whatever the Delta Eagle is. What the fuck's that, anyway,
man, a *Delta Eagle?*"

Good woman, Tamara; she seeks, she ventures. Lots of
strong fibers there. She tries. Make one hell of a good heifer.
Tough broad, but gentle, really. Deeper than I had imagined.
We'd make it if we just would. I knew we could. *Oh Tamara,
Tamara, let's . . .* but "What the fuck's a Delta Eagle?" she has
demanded, and I popped:

"A *choo-choo* train, woman. Look, we're finished, you and I,
okay? Can I help you pack and take you home—or someplace?"

3

DR. KOCHBAUM had been a voice in a hank of black hair done in a bun, thick-rimmed shades and a moss-green pants suit on my first visit. Now she answers the door high-heeled, miniskirted, too tightly bloused. She wears rhinestone-framed chocolate-colored shades, looking kind of tacky. I said that my truck was double-parked, a way of saying that I wasn't staying. She nodded me toward the couch; I handed her the box of fragments which Tamara had banked off my den door, spilling out of order, when she fled, and slouched to the couch.

I had always been without direction, open to suggestion, for up to a fortnight behind a breakup; melancholy, but with a deep pervasive thrill of being free. But I had really come untethered with Tamara gone. It was like floating, only heavy. Heavy but floating—an ugly paradox, like Milton's hell: *darkness visible.* I stretched out on the couch, breathed deeply and let a sigh. The smell was still here; it was a kind of musky incense. Who was it, Ossie Lee, once told me that he or she liked the smell of burning incest? The music was still playing too, in the walls; a Stravinsky string quartet.

"What shall we talk about today, Mr. Hanks?"

"We broke up," I muttered, squirming deeper into the big wide sea-green couch.

"How do you feel about the breakup?"

"Bad."

"Do you still love Tamara?"

"As a fellow sufferer. Still feel for her with whatever *agape* God's grace provides. Eros has fled us, though. Read *eros* backward, Dr. K."

"Do you think you were in love with Tamara?"

"I have never been *in* love with anybody. I don't even believe there is such a thing as *in* love in the way you mean it."

"Isn't that unusual for a man of your age not to have ever been in love in the way that *you* mean it, Mr. Hanks?"

"I have never run down what is usual for a man of my age."

Dr. Kochbaum opened my box of poetry fragments and commenced to leaf through them. "What does this mean: 'Poems are tales of poetry lost'?"

"Aw, you know."

"How is Tamara?"

"I don't know. She won't come to the phone where she's staying. Look, I'm double-parked with a cord of seasoned cedar out there. It's soft, not hard wood, but it smells good burning, and is light. Just use a fire screen because it pops a lot. Where do you want me to dump it?"

"Are you ready to go now, Mr. Hanks?"

"I guess so."

Silence.

"You're not budging, Mr. Hanks."

"This is the most comfortable couch I ever fell into. What's it stuffed with? Old money?"

Silence.

I closed my eyes. The couch was deeply comfortable, but nine degrees too warm, suffocating, like a mother's lust. It oozed up around me just like that, warm and cloying. I was sinking. The couch was stuffed with Paleozoic ferns and the pubic hair of vestal virgins, wishes, dreams, smoke, mothers' milk cheese, archetypal stuff, empty spaces . . . "This is a bog," I said.

Silence, but for the distant string quartet in the walls, the slow, creepy slither of my descent into the couch.

> " 'A girl in a white coat on the Delta Eagle
> Sped by in the lonesome night,
> And I loved her at once and forever;
> Delta Eagle tore the heart from in me out
> And down the tracks' "

Dr. Kochbaum read in a hard, high voice, but with the meter right. "The Delta Eagle, I assume, is a locomotive?"

"Was," I nodded, struggling up for air. Slipping into my shoes, I said, "First diesel on the Missouri Pacific passenger run through east Arkansas, now out of service."

Dr. Kochbaum and I meet mid-carpet. I take her hand; feel for but find no wedding band. Am I happy, do I care that her finger is naked? "Do you have eyes?" I say into her shades. She is a sex therapist. *The rapist.* I am here for *the rapy.* Maybe I'll just knock me off a piece on the big wide couch, in that bog. I am not afraid now, am aroused in fact, by the vestal virgin in Dr. K; I will lay her in the bog, make love with her, reach into her and find that little girl and we will sink blissfully into the bog together. And tomorrow? Fuck tomorrow. Today is tomorrow's maidenhead.

"The girl in the white coat, Mr. Hanks, were you in love with her?" said Dr. Kochbaum, getting her hand out of mine.

WE HAD COME to a sudden, jolting stop when we heard the whistle blast; stopped with screeching tires, a mother's yelp, a father's curse. It hadn't bothered me that the call had been a close one. I figured we would have made it across. If we had zipped on across the tracks I would not be writing this, however. My parents were in front, my father at the wheel; I and my little brother in the back. World War II was on then, and

I was twelve. We had been to a picture show in McGehee. The Delta Eagle only had two long cars, so it passed by very quickly. I see it now, plain as day, always will, the long rows of lighted windows flashing past, and the girl in a white coat framed in one of them. I loved her as soon as I saw her, and my head spun to follow the vanishing train, and the girl was gone as soon as I loved her. The memory seemed no more nor less important, however, than innumerable other memories; oh it remained one of the most vivid, but nothing to strike a medal for, to build an altar to. I told this to Dr. Kochbaum; I told her that I realized that the telling of it elevated it to unwarranted prominence. I told her about other memories I had, to crowd that prominence, so as not to leave the girl in the white coat sticking out up there like a graven image, a bleeding heart. Take the Simmons Sonny pocket knife I dropped into a beehive and grieved over so much I threw away a better knife, a Barlow I'd traded a cigar box of marbles for, and a year or more later I told a lady visiting us about my lost Simmons Sonny, and she chopped open the beeless hive with an axe and found my little knife. It was rusty, and much smaller than I remembered it. I lost a Mickey Mouse wristwatch in a privy and never got it back. I had equally vivid memories of things not lost, but they didn't come to mind then. Dr. Kochbaum seemed pleased to have gotten so much out of me. She told me to get back on the couch, and I did so, in earnest. Now maybe I would get to lose myself in *the rapy.*

"Tell me what you think it means that a kind lady found your little knife but that it was quite small, and rusty?" said Dr. Kochbaum, sitting primly in the upholstered armchair, smoothing out her miniskirt.

I came up on my elbows in the couch. "It only means that it happened. What else? It's a memory, not a dream. Don't go looking for Freudulent symbols in a *memory.*"

Dr. Kochbaum said, "Memories are fully as revealing as dreams. The same censor that codes our dreams selects the memories we recollect, and *your* interpretation of them is what is most important. Whatever a dream or memory might really mean, or how I might interpret it, your interpretation is at least of equal significance."

"Meaning that even if I interpret a dream wrongly you can read something into that, right?"

Dr. Kochbaum remained silent, looking wise, without looking too wise. I asked her if she was married. Her lips formed a silent "no," which looked like, ironically, a kiss pucker. I stuck out my lower lip and nodded. I told her that I had been married, then quickly amended that to, "No, not married. We had a wedding. After the wedding ceremony we shared rooms until the arrangement was terminated nine months later. Long enough to gestate a baby, must be a metaphor for what we gestated. A euphemism." Dr. Kochbaum remained silent, looking wise, bland in her wisdom. I went on, "Why am I telling you this? Tamara is gone now, the deal is off. What am I doing here?"

I began to laugh. I laughed a while and then stopped abruptly. I had stopped laughing facing the wall on which Dr. Kochbaum's diplomas hung. I read each of them carefully, and said, "Well they look legitimate. Accredited schools. Ph.D. in clinical from Columbia. You've got a valid license to jump into people's heads, and other organs, with both feet for high fees in the name of science. Never thought I'd come to this."

I looked up and said, *"My God, my God, why hast thou forsaken me?"*

Then I turned, stood on tiptoe, and boomed down, "THOUGHT YOU'D NEVER ASK."

"Why did you leave the ministry?" said Dr. Kochbaum, instead of laughing.

"What *didn't* Tamara tell you?"

"Oh, you have all the symptoms."

I looked back at her framed ordination papers, her licenses to preach the gospel of the top secular god of this day and age, a god I didn't trust and couldn't. But I dallied with the temptation of the magic of idolatry, erotic flirtation with the gods.

The false gods. "Think I'll answer that," I said to her Ph.D. in Clinical from Columbia. Talk to it. Musn't face the goddess's naked countenance and risk reduction to a pillar of euphemism. The Diploma glowed evilly in its frame there on the wall when I spoke to it, a graven image in its own rite, a little god; even the images of the gods become gods; no getting away from graven images when you're hell-bent on absolution but nowhere near repentance. "I had a heart full of love of God and his message for humankind through Jesus Christ our Lord, O Ph.D. in Clinical from Columbia, but I wasn't satisfied with just a heartful. I had to get a headful too, so I went to a seminary, and the more I studied the more I thought and the more I thought the less I felt, and the less I felt . . . well as you know—I can tell by the way you glow—that's partly the reason and it's only partly true.

"Too many unbelievers in the world, that got to me. Too many people going to hell, and too few believers really caring; it got too difficult to keep the faith. That's part of the reason, and partly true too . . . Ah but you glow so hotly on the wall now O Ph.D. in Clinical from Columbia, impatient for the *real reason*, are you? Well I met a girl at the seminary, a religious education major taking a minor in sacred music, and we thought we were in love. No we didn't. We were both losing faith, had grown weary with the seminary, and we were very horny, and we got caught relieving ourselves of our horniness one Sunday afternoon, in the very act, in her dormitory room, by her house mother, and we got kicked out of the seminary, and that's the real reason I left the ministry, O cynical Ph.D. in Clinical from Columbia, ya fuckin' A."

"What did you do when you left the seminary, Mr. Hanks?"
I spun to face her, and announced, "Messed around."
Silence.
"Messed around?" said Dr. Kochbaum, finally.
Silence.
I said, "You're Jewish, aren't you?"
Dr. Kochbaum's lips parted in an unarticulated "Yes."

"Tamara was Jewish. I thought she was Egyptian, but she turned out Jewish. Didn't believe in God, though. Do you believe in God?"

"I have an open mind. How long did you 'mess around,' Mr. Hanks?"

"I'm still messing around. Come on now, with this 'open mind' bullshit. That means you *don't* believe in God. I believe in God. If you're gonna help me you're gonna have to believe in God. Right now our world views are so basically opposed that you'd never get to the bottom of my problem."

"Believe me, Mr. Hanks, your problem goes nowhere near as deep as ontology. What you've got all men have got to some extent, be they Christian, Jew, Muslim, atheist, or Hottentot."

"Maybe so, maybe not," I muttered. "First fight Tamara and I had was over what being Jewish meant. Couldn't pin her down. She insisted that it didn't mean a race or a religion, that it meant a *people;* but she couldn't define what a *people* was, either, except by the same method she used on *Jewish,* saying what it wasn't. Say everything that a Jew isn't and you've defined a Jew, apparently. What do you think? You claim an open mind when I ask if you believe in God. Is that what being a Jew is? Having an open mind? Plenty of Jews, whatever one is, would say that. That's a very Jewish answer to what a Jew is. But I say you've got to believe in God to be a Jew. Yahweh God. The fight broke out when I told Tamara that it was I, not she, who was the true Jew, a spiritual Jew who accepts as savior the messiah foretold by the Hebrew prophets. Turns out that Tamara was something of an anti-goy. It offended her that I had the temerity to call myself a Jew."

Silence.

I went over and leaned with my fists on Dr. Kochbaum's desk. I said, "I feel stupid bleeding here in front of you, woman. Sit there with your open mind and your pregnant pauses, a place for everything and everything in its place. You can't engineer me, so get off it. Let's see you get mad."

"Why do you want me to get mad?"

"Forget it, lady. Just working off a little hostility, obviously. I'm ashamed of myself, you see. I admit my prejudice against this secular religion of yours, and I'm ashamed for being here. I feel like a man with a good wife, who just woke up in a whore house."

I took a Steuben glass banana paperweight off Dr. Kochbaum's desk and sighted it at that damned framed Ph.D., iconoclasm in my heart and mind; I might have thrown it, I'm not sure, but anyway I didn't.

"*Talk* as hostile as you please, Mr. Hanks. I encourage it. But no violence. I have a gun in my desk, and I've got the ovaries to use it."

Frankly shocked I dropped the glass banana back on her desk. "You'd shoot a man just for breaking that, that . . . ? You're . . ."

"First it's my things, next it's me. It's happened, Mr. Hanks, and I shan't tolerate it. Now that'll be all for today. This has been a good session. I see improvement, rather quicker than I had expected. That 'waking up in a whore house' simile was very good. Perhaps soon you will have the courage to go back to that 'good wife,' find forgiveness, and begin life anew. Next week, Mr. Hanks, same time."

"Do you really believe I'd come back to this one-woman nut house, after being threatened with a gun? You're crazy, Kochbaum. You're a vine-ripe idiot. Hell, I'm not even going to *pay* you. Sue me."

I HIGHBALLED MY TRUCK down Second Avenue, from the Upper East to the Lower East Side, hitting each light green, the only thing to go right that day. I turned left onto East Fourth, then quickly right into the alley behind an old abandoned Yiddish theater where I kept a few cords of cedar on hand for city customers. While relocking the iron gate I noticed that about a quarter of the wood I'd loaded on my truck for Dr. Kochbaum had been ripped off while double-parked on her fancy block. I went up to my apartment, second floor, in the building standing a squat four stories of flaking green and gray on the other side of the alley.

I set a Beethoven sonata spinning on the stereo and got my chainsaw from under the harpsichord I had built from a kit but never tuned. I sat at the kitchen table with my chainsaw and a rattail file. An old girlfriend, a meringue-brained cornflower from Alabama, had given me the kit and helped with the construction, and my failure to tune the harpsichord, or get it done, had been the real reason we broke up. I filed the teeth on my chainsaw in time with the sonata. A hint of fall was in the air; I had caught it along with the airborne debris when charging down Second Avenue. It was time to head for the woods, to lay up a few score cords of firewood before the busy season. Tamara had planned to winter with me in the woods, and I had not thought much of that plan. I had wintered with women in the woods, and knew that two have to be very young, or very much in love, for that to work. It would be good to get back to the woods for days of hard work, evenings of good reading, nights of short but intense prayer, and sleep deeper than the deepest thought. Ah, the woods, at ease in Zion in the woods, blind to the jungle in the woods. When I finished filing the right row of teeth I got up to phone Tamara, see how she was faring.

A man answered the phone. I asked for Tamara. He said that if I was who he thought I was, Tamara did not want to speak to me. I told him that if I was who he thought I was and if he was who I thought he was, it was probably he, not she, who didn't want me to speak to her. He said don't worry about it and I said okay, and we hung up. I returned to the left teeth on my chainsaw, visions of Tamara in bed with another man drifting slowly through my head. The real hurt in jealousy is that the usurper is reveling in what is no longer available to you, no longer exists for you, has been used up by you; he has Tamara fresh off Fifth and Forty-second Street now, is being swept by those Mediterranean eyes deep into the cradle of it all, in ecstasy . . . the telephone rings and I rise like a Roman candle. If it is Tamara I will not ask who that man was; if the man was her brother, I will still countenance no talk of us getting back together, unless it's just for the night. I will be nice to her, but firm; distant, but not uncaring; friendly but practical; anything, but nothing.

"Um?"

"Bud Hanks?"

"Me."

"Karen Kochbaum. Hey, I'm in your neighborhood, on the way to my place on Long Island. You left your box of poems —want me to drop it off?"

"Karen?"

"I'm just around the corner."

"Well. Yes. Okay. Sure. I'm."

She was up in a minute. I didn't even have time to consider tidying or rearranging anything, or to decide to leave things the way they were. The lady blossomed in behind a nice warm smile, handing me my box while looking past me down the hall at my digs with unabashed expectation. I said to come in. I was shocked at how beautiful she was. Absolutely gorgeous if one allows a prominent Semitic nose into one's standard of feminine pulchritude. She had on jeans, a paler blue cotton turtleneck, and sneakers.

"Karen, you said."

"Anna Karenina for long, Karen to my friends."

"I like Anna."

"Then I'm Anna. Bud?"

"I dropped the -weiser when I came East."

She chuckled. I grinned. She stepped in. In the kitchen she said, "That's a chainsaw." I said, "Uh-huh," and we trekked on to the living room where the Beethoven sonata was too loud; I turned the volume down. Anna glanced about with a smile that could have been approving, amused, or just polite. She asked what I did with the chainsaw.

"I saw trees down and up with it. Firewood."

"O-oh," like she had never heard of such a thing. "And that's a harpsichord. May I try it?"

"It's out of tune. Never been in, in fact."

Clearing the top of assorted clothing, newspapers, and magazines, an unopened can of motor oil, a bust of Beethoven with a story of its own, handing these things in handfuls to me, Anna raised the top and looked inside. "Have you pliers?"

I got a pair from the kitchen, turned off the stereo, and Anna tuned the harpsichord by ear. Then she played it. Handel's Harpsichord Suite Six in F-Sharp Minor. Flawlessly. With genius for all I knew, heard. Lovely music, and she so lovely making it. That familiar piece of furniture I had built with my own hands and a little help from meringue brain and never bothered tuning, that rack for coats and hats and papers, a pedestal for blunt instruments, a thing to stick a chainsaw under, that conversation piece found itself under Anna's hands and lived. Pure gold beneath the Maltese Falcon's leaden surface after all. When Anna finished playing I said, "That was very good, really excellent. Lovely, indeed. What can I say? The harpsichord is yours."

"Why thank you," said Anna, getting up and craning her neck toward my partly open den door.

"I'm giving you the harpsichord," I rephrased emphatically, lest she hadn't understood.

"And I really appreciate it," said Anna, going to my den door. 'Depot,' she read off the wall over the door. Depot. Printed in black shoe polish by I forget or never knew who some years back, a medium and message that had bled through two subsequent coats of white latex. *Depot* over my den door. "What do you do in here?" said Anna.

"Not much." Wait. It's a depot. "I wait in it."

Anna turned. "Well, I must be going." She glanced at the harpsichord. "Okay if I wait until after the weekend to pick that up?"

"No charge. Say you've got a place on Long Island?"

"Uh-huh."

"I cut cordwood out there. North shore."

"Smithtown area?"

"Small world. Have you wheels?"

"I was going to take the train. When do you plan to leave?"

"Not before right now. Want a lift?"

"Sure."

We stood there looking at each other, she still smiling. I excused myself and went into the bedroom where I stood with my hands pocketed, to let my head catch up with events. Anna poked her head in and said, "Your bedroom." I nodded. Will she ask what I do in this room? She did not. She strolled in, stiff-fingered the mattress with the casualness of a tire kicker on a used-car lot, then abruptly turned and did cartwheels all the way to the kitchen. Very well-executed cartwheels. About five of them. I followed her, one foot after the other, flat-footed. She was running the tap cold for a drink when I caught up. I got a bottle of Vichy water from the refrigerator and poured two tall glasses of that. We might have toasted but we didn't, not even silently, not even the suggestion of a gesture of a toast. We simply drank our glasses of Vichy water and put them down. It was an intimacy. I picked up my chainsaw and asked her if she was ready.

"That's all you're taking?"

"It's all I need."

She picked up my box of poetry fragments. "May I take these along and read them again over the weekend, while we're on Long Island?"

I nodded. While *we're* on Long Island, she had said. I felt a sap for feeling it, but that excited me, warmed a hypersensitive region of my heart. The *cockles,* that space is called.

Down in the alley I started the truck, which had a dump bed, and was amused to watch Anna watch in amusement while I dumped what was left of the load owed Dr. Kochbaum. We took the upper roadway of the Queensboro Bridge because it is free, and because neither of us liked tunnels, and because that way led to a shortcut to the Long Island Expressway which I thought only I was privy to, but Anna knew. Once on the L.I.E. she went to sleep. She did not wake up until I turned off onto Sunken Meadow Parkway and the moon broke in large and orange yellow, dousing her face in a light that would have made a piss-in-the-pants romantic of a lesser man than I. Anna sang,

> Say it's only a paper moon,
> sailing over a cardboard sea,
> But it wouldn't be make believe,
> if you'd be-lieve in me.
> Yes it's only a canvas sky
> Hanging over a muslin tree,
> But it wouldn't be make believe,
> If you be-lieve in me.
> Without your love, it's a honky-tonk pa-rade,
> With-out your love, it's a melody played in a
>   penny arcade,
> It's a Barnum and Bailey world,
> Just as phony as it can be,
> But it wouuuuldn't be make believe,
> if you'd beeeeelieve in me.

She began in a hauntingly beautiful choirgirl voice that grew progressively jazzier and ended on a right funky note, but mellow, deep mellow.

"You play the harpsichord well, you sing well, you turn a mean cartwheel."

Anna laughed. Her laugh was talent-riddled too.

We drove on in silence. Presently I said, "I turn left off the Jericho Turnpike onto Edgewood Avenue, cut a left onto Fifty Acre Road, on into Head of the Harbor. I cut wood down in there on a big old estate."

Anna said, "I can't wait to see it."

I looked at her. She was looking eagerly ahead, like a child almost at camp. When I turned off Moriches Road onto Cordwood Path I said, "Hey—Cordwood Path," but got no response, or missed it. Off Cordwood onto Harbor Road we bounced. An empty dump truck makes a lot of noise on rough roads. Now and then I would hear Anna's voice but miss her words; I had to nod and let them pass into that void where probable banalities fester in the memory as great nagging mysteries. Two and a half miles down Harbor Road and I turned left onto the private road that winds through Eastern white pine, locust, black walnut, cedar, oaks as big as forest dreams, past a vast umbrella of a linden beneath which the Buddha sat out his enlightenment, on by a sprawling, slightly asymmetrical, but very elegant cedar of Lebanon, and thence into the circle drive of the big house, the manor house of the estate I sort of oversaw. There was one aging, battered car there, which I pretended not to notice. I circled the circle drive and drove back down and into the rear service driveway and parked by my old woods pickup truck.

We entered the big house at the rear, which brings one through the basement up a short flight into a narrow hallway on the left of which is a huge pantry, on the right the equally huge main kitchen; straight ahead a narrow flight up to the servants' quarters. In the kitchen I asked Anna if she was hungry; she wasn't. I led her on through the butler's pantry and out of that by swinging door into the main dining room, thence to the library and through that through French doors to the right into the vast main entrance room where I pointed out a table made of rhinoceros hide. From there we entered the vaster drawing room and went out onto a veranda from which, when the light is right, one commands a grand view. Straight ahead the two branches of Smithtown Bay, one named Porpoise Channel, the other I don't know. Long Island Sound to the north. We strolled across the front lawn, if struggling through grass left unmown most of the summer can be called strolling. We took a twisty path up a steep knoll to a prominence where a grander view of the world below is to be had. There was a rotten wooden bench there, nailed to a big dead red oak, but we didn't sit. We turned and strolled back down, then up toward the big house. We had left some lights on on the first floor. The second floor was dark. From high arched windows of the third-floor room facing us a dim light shone. The owner of the junky car out front was home.

"Beyond the big house and a little to our left are the farm house and barns, which you may have noticed when we drove in. They are rented to a homosexual couple, both of whom teach electives at the State University at Stony Brook." Pointing to our right, I said, "Yonder near that cedar grove is what was once a squash court. Beyond it, bounded by the bay, the next estate, and Harbor Road, are about forty acres of woods that I work." Pointing up, I went on, "And there are the Pleiades. I once knew a Baptist preacher who believed that heaven was in the Pleiades. It sure isn't anywhere else I've pointed out. Not yet, anyway."

"Some spread," said Anna. "Big house. The style eludes me."

"Turn-of-the-century eclectic."

"Beaucoup rooms."

"Thirty-odd. Forty-odder, counting servants' quarters, basement, attic, torture chamber. Nine baths, eleven fireplaces. A thousand closets, beaucoup skeletons."

At the veranda I took Anna's hand and said, "'Taint mine, case you're salivating. It belongs to my ex-father-in-law, Jesse James."

Taking back her hand, she said, "Then I shan't marry you —hey, I'm hungry now."

It was the second time I had touched her, and though she had quickly got her hand back, the effect lingered. How long had it been since I had got a hard-on just holding a girl's hand, I wondered.

We made cheese sandwiches and ate them at the kitchen table, listening to CBS news on an old churchhouse-shaped radio. This scene will be filmed in the big dining room where we will eat our cheese sandwiches under candlelight seated at the ends of the mahogany table with all its leaves inserted,

Mahler's Symphony No. 4 in G for mood. When we finished eating, Anna wangled a tour. We set out up the back stairs to the servants' quarters, where no servants had been quartered for a decade. We ended up outside the door of the master bedroom, still on the second floor. I said, "And this is the master bedroom."

Anna nodded, "And where do I sleep?"

"How about in the master bedroom?"

"And where do you sleep?"

"Sometimes, when the owners are away, in the master bedroom."

"And where are the owners?"

"In Africa."

"Then you, too, intend to sleep in the master bedroom?"

"I can sleep where I generally sleep if you'd rather not share a quarter-acre canopied four poster."

"And where is that?"

"In the master bedroom."

"Not the big bed, One Track," laughed Anna. "In what room do you generally sleep?"

"In the squash court."

She laughed again. "I've seen about a dozen empty bedrooms so far, and there must be that many more on the third floor—who's up there?—so you have lots of choosing to do before resorting to the squash court."

"The squash court is mine. I have a bed in it. Mary James might be upstairs; that was her light we saw on from out front, and her beat-up old car in the driveway."

"Oh, well, if you have a bed in the squash court, might as well sleep in your own bed. Who's Mary James?"

"Do you believe in ghosts, Anna?"

"I have an open mind."

"Then I'd better sleep in the room adjoining the master bedroom. We'll be connected by a bath. This house is haunted."

"Mary James?"

"She's the daughter of Mr. and Mrs. Jesse James, the present mortgagees of these digs, who are in Africa. I thought Mary James went with them but maybe not, not that it matters."

"Well, good night," said Anna.

I shrugged. She went into the master bedroom and closed the door. I went upstairs. The third floor is a hallway with the attic at one end, which is lower than the rest of the floor because it is over the servant's quarters which rooms are eight, not twelve, feet high, and a huge vaulted room at the other end, while on each side of the hallway are four small bedrooms, a bath, and closets, each bedroom funneling into a dormer with inoperable casement window. From the high vaulted room, through high arched windows, one commands the grandest view of the salt marshes, the bay, the Sound, and Connecticut on a clear day. The third floor of the big house was built to contain the young and insane members of the founding family, the Smiths of Smythetown.

The door to the high vaulted room stood ajar. I peeked in and there she lay, my ex-childhood sweetheart. Mary James, multi-divorced daughter of Jesse and Bessie James, in there instead of Africa. She was supine, flatly amorphous in a bluish robe or gown, smashed, with an open law text rising, falling, on her flat bosom; empty Cointreau bottle with a bent, lip-sticked straw in it on the floor in a litter of filter butts, burnt matches, ashes. Mary James was enrolled in a correspondence course in law; was dreaming of admission to the law school at Stony Brook. Story book. Before drifting into law Mary James had studied medicine through the mail, until the school was closed by order of the courts. Back in those days her flat bosom heaved beneath a heavy paperback on pathology as she lay stoned, and I lay stoned beside her, getting my degree in the marital arts. Mary James' last married name was Hanks, but she had never used it; had gone back to James some marriages back, to be professional. I went down to the library.

When the Smiths lived here the library had been stocked with handsomely bound books, many first editions, in mint condition, all locked in glass-doored cases, the key grown green in a locked desk drawer. When the Jameses bought the estate, the books and all other movable valuables had already scattered under the auctioneer's hammer, so now the book-cases were bare but for some early issues of *Life* magazine found in the attic, plus a few feet of Reader's Digest condensed books and a few inches of drugstore paperbacks that came with the Jameses.

I fell into a rotten old leather easy chair that to move would have to have been taken out piece by piece, and commenced to thumb an old *Life*. I got morbidly absorbed in the faces of two youths moments before they went to the electric chair for killing a small-town cop, just as Anna appeared like a theo-phany, with my box of poetry fragments. The youths were laughing. Anna was barefoot. On the facing page the photog-rapher had caught the lads yet laughing while shaving each other's heads, and when they frolicsomely slit each other's trousers to give the leg-shackle electrodes access to their naked ankles. Two crazy kids headed for the hot squat. About to ride the lightning. Panning, stagestruck stars all of a sudden, in the bright flashes of a *Life* photographer. About to die nastily. *Life* didn't show the end of their kicks. I would like to have seen the face of the one standing in line for sloppy seconds. That would have been a public service, but *Life* was romantic in the forties.

"The one about the girl in the white coat is very touching," said Anna.

I closed the old magazine and looked at Anna's feet. They were long and slim, like mine, but delicate, clean, exquisitely proportioned, unlike mine. A car pulled up out in the circle drive and we heard somebody burst in the front door, some-body with big feet on long legs, up the stairs four at a clip, all the way to the third floor. No image formed of Mary James in bed with another man, and no need of it, for none could pain me. No jealousy, no hurt, never a moment of ecstasy with the Mary James up there that fool is running to. Nothing much for Mary James but a little pity for the sot I had had a wedding ceremony with, and nine long months upstairs. The Mary James I loved was still twelve, still my childhood sweetheart, a virgin yet and always would be; she was still in my head, still pure, just like you know who. Inviolable.

"Ghost?" said Anna.

"Somebody going up to service one."

"Mary James."

"Yep."

"Your ex-wife."

"Uh-huh. Have you an ex-husband?"

Anna shook her head, looking at me inquisitively.

"Here's how it happened, Anna. The Jameses are from my home town. They moved away a long time ago. A few years ago I ran into Jesse in New York and he invited me out for a visit. Mary James was here. We had been childhood sweethearts. She had just got divorced. We got married. I did a lot of work for Jesse here, work he couldn't afford—he should have bought in Strathmore or Levittown, but naw, he's upwardly mobile—so a deed to the squash court was the fruit of my labors. Mary James and I got divorced. But I still own the squash court, and still work the woods out there, my livelihood. Still keep an eye on the place for Jesse."

"What is Jesse James doing in Africa?" said Anna, apparently faintly amused.

"Peddling chocolate-colored sunglasses to the blacks and coloreds in, I believe, Rhodesia. Or is it the Union of South Africa? He's an optician."

"Ought to help with the color problem there," said Anna.

"That's the idea," I said. "It's rare, the way we understand each other. Really rare."

"When you consider the number of sperm in a spurt, and that only one of them makes it to the egg which is only there one day out of the month, you realize we're all rather rare," said Anna.

"I've got a poem about that very rarity," I said.

She said, "I'm not surprised. Let's go to your squash court."

Through moon-bathed thigh-high dew-wet grass we threshed to the squash court which is on the bay side of the cedar grove, nestled back in locust and wild cherry crawling with ivy, much of the latter old three-leaf. The squash court was in a state of stalled renovation. I had installed a kitchen and bathroom on the spectator's gallery and put in the beams for a second floor, right after Mary James and I had taken the vows, and had gone on renovating awhile behind their breakage. I owned the squash court free and clear, it and the two acres required by local zoning. A small beach cottage had been gerrymandered out of my deed by Jesse James' lawyer for, I suspect, small favors from my ex-wife, all of whose favors were small. The squash court was my payment for fifty thousand dollars worth of carpentry, plumbing, wiring, roofing, and odd jobs I did on the big house for the Jameses, keeping them afloat. Mary James called the squash court my dowry, in a tone that made the term unmistakably pejorative. I had a mattress, three-quarter-bed size, on the hardwood floor of the court, beneath a huge skylight that could be cranked open, with great effort. I was a poet.

I got a bottle of Madeira Rainwater from the refrigerator and poured us each a glass. I sat on the mattress. Anna strolled around, looking up and about. She sipped and said, "Cold sherry. Interesting." "The Italians," I said, "chill everything they don't heat." "You aren't Italian, and this is Spanish," she said. "I ate in an Italian restaurant where they chilled red wines, and that's not Spanish, it's Portuguese, and it's Rainwater, not sherry," I said. "Our first fight," said Anna, sitting on the mattress.

There we were, sitting on the mattress, Anna and I. It seemed too low. It had never occurred to me before, how low a mere mattress on the floor seemed. I resolved to build a frame for it, get it higher. It would be nice having a high mattress for a change, one just low enough to board without having to

get a running start, or stepping on a box. I lay back on the
mattress, nesting my head in my hands. Pretty soon now, if
Anna just lays back too, I can relax. That will signal that it is
understood between us that the sexual act may be in the offing,
at least not out of the question, before the cock crows. I had
to know if I was going to get some, before I could relax with
a woman, unless she was my mother, or otherwise morally or
legally, or aesthetically taboo. A consummated sexual exercise
with the woman had to be past tense before I could get down
to whatever else there was to be gotten down to. Everybody
is more or less like that, of course. I am not spilling anything.
The penis in the vagina is the train in the tunnel to getting to
know you/getting to know all about you de do de do de do do
. . . Anna lay back and held up my box of poetry fragments.
It was an orange box with black lettering, "Buff Town Bond
Columnar Pads," Anna reads aloud. "What are columnar
pads?"

"You know, pads with big columns, the colonial style. The
ones that came in that box were town, rather than plantation
pads, and they were naked. Buff. Get it?"

"Did you really see a girl in a white coat on that train and
fall in love with her, or was it just a silly dream?"

"Is your place near here?" I said.

"It's over an old brick pump and ice house on the Nissequogue River where it flows into the sound."

"Right at Short Beach?"

"Ah-hah."

"That's only a couple or three miles from here."

"Less than one, according to the crow," said Anna, putting
aside the box, laying her empty wine glass on its side beside
the box. She nested her head in her hands. I came up on an
elbow. Anna's breasts still rose firmly inside the pale blue
turtleneck sweater, even as she lay supine, and they weren't
harnessed, either. I could see the darker prints, on the pale
blue fabric, of her nipples. There are those certain exquisite

women that other men get, not you, for whatever reason—be they too beautiful, too remote, too political, too particular, too tuned to other wavelengths, or a combination of toos—and here lay one of them on my mattress. Anna turned her head away, toward the far end of the squash court. "What's the painted line on that back wall?"

"That's the wall they socked the balls into. It's hardwood, like the floor. Balls had to hit below that line to be in bounds. I have plans for three narrow floor-to-ceiling stained-glass windows in that wall; frame the area off about fifteen feet thisaway for a grand floor-to-rafters den, living, family room maybe."

Anna looked back up. "I like the skylight. Wonder what stars are showing now?"

I got up and turned off the light. I took off my shoes before returning to the mattress. Also my shirt, pants, underwear, and reserve. I floated down upon the mattress for the opening kiss, then all out loving assault upon the myth, and bliss, but the mattress was bare of Anna.

"Anna?"

"Where's the bathroom?" she called out, distantly.

I stumbled back into my pants and turned on the light. Anna stayed in the bathroom for a long time. When I had to go I went outside. When I came back in she was on the mattress, facing the back wall the balls once smashed into, covered to the earlobes. I got under the cover too, facing the other way, leaving space enough between us for a masturbating spastic.

Some time later Anna said, "Wonder who she was?"

"How would I know? It happened thirty years ago, and we never met."

"Haven't you ever wondered?"

"Sure enough. I wonder about the salesgirl in Morgan & Lindsey's Five & Dime toy counter too, who said to her co-salesgirl, 'That's the cutest little boy I ever saw.' I was five."

"Did you write a poem about the Morgan & Lindsey sales-girl?"

"Shucks, woman, I wrote poems about things that didn't happen, too."

"Things that don't happen can be very important," said Anna.

"And things that can't happen?"

Silence. I thought I heard a sigh. I rolled over and reached, finding but a warm dent in the mattress.

"*Now* where are you?" I whined.

"Meditating."

"In what position?"

"In what position do you pray?"

"The missionary position."

"Do you really believe in God?"

"Sure I do, don't you—down deep?"

"I believe God is music."

"I've heard worse theology. What kind of music? A harpsi-chord concerto?"

"Not just any concerto, and not always the same one."

I said, "Hmm," and lay back with a timber rattling sigh.

"Did you enjoy being a preacher, Hank? I mean while you were actually preaching, behind a pulpit."

"Enjoy? If the ministry is a marriage, preaching is marital relations, the conjugal act. Sex. Even when the ministry turned sour, I still sort of enjoyed preaching. I loved to preach. Who was it, some actress, said about sex that even when it was bad it was good?"

"What did you preach about, mostly? What was your favor-ite sermon topic?"

"That God was in Christ, reconciling the world unto Him-self. Have you ever been in love, Anna?"

"Not really. Do you still believe that God was in Christ?"

"Uh-huh, and you ask me one more question, I'm gonna jump square in the middle of you."

"Why don't you pray?"

"You're right. I ought to."
"Then do it."

✿

MY EYES blinked open to pale dawn in the skylight. A colony of raccoons fighting and/or mating in the attic had awakened me. I was adrift alone on the mattress. I called her name. No Anna. I checked bathroom and kitchen. No Anna. I went down the path to the beach cottage and caught her coming out of the high tide, naked and unfazed. I said, "Good morning."

"Good morning, have you a key to the beach house?" said she, dripping, shivering, naked. I could have just swallowed her whole, let her shiver slowly, deliciously down. My head shook. "I didn't bring a towel," she said, hugging herself.

"Want my shirt?"

"Thanks."

Stepping toward her, unbuttoning my shirt, I said, "Okay if I stay in it?" keeping my shirt on.

Laughing, Anna scooped up her clothes off the beach-house deck and lit out suddenly past me and up the path. She was very fast; like a deer she sped up the twisting path through locust, birch, and wild cherry. I couldn't catch her. She was drying her hair up on the spectator's gallery when I burst in. The heaving of her chest from the run further took my breath away.

"Anna, you look real good, naked."

"I'm nude," she said.

"What's the difference?"

"Nude is bare, naked is raw."

"Naw, Anna, naked is when you get caught in the nude. Come on down."

"What do you want for breakfast, Hank?"

"You."

"Then what would I have?" she smiled, bending to step into her panties.

I turned around while she dressed. She made breakfast. It was a real good breakfast. I wasn't hungry and enjoyed it. She did the dishes while I walked back up to the big house for my chainsaw and old woods pickup. I drove back down, picked Anna up, and drove into the woods. She rode in the back because she hadn't ridden in the back of a truck since she was a little girl. Deep in the woods we stopped and I got out. Anna handed me the chainsaw, splitting ax, chopping ax, wedges, plastic bottles of gas-oil mixture, and chain lubricating oil, one by one, fast as I could take them and put them on the ground. She watched me oil and gas the chainsaw, tighten the chain, and start the motor. She watched carefully as I zapped down a small dead locust. Anna screamed "TIMBER!" when the little tree fell. She watched me cut it into twenty-four-inch cordwood lengths and halve them with the splitting maul. She helped me stack them in the back of the pickup.

Anna wanted to cut a tree down and cut it up. She selected a chokecherry that was almost two feet through at the base, and which towered. She got my assurance that the tree was hopelessly dead. I showed her how to first cut out a wedge on the side of the tree in the direction she wanted it to fall. I showed her how to start and hold the chainsaw. She didn't do badly for a novice woodsperson. When the tall cherry started to tilt, Anna quickly pulled out the saw and shut off the motor, so as not to spoil the music of its fall. The chokecherry ticked loudly as it tilted farther, faster, and Anna was thrilled. When it crashed she whispered in my ear, "Timber," and I grabbed her, hugged and kissed her, almost falling.

4

ANNA left for her place around noon. I wanted to drive her but she elected to set out afoot, alone, on the beach. Said she'd call if she wanted a ride back to New York Sunday afternoon. I had not planned to return to the city for at least a month, but that plan was flexible. Then, after twenty-four hours alone with Anna rising nude from the high tide in my head, that plan was scrapped. When she had not called by noon Sunday, I drove to Nissequogue; parked on Short Beach Road at a wet spot where a fountain overflowed. The fountain was built into a rock wall at the base of a steep hill. About forty feet up, set in the side of the hill, was the red brick building with a slate roof, a familiar ruin on this road. Quickly I scaled the rock wall, the steep bank to a narrow dirt road overgrown with weeds and grass; stood there in the weeds and grass, staring at the brick pump and ice house for a puzzled moment before knocking.

Even as I knocked I knew something was amiss. The green paint of the double doors was chalky, cracked with age; the extant windows opaque with a patina of years of dust. The door opened at my knock, creaked open unlocked; it would open to anyone, even to an ill wind. I stepped in. Into a ruin of Baroque turn-of-the-century machinery. Old cast-iron pumps robbed of their brass fittings, some still standing, one lying in pieces. Rusty pieces of metal, shards of glass, beer cans, barrel staves, oily rags, rusty broken tools. There was a tiled pool at one end to receive the water from the deep artesian well; the overflow water from the well vented into the fountain in the rock wall on the road below. The fountain is a favorite of beachgoers, campers, and Sunday drivers, who stop to drink from it, fill their bottles, thermos jugs. The pool was very clear. I could see with magnified clarity pop bottles, beer cans, a shoe, a condom, the bones of pigeons, rats, and raccoons on the white tiled bottom. A modern automatic submersible pump lay down there amongst the junk, sucking water through copper tubing into a pressure tank that stood tall, fat, and galvanized amongst the junk, the rusty relics of more affluent times. Anna?

But Anna had said she lived *over* the pump and ice house. I went out and climbed a rusty iron ladder and opened the door to the ice house side of the building. I spat into a cavernous space of crumbled cork, dry coon shit, and darkness. *Over* the pump house? Over the rainbow, maybe, Anna spent her weekends.

I drove on down to Short Beach and asked the gatekeeper if there were any other brick pump and ice houses with slate roofs anywhere about that somebody might be living over on weekends; naw, there wasn't another like that one anywhere else and nothing but coons inhabited that one, which belonged to the widow lady who lived in a big pink house way up on the hill.

There are no A. K. Kochbaums listed in the New York Telephone directory. Their numbers are unpublished.

On Monday morning I drove to the Smithtown station and took the L.I.R.R. to New York City. Cabbed from Penn Station to Dr. Kochbaum's building on The Upper East Side, and would have entered her office as I had the pump house, but the door was locked, so I rang and took a seat in a bright green vinyl chair with chrome arms and legs.

Dr. Kochbaum's tiny (two-man) waiting room was everything her office wasn't, and wasn't anything her office was, at least on the surface. It was done in Early Movie Theater Men's Lounge, too tacky even for the best low camp. Seated in the bright green chrome and vinyl chair across from me was somebody behind a *Hustler* whose cover bore an almost completely unclothed female person in a pose suggesting rut. Sliding aside a bird-bath-sized green-glass ashtray on a tall fake bamboo stand, I perused the matching fake bamboo magazine rack servicing my chair. It was stuffed with *Playboys*, *Penthouses*, *Ouis*, *Swanks*, *Cavaliers*, *Hustlers*, *Clubs*, and an old *New Yorker*. I pulled out a *Club*, which had the biggest format, and gazed at the dreamy looking girl in a white undershirt masturbating on the cover. I glanced up to catch a pair of quick brown eyes going down again behind the *Hustler*. The rutting girl on its cover still sights me between her knees. She has mean green eyes. I rub my eyes and see nude Anna rising from the high tide, shimmering wet, laughing, outrunning me . . . I get up and ring the bell again.

"She won't answer until the person in there's time is up and *I'm* next," my waiting roommate snapped, high-pitched, small-footed. "You come here often?" I snapped back, sitting again.

The fellow looked away with a cluck and a blow. I gave him the even eye. He was a tall, thin, light-brown fey creature, a little light for his feet, soft as a toadstool, I divined. There are three hundred million active sperm in an ejaculation, each boasting a length of one five hundredths of an inch, and a post-ejaculation speed of three inches per hour. About a hundred of these athletes complete the twelve-inch wiggle to the egg; another hardy hundred having struck out up the wrong oviduct; and then there's no guarantee of an egg in either oviduct. Only one egg a month is sent down for fertilization and birth or abortion, and for just one day from nine to five at that, and then just one teensy-weensy wiggletail out of that whole three hundred million gets let in before the egg grows impervious to further intrusion. The ratio of spermatazoa to boys and girls is a number huge to one. Astronomical. How rare we are, Anna, and yet sad, stuffy little assholes like this creature sitting across from me in Dr. Kochbaum's tacky waiting room made it to the fucking egg. *How come?* I said, "What's your problem, fellow? Queer? Impotent? Both?"

He said, "Who are *you?*"

I closed my eyes. I saw Karen Kochbaum on that wide peat bog of a couch with . . . not me. I opened my eyes and dug down into the magazine rack again, brought out the old *New Yorker;* sought balm in the cartoons until the doctor's door opened and a critter seven feet tall with canoes for shoes loped out looking satisfied. The Afro-American faggot across from me popped up erect.

Dr. Kochbaum in the doorway in severe greens and grays, hair in the tight bun, not one strand askew, so why do I even now with my eyes closed see her in the mini, tucking in the tight blouse, her black hair all over the place? The doctor had on opaque shades today. She said, "Mr. Kimberly."

I said, "Got a minute?"

"Mr. Hanks, do we have an appointment today?"

"A minute will be plenty."

"I can't squeeze you in today, Mr. Hanks."

Mr. Kimberly hiked his narrow shoulder at me as he swished in behind her. The door closed behind them, fanning out that musky incense. There was a heavy hint of estrus and semen in that smell, my imagination screamed. What is that pagan priestess running in there, a fertility cult? I got up, not knowing which way to kick. The door opened again and I heard, "Your appointment is Friday at four thirty, Mr. Hanks."

I cabbed down to the newsstand in my neighborhood, bought a *Village Voice,* went up to my apartment. I checked out the activities calendar in that high-camp rag for open poetry readings. Three were scheduled for that evening, one in an uptown library out of the question, one in a Bowery loft no longer my jug of wine, and one on Bleecker at the eastern fringe of Greenwich Village, about what I had in mind. I put down the *Voice* and got up, floating heavily. I picked up the telephone and put it down undialed. I opened the refrigerator door and closed it. I had to be careful now, things were getting alien. This had happened to me before, and I knew how to handle it, but I did not want to have to handle it, because I was not supposed to have it any more. It was what I had so glibly reassured Tamara about. The sun was setting in my soul, dark old anxiety was rising. I thought to pray, my usual way of coping with the rising terror, but I couldn't pray and knew it; the night had come down finding me unready, the attitude for prayer as difficult to attain as God's kingdom on man's terms. I simply stood there for a moment, alone in my living room, floating heavily, the terror mounting, feeding on itself, and I said to it, "What can you do? Hit me. Hit me and go away," and it was gone as quickly as it had come, gone without a prayer.

I went down to the alley behind the abandoned theater and spent the afternoon quartering cedar rounds with a ten-pound splitting maul. I let a Bowery bum sleep back there. He got in and out under the iron gate. In the winter he built himself a cabin out of cedar. He built it just high enough to crawl in, wide enough to D.T. in, calked it with newspaper. I gave my bum a dollar whenever I saw him. He took the dollar as his due for guarding my woodpile. Some people question the ethics of giving money to bums because they're only going to buy wine with it. Why shouldn't they buy wine with it? If a bum did an honest hour's work for you would you not pay him because he would only buy wine with the dollar? I question the ethics of not giving money to bums since wine is what they want most in the world and money is what they have least, unless it's love, and how many people do you run into in a day to whom you can give what they want the most, without much sacrifice on your part? A dollar. A bum only wants about a dollar at a time, so he can die a little while at a time. A five could be fatal for a bum, either by his own hand or that of another bum. If you think you have more love than money for a bum, don't tell him that until you've gone to the liquor store for him and proven the liquidity of your love, its legal tenderness, to that realist behind the counter. If I could get my Bowery bums—and I've had a few—to accept something better for them, and it was mine to give, I would throw it at them. Most bums claim to pray, especially on a freezing night, and a few survivors say it helps. But they all want that jug more than anything in the world, next to dying in their sleep, or they wouldn't be bums. I went through about a dozen Bowery bums in four years in that alley, while a less sensitive man might have used up a gross of them, or none at all. On the morning after Mary James and I got wedded on Long Island we stopped by my apartment, for something, and looked in this alley to give my Bowery bum a bonus. We had a quart of real booze, a wedding gift, to spare. We found him frozen stiff. The neck of the wine bottle broke off in his mouth when the meat truck driver's helper tried to pry it out. Mary James and I were on our way to a Florida honeymoon, but we were drunk and didn't make it. The sight of the frozen bum seized Mary James with the whim to turn the big house her father had just mortgaged his life for into a home for Bowery bums some day after we had moved into the renovated squash court and her parents into the hereafter. That was the most solid plan we ever courted.

At dusk I quit my splitting and went up for a bite. I wasn't floating any longer; I just felt heavy now. I didn't shower or change, because some women like the smell of a working man, and some women like to pretend to, and I had no stomach for any other kind of woman. At the open poetry reading I might meet me a mate, a poetess, amenable to a tender loving one-night flop with a heavy, smelly man.

The Bleecker Street reading was in a basement coffee house called Hannah's Catacombs. Hannah was a very proper witch of old acquaintance, a fine, obscure poetess who wore a gold cross on a gold chain around her long, dry neck. Hannah took in stride the witch brand, because she looked like what witches were popularly supposed to look like during the period of screen history beginning with *The Wizard of Oz* and ending with *Rosemary's Baby*. Hannah wrote long, difficult poems about witching, but with a Christian twist, because she was a confessing Christian. She was a member of Jews for Jesus, and the cross around her neck was superposed on a Solomon's seal, mistakenly supposed by pagan ignoramuses to be a hex sign. A young black female person with a big Afro and much hubris was shouting unscannable revolutionary cant when I stepped in. When she sat down to polite applause Hannah introduced me to the audience, which was mostly young, white, off-the-street suburbanite doing Greenwich Village. I was introduced as the best nonpracticing poet between the planets Venus and Mars, and asked to give a recitation.

I found myself behind a pulpit. It was an honest to God pulpit Hannah had got from a church house no longer a church. I cast a sweeping glance at the audience, which was mostly female person, with no attempt to focus, to distinguish the sticks from the woodpile. I told them that like Hannah had said, I no longer practiced the craft; that oh some poetry ran through my head now and then, but I didn't damn it. I said, "The only bit of verse I recall off hand is an old piece, a fragment that goes . . . ," and with a faraway, misty look in my mind's eye I quoted it and sat down.

For a moment you could have heard a coffin opening, and then the applause was thunder. I got out quickly at intermission and waited in the shadows on Bleecker Street. Waited for her, my own bait and my own trap; waited for whoever she might be, the first broad to come out bubbling at the best nonpracticing poet lurking in the shadows between the second and fourth planets from Old Sol. Like my little poem do you? Splendid. I have more, lots more . . . Let us go then, you and I, to my place for a little poetry, a little sound, a little wine, a little gab about what we like and don't like, and cap the evening with a little making like.

Two broads came out and seized me. Identified themselves as publishers of a new poetry magazine yclept *Gabriel's Horn*. They wanted to publish "The Girl in the White Coat" and anything else I'd care to lay on them. I nodded thoughtfully, thinking of Ossie Lee Somebody's favorite joke: seems there was a priest who got a nun to perform fellatio on him by conning her into thinking that it was Gabriel's horn he wanted her to blow, that if she blew it the angels in heaven would hear the music and dance for joy. I invited the publishers to my place. I asked them if they were poets. Of course they were. Well, we'll write a group poem. Oh that will be fun, writing a group poem. And so it happened that a trinity of poets went up to my place to make some poetry together. We made a pit stop en route, and I bought a case of cold duck. Who ever heard of a dry-launched orgy?

John Coltrane's arrangement of "My Favorite Things" spins on the stereo. We three poets sit on the rug between the speakers, on the spot where the phantom speaker speaks, drinking cold duck out of tall iced-tea glasses, nobody but the phantom speaker speaking—*"These are a few of my fa-vo-rite things . . ."*

I broke the ice with old Ossie Lee's joke about Gabriel's horn and the joyous dancing of angels in heaven. One of the publisher-poets thought it funny, the other thought it gross. The one who thought it gross asked to see some more of my poems for possible publication. The one who thought it funny wanted to know who would start the group poem. I told the one who thought it gross to go start the group poem.

When she had gone into my den, my depot, to start the group poem, I commenced to hug and kiss the other publisher-poet; had her almost undressed when the other one came out of the depot and said, "Next." The almost undressed publisher-poet got up giggling and went into the depot while the one who came out joined me in the phantom speaker for some hugging and cold duck and kissing and partial undressing. The needle reached the end of "My Favorite Things" and the automatic changer began it again somewhere near the middle where a 45 rpm would commence, because there wasn't another 33 rpm on top to drop and trip the lever. The publisher-poet I have almost undressed (the one who thought the joke gross, recall?) suggested that I change the record, and that I needed some deodorant. I got up and put on the flip side, "Summertime," and went to the bathroom. I was also almost undressed.

In the film I will stalk resolutely from the bathroom naked as a knife blade, with rhinoceros musk in my armpits, and the publisher-poet will be as born too, and we will fall just out of the frame onto the rug there in the phantom speaker, locked in instant copulation, and then the other publisher-poet will come bouncing from the depot a comely stack of naked tits and ass, reading out loud, drowning out the phantom speaker, a rank bit of lesbian doggerel, and the publisher-poet with whom I am humping will take an instant shine to her. We both will. To avoid a tasteless triple X, the three of us will mesh in the lens of a kaleidoscope with "Summertime" ending and "But Not for Me" beginning—which is actually the way it is; I am not composing this: it's right there on the record label, Atlantic stereo #SD-1361. When I've petered out and that pair continue in a Sapphic grope, the "Nutcracker Suite" will cut in on the track and I'll go get a sharp butcher knife in the kitchen, throw on a robe, go out and buy a watermelon. I shall stroll the Bowery, doling out slices of warm watermelon to freezing Bowery bums with *Also spracht Zarathustra* ejaculating from all the phantom jukeboxes on the Bowery. I will tell each bum who takes a slice that God is not music. There will be Latin subtitles.

When I returned from the bathroom with deodorized armpits the other publisher-poet had finished her part of the group poem and had joined the one who thought Ossie Lee's joke gross on the rug. An empty cold duck bottle lay on its side between them, dead soldier, ready for spinning. Both of the young ladies were naked and giggling. I finished getting naked too, but they said *"Next"* in unison, steering me into the den, my depot.

Their page of typescript was still in the machine. The first one had written something too awful to quote or to forget, entitled, "The Man in the Black Coat on the Carrion Vulture."

Crammed in at the bottom of the page was the other publisher poet's contribution:

> DON'T LOSE YOUR HEAD
> I can't compete with your whiteclad fantasy
> flying a greek lettered bird who took away
> your heart (or was it your balls she dragged
> off down the track?) and yet I've lost my head,
> God help me I think I'm in love with you!

which at least had the virtue of brevity.

There are no rules for the writing of group poems, or if there are the rules are the same as those for orgies. I cranked a fresh page into the typewriter. I reread the above and my eyes closed. Which one was she, the one who has fallen (I'm frankly flattered) in love she thinks with me so soon, for so little reason? I try to conjure them but all that forms are the fuzzy images of two naked female figures on a rug—faceless figures, indistinguishable, except that one had on wide jade bracelets that did not hide the ugly scars beneath them. Long white scars on jade-braceleted wrists steering me into here; I had looked away quickly when I saw them, that nakedness I was not supposed to see. She had not been bluffing; life had once got too heavy for death to be a threat, but which of them was she?

I opened my eyes and stared at the blank page awaiting my contribution to the group poem. The grope poem. What will I write? I think of scars, jaded scars on a female figure's wrists. I think of guilt, or rather the feeling of guilt. The nourished feeling of guilt. I arrive at the notion that it is an advanced hubris that nourishes the feeling of guilt. Gilt-edged guilt. I don't know what to write. My eyes close again.

The girl in a white coat on the Delta Eagle goes by and I blurt out loud, "Hey, what's your name?" A thrill ran the length of me when I asked her that. Why? I wondered, then it occurred to me that it was the first time I had ever spoken to her. I had always let her speed by unspoken to. Again I asked her name, not out loud, but inwardly, though my lips formed the words, and again I felt the thrill. I tried to imagine her answer, but couldn't; neither a name nor a voice for her could I imagine, for the names and voices I could imagine were names and voices I already knew, and these plainly would not do. There seemed to be no proper name nor voice for her. When she came by again I did something else I'd never done before; I zoomed in on her, large as life, but she went all grainy close up, out of focus, misty. I let her recede to the proper distance and go on by, and when she returned I spoke to her again.

I asked the girl in the white coat where she had come from and where she was going. Had she married, had she children, was she still alive? I addressed her as "O girl in a white coat," at first, and then as "O Girl in The White Coat." I told her things like, "O Girl in The White Coat, I am sorry for exposing you to others, I'm ashamed of myself for violating our sacred and private relationship by reading that poem about you, letting Tamara and others see it, so that now strangers know about you, talk about you, even write bad poems and worse parodies, blaspheming you . . . ."

As I talked to the girl in the white coat I realized that I was talking to her in earnest, with my head bowed and my eyes closed. It gave my heart a start to realize that; a strange thrill suffused me. I got on my knees and prayed a deliberate, conscious and earnest, agonized prayer to The Girl in the White Coat on the Delta Eagle going round and round on the circular track in my skull. I begged her to stop the train and let me on with her, so we could find a spur line out of my head into forever. I prayed real hard to The Girl in The White Coat on the Delta Eagle in my head, and I got a big hard-on doing it.

There was a knock on the depot door, but I stayed on my knees with my face buried in my hands in the swivel chair, and prayed on, close to climax. I heard the door open and quickly close. I heard whisperings, a giggle, the rustle of bodies getting clothed. I heard the outside door close, and a little while later I said aloud, "Aaaa—*women!*" and the naked man on his knees abandoned, got up, at least the end of his prayer answered. I commenced to type:

> Dr. Kochbaum's office was small enough to be called cozy, but it wasn't. It was leathery, walnutty, woolly, a little universe too tastefully furnished for the best taste. It was dimly lit, the sunlight veiled away behind cloud-colored drapes. I was admitted on the second ring and ushered to a heather-green stuffed leather couch which was twice the width of my idea of a doctor of psychology's couch. "Why have you come . . ."

An hour later, maybe three, I went to the bathroom and then to the kitchen for some cold duck, prepared to write all night, as long as it took to finish. In the kitchen I found a handwritten note on a napkin on the table: "I never met a man who prayed, certainly not when nude. Are you crazy? I am. I must see you again. Seriously. Please call. Stella." There was a number. I scrutinized the handwriting. It was fast and heavy handwriting, but very legible. "Stella," I muttered. "Stella," again. It weighed on me that somehow I should know which of them was Stella, that I owed her that much anyway.

5

"MR. HANKS."

I remained, fixed-focus, on the centerfold of *Swank*.

"Mr. Hanks?"

I had been staring at it for a long time, until it had become but a picture of a piece of meat, like a word said over and over and over and over becomes noise. It was a spread of the girl of most men's dreams, spread, spreading it with her own fingers in good light: the detail was sharp. Not a fold, a follicle, a membrane, a droplet, a hole was left to the imagination. The fields of gynecology and proctology in descending order textbook correct in one color photograph in the centerfold of *Swank*. What next? A tiny camera in a clear plastic dildo, two of them, up both tunnels, looking for the lights at the ends of them?

"Mr. *Hanks.*"

I turned the magazine around and held it up for Dr. Kochbaum to see. She had a tweedy look today, hair in a sort of pompadour with a slender bone run through it. She glanced at the centerfold through slanty lavender shades.

"What do you want me to see, Mr. Hanks, and say?"

"Oh say what you see."

"An ink blot," said Dr. Kochbaum, turning and returning to her office.

She sat at her desk and I sat in a chair beside it, in loan-applicant juxtaposition. "I want to see Anna."

Dr. Kochbaum waited silently, impassively, for my reason.

"She lied to me. She doesn't live over any pump and ice house in Nissequogue."

"Would that not be between you and Anna, Mr. Hanks?" said Dr. Kochbaum, nodding.

"Also I want to tell her a secret."

"Would you like to tell me your secret?"

"It's a secret."

"Well, it is no secret that you have a secret," said Dr. Kochbaum, pushing her shades up just enough to rub her eyes, a necessary gesture behind that kind of sophistry. "Do you feel that Anna wants to see you again?"

"If she wants that harpsichord I gave her and would like to play with my chainsaw some more and holler *timber.* "

"Do you feel that Anna is charmed by men who give away harpsichords and play with chainsaws, Mr. Hanks?"

"All of them, yes. Do you fuck your clients, Dr. Kochbaum? Tamara intimated that you did."

"By 'fuck' do you mean sexually or metaphorically?"

I made a circle of one index finger and thumb and jooged the other index finger in it.

Dr. Kochbaum made a note, and said, "Why do you ask, Mr. Hanks?"

"Well I wasn't hinting, if that's what you mean by asking why I asked."

"What would I assume you were hinting?"

"Answering questions with questions, you ought to be a rabbi," I muttered, looking away. "I'd rather hear Anna whisper 'timber' in my ear again than get any *the rapy,* metaphor or otherwise, from you, Sister."

Dr. Kochbaum closed her notebook and got up. She went and got on the couch. Her passage across the deep dark rug was accomplished without a sound. The couch let but a faint sigh when she stretched out on it with her hands behind her head.

"What did you do for a living before you went into wood, Mr. Hanks?"

"I taught."

"What?"

"Look, this is a waste of time."

"And who, and where?"

I got up and went to the couch. My footfalls made a little muffled noise on the rug; must take practice, or something terribly insubstantial in one's being, to cross it like a cloud. I sat in the upholstered armchair by the couch. Dr. K had on black knit hose. I could see her raising her knees, the tweedy skirt sliding down, bunching up about her thighs. She would have on plain white cotton panties with red garterbelt . . . not that I have ever been driven all that frenzied by such trappings.

"You're unreal," I said.

"Who is real, Mr. Hanks?"

"I want to talk; okay if I talk?"

"Talk."

"My childhood sweetheart was Mary James. Her father was a pulpwood cutter, her mother a fat housewife who grinned a lot and had dyed black hair. The Jameses lived in a shotgun house on the edge of niggertown. Like poor white trash. Maybe they were poor white trash, maybe they really weren't. It was the depression and lots of folks got trashed. I loved Mary James. She was real pretty and delicate, and said things like, *well personally* this and *well personally* that, and *I couldn't personally for the world* do or think this or that, and this is *just personally* something or another. A month later and *well incidentally* this and that and *incidentally* whatever, off the wall, followed by a month of *positivelies*. Mary James drove us all crazy with two weeks of *lawsy*. Yaknow, *lawsy me, well lawsy.* People with pretensions have always found a big empty room in my heart to let them echo in. An echo chamber for other people's pretensions in my heart. I like that, whatever it means. Hey, Dr. K?"

"I'm listening, Mr. Hanks."

"I like pretentious people better than your simple, self-satisfied souls. I find them more intriguing, interesting. I met a lady in a bar one time whose face was landscaped in enough makeup for live TV, but underneath it you could see she was as plain as yesterday. I asked her what her name was and she said it was Evelynette LaMouré, or something equally unlikely, and I bought her a drink, a champagne cocktail, but she wouldn't leave with me because she couldn't do that and still keep her pretension, and she must have known that her pretension was all I wanted to take home with me. One time Mary James and I took off our clothes in a hayloft and looked at each other. She had started growing pubic hair and I hadn't. We got dressed again real quick and ran. Twenty-eight years later we got married. We have yet to bring up the hayloft incident."

I got out of the chair and sat on the edge of the couch. Dr. Kochbaum got off the couch and sat in the chair. I went on.

"Wasn't long after the hayloft that the Jameses moved. That was back during World War Two. About five years ago I ran into Jesse James on Times Square, where it's said that you'll eventually meet someone you know or knew. One of us was going down, the other up the steps of the IRT subway station. I recognized him at once; he had to take me on faith at first, since you change a lot more from twelve to forty than you do from forty-odd to close to seventy. But soon it all came back to him, what little there was of me in his memory. We went to an Irish chain saloon with a mile of blue-collar crowded bar, a doghouse-sized TV, two-for-six-bits drinks out of shot glasses thick as crystal balls, and had a few.

"One of the best times I ever had in New York City, Dr. Kochbaum, was getting drunk with old Jesse James in the Shamrock Bar on Eighth Avenue and Fortieth. Jesse told me he was an optician now, that he owned a chain of eyeglass stores on Long Island, and had just bought a famous old estate out there, a 'showplace home' he called it. Jesse told me how he had risen from pulpwood cutter in southeast Arkansas to correcting vision on Long Island. It was a long and fascinating tale and it made me proud of him. I told Jesse how I had once felt about his daughter Mary James, and that made him proud of me. Jesse told me that by the way Mary James had just got divorced from her husband and was at home with her parents again, at the showplace home on Long Island. Well that was just too personally much.

"Jesse James said that I just had to come out and visit, that he would not take no for an answer. I told him I would come out for a visit even if he told me not to come out for a visit. We drank to that and he went to the phone booth and called home to prepare the way. We drove out in my car that very afternoon. Mary James met me at the door. Her daddy had sent me in that way while he went in another way; they must have planned it that way. Mary James was an alcoholic chain smoker now, a little dried around the edges, but otherwise unchanged; pretty much the same as I remembered her. I moved in that very night, into a guest room, and soon after we got married."

"Why, Mr. Hanks?" said Dr. Kochbaum.

"If I knew why, would I need you? Would I need anybody? If I knew why I probably wouldn't have done it. If I knew why, why I'd, I'd . . . if a frog had wings he wouldn't bump his ass behind the second hop. I saw Mary James one time between our twelfth and fortieth years. When we were nineteen. I was home for the summer after my freshman year in college, and she was back to visit an aunt or uncle. She was engaged to a crop duster in Greenville, Mississippi, which is where the Jameses had been living ever since they moved. Can you imagine, Dr. Kochbaum? Greenville is across the river, about forty miles from Arkansas City. My childhood sweetheart had been only a couple hours by bad roads from me for seven years and I didn't know it?

"Oh Lordy, was Mary James pretty when she was nineteen. She was a little bit too thin, but O so very pretty. Oh it was absolutely intolerable, said she, that here she was engaged and we hadn't seen each other in seven years, and her fiancé was coming down for her that very night. But we would have the afternoon together. I borrowed our family car and drove Mary James down to the river where we hugged and kissed some. They called it smooching then. We smooched for a little while in the front seat. Mary James wouldn't let me get my hands into her blouse or up her dress. When we got back to her aunt or uncle's she'd got a phone call from Greenville. I stood by while she returned the call. Mary James found things absolutely intolerable maybe twenty times during a ten-minute conversation with her fiancé, and when she hung up she fumed at me to come pick her up at eight. She told me that she was going to make it up to me for all the time that had passed, that she'd show *him*. Not very flattering, but talk about pretension. 'I will make it up to you for all the time that has passed,' her exact words. A humble girl couldn't have said that. We kissed then, I sweetly, she fiercely, and I went home, shaved, shined and showered, dressed to kill, talked Dad out of the car again, and was back at the aunt or uncle's house at eight flat. Mary James was gone."

Dr. Kochbaum allowed a proper pause before she said, "And you made no effort to contact her after that?"

"No. Never was very much between us, really. Still isn't."

"How did you feel when she stood you up?"

"Bad."

"Do you feel that her standing you up, without making some excuse, has affected the way that you relate to women?"

"I take each woman I meet on her own merits," I said.

"Consciously, perhaps."

"Well I can only be held accountable for my consciousness."

"Come now, Mr. Hanks. You are conscious of the fact that you have an unconscious mind that affects your behavior, are you not?"

"Unconsciously, perhaps."

"You're being flip, Mr. Hanks."

"You're in a flip profession, Dr. Kochbaum."

"Who was the girl in the white coat, Mr. Hanks."

"I don't want to discuss her."

"Why not?"

"Because she's—it's getting out of hand, all this talk about her. I'm being talked into a problem I don't have or, if I do have, is no worse than anybody else's problem. I've even started talking *to* her now, and I never even thought about her all that often until you broads all started getting off on her, I mean that poem I wrote about her. First Tamara, then you, Anna, Stella and her friend, a whole bloody poetry reading . . . Ask me, Dr. Kochbaum, the girl in the white coat isn't my problem—she's *youall*'s."

Dr. Kochbaum made a note.

"What do you say to the girl in the white coat when you talk to her, Mr. Hanks?"

"Come on, this is silly."

Dr. Kochbaum nodded, waiting for an answer.

"I only talked to her *once*, the other night. I apologized to her for dragging her into *mutability*. She was pure, serene, and sublimely aloof on that train, going around in my head, and now I've soiled her, letting her get into other people's heads. I've cracked the Grecian Urn, or let it get duplicated, whatever, mixed metaphors."

Dr. Kochbaum nodded thoughtfully, making more notes. "Well now that she's out, cracked, or duplicated, Mr. Hanks, why don't you tell me who she really is?"

"You really want to know, don't you? I won't get a moment's rest until I tell you, right?"

"It would be helpful for you to speculate."

"Okay. He was a transvestite ex-bauxite miner from Sweet Home, Arkansas, en route to Jackson, Mississippi, to accept the chair of psychology at the magnolia state's university. Rumors that she was a purloined department store dummy with the face of Karen Horney, constant companion of Anna Freud, on her way to upholster the chair of psychology with the white coat at Bob Jones University have been shot down and stuffed. Mounted. Bob Jones isn't on the Missouri Pacific line. It's on the narrow gauge tracks of the Gospel Train."

"Then you realize that the girl in the white coat may have been a wizened grandmother, or perhaps a coat on a hanger in the window? The train was speeding by, was it not, and you were an impressionable child some distance back in the night, *looking* for something?"

"Oh yessum, that realization has been run up the pole and saluted. And the Delta Eagle may have been a trick, too. Delta Eagles are very rare, you know. Most of them are omega shaped. Stella or her friend think it was a carrion vulture, a redundancy. Who knows?"

"Mr. Hanks, have you ever considered the possibility that you have been wasting your life and hurting those who get close to you, not in an honest search for this girl, symbolically or otherwise, but by just using her as an excuse for irresponsible behavior?"

"Waste? Hurt?"

Dr. Kochbaum waited. So did I. There was a long silence. Then she tacked. "How are you getting along now that Tamara is gone? Have you found someone else?"

I shook my head.

"You have twice mentioned a Stella."

"Stella? Oh she's just some nutty poet trying to launch a new poetry magazine called *Gabriel's Horn.* Last Friday when I left here pissed off after you wouldn't give me a minute I went to an open poetry reading, quoted you know what, and ended up with these two female people in my apartment. We came just shy of an orgy, but we wrote a group poem instead." I took a wadded quarter page of typescript from my pocket and smoothed it out on the couch, handed it to Dr. Kochbaum. "Read that and tell *me* whose problem the girl in the white coat really is."

When Dr. Kochbaum had finished reading it she said, not looking up, "She says she loves you."

"That's poetic license. It and five dollars will get you a marriage license. Throw in another fifty and you've got a wedding band, a grand and it's a honeymoon."

"What was written above this, Mr. Hanks?"

"What the other girl wrote. It was embarrassingly bad. I threw it away."

Dr. Kochbaum gave me back the piece of paper. "And Stella authored this?"

"I don't know which of them was Stella. There were no introductions. The only reason I know one of them was named Stella is that she left a note."

Dr. Kochbaum nodded, got up and went to her desk. I followed her, sat in that chair beside it. She said, "What did you mean that you came 'just shy of an orgy'?"

"I don't want to discuss that part, because you'd tell Anna and I prefer that she learn the good side of me along with the seamy."

"I should think, Mr. Hanks, that now that you have found a woman who loves you, that you should grasp that opportunity for getting mothered and forget Anna."

"I'm gonna let that go right over, Dr. Kochbaum, show you how big I am."

"Tell me about this Stella, Mr. Hanks."

"I told you I don't know which of them was Stella. We were full of cold duck and I'd had a bad time of it earlier that day. I was feeling very heavy. We were naked—there, it's out—but the only distinguishing feature I recall was that one of them wore jade bracelets to hide scars on her wrists."

"Scars on her wrists? Have you the note she left?"

I gave Dr. Kochbaum the note, saying, "Like I said, I don't know which of them was Stella, so don't go matching the author of this note with the one with the scars on her wrists."

"Says she's crazy, and very likely is—have you called her?" said Dr. Kochbaum, taking off her lavender shades to look at me. I had been hoping she would denude her eyes, so I could see if there was any Anna in her eyes, but there was little of Anna there beyond crass physical resemblance, at least in the eye of this beholder. "I would match, Mr. Hanks, the author of this note with the one who loves you, wouldn't you?"

"Not necessarily."

"She is desperate. I suggest that you call her."

"Come on, you're too used to emergencies. I doubt she's all that desperate."

"Mr. Hanks, any woman who will pray nude with you on the first night you've met, then leave you a note saying she must see you again, has *got* to be outstandingly desperate. You may use my phone."

"She didn't pray nude with me, I was alone nude, nude alone in my depot. God, this is getting too . . . that's why I didn't want . . ."

"I don't understand why you haven't already called her. You call yourself a . . ."

"God, woman, I would have—I *intend* to—but it's embarrassing that I don't know which of them she was. I feel like I owe her that much, and I haven't figured out how to figure it out without asking. I have a tin ear for voices, the chainsaw's done that to my hearing, dulled it."

"Apparently that's not all it's dulled," muttered Dr. Kochbaum, writing something on a small pad. She tore off the note and shoved it at me. "Deliver the wood to the alley behind that address, Mr. Hanks. A full cord you owe me now. Nicely seasoned hardwood, neatly stacked, and be sure to tell the doorman when you have finished so that he may relock the gate."

The doorbell rang.

I looked at the note. The address was this address. Queer.

Dr. Kochbaum straightened in her swivel chair, elbows on the arms, her fingertips touching. "First thing that pops into your head, Mr. Hanks: *White.*"

"Coat."

"White."

"Pure."

"White."

"Uh-girl."

"Girl."

"Uh-uh-love."

"Love."

"You-*agggh*—not *you*, Anna.*"
"Delta Eagle."
"Death."
"Death."
"Life."
"Anna."
"Crazy—both of you."
The doorbell rang again.
"Love."
"God."
"Quickly now, tell me: Who *is* the girl in the white coat?"
"My angel, she's an angel of the Lord."
"Who else?"
"My mommy?"
"And?"
"Girl next door."
"And who else?"
"My reflection in a pond?"
"Go on, Mr. Hanks."
"God. Of course she's God."
"Many a truth is spoken in Jest, Mr. . . . ."
"Shakespeare."
"Chaucer. Why don't you call Stella now?"
"The girl in the white coat is Stella," I said.
Silence.
"The girl in the white coat is the bluebird of happiness, Dr. Kochbaum."
"Who is Mary James, Mr. Hanks?"
The doorbell rang again, a long time.
"The bluebird of happiness in the white coat is swinging in my back yard right this very minute, on my swing, if I would but go and swing with her."
"Your time is up, Mr. Hanks," said Dr. Kochbaum, with emphasis, turning the phone around for me.
I dialed the number left to me by whoever Stella was. There was an answer after the first ring, a "Hello," pitched more like

good-bye. I asked to speak to Stella. I was asked if I was Malcolm. I replied that Stella did not know me by name, far as I knew, that we had met last week at a poetry reading. I gave my name, and my name was informed by an unnamed stranger that Stella had passed away in a fall from her apartment window yesterday and the body had been cremated this morning, that he or she was sorry. My name said that it was sorry too, and we hung up.

"She's out," I told the female person with degrees and lavender shades behind a desk I stood sick in front of.

The doorbell started to ring again.

"Out?"

I nodded, closing my eyes. Behind the doorbell's ringing I heard, in that dimension encompassing the darkest darkness and the brightest light, Gabriel's horn ablowing.

"Then she's all right?"

"God knows."

The doorbell was still ringing.

Dr. Kochbaum reached under her desk and at once my phone conversation replayed from under there for both our ears with the doorbell ringing. Dr. Kochbaum got up and did some rearranging on her desk—a gesture of termination. The doorbell kept on ringing.

"That's all, Mr. Hanks. That's it. We are finished. I cannot help you. Go find her, or whatever it was on that train that is dragging you and God knows how many other poor Stellas down the drain. I mean *really* look for her. Actually. Go. Bye now, and . . . she glanced desperately at the door, the bell of which was still ringing. "Please go now, Sir. I have a patient ringing."

I lunged for the door and yanked it open. The bell ringer's finger stayed hard upon the button. His lips were in an asshole pucker. His nostrils flared at me. His finger, bent back almost double, stayed hard and fast upon the button. The bell was ringing, ringing, ringing. I put the heel of my hand on the fellow's button finger and mashed the whole works clean through the switch which fetched us both a stimulating jolt. The bell ringer shrieked and sucked his finger, spit on my fly, stomped my foot. I grabbed a handful of his hair and jerked his head down to wipe the spit off my fly, but he butted me in the fly, bowled me over one of the big ashtrays, breaking it. The bell ringer dumped a rack full of dirty magazines on me while I was down, and tried to escape into Dr. Kochbaum's office, but I caught him in the middle of the deep dark carpet and fetched him a real swift kick in the ass. He was a big, slope-shouldered fellow looking for himself in the good orifices of Anna Karenina Kochbaum. My kick was disproportionate to his crime, but in harmony with my need for justice at the expense of it; it was a real hard kick in the ass; it almost left my shoe in it; it raised him to his toes and he was launched headlong in a stagger; he landed in a toddler's sprawl across the neat little desk in the corner, scattering papers, pens, clips and notes, appointment book and calendar, glass banana paperweight, and startled Occupant. The bell ringer rolled off the desk and stalked me flat-footed in a spluttering rage, shucking his coat and tie, as did I, and we squared off for Fist City.

The doctor stepped between us with a big shiny pistol pointed at my feet.

"Mr. Hanks, I don't fire warning shots. The first one goes through your foot."

I SPENT most of the night in the depot, telling myself that it was just another day, and wondering who Stella had been. I tried to write, tried to pray, but I just sat dumbly in my depot, waiting, lying to myself that any day is just another day. I tried not to think, tried to pray, and nothing came of it but tears.

6

I WAS awakened at dawn by a crowing rooster. I got up and fried two eggs. The rooster was still crowing. Deed holder of a squash court in the country where raccoons were my alarm, where I had no chickens; I had to rent an apartment in a New York City slum to get crowbarred from my dreams by that announcer of new days and an old betrayal. The cock was still crowing when I left my dirty dishes in the sink and went down to load my truck with Dr. Kochbaum's fee, forgetting that I had left my truck on Long Island. I came back up and dialed the Mother Truckers who operate out of Greenwich Village. The Mother Truckers hadn't opened yet. I sat in the depot with a fresh page cranked into the machine, seeing white, scar white. The rooster crowed. He was a fighting game cock who lived in a box on the fire escape on the building across the airshaft from my kitchen window. His master was a Puerto Rican bodega operator who operated an illegal cockpit beneath his bodega. I could see the crowing cock popping and hissing on a spit in an open fire, then in a bubbling pot of rice and onions and cheap red wine. I commenced to type:

> Dr. Kochbaum had been a voice in a hank of black hair done in a bun, thick rimmed shades and a moss-green pants suit on my first visit. Now she answers the bell high-heeled, miniskirted, too tightly bloused, hair down to her shoulders, rhinestoned shades of a chocolate hue. Looking kind of tacky. Pointing to the couch she asked if I'd brought the poem. I am without

direction, open to suggestion, for up to a fortnight behind a breakup. I . . .

Went down to my woodyard and woke up my Bowery bum. Gave him five dollars and asked what his name was. Said it was Ed. I said Ed I'm going to the woods and won't be back until spring so after I haul out what I need of this wood to pay a debt the rest is yours to sell. Ed shrugged and gave me some advice. I went back up and called the Mother Truckers again. Move a cord of cedar? First time for everything. Said they'd be over in an hour. I spent that hour writing the following:

> Sometimes I lose the thread. Sometimes I lose the direction four decades have not dictated so much as demanded, not demanded so much as directed, not directed so much as doomed. If I didn't lose the direction, the thread now and then, the doom, I wouldn't be free, would I?

Then I Xed out the above and filed it.

The Mother Truckers buzzed. They were two, one of whom looked like she would make a good all-round hand in the woods. After they had loaded a cord on their truck and got my directions, I asked what I owed and they asked what I got for the cedar. The Mother Truckers had gone apeshit over the pretty, sweet-smelling cedar and wanted some. We decided that the rest of the cedar in the alley would square us, and they loaded it on, all of it, including my Bowery bum's log cabin. Ed. When the Mother Truckers were gone, I wondered why I had let them take every last stick including Ed's little cabin. I guessed it was because Ed was an ingrate and I didn't like him. I give him a good gift of a five dollar bill and over a hundred and fifty dollars worth of wood and he gives me not one word of thanks; he gives me advice. What was Ed's advice?

Who knows? Who cares? Who remembers advice? It was probably good advice. What else does a bum have to give you but advice? Thanks are cheap. Advice at least takes a little thought. Ed must have had a little pride. I went looking for him. I had given him the wood and ought to pay him something for it. I walked the length of the Bowery and back, going in and out of bars and flophouses, but couldn't find him. I hung around the alley until afternoon, but he never came back. How long do you wait around for a Bowery bum? He must have gone so far on that five dollars I gave him that he couldn't make it back. So whose fault is that?

I was all set to leave a second or third time, and the harpsichord got in my eye. Should have had the Mother Truckers take it too, but then I had not given it to Dr. Kochbaum. The harpsichord was Anna's. I wrote a letter to my parents:

Dear Mom and Dad,
Got to thinking the other day about one night back during the war (WW II) when we were returning from McGehee or somewhere and had to stop for the train where it crosses State Road 4 just around that bad curve where Hamilton Pike got killed. We had the blue '41 Chevy. Seems the moon was full that night and Dad had already stopped once, just before Pike's curve, and made us all get out and look at the moon. He had been drinking. We almost hit the train—but that may have been another night. It's just one of those funny things that sticks with you, and I wondered if either of youall remembered it. Especially when the train went by, the lighted windows. People in the windows as the train sped by. Either of youall remember any particular people in the windows? I remember a girl in a white coat. Did you notice her? Not that it's all that important. Just a bug in my britches. I'd just like to know what night it happened.
Well, I'm off for the woods this afternoon, plan to stay

there until spring. Got your birthday letter, Mom, and would have answered sooner but I lost my hand in a chainsaw rebellion and the new one has only now grown out enough to hold a pen. Love to both of you,

Bud

I mailed that and walked over to Hannah's Catacomb Coffee House. It was empty save for Hannah and a fat girl with hairy arms in a corner with a paperback. Hannah did not know a Stella, nor recall who had followed me out at intermission, if anybody. She had never heard of a magazine called *Gabriel's Horn*. No *Gabriel's Horn* was listed in the phone book. I strolled back toward my block. At Second Avenue and Fourth I had the green and started across. Stopped for the red on the east side of Second with its left signal blinking was a moss-green Dodge van with Dr. Kochbaum in the cockpit. If we recognized each other we gave no sign, except that I may have quickened my pace when crossing in front of her van.

I waited in a doorway across the street from my building while the van was expertly jockeyed into a parking space that left just room enough for ghosts to squeeze through at either end. The driver took off her shades, brushed out her hair, and so forth with the rest of the ritual performed by female people before springing themselves upon you. When Anna got out of the van I crossed over and stood behind her. I let her ring a second time, and said, "He's not home."

"Oh Hank," with a gleam of even white teeth just visible in her smile, her smile a dewy rose, her breath sweet as one. I sucked wind and looked away. "Or would you rather *Bud?*"

"Your choice," I muttered. "Here for the harpsichord?"

"Thought I'd put it in my country place."

"Over the pump and ice house? The red brick one with a slate roof and raccoons on Short Beach Road, only one of its kind on the planet?"

"Uh-huh."

I unlocked the door and she followed me up. We stood by the harpsichord.

"Well, here it is. Waiting for you. Like a glass of Vichy water? Or some cold duck? Lots of cold duck in the fridge."

"Thanks, but I have to go."

I took the keyboard end of the harpsichord, she took the back, and we toted it down the stairs, shoved it in the van. I guyed it with sash cord. There were the parts of a windmill boxed in the van.

"Thanks again for the harpsichord," said Anna, sliding behind the wheel.

"You're welcome."

"Going out this weekend?"

"Yeah, until next spring."

"Don't blame you. Well, gotta roll."

"I'm taking the train."

"Oh, you don't have your truck in town? Wanna ride?"

WE TOOK the upper roadway of the Queensboro Bridge, our short cut, and the middle lane of the L.I.E. Traffic was heavy to absolutely intolerable.

"Got a letter off to my parents today," I said.

"Oh?"

"Asked them if they remembered the night we stopped for the train, when the moon was full, and the girl in the white coat came by. On the train," a shrug in my voice. "Start somewhere looking for her."

"You're really going to look for her?"

"Hard to say."

"How can your parents help?"

"Pinpoint the night, maybe. All I remember is I was twelve, we were in World War Two, and that it *might* have been the night we saw *The Bluebird* at the Ritz in McGehee—funny, I just remembered that. I believe it was the . . . naw, *Mrs. Miniver* was the movie we saw that night. I *think* . . . it was very sad, we all cried, all but my father. It was either that or *The Blue-bird.*"

"Anyway the moon was full," said Anna.

"Uh-huh."

Traffic came to a halt. I went on, "Know what? I was just thinking, I probably don't actually remember that girl in a white coat. I only remember the memory. Lots of my earliest memories are of memories, I'm positive of it."

We moved an inch, halted, inched, halted, crept. Three lanes of cars in front and three behind, far as the eye could see. It was 6:00 P.M., a time for masochists to be en route to Long Island on the last warm and sunny Friday of the year. Anna turned the radio on. It was tuned to WLIX which broadcasts oldies and the Gospel. A running nostalgia kick. Fats Domino was singing "Blueberry Hill." Anna sang along with him. I hummed. During a commercial for WLIX bumper stickers I said, "Traffic gets any slower it won't be traffic. Be a parking lot." Anna said, "World's longest." I said, "Quickest way to travel at this hour is to sell your car to the guy behind you and buy the one from the guy in front of you, all the way home." Anna laughed and I relaxed a little. I said, "Ever see the analogy of highways to the blood-stream?" She said, "Uh-huh." "The Island's suffering a stroke," I persisted. She went, "Uh-huh," again. "Not the best analogy," I guessed.

The Platters came on with "The Great Pretender." O-o-o yes, I'm the great pre-e-tender, a-drift in a world not my own. I played the game, but to my re-e-al shame, you left me to dream all alone, and now I'm wearing my heart like a crown, pretending that you're still around, something like that. Too real is this fe-eling of make be-lieve, something about what my heart can't con-ce-e-e-e-eive, o-o-o yes, I-I'm the great pre-e-e- . . .

"Good tune, dumb lyrics," said Anna.

"Oh I don't know, if you don't listen too closely, enough of the lyrics get through to give me a haunting, melancholy message. Agree though, good tune. One of my favorites."

Next came "Blue Tango" and we fell silent. "Canadian Sunset," "Red Sails in the Sunset," and Johnny Ray sang "Cry." WLIX went off the air. It didn't go off on the "Star-spangled Banner." It spun us a neo-rococo arrangement of "America the Beautiful," sporting a full orchestra with thousand-voiced choir and a rainbow-sized pipe organ with fifty million pipes and all the stops made use of and then all pulled out for the finale that scoured a kitchen sink whiter than white. Anna let a few seconds of off-station static clear the air, then switched to a Benjamin Britten symphony I never heard and that scored the rest of our trip to Smithtown.

"Let's go to your place first and I'll help unload the harpsichord," I said.

"Thanks, but a friend who is waiting will help."

" 'Who,' " I muttered.

"My friend."

"Wasn't prying, just repeating. Most people would say, 'I have a friend waiting and *he* or *she* will help,' that's all."

Anna laughed. When she pulled up at my squash court, that laugh was still in my head since not a word from either of us had followed to flush it. I got out of the van and looked back in.

"Vots mit der vindmill?"

"It's a secret."

"Set it up and I'll bring over my lance and shield and work out."

Anna nodded, smiling, easing the van away. "Luck with your search," she said.

I shouted after her, "Did Dr. Kochbaum get her load of wood?"

"She's annoyed that the pieces are too big, and you didn't stack it," Anna yelled back.

"Good," I shouted.

I WASHED a cheese sandwich down with Rainwater and crapped out around nine thirty. The sound of rock woke me up. I slipped on my pants and shirt and walked up to the big house, stopping just short of the veranda, in the shadow of the biggest white oak on Long Island. A man was pissing on it. The big house was lit up like a cruise ship. Mary James was having a party. A jukebox had been trucked in and dollied onto the veranda. Two or three people were dancing and two or three were watching them; two or three slouched in aluminum and plastic lawn chairs, two or three lay in the high grass just off the veranda, sucking weed. Two or three were fingerfucking off in the shadows up on the bluff with that grand view. Pot and tobacco smoke lay stratified in the yellow-lit unseasonable warmth of a humid last night of summer. Eight or a dozen mosquitoes were having a party. A bubblegum rock side ended on the jukebox and began again. In the brief blessed interval of its silence, shouts and laughter and the din of breakage emanated from the big house. The Social-Registered founding family raised eyebrows in their graves. An unregistered party was having the Jameses.

A girl in a white coat stepped from the drawing room onto the veranda, and the memory of the memory was subsumed in pure memory. I heard the big diesel, felt its thunder, smelt the burning fuel, got with the steel of it whipping by in the night, knew the loneliness of a boy looming toward manhood in the back seat of a '41 Chevy in a war year, and then the sight of her in the lighted window carving out a need in me in that one glimpse, and then she was gone. Oh, the silence behind her vanishing, the emptiness.

The man pissing on the tree said, "Some fukkin' party."

"Who's that girl in the white coat?" I said.

"How the fuck'd I know? Some fukkin' broad. Some fukkin' house, huh?"

I grunted. The fellow kept on pissing on the tree. The girl in the white coat took a step off the veranda in our direction. I couldn't see her face clearly, or didn't. But it lit a memory.

Mary James and I one night, walking home from the picture show together, passing the house of the widow who owned the liquor store. A loud party was going on in there. We slipped into the yard to peek in on the party, and almost stepped on two half-naked grownups in the grass behind a privet hedge. One of the grownups was on top of the other one, moving up and down real fast. We fled. Not long after that we took off all our clothes in the hayloft and fled again. Not long after that the Jameses moved.

"Some fukkin' tree," said the pissing man. "Nuff board feet in this fukkin' tree to floor every fukkin' house between here and the fukkin' Sunrise Highway."

The girl in the white coat took another hesitant step and called out, "Lonnie?"

"Is that Mary James?" I asked the pissing man. She was about the size of Mary James. Girl-sized.

"Who the fuk's Mary James?"

"Mary James is your hostess, Fuck Head."

"Lonnie?"

The man grunted. The girl in the white coat moved closer. She wasn't Mary James. She was much younger.

"Aw *that* fukkin' skinny broad, naw I dunno her."

"Lonnie?"

"Hah? Yeah, c'mere, I've gotcher *lonnie* hangin'," went the pissing man.

"Not you, Asshole-Creep, *him.* "

"I'm not Lonnie either," I said. "Who are you?"

She gave a wave of dismissal as she turned and disappeared. I returned to the squash court, put on some shoes, and drove into Stony Brook. The liquor store was closed. I went to a bar and ordered a beer mug full of bourbon, which came to twelve dollars measured out in shot glasses. I ordered a mug of beer to give it chase. I got drunk infrequently, irregularly, deliberately. Some citizens moved closer to watch me make a fool or corpse of myself. I quaffed the bourbon, put out the fire with the beer, told them, "Jesus saves," and went back to my truck.

Drove to Nissequogue and parked at the overflowing fountain. Got out and vomited. Washed and gargled at the fountain, took a long cool drink from it, and went over the wall. Stood in the weeds before the brick building with slate roof, dark and empty. Listened to the automatic pump go on and off at one minute intervals. It was a cloudy night, dark. It was dark as the inside of a rubber boot on a nigger's foot buried in a swamp in Arkansas, midnight 1931. Where was Anna, who was she, and why? How come she to lie? I looked up, into a black canopy of treetops that blotted out the sky. I heard a harpsichord. From up there in the dark somewhere, Bach's Concerto in D Minor for Three Harpsichords. A fukkin' harpsichord playing up there in the darkness darker than the devil's heart. I slid down the bank and went home.

The big house was still lit up, but quiet. A girl in a white coat was sitting on the fountain which is in a sunken garden midway between the squash court and the big house. The sunken garden was taken now by weeds and beach peas, a few sickly little cedars and a small growing stand of locust saplings. It would have been amusing to turn the fountain on, but it had never worked for the Jameses. I parked my truck at the squash court and walked back up to the fountain.

"Find Lonnie?" I said.

"Lonnie?"

Odd, two identical girls in identical white coats at the same sad little party on a warm night.

"Is this some occult thing, sitting on a fountain at two A.M. in a white coat?"

"It's the first day of fall," she said.

I said, "It started out the last night of summer. Where'd you get that coat?"

"Found it in the house."

"Looks kind of heavy for the weather."

"It's all I've got on. Somebody wet me."

"One in every party. Seems quiet up there now, though."

"Yah, somebody called the police."

"That's nice. Well, I'm going to have some buttered toast and milk before beddy-bye. Want some?"

We sat at the kitchen table making toast, buttering and jamming it, washing it down with milk fast as the toaster humming hot between us could pop it. The girl cast sporadic, unselfconscious glances at my unfinished restoration project while we ate. "Funny house," she muttered more than once. She had long, blondish hair, brown eyes, a slender oval face. Not especially pretty, just very young. I asked how old she was. "Old enough to miss a period."

Ten-thirty San Quentin Quail, we used to call her. Takes ten minutes to get in, thirty years to get out of San Quentin. Abridged version: Fifteen'll getcha twenty. When the loaf of bread and jug of milk were finished we got up and stood at the rail. There was my mattress down there on the floor. Also a big worktable loaded with things to work and things to work with, a stereo, record cabinet, books in their cases, a black walnut dining table for Occasions, chairs, a couch, the usual stuff one gathers—plus empty spaces where one has not gathered. Like the absence of a potty chair, for instance, a teddy bear, the absence of a stack of *Better Homes & Gardens,* or the *Journal, Ms.* even. Those empty spaces also make up the furnishings of a house not yet a home. It was all arranged, all my furnishings and empty spaces, in maze formation leading inevitably and without a lot of complication to that mattress on the floor. The only way out. Ye olde in & out. I had never noticed that before. How many had there been, how many female people? Not that many really, about as many as I had fingers, toes, not many more, not a lot for a healthy man fresh on the epitaph side of forty. The girl was looking at the mattress too. The white coat was too big for her. The cuffs hid all but her fingertips and the hem hung way below her knees. Too big, too big for the both of us.

"What's your name?"

"Marsha."

"Bud Hanks."

"Hi."

I looked at my watch. It was after three. "Tell you what, Marsha, before I take you home . . . " I paused to let her say something like, "Let's not plan it, let's just see what happens," or, "You'll have to pull out because I didn't bring my diaphragm," or, "Sorry, but it's my period," or, some joke about it, but the girl's face was absolutely naked. A *tabula rasa.* I concluded, "Let's pray together."

"Christ, I never got asked to *pray* with a guy before."

"Nothing to it, it's one of the oldest kinks. We just get on our knees, bow our heads, and close our eyes. The conventional position. Then we say . . . "

"You're kidding me, aren't you? Well I don't like jokes about religion."

"In that drawer over there on the left is a very sharp butcher knife. If at any time while we're praying you think I'm joking, you have my permission to get that knife and cut off whatever you think will remove the joke."

We got on our knees at the rail. I told her she must be religious since she didn't like jokes about religion. She said she didn't like jokes about sex either, and she was a virgin. I guessed that meant she wasn't religious. She asked me how to pray. I said to repeat after me the Lord's Prayer, which was the one Jesus composed to teach his disciples to pray, not that I'm forging an analogy here. I told Marsha that after we said the Lord's Prayer out loud we could just pray on silently as long as the Spirit moved us. A good while after we had finished the Lord's Prayer Marsha got up. I listened to her descent of the steps; intuited her retirement on my mattress. I kept on praying. No I did not. I asked myself did I realize that I had stayed on my knees this long so she would get on my mattress without my having to further finagle her onto it. I opened my eyes and peered over the rail. She was covered. The white coat was not in evidence. She was sleeping in the white coat which was all she had on. I turned out the kitchen light and groped down the steps, passed the mattress, and fell onto the couch

where I groped on into sleep. I don't recall my dreams, but the
movie version will.

I awoke to a knock on the door. Anna. The sun was over the
woods behind her. It must have been after ten.

"I brought you something," Anna said, looking past me at
the mattress. At the thin but definable lump with a mess of
blondish hair fanned out on the mattress.

"Girl I put up for the night."

"It's in the van," said Anna, turning.

"She's got on a white coat, funny huh?" following Anna to
the van. She opened the side doors. There were the boxed
windmill parts. She opened the rear doors. There was a fully
assembled cordwood saw, complete with flywheel, pulleys,
and a belt, old but in mint condition and ready to buzz but for
a power unit. "A windmill-powered cordwood saw," I said,
reverently.

Anna pointed. "Down in the valley where they grow tall to
get the light you cut three young locusts for a tripod tower."
Looking another way, she pointed, "That rise would be the
best place to set it up." She took a folded piece of paper from
her shirt pocket and stuffed it in the box containing the vanes.
"The directions for assembly, but consider them suggestions,"
said Anna, hefting the box of vanes out of the van.

"I'm really touched," I said. "Oh, uh, *I* slept on the *couch.*"

"You can help get the saw out, it's quite heavy," Anna said,
dragging out the box of gears.

A girl in a white coat appeared in the doorway of the squash
court. Nobody spoke. She looked at Anna and Anna looked at
her. I looked at my feet. My feet said, "Don't look at *us.*" Anna
and I slid the cordwood saw out the van's back, until it tipped
to the ground. Anna got in the van, started the motor, and
drove out from under it. The saw went *blump* on the grassy
ground; I felt it in my feet. I went to shut the van's back doors
and to thank Anna profusely, invite her in, introduce her to
. . . but Kochbaum kept on truckin'. She spun out a fast U and
sped back up the lawn with wheels aspinning; swerved onto

the rear drive of the big house and sped away, gone, those back doors flapping open and shut like hands fanning away a fart.

"Come on, I'll take you home," I said to Marsha.

"That's okay, I'm staying up there for the weekend."

"Oh? You a friend of Mary James?"

"She's my father's girl friend."

I nodded, glancing up at the big house. "Where's your mother?"

Marsha shrugged.

"Well," I said, looking around, "I've got traps to run."

"What kind of traps?"

"That's an old Arkansas expression for I've got things to do."

"Like I've got a cake in the oven?"

"Something like that. Well."

"Need some help?"

I shrugged.

We got in my old woods pickup and drove down into the valley where the trees grow tall to get the light. Marsha stayed in the cab while I zapped off three strong young yellow locusts. They were about ten inches base diameter, shooting up to almost sixty feet. I trimmed their limbs off, peeled the bark, chained them to the trailer hitch, and snaked them up to the rise. Marsha wasn't much help. It was noon by then, and we hadn't eaten.

"Go fix us some breakfast, okay? While I dig holes for these poles."

"What's this gonna be?"

"See if you can guess as it goes up." I took her arm and we walked down to the squash court. Marsha went in to fix the food and I got a posthole digger from the cellar, Anna's instructions from the vane box, and went back up the rise. I cut the two longer poles to the shortest one's length. I scratched an equilateral triangle on the rise and dug a hole at each point; walked in the locust poles. I pushed each pole inward until their ends met at the top, then filled in the dirt at their base and tamped it with my feet. Two people were strolling down from the big house, a man and a woman. A girl in a white coat came out of the squash court and hollered, *"Breakfast!"* The woman coming down was Mary James. I went in, washed my hands, and sat down to breakfast with Marsha.

"Your father tall and skinny?" She nodded. "That must be him, then, coming down with Mary James." Marsha shrugged. She had whipped up a big bowl of scrambled eggs. We had eaten all the bread before going to beds, but she had found a box of crackers. "Do you say grace before meals?" Marsha asked.

"Want to say grace?"

There was a knock on the door.

"I remember a prayer from when I was little," said Marsha, bowing her head. "My baby sitter taught it to me." I bowed my head. There was another knock. Marsha said her little baby sitter's prayer. The door opened before she finished it, but she finished it, and I looked up at our guests with a hearty, "Amen!"

My ex-wife and Marsha's father, a Mutt-and-Jeff-looking couple in the doorway. A dog stood behind them. Mary James looked from us to the mattress on the floor and hipped her hands. Marsha's father glanced about at my digs with an eye for structural detail. Looking for the best beam from which to string me, I guessed. The dog, grown impatient, pushed through their legs and trotted up the steps to where we sat. He wagged his tail. Marsha poured our coffee and ladeled herself a plateful of scrambled eggs. I dipped myself a plateful and scooped some into a saucer for the dog. Marsha had scrambled almost a dozen eggs. There was plenty for the three of us. They were pretty fair scrambled eggs, a shade dry and too salty for my taste. The dog loved them. He was my dog. That is to say, he came with the place, a stray. I called him Joe, because he looked like one. I sweetened my coffee and took a sip.

"Well?" said Mary James.

"Look, let's come back later, they're eating," said Marsha's father.

"Don't let that cool act of his fool you, his ass is chewing buttonholes in that chair," my ex-wife said.

"Your father seems nice," I told Marsha.

"He's okay," she said.

Joe asked for more eggs. I gave him the rest of them, plus a handful of crackers. I said to Marsha, "Why don't you introduce us, because it seems Mary James isn't in the mood."

"Oh I'm in the mood, positively in the mood. Lonnie, that's Bud Hanks, my ex-husband, having breakfast with your fifteen-year-old daughter. Wonder where she *slept* last night, don't you?"

I looked at Joe, just finished with his second helping of eggs and looking up for more. It would take a whole hen house to satiate Joe. Dogs are like that. All appetite. And yet Joe could go for weeks on his own with me in New York City. How did he manage? I don't know. Maybe dogs aren't all appetite. I said, "Joe, you're just a dog, you know. Come to terms with that fact and you'll be a man." Joe turned around and walked right out, before my homily could tempt him. One could say he fled.

"You used to be married to Mary James?" said Marsha, a forkful of eggs about to pop into her pink rosebud mouth.

I swallowed a bite whole and said, "That *was* you last night calling a Lonnie."

Marsha went on eating.

"You remember. I was under the big tree. Another guy was urinating on it. You called . . . "

I gave up. She wasn't going to answer me, I could see that. She went on eating, dribbling scrambled egg on the white coat. I let her get away with it. Let people have their little mysteries. Leave them that. I went on eating. Then Marsha said, "I don't call my father anything but Daddy."

I said, "I wasn't going to suggest that if that girl in a white coat wasn't you that the Lonnie she was looking for was your father, since your father, obviously, has a girl friend. Guess there was another Lonnie at the little party, and another girl in a white coat who could have been your twin."

"What *is* this?" said Mary James.

"Shit, Daddy has lots of girl friends," said Marsha.

"That's okay. That's liberal. That's modern. That's fair. That's warfare. I have a squash court and a dog. You are fifteen, have a hymen, and ripped off a white coat last night. Mary James has lots of boy friends, too. Service it."

"Listen to them. Don't listen to them. See what they're trying to do?" Mary James told Alonzo.

"Why don't we go now, take that boat ride," said Marsha's father.

"Go? Boat ride? Don't you want an expla*nation?* Personally I think this is absolutely intolerable."

"When I'm ready for an explanation I'll ask for it," said Lonnie.

I got up and said, "Good breakfast, Marsha."

"Just like an old married *couple*. The *nerve!*" said Mary James.

Muttering, "Traps to run," I squeezed past the couple in the doorway and walked up to the rise where the three locust poles hove high. I got in my old woods pickup and backed it down to the cellar door.

"And another thing, Bud Hanks, what's that you're making up on that hill, a *derrick?*" Mary James demanded, with proprietary indignation, and it my hill. "Three crosses," I reply, opening the cellar door. "Hear him blastphim [*sic*], and he used to be a preacher, some goddamn hypocrite preacher," I hear my childhood sweetheart tell the world. I gathered up an armload of scrap lumber and loaded it on the pickup, went back for more and loaded that. I got a good load on, and got back in the truck.

"Want me to close the cellar door?" hollered Marsha.

> O no no doncha climb up the apple tree
> With anyone else but me,
>> Anyone else but me,
>> Anyone else but me,
> O no no doncha slide down the cellar door
> With anyone else but me,
>> Till I come mar-ching hoooome . . .

I hear. Mary James would remember it from our childhood days. Anna would know it too, from WLIX. Anna would know who the authority was who proclaimed *cellardoor* the most beautiful sound in the English language. Or is it *celladore?* The next poem I write will have a *sellador* in it. It will be spelled in all possible ways throughout the poem, and that will pose a challenge to the film director.

I popped the clutch and spun off up the rise in the soft turf. A girl in a white coat chased me in the rearview mirror. The white coat flapped about her thin calves. The girl in the white coat on the Delta Eagle had no calves. Up on the rise I got out and commenced at once to saw and nail struts to the poles. Marsha stood by, her hands held tentatively in front of her, looking in need of being needed. I told her she could hold the can of nails for me. Pretty soon she started handing me the two by fours. Marsha caught on fast. She suggested that I just nail the two by fours on without measuring them, and then saw off what I didn't need, which turned out to be a workable, time-saving, two-by-four-wasting idea. As the struts rose and I had to climb them, Marsha kept a supply of raw materials ready at my feet. I began to feel fatherly toward her; I began to feel more. Mary James and Lonnie remained framed in the doorway of the squash court. Lonnie was watching the growing tower. He nodded absently, and only occasionally, as Mary James harangued him with much gesturing of hand and foot. Poor Lonnie. Whatever he suspected had happened between Marsha and me during the night he had come to terms with, with a show of grace. The worst we could have done, he no doubt thought, was to have fucked, and in this day and age that was to be expected. He might have allowed himself a little show of outrage, for old values' sake, but not *jealousy* . . . but this was something else, and poor Lonnie was eaten up, watching me doing something with his little girl that he could and should have done with her—building something. And Mary James down there in that doorway, from this distance, looked as young as Marsha—a lot like her, in fact, a lot like my old childhood sweetheart.

When we finished with the struts and got the platform nailed down and braced, Marsha and I sat cross-legged on it and congratulated ourselves on the tower we had built. We shook hands. In the heat of labor Marsha had undone all but the middle button of the white coat, and now it was open here and there, revealing a bit of tit and hair. She seemed completely unaware, or didn't care. Catering to new values, over my protests, the film will make us fuck at this point. We will make it as symbol-ridden as possible, however. Marsha will shuck the white coat without fanfare and fling it at her father and my ex-wife. It will flutter down on them in slow motion like a shotgunned snowgoose, and Marsha and I will make sweet passionate grainy-filmed love up there on our windmill Babel altar under God and over everybody, quick fadeout.

"I guess you know, Bud Hanks, you've done violated the zoning laws, you can't stick up something like that in *this* neighborhood," hollered Mary James.

"This is a sixty-acre estate in Head of the Harbor and she calls it a neighborhood," I confided to Marsha, who didn't understand. I hollered back, "Mooka hokem hocha yakka dickie loco printems," but nobody got that either. Anna would have.

"You think you can do anything you want to, do it to fifteen-year-old girls and drill for oil in the middle of Head of the Harbor without a license, well we'll just see, Bud Hanks," bellowed Mary James.

"*Tais-toi, s'il vous plaît!*" I shouted at her.

"Kiss my ass you fucking idiot!" she screamed back, *"I'm gonna call the po-lice!"*

You can take the person out of the country, but you can't take the country out of the person.

"She's still in love with you," observed Marsha, not trying to be funny, nor wise even, just seeing something that female people think they see.

When the law arrived Marsha had climbed down and gone up to the big house to see if her clothes were dry. Her father had climbed up the tower for a chat. He looked to be a few years younger than I. He thought the windmill-powered cord-wood saw a way-out idea. Said he'd always wanted to make things like this but was always too busy. He was in real estate, as I recall. Said he made a good buck. I told him, case he was interested, that the only time I had touched his daughter was when we shook hands up there in front of God and everybody, that I had given her the bed and slept on the couch. He said, "Did I ask you?" I said, "If I was you, I would." He said, "Would you tell me if you had balled her?" I said, "That's more information than you've got coming, Dad." He said, "If I thought you had balled her, I'd knock you off this tower." I said, "That's the spirit." We were discussing the cordwood business when Head of the Harbor's black-and-white patrol car pulled up. Mary James had stopped it up at the big house and got in. When it stopped at the base of the tower, she piled out like a deputy. The police officer, an elderly white-haired gentleman who has since retired, got out and looked up at me, squinting in the sun. He said, "Hey Hank, what's this thing?"

"'Lo, Hopalong. So far this here is three locust poles strutted together with a platform on top."

"Sure is what it looks like, Hank," said Officer Cassidy. "Miss James here says it's an oil rig you put up here. Ain't no oil on Long Island, is there?"

"Well now she's the daughter of Jesse James, Hopalong, so I reckon you better take anything she says with a big dose of salts."

"Awww *you* . . ." splutters the daughter of Jesse James. Good thing for me she wasn't Annie Oakley about then.

"Fact is, it's gonna be a windmill connected to a cordwood saw," I went on.

"Don't say," said Hopalong Cassidy, "Well a windmill cordwood saw, that's between you and the zoning people, Hank. Miz James here also mentioned an underaged girl staying over at your place."

"Don't say," I said. "That Mary James, she sure likes to keep people half-informed. Have to take her over to the *Three Village Herald* one of these days, get her a cub reporting job. Yep, this young girl was down here last night for some toast and milk, oh about two in the morning, I guess. Then we said our prayers together and I give her a bunk, and I took a bunk. This here is her daddy up here with me on this tower. Name of Lonnie —what's the last name, Lonnie?" "Greer," said Lonnie. "Lonnie Greer, Officer Cassidy down there. We call him Hopalong, I don't know why. Name's shrouded in mystery and he aims to keep it thataway."

Officer Cassidy saluted, Lonnie Greer waved. Then Hopalong looked at the daughter of Jesse James and shrugged. It was plain she had no case against ol' Hank. Mary James she spun around in a huff and hightailed it back up to the big house. Ol' Hopalong he saluted again, got on his mount, and rode off into the sunrise, grin on his face big as the crescent moon.

7

SUNDOWN. The windmill is bolted to its platform, the bevel gear meshed with the drive-shaft bevel, the drive shaft connected to the pulley gear on the flywheel shaft, the belt connected to that pulley, and the pulley on the saw shaft. I'm waiting for the breath of the Lord. It was dead calm.

Marsha knocked while I was eating supper. At first I didn't recognize her in a striped sweater and jeans, without the white coat. I invited her in to potluck but she was going out to dinner with her father and Mary James. What she wanted was to come down after they got back from dinner and maybe a movie. I said, "No way."

"Just to pray?"

I gave her a long one-eyed look and said, "But not all night, awright? How long are youall going to be around, anyway? You and your old man."

"We're going back tomorrow afternoon."

"To where?"

"To Babylon."

"Ask your daddy before you come down, okay? Tell him what our activity will be limited to."

Backing out the door, Marsha said, "He'd sooner we screwed."

"Where's that white coat?" I yelled.

"Whoever owned it came back and got it," she yelled back.

I sharpened saw chains, filed axes, read the paper, swept, fooled around outside, came back in, and fooled around. Opened some books to their bookmarks, read some paragraphs, replaced the bookmarks, the books. Picked up the phone book. There are no Kochbaums in the Suffolk directory; an A. K. Kochbaum's number is unpublished, the operator advised. I went out and gave the flywheel on my new Trojan horse a spin, wishing for a wind. Around 11:00 P.M. a car pulled up at the big house and the lights came on through the house, up to the second floor. They went out first in the master bedroom. Adultery would be committed tonight in the master bedroom, on the big old fourposter with canopy, that ex-Smith rookery. I went up to the sunken garden and sat on the fountain to wait for Marsha. We'd pray there in the sunken garden, a cool neutral ground with no mattresses around. Half an hour passed. I guessed her daddy had taken a stand, slid off the fountain and went back down, retired. And then there was a knock. I stage yawned and the door opened.

She was briefly silhouetted in the deep blue of midnight before the door closed again.

"Sneaked out, didn't you?"

"*Aeunh*, I just waited until I heard their bedsprings, and then I could have stomped out."

"Thought you were going to ask your father."

"Why rattle his cage when mine's not locked?"

I couldn't see her. The windows in a squash court are twelve feet above floor level, so the balls won't break them. One day I would get around to cutting in some windows at my level.

"Ready to start praying?" Marsha said, sounding a little closer.

"That's what you're here for, isn't it?"

Silence. Then she said, "Let's pray for something tonight, something special, see if it works."

I thought for a moment and said, "Okay, let's pray for wind."

"Are you making a joke?"

"It's dead calm, we haven't got to test my new machine yet."

"Oh, awright."

Silence.

"Are you kneeling?"

"Sometimes I pray lying," I muttered.

"Well I'm kneeling."

Silence.

"Want to start with the Lord's Prayer again?"

I commenced the Lord's Prayer aloud, and she joined in at once. She had memorized it. Must have found a Bible in the big house. When we finished the Lord's Prayer we prayed on in silence, like we had the night before. How quickly rituals are established. I felt silly, praying for wind, even praying silently for it, but we had agreed to pray for it—*to see if it works* —Marsha's words, not mine. I knew it wouldn't work. God doesn't change things, he changes people, Marsha, I will explain in the morning. God will help us to adjust to no wind if we pray for wind. Of course there will eventually be a wind, but in God's own good time. That's what prayer is all about, Marsha, learning to cooperate with the inevitable, to take shit from the cosmos and be thankful for it.

I heard soft mutterings as Marsha prayed, within my reach, and grasp. After a while I fancied I heard her heart beating, but now I realize it must have been my own. The way I generally prayed was to sweep away as much thought as possible and fix on a small point of light back in the boondocks of consciousness. That light is a little flame rising like swamp gas, like foxfire, out of the unconscious. Sometimes it bubbles up a fountain of light and forms images, images of people, places, things, images beautiful and images grotesque; clear sometimes but often through a veil. The foxfire of consciousness rises formless sometimes, a benign chaos. And there are times when it doesn't rise at all, and I slip down through the hole, into unconsciousness. Whatever happens happens, and that has to be God's will, because I give up in honest prayer. I surrender. It's a kind of suicide with built-in resurrection, and it isn't all that easy. Nor always pleasant. The thought must be abandoned, the scheming. You have to be receptive to what happens, knowing that it might be bright handwriting on the wall of consciousness, a message you would not have authored. Honest praying is hard enough to slip into alone, or with someone whose flesh does not get under yours. Try it when there's a strange nubile girl a heartbeat distant in the dark, open, probably, to anything, and you really have to pray.

The foxfire rises like a jet of burning gas and forms her in sharp relief; she creeps toward me on her knees, naked as a jet of burning gas . . . I suppose that sexual intercourse is not inimicable to prayer, that the two acts are fusable in a single act of worship, but such an ecstatic act would constitute a real made-in-heaven marriage which is as rare as perfect peace to my way of thinking. I gave up long before Marsha finished whatever she was doing over there; I rolled over, played Onan quickly, quietly, discreetly, and drifted off to sleep.

I woke up to the roar of the wind and a hum with a high whine just beginning in it. Leaves and twigs streaked across the skylight, the panes were rattling. A gale was blowing up from off the Sound. The high whine in the hum augmented to a metallic shriek, then came the sound of creaking timbers, struts stressing to their limits. I leaped up and ran to the door, out into the storm. I had left the windmill in gear and the gear to the cordwood saw engaged. My gift from Anna was already doing twice the rpms it was built to handle, and God was just beginning to give his answer to our prayers. It was too late to try and brake the thing, too dangerous. The big circular blade had revved to a high whine, severing the wind; the flywheel was starting to spin eccentric on its shaft. The shaft ends of the flywheel and saw turned in babbitt bushings which needed frequent oiling. The oil had burned out and the babbitts were melting down, vaporizing, and then raw steel spinning red hot on steel, the wood housings spewing smoke and orange fire. The wind blew harder, a mere sigh yet of the Almighty, and the earth shook; the sawframe shuddered violently and commenced to dance. It danced a dance to answered prayer.

Thou prayest for wind o man, and wind thou hast received,
Wind and more wind, and wind in overplus.

The belt broke about then, with a cannon's crack, and the shaft ends seized in their sockets and the thing exploded in a spiral of flying splinters and metal shards, blue-green and orange sparks. The flywheel barreled off across the fields and into the woods, the sawblade spun off its frozen shaft, zinged once off the ground, and frisbied in a corkscrew trajectory, topping out an English laurel and burying itself high in the bole of the cedar of Lebanon where it remains to this day, in the Name of our Lord and Savior, Jesus Christ, amen.

Freed of its burden the windmill wound up at once beyond its capacity and commenced to go to pieces. It shimmied and it shook, it sparked and threw a vane, went eccentric on its shaft—*ratatatatatatatatatata* on the platform, splitting that, and threw another vane; the windward pole of the tripod uprooted, twisted, and over she arched, driven by the remaining madly spinning blades to sock into *terra firma* like a kamikaze, bottom ending up, struts aflying everywhere, poles cavorting, falling, pickup sticks—and the wind blew on, harder and harder, amen, Lord I *said* amen: Amen again. *Amen!*

I spun, looking for Marsha, around and around. Ran back in and yelled for her, tripping switches, but the lights were out, the lines down. Anyway, she had left, gone back up to the big house and gone to bed. She had missed the miracle. Tomorrow there would be but the evidence of it. But then Marsha didn't need miracles, nor the evidence of one, which is never quite enough to be conclusive, unless one believes in miracles enough to pray for one, with no questions asked, and with no ready answers just in case.

ABOUT MID-MORNING I drove to Nissequogue. It was a dark and rainy day. Where Short Beach Road crests the last hill before descending to the river I turned right onto a white graveled private road which runs through the hilltop estate of the widow lady who owns the brick pump and ice house. Her private road goes on by her salmon-colored mansion, veering right after a hundred yards and proceding down that much farther to a bluff right over the Sound. Where the white-graveled road veers right, a narrower, macadam road continues straight ahead for a ways, trailing off into a two-rut dirt road that ends in a cul-de-sac, from which on a clear day one could see the Nissequogue flowing into the sound were it not for the jungle there. A green Dodge van was parked in the cul-de-sac.

A footpath through the dense foliage wound a short ways down the slope, ending at an outcropping of rock. The path was a muddy little creek in the rain. I climbed the outcropping of rock and peered into the luxuriant gloom, barely making out a patch of the slate roof of the pump house about fifty yards below. Somewhere between the rock I stood on and the pump house there had to be a small cottage, cabin, shack . . . cave?

The rain ran down my collar, a chill up my spine. I *had* heard that harpsichord. I had *not* been all that drunk. I slid off the rock, selected a wieldy branch, and beat a virgin trail down through the brush to the pump house. Beat another virgin trail back up to the rock. I had crossed a couple of animal trails going and coming, the only signs of fauna. I leaned against the cold rock, out of breath, soaking wet, freezing, my clothing torn, my body scratched and bleeding from the thorns and briars of outrageous nature.

I had passed beneath a gigantic tulip tree going down. It was rooted about midway between the pump house and outcropping of rock. It soared a hundred and fifty feet high, at least, and didn't branch below eighty feet. Wild grape and poison ivy vines as thick as the trunks of smaller trees wound around the great tulip and mingled with its branches in a tangled chaos of ivy, grape, and tulip leaves. Plenty of hidden room up there in that tulip tree. But there had been no sign of a ladder, nor where one had been, down at the trunk, and no path to be sure. Once more I scaled the outcropping of rock. It was, from above, but a gentle grade, and at the top of it, it was but another step onto a branch of the tulip tree. The branch, though small this far from the trunk, was surprisingly sturdy. It was sturdy because it was guyed by wild grape vines to higher branches, grape vines that had been tamed, trained by human hands. The branch was sturdy enough to support the gyrations of a pair of agile harpsichord toters. Another trained grapevine trailed conveniently alongside and three to four feet above the branch, all the way to the trunk, a handrail.

I stopped at a narrow, doweled ladder hewn from native wood and stained the color of the tulip's trunk. It rose from the branch, just back from the juncture with the trunk, eight feet up to a trapdoor in a deck which completely encircled the trunk. I judged the deck to be at least eighty feet in circumference. It was underpinned by other limbs, struts of log lug bolted to the trunk, and was guyed from above (a detail I learned later) by steel cables. Grape and poison ivy vines twisted in profusion around the base of the deck and over its rail. Even in the dead of winter, when the tree was leafless, one would have to be looking for it with a sharp eye to see this masterpiece of camouflage.

"Only God can make a tree, and only a person can build a house in one," I called out, with trepidation, knowing deep down and dreading it, who would be at home in this cuckoo nest.

The trapdoor cracked up an inch, and in that crack a pair of shaded eyes peered down at me.

"Mr. *Hanks.*"

Pause.

"Well?"

"Anna told me where her place was, so here I am. A woman doesn't tell a man where her place is unless she wants it visited. I'm soaking wet and freezing, to begin a list of woes."

"My office hours are from ten to four, Monday through Friday, at my office in the city, and you are no longer a client of mine. Two good reasons why you have no earthly excuse for being on that limb down there."

"You tell Anna that the girl she saw on my mattress went to sleep there while I was praying, and sleep was all that happened to her unless she had a wet dream. She's my ex-wife's boy friend's daughter. Also, I am grieved to report that the lovely gift Anna gave me, and which I assembled yesterday, was destroyed by an Act of God—the storm—last night. Unthinkingly I had left it in gear. I wish Anna knew me well enough to know that what I have just said inadequately expresses how sorry I am, for I truly appreciated both gift and giver. Good-day, Bitch."

As I slipped and slid back down the wet limb there came the sound of something kind of hollow, resonant, tenderly constructed and fragile to a fault, full of tunes banging out of them, crashing through the branches and smashing on the hillside far below. It sounded just like a harpsichord gone to hell. I sneezed.

Marsha was standing in the wreckage when I got back. She looked at me accusingly. I told her that it had been *her* idea to pray for something special, that I didn't want to discuss it, and I went on inside. She followed. "We didn't even get to try it," she said, about to cry. "That's life," I said, suddenly noticing her.

Marsha had on a blue jumper that hemmed off a ways above her knees, and a long-sleeved cotton blouse of a paler blue. She stood five feet three inches tall in polished saddle oxfords. She had on white knee socks. I hadn't seen saddle oxfords since way before Marsha was even a gleam in her old man's eye. She must have got them at a yard sale. I hadn't seen a dress on a young girl in a long time, either. Her hair was brushed, and with just the proper inept touch of makeup she was prettier than any little sweetheart a sensible man would pray for.

"Where do you go to church?" said Marsha.

"Well, I don't go regularly."

"I'm sorry, but I've forgotten your name."

"Bud Hanks. Yours is Marsha Greer."

"You haven't called my name since we met," she said.

"Marsha," I said. "Marsha Greer."

"Bud Hanks," she said. "Were you really a preacher like Mary James said?"

"Not like Mary James said, least I tried not to be. When are you and your dad leaving for Babylon?"

"Not until late this afternoon. But you *were* a preacher?"

"I got committed once."

"How long?"

"Couple, three years."

"What kind of church?"

"Baptist."

"I've never been to church in my life," said Marsha.

I looked at my watch. "Well, if we hurry we can just make it to a close one. I'll have to change clothes."

"That's what I came down here for."

Marsha wanted to go to a Baptist church. We went to the one on Smithtown's Edgewood Avenue. It is housed in what had been a private mansion. The people were friendly, the preaching was good Gospel, the singing was spirited, the world of Smithtown Baptist was both down to earth and otherly. I came out with one foot in the past, the other feeling for a good solid metaphor. Marsha loved it. Why hadn't anybody told her about church before, except the usual shit? Church was beautiful, she said. How come I had quit it? I said it had been too pat. She said so was my answer.

"It's difficult, Marsha, very difficult," turning west off Edgewood onto the Jericho Turnpike, "to explain it unpatly."

"Where are we going?" she said.

"I'm running away with you."

"I'll go," she said.

Oh Christ don't tempt me . . . we fell silent. A short while in a motel somewhere west of here might give her time to change her mind, or me mine, perhaps. I drove faster, braked hard in Commack, swerving into Colonel Sanders' Kentucky

Fried. Stiff-legged inside and came out with two boxed dinners and root beer. My destination all along. We ate in the truck. I had turned it around to point east when I parked, so I could relax and digest my chicken.

On the way back to Smithtown, I said, "One reason I quit preaching was, well, all the other things expected of and not expected of a preacher other than preaching. It's sort of like being married. There are parts of married life that are fine, but the rest of it some people just can't cope with."

"What was it you didn't like about being a preacher?"

"Well, the Baptists think a Christian shouldn't drink, smoke, cuss, gamble, or engage in pre- or extra-marital sex; now the average Baptist is pretty lax when it comes to practicing his dos and don'ts, and he'll let his Baptist neighbor get away with a bit of laxity, but they all gang up on the preacher. He's got to be better than everybody else."

"Well, I think preachers *do* have to be better. The best people ought to be preachers, shouldn't they?" said Marsha.

I went "*Aeunh.*"

"Preachers are different, they have to set good examples. They have to do and not do things even if it doesn't make sense to them, if other people are going to think those things are sins. Like Abraham Lincoln said, 'If you can't take the heat, get out of the kitchen.' "

"Harry Truman said that."

"One of the old-time presidents."

We drove awhile in silence. Then I said, "There's a lot of truth in what you said about preachers, Marsha. Guess there are truths one sees clearly as a child, muddies as a youth, forgets as a young adult, and returns to, with great reluctance, in one's forties."

"You're in your forties?"

"Kind of deep."

"My father's thirty-four, but he seems older than you, a lot older," she said, and I loved it. "Hey, if we got married, our children's father would be older than their grandfather."

"Things like that happen," I muttered.

We stopped at a small shopping center on Route 25A and I bought a cassette of Super 8 movie film. Next stop the St. James railroad station where I checked the schedules. I cruised the residential streets of St. James, looking for yard sales. Marsha wanted to know why.

"I want to buy you a white coat."

"I don't need a white coat."

"Humor me."

Three yard sales behind us in half an hour and no white coat. I was about to give it up when Marsha said that she knew where there was a white coat if I had such a kink to get her into one again. It was in a trunk in the attic of the big house. Of course one was. It would be a moth-eaten old ermine left in a steamer trunk with round the world stickers on it in a remote corner of the attic by the Smiths' descendants' executor's movers. But it warn't. It was rabbit. Well-preserved bunny rabbit fur wrapped in cellophane in a cheap unlabeled tin trunk with nothing else inside but a heavy hint of camphor.

"Two or three wonders," I said to Marsha as we took the servants' stairs back down, "Whose coat this is, or was, and why you were poking around in somebody else's attic."

"What else is there to do in a big house like this if you're not getting poked around in?" said Marsha.

"That leaves one or two wonders."

"Who cares?"

We drove to the St. James station and parked. I loaded my movie camera while Marsha tore the cellophane off the white coat. Before she slipped into the coat, I said, "You look real pretty."

"I'm glad you like me."

My mind reran that interchange a couple times—*you look real pretty/I'm glad you like me*—and then I told Marsha that it was a minute until train time. She leaned over with a sudden smile, kissed me, and jumped out of the truck. I drove east the couple of miles to the grade crossing on Mills Pond Road, parked on the shoulder. Marsha's kiss was typical of a fifteen-year-old girl's impulsive kiss. Too wet and too short. It lingers on my mouth yet, fresh as a morning glory, wet as a tear.

Pretty soon the bells began to ring, the red lights flash, and the cross bars came down. Too bad it wasn't a full-mooned night in 1943, me in the back seat of a blue '41 Chevrolet, but one can't have everything. I got out of the truck and sat on the hood with my feet on the bumper, and here she came. The L.I.R.R.'s boxy, filthy, prosaic, characterless old # (illegible), black smoke aspouting; no elegant Delta Eagle nor the progeny of one, this ugly huffing monster. I raised my Super 8 and started shooting. Through the lens and through a glass darkly, dark with rain-streaked soot and dirt, and what looked like a splattered egg, I shot a white coat speeding by. Marsha might have sat by a cleaner window. I drove to the Stony Brook station and picked her up.

Back at my place I got a ball of twine, a rock, and a long rope, and we walked into the woods. When we found the right tree, I tied the twine to the rock and threw the rock over the right limb. Tied the other end of the twine to the rope and with the twine pulled the rope over the limb. I tied the ends of the rope and stuck a short, sturdy branch in the loop over the knot. Marsha sat on the branch and commenced to swing. I filmed her swinging in the white coat in my back woods, until the film was used up. We walked down the steep path to Porpoise Channel. It was ebb tide, the sun was out now, the marsh grass just beginning to turn from deep summer green to autumn gold. There wasn't another soul in sight.

Marsha hopped up on the porch of the beach cottage and peeked in a window. She went *tch-tch*, and beckoned me conspiratorially with one finger crooked and another to her lips. I mounted the porch and peeked in too. Nothing. Marsha jumped, laughing, off the porch, kicking off her saddle oxfords; she ran out across the wet rocks to where a small swift current of Porpoise Channel still ebbed. I never went much for games like this, but I kicked off my shoes, rolled up my pants, and followed her. She stopped wading when the water reached her hemline. I had fancied she would keep on wading, pulling the dress higher and higher as she got deeper and deeper, which is what any director would have directed, unless he was Billy Graham. Marsha stood there in the knee-deep water, which wasn't yet cold enough to turn one blue, snug in the white coat, her arms folded and with a reflective set to her jaw.

"Like clams?" I said, digging my foot into the sandy bottom.

"Fried."

My foot found a bed of clams. I reached down and brought up a pair of cherrystones and one quahog. I let the quahog go to reproduce, and gave Marsha one of the cherrystones. I reached under the water again and brought up a good-sized stone. I cracked my clam on the stone, sipped the juice out of it, and ate the meat. I said, "Ahh," took Marsha's clam, cracked and handed it to her. She held the clam over her tongue and let some juice trickle on it. Her tongue was slender, red, and pointy. It twitched in the clam juice.

"Good?" I said.

"Salty."

"Eat the meat."

Marsha pulled off the cracked half of the bivalve and sniffed the meat. She took a wee nibble.

"You're supposed to gobble it whole."

She scooped the clam from its shell with her teeth, chomped it three times, and gulped. I watched the waves of peristalsis on her throat win after a brief tug of war with her gag reflex.

"Good?" I said.

"Guess it takes some getting used to, like French kissing," she said. I felt around with my foot and brought up two more clams.

"I don't want any more raw clams," said Marsha.

I told her we'd take some home and fry them, handing her the two clams. I stooped again for more. I wondered if she had French-kissed very much, and if she liked to do it, and exactly what she meant by that term. When I was her age it meant sticking your tongues in each other's mouths. I guessed it meant at least that much, and hoped it meant no more. I brought up a double handful of clams. Pretty soon I had found more clams than she could hold in her hands and arms, and she had to hold up the hem of her skirt in both hands to hold the clams, while I kept digging around in the sandy gravelly bottom with both feet and hands, coming up with double handfuls of clams to dump into her skirt. When I was down for clams I could see Marsha's panties. They were pink. In the tight crotch of Marsha's panties I could see the outline of the soft unopened clam in there. Each time I stooped I had to quell the urge to bump it with my nose. Back in the squash court I had Marsha once more hold the clams in her skirt like that while I took some still shots with an empty camera.

A horn honked in the distance and Marsha ran up to the kitchen, dumped the clams in the sink and paper-toweled her skirt. "My father—I have to go," she said, taking off the white coat as she came down from the kitchen. She opened the door, draped the coat over the knob, said "Bye," closed the door and fled.

I sat on a beam of the unfinished upper floor, so as to see out the window, watch Marsha running up to the big house. She wasn't running to her father, she was running away from me, I felt. "Marsha Greer," I muttered, and sat there on the beam awhile after her old man had driven her away. Sat there on that beam until it seemed that the weight of my heart would bring the beam, the whole house down.

8

DEAR SON,

You finally wrote. Good to hear from you. Your Mom is in El Dorado. Your Grandmaw who is ninety-seven is doing poorly. She will be glad to know you wrote. Write your Grandmaw before it's too late.

Business was better this year but expenses were up. They raised our taxes again. The garden was good but it rained too much, busted a lot of tomatoes. Mel Haggard died. Molly Leach died. Her husband died last year. Looks like Sid and Frannie are about to break up again. You might write them. Your sister and her husband have got back together. I don't know why. He's a nitshit, always was, always will be.

Have you been drinking too much again? All you wrote about was the train crossing the road back during the war. How the hell would I remember something like that? And you never saw me drunk, not once in your life. I read in the paper the other day that too much alcohol makes wet spots on your brain, so don't drink so much. Find yourself a good woman and get married, have some babies. Forget that James girl. She never was any good. Go back to your teaching, you can't cut cordwood all your life. You must be damn near forty-five.

Love, Dad

P.S. Your Mom got back before I got this mailed. Your Grandmaw died. If you can't make the funeral which will be Friday, call.

Dear Buddy,

It was so nice to hear you on the phone, but you sounded tired. Are you working too hard? Dad thinks you've been drinking, but you aren't drinking too much are you? He read about people with wet spots on their brains from drinking too much.

I wish you could have made it to Mama's funeral. There was a big family reunion the next day. Your Dad photostated the pages of the guest book, which are enclosed, so I won't have to use a ream of paper telling you whoall was there, ha ha. Gracie, Tom, and Mona Beth were up from Montgomery. Allen and Tracy down from Kansas, and that awful Billy Bob . . .

The only night I remember almost hitting the train we were coming back from the Ritz after seeing The Bluebird, and you and your father got in a big argument over what it was about. He was looking back at you and the whistle was all that saved us. I don't remember getting out and looking at the moon. Are you writing poems again, Buddy?

Dear Mr. Hanks:

The New Ritz Theater has been under new management since 1969, and prior to our takeover I understand the old Ritz changed management three or four times since the 1940s. So, understandably, we wouldn't know when *The Bluebird* played here. Frankly, I never heard of it.

If you're ever in McGehee again, the New Ritz Theater has been remodeled inside and out. We boast a marble-like façade of purple and buff colored plastic squares with chrome trim. Enclosed is a photocopy of the McGehee Times writeup with picture. First-run films, double feature and matinee on Sat & Sun. Adult Features late Sat. nite.

Best Wishers [sic]
Howard Bennet, MANAGER
New Ritz, McGehee, Arkansas

P.S. You might write to Miss Mona Hankins, our local film buff who hasn't missed a movie in forty years. Don't know her address, but she'll get it in care of us. Say, would you be the same Bud Hanks who used to play left end on the Ark. City six? If so, we butted heads more than once. I was right end on the Kelso Six. We generally won.

Dear Mr. Hanks:

Enclosed are Xeroxes from the January and May 1941 issues of *Missouri Pacific Lines Magazine.* Respectively they report the construction and maiden run of the Delta Eagle. Also enclosed is an 8 x 10 glossy of the thousand-horsepower diesel-electric three-unit beauty which was capable of speeds in excess of 65 mph and made daily runs between Memphis and Tallulah. She carried 48 passengers in the rear car which had two attractive and commodious lounge rooms. The forward coach had seats for 60 colored passengers, with rest rooms at the front, and had a fifteen-foot section for the U.S. mail.

Unfortunately specific schedules are not available, and then they were subject to frequent change during the hectic war years when the railroads enjoyed their peak period of passenger miles (over 95 million in 1944). Hence we cannot tell you on what nights the Delta Eagle may have pulled out of McGehee during a particular phase of the moon.

The Missouri Pacific Railroad Company is today a progressive, diversified . . .

Dear Mr. Hanks:

Information Please Almanac was first published in 1947, so we are unable to comply with your request. However, you should be able to compute the phases of the moon on any particular day as far back as you please simply by using the 1971 issue you say you have, keeping in mind that the lunar month is approx. 29½ days.

You state that the moon was full on the night in question, and we would only like to remind you that it is common to mistake a late first quarter or early last quarter gibbous moon for the full moon. The new moon phase occurs when the moon is between the sun and the earth, a full moon when earth is between sun and moon. Interestingly enough, the new moon cannot be seen, hence the old popular song, "There's a New Moon over My Shoulder and an Old Love Still in My Heart" is either based on a misconception, or is quite poignant indeed.

The new 1977 *Information Please Almanac* is available at . . .

My Dear Mr. Bud Hanks,

It was so sweet to hear from a fellow picture show aficionado. I love 'em. Even the modern ones that don't make any sense. Love 'em all. I love the smell and sound of popcorn munched, I love the cushiony darkness except on weekends when the brats are there. I haven't missed a picture show since I was a little girl in the silent days. They have been my life, Mr. Hanks. Them and my job at the ice house where I keep books and do the bills and correspondence. Miss Mona they call me there, Miss Mona she runs the ice house. They're a bunch of nincompoops, but I love 'em too. Would you believe, Mr. Hanks, that people still buy ice? We sell ice cream wholesale, too. I sing in the choir at the Presbyterian. That's the rest of my life. Well, I'm a maiden lady, never been married nor had a beau worth taking dinner with. How about you, Mr. Hanks? The picture show, The Bluebird, was made in 1939 in Technicolor and cost $200,000 for sets that would cost a million today. It was produced by Darryl F. Zanuck and directed by Walter Lang. It starred Shirley Temple, Gale Sondergaard, Eddy Collins who played Tyltyl, Shirley's cute little brother. The February 5, 1940, *Time* magazine gave it a snotty review. I have every issue of *Time* magazine ever printed, but I don't agree with all of them.

Mr. Hanks, what romance I have found in my life it has been with strangers who sat next to me in the picture show. I feel I can tell you this because we have never met and never will and you don't sound like a blabbermouth. Maybe some night when I have had a glass of wine I will tell you about one of them. The Bluebird was adapted from Maurice Maeterlinck's story which had characters named Milk, Fire, Bread, and Sugar which the picture left out. Mr. Maeterlinck was a Belgian. It played at the Ritz Theater in December 1940 and again in November 1943, the exact dates I don't remember. I saw it both times, so once we saw it at the same time. Who knows, maybe you were sitting by me, Mr. Hanks! It was about finding happiness. The bluebird turned out to be in Shirley Temple's own back yard. The bluebird stood for happiness.

Maybe when I write about that romance in the Ritz one night I'll tell you what's in my back yard, Mr. Hanks. Do you know you are the first to ever write to me asking about picture shows, and I know more about picture shows than anybody I ever heard of. My address is 14 South Walnut when you answer this. Yes indeed I will tell Mr. Bennett that Kelso never beat Arkansas City when you were on the team.

As Always,
Mona Hankins

Dear Mr. Hanks:

Considering the date of your letter and the nature of your request, we suspect a Halloween prank. Nevertheless, we have researched our morgue and exhumed the following:

According to the *McGehee Times* of November 11, 1943, The Bluebird was playing at the Ritz, and the moon was full at 7:26 P.M. C.S.T. on that date. The southbound Delta Eagle was scheduled to depart the McGehee station at 9:06 P.M.

The *McGehee Times* can only attest to the accuracy of its reportage of the moon's phases, since neither the Ritz Theater nor the Missouri Pacific Railroad are under direct control of the Almighty. However, it is entirely possible that you could have seen The Bluebird at the Ritz, and then been at the grade crossing on Highway 4 in time to see the Delta Eagle pass. The Bluebird came on at 7 and 9 P.M., according to the published schedule, and the Delta Eagle was almost always late during the war years.

Enclosed is a bill for our research fee, plus the bill for the subscription to the *McGehee Times* which you requested. We took the liberty of putting you down for a five-year subscription, which represents a considerable savings.

The McGehee Times has enjoyed a long and . . .

Dear Bud,

My father broke off with Mary James so I guess we won't be back. I have gone to church the last two Sundays and have found Jesus. It is an experience I don't know how to describe. My life is changed. My father thinks I am sick. I miss our prayers together. I didn't know how few real Christians there were in the world until I became one. I pray every night at ten and mornings at eight. I read the Bible a lot. Please pray at those times too so I will know we are praying together. If you write to me don't put your name on the envelope for my father to see it. I love you.

Marsha Greer

Dear Miss Mona,

You have been more helpful than the Missouri Pacific Railroad Company, the *McGehee Times, Information Please Almanac,* and my parents put together. Muchos gracias. And any time you feel like telling me about that romance, I will bend a discreet ear. As to what you have in

your own back yard, Miss Mona, I don't want to know.
I want to wonder.

Your Friend,
Bud Hanks

Dear Anna,

I'm writing to you since Dr. Kochbaum won't talk to
me on the phone, and won't put you on. She hangs up
on me. Why is she being so unprofessional, not to mention rude? Because she's opened up a box of worms and
can't get the lid back on? Is she in love or something?
Here's what's happening.

My research has turned up enough information to
nail down the night I saw the girl in the white coat.
I'm about to get off a note for the personals in some
newspapers along the old Delta Eagle line. How does
this sound:

"Will the girl wearing a white coat on the southbound
Delta Eagle on or about the night of November 11, 1943,
or anybody knowing her identity and present whereabouts please contact B.H., Harbor Road, Stony Brook,
L.I., N.Y., (tel: 516-751-0469)?"

I feel like a fool. For over thirty years the girl in
the white coat was just my private memory, and not a
threat to anybody. My private reminder that there are
needs in life that life can't fill. There were two girls
in white coats. The one who stayed in my mind and
the real girl who went on down to Tallulah or wherever and is probably somebody's grandmother now.
So why am I doing this? Why has Dr. Kochbaum
opened the doors to temptation and got me looking
for the myth incarnate—my Eve?

I am an Adam. Adams are dangerous. An Adam wants
his Eve. Not just any woman, but his own Tailor-made
Eve. He is adamant about that. Most women hope to be
some Adam's Eve, and when they spot an Adam, they try
out for the role, and generally fail. Most women can spot
an Adam a mile away, and a smart woman will head for

the nearest convent before she gets mixed up with an Adam. A smart woman is one who has been mixed up once with an Adam. Of course Adams have found their Eves and Eves their Adams. In old movies. I quit looking for my Eve a long time ago. When I was a child I thought Mary James was my Eve, but turns out she was any Adam's Eve, and still is. When I finally married her she'd already played Eve to three or four Adams of record, and God knows how many off the books, but I married her anyway like a damn fool, not because I thought she'd be my Eve, but because I wasn't thinking. I married a memory.

Dr. K got me into this present madness and now she's abandoned me. I was doing okay before I met her. Stella was doing okay. Tamara was doing okay. Marsha (the girl you saw on my mattress, who is still a virgin) was doing okay. Even Mary James in her own screwed-up way was doing okay. I reckon even Dr. K was doing okay. Doing okay means getting on through your life without making too many waves. People up to their lips in water, or worse, not ready to sink and scared or unable to swim, ought not to make waves. Dr. K made waves when she made more of the girl in the white coat than ought to have been made of her. What was my own private myth is now out, and here come the candidates for Eve, the girls in white coats, tidal waves.

First it was you. Dr. K is chickenshit so she invented and sent you to my apartment as soon as Tamara was out of the way. Next was poor Stella. Now I've got a letter on my desk I don't know how to answer from Marsha the virgin who says she loves me, and that Mary James and her (Marsha's) father have broken up. That means Mary James is going to be Eveing around again, making ripples. I can handle that, but Marsha is dangerous. I'm liable to get swamped. She's found Jesus since we met and she's young and pretty and malleable and I'm tempted. Trouble is, she's too young and innocent. She's not looking for an Adam, she's looking for a daddy. She's got one, but he's a shithead. Anybody who would go for Mary James without a childhood memory of her to warp his perspective has got to be a shithead. Why am I telling you all this?

Because you tuned and played my harpsichord
like you had created harpsichords and music,
because you touched my bed, looked at my feet,
and cartwheeled from bedroom to the kitchen,
wheeled away without my axle in your hub;
because face to face we drank pure water
without smiles or pretense of a toast,
because a pumpkin moon lit up your face
on the Sunken Meadow Parkway and you sang
Paper Moon but would not mate with me;
because we slept together, only slept,
and in the morning you were gone.
Because I found you, Venus rising
naked from the high tide
and you eluded me again,
running faster than the Delta Eagle ran,
without a white coat on;
because I taught you to fell a tree
and watched you fell a tall chokecherry
and when Earth shook with its fall
you whispered *timber* in my ear,
and I held and kissed you, almost felled.

Because you live in a tree house and I live in a squash court, and if ever an Adam and Eve were forged for one another, the pair is us. Trouble is, you're a forgery of Dr. K and I'd have to go to her to redeem you, and then I'm a forgery too, and she'd have to go to Christ to redeem me.

Guess I'll get that note off to the personal columns now. I can just see the film version of what that's going to lead to. Me with a squash court full of aging Eves in white coats.

Once I wrote a note, unsigned, to Mary James (back in 1942): "I love you." But I've never volunteered that remark out loud to any girl or woman (except my mother).

Isle of view.

Bud

PERSONALS

Will the girl wearing a white coat aboard the southbound Delta Eagle on or about the night of November 11, 1943, or anybody knowing her identity and present whereabouts please contact . . .

9

I HAD hit iron deep in the bole of an old cottonwood, and was at my worktable fitting a new chain on the saw bar when Mary James came in without knocking, like there was or had been or would be enough between us to justify the intrusion. She looked to have just fallen out of bed and into the pink robe and black rubber boots she wore. She folded and leaned against the wall a holey old beach umbrella that had come with the big house. It commenced to drain off a small pond on my hardwood floor. It was raining and too cold for comfort, 11:00 A.M., a mid-November Sunday.

Mary James made for the 55-gallon oil drum I had converted into a logwood heater. She said, "You woke me up, the noise of that thing." I made a that's-the-way-it-is gesture while going on with my chain change. I had not just hit the iron, I had leaned on it, my mind elsewhere, and ruined the chain. I cut around the spot with my spare saw and found a horseshoe in there, on a railroad spike, deep in the heartwood of the cottonwood. I counted one hundred and eighty-eight annual rings.

"How come you don't build a fireplace in this place?" said Mary James.

"Ninety percent of your heat shoots up the chimney into the cold world out of a fireplace," I said.

"Well they're a damn sight prettier than an old iron barrel, that's conclusive," said Mary James.

"My sense of aesthetics pales when my butt is freezing," I replied.

Mary James was facing the heater. Men stand with their

backs to the fire, women face it. That is a simple observation of a number of men and women before the actual fire, for warmth, may not be statistically true at all, and is not necessarily published for symbolic content. Mary James came over and put her elbows on my worktable, dropped her chin in her hands. Her big blue eyes with the long, delicate, wispy-ended lashes that once brushed my heart with each flutter were much the same, except that they no longer brushed my heart, and the skin around them though still fine at a distance took on the appearance of graph paper close up. Mary James was an old twelve. I asked her how her legal studies were progressing. She went, *"Aeunh."*

Mary James picked up the horseshoe. She examined it minutely, tracing a fingernail through the bright cut my chainsaw had made in coming out second best. Mary James had the same long, exquisitely shaped fingernails she'd modeled in her youth. She would sometimes threaten to, but to my knowledge never did, scratch somebody's eyes out with them when irked. She placed the horseshoe back on the table, like it was a Steuben-wrought crystal crescent. She asked me why I didn't nail it over my door for luck. I reminded her of her father's favorite shibboleth: "A man makes his own luck," Jesse James will tell you. Mary James went *"Aeunh,"* pushing off from the table. She sauntered toward the kitchen. I had wondered how much longer she would stall before making that move.

I tightened the last bolt on the saw bar, amusing myself with the thought of giving the motor a quick crank and revving it, to see Mary James jump shrieking out of her gum boots and wrap around a beam. I picked up the railroad spike and leaned back, my feet clearing themselves a place to rest on the table. By ring count the spike had been driven into the tree when it was twelve years old, by Obadiah Smith or Smythe, of the Smithtown Smiths or Smythes, same age. Obadiah did it one mid-November day when there wasn't much for a boy to do on Long Island but be creative or abuse himself. After driving in the spike little Obadiah amused himself with tossing the horseshoe at it. When he grew bored he left a ringer on the railroad spike in the little cottonwood, back in November of 1811, for me to ruin a thirty-dollar saw chain on in the bicentennial year, and ducked behind the barn and abused himself.

Mary James in the kitchen, opening doors and drawers and closing them, her big blue eyes casting thirstily about. It was after eleven on a Sunday morning and she had polished off her booze supply the night before and needed a transfusion now. Let her suffer, I reasoned, returning to my study of the railroad spike. Mary James returning, fishing a cigarette from her bathrobe pocket; she lights it with, I note, steady fingers, French-inhales. I tossed the railroad spike aside and let my feet drop to the floor.

"Mary James, remember when we took off our clothes in that hayloft?"

She gazed dumbly at me through her smoke, then she frowned, picked up the horseshoe and sighted me through it. "Maybe with Dwight Brown I did that."

"Dwight Brown? You're kidding."

Mary James fit the horseshoe over her forearm. "I'm s'prised he didn't tell you."

"Why I'd of beat his butt, you were *my* girl friend."

"You couldn't of beat Dwight Brown's butt, Bud Hanks. No way."

"For that I could have. I'm really surprised, Mary James. You and Dwight Brown really took off your clothes in the hayloft?"

She took the horseshoe off her arm, made a yucky gesture at the rust it left on her pink robe sleeve, and sighted me through the shoe again. "All of us kids used to take off our clothes and maybe touch each other once in a while in the hayloft, Bud Hanks, what's the big deal?"

My childhood sweetheart, my own true love, too pure to touch, too pure for *me* to touch. In *my* simple mind too pure.

"Anyway, I wasn't your girl friend," she concluded.

"Well I sure thought you were."

"Well it wasn't con*clusive.*"

"Well, do you remember the night we were coming back from the picture show and caught that couple fucking in the Widow Vick's side yard?"

Mary James laughed, "Was that you with me that night? I thought it was Floyd Scott," trying to fit the horseshoe around her neck. "Now, wait a minute—it was Junior *Proctor.* He was real cute."

I let a heavy sigh and told her, "Get your neck stuck in that thing and it's yours."

Mary James laughed.

I thought a moment and tried again. "Mary James, 'member the revival meeting when we went every night together, and how we'd hold hands under the hymnal? That was the revival meeting that we both got saved at, and were baptized."

Mary James made another yucky gesture at all the rust she was getting off the horseshoe. She said, "Every time you turned around the Baptist church was having a revival meeting."

"Mary James, you don't remember a single thing I married you for. No wonder we failed."

She gave the horseshoe a toss on the table, saying, "Those things are collector's items, people will pay good money for a rusty horseshoe."

> *Omega, omega you horseshoe in the future*
> *with hoofprints in the present*
> *and the thundering hoofbeats of the Great Horse Silver*
> *way back there reminding:*
> *From Alpha to the Arch is a long long way awinding.*

"That's how come I didn't like you all that much in grade school, Bud Hanks, always saying crazy things."

"Junior Proctor said crazy things as I did."

"All the same," said Mary James, looking away.

"My own childhood sweetheart didn't like me," I muttered.

"Well now I wasn't exactly your childhood sweetheart, Bud Hanks."

"Then how come you married me?"

"Are you crazy? Nobody gets married just because they were childhood sweethearts."

Mary James glanced back toward the kitchen, her mind suddenly back on why she was down here, back to basics.

"Hear you and Lonnie Greer broke up," I said.

"His little whatchername told you, huh? She still sneaking down here?"

"I got a letter from her. Says she found Jesus."

"Didn't know he was lost," grunted Mary James, going to the front door to throw out her cigarette butt. "You better hope she doesn't miss her period, that's all."

Mary James took note of the white coat on the knob when she opened the door. Marsha had left the white coat on the knob when she left and I had left it there because Marsha had left it there. Mary James threw out her cigarette. Funny how men thump cigarettes away and women throw them. Probably because boys get their start playing marbles. I might have brought this up with Mary James but why get called crazy for nothing? I said, "It's none of your business, but I haven't touched Marsha Greer."

"Uh-huh, sure," said Mary James, still looking at the white coat. "This looks like my old rabbit coat that used to be Mama's."

I got up and went to the kitchen. "How about a cup of coffee?"

"Naw. But if you've got some brandy, though. Or whiskey? Hell, Bud Hanks, long as it burns if you stick a match to it— but doncha pour me no *gas*oline, haha."

I fetched what was left of the Madeira Rainwater from the refrigerator. It was only 20-percent alcohol, unburnable, but dipsomaniacs will quaff flat beer on the rocks in lieu of higher proof. "Lonnie seemed like a nice enough fellow," I said, pouring the last of the Rainwater into a coffee cup. Mary James

took the cup and held it in an offhand way, saying "Oh . . ."
as though she was sorting the complexities of her relationship
with Lonnie and not anxious to get that wine past her lips,
". . . he was too kinky."

I chuckled.

"One example," said Mary James, casting about for a conve-
nient place to set her yet untouched cup, quickly failing, and
with a shrug quaffing its contents, running her finger through
the handle while untying her robe with the other hand. She
turned as it slid to the floor over her arms and empty cup. She
stood there naked as a peeled banana, but for the rubber boots.
There were some long purplish welts on her ass and upper
thighs. That plump little untouchable butt of my pubescent
sweetheart in the hayloft wider now, and flattened some, and
beaten.

"Lonnie did that? Why?"

"We were out in the woods making nookie under that tree
with the long funny beans on it. Alla sudden Lonnie jumped
up and snatched off one of those beans and he like to burnt me
up with it . . ." holding out the cup, "hey you got some more
of this? It's nice. Personally I prefer my wine a shade drier, but
it's got a good *boo-kay*, all the same. Hey, you got some brandy
or whiskey, Bud Hanks?"

"How come Lonnie to whip you with a catalpa bean, Mary
James?"

"'Cause he was losing his hard, why else do men get kinky?"
she snapped, still standing there naked with her back to me,
in black rubber boots, waving that fucking empty cup. Why
doesn't she put her robe back on before Anna or somebody
busts in here, Marsha Greer, her parents, my parents, Alonzo,
my dog Joe . . . Mary James turned around, her eyebrows
raised, mouth screwed into a that's-the-way-it-is expression.
Her tits were always small, a bit too close together. They had
commenced to sag now, like testicles. How sad, what happens
to children.

"Funny thing, Bud Hanks, but the tree we were under, way

up in it I saw strands of barbed wire sticking out. High up as those beams up there, wonder why?"

"That's easy. Back in about eighteen hundred and forty-three, Anno Domini, a fellow named Obadiah Smith, one of our Founding Fathers, cut down a catalpa tree and split it into posts, made a barbed-wire fence. The posts took root and over the years the fittest of them grew into new catalpa trees, taking Obadiah's barbed wire up with them. Next time you're on your back down there in the woods, Mary James, open your eyes a little wider and you'll notice a whole row of catalpa trees with barbed wire hanging out of them as high as my beams. Old barbed wire is a collector's item too."

"I only saw the one tree with the wire hanging out of it," she said into her empty cup.

"And one catalpa bean," I said.

"That wasn't the only thing caused me to break off with Lonnie. That monkey business between you and his daughter didn't help. A man who doesn't care any more about his own daughter than to let her sleep with a man old enough to be her father is not the next man I'm gonna marry, Bud Hanks, and that's conclusive. Shoot-heck, I might want to have some children myself, and with a man like that, who knows? Let's have a drink together, Bud Hanks, whacha say? Old times?"

Old times.

I was teaching in New York City, writing poetry, giving readings, getting a little published, considering marriage with a fine attractive woman ten years my junior. I was just about to settle up, and who do I run into but Jesse James on the steps of the Times Square subway station. We get drunk together over old times and I'm invited to his showplace home on Long Island and who answers the door but my old childhood sweetheart with a drink in her hand and several in her head—"Why it's Bud Hanks, *lawsy me!* I can't believe my eyes, this is personally too too much. You come in here Bud Hanks and let's have a drink together for old times! *Lawsy me . . .*"

I said, "Mary James, I just dropped by to ask how come you

stood me up that night back in nineteen-fifty?"

"Bud *Hanks!* I can *explain!*"

And Mary James grabbed my hand, dragged me in, and sank me. We sat out on the veranda, drinking, she explaining. She explained and explained, she continues to explain. We drank and drank while Mary James explained. Along about sundown we had got engaged to be married, still sitting out there in old wicker chairs since gone to pieces, neither of us having gotten up except to pour drinks and piss. We hadn't even kissed yet, not since that brief afternoon of not even French kisses twenty-two years earlier, and here we sat engaged to be married after three hours and fifteen minutes of pre-pubescent reminiscences while getting wrecked on her daddy's mortgaged Long Island veranda.

I don't know what possessed Mary James to marry me, other than it happened to be me on hand that day to catch her on another rebound. I know what possessed me. It was plain as sundown sitting there on the veranda. The grass grown wild down to an untrimmed privet hedge beyond which stretched the salt marshes beyond Porpoise Channel at ebb tide beneath rosy-bottomed clouds, a flock of pterodactyls winging over in the old-time stillness. The big house at our backs. A weariness with New York City, with poem making, a bone weariness with sophisticated cant and cunt. I moved into a guest room that very night, came to terms with Jesse James on the matter of my dowry the next day.

The wedding and reception happened in the drawing room when and where we had our first fight, over the etymology of *drawing* room. My contention was that it was short for *with*-drawing, while Mary James was positive that it was for like artists' drawing, or for drawing together, she wasn't absolutely positive exactly which, but that one or the other was the truth she was sure was personally conclusive and it was absolutely intolerable that I should argue with her. There wasn't a dictionary in the big house, but in our search for one somebody found the big house blueprints in a secret drawer in the library along with an antique nickel-plated Quackenbush air-gun, and sure enough there the room was in blue and white, WITHDRAWING ROOM. *"You always did have to be right different, Bud Hanks!"* my bride screamed at me.

We honeymooned in a rented camper on Montauk or Orient Point, having missed the turn for Florida after discovering my frozen Bowery bum and heading back out on the Long Island Expressway drinking Early Times out of the bottle, realizing that we probably weren't Florida-bound along about the Babylon exit of the L.I.E. We had waited until our wedding night to consummate the thing, because that was the way I wanted it, and then we didn't because I couldn't, being swept back to the hayloft on a flood of Early Times, to the untouchable ... I simply could not get it up. When we did consummate it, Mary James asked me what I was thinking. She asked that while we were consummating it, in the missionary position. I had to think for a moment, and then I said, "I am thinking about thought," and Mary James came back with, "Don't get eso*teric* on me, Bud Hanks."

She shook my arm, naked in her father's black gum boots, a *Lampoon* centerfold. "Bud? A drink for old times?"

Mary James and I stayed drunk for the better part of our for-worse union. Between hangovers I worked on the big house, commenced the squash court renovation, and launched my firewood business. We lived in the big high vaulted room with the arched windows and the magnificent view. We were strapped for money and had loud arguments. We would have a drink and make up, make large promises and small efforts to do better. I sold my car and bought a cheaper and more useful truck. Mary James enrolled in a mail-order medical course to cut down on doctor bills should they come up. We set aside nondrinking days to economize, but I became a secret teetotaler, while Mary James openly vowed to quit. In an economy move one day Mary James, secretly drunk, tweezered dead flies off the flypaper while I watched, secretly sober, laughing on the inside and crying in there too. Stuff like that was the fabric of our marriage. We didn't break up in a neat sense of the word. We just came apart, like a pissed-on cigarette. Some marriages are made in hell.

"Doncha want to have a drink with me for old times, Bud Hanks?"

"I want you to put that robe back on before you get a cold in the ass, Mary James."

She put her robe back on and drew it tightly; almost cut herself in two. Mary James' waist wasn't much bigger than my arm. She turned up the collar and went back to the kitchen where she rummaged under the sink and found an unopened bottle of Southern Comfort. To this day I do not know how that bottle of Southern Comfort got under my sink, unless it was put there, in a blatant intrusion on my medium, by Special Effects. Mary James got down two iced-tea glasses, dropped a cube of ice in each of them and brimmed them with Southern Comfort. To cut down on the sloshing she sipped from each glass en route to my work table. She set the glasses down amongst assorted hardware. I bowed my head and shook it over life's ambiguous gifts. That act reminded me that I had forgotten, these past few days, to pray at 8:00 A.M. and 10:00 P.M. with Marsha Greer across the gulf that separated us.

As with Anna there was no toast when Mary James and I bent the old elbow, but this was no intimacy; it was simple neglect of an unnecessary gesture preluding a binge. I took a sip of the too sweet, lemony hundred-proof liqueur, and set my glass well to one side—a gesture I hoped Mary James would fathom and respect, if not imitate. She took a sip and said, "I'm not as dumb as you think, Bud Hanks."

"How dumb do you think I think you are?"

She laughs and sips Southern Comfort. She muses. She wears a wiser look than Dr. Kochbaum; she flaunts it. " 'Member in the sixth grade, Bud, when Miz McCain asked us each and every one what we wanted to be when we grew up?"

My head lolled wearily, warily.

"You said, 'I want to be a mysterious stranger.' Those were

your exact words. Oh Bud, that's the easiest thing in the world to be!—a mysterious stranger!"

"Did you realize that back in the sixth grade, or later? It's a good rejoinder, Mary James. Bet somebody helped you to realize it."

"You like it, stick it in a poem," said Mary James, taking another sip of Southern Comfort, cooking off another batch of brain cells. She was gazing at me with a darkened, plaintive countenance. She went on, of course:

"Oh Bud, where did we go wrong?" Organ music rises, fades, and we pause briefly for an Ivory Snow commercial. Fade back in with organ, same scene, softer lighting, Mary James: *"Oh Bud, let's pick up the pieces."*

I said, "Look, I'm going to laugh. Please don't take offense. Be big, expansive, be above it, this laugh I'm about to laugh."

"Laugh your ass off, Bud Hanks."

"Mary James, what happens to a bottle of booze you leave open long enough?"

"It gets drunk."

"Barring that, though, it evaporates, right? Its little molecules bounce out of the bottle and into the surrounding space. Pretty soon those molecules are spread all over the place in a state of thermodynamic equilibrium. Those are the pieces, Mary James, of our marriage: those little evaporated molecules of booze, spread thin as a day-old sneeze. They never go back into the bottle, no more than you can run time backward. You can't pick them up or herd them back in. No way. Our marriage is an empty bottle, honey. Dead soldier."

"But we didn't let our marriage evaporate, did we, Bud? Naw, we pissed it away."

"Very good, Mary James. You're not so dumb."

"Then how come we can't get back together?"

"Wasn't your brains, or lack of them, I married you for, Mary James."

"I know why you married me, and I'm not holding it against you, not anymore anyway," she muttered, lighting another cigarette, blowing an aggressive cloud of smoke.

"Why do you want us to get back together?"

"Shit man, I love you, what do you think?"

"Shit."

"That's all you've got to say to me, Bud Hanks, when I say I *love* you? *Shit?*"

"Scented shit."

"You don't love me, Bud?"

"In a way, but not enough to explain it, certainly not enough to mouth it without explaining it, and in no way enough to share rooms with you again."

She shrugged and took another drink. She didn't break into tears. Fact was, I couldn't remember ever seeing Mary James in tears, though certainly I must have at one time or another. She said, "That poem about the *omega,* show you I'm not dumb . . ." she picked up the horseshoe, held it up like Exhibit B, "Omega is the last letter of the Greek ABCs and it's shaped like this horseshoe, right? The poem is about the Greeks. The old-timey Greeks, back in the Roman days. Don't forget, Bud Hanks, I studied medicine and Hippocrates was the father of medicine, and he was a Greek, Hippocrates was. *Alpha* is the first letter of the Greek alphabet. Head of the class, huh?"

What would you ship hippos in? Well that's how Mary James pronounced Hippocrates.

"What's so doggone funny, Bud Hanks?"

Pretty soon she was laughing too; we got down laughing until tears flowed fast and free, and she never found out what I was laughing about, but no matter because pretty soon we were just laughing at laughing. That we could share.

After we had dried up laughing, and fallen silent, Mary James said, "That poem *Omega* wasn't really about the ancient Greeks, was it? It's like dreams, what you dream about isn't really what you're dreaming about. Mean to say, everything means something else in a dream. It's all sym*bolic,* right, Bud? Hell, I wasn't born yesterday. Born in Arkansas, but not yesterday." She laughed. " 'Member when Miz Payne told you that you weren't born, that a buzzard laid you on a rock and the sun hatched you?"

A very salty lady, Miz Payne, our seventh-grade teacher with whom I often engaged in repartee. It was in the winter of our seventh grade that Mary James had moved.

"And when you spit on the dictonary and Billy Matthews was gonna hit you for it, but you convinced him it was the Bible you weren't supposed to spit on?"

"That was Lee Edward Whittaker," I said.

"All the same, you could talk your way around most people, Bud Hanks."

"Lee Edward Whittaker had inordinate respect for books, because he couldn't read," I said.

"He was cross-eyed, I remember," said Mary James. "Last I heard of him he was making lots of money down in Mississippi somewheres."

"That Billy Matthews was an ornery little cuss. Remember his little redheaded cousin? Billy and I diddled her in an old cabin boat dry-docked in the vacant lot by his house."

"I heard it was Floyd Scott's cousin youall diddled," said Mary James.

"You *heard?* You weren't supposed to hear things like that, not about *me*, Mary James. I'd of died of shame to know you knew that then. Oh well, we diddled her too, Floyd and I did. And Billy and I diddled Billy's cousin. All my cousins lived and diddled elsewhere."

"Where did you and Floyd diddle his cousin, Bud?"

"Over the levee."

"That's where I got diddled the first time, over the levee."

Again that kick in the heart. Were we *never* innocent, Mary James? "Who *didn't?*" I blurted, hoping she wouldn't tell me who it was, "First time I diddled myself was over the levee. *Over the levee* was a euphemism for diddling."

"It was Jimmy Bowden," said Mary James, la sacrée dame sans merci.

Jimmy Bowden, for God's sake, was older than we were.

That must have been a serious diddle, a penetrating one.

"Those were the days—hey Bud, you're not drinking your drink."

"Diddle it."

Mary James glanced pensively into her glass. There was a moment of silence while she read the cue card in her glass, then she said her line, about as well as could be directed: *"Bud, what do you want out of life?"*

I started my chainsaw and revved it high. Mary James laughed uproariously in the din, though I couldn't hear her laughter for it; I watched her with a grin, and when the smoke commenced to choke us I shut it off.

"That chainsaw, that's a phallic symbol to you, isn't it, Bud Hanks? Cutting into all those trees . . . well isn't it now? Tell the truth?"

"What *isn't* a phallic symbol that isn't concave, gaseous, abstract, or a phallus?"

"Anything that makes you think of a stiff dick is a phallic symbol, that's all I know, Bud. That's what Freud said. Like a serviceman at attention, f'rinstance, now that always made me think of a stiff dick, a phallic symbol, seeing a serviceman standing at attention."

"You ought to become a poet, Mary James. Write poems. There's a rough-cut, not-half-bad poet diddling around in you."

"I used to write poetry every once in a while. I wrote a poem the night I left on the train, Bud Hanks. When we moved to Greenville when I was twelve. It was about how sad and happy I was, leaving Arkansas City, as best I remember it. I've got it in a notebook somewhere. My poems rhymed. Poems don't rhyme anymore. Shoot-heck, I wouldn't know if I had written a poem unless I made it rhyme. I love rhymes. You had a beautiful rhyme in that poem you said by heart while ago. That was a beautiful poem, Bud, though to tell the frank truth I really didn't understand it. But it *did* give me the shivers and it wasn't crazy sounding like I said. Say it again, Bud, okay?"

"Omega, omega, you horseshoe in the future with hoof-prints in the present, and the thundering hoofbeats of the Great Horse Silver way back there reminding: from Alpha to the Arch is a long long way awinding."

She was nodding, nodding to my voice, its words, the Southern Comfort. "I know Silver was the Lone Ranger's horse," she said at length.

"The Book of Revelation in the Bible calls Jesus Christ the Alpha and the Omega—the beginning and the end, Mary. That's a way of saying that as the Christ, the *Logos,* he always has been, always will be; he is the power of creation and of salvation, the *new* creation, and he will be and is the consummater of time in eternity. Okay? The Great Horse Silver is the action, evolution, the unfolding of history, Revelation and response, the Trip. And who rides the Great Horse Silver, Mary?"

"The Lone *Ranger.* "

"And who is the great lone ranger of all great lone rangers?"

"Jesus Christ?"

"Star in your crown, Mary James. You're not so dumb at all."

"Oh Bud, quote it again, I want to hear it again."

We looked at each other while I quoted it a third time, and my voice trailed off at the end, caving into silence. In the silence we went on looking at each other's eyes until Mary James' eyes dampened and she looked away, a new memory of her arising. It was not just the memory of a memory, but a fresh one, virginal, brought to light by that look in Mary James' eyes when she was touched.

Once when we were ten or eleven I wrote "I love you" on a piece of paper and left it under a rock on Mary James' bicycle seat. I hid behind a pecan tree by her house until she came out and found the note. I watched her face while she read and reread the love note I had not signed, and I fancied that she was brought to tears, knowing who had written it, but it was getting dark and my imagination leaped with light. Mary

James got on her bicycle and rode away with the note in her little coin purse, and I went home. That was the only time I ever told Mary James that I loved her, and she had never told me until this Sunday, when my response had been "shit." Not even when we got engaged, not on our wedding day, nor the early morning hour when we consummated it, not ever, had we said aloud, "I love you."

Dabbing at her eyes with the pink bathrobe sleeve, Mary James said, "Sometimes I hate love."

"God is love, mustn't hate God," I muttered.

"That's not the kind of love I hate. I hate the kind I'm always falling into."

She went to the door, paused, looked back. At the bottle of Southern Comfort, I supposed. I made a gesture that she take it, but she shook her head. "I'm gonna quit."

Mary James looked back at the door, at the white coat hanging on the knob. She untied her robe and let it slide to the floor. She put on the white coat and buttoned it. She turned again and looked at me. The hemline of the white coat reached just below her knees. Mary James came back to me then, in the white coat and the black rubber boots.

> That night, God forgive me,
> Mary James beneath me,
> I pretended she was Anna.

Dear B.H.,

Regards to your personal ad in the Commercial Appeal, what got my eye was the Delta Eagle. My father was a brakeman for the Missouri Pacific Lines (he retired in 1951 and passed away the following year) so we had passes. I used to make the run every now and again from Memphis to Tallulah and back just for the heck of it, you know a little horse play, ha ha. I sure saw a lot of hot numbers on the old Delta Eagle, tell you that. What they were wearing I don't remember for my eye was out in those days for what was *under* what they were wearing, ha ha. Well, sorry I can't help you, but good luck in your search for that gal in the white coat. If you're really lucky you'll meet her *daughter*, ha ha.

> Keep it up (ha ha)
> Harold Dean Sykes
> Memphis, Tenn.

Dear B.H.,

Would you be the soldier boy sitting across the aisle from me from Marianna to Watson where I had to get off? I never will forget. I got on at Helena where I still live and he got on at Marianna, and the whole time from Marianna to Watson we would catch each other looking at each other and look away with red faces. I have often wondered whatever happened to that soldier boy. I have always worried that he got mixed up in that awful thing that happened between Lake Village and Eudora. I have always hoped that he got off before it happened. I don't believe he was the kind of boy that would have anything to do with anything that awful. He was so nice and shy. Soldier boys sure aren't shy these days. I know, I've got a daughter married to one and I lost a boy to the marines in Viet Nam. If you are that soldier boy I would just like to know that's all. Yes I may well have been wearing a white coat that night. I just wonder why you put that ad in the paper. If you write to me, write at the address where I work, as my husband wouldn't under . . .

B.H.:

Who are you? Were you one of us? Is this a trick? For God sake man its been thirty-three years. Let sleeping dogs lie. Don't you know she died? Don't you know we killed her God knows who? I for one have suffered 33 years of nightmares and bad conscience. Now I have to live in terror for my life. Right after it happened I volunteered for overseas duty and served my country in the Pacific Theater. I earned the Purple Heart. After my Honorable Discharge I returned to the States only to learn that somebody was tracking us down and killing us. God knows who he was—one of us or one of them. A buddy of mine had been tracked down and shot and left for dead by him, said he was looking for a box the dead girl had that one of us was supposed to have taken. I don't know about any box. All I know is I grabbed my gear and jumped off the train and ran like hell. If anybody got her box it must have been a civilian. I moved to Canada and changed my name and have been an honest hard-working law-abiding citizen living with my bad conscience and my nightmares. I've got a family. I've got grandchildren. And now you've put that ad in the paper. That's not bad enough I have to get it clipped out and mailed to me from God knows who. I've been somebody else somewhere else for thirty years, and now somebody's found out or knew all the time. This is driving me crazy. What if that box hunter is still looking for the dead girl's box? Do you have it? Is that it? Did you think maybe she wasn't dead and you want to give it back to her? For God sake put *that* in the papers before you get the rest of us left alive killed. I'm too old and settled to change my name and move again. I've got a responsible job, up for retirement next year. I stand to lose everything. Why some ambitious D.A. or nosy reporter could start prying and ruin us all. Nobody was ever prosecuted you know. For God sake put another ad in the papers and be more specific. Maybe it was another girl in a white coat you were looking for, who's still alive? If you are a black man, and there's a thought, the car right behind the engine was for black citizens. Unfortunately there was segregation then. I bet there was a black girl in a white coat in that car. That would solve everything for us before this thing gets out of hand and that Box Hunter starts tracking us down again. And for God sake if that's who you are, Sir, I for one know absolutely nothing about any box and have served my country honorably and well (Purple Heart with Oak Leaf Cluster) and have been the prisoner of my conscience for thirty-three long years, a fate worse than death, and have three grandbabies. If anybody took her box it was a civilian. They stayed on the train. Have you checked out the civilians who were on the train that night? Whoever you are for God sake let's be reasonable and let sleeping dogs lie. I am too old and sick to run any more. I have got nothing to lose now. I have written up a full account of what happened that night, naming names. It is in the hands of a trusted friend. If anything happens to me it goes to the D.A. and the papers. If I have to face the music I won't face it alone.

One who has Suffered Enough

Dearest darling Dad,
   You noticed. How quaint of you. Love & daggers.

Griselda

Dear Lost Sinner:
   Seek ye first the Kingdom of Heaven.

An Apostle of the Lord

Dear B.H.,

How strange that you should try to find me after all these years, or have you been searching ever since that night? It has to be you, the boy who was sitting behind me on the train, and it must be me you are looking for. I was the only girl with a white coat on the train. It was new and I was very proud of it. It was a Christmas present from my father; we had our Christmas November 10 because my father, an Army captain, was to be sent overseas the following night. We lived in Memphis then. My father (who did not come back alive) took us to the picture show the next day before he left. After the picture show they saw me off on the train which I took down to Tallulah where my grandparents met me and drove me on down to their home in New Orleans where I stayed through the Thanksgiving holidays.

It was my first time to take the train alone. It was a fateful night indeed. I boarded the Delta Eagle, a child with a woman's heart, and I got off a woman who had lost her heart. I don't know when you boarded, but you first spoke to me just south of St. Charles. You leaned over the seat and asked if you could sit by me. I had put my suitcase on the aisle seat so nobody would sit there. I wanted to be alone on my first train ride alone. I'm afraid I was rude to you. You were smiling. You had a nice face, but you frightened me. You were a few years older than I, and lonely looking. I looked away from your face, looked out the window.

The night was cold, the moon was full. I pressed my face against the cold window and watched the moon-bathed countryside sweep by. You kept on talking to me, but I couldn't hear what you were saying for the roar of the train. I was sorry I had been rude, and decided that at the next stop I would move my suitcase, so you could sit by me, but at the next stop—McGehee I think it was —a lot of people came aboard. A lady got the seat by me and you gave yours up to another lady. You stood in the aisle next to us. I could see your face reflected in the window. Not far out of McGehee I was looking again at the moonbathed countryside sweeping by—looking at it through the dark image of your face in the window. There was a highway ahead that crossed the railroad tracks, and I saw a car just barely stop in time before it hit the train. As we passed by I saw a boy sitting in the back seat of the car with his face bathed in the full moon, pressed against the window just like mine. He was looking at me as I sped by, and he didn't look like he even knew or cared that he had almost crashed into the train. He was looking at me like he knew me and had been looking for me all his life, and it seemed I knew him too, had been looking for him, and then he was gone. My heart leaped with love at the sight of that boy, and then the Delta Eagle carried me away, and my heart was gone. You got off at the next stop. As you were leaving you asked my name, but I couldn't speak. I was crying. You asked what was wrong. I buried my face in my hands and didn't look up again until the train was moving and you were gone. I was a different person. A whole lifetime had passed in that one brief moment when I loved and lost my heart. The Delta Eagle had sped me from childhood with my woman's heart to womanhood without the heart to ever love another. And whatever happened to him? The boy in the blue car by the Delta Eagle's tracks? In my mind he still waits there for me. I can still see his moonlit face pressed against the window.

This must sound very foolish to you, B.H.—but then again, perhaps not. You did remember me, and think about me enough to place that unlikely ad! Am I to you what that boy is to me? How ironic life is. I have often thought about you. The picture show I saw with my family that afternoon was *The Bluebird*. Did you ever see it? It is about happiness being in your own back yard. No matter where you roam, that is where you must look for it. You were sitting behind me on the Delta Eagle, and wanted to move up beside me, but I looked away—and lost my heart to a . . . what does "B.H." initial? Bluebird Home? Should we meet? My heart is suddenly back now, literally, in my throat! Perhaps I will call you in a day or so after you have received this letter, after you've had time to think.

As never,
The Girl in the White Coat on the Delta Eagle
(Kim)

Dear Mr. Hanks;

A serious matter has come up that we must discuss. First I wrote you a letter (in partial response to yours), and then it occurred to me that we should talk. Unable to reach you by phone on Long Island (you must be busy in the woods), I tried your number in New York, and was advised by the friend you have staying in your apartment (rather nosy for a friend, I might add) that you were "out of town." Hence this note.

Would you mind coming to my office, rather than calling? Call it an informal session—on me. Come as soon as you get this note, if at all possible.

As ever,
(Miss) A. K. Kochbaum

11

I TRUCKED to New York, stopping first at my apartment. It had been ransacked. I trucked up to A. K. Kochbaum's building, double-parked. It was after office hours. The waiting room was empty. She opened the door before I had finished ringing.

"You're faster than the mail," she said.

"Faster than a speeding locomotive," I exhaled, handing her my mail. "Read this if you think you have a serious matter to discuss."

I followed her across the deep pile carpet to her desk; she sat behind it, I sat on it. The cloud-colored drapes were parted a crack, letting in a thin shaft of sunny city. Dr. K had on an autumn-leaf-hued pants suit, a matching ribbon in her long black hair. Holding the letters, she glanced up at me with an expression I hadn't seen before; it had in it a kind of suspicious curiosity, like maybe there was a seamier side of me than she had heretofore suspected. At length she glanced away, toward the far wall where her diplomas hung. All but one. The Ph.D. in clinical from Columbia was missing. Our eyes met again. Her expression had not changed. She glanced down at her desk, at her Steuben glass banana paperweight, which was cracked. Abruptly she took an unenveloped letter from her desk, hand-delivered it. She then commenced to read my mail, while I read her unmailed letter to me.

Dear Mr. Hanks,
My office was broken into sometime over the weekend. I went out to dinner and the theater Friday night, and

on Saturday morning went away for the weekend, not returning to my office until this morning. After a thorough inventory all I can find missing is your file. There was also an act of vandalism. The glass on my Columbia diploma had been smashed with the glass banana paperweight. The police were here. In order to spare you the embarrassment of being questioned as a suspect, I reported to them that nothing of value was missing.

The fact that only your file was taken, and that the act of vandalism was one you threatened once in my presence, makes you a logical suspect—or would to the police. My own opinion is that you are the kind of man who would come in and ask for what he wanted, and then perhaps try to take it anyway, if I refused. Whatever you are—and I find much in you that is offensive—you are not a sneak. And if you were, you are too intelligent to have made yourself a logical suspect by just taking your own file, and doing that piece of malicious mischief. That leaves us with this: Who did it and why?

I have wealthy clients whose files would be attractive to potential blackmailers, but you have no money. I have clients in important business and government positions, but you have no position. I have famous clients—celebrities—whose secrets, if any, some prurient fools would get off on, but you have no fame.

I believe the perpetrator is one of my clients, or an ex-client. Most of them are men with sexual problems, some mental, some physical, a few feigned. This was not my intended area of specialization, nor is it my major interest, but being a female psychotherapist whom most men find an exceptionally attractive female, I have ended up with a hard-core clientele of lechers, built largely on word of lying mouth.* They tell tales to their friends about the beautiful, sexy sex therapist, and here come their friends, expecting to pile on the couch with me. I've had men come in here and actually expose themselves, some whose problem obviously was not sexual potency.

*Your Marsha, for what it's worth, is not the only virgin in these parts.

Men come in here thinking that my fee entitles them to sexual intimacies, as though I were a prostitute with a degree. I try to help them all to face and overcome whatever their real problems are, and if I can't help them I tell them so. My clients fall in love with me, or say they do. They fly into jealous rages because they're not getting what they think the others are getting. They come unscheduled. They hang around in the waiting room. They get in fights with each other and with scheduled clients. Some of these men are dangerous psychotics. One of them may be the man who broke in here and stole your file. His motivation would be to find out what went on between you and me, to make you the suspect by taking your file, which he undoubtedly read first—then smashed my diploma as you had threatened, to further incriminate you. God only knows what else motivated him or what his plans are now.

Since I never give the name of nor any other information on one client to another, he had to learn your name through you, or from a mutual acquaintance to whom you've talked about me. I am not suggesting that you have told any tales, quite the contrary, but to a man insane with jealousy a denial is an admission of guilt. Neither the man with whom you had the fight on your last scheduled visit, nor the man with whom you had words the day you came unscheduled, are the kind of men who would have done this, in my opinion. Were you in my waiting room, unscheduled, at any other time?

I cannot respond in full to your letter, having read it but once, and hurriedly (my date was waiting) and filed it (in the now stolen file) before going out to dinner and the theater Friday evening. I recall enough to offer the following remarks: First, does not the New Testament teach that there are two Adams, and that the Second Adam taught, "Seek ye first the Kingdom of Heaven, and all these things will be added unto you?" And would not an "Eve" be among those "things?" Second, it was you, not I, who "invented" Anna, though I admit complicity in the forging (not "forgery") beneath your dead chokecherry tree, as well as in the previous games we played. I might have fallen too (you're not the first, not even the first client, who has brought out the Anna in me), but I know men far too well to fall for one.

> When I let me love a man,
> the whole me will love him,
> and the whole man will love me,
> and we shall rise in love,
>   not fall in it.
> A living, growing tree impresses me.
> What is the view from your isle?
>   *(Miss) A. K. Kochbaum.*

Anna had finished reading my mail and was looking at me when I finished reading that (see I said "Anna"—well, let it stand). I said, "My apartment was broken into, also. Whoever answered when you called was no friend of mine. I gave nobody leave to stay there. You should see the place. Everything emptied out on the floor."

"What was taken?"

"That's the strange thing. Looks like he left more than he found, if anything, the mess the place is in. It wasn't a junkie job, for sure. Typewriter, stereo, suit, everything hockable, he left. Looks like he camped there awhile—empty pork-and-beans cans in the kitchen, cigarette butts on the floor. Another thing, the door wasn't busted open; he either picked the lock, or had a key. I keep saying "he"—you have a way of not denoting sex when you talk about "friends.""

"It was a man, with your southwestern accent. At first I thought he was you. As I mentioned in my letter, he was quite nosy, asking a lot of questions about you."

"Did you answer them?"

"No. Have you called the police?"

"No." I slid off the desk and went to the door, checked out the signs of repair, and glanced back at Dr. K. "If we've shared the same intruder, he couldn't pick your lock, apparently.

'Pears I was the victim of a pro—or maybe a pair of them: he or they smoked two different brands, Camels and Lucky Strikes, both unfiltered."

Dr. K was looking at the envelopes of the mail I gave her. "Little Rock, Quebec, New Orleans. This madness has become epidemic." She looked at me, shaking her head, "Whoever was in your apartment was never a client of mine. I would have recognized his voice. If it wasn't you, it was nobody I ever heard before. And of course it wasn't you."

I let that addendum slide by and said, "Did you give him your name?"

"I don't recall."

"You probably did, and he looked your address up and hit you next, looking for whatever he was looking for on me. He could have had a key to my apartment. I've given, uh, *friends* keys from time to time. Wouldn't be surprised if it was Tamara's new servicer, or an old one. She was a patient of yours, and nosy as a cat. I wouldn't put it past her to be behind something like this."

Dr. K pushed back from her desk and put her hands behind her head. "I doubt it. I think Tamara knew more than she wanted to know about you. Nevertheless, in both break-ins you were the target for not what you have, but who you are. Is there something about you I don't know? I know very little, actually."

I returned to her desk, leaned on it, and took one of the hands from behind her head. It stiffened in my hand, but did not try to free itself. Her other hand came down and positioned itself, much like a guardian, in her lap.

In a voice I hardly recognized I said, "Anna, aren't we avoiding the subject of real interest to us? That letter?"

She got her hand back, got up and went to the window for a peek out through the partly parted drapes.

"Which letter? The one from your alleged myth-in-the-flesh, or the one from the ex-soldier? Those letters come from two different worlds, Hanks, and only one of them from the real world."

She turned suddenly, nailing me with her big brown beautiful wise eyes.

"The veteran's letter has the weight of reality in it. The poor man relived his life just writing it, and the letter from that silly woman also on the train that night verifies what he said. Something awful happened. The girl got killed. Your girl in the white coat is . . . "

"She is *not!*" I demanded, pushing away from the desk and pounding it. "She's *alive!* You read her letter, postmarked New Orleans, Louisiana. You read what she said. She said things only *she* could have known. The thing we've got to face is that I've actually found her. The impossible has happened. She even saw me in the back seat of the blue car at the highway crossing south of McGehee, *and*—even God would not have dreamed it—she fell for me in that moment that I fell for her! It's too strange for truth. She even saw *The Bluebird* that day too. And get this—the iron of this is too thick to mine—she thinks I'm that lug trying to make time with her from the seat behind her on the train, and now she wants to meet *him!* To settle for him after all these years of saving herself for me. What's she gonna say when I tell her I was the boy in the blue car by the Delta Eagle's tracks? Why she's not gonna *believe* me. Why I . . . "

I raved on until Dr. K picked up that letter again, and then I gladly fell silent.

"Of course you are going to meet her if she calls."

"Are you kidding me? I've got to get to the bottom of this."

"Oh, I think you should. I also think you should temper your anticipation with these other letters. Something 'awful' happened on the train that night. Apparently a murder was committed. Apparently someone known as a 'box hunter' is murdering the murderers of your poor dead myth, looking for some box she had, God rest her soul. You could be in real danger. This letter from the person claiming to be *her* could be from that *Box Hunter*. Have you thought of that? He could have been sitting next to her, talked with her, and have seen everything she saw—enough to con you with this letter."

"Come on now, Karen, would a killer Box Hunter write a letter like that? If he'd read my ad, assuming there is such a myth as him, why hasn't he just shown up unannounced and done his thing?"

"Hey Bud, this is out of my area of competence. I'm not Agatha Christie. Call the police and tell them about this odd break-in you've had, and show them this letter from the desperate veteran, let them do the detecting. Maybe nothing is missing from your apartment because you didn't have that box there that he was looking for."

"Anna, on my worry scale, the Box Hunter doesn't even register. (Kim) is far more of a threat to us."

"Who?"

"That's the name of the girl in the white coat on the Delta Eagle. (Kim)."

"Oh. Yes," muttered Anna, glancing at the letter, then back at me. "What do you mean, 'to us'?"

"What if she's real?"

"Then you have found what you're looking for."

Suddenly I have Anna in my arms, and we hear me say, in a voice strange to us, "Nobody's real but us, let's run away together. Right now."

"If we're all that's real, why run—and where?" said Anna.

Then I am standing at the window, looking out and down, sorry for that disgusting display of solipsism for two. My truck was being ticketed by one of New York City's Finest. Black she was.

"How many cars did the Delta Eagle have?"

"Two."

"Which one was your girl in the white coat on?"

"One of them is all that I remember. Why?"

"Was she white?"

I turned and frowned. "What else? I mean . . . oh, I get what you mean. Can't swear to it, but I've always thought of her as . . . come to think of it, her color never occurred to me, just the color of her coat. Of course being white I guess I would guess she was too. Hmmm. Reckon I would have noticed if she was black."

"The veteran, Suffered Enough, points out that the car behind the engine was for blacks," said Anna. "That there could have been a black girl with a white coat in that car. Perhaps (Kim) is real, and black. If the riot broke out in the car for whites and a girl in a white coat was killed, (Kim) might never have known that in her segregated car. That would explain the apparent discrepancy in their letters regarding what happened that night."

I nodded, and muttered, "That's a point all right. Makes no difference to me though if she's black."

"I'm not suggesting that it does."

"I've had black female friends."

"I'm sure that if females came in dots and stripes that you would have sampled them too."

"Maybe in the dark. Say, it just occurs to me that I better get back out to Long Island before my squash court gets ransacked too."

Dr. K had that suspicious look again, but with some pain in it now.

"Mr. Hanks, would you please sit in that chair for just a moment, and listen—and then talk?"

I sat. She said, "Most of my clients are liars. Some of them don't even know it they've been at it so long and in so deep. Those who believe their own tales can be very convincing."

"I suspected as much. How deep and long do you think I've gone in my lie, Doc?"

We had some silence. She would not be stared down, but she softened about the lovely soul-probing eyes. She was in pain. I had directed my question to the wrong person. This was Anna. My focus shifted to her lips. I could see the gleaming tips of teeth in them. I pined to kiss her. Her lips began to move.

"Put yourself in my position," her luscious full lips said.

"I'd like that a whole lot."

"I have to be skeptical in this profession. Men bring me their fantasies. If I believed them I'd need help myself. Now you must admit that much of what you've told and shown me," touching the mail on her desk, "would strain the credulity of even a gullible person."

"I know just what you mean, but dual-personalitied shrinks who live in tree houses shouldn't stow thrones—throw *stones*. Guess you think I sacked my own apartment, wrote those letters, flew to New Orleans, Little Rock, and Quebec to mail them, or had it done. How many confederates do I have? How far back does my lie go? To the night of November the eleventh, nineteen hundred and forty-three, Anno Domini? Did I make up the girl in the white coat?"

"I almost wish you had."

"Then we'd never have met."

A. K. Kochbaum sighed and rubbed her eyes; "That's a chance I'd take." She looked at her watch and got up. "I have to go now. I have a—I'm going out this evening."

"Date, huh?" I said, getting up, "Same guy you spent the weekend with?"

"I didn't spend the weekend with anybody. I went to dinner and the theater with a date, and spent the weekend visiting my . . . "

"Uh-huh, sure. I got your footnote in that letter. First time I ever saw a footnote in a letter. How old are you anyway, thirty? Thirty-year-old virgin with your looks and occasional personality and not raised in a convent? Talk about a credulity strainer."

"Only one man will ever be convinced of that," said Anna.

I went to the door, started out, then turned with one foot in it. She was standing with the light at her back, her face obscured in shadow. She could have been Ann Landers then.

"You got me into this, said look for her. I did, I found her, we're going to meet, and now you don't believe me. Know what's gonna happen? I'm gonna fall—not rise—in love with (Kim) and she'll probably turn out to be another Mary James or worse. I need you now, to help me not make another big mistake. Come here and give me a kiss, at least."

She faced me in the partly open doorway; she said, unsmiling, "A kiss to build another dream on?"

She stiffened when I held her. "Don't tell me you've never even been *kissed?*"

"Oh I've been kissed, all right. I've been kissed real good."

She kissed me then, real quick, and pulled away. It was a kiss to build the dream of a real good kiss on, at best. "Keep me posted," she said as I departed, and I left her with the tasteless, "I'd love to."

Speeding eastward on the L.I.E. it occurred to me that Dr. K could have engineered all this herself, lured me to New York to leave my squash court unguarded, for reasons as obscure as she suspected mine were.

I found the squash court as I had left it, except for a note under the door, that went, "Dear Bud, an old friend of yours from Arkansas was by to see you today, and said he'd be back. He wouldn't give his name, said he wanted to surprise you. Give me a call when you get back, okay? Love ya, MJ."

I dialed the big house and got no answer; took a walk up there, found it empty. I was startled to find Mary James' room hewing fast to our sixth-grade teacher's injunction which she periodically had us chant: "A place for everything and everything in its place." Not an ash, a butt, an empty bottle on the floor, the bed made with clean linens, her two-volume law library neatly arranged next to her two-volume medical library in their little case. I felt watched, returning to the squash court.

I reached it in a sprint—the telephone was ringing. When I slammed the receiver to my ear it fetched me the dial tone. I sat at my worktable, going over cordwood orders, nipping

Southern Comfort from the bottle, going over good solid unin-triguing down-to-*terra-firma* cordwood orders, nipping. Some-thing sinister was afoot. Cordwood orders aside, I went through my mail, then through my pockets. It would have been good to go through the letter from (Kim) again, and the one from Suffered Enough, but I had left them with Dr. K, unwittingly. It was getting dark, but I didn't turn on the light. I felt like a target. Nip and tuck. The telephone rang.

"Yeah?"

"BH?"

"Speaking."

"Hi. It's me. (Kim)."

"(Kim)," I said, and "(Kim)," again. My heart had shot up and wedged between my vocal cords, tuning them to preado-lescent register.

"Did you get my letter?"

Her voice was a rich alto with a touch of the Old Southwest, a taint of something else.

"Yep," I got out, trying to swallow back my heart, sound like a man. "Where you calling from? Sounds like next door."

I heard her catch her breath—"Kennedy."

She heard me catch my breath.

"I've been wanting to come to New York for some time, anyway, and see *The Wiz.* The old Judy Garland film was one of my favorites. I have a seat reserved for tonight, and I'll be staying over with a friend. Tomorrow I plan to do some shop-ping, go to the Museum of Modern Art, and—are you free tomorrow evening?"

"I'm free right now."

"Then tomorrow afternoon I'll catch the Long Island train to Stony Brook, and we'll meet, okay? What's your name?"

"Bud Hanks. Look, I . . . "

"Let's not talk any more on the phone. How could we know what to say, anyway, until we've seen each other? Seeya in twenty-four hours or so—bye for now, Bluebird."

12

I was in the bed of my old woods pickup, unloading the last rick of a two-cord delivery onto the one-ton dump when I saw her coming down the path from the circle drive behind the big house. It was not yet 5:00 p.m., misting rain, darkening on a cold late November day. I wore a yellow slicker. She wore an off-white raincoat with the collar up, a matching vinyl hat cocked at a jaunty angle, sneakers. I had not heard the train pull into Stony Brook Station, and I had been tuned for it. One eye on the female figure coming down the path, I continued the unloading of one truck onto another.

And then I spied another female coming down the path, not fifty feet behind the first. She had on a light tan raincoat, matching rubber boots, and held a yellow umbrella. I continued to empty one truck into another. The real difference between dreams and reality, if any, had been on my mind all day. All day my mind had been twilit in the afterglow of a nightful of dreams. When I rolled out of bed late that morning I staggered like a man emerging from a movie theater behind a marathon of features old and new plus intermittent previews of features yet to come. One that lingers yet was a dream of entering Heaven's gates. The gates of Heaven were three-quarter-inch plyboard painted white, and stood ajar. Inside I found a ghost town, not a saint in sight, and then I heard a train departing from the far end of town which was an old Western movie set, and the gates were banging in a dusty wind, and as I awoke I was saying out loud, ". . . and then the dream abandoned me in the House not made with hands within."

I kept to my work as the two females approached, one behind the other, the first one unaware of the one behind her. In the film the third female will appear in a flash forward just as the first one arrives and the second one is in recognition range, and the three will fuse into one mysterious stranger. There is a place in reality for celluloid miracles. Dreams are real. They are really dreams. Theater is a necessary evil. I would have been drummed out of Plato's Republic. My different drummer well nigh drummed me out of this one. But dreams will be redeemed in the House not made with hands.

The first female breaks into a run just this side of the fountain. Her hat flies off. She skids to a stop at the back of the old pickup and looks up at me with a big ingenuous smile. She looks taller, more filled out. She has become a budding beauty in just a few weeks time. Her face is rainstreaked beautiful.

"Trouble at home, can I stay with you for a while?"

As she reached the dry fountain, I recognized Mary James who did not break into a run, though she quickened her pace. She must have spied Marsha coming down the path, and fell in line to thin the plot.

Marsha climbed aboard the dump truck's bed and commenced to receive from me and stack the cordwood splits. Mary James stood by in the rain under her brand-new yellow umbrella and watched us, reserved in comment. When Marsha and I finished loading the dump truck, I heard the train. I jumped off the empty truck, Marsha off the dump; we landed in a triangle with Mary James. We stood in that configuration, in the rain, listening to the whistling train braking into Stony Brook Station.

"Have a good visit with your old friend?" said Mary James.

"Haven't seen him yet. Saw your note and tried to call you but you were out last night."

"Oh, he took me out to dinner. He's real nice."

"That's nice. Exactly who is he?"

Marsha said, "Why are we standing here in the freezing rain?"

They looked at the squash court. I got in the dump truck, behind the wheel. Marsha and Mary James, in that order, got in on the other side. I started the engine. Marsha, crowding close to me, got my eye.

"My father wouldn't let me go to church, wouldn't let me say grace at the table, and blows up when I try to tell him about Jesus."

"He said he was coming down to see you, 'bout ten this morning," said Mary James. "Oh, he had no place to stay and since you weren't home, I let him have a guest room. He hasn't been down to see you yet? That's funny."

"I was home all evening and all night and all day today."

"I know the Bible says honor thy father and mother, but what if they don't honor you? So after school today I hitched here instead of going home. I hope I can stay with you until the Lord tells me what to do next."

"That's real funny, because his car's still parked up in the front drive."

"I'll sleep on the couch."

"Funny, huh, Bud Hanks?"

I rolled down the window in time to hear the train whistling out of Stony Brook Station; I shifted and commenced to pull away.

"Where are we going, Bud Hanks?"

"I have a delivery to make. You say this friend of mine came down this morning, and that his car's still parked up there? He didn't come down. Say he stayed in a guest room? Did you check his room? He might still be in it."

"I know what you're thinking, Bud Hanks, you're thinking I slept with him, I know how you think."

"I'm not thinking that either of you slept, Mary James. What's his name?"

"He wants to surprise you."

"He's already surprised me."

"Are you taking both of us on this delivery with you?" said Marsha.

I drove through the front circle drive of the big house. The only car there was Mary James' beat-up old Ford. I parked in front of it.

"Now that's funny enough to beat the band. His car was still here when I walked down to your house a minute ago. I thought he must of been down visiting with you all day. Now that's real . . . "

"Who is he, Mary James?"

"O. L. Smith. He was in school with you, back in grade school."

"I knew a Buddy Smith, an O. B. Green, an E. J. Weehunt, a T. C. Lambkin, but no O. L. Smith. What's he look like?"

"Good lookin'. Shorter than you, but good lookin' enough. Looks kind of like Humphrey Bogart. Solid built like James Cagney. Ugly good lookin', if yaknow what I mean. Same as you. Ugly good looks."

Marsha said, "Bud's not ugly at all. He's beautiful."

"You were in grade school with me too, Mary James, same grade. Did you remember this O. L. Smith?"

"I don't claim to have the memory you claim to have, Bud Hanks. Anyway I left Arkansas City in the seventh grade. Naw, he didn't remember me either. We didn't talk about the past, anyhow. Who cares about the past? That's over and done with and finished and through, the past is. It's the future we've got to watch out for."

"Are we going to make this firewood delivery or are we going to sit here all night talking about the past and the future?" said Marsha.

Taking Marsha's hand, I said, "It's getting too dark and it's too cold and rainy to deliver wood tonight. You need a place to stay for a while? Okay. I got your letter, and I think we ought to talk about it."

"Stay with you? Why that's not necessary, Bud Hanks, all the room I've got here, thirty rooms. Marsha you can sleep in the room you slept in when your daddy and I were seeing each other."

I squeezed Marsha's hand; "That's a good idea, your own room here in the big house. I'm tired now, didn't sleep well last night. I'm going back down and sack out early—see youall tomorrow."

"Hey Bud Hanks, I want to talk to you tonight."

"Tomorrow, Mary James, not tonight."

I got out of the truck and opened the door for them. Marsha slid out on my side, though. They sandwiched me at the front door of the big house.

"Mary James, if ol' O. L. Smith shows up again tonight, give me a call on the telephone. Marsha, maybe you and Mary James could pray together tonight. Pray for a better present. Mary James, lock the doors, all the doors. You left the house open today. You're too trusting or negligent. You've got to realize, both of you, that this house and all our houses lie way east of Eden. Good night, youall."

"Good night Bud (Hanks)."

I sprinted down the path to the squash court. I did not drive back down because, though I knew not at the time, it was in the Script of Living Theater that my firewood-loaded dump truck be ready and waiting where it was. I quickly shaved and showered, dressed in comfortable clean old clothes. I had already tidied up the place that morning, sliding the mattress into a far corner, and there had undergone a crisis.

To change the sheets or not change the sheets. The girl in the white coat had never been on the sex track in my mind. The Delta Eagle had never routed her into a masturbation fantasy. Not so much as a quick kiss on her cheek had my imagination planted. She did not exist from the waist down, for all I ever saw of her was from the white-coated shoulders up; breasts, if she had them (my imagination never sought them) were as much inner organs as was her heart, untouchable, and the white coat that covered them was all I ever saw or sought, as much a part of her as an angel's folded wings. To change the sheets was to admit a possibility I had never entertained, that we might meet and mate, while not to change the sheets meant that we might end up mating on (unthinkable) dirty sheets; to change them in her presence would be a crudity before that perfect union on the order of rolling on a rubber at your wedding even as you slip your bride's ring on.

Since clean sheets were better, in any case, than dirty sheets, I changed the bloody sheets, feeling like a premeditating rakehell of the basest sort, a defecator into monstrances, while doing it.

Even stuck off in that far corner my mattress seemed to dominate the room; when she arrived, my mind's eye saw, it would commence to glow evilly, like a giant television screen, and rerun all my carnal sins at full volume and in living color . . .

When she did arrive, however, I was ready to greet her with that peculiar peace of mind that rises out of healthy skepticism and total resignation to whatever. Once shaved, bathed, and dressed, I climbed the beam from which I'd witnessed Marsha's departure some weeks earlier; no sooner up there than I spied the dome and tail lights of one of Stony Brook Station's Tootsie Cabs moving out of the service drive behind the big house. Moments later, a white raincoat, white boots, and umbrella materialized in the rain this side of the now-overflowing fountain, moving down the path. I slid off the beam and waited by the door; waited a few breaths to open it after she had knocked. I cannot imagine a film version being any different.

She ducked smartly in out of the rain, folding her umbrella. "(Kim)?"

"In the flesh."

A little puff of steam came with that. Only two lights were on, a low-watt reading lamp over the couch and a flickering spiral of fluorescence over the kitchen table, both distant. I could make out the ivory teeth of a smile, the whites of eyes. She was my height exactly. She turned, placing her folded umbrella just outside the door, then moved farther in. I shut the door. She unbuttoned her raincoat and I helped her out of it, held it while she took off her hat; I took her hat. She shook out her hair and smiled again, in better light, a lesser smile, and it was as plain to me as a color chart that she might well be the authentic Girl. She had on an eye-white white fur coat. She looked around, up, back at me, inquisitively.

"Have any trouble finding the place?" I ventured.

"None at all. The cab driver knew where you lived."

"I would have met you at the station, but you hung up without telling me which train."

"I wanted to meet you this way," she said, in a softer voice, moving toward the stove. She had the fluid way of walking of a dancer born and bred.

I hung her things on the back of a chair and joined her by the stove where she was pulling off her gloves, also white. She stuffed them in the coat pocket, unbuttoned the coat.

"It's not this cold in New Orleans," she said, holding her hands over the stove. She had long slim fingers; she was long and slim, high-breasted.

I merely nodded, determined not to get off on the weather. We had our first awkward silence, with not even a platter spinning on the stereo, a golden oldie, to smooth us through it.

At length I blurted, "Can I fix you a drink or something?"

"No thanks, but if you want one, go ahead."

"Naw, I don't need one. Hey, why don't you sit down, if you want to?"

With an amused smile she moved around the stove, slipping out of her white coat which she lay over the couch arm and sat beside. I sat beside her. She leaned back, looking up at the rainstreaked skylight.

"Where did you see my ad, anyway? Just curious."

"My mother clipped it and mailed it to me from Memphis, with a big question mark on it. Of course she remembers that night well—last night we saw Dad alive," she said to the skylight.

"I placed that ad in a Memphis paper all right. The *Commercial Appeal.* I was just curious, since I didn't place it in a New Orleans paper."

"I'm skeptical too, Bluebird."

"You've got a right to be. Another point I'd like to clear up. You say you *saw* the boy in the blue car. I don't recall . . . "

Her eyes snapped from the skylight to mine, and she spoke quite frankly, "You aren't—weren't—the boy sitting behind me on the train that night."

"No."

"And if you were on the train, you wouldn't have been in . . . "

"I wasn't on the train."

She caught her breath. I reached under the couch and brought out my box of poetry fragments, set it in her lap, took off the lid.

"These are fragments of poetry I've written over the years. Read the scrap on top. I hope you're ready for it."

When she had read it through a few times and looked back at the skylight, I said, "We had been to McGehee to see *The Bluebird* and were on our way back home. The highway—State Road Four—crosses the tracks southeast of McGehee. There's a cemetery there, north of the road, west of the tracks. My grandfather Hanks is since buried in it. There was no light or barrier at the crossing in those days, and we almost hit the train. I was in the back seat, on the left, in our blue forty-one four-door Chevrolet. The moon was full. As the train went by I was watching the faces . . . "

"My God!" said (Kim), looking at me, finally, "I remember the cemetery now—the moonlight on the gravestones!"

She gasped, moving closer, her big brown moistening Nefertiti eyes on my eyes also misty.

"I can't believe it."

"Neither can I."

We embraced, the box of poetry pressed between us. We embraced the box of poetry pressed between us.

Then we turned each other loose.

"What shall we do?" said she, taking hold of my hands, glancing back up at the skylight.

"Talk? I don't know. Talk I guess, awhile? We have everything to talk about."

She squeezed my hands, real hard—"I'm too stunned to talk, Bluebird," she told the skylight. "I don't think I could even talk to God right now, because the prayer I never had the faith to pray has been answered." Then her eyes returned to mine. "Bluebird?"

"Yes, (Kim)?"

"Do you want to fuck?"

I near 'bout fainted. My mouth came open and nothing came out; wind came in. I had no precedent as guide to word or deed, not even from Hollywood. Slowly she released my hands and looked down at her feet, a martyr's smile etched about her lips and eyes.

"Is it because I'm black?"

Actually she was the color of new copper, moderately thick of lip and wide of nostril, with off-black hair of curls, not kings, I mean kinks, and could have passed for Indian, for the enlightenment of all you good white people out there in literary land who number knee-grows black or of whatever ratio of cream to coffee among your best friends and lovers, real and fancied.

I shot back: "It's because I never thought of you as a sex object, or subject, and because I don't know if you asked me that because you want to do that or just because you think I might want to, or simply because we live in times when people do that at the drop of a pant and think it's the thing to do, a howdy-do."

She put the poem scrap back in the box, closed the box and slid it back under the couch. She assumed the following position: legs close together, feet on the floor at a tilt, body turned from the waist up, facing me—have I mentioned that she wore a close fitting burnt-orange dress of a length I don't recall?—

and ventured again, "Then you aren't disappointed that I'm not white?"

"The color of your coat is all I care about."

She started laughing.

"And anyhow, aren't you sorry I'm not black?"

"Your soul's as black as mine, Bluebird," she laughed, throwing her head back for a good, thigh-slapping one, but musical. We made a duet of it, her alto, my baritone, rising from the couch together, risible, laughing dithyrambically as we undressed, falling back on the couch still laughing, limbs entangling, and then falling silent in a kiss. A soul kiss, to be sure.

A little later, at her request, I reached up and turned off the reading lamp, leaving us in the faint flickering glow of the kitchen fluorescent, a spiral nebula light years away . . . A few silent, groping minutes later, "Please don't be disappointed in me, be patient, I've never done this before," she whispers in my mouth, and I whisper back, "I'm a stranger in paradise, myself," unsure of my bearings.

Positioned for the coupling, I heard the distant rumbling and whistle of the train headed east or west, and I saw *her* in her lighted window headed south and gone, never seeing me, and my mind could not or would not make the connection between *her* and she beneath me, and the flesh pressed on, and the Delta Eagle, on a spur line, limped into a tunnel . . .

> How can I tell you how it went,
> two dreams meshing in the flesh?
> (where went the perfect shapes this omelet were?)
> How does bold lover mate unravished bride
> (soft pipe playing in and prematurely out)
> except the urn they shared apart be broke
> and their potsherds forced to a mating?
> (Heard melodies are sweet, but those unheard . . .)

A respectful period of postcoital caressing was observed. Then I got up and stuck another log in the stove. When I sat back on the couch (Kim) had turned on her side, facing back. I got my shirt off the floor, fished out my makings, and rolled a cigarette by the light of the spiral nebula.

"Smoke?" I muttered, glancing back at (Kim).

"Uh-uh, thanks, but I'll have that drink now."

I went to the kitchen and poured what was left in the Southern Comfort bottle into two glasses; dropped a rock in each of them. She had covered herself with that white coat when I returned.

"Here you go. It's a bourbon liqueur, all I've got. Hope it's okay."

She took a sip and held the glass in both hands, over her white-coat-covered breasts, her eyes on it, the glass. I drained my drink and lit the cigarette.

"Were you disappointed? Was I . . . was I like a *woman* to you?"

"What kind of a dumb question is that?"

"An honest question. Two of them. I didn't satisfy you, did I?"

"What you're saying is that I didn't satisfy you. Look, it happened too quick. We rushed it. That's what."

"I told you it was my first time. Guess you believe me now. I didn't know what to expect. Imagined, but didn't know."

"And it wasn't what you imagined, was it? I know."

I dropped my cigarette in the glass of ice and set it on the floor. I started to take her glass but she held onto it, sipped at it while I expostulated.

"We should have got to know each other first. We've been living with dreams of each other all these years, based on single sightings, but my dream of you can't be what you really are, nor your dream of me. We're just symbols to each other, and what happens when cymbals meet? They clash."

"I don't get your drift, man," said (Kim), over the rim of her glass.

I drifted on, tacking, "We loved what we saw but for a second, thirty-three years ago, and we've held on to what we saw and loved all these years. That's a rare order of tenacity we share. I think that just about any two strangers could meet for the first time and say 'Hey let's fall—or rise—in love,' and do it. Unless, of course, one of them was a freak or just plain repulsive to the other. But in our case . . . "

"Do you find me repulsive, Bluebird?"

"What's wrong with you, anyway? I won't dignify that with an answer. Look, (Kim), I think we could probably make it if we wanted to and tried, but first we've got to reconcile what we've held onto all these years with what we are now. We've built up expectations that no two mortals have a right to expect of each other. We've dreamed of each other all these years, never dreaming that we'd actually meet, but we did, and it's like finding yourself at Heaven's gates after a lifelong pilgrimage. So close. But once you've reached Heaven's gates do you storm them or do you wait until you're ready to be admitted? Heaven isn't Heaven until you're ready for it. It's just another old movie set. Milk first and then meat. The Apostle Paul said that. Babies thrive on milk, choke on meat. We should have had ourselves a glass of milk first, (Kim). What I'm saying is . . . "

"Cut the jivin', Bluebird. You think I'm a freak, don't you?"

I got up and looked down at her. "You weren't even listening."

"I don't want to lie here all night talking about why we didn't satisfy each other. Let's satisfy each other and then talk about that."

I turned away and sought out the darkest corner of the house for my penetrating gaze, and this: "Finding a mate is simple enough for animals, why not for us? How come we homo saps have to marry God? There's no marriage in Heaven, anyway. Says so in the Book. Why can't I just settle down with the next woman I meet, or the last woman I met, and get on with what I'm here to get on with? Surely I'm not here merely to get on with procreation? If so, I'm failing. I'm failing anyway, because I'm preoccupied with procreation and all its lovely trimmings, none of its loveless trappings. 'O wretched man that I am, Who will deliver me . . . ' "

The phone rang. Saved by Ma Bell. It was Anna Karenina Kochbaum.

"Mr. Hanks, I think I have identified the person who broke in here and stole your file."

"No shit."

"On a hunch I went through my files and compared the handwriting of my female clients with that of your letter from (Kim). By the way, has she called yet?"

"Uh-huh."

"And?"

"We agreed to meet. So what did you turn up?"

"None matched, which didn't surprise me. Breaking and entering is a male enterprise almost exclusively. So next I began comparing the handwriting with male clients I considered likely suspects, and then a bizarre thought struck me. I have a few male to female transsexual clients."

"Oh shit."

"I will be violating a trust in giving you this information, but since he—or she now—broke in and stole your file, you have a right to know, especially since you have agreed to meet her. Do you recall the black person sitting across from you the day you came unscheduled, the one with whom you had words?"

"You said he wasn't that kind of person."

"Apparently I was wrong. He was, after all, becoming another person."

"Yeah—a woman, capable of anything."

"He must have heard me speak to you by name. I recall that he asked a number of questions about you during our session. Whatever passed between you two in the waiting room must have made quite an impression on him-her; so much so that he-she was obsessed enough to break in here and steal your file. This may solve the mystery of your own break-in. I should have realized when I read that letter that the information in it could only have been known by you and me, and the person who stole your file—and, of course, if she existed, the girl in the white coat."

"We all have twenty-twenty hindsight, Agatha."

"His name is Horace Kimberly, Mr. Hanks—or was. It's a good guess that she calls herself *Kim* now, and I strongly suggest that you call off your meeting with her, politely but firmly."

"Too late for that."

"I see. Very well, but I urge you to be careful—for her sake, not yours. She is an intelligent and sensitive person, and you could do her a great deal of harm by being insensitive. Transsexuals are very anxious about their first contacts with the opposite sex. Unless they are public figures, they often move and begin life all over again with new identities, and their deepest fear is that they will not be accepted as authentic, that somehow people, especially members of the opposite sex, will detect that they've made the switch. Mr. Kimberly as Kim will be looking for . . . "

"Is telling me all this going to help things? I might have been fooled."

"Mr. Hanks, you've been a fool too long—I'm trying to help you too. Now just remember that Kim is looking for love. You will very likely be her first contact with a man since her operation. She will be very anxious, very eager to please. She will be looking for love—to share. She will behave like a virgin —and as a woman now she is, of course, a virgin."

"Look, I'll be real, real sensitive. Real gentle with her."

"I am not suggesting that you have an affair with her, if that's what you think."

"Why not? I'm not . . . "

"Do what you please, Mr. Hanks, but keep in mind that you're in a position to take unfair advantage, that she's not to be treated as just another lay. Frankly, I don't think you're capable of treating a woman any other way. That poor creature deserves a warm, tender, loving, sensitive man with whom to share her first sexual experience."

"Look, I'll keep you posted."

"Don't ever speak to me again."

Her hang-up crashed in my ear, reverberating off the far drum. I glanced over at our poor creature, that fey high-yellow spermataozoon that had eyeballed me over a *Hustler* in Dr. Kochbaum's tacky waiting room, and went to the bathroom. Baptized my member in hot soapy water, rinsed out my mouth, avoiding the face in the mirror, rummaged around in vain in the kitchen for a bottle of consciousness lowerer, came down and jammed another log in the stove, and faced again the couch.

It was still there, sitting up, with that fake fur white coat covering its silicone-injected titties and that cock-skin-lined man-made hole between its legs. Guess I was just prejudiced.

"You seem more upset than ever—hope it was the phone call."

"It was the phone call all right."

"Girl friend?"

"Ex. Look, (Kim), I don't know. What do you think?"

"Do you want me to leave?"

I let a heavy sigh and sat beside her, saying, "No." It was the Christian thing to say. Also the Jewish, the Moslem, the humanist, and the easiest. Since she thought I thought she was the girl of my dreams, what else could I say? What kind of a man would she take me for if I sent her out in the rain behind a quick lay? Besides, she was, whatever he had been, a sensitive soul, eager to please, gorgeous, and I owed her at least all the sensitivity the doctor ordered; come the morrow I'd get rid of her in a reasonably sensitive way.

I leaned back on the couch with deep relief that this really wasn't *her*, that *she* was still on the Delta Eagle, unviolated. Kim's head lolled over on my shoulder, her hand settled in my lap. I had plumb forgot that I was still naked. She whispered in my ear, "Where's the bed? Let's try again."

See here now, I had a prejudice to overcome.

We were well on our way to a no complaints climax, Kim on top, when came the knock; we froze thus juxtaposed. The knocker knocked again—a rapid series of blows a bit hard for Mary James, more like a Gestapo knock in a World War II B grade black and white hair raiser, a detumescer, a setter-off of vibrations in the windowpanes. We waited breathlessly for the knocker to go away, but no, a sudden wind came in then stopped as suddenly. I had forgot to lock the door.

Soft footfalls in the room. I slipped from under Kim, covered her, and crept to the couch where I slipped quickly into my trousers. One feels so naked naked when there's an intruder in the house.

"Who's there?" I demanded.

"That you Bud Hanks?" came a male voice from the old southwest.

A squat shape hove into view in the kitchen light behind it. I angled the reading lamp toward it and turned it on. He shielded his eyes, holding the other hand out in peace. He had on a khaki trenchcoat with the collar up, a snapbrim low over his eyes.

"It's me all right. Who in the hell are you?"

"Din the lady up in the mansion up there tell you?"

He moved out of the light. I followed him with it, keeping him in the spot to my worktable, where he stopped with his back to me, hands behind his back.

"We go way back, me and you, Bud Hanks. Arkansas City, Arkansas." He moved one hand from behind his back to give my chainsaw a nudge, then turned, shielding his eyes again. He glanced toward the mattress corner, which was getting some of the light.

"'Pears you've got company with you on that there mattress. Sorry to interrupt. Kin she wait in another room while me and you visit? Hit won't take long."

"The lady is indisposed," I muttered, buckling my britches, "Go up those stairs over there and wait for me in the kitchen. I'll be a minute."

"Aw you lead the way."

I glanced over at the blanketed lump on my mattress and, shirtless, barefoot, irked, led the way. We faced each other, not sitting, across the kitchen table. He looked like Humphrey Bogart on a James Cagney frame.

"Mary James said your name was O. L. Smith, but I don't remember you, name nor face."

" 'Indisposed,' now that's a funny word. What's that mean?"

He had Peter Lorre's milk-curdling smile, though like Bogie's it worked independently of his eyes.

"Maybe it was Arkansas City, *Kansas,* where you used to know another Bud Hanks."

His smile went out like a match in the wind.

"Believe I told you *Ar*kansas. The town in Kansas they call Ar*kansas* City. Now that one, hits a real city. One in Arkansas hit aint nothin' but the wide end of a narrow road. *Indisposed,* don't that mean sick? The lady get her monthlies? Now they don't learn you words like that down in Arkansaw City Arkansaw. A feller's got to come up to Yankee land to get somethin' like that in his head."

His hand shot suddenly across the table, startling me.

"Christian name's Ossie Lee. That ring a bell?"

Pure old habit, not courtesy, stuck my hand out and took his, which hung in mine limp as a fresh corpse's, but colder, while the rest of him stood rigor-mortised—an effect hindsight tells me he intended. I let go of it real quick, and it sprang back as it had sprung forth. I gave him the squint-eye, trying to recollect. 'Course I remembered Ossie Lee, but not his last name, nor even the face of his youth. But Smith? I would have remembered that.

"I knew an Ossie Lee, okay, but you don't ring his bell. Look, pal, if this is a friendly visit . . . "

" 'Member that old nun I told you about, the one I pulled her habit up at the train station, and didn't see nothin' underneath? Reckon you 'member me telling you 'bout that, 'bout that old nun didn't have nothing underneath?"

My eyes went out of focus, the short hairs on my neck erect. I saw this freak in my apartment in New York, going through the first few pages of the first draft of my manuscript of this, tossing it page by page, over his trench-coated shoulder. My eyes refocused. 'Pears I stood face to face with Suffered Enough's Box Hunter. I gave him a little test, just to be sure.

"Guess you're Ossie Lee, all right. Nobody but him would have done that, and talked about it. But it comes back to me now that you were a Culpepper?"

He took out a pack of Luckies, picked one out, wet his lips, and glued it in; lit it with a Zippo automatic, its chrome finish worn down to the dull brass. The smoke had collected under his hat brim before he spoke.

"Jus' used Smith to test you," he muttered, glancing about. "Reckon you're ol' Bud Hanks, awright. Whatchu runnin' here? A sawmill?"

"And you're ole Ossie Lee Culpepper, for sure. Son of a gun. Hey, Ossie, let's get together tomorrow for a good visit."

I threw him a conspiratorial wink toward the mattress corner, instead of a punch; the chiefest regret of my life is that I didn't punch him out right there, hogtie him, and call the police. I thought I still had time.

"I'd like to do that a whole lot, podnuh, but I've got to be back in Washington, D.C., tomorrow. Yep; the nation's capital. Get rid of the girl, whacha say? Old friends they come before new girl friends in a Christian nation. Now am I right? If the girl's from out of town, send her up to the mansion up there. The lady there, that Mary James, she's got rooms enough. Reckon you know that. She put me up in one of them last night. I tuk her out to supper first. She can sure eat. Sure drink, too. Real loose lady, tell you that. Real charmer when she's a sheet in the wind. Come into my room thataway and crawled in bed with me. Only I don't do that, not when I'm on duty. Turns out she passed out anyhow, and I went and got me another room. Now I'll git right to . . . "

Kim appeared at the top of the steps, buttoned up in the white coat, the rest of her apparel in her arms. She passed by us, looking straight ahead, and disappeared in the bathroom, slamming the door behind her.

The man went through a metamorphosis, not exactly a Jeckyll to Hyde or a werewolf to Chaney, just a something weird to something equally weird. He *was* Bogart on a Cagney frame. His lips tightened on the glowing Lucky, bringing it erect, and then he spat it out, ground it out on the floor with the toe of a black military-type shoe. Hands interred in the trenchcoat pockets, he descended the steps and ambled off toward the worktable.

I followed, about to pounce when he spun suddenly.

"Hey, who *was* that girl in the white coat?"

"That was the girl in the white coat."

He nodded, breaking into a smile to freeze the curdled milk. "Very funny, Mister. I'll remember to tell Mr. Roosevelt that you had a sense of humor."

He cast another glance up at the bathroom door, backing away, then took a stroll around the worktable, like an idler at a garage sale, giving the chainsaw a heft. He took out a pack of Camels, beat one out, screwed it dry into his lips, and lit it with a kitchen match struck off his thumbnail. We faced.

"It's time for business, Hanks. Where's the box? The darkie in the white coat in on this? Did she come to get the box or give it? Don't tell me she answered your ad for romance. My constitution can't take more than one joke per customer. One more and I erupt in violence. That ad in the personals was your code, wasn't it? Where's the box, Mister?"

He blew smoke in my face, and again I was all cocked and primed to light into him, only I didn't. Guess I was just too incredulous to be alarmed, being one generation removed from that audience that ducked from fists and locomotives and things coming at them from the silver screen. All I did was blow his smoke back at him and pursue the foolish course of sweet reason.

"It's none of your business, but since you've taken the trouble to bust in here and intrigue me by asking, I placed that ad because I wanted to meet the girl mentioned in that ad, and nobody else, and the lady you just saw answered that ad for the same reason I placed it. For romance. Box? Code? You're barking up the wrong tree, fellow."

He removed his cigarette with thumb and forefinger. He pulled on his earlobe and showed his teeth. One eyelid half-masted. His feet slid wide apart, his knees bowed back. Bogart-Cagney incarnate. Only his voice I couldn't place.

"If it's none of my business, why are you standing there making it my business? Because you're as guilty as you are yellow, that's why. You know I'm not Ossie Lee whoever, so how come you let on I was? *Hoover*'s the name. J. Edgar. Does that ring a bell?"

"An asylum bell."

"I didn't hear that, yet. Now let's be smart, Mister. Are you gonna tell me again that that shine in the white coat was the one on the train that night? That's the same as saying my mama raised a fool. The girl on the train was *yellow*, and she got croaked. I know that, and you . . . "

"Yellow? Why so's the lady that just passed by us in the white coat yellow. Croaked?"

"She's a *high* yellow but she's black, or my mother raised a fool. Aiko Abé, the girl on the train, was a *Jap*, and got what was coming to her. Maybe your high-yellow tomato up there was on the train that night, but she wasn't in the car we were on because we were in the *white* car."

"I wasn't even on the train, fellow. 'Aiko Abé?' That was the girl in the white coat's name?"

He dropped his Camel, unbuttoned the trenchcoat, and hipped his hands. He had on a double-breasted blue serge suit with wide lapels, circa 1943.

"Hanks, I've been on this case for thirty-three long years, and I've got about another thirty seconds of patience left. Just give me the box and I'll be off to Washington on the next flight and you can go back to your blackbird of happiness."

A laugh stormed up from deep within me, the deep gut laugh of the absurd, the laugh of Abraham and Sarah at the news of Isaac, the treasured laugh of those prospectors watching their gold dust blow back up the Sierra Madre, a laugh I knew would be dangerous in this scenario and I tried to vent it, bursting *"Box!"*—and out it came, bigger than the both of us. I fell back on the couch and almost laughed my head off.

Hoover reached into his trenchcoat and blue serge suit, on into his armpit, and whipped out a revolver, and my laugh was gone like a good dream.

"Git offa that sofa, boy."

The phone rang.

I got up. This wasn't real. It was a movie. A gun was pointed at me. It was a .38 mounted on a .45 frame. The phone was ringing.

"Now *git* that box."

"Man, I wasn't even *on* the train, I've done *told* you, why I wasn't but twelve years old in nineteen forty-three, now stop pointing that . . . "

"And my mama she raised a fool. Gimme the box or Imo blow a hole in you of a size to git my foot in."

I looked at the ringing phone, a straw—"I better get that phone."

"Let it ring."

The phone rang and rang. This was a Woody Allen movie. I was Woody Allen. The audience was laughing its ass off at this mess Woody Allen had gotten himself into. Woody Allen heard himself laugh, hollow as Bud Hanks' head, "Hey fellow, come on now, I don't like having guns pointed at me."

The audience booed and hissed and left the theater. The phone stopped ringing.

"You don't have to like it. Congress hasn't passed legislation making it mandatory for a man to like a loaded gun pointed at him, and if it did, Mr. Roosevelt would veto it, because a man is not supposed to like it. There would be no progress at all in this world if men liked guns pointed at them. How would you like for me to reholster it smoking? And then pluck your blackbird of happiness before I take this barn apart to find that box? I know it's here, sure as God made little green apples, and you've got the time a man can hold his breath to come up with that box, or you can try breathing through the holes I made in you."

My palms went up in helpless emptiness, in empty helplessness, my eyes crossing in focus on the advancing black hole of his pistol muzzle and cylinder of naked lead balls. I did not like the sight of that at all. Words fail me, how I felt about that pistol pointing at me. Why if I could just get mad I'd take that pistol from him and shove it in, depending on how mad I got, an aperture of his to get us a rating anywhere from PG to X. Could I not recall instant replays of Bogart, Cagney, Mitchum, Wayne, Cooper, Peck, Scott, Cameron, Jones, Holt, Starrett, Autry, Rogers, Steele, Canlaster—I mean Lancaster—Poitier, Raft, Robinson—oh they are legion . . . hell, Woody Allen even —getting mad enough to steal this scene? But I couldn't get mad. All I got was scared. I was paralyzed with fear. I was so scared I was about to wet my pants, water sports in a 42nd Street jackoff booth, two bits a minute. I looked at my feet, my naked feet; their toes had crawled under them. I spied the orange Buff Town Bond Columnar Pad box stuffed with poetry fragments sticking out from under the couch, behind their heels.

"Box," squeaked the boy in the blue car, 1943.

"Reach it out real gentle and slide it crost the floor. Use yore foot. Keep them hands in sight. Up high with them hands. Take holt of a cloud. There you go—now slide it on over here real easylike. What size a shoe you wear, anyhow, boy?"

The Box Hunter held the box against his side with the arm of the hand holding the pistol pointed at my bladder. His free thumb thumped off the top, peeled up some pages, letting them sally off onto the floor, without even scanning them.

"Ast you what size shoe you wear."

"Thirteen."

The Box Hunter gouged up the rest of the pages, riffed them, and tossed them box and all over his shoulder. Rejection.

"Thas all? Thirteens? How wide a foot you got? Don't look no wider than a shake."

"A. Hard to get a fit."

"Hit don't mean nothing, the size foot a man's got. All it means is he'd of been a taller man, hadn't been so much turned out in foot. Me, I wear a size six shoe and proud of it, and mine's a heap wider than yourn. Quadrupple E. That wasn't nothin' but poems in that box. I don't like poems. Man writes poems, he's a fruit."

He was right under my face, behind that, looking up in my bulging eyes out of the slits of his. He was a foot shorter than I, a confident little rock prepared to play Procrustes, mad as a hatter, need I say? He was going to hit me with his gun, low down. I could see it coming. Literary criticism run amok, with an absurd footnote.

"That was not the box, Hanks. I remember the box plain as my mother's face. I observed it as soon as the Jap tomato boarded the train. I got a seat across the aisle from her and kept my eye on it, because I knew what was in that box. I put two and two together, see? That's my profession, putting two and two together. And subtracting one from one."

The pistol wiggled in his hand.

"It wasn't an orange business box full of fruity poems. It was a white shoe box full of *high I.Q.*"

"Full of *what?*"

"*High I.Q., ya stupid big-foot fruit!*"

Like the connecting arm on the drive wheels of old steam locomotives his gun arm jerked back—for a groin jab with the gun I thought, and moved to block it, but his right (he was a southpaw) connected in a swift jab with my chin; not hard enough to deck me in the open, but with my legs back against the couch I was sat hard on that—him yelling *"Timber!"*—in no position to retaliate. Nevertheless I bounced and pounced.

Next thing I remember I'm on my hands and knees, picking up my scattered pages, stacking them back in the box while the Box Hunter sits on my worktable, his short legs dangling, watching me over his gun muzzle which he holds under his nose, sniffing in the smoke. My ears ring and I'm talking fast, hoping his ears aren't ringing too loud too. When I bounced the shot must have passed between my legs. There's a hole in the couch where my heart was. My pounce landed me on all fours on the floor. What I was saying went about as follows:

"The box wore out, Mr. Hoover, don't shoot again," or more probably, *"Don't shoot again, Mr. Hoover!* This is what you're looking for! The white shoe box wore out and I transferred the *code* to this orange business box. It's not poems it's *code*, just what you were looking for—now don't fly off the handle, it was *my* mama who raised the fool—*here, here,* these were *hers,* Aiko in the white coat's, and they're all yours now, all this *code!* I don't understand it and I've spent thirty-three years trying, but . . . " and so forth, more or less.

I held out the box to him, refilled and with the lid back on, on shaky legs. I could see in his face not whether he believed me, but that he was beyond belief. The box I held could have metamorphosed into a white shoe box and he would still have rejected it, no matter what was in it. The Delta Eagle could have pulled in then, and the Girl in the White Coat leaned out her window and handed him the Real Box with the Holy Grail in it, and he would have given it a glance and tossed it box and all, and come on with his gun, and gone on looking. The man was all means and no end, like the lostest kind of poet, glued to a single theme, only he was his own effort, literally, an incarnate scrap of bad poetry with both ends ripped off, a fragment . . .

He shoves back the hat on his head, letting loose a lock of red hair to drop down on his low forehead and swing there like a bloody sickle.

"You say the shoe box wore out? Where's it at?"

I came a heartbeat of saying I'd thrown it out, but the Good

Lord whispered in my inner ear that long as I was lying I'd better lie smart, so I said, "In the cellar."

"Howja git it in the first place, if you weren't on the train?"

"I've never admitted I was on the train. You know why."

He laughed, not like movie madmen laugh, but humorful, and touched his forelock with a stubby finger, and pulled his hat low again, cocking his head back, that pistol pointed steady at my crotch.

"And you was only twelve, you say? I thought you was sojers on that train. Must of been a boy scout troop. You boy scouts are all the same. Feared to admit you was on that train. Whacha think you done on that train worse than gang-bang Miss Rising Sun? Imo give you a merit badge for that. But you don't get no medal for the execution. Mr. Roosevelt, he's gonna pin that one on me. You boy scouts tucked tail and jumped off the train fore hit had stopped. I've done had to splain this to ever one of you I done tracked down and paid off for actin' like boy scouts stid of sojers. I seen her tuck that shoe box up in that white coat she had on when you scouts commenced to grab at her, and when you tucked tail and left her lyin' spreddylegged in the aisle, I got down and felt up inside that coat to git that box for my country. I—I . . . "

A tremor went the length of the maniac and his pistol, and through me, likewise, a twin tremor went.

"I had not suspected, Hanks, that anybody but me was after her box, that one of you soldiers was a traitor to his country. Otherwise, I would not have wasted time searching the girl. I would have been on you before you got off the train. That mistake cost me—and my country—thirty-three long years. When it became apparent that the box wasn't on her, I . . . "

Again we have our tremors.

"I tuk her by the throat an I said to her, *What was in the box them sojers tuk?*, and she croaked back at me, her eyes bugged out like yourn are now, *High I.Q.!* An' then I knowed what I had done suspected. I knowed for shore. An' then I squeezed and wrung the eyes and tongue plum out of her head, for God and Country, Mister . . . and here's *yore* merit badge . . . "

I didn't try to knock the gun out of his hand with the box. In his own way he had more grip than I did. I shoved the box into the gun, and kicked him in the nuts, gun going off one shot tunneling through those few inches of more years of my efforts to find ends, my obscure code, my (some purists call it poetry) fragments. They slowed the bullet down enough that it petered out in my palm, kind of deep, but boy did I kick the Box Hunter in the nuts. Hit turned him a backward somersault, my naked size thirteen-A did. And then I passed up my last chance to give this a real Golden Oldie ending—

I ran.

CUT! CUT! FOR CHRISSAKES CUT! HANKS YOU SON OF A BITCH, YOU WERE S'POSED TO GET HIS GUN BEHIND THAT KICK, NOT CUT AND RUN!

I locked myself in the bathroom. I could lie and say I ran in there to save Kim, and the film might well give me benefit of the doubt, showing me flying by the quickest way out—the way in—and up the steps in two leaps, bounding past the kitchen like a kangaroo and ducking into the bathroom (empty, by the way, the window opened wide; I never did see Kim again; she left lipsticked on the mirror, in coral ice, a railroad track with a bird on its back, feet up, Xs for its eyes, between the rails) like a fool.

Through the bathroom door—flush plyboard, pervious to real bullets—I heard the Box Hunter moaning and threshing about on the squash-court floor. I plucked his slug from my left hand and pocketed it. I looked out the window, down on a two-story drop, and made it (too).

UP IN THE BIG HOUSE, Mary James and Marsha are spending a quiet rainy evening at the kitchen table. Getting acquainted. Mary James sips brandy from the bottle through a straw while Marsha reads to her from a pocket-size New Testament. I saw them through the window, see them yet, side by side, still in their raincoats in the big drafty kitchen, old Seth Thomas clucking on the wall over the sink, true to the minute. Marsha reads from John's Gospel, Chapter 3 ("For God so loved the world . . . "), and Mary James sips and nods, doing her best to be all ears; they are at peace, and my mind reins in as I burst in and runs me back, backward down the rain-puddled path to a sprawl from where I levitate into the squash court's bathroom window and back on the fly, backing down and in a spin to face the somersaulted Box Hunter . . . then on with time according to the Script of Might Have Been . . . O to run time back and end it there for one or both of us, the guilty and the mad, anything to spare the innocent, as I burst willy-nilly in again on them, bringing down what was and was to be.

"No time to explain, we've got to get out of here, the man's a homicidal maniac," I explained, dashing for the wall phone, limping on my right foot, bleeding from my left hand, naked from the waist up and cuffs down, sopping wet, "Out with the lights, we've got to get out of here, he'll be up here after me . . . oh shit!"

The phone was dead.

"Bud Hanks, are you *drunk?*"

"He's *bleeding.*"

"He who?"

I herded them out, over their questions, into the front circle drive where I expected the Box Hunter's car to be parked for me to rob of its distributor, but his car wasn't there; we piled into the dump truck, and as I turned the key there came the glow of headlights aglittering in the rainwet trees down the drive and growing brighter, a quiet explosion.

He had driven down and parked outside my door, while I was on the mattress, coupled with a transsexual, tuned to a distant train.

We locked the truck doors and scrunched down, behind my reasoning: when he sees the truck and Mary James' car still there, he'll search the house, and once he's inside, we'll speed away. And so we waited, down in the dump truck cab. Years went by, all the same season, rainy, cold, the same questions hissed and shushed, my shot hand not healing, throbbing through the years. Finally I sat up for a peek out—no headlight glow ahead, just rain and darkness.

I started the engine and the windshield went spiderwebby with a bark of manmade thunder. And then again, the bark, the bites of flying bits of glass, and yet again, the engine high, low gear engaged, clutch out, my head below the dash, Mary James screaming, we're off like an overstuffed arthritic rabbit. One hell of an escape vehicle, a one-ton dump with two tons of cordwood in the bed—a blivet by any other name.

At the end of the long narrow winding drive lights hove into our outrigged side mirrors, bright, brighter, blinding. I was going to swerve left on Harbor Road into Stony Brook with its cops and magistrates, civilization and sanctuary, but he passed us where the drive widened into Harbor Road, power-skidded around and cut us off. I rammed him, almost cleared the road of him, backed up to ram him real good, but my side window went KAARAK—spiderwebby, and I wheeled right, wrongly, and lumbered off down narrow, winding, potholey, hilly Harbor Road.

The windshield was laid out in a mosaic over the dashboard like ruined, sequined old lace. Needles of cold rain blew in our faces—two of them; Mary James was under the dash. The outrigged mirrors tormented me with light—the lights that chase, the lights I face in flight, the heatless, blinding light of Lucifer pursuing. I dreaded the hills of that hilly road, where I had to downshift, where he might shoot out the tires. Barreling down one hill we ran an oncoming car up a steep bank into the bush; ahead was Cordwood Path where I hoped to turn left into St. James, but our pursuer passed us at that intersection, spinning around in it, there to meet us head-on, hanging out the window like an engineer of yore, but with that pistol pointing—

I swerved right, the load shifting, almost tipping us, and

ground off up Cordwood Path, up the steepest longest hill in the East. The lights got so close behind they dropped out of the mirrors, like suddenly setting suns. The same thought came to the three of us:

"If we just didn't have all that weight behind," said Marsha.

Mary James: "This here's a dump truck, Bud Hanks, dump that firewood off!"

Bud Hanks: *Dump the load on him.*

For a split instant the bright lights appeared in the mirrors again—then up and out in two hundred and fifty-six cubic feet (air spaces included) of cascading locust, maple, oak and hickory; by the time the dump bed was back down we had crested the hill and were rattling loud and fast down the other side. We met headlights coming up—I blinked mine and blew the horn in warning of the blockade. Not far from Moriches Road I pulled into a driveway and cut the lights and engine.

"How come we're stopping here, Bud Hanks? he might of got through."

"We have to call the police, somebody could get hurt back there," said Marsha.

Confident that it would take a bulldozer to get through back there, I got out and went to the door and knocked, Mary James behind me, raising hell. Nobody was home, and a yearling-sized Doberman inside, louder than Mary James, dissuaded me from breaking in.

I turned the truck around in the drive and headed back out. At the intersection of Cordwood Path and Moriches a car was in front of us, making a left turn toward St. James, my intended destination; I signaled left.

"That was the car coming up the hill when we were going down," said Marsha.

I turned right. The car, a yellow Volvo station wagon, seemed to slow down.

"It's *him*—it's *him!* He comman*deered* that car!" shrieked Mary James.

I watched the Volvo's taillights in my mirrors until they

curved out of range, then turned my lights off and felt our way around the next curve and over a hill, then lights back on, I gunned her. A mile down the road and lights appeared again in the mirrors, and headlights loomed ahead. Any light now was the enemy. I was going to take a left on River Road and ball the jack for Smithtown, but I missed River Road for watching the rear in the mirrors. There was only darkness in them. My fear turned into a foolish feeling. The Box Hunter was buried under cordwood. We were safe. We were on Short Beach Road now, the Nissequogue River on our left; in the last house on the right, a semi-converted brick barn and carriage house, lived an obscure novelist of my acquaintance. We'd pull in there and call the cops. Marsha thrust herself head and shoulders out the right window and looked back.

"That yellow Volvo is following us without lights on."

Yelling at her to get back in, I drove on toward Short Beach, Mary James yelling. Around the last curve before the beach I stopped, shifted into reverse, turned off the lights, and waited. The tide was high, the river almost on the road. We were in the lights of Kings Park Marina, across the river. I kept my eyes on the mirror. I would see him come creeping around the curve, and I would ram him, full throttle, right into the river.

"He's not following," said Marsha.

"Get back in!"

Mary James popped up from under the dash.

"Where in the hell are we—oh hell Bud Hanks that's Short Beach over there, this here's a *dead end*, he's got us *trapped!*"

"Maybe it wasn't him after all, maybe it was just some kids fooling around, he's still not following," said Marsha.

I reached over and pulled her back in. And then I saw that landmark fountain built into the rock wall just outside her window. Above was the old brick pump and ice house, and above that, nesting in what only God could make—*sanctuary*.

13

MARSHA went right on up the limb, taking my word on faith that there was a comfortable house up there, but Mary James sat down on the outcropping of rock and wouldn't budge, not caring if the Kingdom of God was up there, because, she announced, she got hysterical and peed in her pants in high places. I told her to hush and pee on the rock before we took to the limb, and she repeated, hysterically, that she got hysterical and peed in her pants in high places. She kicked and scratched me as I tried to drag her onto the limb, yelling a third time her incontinence in high places, so I had to bop her with the ham side of my fist atop her head and haul her up on my shoulder, kicking and screaming and peeing on me.

It was very dark and the rainwet limb was slippery, and longer than a dream, and I was visited with the terrifying thought that I had dreamed the house up there.

Marsha was awaiting us on the ladder to the trapdoor which was padlocked. Mary James had dug in on me and couldn't be removed without leaving part of her clinging to me or part of me on her. Marsha took off her tattered, splattered new raincoat while I wrestled Mary James over onto my left shoulder. Marsha wrapped the coat around my good right hand while I got a grip on the ladder with my wounded left. Marsha held onto my left arm and the ladder, to steady me, and I used my woodsman's muscle and the strength born of desperation to punch the trapdoor open. Once on the promenade deck I busted the treehouse door in with my ass, being barefoot.

Marsha found a light and drew the drapes. MJ beelined off me for the bar.

If one can come to terms with a treehouse built for serious adult human habitation, then a treehouse furnished in Early American need not strain the credulity, if one keeps in mind that which is stranger than fiction. It was two-storied, and boasted most of the Late American conveniences. Living and dining areas, kitchen and bath on the first floor, then up a spiral stairway lugbolted round the tree trunk, one happens upon a den, a bedroom and a second bath. The wreckage of a harpsichord given up in futile mid-repair was in one curve (the house was round, tank-shaped in fact, with a cedar shingled conical roof, and looked not unlike a Middle American tank town's trackside water tank—with windows and a promenade deck) of the den, while in my squash court's cellar lies to this day the remains of a windmill powered cordwood saw, sans blade. The floors were carpeted in deep pile moss green. The electrical heating panels were adequate. The sewer system was the hollow heart of the tree. It was relatively odor free.

Marsha and Mary James headed for the showers, I for the telephone. Then I showered and Marsha nursed my wound while Mary James pumped me for what had happened on the phone, while patching herself back together with a quart of Johnnie Walker Black. We were decked out in clean dry garments from our hostess's wardrobe. Mary James and Marsha looked a little lost in the bigger woman's pants suits, while I felt a bit closeted in her bib overalls and bright blue cotton pullover. Here's what happened on the phone:

Nissequogue's police dispatcher told me to call Head of the Harbor if that's where the incidents took place. Head of the Harbor's dispatcher said their patrolman on duty was tied up at an accident on Cordwood Path and to call Nissequogue if that's where the man chased us. I told her that the man who chased us was in the accident on Cordwood Path, and was he still in the car? She didn't know. I told her it was important that I know. Where was I calling from. A *what?* She hung up on me. I called Nissequogue again and was told that the Nissequogue patrolman had responded to an accident on Cordwood Path at request of Head of the Harbor. I called the Suffolk County cops and was told that I was out of their jurisdiction, to call my local police, whereupon I hung up and took that shower.

When Marsha finished bandaging my hand, Mary James said well for godsake Bud Hanks call the po-lice back and tell them what happened and where we are. "What happened? Where are we?" I muttered, picking up the phone again and dialing the tree house's local police. I told the Nissequogue dispatcher to listen carefully, that if she hung up on me I'd have her brought up on serious charges, got her attention, and explained our whereabouts and situation. She asked for a description of our pursuer and his car. I described the man, without resorting to any likenesses, and put Mary James on to describe his car since she had been out in it the night before and I had only seen bright lights. Mary James told the dispatcher that the car was a black '40 Dodge two-door that looked brand new, and put me back on. The dispatcher had two more questions: the number I was calling from and the number of the house. Well the phone was unlisted, without a number on its dial, and the house was numberless. I would have to call back in ten minutes to get a report.

Marsha started supper, Mary James drank and worried, and I stood guard out on the promenade deck, a black new-looking '40 two-door Dodge tooling through my mind behind our old '41 blue Chevy. When the chill got to me out there I returned to the telephone.

"Mr. Hanks, Officer Egan reports that the driver of the antique Dodge suffered a severe concussion and is being taken to Smithtown General. There was no identification on him, but a number of firearms were found in the car which has Arkansas plates, so it looks like we have your assailant. Chief Lynch said to tell you to come over to the hospital and identify the man. Head of the Harbor would like to speak to you about that firewood you dumped on Cordwood Path. They understand that you must have done it to thwart your pursuer, but still it's a formality."

"Thank you, ma'am."

"Not at all, Mr. Hanks."

We sat down to a supper of broiled shell steaks, baked potatoes, boiled asparagus tips, tossed green salad with bleu cheese dressing, and a superior red wine which Mary James judged "puckery." For desert we had apple pie with melted cheese on top ("Apple pie without cheese is like a kiss without a squeeze," MJ), topping it off with demitasses of espresso coffee (MJ's laced with JW Black). Marsha said grace before we ate, giving thanks for our escape, praying for the Box Hunter, along with calling down a blessing on the meal, "for the good of our bodies and the nourishment of our souls"—that dogged old Platonic dualism done crept into her theology.

It was a real good supper and we enjoyed it in that buoyant spirit born of relief against suspended doubt. The unanswered question we let go begging until we were through. We shared some laughs—Mary James: "Hey Bud Hanks, you never did tell us whose cuckoo nest this is?" "Belongs to person or persons yclept A. K. Kochbaum, Ph.D." "What's he doin' with all these women's clothes?" "Dr. K has a thing for women's clothes." Marsha: "And that man tried to kill you because he didn't like your *poetry?* And the size of your *feet?*" "He said my poetry wasn't high I.Q., and my feet . . . " "Bud Hanks's a poet and his feet show it—Longfellows!" (MJ), and so forth . . .

We dragged it out, that Last Supper, savoring the grounds in our espresso cups. Then Marsha said, "Then who was in that yellow Volvo?"

"Like you said," I said, "Probably some kids . . . playing chicken. Well, guess I'd better get on over to Smithtown General and make that identification."

"And what if it *ain't* him, Bud Hanks?"

"Least we'll be there, with cops and doctors, and not here."

"Uh-huh, if it ain't him there we'll be there all right, to get pronounced dead."

"If that's not *him* on the way to the hospital, with a severe concussion, then who is it?" I asked defiantly, Socratically, knowing the answer.

Mary James put the bottle to her lips. I got up and got myself a glass. Marsha said, "The owner of the yellow Volvo."

I left my glass empty on the table and went back out on the deck to take up my post again. I could see it plain as the full moon, the yellow Volvo screeching to a stop at my firewood barricade, the driver getting out as *he* climbed out of the wood-pile with a stick of it, the crack across the head, the switch, the chase resumed. The rain had slackened to a heavy, windblown fog, a couple of degrees too high for a blizzard. Cold wet leaves blew off our cover, pasting on my face. After three turns around, five peers down the splintered trapdoor, I deemed it not a fit night out for man nor madman and went back inside.

I sat at the kitchen table with a glass of Scotch, longing for my tobacco makings, for bourbon instead of Scotch, for my squash court and sweet solitude, for a warm hearthside and one good woman, kids, for miracles, while the women finished doing the dishes, Marsha humming "Amazing Grace."

"Bud Hanks, we decided while you were outside that we've had too hard a day to think clear tonight. 'Course that's *him* they found in the old Dodge—yaknow, its a funny thing I remember now but I asked him last night at dinner, me think-ing he was your old friend's why I took dinner with him, yaknow, how come that old forty Dodge looked so new, and you know what he said? He said hell hits only three year old, and then again I got to take good care of it for its a war on you know, and I got to make it last. His exact words. I didn't make nothing of it then, thinking he was just a funny talker, like you. Anyhow, what we decided, Marsha and me, we'll just spend the night here tonight, the three of us, just to be on the safe side. Nobody could find us here, not even the po-lice, ha ha."

"Have you and Marsha also figured out to your satisfaction why that yellow Volvo was following us with the lights out?"

"The driver saw us in the dump truck leaving that load of wood on the road, and had to turn around anyway, and then when he spotted us coming up behind him he figured we had been hiding, and he turned around and followed us with his lights out so we wouldn't see him, and he's probably got your license number and called the police, like a good citizen."

"Now don't that make sense?" said Mary James.

I nodded and gagged down the glass of Scotch. "Makes real good sense. Too good to fit in with the rest of the day."

"Aw Bud Hanks you've seen too many movies," laughed Mary James.

She gave me a bald look then and said, "Imo go up now and see to the sleeping arrangements."

She staggered up the spiral staircase, taking Johnnie Walker with her. Marsha joined me at the table. She took my bandaged hand in hers and looked with concern at a half-dollar-sized blood spot that had stained through the gauze.

"Sorry I got you into this, Marsha. I got your letter, and was going to answer it. I'll answer it now. I'm very happy that you've found Jesus. Now about that trouble at home you mentioned, I guess you see now that you're better off with your father than with me. Hang in there with him, he'll come around. He's just jealous that you've got your head on straight. Also he probably feels guilty, but he'll . . . "

"Let's not talk about him. I'm glad I'm here with you. I meant everything I said in that letter, Bud. *Every*thing."

She gave my injured hand a little squeeze. I didn't flinch.

"Let's hear you answer the rest of my letter."

By 'the rest' she meant, of course, her closing—"I love you." I said, "I don't know how to answer any more of it without saying too much, Marsha," realizing that that was saying too much.

She smiled a saintly smile and let go of my hand. I put it in my lap. She interlocked her fingers on the table.

"I love Jesus more than life. And what real love He has. I was reading to Mary James from the Gospels tonight. When they crucified Him, He asked God to forgive them, because they knew not what they were doing. There's no greater love than that, is there Bud?"

"None realler."

"How hard it must be to love your enemies."

"Hard enough, sometimes, to love your friends—and relatives."

She got my eye, with a look I can't describe, except to say that if she'd just walked in with that expression I would not have recognized her, no more than the torchman would have recognized Jeanne d'Arc, even had he flirted with her prior to her trial.

"To hate is to commit murder in your heart," said Marsha.

"That's what Jesus said, all right."

"How do you feel about that man down there, Bud?"

"Feel about him? You mean do I . . . I'm not Jesus, Marsha."

"Do you hate him?"

"Don't believe I do, but I don't love him, either. You can't love somebody you can't hate, or vice versa. Hate's the flip side of love. The third—and worst side—is indifference, and I'm not even indifferent to him, far from it; guess you could say I'm right pissed off at him. He's got me scared, and I hate that. Don't know just how I feel about *him.*"

" 'Hate the sin, love the sinner,' " said Marsha. "Whatever happens, you must forgive him, Bud."

"Nothing's going to happen to require any further forgiveness. I forgive him, insofar as he has my forgiveness coming, for what he's already done, okay?"

Again that look of incipient sainthood, intensified, on Marsha's stranger's face.

"He's coming, Bud. I know it. I feel it deep inside of me. And you must for . . . "

"Marsha, I know my theology well, and I know the world that doesn't, and I'm just enough a part of that world to doubt that even God can forgive a fellow who's not interested in forgiveness. Christlikeness is a mighty hard row to hoe."

"It's the only row worth hoeing. Promise to forgive him, Bud—no matter what he does."

"All right, all right, but let's get out of this rut. Suppose he does bust in here? We're not going to be impractical, are we? I'm sure not. I'm going to be Christlike and clean out the Temple. I'm not going to face that maniac with folded hands and bleat, 'Beloved Enemy, I forgive you for you know not what you do,' because in his twisted way he knows damn well what he's doing, same as those crucifying Romans did—why are you looking at me like that?"

"Did you tell him about Jesus when he was in your house?"

'Fraid I laughed.

"Maybe if you had told him the Good News none of this would have happened."

"He's *heard* about Jesus. He's from where I hail from, where every Ku Klux redneck off a two-rut road claims to be a Christian, where everybody but the deaf has heard, and they've seen the Word in sign language. The Gospel's not a magic formula for purifying evil hearts without the mind's consent. Pontius Pilate had a talk with Jesus in the flesh. Nero knew about Jesus, and Torquemada, and Jack the Ripper, and Adolf Hitler. There's not a soul in hell who hasn't heard the Gospel, and that includes Hell's Prince who heard it first. Most of the civilized world has heard about Jesus Christ, and all history has happened anyway. If that God-damned Box Hunter finds us I'm gonna pounce first and talk Good News later, if he's still got an ear to hear. I'll even have a heart full of forgiveness for him, once I'm on top of him. Stop looking at me like that. Charity begins at home. Our own selves are people, too. We owe ourselves. The Bible says 'Love thy neighbor as thy*self.*' Martyrdom has been bled white."

I got up and retired to the withdrawing room, which was in the western hemisphere of the treehouse, and flopped on the couch. Presently Marsha joined me there.

"I've been praying for that poor Volvo owner."

"Good."

"Bud, what's the real reason that man is after you? I've been praying for him, too."

Whereupon I told Marsha about that night so long ago and how it led to our presence in the tulip tree (skipping over Kim), concluding by quoting the poetry fragment inspired by the girl in the white coat. I watched for the face of the saint to become that of the skeptic, but it never did. Never did.

"I guess I understand now why you had me put on that white coat and took that movie of me on the train. Is it developed yet?"

"I'll get it out of the shop tomorrow, and we can watch it in the squash court, see how it came out."

Marsha looked away. "It'll just be me going by on the train, like *she* did. Is that all you want?"

Out of the mouths of babes and sucklings thou hast ordained painfully wise questions, O Lamb of God.

"Guess I better get back on the phone, call the hospital and the cops, tell them what our suspicions are."

Mary James hollered down the spiral staircase, "Hey Bud Hanks, what kinda tree is this we're in, one of the Oaks, maybe a black oak—the *quercus velutina,* La Mark?"

"It's a tulip," I stage whispered back, "and keep your voice down."

"A tulip's not a tree, it's a flower. Whachayll talking about down there?"

"The situation."

"Yeah, well our bed's ready, Bud. That's the situation. Marsha can sleep on the couch down there. *Tulip* tree. I *say* tulip tree."

"She's found a tree book in the den," I whispered to Marsha. "Hope *tulip tree* is in it. We'll see what she's made of tonight."

"You better make that call, Bud. If he killed that poor girl on the train, and those soldiers he tracked down, and the Volvo owner, it's not just us in danger."

"You're right, but then we might be wrong. It *has* to be him they found hurt, and I didn't say whoever he was was dead. Mary James is probably right. I've seen too many movies. We all have."

"Hey!" from the spiral staircase, "there *is* a tulip tree! Whacha know about that?"

"She's growing," I told Marsha. "You call the police this time. Maybe they'll believe you."

While Marsha got on the phone, Mary James hollered down from the spiral staircase, "Hey, listen to this, this is interesting. Listen: 'One of the largest and most valuable trees of the eastern states, the *tulip tree,* is found in the region bounded by southern New England through New York to . . . "

Marsha was doing more listening than talking on the phone. When she returned to me her face had taken on a prophet's cast.

"The man they found in the old Dodge reached Smithtown General D.O.A. The police found your dump truck at the squash court, and no yellow Volvo anywhere. They don't know about any treehouse around here, at least not one with a telephone in it. They told me to tell you to sober up and come down to the station before they get a warrant out on you for everything from littering that road to involuntary manslaughter. Bud, they don't believe we're here, nor that *he's* still on the loose. It's like this isn't *real.* "

". . . It reaches its largest size in the deep rich soil . . . "

I had got up, reaching in my pockets, which weren't my pockets anyway—"I even left my key for him." (I hadn't, my key was in my pocket; he hotwired the truck.) "In the truck. He must have dumped the Volvo and driven my truck back to the squash court to find the *real* box."

". . . a height of over one hundred and fifty feet and a diameter of eight or ten feet . . .' "

I ran to the phone, but reconsidered. I might get a good cop just curious enough to amble over there, and get shot. I rejoined Marsha on the couch.

"Well here we sit, safe but unsound, in a tulip tree."

" ' . . . while the Onondaga Indians of central New York called it the white tree, Ko-yen-ta-ka-ah-tas . . .' "

I closed my eyes and let a heavy sigh.

"Did he say *why* he killed her, Bud?"

"Huh?"

"The Japanese girl on the train."

"I don't know, Marsha. He said she 'deserved' it. I don't know if he really killed her, if she's really dead, or Japanese, or if he was on the train. He's the complete psychotic. One minute he talked like a redneck and the next like a nineteen forties' movie cop, and a change would actually come over him with each voice. There are probably more of him than that. He claims to be J. Edgar Hoover. He could have written all those letters to me himself, except one, and I wish he'd written it. All I know for sure is what I saw that night in nineteen forty-three."

"You really fell in love with her, Bud?"

"Fell? Yes, definitely *fell.* "

"Well if you saw enough to fall in love with her, you must have seen a lot—enough to fall in love with."

" ' . . . It is characterized by the clean-cut, glossy, fiddle-shaped leaves, which the botanist describes as truncate, or ending abruptly, as if cut off . . .' "

"I only saw what I saw, Child—my God!—a female figure flicking by like a silent old one-reeler in the night, in profile, from the shoulder up. A cameo."

"Then you didn't see enough to know what you're looking for, much less to fall in love with, and I'm not a child, I'm a woman."

"Hey, are youall *listening?*"

"Falling in love is a downer," I muttered, arising, "You're supposed to rise in it. I've got to call Anna."

The phone was dead. Crediting its death to a wind-broken line I returned, with shrinking scrotum, to the couch. I spied small naked feet up on the spiral staircase.

" ' . . . The tulip tree belongs to the magnolia family, which is far removed from any of the poplars and cottonwoods, but because of its soft wood it is frequently called yellow poplar . . .' "

"Maybe he thought she was a spy, Bud, and it was microfilm in the box. Wasn't World War II going on then, after the Japanese bombed Pearl Harbor December the seventh, nineteen forty-one? I learned that in history."

"Head of the class. Did you learn that the east coast of Arkansas was full of Japanese spies in forty-three, with shoe boxes full of microfilm, and what great photographers the Japanese are?"

"You don't have to be sarcastic. Why don't you go back and call *Anna* like you said you were going to do, whoever she is."

Then suddenly it hit me. I took Marsha's hand. "Maybe you *are* right. Arkansas *was* full of Japanese in nineteen forty-three. Not spies, but American citizens rounded up from the East Coast and stuck in relocation camps in the most godforsaken jerkwater towns in the hinterlands of the nation—two of those relocation camps were in Arkansas, in Jerome and Rohwer. Rohwer is only a rifle shot from McGehee where Aiko boarded the Delta Eagle that night."

"Why that's *awful*," said Marsha. "Put in concentration camps just because of their *race?*"

" ' . . . Lirodendron is from two Greek words describing a tree with lilylike flowers,' " Mary James reads on, her thin naked thighs in sight now on the spiral staircase. " '*Tulipfera* refers to the tuliplike blossoms. It is a tree of ancient origin and with its close relatives is geologically recorded in Europe and Asia as well as in North America, where it once . . .' "

"But weren't we at war with the Germans and some other country, too? Were the loyal German Americans stuck in concentration camps?"

"Do you know a German when you see one?"

Marsha scratched her head. The beginning of education is marked by the scratching of the head.

"High I.Q.," I said. "He said she said she had high I.Q. in her box. That could be spy and FBI jargon for *intelligence*—top secret. Maybe she *was* a spy and he's telling the truth, and one of the soldiers did get her box, and he's spent all these years going crazy looking for it. He doesn't even know that war is over. He thinks Roosevelt is still president."

" '. . . The nineteen-forty-six lumber cut was approximately seven hundred and . . .' bunch of zeros, millions I guess, ' . . . board feet of which three hundred and thirty six . . .' shittin' zeros again, how come they can't write it out for people who aren't sober mathematicians?, '. . . feet came from the Appalachian . . .' "

"If you ask me, that poor girl was crazy too. Maybe being put in that concentration camp because she might be a spy made her imagine she really was one. Whatever she had in her box, I bet it wasn't anything the government would be interested in, certainly not now, this long later, and anyway what kind of *intelligence* would she have found in Arkansas?"

Well I smiled at that. It was the last smile I would enjoy, free and clear, until my wedding day.

Mary James goes on, " '. . . The wood is light yellow to brown with a creamy white margin of sapwood. It is soft, easily worked and takes paint well. When air dry it weighs only about twenty-six pounds to the cubic foot. It is used in many kinds of construction . . . ,' " standing halfway down the staircase in baggy yellow panties and matching bra of Kochbaum's that I see the latter filling out so perfectly. MJ leaned against the tree trunk for another step, tree book in both hands, and it dawned on me that every light upstairs was on.

"You idiot, get back up there and turn out those lights before they get shot out!"

" ' . . . boxes, crates, baskets and woodenware, for excelsior, veneer wood, and also as a core upon which to glue veneers of other wood. Small amounts are cut for pulpwood to make paper.' Hey, my daddy used to be a poor pulpwood cutter, 'member that, Bud Hanks?"

Paper. Of course, paper. I had calmed the Box Hunter momentarily with my orange box of papers, my code, *code.* Secret papers. Secret papers was what he thought he was looking for and mine had stalled him in a brief moment of lie, long enough for me to get off my hands and knees and save myself.

"Hey listen, yall, just listen to *this:* 'The inner bark of the root and trunk is intensely acrid, bitter, and has been used as a tonic and stimulant. It is a source of hydrochlorate of tulipiferine, which is an alkaloid possessing the power of stimulating the heart.' Jesus Christ you guys you know where we are? We're up in an *upper!*"

Marsha got up and went into the kitchen, and then on around, disappearing around the tree trunk.

"Hey Bud Hanks just listen to *this* . . . "

"*Marsha!*" I said, getting off the couch, "*don't go outside!*"

"*Listen, Bud Hanks, forget the teeny bop*—'The tree is moderately free from pests, but frequently unsightly brown spots cause a gall, I mean caused *by* a gall insect, cover the leaves. Also they may turn yellow and drop during the summer.' And somebody's done wrote after that, '*So may your pants!*' "

I started after Marsha and Mary James stopped laughing and let a yell, no less theatrical, and here she came atumble down the remaining arc of spiral, all flying limbs and fluttering leaves of *Knowing Your Trees* (Collingwood & Brush, A publication of the American Forestry Association, Washington, D.C., Fourteenth Printing, October 1954).

Marsha returned on the run, to observe, with compassion, me scooping up my ex-wife off the carpet. I carried her back up the corkscrew way and into the bedroom and dumped her on an Early American bed, covered her with a quilt of that same period. It was a narrow bed, twinless, a child's dream sack in days of American yore, wide enough for Dr. Kochbaum and Anna K, and what good kisser too, too close? Mary James let a whimper when I covered her, the only sound she'd made since yelling before falling, and then she fell silent again. Her whimper, between two tell-tale silences, including them, indicted me for deliberately not catching her. I could have caught her, and probably should have; the fall she had not expected; she had yelled before letting go, expecting me to catch her, but I was tired of that.

Mary James is not nor never was nor never will be—it's just not in her system—a martyr. Nevertheless I had betrayed her. So be it. I took the quart of Johnnie Walker Black off the nightstand and tucked it in beside her—driving in nail number two. I turned off the light and went back down to Marsha —the third nail.

Before turning out the light and going back down to Marsha, I poked into Kochbaum's wardrobe again. I had seen a white box on the shelf over the clothes rack when selecting my evening's wear. It was about the size of a seven-league boot box, or a coat box. It had not been opened. The coat in it had not been worn. The price tag was still on it, the price astronomical; the coat, of yeti fur, was mother pearly white. I came an inch of falling down the steps myself. Marsha met me at the bottom.

"You still love her, don't you, Bud?"

I rolled my eyes and headed for the bar. I was ashamed of Mary James, and for her, and of myself. Ashamed for having been and still being yoked with her; yoked to that pretentious little clown, thrice-yoked: by God's single-tree marriage vow and man's double-crossing guilt and childhood memory's long reins. Yoked to an aging sot shorn now of her prettiest pretensions. A self-made fool yoked to a natural clown, now there's a pair. I fell on my knees before the Early American bar.

"Are you going to marry her again?"

It was a night for foolish answers, not foolish questions. I reached in and took a Wild Turkey 101 out by the neck. I hated Mary James. Suddenly and with a little passion. To be true to my theory of human yoking, that to hate her I had to love her or be studiously indifferent to her, I must have hated her—like a cancer in the gut.

"Bud, if you're going to get drunk too, I'm leaving."

I hated Marsha too, all of a sudden, and Kochbaum—both of them—and, yes, I hated *her* . . . she whom I had most loved, who strung out my entrails down those long tracks. I spun on my knees with the bottle in my hand and arose to look down on a slim young nubile girl in an outsized green pants suit not her style, a green New Testament in her hands—a blooming saint dressed like a clown, and it hit me then who else I hated at least as much as these.

"Bud . . . "

"Marsha, thou shalt hate thy neighbor as thyself."

The chickens were coming home to roost, in that tree house. I could feel it in my marrow, cooped up in that tulip tree. I set the bottle on the table, sat and looked at it, the best distillate of the golden grain ever bonded. The seal had not been broken. Who was this Kochbaum, anyway, the best of everything and all untapped?

"Bu-ud, when you comin up?" Mary James whined down.

I went out on the promenade deck. The cold driving mist was coming straight out of the west. Presently it chilled off the brief luxury of hatred in my breast. I heard the train pulling into St. James, and I could see her again as usual, as always. How could she be dead? Eyes wide open in the dark I saw her in her bright window, and gone again, and then appeared not the face, for I could not recall it, but the signature "Stella," and her jade bracelets and white scars, and as Stella fell away my no-name Bowery bum appeared, frozen in the pose of prenatal bliss, broken-off bottle neck in his lips. The train whistled out of St. James and *she* returned, and then my arm was touched and I jumped out of my skin.

"Sorry—I thought you saw me coming," she said, her fingers interlocking with mine. We moved around until the floodlights of Kings Park Marina reached us through the foliage, refracted in the mist, with fuzzy rainbow rings around them; the lights touched her face with an eerie just this side of heavenly glow.

"Why did you say that, Bud? 'Hate thy neighbor as thy-self?' "

"Because I hated myself, all of a sudden."

"I love you, Bud."

"Marsha."

Hand in hand we gazed across the choppy white-capped Nissequogue at high tide, at the lights, the marina lights, and to the southwest of them the lights of Kings Park Psychiatric Center looming high and full of nightmares day and night.

"Bud, do you believe God has a will for everyone?"

"Generally speaking. He prefers that we be good, but how we be good He leaves up to us. Else why have we minds?"

" 'Let this mind be in you that was also in Christ Jesus,' " quoth she.

"Paul also said, 'I can will what is right, but I cannot do it. For I do not do the good I want, but the evil I do not want is what I do . . . I see in my members another law at war with the law of my mind . . . Wretched man that I am!' " I said.

"Paul also said, 'It is better to marry than to be aflame with passion,' " said Marsha, squeezing my good left hand real hard.

More light radiated from her face than seemed natural. My arms closed, naturally, around her. We heard Mary James up there yelling down again for me to come on up now.

"You can kiss me, Bud, but that's all."

"When will you be sixteen?"

"I was sixteen a week ago. And I'm still a virgin."

She waits for that kiss with her eyes wide open, her mouth half open, and I ask her if she likes poetry, unable to eat just one sweet ripe cherry from a bowl of them without gobbling the whole bowl, without getting bowled over, sure as God made little green apples. And sour grapes.

"I liked your poem about the girl on the train, only it was too sad. I love poetry. The Psalms are my favorites. My favorite one goes, 'The Lord is my shepherd, I shall not want. He maketh me to lie down in green pastures . . . ' "

She quoted the Twenty-third Psalm like King David had just penned it that day for her, not like it was the most widely mouthed poem in most languages, next to the endless one beginning, Roses are red/Violets are blue . . .

"Hey, whachall doin' out here in the cold?"

Mary James, her long blond hair and AK's flowing blue robe blowing in the wind, looking like a ghost. Marsha and I let go of each other.

"Talking about poetry."

"Roses are red/violets are blue/piss on poetry/who wants to screw?" says my ex-childhood sweetheart.

"You asshole," I said.

"You fukkin' child molester," she said.

Marsha disappeared around the south side of the deck.

"You slut."

"You freak-creep hypocrite shitass son of a bitch."

"You vulgar slip-wit pretentious dried up little slut-sot."

"You phony goddam holier-than-thou shithead sonsybitch-ing Gospel spoutin' hypocrite bastard bum."

"You cock pit. You running sore. You . . ."

Marsha reappeared.

"*Bud*—somebody's down there with a flashlight!"

About then the beam shot through the spaces of our deck planking, creating glorious panels of illuminated swirling mist; we flattened against the shingled side of our cage and slithered back inside.

"Reckon it's the po-lice?" breathed Mary James, white faced, eyes big as bottle bottoms.

We turned off all lights except the hooded low-watt fluorescent over the kitchen stove. If it was a cop down there it was up to him to identify himself and convince us. If it was the Box Hunter, he obviously didn't know the way up, and would not likely find it. I stood guard by the partly opened door, one eye on the splintered trapdoor just in case, armed with that traditional blunt instrument no Real American kitchen is without, a rolling pin. We waited. We waited in silence until Mary

James lit a burner under the coffee pot, and broke it (the silence).

"What were youall talking about about 'the situation' when I was reading to you out of that tree book, something about a girl on a train whose box you got, Bud Hanks and that man wants it? And no more of your jokes, this has done got too serious. I've got a right to know how come I'm up here in this tree, chased up here by that crazy friend of yours down there. Whaja do Bud Hanks, screw his daughter?"

"Mary James dwells on the lowest common denominator. That's the genius of the simple mind, to see all our joys and sorrows and boredoms rising from that position, that commonest denominator, the beast with two backs."

"Screw him—you tell me," she said to Marsha.

I listened in fascination as Marsha retold the tale I told her, with emendations here, omissions there, an old tale made new in the retelling, a new myth in gestation and now out of my control; my mind harked back to oral times, days of the Homeric Greeks and Abrahamic Hebrews, men and their women and children sitting around the fire, building the foundations of our writ—profane and sacred. Of equal fascination was the change that washed across the face of Mary James as she listened, and at the end of it she cast me a glance I'd never seen before, and I thought I knew her like the back of my hand. It was like the back of my hand had grown a whole new map of veins. It seemed Mary James was seeing me—if not through me—for the first time. The coffee pot commenced to rock at full boil.

"Coffee boiled is coffee spoiled," muttered Mary James, pouring herself a cup. She eyed us through the steam of it.

"So Bud Hanks fell in love with a girl in a white coat he saw passing by on the old Delta Eagle, and he put an ad in the papers for her, and that's how come we're in this tree tonight? Well I'll just be diddly-damned. And what night was that s'posed to have happened?

Marsha related the correct date. Mary James stared at me for the longest, then got her raincoat off the chair it hung on and took out a damp pack of Virginia Slims and a notebook also damp around the edges. She stood the notebook like an A frame over the burner and fished out a yellowed cigarette. The front of the tablet had a big red Indian head on it. She held the yellowed Virginia Slim inside the A frame to dry. She did all this with an absent-minded efficiency.

This was Mary James in her Mysterious Act, at which she was marvelous. She could use up a whole half day or more spinning one of these before finally letting you in on the mystery which was nine times out of nine some loose end not worth the effort. But the effort was a kind of poetry; not a poem, MJ's mysterious act, but a poetry fragment—a going, not a getting there.

"This Dr. Cock-whassisname, owns this cuckoo nest, what if he comes out tonight?"

"Kochbaum. She only comes out on weekends, in fair weather."

"She?" in unison.

"Uh-huh. She, as in *sheep*. What kind of friends do youall think I have, wear clothes like these?"

"Well s'pose she does come out tonight and that *man* down there sees her?"

"I've thought of that and dismissed it. It's foul weather."

"All the same it's a weekend."

"Still, it's foul weather."

"Oh—she might get killed!" said Marsha.

"Never mind her. *He* might let her get by him, and then follow her up, and then we'll *all* get killed," said Mary James.

The two of them stare at me for answers, for action. Mary James lights her cigarette with trembling fingers.

"You're the man up here, Bud Hanks. We can't even call for help now, cause I tried to call while ago and the phone is dead. Whacha gonna do, Bud Hanks?"

"The conventional approach to the limb we came up on is down a path from a cul-de-sac to that outcropping of rock you went to pieces on. I'll see her lights if she drives up, then rush down the limb and up and head her off."

"And then what?"

"Head off with her?"

"Be serious, Bud Hanks, unless you *are* being serious. This is serious."

I glanced at Marsha and asked for her suggestion, knowing what it would be, and after she suggested it, MJ said, "Yes indeed, and while we're praying let's pray none of this ever happened."

I did a quick turn around the deck and came back in, reporting that the light was gone, a good sign that the man was gone too, given up.

"His kind never give up, you know that, now I heard the train while ago and I bet *she* was on it and any minute now a cab will be up there in that *culdesack* and *he's* gonna see her comin' down the path with a flashlight and lead him right up here to us, now you've got to go down there with a butcher knife, that rolling pin, or something, and wait by that rock where you can watch for both of them. That's the safest thing for us."

"Me down there with a rolling pin or something and him with a gun? No way. Suppose he sees me coming down. He'll shoot me and come up for you."

"But it's you he wants."

"Don't count on it. He wants the *box,* remember. And he'll be up here looking for it, and no telling what else."

"You're just scared to go down there, aren't you Bud Hanks?"

"You ain't just shittin', kitten."

"But hell Bud Hanks, you saw action in Korea. You know what it's like."

"I sure do. That's why I'm so scared. It's not like in the movies, tell you that."

"All right, Chicken Shit, then *I'll* go down there. You want *me* to have to go down there?"

"Only way you're going down there, Big Mouth, is over my shoulder again, kicking and screaming and pissing, same as the way you came up."

"I'll go," said Marsha, starting to go.

I grabbed her.

"Let her go if she wants to go, somebody's got to go."

"She's too young."

"*Now* she's too young, you say. Old enough to bleed, old enough to butcher, but just in bed, huh, Bud Hanks? You in love with her or something?"

About then Goldilocks burst in pointing a big bright pistol at the label on her bib overalls Papa Bear had on. It was a mother-of-pearl-handled .44 single action iron with notches, like ole Buck Jones usta tote two of as the Lone Ranger for Republic Pictures. Mamma Bear in Goldilocks' blue gown let a yell and dived under the kitchen table. Baby Bear in Goldilocks green pants suit stood her ground like a Christian Soldier. Papa Bear hollered, "Hey—it's *me!*"

"What in the *world?*" our hostess gasped, slowly lowering the pistol.

"We didn't see you drive up or I would have . . . "

"*What* in the world?"

Mary James crawled from under the kitchen table.

"What *in* the world are you people doing . . . "

"If we'll all be calm and quiet I'll ex . . . "

"Who are you?" AK demanded of MJ.

"I'm his ex-wife, and you must be . . . "

"And who are you? His ex-daughter?"

"God willing, I'm his next wife," said Marsha. "And aren't you the lady who gave Bud the cordwood-powered windmill?"

"Millcord-powered woodwind," I clear the air with.

AK, free hand backside to her forehead, went, "Good grief."

"She's not neither his next wife, but the important thing we've gotta know, Miz Cockbum, did a man down there see you come up the limb? It's . . . "

AK spun for a light switch; then froze, spun again. "I saw

no one down there. Mr. Hanks, I want to see you in private."
I followed her at a smart clip up the spiral staircase. We
stood in her den in the dark, at a momentary loss. She fumbled
somewhere and presently a match was struck. The glass chimney of a small lamp lit up with enough light to read gross
expressions by. We sat cross-legged on the carpet, the lamp
between us, a hint of lilac-scented kerosene in the air. AK had
on faded jeans and hiking boots, a fur-lined poplin raincoat.
The flickering lamp flame rendered grotesque her fine Semitic
features.

I explained events. She took my wounded hand and examined the bloody bandage by the lamplight. She went on holding my hand while telling me how she happened to be here.

During our telephone conversation that evening she had
detected a guarded note in my voice, and had assumed that
Kim was already there. But then another thought fired her
imagination, which she had tried to dismiss as the product of
too many movies: the Box Hunter standing by me at the phone
with a gun to my head. The image had nagged her until, even
though she doubted there was a real Box Hunter, she rang me
up again. The phone rang and rang, unanswered, meaning I
was either safe or beyond her help. Nagged by doubts and
fears now, she decided to get to the bottom of this. She called
the *McGehee Times* and persuaded the editor, who was about to
close for the day, to dig into that weekly's morgue for the
edition published immediately subsequent to November 11,
1943 . . .

Midway between McGehee and Lake Village that night
there had been a riot on the southbound Delta Eagle, and an
escapee from the Rohwer Japanese Relocation Camp had been
killed. It was Armistice Day weekend, in the middle of another
war, and the rioters, U.S. servicemen on leave, had been cele-
brating. The riot broke up as the train was slowing down for
Lake Village, and the servicemen jumped off the still moving
train.

According to witnesses, the Relocation Camp escapee,

fifteen-year-old Aiko Abé, had boarded at McGehee, clad in a white coat and carrying a shoe box. One witness described her as "a stunning beauty with flowing black hair, pale buff complexion, dazzling in her attire," who had "at once got the attention of the drunken servicemen and incited them, to a man, to love and war."

A young man in a trenchcoat who had been sitting across the aisle from Miss Abé went to her aid as the train was stopping. Identifying himself as "an FBI agent," he ordered everyone off the car. He had disappeared when Lake Village police arrived. The FBI denies that it had an agent on the Delta Eagle that night.

Desha County Sheriff Howard Clayton, in cooperation with railroad, state, military, and federal authorities, was investigating the incident.

"That squares with what the Box Hunter told me, like I told you," I told AK. "What nobody knows is that the Box Hunter is the real killer, not the servicemen."

AK nodded; "Well the police should be here by now. You have called them?"

"I tried, and tried. They don't believe in treehouses. And then I tried to call you—and the line was dead."

"Oh God," AK muttered, releasing my hand and turning the lamp flame down lower. "Let's pray it was the wind."

Now there was a kind of prayer I'd never thought to try, a faith I'd never entertained, in a god I'd never come to grips with, One who might be persuaded to undo what had been done: Let it be the wind that cut us off from help O Nameless One and not the one against whom we need help . . . and while we're in this fantastic prayer (eh, MJ?) make Eve tell the serpent to fuck off, and leave that Apple hanging on the Good & Evil Tree unbitten.

"Anyway, I made another call," AK went on, taking my unwounded hand in hers. "The current sheriff of Desha County. Robert Moore."

"He's my uncle."

"He mentioned that. He was very cooperative, anyway. He dug into his office's unsolved cases file and called me back. Aiko Abé's death had been ruled homicide by person or persons unknown. She had been strangled. None of the servicemen were ever identified. Incidentally, the girl was molested, but not raped."

"Then she died a virgin."

"That doesn't necessarily follow. But anyway, the young man in the trenchcoat who identified himself as an FBI agent never was identified. Nor was he ever a suspect, it having been assumed all along that one of the soldiers killed Aiko. Your uncle said that if you have a lead on your so-called Box Hunter, he would be mighty interested in questioning him, and wants you to give him a call."

"Must be an election year."

"Don't be a cynic. Sheriff Moore sounded to me like a very fine man. If the world was just half full of men like him, I'd be out of business, and grateful for it. Anyway, here we are. If Suffered Enough is right—and I don't doubt him now—about the Box Hunter tracking down and killing soldiers who were on the train that night, it's easy to see how no authorities would detect the pattern. Out of fear of being brought to justice none of them have admitted being on the train that night, and his systematic killing of them is known only to them. Probably one of them escaped him and warned others whom he knew, and thus the news spread among them. In a way you could call it justice. Their fear of being brought to justice for a crime they think they committed has enabled the real killer to kill them and get away with it. *Poetic justice.*"

" 'The wages of sin is death,' " I muttered. "Looks like we've solved an old case Uncle Robert inherited. Wish he was here to make the collar."

"I made another call, Hank. Your uncle read to me a letter from an Aiko Abé, written some years ago from New York, when Sheriff Clayton was still in office."

"Then she's *not* dead?"

"This is another Aiko Abé who was in the same camp, and a close friend of the Aiko who was killed. She told me that it is a common Japanese name, like Mary Smith is in this country."

"You actually talked to somebody who actually knew her?"

"In her letter to Sheriff Clayton she asked what progress was being made in tracking down the killers of her friend. On impulse, I looked her up in the Manhattan directory. She's still in New York, working for the National Council of Churches. She remembers that night only too well. Her friend Aiko ran away . . ."

The Nisei in the white coat ran away from the concentration camp because she was a poet and the camps had not been built for truth or poetry. She had boarded the southbound Delta Eagle at McGehee, taking with her nothing but a shoe box full of poetry. She called herself a Christian poet, and just like a Christian poet she had no special destination this side of Heaven where all roads end short of the Promised Land. She took the first train that pulled into the depot. Going was the poetry . . . but that night Aiko reached her Destination—she crossed the Jordan.

I glanced from the lamp and spied two heads at the top of the staircase. "To think," I muttered, to any ear that cared to hear, "that I lived not too long a walk from that damned camp during that period of infamy. My Boy Scout troop visited theirs one time. And *she* was there."

"Irony of ironies," AK summed up. "Your girl in the white coat, God rest her soul, was a poet too, and that Box Hunter *has* been looking for a shoe box full of poems all these years . . . and driven us to this! It's enough to make a Platonist of me."

"Bud, I heard a funny noise down there," said Marsha.

I looked back at AK. "What I don't understand is that *intelligence* business. The Box Hunter said he asked her what was in the box and she said 'High I.Q.' The sick son of a bitch had her by the throat and squeezed that out of her.

'High I.Q.,' before he killed her. Why?"

AK got off the carpet and started for the stairs. "What is the popular seventeen-syllable verse form used by the Japanese since God knows when?"

"Haiku."

"Aiko Abé was a haiku poet, her friend Aiko Abé told me. Haiku—high I.Q. Close enough, for a man listening for what he wanted to hear ... shhhh—what kind of funny noise, young lady?"

"It's going ... ," and Marsha produced a few short series of that effect when you vibrate your tongue on the roof of your mouth with bursts of expelled breath. Giving the mechanics of its production is easier than scrounging for a combination of letters of the English alphabet that might mimic it. It was an early sound effect my peers and I used to motorize our bicycles, play rattlesnake, and after December 7, 1941, mow down Japs with. Some troops went *ratatatatatatata* right out of the comic books, while the more creative of us dispatched Tojo's warriors with the esophagal *anh-anh-anh-anh-anh-anh*, sounding not unlike a rutting goat, but a little of that was fatiguing and slurred off into a tired wail, so we war lovers with a real taste for it relied on *tongue on roof of mouth*, from an almost endless magazine. It gives great vibrations, and it tickles. Try it ... Marsha's tongue vibrating on the roof of her sweet mouth conjured for me not pleasant childhood memories, but a noise from my copout profession—a chainsaw being cranked. Soon as she shut up I heard it myself, and fear sliced through me like a chainsaw through a rotten tree.

"Sounds like somebody trying to start an outboard motor," said AK.

"Oh shit!" said Mary James. "Sounds like Bud Hanks cranking up his chainsaw. Oh shit! Oh shit, Bud Hanks he's done gone back to the squash court and got your chainsaw and come back here and he's gonna cut us down. Oh shit Bud Hanks you've gotta go down there and *stop* that man!"

We stampeded single file down the spiral staircase and stuck our ears out the doorway. There was no denying it. *Tongue on roof of mouth* was going on down there. I took the pistol out of AK's hand and weighed it in mine. It was heavier than it looked, like real guns are. Real heavy. I flipped out the cylinder for a check. All six holes were stuffed with lead-nosed brass-assed nastiness.

"You're not going down there—" said AK, her tone in that zone between the interrogative and the imperative.

Tongue on roof of mouth.

I looked at her, at them; this was no Woody Allen movie. I was Glenn Ford now, cowering in the churchhouse with his townsfolk while the challenger, baddest gunslinger in the West, was out there in the saloon about to burn the town down if I didn't come out and draw with him, back in the Fastest Gun in the West, ol' Glenn the Fastest Gun all right, at shooting flipped silver dollars out of the sky, but he'd never even drawn against his own shadow.

"Maybe I can stop him from out on the deck, through a crack in the planks," my voice said, my thumb clicking the cylinder back into its place of business. My body slunk out on the deck.

I took one long trip around, peering over, peeking through, seeing nothing, hearing *tongue on roof of mouth—tongue on roof of mouth—tongue on roof of mouth*—and returned to the women; announced the results of my reconnaissance. As to his getting the chainsaw started:

"It starts for me after about the third crank, so apparently he hasn't found the switch, and if he has he hasn't figured out the primer and the choke. It has to be properly primed and choked to start, or you flood it. He's got it flooded, and when it's flooded . . . "

They had set a ten-gallon clam steamer crock on the stove and were filling it with hot water from the tap. They just glanced at me and went on filling the pot, like I was some kind of a drone. I slunk back out. The noise had stopped. Halfway around I spied the light down there. He would be looking for the switch now, or the primer or the choke. I got him sighted through a crack—or part of him; at least something moving in the light—and cocked, aimed . . . and hesitated.

"Corporal Hanks, General Ridgeway wants that hill. Take your squad up there and take it." "Sergeant Proctor, why does General Ridgeway want that hill? It's too rocky poor to raise a hard-on, and it's full of gooks with machine guns who got it first and want it worse." "General Ridgeway wants that hill because that hill is a symbol of man's eternal struggle against the forces of evil and Communist Aggression. Any further questions address them to God, on your way up that hill, Corporal Hanks."

Tongue on roof of mouth—tongue on roof of mouth . . .

Corporal Hanks got off a shot. A thunderous silence closed in behind it, and the light went out down there. Then down there returned three shots squeezed off fast enough to hold hands coming up and I got off another two at the muzzle fire down there just like up that hill, shooting at shots, belly down, M1 cradled in elbow hollows for another crawl toward thee o enemy, firing at fire, fire fired at, shooting at shadows, shadows shooting back, blasting away at anything that moved, everything that moved blasting back, and between the sound of fire the awful silences and the awfuller noise man makes when he's shot . . . none of your cushiony darkness silver-screened with the sound and smell of popcorn munched—O for the noise of the weekend brats to ruin this show, Miss Mona! . . . and then I hear that terrible telltale click of firing pin against empty casing and I remember the Lone Ranger once getting off two dozen shots apiece from his pair of these without reloading . . .

AK and Marsha met me at the door, flanked and yanked me in. MJ stuck her head out of the bathroom—*"Dija gettim? Dija gettim?"*

I sat at the kitchen table and dropped the smoking pistol on it, trying not to exude too much the miasma of a hero. I had been plenty scared slithering up that hill in Korea, when I was twenty-one, half my lifetime back, and fear increases if not logarithmically at least double half a lifetime. Yep, I was right proud of myself. Courage is not fearlessness. Only fools are fearless; courage is doing what fools do but for the right reasons, and being scared to death while doing it; yessiree I felt like a real hero, unmindful of my years of moral cowardice that had treed me with three relative innocents for an exhibition of overcautious physical bravado.

"Hey, how about a drink?"

And a medal. And kisses, where are my kisses? Strike me a medal. Shower me with kisses. Heap on the garlands.

AK broke the seal on the Wild Turkey 101 and poured me a shot glass almost full. Marsha had her head bowed. Mary James closed the door and put her ear to it. Steam was rising from the clam crock on the stove.

"The police should be here any minute now, after all that shooting," said AK, restoppering the bottle.

I did not point out that only game wardens responded to gunfire in this neck of the woods.

Mary James took her ear off the door and opened her mouth: "Bud Hanks, why don't you go down there now and *see* if you got him?"

"Mary James, why don't you go to hell?"

She went to the stove and relit her Virginia Slim butt off the burner, took a heavy drag, said, "Spit in the pot for luck," and spat in the steaming clam pot. I was so disgusted with her I could have spit in her face. Some spoil of war for a hero to be hung up with; some Bresius, some Helen—some face I face there at the stove: is that a puss to launch one rubber raft for? Mary James picked up that old tablet and riffed its pages yellowed as her cigarette, wrinkled dry around the edges.

"Well least let's somebody read something out loud while we're waiting, like Melanie did in *Gone with the Wind* when the men were out that night on a dangerous mission. 'Member, Bud Hanks, we saw *Gone with the Wind* on our honeymoon? I'd done seen it before four or five times, so had you, but that was

the first time we saw it together. 'Member Melanie reading—
what was that book?—while the men . . . "

It was kind of touching, Mary James playing Melanie for a
change, instead of Scarlett. I let myself be touched by it; after
all, I had done played Rhett, and could afford it.

"You first, Bud Hanks, I want to hear the one about the Girl
in the White Coat on the Delta Eagle."

"Everybody's heard that one."

"Everybody but me, the one who ought to have heard it
first."

"You had your chance to hear it first, and fucked it away."

"Fuck you too, Bud Hanks, right up the . . . "

"I'll read something first," said Marsha, stepping between
us with her New Testament.

> If I speak in the tongues of men and of angels,
> but have not love,
> I am a noisy gong or a clanging cymbal.
> And if I have prophetic powers,
> and understand all mysteries and all knowledge,
> and if I have all faith, so as to remove mountains,
> but have not love, I am nothing.
> If I give away all I have,
> and if I deliver my body to be burned,
> but have not love, I gain nothing.
>
> Love is patient and kind;
> Love is not jealous or boastful;
> it is not arrogant or rude.
> Love does not insist on its own way;
> it is not irritable or resentful;
> it does not rejoice at wrong, but rejoices in the right.
>
> Love bears all things, believes all things,
> hopes all things, endures all things.
> Love never ends; as for prophecy,
> it will pass away; as for tongues, they will cease;
> as for knowledge, it will pass away.

For our knowledge is imperfect and our prophecy is
    imperfect;
but when the perfect comes, the imperfect will pass away.

When I was a child, I spoke like a child,
I thought like a child, I reasoned like a child;
when I became a man, I gave up childish ways.
For now we see in a mirror dimly, but then face to face.
Now I know in part; then I shall understand fully,
even as I have been fully understood.

So faith, hope, love abide, these three;
but the greatest of these is love.

Marsha read that in the tongue of an angel, with love. After
a moment of silence, but for the wind in the boughs that held
us, AK asked to see the passage, saying, "That is the most
profound and beautiful panegyric on love I've ever heard—is
it something Jesus said?"

"Our Lord inspired it, ma'am. The Apostle Paul wrote it to
the First Corinthians, Chapter Thirteen. Jesus talked about
love too, though. He said, 'For God so loved the world that he
gave his only begotten son, that whosoever believeth in him
shall not perish, but have everlasting life.' Paul had been a Jew
who persecuted Christians, until he met Jesus in a blinding
light on the road to Damascus, and then he became a Jewish
Christian.

"Oh yes, Saul of Tarsus, the converted pharisee who took
the Gospel to the gentiles," said AK, scanning the passage. "I
have a favorite Psalm."

And AK quoted from heart her favorite Psalm, also in the
loving tongue of an angel—

Behold, how good and pleasant it is
    when people dwell in unity!
It is like the precious oil upon the head,
    running down upon the beard,
    upon the beard of Aaron,
Running down on the collar of his robes!

> It is like the dew of Hermon, which falls
> on the mountains of Zion!
> For there the Lord has commanded the blessing,
> Life for evermore.

I knew that psalm well enough to recognize a substitution
—"people" for "brothers." AK would later read, in Paul's
panegyric on love, unannounced and suddenly out loud at
Marsha's funeral, "When I became a *woman*, I gave up childish
ways," and later yet, beyond the scope of this chronicle, the
good doctor will have that passage to the Church in Corinth
printed on a poster in her new office, with the phrase finally
redacted to: "When I became a *mature person* . . . "

Emptying a box of salt into the boiling pot, Mary James said,
"It's your turn, Bud Hanks."

I took the New Testament (with Psalms in the back) from
AK and turned to one of my favorite psalms—

> By the waters of Babylon,
> there we sat down and wept,
> when we remembered Zion.
> On the willows there
> we hung up our lyres.
> For there our captors
> required of us songs,
> and our tormentors, mirth, saying,
> "Sing us one of the songs of Zion!"
>
> How shall we sing the Lord's song
> in a foreign land?
> If I forget you, O Jerusalem,
> let my right hand wither!
> Let my tongue cleave to the roof
> of my mouth . . .

"I don't wanna hear about a Jew song, I wanna hear about
that girl you fell in love with on the old Delta Eagle, you
bastard!"

"Oh for crissakes Mary James, it goes like this:

This girl in a white coat on the Delta Eagle
   whistled by one lonesome night
and I fell ass over appetite in love with her,
   and that bad old loco motive hit
dragged the gut from in me out and down the tracks.
   Burma Shave.

"*Burma* Shave . . . you're shittin' me, Bud Hanks."
"And you look it."
"Please, you two," said AK. "It goes like this, Mary:

   Some girl in a white coat on the Delta Eagle
   Crossed me in childhood's lonely night
   And I fell in puppy love with love forever—
   Delta Eagle took my heart and mind
   Down that single track
   And that is why I still speak as a child.

"Ha ha ha," I said. "Highly risible."

Mary James dumped a box of dish detergent into the boiling pot, and stepped stage center with her notebook. It was a Big Chief tablet out of the 1940s, our grade-school years. "And now me," she said.

She read in silence for a few seconds, her lips moving, her hands trembling, her big blue bloodshot eyes moistening. I got the chilly feeling that maybe she really did have some enormous mystery about to pop. She closed the tablet on her finger.

Still looking at the tablet, at the Indian head, she said, " 'Member, Bud, when we were together that Sunday awhile back, I told you about that poem I wrote that night my folks and I left Arkansas City on the train? You had just read me your poem about the Lone Ranger and that horseshoe in the future?"

"I recall."

"Well this is it, what I'm going to read now. I was coming down tonight to the squash court to read it to you, only Marsha got down ahead of me and you took us back up to the big house. I was gonna come down again, but that taxicab pulled up in the back drive and let this woman out and she went down, whoever she was—I wasn't going to ask. Anyway, pretty soon all hell broke loose, so I'm gonna read it now. It's gonna mean a whole hell of a lot more now, this old poem of mine."

I had glanced at AK who glanced away; she glanced back and I glanced away. She says now, "You had another female visitor tonight? Was it *her?* It *was* her, wasn't it? What happened to her?"

"She's okay. She got rerouted."

"Youall gonna listen or not? *Listen.* First, Bud Hanks, you 'member that night I moved away from Arkansas City, doncha?"

"Stop stalling and read your poem, Mary James. Nobody's perfect."

"You remember. I had asked you if you would see us off that night, and you said you couldn't. I had lived in Arkansas City all my life, and we were poor then, and moving away, and nobody cared enough to see us off on the train. We didn't have a car, you remember, and had to ask somebody to drive us to the depot in McGehee. I told my parents let's ask the Hankses because they had a car and Bud liked me a lot, and my daddy said it would be good to ask somebody who liked one of us. I called you up and you said youall were going to see a picture show in McGehee, and couldn't. Bud, youall could have dropped us off at the depot and still gone on to the picture show. It wasn't but a block away."

"You didn't care if I saw you off. You just wanted a ride. Anyway there were four of us and six or eight of you. How much do you think you can get in a '41 Chevrolet? It wasn't a dump truck, it was a sedan."

It started coming back to me then. Guess I had repressed the first part of that fateful night. The climax at the grade crossing on Highway 4 had rendered the first part pale by comparison —or dark, perhaps, is the better metaphor. Yes, the poor

Jameses needed a ride and Mary had called me that afternoon
—on whose phone I don't know; they didn't have one—and
coyly asked if I wanted to see her off, that they were moving.
What a blow: I didn't know they were moving. I told her I
guessed so, and *then* she asked if I'd ask my father to drive them
to the depot, which I did, and my father said, "Hell no." Too
many Jameses. My mother, seeing how upset I was, suggested
that we go see the picture show, and take Mary James with us
to the depot first, and somebody else could take the rest of
them. Well, it was a very special picture show I'd been dying
to see, starring Shirley Temple, whom I adored, while Mary
James was betraying me by moving, so I went back to the
phone and told her we didn't have room in the car, and that
anyway we were going to the Ritz. She asked if I would at least
stop by the depot and see her off, and I said I'd try. But I didn't.
Didn't even mention it to my parents. You see, the train was
always late and I didn't want to risk missing that very special
picture show.

"Anyway Imo read that poem now."

"You do that."

Her mouth opened, her chin trembled, she strove to get the
words out. It was plain that she was going through a crisis.
Then suddenly she began, and as suddenly, *tongue on roof of
mouth* again, but it didn't cut her off, nor did we.

> I have on Mama's coat tonight,
> Her coat as white as snow.
> Mama's coat is too big for me,
> But in it I will grow.
> I asked Bud to see me off,
> To tell me that last good-bye,
> But he had to see The Bluebird,
> So on the train tonight I cry.
> I'm glad to leave that awful town,
> And move to a big fine city,
> Though I won't see Bud Hanks again,

And that's a terrible pity.
And now the Delta Eagle speeds me
Off into the lonesome night,
And I sit looking straight ahead,
Dressed in my coat so white.
Oh Bud Hanks you

Tongue on roof of mouth—Tongue on roof of mouth—Tongue on . . . She threw the tablet on the table and turned her back on us, hugging herself. I snatched up the tablet for bugeyed unbelieving scrutiny. It was of that poor, depression quality pulp, yellowed as a wintered autumn leaf. The doggerel had been written in that soft graphite of those old brown penny pencils, in the pretentious handwriting of little Mary James, baroque with curliques, and circle dotted i's. It was dated at the top, the day, date, year and hour I lost my heart to my own imagination, and it had ended where Mary James had stopped reading, unended . . .

. . . *roof of mouth—tongue on roof of mouth—tongue on roof*. . . Still looking away, the old gal said, "I didn't finish it because all a sudden those servicemen started to hoot and holler—there were a bunch of drunk servicemen on the train—and then a girl screamed and people started crowding the aisle trying to get away from the fracas, and a man hollered for the conductor to stop those servicemen from killing the girl in the white coat . . . Then they were crawling all over us, drunk soldiers, and I was screaming, and one of them grabbed me, and my daddy hit him and pushed me down on the floor, and I just screamed and screamed and screamed."

She turned and faced us then, calm, almost serene, searching faces, and settled on Marsha's.

"When I was down on the floor screaming, it was like I was two different people. I divided myself up. Part of me, the real me, was in the Ritz with Bud Hanks, watching *The Bluebird.* Just my body was there screaming on the floor of the Delta Eagle. I never did see *The Bluebird,* never did. It showed in

Greenville, but I didn't go. I've never told any of this before, except when I was in the mental hospital. They had to put me in the mental hospital for a while on account of screaming nightmares, and I told the doctor, but this is the first time since then that I've talked about it, and the last. There was another girl on the train that night who had a white coat on, and it was her those servicemen killed. I didn't see her, but I read about her in the papers. Mama had saved the paper and I found it one day. She was a Japanese. Her picture was in the paper in the aisle of the train, covered up with her coat so you couldn't see her face. You're a good girl, Marsha. It took me back to when I was pure when you read to me from the Bible in the big house tonight, and talked to me. I wish I was your age and knew what you know now. I'd get a good education, marry a good man, have lots of good children, and not ruin my life."

"It's never too late to start, with God's help," said Marsha.

"It can get too late to finish," said Mary James.

Tongue on roof of mouth—tongue on—splutter-splutter-splutter . . .

"Oh Jesus!" said Mary James, running to the stove, "Somebody help me with this pot!"

The chainsaw spluttered again and screamed to angry life, but died at once, then *tongue on roof of mouth again* with the persistence of pure evil. I picked up the pistol, ejected the spent casings.

"*Anna*—have you any more ammunition for this thing?"

"No."

I dropped the pistol, selected a butcher knife from a rack by the sink, and headed for the door. The knife felt better in my hand than the gun; it felt more a part of me; I felt more a man with it—did not the Achaean spearmen scorn the archers?— and had the awful urge now to get my hands on *him*, to slip down that limb and creep up on him while he yanked that pull cord, and pounce, animal on animal. I could taste blood—no metaphor—for the first and only time since creeping near the top of that Korean hill, not a scratch on me and no longer scared, bone dissatisfied with shadow shooting, a fool now spoiling for a real fight hand to hand, hungry for a kill . . . and never getting it . . . I got honorably discharged never having seen a man go down before my bucking gun, without a purple heart, a front-line virgin.

"No!" said AK and Marsha, as one.

"You can't stop me."

"You can't stop us from following you."

"I looked at silent Mary James; "Let's take a vote. If it's a tie, I go."

"What makes you think I want you dead?" she muttered. "Come on and help me with this pot."

"Let's try talking to him first," said Marsha. "Tell him the truth."

"That Jesus saves?"

"Marsha's right. We should try talking first," said AK. "If we can get him to listen, maybe we can convince him of the truth—that the Japanese girl had haiku in her box and that he misunderstood her, that . . . "

"*Bull*shit, Dr. Cockbum. Puredee old bull*shit*. That man down there's as crazy as Bud Hanks—one's looking for a box he only saw the outside of and doesn't know what's in it and the other's looking for a girl he never met. Crazy obsessed, and nothing but death's gonna stop either one of them from looking and wrecking other lives while doing it. Convince him of the truth? Convince *Pontius Pilate* of the fukkin' truth. I don't know who's the craziest, you or that *man* down there looking for a fukkin' *shoe* box for over thirty years or Bud Hanks lookin' for a girl those same years who's long dead, *both* of them long dead. Convince him of the truth? How'd you like to spend a lifetime, best years of a lifetime, looking for something only to have somebody holler down to you that what you've wasted your life looking for is *nothing?*"

Mary James grabbed up the bottle of Wild Turkey and took quite a slug from it. The chainsaw spluttered again, but she held the floor. She was raving eloquently and we were as awed of her as we were scared of it.

"I've got a lot of sympathy for that fool down there. Same as for Bud Hanks, and my own self. Waste your life looking for a box of poems, or a dead girl, or a good man, and you've got some goddamn *sym* pathy coming. Tell you what. *I'll* holler down and tell that man to come up, that *I've* got the fukkin' box. Hell, I'll go down there and *bring* him up. He took me out last night, and he was nice. He can be nice. Youall go upstairs and wait and leave that fool to me. He couldn't get it up, and I passed out drunk last night but I'm sober now. I'll get that Box Hunter on that couch and get his gun my*self!*"

I cursed and started out, as did Mary James; we came to blows just short of the splintered trapdoor. I had to drop the butcher knife and, from all appearances, knocked her out, but she was playing possum. AK and I picked her up and were hauling her to the couch when the chainsaw bleated loud, revving high, and bore down in the bole of our foundation. We could feel the vibrations in our feet. We dropped Mary James on the carpet and raced for the boiling crock, potholdered our hands and started, staggering, out with it—

"My God! How long does it take?" gasped AK, presenting me a new face, fearstricken, and not all that attractive; guess I looked as bad to her. How could I comfort her? It was a five-cube chainsaw with a brandnew chain and the tulip tree was heartless—an envelope of dumb life around a core of rot and nothing, like some folks of my acquaintance. He wouldn't have far to go before the wind finished his task for him.

We lugged the crock out on the deck, sloshing it, scalding our hands—and suddenly there was silence, but for the sound of Marsha's voice around the bend, hollering down to the Box Hunter, over *tongue on roof of mouth*. AK ran back in and out with the pot lid and two towels, and we started around again with it, *tongue on roof of mouth* now silent too.

Marsha was leaning over the rail, talking to the Box Hunter just loud enough to be heard, sounding crazy talking sense. We set the lethal cauldron on the deck behind her and I kicked off the lid.

"Get back in!" I hissed at her.

"Don't—please don't do that. He's agreed to listen to *the truth*. He says send it down in the *box.*"

"*Which* truth? The poetry or the Bible?"

"About what was in the box—write it down for him, while I tell him about Jesus," said she, and turned from us to lean back over the rail and commence to preach the Gospel to the Box Hunter.

I looked at AK; if she said tip the pot, I'd tip the pot and baptize him while Marsha preached.

"I'll go up and get a shoe box—let her preach to him; she's worked one miracle, getting him to listen. Maybe she'll work two and get him to *believe.*"

AK sits across the kitchen table from me, waiting with a ball of twine and one of her white shoe boxes. I write the truth about the Japanese girl in the white coat on the Delta Eagle and my connection with that train that night. Mary James sits in a blue lump on the carpet, shaking her head in disbelief. Marsha is out there casting her Gospel pearls down to a swine possessed of demons.

I tried to keep it to a page, then two, but it grew to three, with slashed in qualifiers, parentheses, emendations, and a crowd of footnotes, writing furiously and with deepening despair that this work would ever be accepted by the most quintessentially heartless, mindless editor that ever a writer wrote for his life for—

Mary James got off the floor and stalked out as I stuffed my manuscript unproofread in the shoe box and AK slammed on the lid; tied the box with the loose end of the ball of twine—out and around we ran . . . too late.

Marsha was still preaching, Mary James turning over the crock. The scalding brew spilled out in a great cloud of windshredded steam, pouring down the spaces of the deck planking.

A hideous scream arose from down there. Then shots and shouts. Screams and shots and shouts and shots, moans and shots . . . and silence . . . we had scrambled around and back inside. The light had gone out over the kitchen stove. The silence was intense, the darkness of a piece with it.

"My foot, Bud Hanks . . . a piece is out of my foot . . . and I've got splinters in my armpit."

"Serves you right. Marsha, Anna, youall get any splinters?"

"In my head," said Anna, "just splinters."

"Marsha?"

The wind played its old song in the tulip's limbs, but with an offbeat rhythm section, a sharp staccato ticking resonating up the hollow trunk. Otherwise there was silence—a void. Mary James whispered that she was bleeding. I heard some groping about. I wasn't breathing. I whispered "Marsha?" praying that she was praying. The long dark silent wind-addled ticking void grew unbearable.

"Marsha!"

AK struck a match, lit a candle. In its mean little light there were but the two of them—and the void discarnate . . . "MAR-SHA!"

She was slumped over the rail, head and arms hanging down. I lifted her, cradled her in my arms. She seemed to be at peace, in no great pain. When I laid her on the couch, a last "Dear Jesus" had left her lips while she was in my arms, and she was dead. I felt her pulse, listened at her mouth. Listened at her chest. I heard the ticking, louder now, the snapping grains, the dying cry of tall trees before they fall. I closed my ear to that and pressed the other harder to Marsha's breast. She was not alive.

I put my lips to hers and blew in her mouth, filling her lungs. My own breath sighed back in my face.

I stood over her, grasping at air, looking around for help. This was not right, not acceptable.

AK was dressing Mary James' shot foot by the candle light. "Let the dead bury their dead," Jesus said, but I snatched up our only light and returned to Marsha.

She had not moved. She still lay still as death on the couch. She was in a coma. We'd get her to a hospital, and they'd bring her around. I felt her pulse. None. Listened at her chest. The ticking rattled louder up the empty trunk. Blew in her mouth. My breath sighed back in my face. I'd stick by her in her coma, if it took forever. Where was the wound, if she was dead? How could she be dead? No wound . . . not in her head . . . I ripped open the jacket and blouse, tore them off. Not in her chest or back. I ripped off the pants and panties . . . the bloody panties.

Obscenity! Double obscenity! Right through her maiden head his dirty bullet went—and pierced my Marsha's heart! Shades of Byzantium! Triple damned obscenity! I'll kill him with my bare . . .

A sudden light threw my shadow huge and hulking against the concave wall. A voice from out of the South demands the box and I spin to face the light—

"Look what you've done!

The voice demanded the box.

"Look what you've done!

AK passed between us and the light lit up the white shoe box with my manuscript in it. The truth. AK opened a cup-board-sized door in the tree trunk and tossed the box inside. It was where she dumped her garbage, down the hollow trunk down which her sewerage also ran, to feed her tree. The tick-ing rattled out of there like the crackling fire of hell. He lunged for the opening and I lunged and snatched the light from him, stuck it in his face.

Shreds of skin hung from his scalded neck and ears and hands. He was unarmed, shuddering in agony, terrible to be-hold. I collared him and shined the light on Marsha.

"Look what you did!"

He twisted out of my grip and shoved me sprawling, with the strength of the possessed, and lunged again for the opening in the tree; plunged head and shoulders in and groped, growl-ing for the box.

I got behind him and stooped to grab his ankles, dump him into the place prepared for him.

And then I heard in the wind's song Marsha's *promise to forgive him,* and I yelled at Heaven for the strength to keep that promise, even as the wind of answered prayer—God's own redemptive and judgmental breath—tipped the tulip tree.

Ah the justice of pure poetry!

The Box Hunter tumbled down its hollow heart, and the falling tree's own stout branches cushioned our fall against the hillside. We came to rest in a great deal of noise and tumbling confusion, but safer than one has a right to expect outside of Paradise.

14

I T W A S your simple basic Christian funeral. We sang "Amazing Grace." The preacher prayed, preached a short sermon from the text John 11:25–26, and we sang "Blessed Be the Tie That Binds." The preacher prayed again and that was to be the end of it, when lo and behold an angel of the Lord arose unannounced in our midst and began to read unto us from the New Covenant—

> If I speak in the tongues of men and of angels,
>   but have not love,
> I am a noisy gong or a clanging cymbal.
> And if I have prophetic powers . . .

LIGHTS! CAMERA! ACTION!

We are gathered in Dr. Kochbaum's office which is changed. The couch, the desk and chairs, the diplomas on the wall, the cloudy drapes, the deep dark carpet, are all gone. We have the sense of an enormous space, of hyperspace. All is white and full of light, except the carpet we are comfortably seated on, which is of the hue of newly minted gold. Over the doorway, upon entering, we read: "In my father's house are many rooms."

Standing before us, radiant in a flowing white formal gown, Dr. Kochbaum reads from the thirteenth chapter of First Corinthians.

. . . and understand all mysteries and all knowledge . . .

— *233*

Marsha and I and our lovely children are seated directly in front of Dr. Kochbaum. Next to us is Mary James and her first husband the crop duster, and their darling children. I was best man at their remarriage. Nearby with her fine husband and wonderful children are Tamara, and Marsha's father Alonzo (Lonnie) Greer with his dear wife and their prides and joys, and—she would not have missed this for the world—Miss Mona Hankins with her splendid husband Howard Bennett of the New Ritz Theater and their angelic progeny. Why it seems like everyone I might have at one time been indifferent to is here to hear this joyous reading of the Word—

> If I give away all I have,
> and if I deliver my body to be burned,
> but have not love, I gain nothing . . .

—seated in deep comfort and close with room to spare on the golden carpet, looking up, all heads bowed in silent prayer—

The poet-publishers of *Gabriel's Horn* are here, with their sweet offspring and spouses, all bowed in silent prayer. When we got Marsha to the hospital in that coma (Heaven can wait), who did we run into there but one of the poet-publishers whose name turned out to be Susan who told us about Stella's accident, which had not been fatal; the person who had answered the phone when I called from Dr. Kochbaum's office that terrible day thought I was Malcolm calling anonymously and had lied that Stella died just to shock me into the truth, and now Malcolm and Stella who had been separated because Malcolm was unable to really love a woman because he was hung up on a childhood loss, but was cured by Dr. Kochbaum's reading of I Corinthians 13, are blissfully reunited and fecund. My Bowery bum Ed whom I doomed with a five-dollar bill is here with his fine family; when Ed got to the liquor store he felt suddenly so ashamed for being a Bowery bum about to drink himself to death that he went and gave the five-dollar bill to the Salvation Army, in an effort to redeem himself, but the Salvation Army told Ed that he couldn't buy salvation, that it was God's free gift to all who asked, so Ed asked, and today he and his devoted wife and dutiful children are in the Salvation Army helping Bowery bums find salvation. They bring them to Mary James and her husband who have turned the big house into a home for believers in a House not made with hands; Mary James finally got her medical degree, and also her law degree; she needed the law, along with Grace, to wangle the zoning variance needed to turn the big house into a home for bums whose bishop is my unnamed Bowery bum whose name is Jack, whom Mary James and I found frozen in the alley back in the ice age of our lives; turns out that when they got Jack to Bellevue a world-renowned cryobiologist was there and he resuscitated Jack who married his nurse who bore him many fine sons and daughters, all here and bowed now with Bishop Jack in silent thankful prayer.

The big slope-shouldered man whose finger I mashed through the ringing bell when this house was made with hands in those violent days of yore is here right beside the Kimberlys and all their happy host of kinder. Hannah the Jewish Christian witch of Hannah's Catacomb Coffee House and her patron the fat girl with hairy arms who sings like an angel and their handsome husbands and little honeys are here and bowed in silent fervent prayer, and all of my old friends and girl friends and all Mary James' old friends and boy friends and their helpmates and the unblemished fruits of their wombs and loins all bowed in joyous prayer. All Mary James' old boy friends have told me that they never seriously diddled her back in our diddling days, but I already knew that because Mary James was a virgin when we remarried, not that it makes a whit of difference now, for we are as one in our regenerated squash court with our healthy, happy young . . .

> Love bears all things, believes all things,
> hopes all things, endures all things . . .

My beloved wife Anna gives my hand a warm squeeze as Dr. Kochbaum reads, our heads bowed in silent blissful prayer, the fruits of our ecstatic union gathered like the petals of a rose around us. We live in the tulip tree where Anna writes great sacred concerti and I write great epic spiritual poetry. We gather on the Lord's Day with Marsha and her family and Mary James and her family and Dr. Kochbaum and her family at the big house for all-day preaching and dinner on the ground with the Beatific Bums and a happy host of millions stretching further than the mind can reel—

> Love never ends; as for prophecy,
> it will pass away; as for tongues; they will cease . . .

Through the drapeless lightful windows we hear harpsichords, flutes, coronets and lutes, trumpets, clarinets and violins, bagpipes, pipe organs, windmills, harmonicas and xylophones, mirimbas, tubas and mandolins, zithers, clavichords, silver bells and sewing machines, bass fiddles, second fiddles, slide trombones, banjos, pianos, harps and lyres and saxophones, Jew's-harps, drums and castanets, tambourines and French horns, cellos and oboes, glockenspiels and flugelhorns, the bluebird's song and Gabriel's horn, for these are the horns of smoothly flowing New York City traffic, all orchestrated by a grand maestro computer in Central Park in a celestial arrangement of the "Hallelujah Chorus" accompanying the voices from the rainbow choir loft of the Bowery—

. . . . as for knowledge, it will pass away.
For our knowledge is imperfect and our prophecy
   is imperfect;
but when the perfect comes, the imperfect will
   pass away . . .

Miss Mona's movie romancers are here with their splendid families; Miss Mona married one of her movie romancers, the romancer in the dark popcorny Ritz she was going
to write me about over a glass of wine one night, well she
wrote and I wrote back, telling her to put an ad in the personal column of the *McGehee Times* and he would surely answer as surely as my truelove did, and when I saw Miss
Mona's ad I realized that her favorite movie romancer had
been me; just as she had speculated in her letter, it was me
sitting next to her watching the Bluebird in '43 so now
Miss Mona and I are married and beside ourselves and pro-
lific. Oh yes, what Miss Mona had in her backyard that she
was coy about and I was coy about finding out about
turned out to be an immense aviary housing three hundred
million fertile bluebirds. When we got married we set them
free and now there's a bluebird in everybody's backyard in
the whole wide cosmos and even the moon is blue with
them while the original three hundred million bluebirds
are here with us this Day of Thanksgiving without end,
with their leader, the *original* bluebird of happiness, all
bowed in silent prayer, and Shirley Temple is here too still
looking like she does on the purple syrup pitcher; she
hasn't married, being too young, and the Wizard of Oz
with the Wiz and a Mysterious Stranger and the obscure
novelist from the brick barn on Short Beach Road and his
publisher and agent and the penitent reviewers of the dust
jacket of his first novel, and their cute puppies, and his
penitent ex-agent and ex-publisher, all humbly bowed, and
the *original* Girl in the White Coat, and Hopalong Cassidy's
white hat and white-handled pistol, and the Lone Ranger

in his white hat and white-handled pistols, on his white horse Silver, their pistols loaded with gold, frankincense and myrrh, and the Delta Eagle is here on time, and the harpsichord I gave Anna and the windmill-powered cordwood saw she gave me, both resurrected and in concert, and the *McGehee Times* and *Information Please*, the Missouri Pacific Railroad and the New Ritz Theater, and the grade crossing at Highway 4, and all our kith and kin, and everybody who ever rode the Delta Eagle, and the entire casts of all versions of *The Bluebird*, and Mr. Maeterlinck, and a penitent *Time* magazine, and *Prayboy* and *Repenthouse*, all bowed in silent, fervent prayer, and the *original* Bud Hanks who was an old unwashed ragged crazy Arkansas City nigger who mowed lawns and chopped wood for a living and had no home on earth, his head bowed now and smelling sweet, and O God who have I left out—Mr. Kimberly, the unlikely high yellow spermatozoon has come into his own, he's married (Kim) and they've been fruitful to the tune of three hundred million saints of the Blessed Lord and are just too absolutely in too much bliss for speech, and the shoe box of haiku is here reunited with Aiko Abé, united with the Box Hunter and my orange box of effort and they likewise are in that much bliss if not more, and ol' Ossie Lee is here with the nun whose habit he pulled up at the bus stop in his naughty Catholic childhood; Ossie Lee found an even better habit under there and now he and the sweet old nun are married and live and work for the Lord in blissful celibacy, and—oh yes . . .

> When I was a child, I spoke like a child,
> I thought like a child, I reasoned like a child . . .

CUT! CUT! CUT!

Thus endeth the Hereafter According to Hanks. My eyes opened on the coffin, on Dr. Anna Kochbaum standing by it reading from the little green New Testament.

When I became a *woman,* I gave up childish ways . . .

And I said thank you Lord that the directing isn't up to me,
that I still have time to clean up my act, that we all do,

For now we see in a mirror dimly, but then face to face.
Now I know in part; then I shall understand fully,
even as I have been fully understood.
So faith, hope, love abide, these three;
but the greatest of these is love.

Down with the curtain! Up with the lights! Out into the street!

"Follow me, and leave the dead to bury their own dead."

15

A Salvation Army truck was double-parked out front, two soldiers of the Lord loading into it, with great effort, a large heather-green stuffed leather couch. Up on her floor in the hallway outside Dr. Kochbaum's little waiting room the desk and chairs awaited the Salvation Army. The waiting room was piled to the ceiling with crates, leaving only a straight and narrow passage to the open office door. The office was bare as a ghost's hope chest, stripped of everything not in the blueprints; even the deep dark carpet had been ripped up, exposing a parquet floor layered with fine dust that had sifted through, down from her decade of practice.

A brilliant shaft of good morning light from the drapeless window flooded the small room, brought it down to size; to my surprise it was just another small office cubicle, an empty box, in a city flush with them, bereft of the magic of the decorator's art and the ambience created by its occupant and her profession. Anna stood at the window, looking out and up. She had on a faded blue old housecoat and fuzzy slippers, her hair battened with a red bandanna, loose strands twigging out here and there. She heard my feet on the creaky old parquet floor and turned abruptly, stirring up a nebula of dust motes in the bright sunlight shaft. She had never looked so lovely.

"*Bud!* We must be telepathic."

"Remodeling? Moving?"

"Quitting."

She invited me in for coffee. In was through a door I'd never noticed, in the corner behind where her desk had been; it led into her kitchen. She poured two cups of coffee from an old aluminum dripolator. We sat catercorner at a milk-glass-topped table, wrought-iron legs. From where I sat I could see down a short white hallway an open room with a floor-to-ceiling wall of books, and the keyboard of a grand piano. The sweet scent of burning cedar wafted out of there. I took from my shirt pocket the little green New Testament she had left on Marsha's coffin.

"I came in to straighten up my apartment," handing her the Testament, avoiding her eyes, careful not to touch her hand, "and when I got there I decided to give it up. Time I settled down in one place, somewhere. The squash court, I guess. Say you're *quitting?*"

She nods, her eyes on the Testament in her hand. "Wouldn't Marsha rather you kept this?"

"No, she wants you to have it, Anna."

She looked at me, misty-eyed and with a wan smile at my use of the present tense.

"I already have one. Anyway it's supposed to be written on our hearts, says the Prophet Jeremiah, chapter thirty-one, verse thirty-one and following, Old Covenant."

"Done gone back to preaching, Bud Hanks?"

"Words. I don't feel all that close to the Word, frankly speaking."

Anna told me to keep the faith, and took a sip of coffee. I asked why she was quitting. She put down her cup and gave me a look that said her reason was very personal and that to tell me would be a shared intimacy. I let go with an understanding nod. She put down the Testament and got both hands around her cup, looking in it like it was a crystal ball.

"I had a small gift of prophecy, and healing, and was adept at tongues and their intrepetation, but I lacked what Paul wrote about, what Marsha had. I didn't have *love*, Bud. I love my parents, my friends. I even love a man, which I find most upsetting. But that all-embracing love for everyone—including the loveless and unlovable, that *agape*—I've been brushing up on my Greek—without which one is nothing, I simply didn't have."

She pushed away her cup, put her palms flat down on the table and looked straight into my eyes with such tender vulnerability that I dared not blink for fear of shutting her away forever.

"After the funeral I came back to my office to go over the files of clients scheduled for the next day. I always put in a good hour of thought and study for every fifty minutes spent with a client. But I couldn't concentrate. Paul's hymn to love kept going through my mind, and finally it dawned on me that I hated what I was doing, and that I didn't *love* my clients. Perhaps a physician or a surgeon can do her job and remain indifferent to her patients, but how could a psychotherapist who deals with emotional and spiritual problems remain aloof or indifferent, or worse, actually hate some of her clients? Medical doctors treat problems, but psychotherapists treat people, yet I was treating people as so many packages of problems—problems that I held in contempt."

"Well, Anna, Marsha told me the other night, before you showed up—we were talking about my feelings toward our pursuer—'Hate the sin, love the sinner.' Perhaps you're confusing . . . "

"I'm not at all confused, Bud. I was contemptuous of my clients because of their problems. Perhaps contempt is too strong a word for how I felt about many of them. My feelings were alternately superiority, pity, indifference, fear, whatever —anything but *agape.* Anyway, I shoved those files aside and fled in there to my first love—my piano. I began playing aimlessly—Brahms, I think—and not well at all. I had never been so depressed. I could see their faces as I played—hundreds of them—and I had not given them what they needed most— *agape.* Oh, I helped a lot of people in the last ten years, if treating symptoms is any real help, but I had withheld from them that love that is patient and kind, that is not arrogant or rude and does not insist on its own way. I felt so *guilty,* sitting there at my expensive grand piano in my comfortable apartment that *they* had paid for, and I had failed them. And then the worst blow came . . . "

Anna took my hand, my bandaged hand, and caressed it.

"I realized that I didn't have it to give. The capacity for that kind of love just wasn't in me. One face stood out above all the others. A few years ago a client went into a rage while I was questioning him about his problem. He wrecked my office and then tried to rape me; I was saved from rape by the problem he had come to me with—his impotence. After failing, he broke down crying, filled with remorse, begging me to forgive him. I was in a position, finally, to really help him, but I betrayed him. I called the police. I testified against him and he went to prison. After that I bought the pistol."

Anna let go of my hand, picking up the New Testament, and looked at the door to the empty box that was Dr. Kochbaum's office.

"Marsha had that love that does not rejoice at wrong; the love that bears all things, hopes all things and endures all things. She would have forgiven that man, even had he succeeded in raping her. She would have helped him. But I sent him to jail, and bought a pistol to use against any more like him. That pistol became my security. I think it even made me arrogant, made me deep down dare another man to get violent with me. It was like a surrogate cock in my drawer, and with it I secretly rejoiced in the impotence of my clients. I think it ended whatever effectiveness I ever had in healing."

"I think you're being way too hard on yourself, Anna. Martyrdom is a very special calling. Suffice it that the rest of us see justice done, and leave mercy to God and the martyrs. Your would-be rapist's remorse was likely that he had failed, not that he tried to rape you. If you hadn't sent him to prison he might have tried again, and succeeded or killed you."

"Perhaps so, Bud, but I chose a profession that demanded of me some risks, some sacrifice of personal safety, some selflessness—some *agape*. There is real danger in leading people to see the truth of their lives. You were a minister, so you must know that as well as I. I called it sickness, and you called it sin—or were you one of those wise preachers who called it *sin-sickness?*"

"It's a sin-sick world, they say. 'Wise' you say?"

"When you led people into their own selves to see the sin-sickness there, what did you do when they lashed out at you for leading them there?"

"Anna, I must confess that I was just a pulpit preacher. A good one, they said, but that's all. And I didn't last long at that. I never was one for one-on-one soul sessions, unless it was with my own soul, in prayer, or poetry. Or cordwood cutting."

"You're a loner, all right," she said, arising. "So am I. Perhaps we were both in the wrong professions."

She walked by me and paused, her back to me, gazing down the hallway. "I could have been a concert pianist. I was good enough. But I thought I wanted to help people in a more basic way."

She turned her magnificent profile to me, leaning against the door jamb. "Of course music and poetry are basic necessities too, though I doubt that the best art can be produced—created—without *agape.*"

She glanced down that hallway again, at the keyboard of her piano, I divined.

"Do you recall my telling you that time that God was music? I was wrong. God is *love.* But he spoke to me through music, the night of Marsha's funeral. I recall now, it was Brahms' First Piano Concerto I was trying to play. Remember *The L-shaped Room,* with Leslie Caron? That was the background music. Perhaps I . . . but here I go psychologizing. You asked that night, in your country home, if I thought God was a harpsichord concerto, and I said not just any concerto and not always the same one. Brahms' First Piano Concerto used to be one of my theophanies, but it didn't work the night of Marsha's funeral. Then, suddenly, I was picking out—but listen . . . "

Anna went down the hallway into her den and sat at her piano. She did not look back, and I did not follow. She played "Amazing Grace," the first song we sang at Marsha's funeral. But she didn't play it like a church pianist, she played it like a grand pianist, and then she played it through again, like a grand church pianist, and sang the words—

> Amazing grace! how sweet the sound,
> That saved a wretch like me!
> I once was lost, but now am found,
> Was blind, but now I see.
>
> 'Twas grace that taught my heart to fear,
> And grace my fears re-lieved;
> How precious did that grace appear
> The hour I first believed!
>
> Thro' many dangers, toils, and snares,
> I have already come;
> 'Tis grace hath bro't me safe thus far,
> And grace will lead me home.
>
> When we've been there ten thousand years,
> Bright shining as the sun,
> We've no less days to sing God's praise
> Than when we first begun.

In the holy silence that followed that I arose slowly from the kitchen table, saying, "Anna." To say more would have been to say too little, except "Amen."

Still looking at her keyboard, she said, "Would you like to come in, Bud?"

Would I like to come into her most holy place and sing "Amazing Grace" with her until the graves give up their dead? O would I love to, Anna—but I have a wretched promise to keep.

" 'Fraid I can't, Anna."

"How *is* Mary James?" she said.

"I brought her back from the hospital last night. She's okay. On crutches, off the bottle—she says. She got me to promise her we'd give it another try."

"Why?" Anna asked of her keyboard.

"Because I never really tried. I married the memory of my childhood sweetheart, not the woman she'd grown up to be. Guess I owe the woman one good try."

"You've got *agape,* Bud, hand you that."

"Must be. It's sure not *eros,* tell you that. Tell you what I really want to do. I really want, more than . . . "

"You better get on out of here, Bud Hanks, before you break a promise and at least one heart."

"What are you going to do, Anna?"

"Tomorrow I'm going out to the island and salvage what I can from my fallen house. Then I'll take a trip, come back, and figure out the rest of my tomorrows, one day at a time. Don't worry about me Bud. Like you, I'm a born survivor—*re*born."

"Praise the Lord, Anna. Let's keep in touch."

"Seeya round, Hank."

16

WELL, I drove back out to Long Island, thinking what a filmy ending this, not like those good old wholesome films where duty wins out over romance, but wholesomer yet, where duty (read *agape*) wins out over true love (read *eros* in its biblical Greek sense). This was *An American Tragedy* I was in now, only Montgomery Clift was *saving* Shelley Winters from the drink, losing Elizabeth Taylor, for a life sentence with ol' Shell. Now there's a *real* tragedy raised to the sublime, transcending tragedy, elevating ol' Monty (me) beyond the tragic hero to just this side of Heaven of that lonely soul nobody finds catharsis in—the Knight of Faith! A fool for Christ sake nobody cares to emulate—or film.

That night Mary James and I watched home movies in the squash court. Our film ends with me running the film I took of Marsha on the train and on the swing. It was the first run of the film. The LIRR's windows were too filmy with filth, though, and I couldn't make out the girl in the white coat's features. Even on the swing she was a blur. It could have been anybody. It looked like a ghost. I took hold of Mary James' hand and we watched it running backward. Her hand was warm and moist, and she had brandy on her breath. When the film had finished running backward and the loose end commenced to flap around the reel, and the screen glared white as a square full moon at us, and Mary James was laughing, I let go of her hand, got up, and burned the film, smashed the projector with the movie camera, and Mary James and I said our prayers, at my insistence, and went to bed. After she passed out, I prayed on and on—"Father, if thou art willing, remove this cup from me; nevertheless not my will, but thine, be done," until Morpheus brought his gift.

IT WAS a clear bright morning, cold as Nordic hell. I stoked up the stove and knelt over Mary James, shaking her awake.

"Mary, listen: It would be what men call 'noble' to keep my mouth shut about how I feel about and what I think of you. But I've got to tell you the truth, even at the risk of using the truth to get myself out of this commitment. And God knows I want out of it. The truth is, as I see and feel it: I don't want to live with you. I don't want to try. I'm not even sure I want to want to. But I feel I owe you, and I believe that any two people can make a marriage if they try—even learn to love each other. I don't love you. I don't like you. I think you're a hopeless mess. And if you feel any different about me, we sure don't have a chance. We've got to start from scratch, like Adam and Eve fresh kicked out of Eden. I do love you, Mary James. With that special love the Greeks called *agape*. I've got as much *agape* for you as I do for any Bowery bum. But don't worry. That kind of love doesn't thin out in the spreading. We've got a long hard row to hoe. You've got to help me get over another love I have. The love I've been all my life looking for. A love that spreads thin in the sharing. Are you awake, Mary James? Are you listening?"

I gave her another shake. She backhanded matter from her bloodshot eyes, blinked at me, and I almost kissed her and said it all again, but, blinded by the skylight, she closed her eyes and said—

"Lonnie?"

I PARKED BY the fountain, climbed the bluff, and made my way to the stump. Just in time to see her disappearing over the outcropping of rock, with a white seven-league boot box under her arm—all she had chosen to salvage. I started to yell, but no, I had burnt that bridge too, right down to the running waters. Suddenly I felt free. Free as a spore in the wind. I set out for New York City on the L.I.E., but traffic was too heavy for the freedom I felt, so I pulled into Huntington Station and waited for the train. While waiting for the train I took the plates off my truck and threw them in the trash. Burn another bridge. Settle down? No, settle up. When I got on the train, I had settled it: get together the rough draft of this from my apartment in New York, catch a cab to Kennedy, catch the first flight to wherever it was warm the year around, and polish up the story of my life. Then, maybe, write a poem.

O how heady freedom is when it's all in the head.

Once aboard the train, I walked from car to car, driven like a slave, driven like the Israelites from Egyptian bondage to the Promised Land. I spied a woman in a coat as white as pearl seated in the nonsmokers' car, her face pressed against the window. A gentleman was seated next to her. I said to the gentleman, "Excuse me, sir, but you have my seat", and the gentleman, a true gentleman, relinquished it, without a fuss or loss of face.

Her face turned from the window and the Red Sea of her Near Eastern eyes closed over mine. The train whistled at a crossing east of East Northport, the train's rumbling the tumbling of the walls of Jericho.

"My given name is John Wayne," I said. "They've always called me Bud."

"Ruth," she said, "Naomi Ruth. I switched to Anna Karenina somewhere along the way and off the track."

"Ruth," I said.

" 'Entreat me not to leave you or to return from following you; for where you go I will go, and where you lodge I will lodge; your people shall be my people, and your God my God; where you die I will die, and there will I be buried.' "

"Marriage is not an end," I told her. "It's just a good carriage to get you there."

"It's the driver of the good carriage," she said.
And the woman took my hand.

> Then the Lord God said, "It is not good
> that the man should be alone; I will make him
> a helper fit for him."

THE CRISIS OF
THE MIDDLE CLASS

The CRISIS of the MIDDLE CLASS

by Lewis Corey

COLUMBIA UNIVERSITY PRESS
NEW YORK

COLUMBIA UNIVERSITY PRESS
MORNINGSIDE EDITION

COLUMBIA UNIVERSITY PRESS

New York   Chichester, West Sussex

Library of Congress Cataloging-in-Publication Data

Corey, Lewis.
The crisis of the middle class / by Lewis Corey.
p.   cm.
Reprint. Originally published by Covici Friede
Publishers, 1935.
Includes bibliographical references.
ISBN 0-231-09976-2 : ISBN 0-231-09977-0 (pbk.) :
1. Middle class—United States.   2. United States—
Economic conditions—1918–1945.
3. Collectivism.   4. Socialism.   I. Title.
HT690.U6C67   1994
305.5'5'0973—dc20   94-13654
CIP

c 10 9 8 7 6 5 4 3 2 1
p 10 9 8 7 6 5 4 3 2 1

CONTENTS

FOREWORD TO THE
MORNINGSIDE EDITION
by PAUL BUHLE

HAILING *The Crisis of the Middle Class* at its 1935
appearance, Columbia University economic historian Louis Hacker described this "Addresses to
the Middle Class" as both a foremost intellectual
accomplishment and an important political challenge. Corey, now "undoubtedly the most important Marxist writer in the United States today,"
had the independence to "pursue his thought
wherever it may lead him" and the skill to jettison
Marxist "official seminar terminology" for a lucid
style so that masses of ordinary Americans could
understand his work. Alan Angoff wrote similarly,
in the *Boston Evening Transcript,* that the book
proved Corey to be the "best informed and most
thoroughly communistic of all current American
economists." Playwright Clifford Odets, then at
the height of his precocious renown, was quoted
as saying the book seemed to be a "statistical version" of his *Paradise Lost.* The publication of *The
Crisis of the Middle Class* actually made the front
page of the *New York Post* and it briefly reached
the best-seller list. A bright future evidently

vii

awaited the author.[1] Few readers guessed that Lewis Corey had been, a generation earlier, a leading cultural avant-gardist and a major figure in the proto-Communist Left. Still fewer of his army of admirers suspected that Corey's days as a celebrated author were finished.

Yet this volume, originally published in 1935, remains a landmark popular study of American life. Never previously reprinted, it reflects not only its moment of creation but also the work of an enormously fertile intellect, wrongly neglected by intellectual historians of the twentieth century. Corey's insights into the problems of society were contained, but not exhausted, by the expectation of capitalist collapse. He read history, especially American history, as if a climax were at hand. For these reasons, the book naturally seemed for several decades after the 1930s to have been outstripped by the resurgent U.S. economy and by the Cold War between two mighty military states for pre-eminent world influence. Corey personally renounced any faith in the future of communism long before it collapsed. Now, the end of Communism has caused many key problems raised by *The Crisis of the Middle Class* to undeniably return to view.

Although many of the book's particulars have been proven wrong, its thesis remains intact. The fate of a troubled democracy is tied to a middle class both hugely variegated and deeply conflicted. As a group, this middle stratum admires

viii

or envies those formations above even though it sees the damage wrought by the continuing concentrations of wealth and influence; it fears those multitudes below even as it perceives the demoralization of society at large through the spread of poverty, hopelessness, and violence. Acutely aware of vapid materialism yet craving security, it drifts to apathy, pessimism, and escape into a personal life. Despite the wide range of sociological and historical literature touching on the middle class, none has focused upon the basic dilemmas more clearly or eloquently than this volume.[2]

Corey saw the crisis as perhaps only an outsider can. He spent his early life rising out of the severe conditions that beset the immigrant poor and grappled his way upward to become a clarion of the masses' presumed part in an impending great social transformation. He wrote stirring manifestoes, traveled across the world, huddled with Lenin, and returned to anonymity of the ordinary American. Self-educated but enormously erudite, he then set out to learn what was unique about American life. To understand him better, then, is to gain a view into the book at hand.[3]

* * *

Corey was born Luigi Carlo Fraina in Galdo (Salerno), Italy in 1892. Brought to the U.S. at an early age, he grew up in the slum section of Manhattan known as Hell's Kitchen. An undersized and often sickly "Louis" Fraina went to work selling newspapers at age six, later assisted his mother in a tobacco factory, and still later worked as a boot black. In slightly more favorable conditions, the brilliant boy—an autodidact novel-reader and valedictorian of his grade school class—could have risen swiftly upward through formal education. But, life cheated him. His formal schooling ended when his father died and he was forced to become the main breadwinner of the family.

An instinctive rebel and truant against repressive parochial school authorities, Fraina repeatedly turned misfortune into radical idealism. Hired as a stage-hand, he found himself physically unequal to the demands of the job. But he solicited the assistance of his fellow employees to "cover" his work, suggesting a key insight for his evolving work view. Leaving school at seventeen and seeking intellectual outlets, he began contributing to the *Truth Seeker,* dreaming aloud in that free-thought weekly of a better world, free of prejudice and superstitions. Meanwhile, he filled his time with a furious drive for intellectual self-improvement, not only to make up for his lack of formal education but to prepare himself for a life worthy of his growing visions. The same year, 1909, he became a socialist.

It was one of those rare, optimistic moments for American socialism. For nearly a decade the Socialist Party, under its beloved leader Eugene V. Debs, had worked to educate ordinary Americans not to fear socialist doctrine. In its modest success, the party published dozens of newspapers in many languages, gained a foothold in factory towns and in many large cities outside the Old South, and cultivated a large rural following in the Southwest. It elected tens, then hundreds of local officials to office. But according to its critics—and Fraina was quickly one of them—the Socialist Party had made too many concessions to the presumed sources of membership so as to compromise Marxian doctrines and methods of organization with middle class tastes and (Protestant) religious inclinations. A true proletarian organization would do better. The "new immigrant" workers from Southern and Eastern Europe who engaged in widespread strikes from 1909 onward seemed to him the key constituency in every way, if only the proper political-industrial vessel could be found for their mobilization.

Fraina converted to the small and sectarian Socialist Labor Party, staying until 1913. Rising through its thin ranks as a street-corner agitator, he joined the miniscule staff of the party's newspaper, *The Daily People,* working almost literally at the right hand of the charismatic party leader, Daniel DeLeon. In this capacity, Fraina became heir to a very particular leftist tradition. DeLeon, an outstanding socialist figure during the 1890s but now badly reduced and in his final years of life, had palpably failed to build a political organization. He had however developed a remarkable quasi-anthropological view of modern society. According to DeLeon, history of socialism to date had been mere prologue. Where modern industry had organized society around itself—above all in the United States—the political form of the state had been outmoded and the effort to capture it a fruitless task. The modern working class was uniquely constituted to supersede the state's present function through a government of freely-constituted governing councils. The ordinary masses, taught to understand their own power, were being prepared by life and the help of a socialist educational body to liberate all society, all art, indeed all creative impulses, from their historical integument.[4]

Although Fraina could no longer be constrained within the narrow boundaries of the Socialist Labor Party, he retained for the rest of his life certain elements of his experience. He moved on swiftly to a variety of pursuits, which allowed him to elaborate a vision of a freer future order and to gain an increasingly precise view of the society at hand. As a staff member of the *New Review* magazine, arguably the first American leftwing publication specifically for intellectuals, Fraina rubbed shoulders with Columbia University intellectuals and Greenwich Village bohemians, anthropologists, psychologists and cultural critics, from Robert Lowie to W.E.B. DuBois. As a managing editor and contributor to *Modern Dance* magazine, he found himself exploring the social role of jazz and popular arts, enraptured with performances of the "Divine Isadora" Duncan, and enraged by the high-brow critics' indifference to the most creative elements in vernacular American culture.[5]

His remarkable volume, *Revolutionary Socialism* (1918), explicated the more sociological element of this broad perspective. This volume also best predicts *The Crisis of the Middle Class*. Capitalism, Fraina argued, was passing through its laissez-faire, competitive period into a newer epoch of regulated capitalism and expansive empire. In the "progressive" or regulatory politics of Theodore Roosevelt and Woodrow Wilson, he found the "clear and consistent formulation of the requirements of the new era of controlled industry and collectivist Capitalism." Centralization of the executive apparatus and the national government at large and coordination of all forces including labor and capital had rendered the old socialism of Debs's party utterly obsolete.

Fraina acutely saw that, contrary to widely-held expectations, capitalism was not about to collapse from its own anarchic tendencies. The middle classes, rather than disappearing, had divided into the fading small proprietor section and the rising army of white collar employees. Like the skilled working class, this last sector had far more to lose than its chains. It increasingly looked upon itself as part of America's economic empire which overpowered and steadily replaced European-style colonialism and recycled a considerable portion of the profits on the home front.

The self-trained thinker Fraina, painfully aware

xiii

of the elite backgrounds and personal connections which brought young men to the *New Republic* and the other liberal opinion magazines, was especially critical of the intellectuals' muted criticisms of the system. Socially, the cultural climate had grown more emancipating for the individual and especially the new middle class. But politically, it rewarded the loyalty of those who supported the U.S. entry into World War I.

Fraina saw his subjects clearly, anticipating in many respects the objections that Lewis Mumford, Waldo Frank, Randolph Bourne and a bevy of other thinkers would soon levy against the defects of a business-oriented liberalism.[6] He considered the issues of democracy more deeply than they did in important areas for he concretely posed the questions of mass participation in the present and future order. He had very early glimpsed the promiseful emergence of what he called a "new racial type," a multicultural figure of the Americas, free of Europe's historical constraints and prepared by experience for a truly democratic transformation of society.[7] His writings on subjects ranging from free verse and graphic Futurism to the social possibilities of dance often hint at a fuller development of this idea with the intersection of popular culture and modernism as the key juncture. These contributions remain stunning for their precocious premonitions. But Fraina, the immigrant boy, was above all committed to socialist revolution—and in 1917, Russia called.

xiv

Here lay the chief tragedy of Fraina's life. For the vigorous young journalist, critic and activist as for millions around the world, the initial reports from Russia presented a vision of proletarian revolution fulfilled. After all, veteran radicals observed that the Soviets ("workers councils" in Russian) had the look and sound of the Industrial Workers of the World. John Reed, Fraina's sometime associate and sometime political rival, said so with special elegance in the reportorial *Ten Days That Shook the World.*[8]

Fraina gave himself to this moment in history, heart and soul. Decades later, after the most severe disillusionment, he still had not shaken the incubus which directed him away from his own unique analytical approach to economics, politics and culture. Even as Communism's fierce opponent, he remained locked into the narrowed logic of the intellectual debate between liberalism and Stalinism. To this dilemma we trace, below, some of the weakest elements in *The Crisis of the Middle Class.*

Fraina edited the *Socialist Revolution in Russia,* the first collection of documents to appear in English about the Bolshevik Revolution. He also edited, during 1917 from Boston, the first newspaper in the English-speaking world which could claim to be the voice of the Bolsheviks (not only in ideas but personally, by way of the paper's sponsors, Latvian exiles close to Lenin). He lectured and wrote furiously, attracting wide interest within Left circles. He also heroically went to jail, if briefly, for avowed draft resistance. When the Socialist Party membership voted for a new slate of executive officers in 1919, Fraina who had only recently rejoined the organization finished at the top of the list. He seemed, more than ever, to have a brilliant future before him.

But this was an altogether misleading picture of reality. Fraina's supporters, the immigrants from Eastern Europe who streamed into the Socialist Party, looked mainly toward world revolution and especially the events in their various homelands. Neither he nor they had much appreciation for the complexity of developments on the American domestic front, where both anti-war sentiment and labor activity surged forward—but not toward revolutionary ends. From 1915 to 1920, Americans staged a grand rehearsal for the 1930s, that is a multi-faceted campaign to redress the imbalance of the social order. In the glare of the events in Russia, it looked not so much like a large-scale adjustment as the merest premonition of incendiary uprisings soon to follow.[9]

Disoriented, Fraina stumbled badly. He fell captive to enthusiasts who compulsively created an imitation Russian Bolshevik party, indifferent to the political costs along the way. He looked superficially impressive as one of the most Americanized figures and precocious intellects among the leaders of the Communist Party in 1919. (It is this particular image of Fraina that actor Paul Sorvino captured in the epic film, *Reds*.) But his chosen movement, torn by its own internal wrangling as much as by the unprecedented wave of political repression from federal and state authorities, collapsed as the ranks of radicals shrank within two years from more than a hundred thousand activists to a few thousand who were mostly at each others' throats. While communist publications spent their energy in polemical internecine warfare and the government swept in to close newspapers, wreck offices, and prepare cases for imprisonment and deportation, the demoralized radical ranks let slip their chance to consolidate their wide influence among the restless workers, farmers, African Americans, European ethnic groups, and others.[10]

Bad quickly went to worse amid the climate of false expectations and ubiquitous federal infiltrators. Fraina was accused, by an admitted former government agent, of being a police spy! In a thoroughly bizarre twist, Fraina found himself also defended by another federal agent. This strange set of circumstances meant that his usefulness had all but vanished. One last hope remained in the Mecca of revolution: Moscow.

A trip to the Soviet Union to see things for himself and to clear his name brought him moments of unforgettable intensity. Lenin, in a personal interview with Fraina, agreed to collaborate on a Russian edition of DeLeon's essays. Fraina boldly addressed the Comintern that was still operating at fever pitch of world-revolutionary expectations. Bedeviled by controversies at home and increasingly aware that his positions could not be sustained, he lost badly. Intuitively, Fraina anticipated the degeneration of internationalism that the consolidation of Stalin's grip would make final in a few years.

Shunted aside by Comintern leaders, Fraina was sent on a fool's errand to Mexico. Ordered to guide a non-existent communist movement there into a fantasized revolutionary climax, he marked time and badly missed a Russian Jewish wife he had left behind in Moscow. He joined her in New York, crossing the border under an assumed name and abandoning his career as professional revolutionary. He worked as a copyeditor for *The New York Times* and elsewhere under the name of "Joseph Skala" and eagerly embraced something he had hardly known previously: a private life. With the birth of a beloved daughter, he had become a family man.

Here, a crucial phase for his new life and for the later creation of *The Crisis of the Middle Class* began in several different ways. As he recalled in unpublished memoirs, he looked at American life anew through both his wife's eyes and his. What he saw was not by any means an ideal society, but a society with great democratic energies. It blindly denied itself, however, the potentialities it might achieve with foresight and planning. The writer "Lewis Corey" (as he called himself, using initials

xviii

from his name), emerged as if from nowhere in 1926 to expose the shallowness of capitalism's "New Era," and to suggest better alternatives.

In the pages of the *New Republic* most prominently, and in smaller venues like the Amalgamated Clothing Workers' weekly paper, *The Advance*, the self-taught economist Corey carefully used statistics to show that prosperity was based on speculation, its fruits barely reaching the poor. "The ideology and practice of individual acquisition, accumulation and concentration are now ascendent," he warned, adding sarcastically, "Let us produce and accumulate: there are no social problems! But there is an awakening coming."[11] Better than any professional economist, he had predicted the causes of the coming Depression, anticipating by several years the famous volume by Adolph Berle and Gardiner Means, *The Modern Corporation and Private Property.*[12]

Lewis Corey had placed himself, one would think, perfectly for the economic crash and the rise of social movements to follow. Indeed, while he made a meager living as a writer and lesser editor at the *Encyclopedia of the Social Sciences* between 1931 and 1934, his reputation grew sufficiently for him to go on the road as a modestly successful public lecturer. *The Modern Monthly,* an outstanding independent voice of radical intellectuals, enthroned him during these years as a leading political contributor. An intelligent historical study, *The House of Morgan* (1931), received good notices as a fair-minded interpretation of monopoly's rise in post-Civil War America.

But Corey had several almost overwhelming frustrations. His magnum opus, *The Decline of American Capitalism* (1934), was greeted as "Radicalism's Complete Handbook" or the volume which demonstrated the adaptability of Marxian ideas to U.S. conditions.[13] Noted labor economist John R. Commons further described its author as the "first Marxian economist to reduce the Marxian theory to quantitative terms."[14] He had managed only to get a small commercial house to publish the volume, and readers found the book too overwhelming in length and too turgid in prose to swallow whole. Most also found its thematic finality, predicting absolute capitalist breakdown, far too pessimistic a few years later, when the New Deal and the fear of Fascism made "bourgeois democracy" look much better than before.

Corey also inevitably failed in his efforts to reconcile with the Communist Party. Expecting to re-enter at a leadership level, he made himself the outstanding figure in the League of Professional Groups for Foster and Ford, the Communist presidential slate in 1932. Seeking to create an independent-minded milieu of intellectuals, Corey ran into the sectarian roadblock which stymied so many others. Communist leaders usually tolerated a limited degree of organizational latitude during some historical eras. But during this early 1930s moment of renewed revolutionary expectation (reminiscent, ironically, of Daniel DeLeon's approach decades earlier), they deeply feared potential competition and practically demonized any suspected free agents. Unlike a group of younger intellectuals who navigated through Trotskyism into the prestigious circles of the New York Intellectuals, Corey had no interest in lesser political entities and had no such potent alliances. Despite his accomplishments, he found himself surprisingly alone.

* * *

Yet all these experiences, good and bad, had been perhaps necessary for the unique effort to create *The Crisis of the Middle Class*. Unbound to any chiliastic revolutionary ideology and pursuing his own intellectual leads, he interested himself increasingly in what European socialists had traditionally called "American Exceptionalism." Existing Marxian models, he concluded, could not really explain the particular trajectory of U.S. society. Although Corey clearly held back from jettisoning Marxist methodology, he sought to make an original analysis with the proletariat no longer at the center of the picture.

His perspective was less strictly original, in some respects, than he might have believed. As he moved from economics to history and especially U.S. history, Corey assimilated the "Progressive" historiography which had been predominant since the 1910s. Highlighted by the writings of Charles Beard, it had framed the American saga in terms of "interests," less like permanent class formations and more like competing and often geographically-based strata such as merchants and farmers. In Beard's model, egalitarian-minded settlers had continuously resisted the imposition of European-style rule by monopolists based in Eastern cities. Toward the end of the nineteenth century—coinciding with the end of the frontier—the emerging banking and industrial capitalists had quashed the last major agrarian threat. But, the middle and, to a lesser degree, the lower classes shocked by the growing inequalities, waste, and corruption of society began the long road back to modern liberalism. For Beard's intellectual history counterpart, V. L. Parrington, the sparks of liberation had similarly passed from Jeffersonians to Concord litterateurs and Abolitionists to the literary realists and finally, the radical intelligentsia—all of them based fundamentally in the middle class.[15]

In *The Crisis of the Middle Class,* Corey sought to sharpen the class analysis of this perspective without falling back into the vulgarizations of garden variety American Marxism. The middle class, its general situation continually shifting with the stage through which society was passing, had revealed internal fissures from the beginning of capitalist hegemony. Those in the lower stratum became petty-bourgeois radicals, continually waging war against monopoly for the right of everyone to be small property owners. As such, they constituted the driving force of the bourgeois revolution (*i.e.*, the Revolutionary War). But as an intermediate force, they could not hold power. Adopting the most iconoclastic view of the Progressive historians, Corey insisted that the Constitutional Convention of 1787 had been a sort of self-legalized *coup d'état* to consolidate the influence of large property owners. Thus the ideals of equality and democracy, just as elsewhere in the Western world, were realized only in part and threatened with further degradation by newer requirements of capitalism.

Developing his argument historically, Corey continued one particular thread from *Decline of American Capitalism*. As the inevitable economic crisis of capitalism had in his earlier book been dramatically delayed by the existence of the frontier, so here the various ill effects of monopoly had been postponed and even reversed, for several generations, by a frontier-based middle class whose rise made the "struggle for democratic rights irresistible." (115). The delay of U.S. entry into global imperialism that Corey had earlier seen as a byproduct of the frontier experience became here something very different. The vitality of frontier democracy made the related delay in the rise of working class awareness considerably less important than the activities and consciousness of "the people," a far more general category. Democracy, strengthened by the frontier experience, stood against Empire.

Yet class had not disappeared, it had only taken

on new dimensions. The consolidation of industrial capitalism inevitably eroded the old, small property-owning bourgeoisie and created the "new" middle class of propertyless white-collar workers, as in Fraina's *Revolutionary Socialism*. The failure of Populism and then Progressivism—which Corey styled the "final expression of middle class revolt" (135) posed the current dilemma. Further resistance against monopolism required alliance with the working class, which had previously played only a slight role in Corey's narration. Once on the stage, it occupied a curiously sudden and crucial yet largely inert role. The contradictions of fully-developed monopoly capitalism in the 1910s had prompted the upper ends of the middle class toward their social betters for regulation of the system and, if necessary, repression of the restless workers. The lower element looked more toward its "natural" ally, the rapidly increasing mass of factory operatives.

Corey made a noticeable argument for optimism, while decisively reframing Fraina's insights about this very worker. As individualism and freedom of enterprise became outmoded ideals, collectivism had grown organically within daily life. If ordinary people already engaged in productively socialized (if privately owned) production and distribution, the alteration necessary lay more and more obviously within the particulars of social relations.

But this was a troubled thesis. The pre-revolutionary freedom of ideas and mass behavior that he thought he had glimpsed in *Modern Dance* magazine had slipped away, as they did to most observers keen to the cultural conservatism of the 1930s.[16] Borrowing from a favorite source of the 1930s, William Ogburn's thesis of a "cultural lag" in social consciousness, Corey insisted that impending cultural changes *could* liberate people to enjoy qualitatively different lives—but only after resolution of the economic-political crisis allowed them the opportunity to do so.

He also tempered yesterday's optimism with warnings. A democratic socialism did not come from economic equations alone. If the Left failed to appeal to the new middle class as it had failed in the past, this class might well turn toward fascism. The outcome depended substantially upon the historical bearer of socialism in Europe and elsewhere, the working class. But it depended— one would gather from the emphases of Corey's argument—even more upon the general reassertion of Enlightenment ideals, the challenge to society to move forward and not backward. Although Corey did not quite say so, this challenge would best be understood by the middle class intellectual such as himself.

The Crisis of the Middle Class is fascinating for its conglomeration of intentions, its vaguely articulated or (as a later generation would say) "undertheorized" attempt to combine Marxist and traditional liberal goals with historical materialism and

Beardian notions of American progress. Another self-trained economist, William Blake, shrewdly suggested that Corey would have done better to have reorganized facts and arguments, combining the book with *Decline of American Capitalism,* for "in that changed setting his two books could become extremely valuable for the American scene." [17]

That possibility would probably never have occurred to Corey, racing from one class subject to another within a few years. *Decline* had, after all, been written to prepare readers for capitalism's ultimate decline and for a revolutionary transformation; *Crisis* suggested a less-than-final crisis in the system, with a protracted "war of positions" until the issues could be resolved. Similarly, he had pursued to their logical conclusions the least Marxian strains of his economic analysis in *The Decline.* He dropped the earlier argument that the downward slide of profits even indirectly resulted from the smaller amount of variable capital (*i.e.,* labor power) in modern production, as in the orthodox Marxian schema. Rather, the crisis of capitalism was—just as the orthodox liberal economists believed—a crisis of abundance, from an excess of profits which could not be invested profitably. Corey's argument now differed from theirs mainly in the prediction of the outcome. [18]

Finally, Corey had practically abandoned Fraina's vision of a revolution which replaced the political state with a non-coercive, administrative apparatus. As a Fraina-like theorist would com-

xxvi

plain in a few years about Communist thinkers, Corey had substituted critiques of *property ownership* for critiques of the *process of production,* and thereby shifted the situation of the working class from the subject to the object.[19] This view of socialism as the fulfillment of an old and even bourgeois dream was not, in fact, very far from Communist leader Earl Browder's description of socialism as the "Americanism of the Twentieth Century." Corey had joined a broad intellectual current which shared many of the predilections of the Communists' Popular Front without adopting its credulity toward the Soviet Union or its faith in domestic communist leadership.

Coming in 1935, as fears of fascism spread like wildfire, *The Crisis* struck just the right note for most reviewers. One might say, indeed, that the books' weaknesses were strengths in the eyes of readers. Themselves quietly abandoning chiliastic views of revolution and along with them most of the Marxian pretensions, middle class radical intellectuals grasped Corey as an ideal link between the ideal of the Left and the legacy of American liberalism.

Amidst the enthusiastic responses to the book, a few critics offered more cautious or ironic observations. *The New York Times'* John Chamberlain, reviewing *Crisis* with the counterpart volume, *Insurgent America,* by the radical but anti-socialist Alfred Bingham, reflected that for the last few years Bingham had been "running away from the communists, [while] the Left theoreticians like Mr Corey have been running towards Mr Bingham." [20] If revolution was off the agenda, moral appeal to the middle classes was on.

* * *

For just a moment, it seemed the Communists themselves had been converted by Corey. Shocked by Roosevelt's growing appeal among the ethnic working class and impelled toward liberalism by the Comintern's declaration of a Popular Front against Fascism, they greeted *The Crisis of the Middle Class* warmly. The *New Masses* called it "a book you should get at once and one you should persuade all of your middle class acquaintances to read." [21] In a marvelous stroke of irony, *Crisis* was given away free in a special offer with *New Masses* subscriptions, while Communist bookstores now offered copies of *Crisis* for sale with a pamphlet attacking *Decline of American Capitalism* added as a combination bonus and advanced antidote for that book's errors.

But this moment of amity proved as false as the rest. Inviting Corey to serve as a guest editor of a special "Middle Class" number of the *New Masses,* the editors pulled the rug out from under him in the process of production, making him a nominal "chairman" of the editorial committee for what was a disappointingly narrow issue.[22]

This incident along with world events precipitated a final disillusionment with communism. Corey, Louis Hacker, self-taught historian Bertram D. Wolfe, art historian Meyer Schapiro and others set out to create an independent Marxist theoretical journal, the *Marxist Quarterly*. After several provocative issues, it floundered in 1936-37 upon the rocks of the Moscow Trials, with its pro-Russian financial angel removing his subsidy. Corey's own Marxism had already virtually expired, and he grappled to find a place for himself. Working a few months at the Works Projects Administration in Washington, he signed on as Educational Director of Local 22, International Ladies Garment Workers Union in New York, a particular bastion of anti-communist union leadership. Growing increasingly restless during several years there, he pursued other possibilities and by 1940 published in the *Nation* a three-part manifesto, "Marxism Reconsidered." [23]

He now proclaimed views immanent but unarticulated in *Crisis*. Marxian doctrine had disguised the vital importance of appealing to all functional groups, blue and white collar workers, technicians and farmers alike. Capitalism could be peacefully transformed if only Americans learned "to use the democratic state, overcome its class nature and limitations, democratize it still further with greater popular controls, and increase its constructive services." [24] An unsympathetic critic commented that if Corey promised to put teeth into the doctrine of "gradualism," in reality "Mr. Corey's teeth, and those of most middle-class radicals, are chattering with fright in the growing totalitarian darkness." [25]

This comment was uncharitable, but not entirely unfair. At first polemically opposed to U.S. entry into the Second World War, Corey (like many other intellectuals) swung around to an extreme pro-interventionist view and into alliance with others who shared his perspectives. Joining theologian Reinhold Niebuhr, union leader A. Philip Randolph and others, Corey established the Union of Democratic Action in 1940. By now a veteran author of manifestoes and organizer of intellectuals, he played a key role in this fledgling organization until it faded a few years later. He also prepared a volume of essays, *The Unfinished Task: Economic Reconstruction of Democracy* (1942), summing up his thoughts since *Crisis*.

The lack of reception for this book showed how far the political climate had shifted in seven years. Intent upon the war itself and losing focus on the once-numerous proposals to construct a post-capitalist economy, intellectuals met *The Unfinished Task* with indifference. Corey had apparently been the first to coin the phrase "mixed economy." But it was an idea never credited to him, perhaps because he had meant a "socialist" mixed economy with the cooperative sector firmly in control, a vision that centrist-drifting liberals steadily abandoned. As in the case of Corey's role in the UDA, he also seems to have been denied credit by virtue of his unsavory "red" past which had by this time become fairly common knowledge. Histories of the Americans for Democratic Action, the UDA's influential liberal successor, simply discarded him from memory.[26]

Corey, who had always lacked a stable occupation, found a home at Antioch College, teaching there until 1949. A sometimes controversial campus figure, he was also a dynamic lecturer, especially when recalling the joy and naivete of the 1910s radicalism that he had experienced in a far more hopeful moment of the century. Although suffering a stroke in 1943 and warned against overexertion, he threw himself back into the political fray in 1946-47. Appealing for a people's party to the left of the Democrats (but rigidly excluding the communists), he led the creation of the National Educational Committee for a New Party. Its honorary chairman, John Dewey, had during the 'thirties headed a similar third-party effort that Corey then regarded as too moderate. By now, with the resurgent economy and the rise of the Cold War, the same idea had become too radical by far. In 1948, only former vice-president Henry Wallace—along with a handful of conservative Republicans—opposed Harry Truman's combining military build-up and economic expansion in a plan that sounded curiously like the State Capitalism that young Fraina had lambasted. Corey regarded Wallace as a disguised supporter of communism, and conservatives like Robert Taft as hopeless isolationists.

Corey spent the last years of his life in turmoil. Writing *Meat and Man* (1950), an exuberant history of the meat-packing industry and its workers, led Corey to leave Antioch for the familiar post of union educational director at the Amalgamated Butcher Workmen in Chicago. This time, however, he seemed almost immediately unhappy at work he considered routine and limiting. He poured his energies into journalism, mainly in the *New Leader*, articulating harsh views which seemed increasingly the mirror-image opposite of Louis Fraina's perspectives on capitalism and empire. He outlined never-to-be realized book projects, such as a dictionary of American labor biography. Most telling of all, he devised a book-length manuscript for a popular history of Frances Wright, the nineteenth century woman's rights activist and utopian socialist long considered the historic avant-gardist who most greatly resembled those gentle bohemians of the 1910s.[27]

Then McCarthyism's axe fell. This ardent anti-communist with more than a decade's polemics to demonstrate his loyalties faced a battery of government officials more persuaded by testimony against his pre-1923 activities. Never officially naturalized (he had decided against filing because of his 1917 arrest and conviction as a conscientious objector), he seemed destined for deportation to Italy. Against this prospect, he furiously gathered evidence. He also suffered a mild heart attack, premonition of a second stroke to follow. On Christmas Day, 1952, he received an announcement of an impending deportation order; the following month, the butchers' union released him, adding greatly to his stress. On September 15, 1953, working at his desk, he lapsed into a coma, and died the next day. Two days posthumous, a Certificate of Lawful Entry arrived along with a notice from a publisher of a proposed contract for yet another book he wanted to write, *Toward an Understanding of America*.

* * *

A central category in young Louis Fraina's *oeuvre* and a large missing element in *The Crisis of the Middle Class* helps explain the obscurity into which the book and the life behind it have fallen. The group of intellectuals who, at the end of Corey's life, set the pace for the changing framework of the era to come were not far from Corey's political inclinations. Mostly former socialists and communists, noted liberal figures like Daniel Bell, David Riesman, and Richard Hofstadter now paid homage to the "capitalist revolution" which outmoded the old socialist anticipation of class warfare and protected the West against the ideological appeals of communism. But these critics had, unlike Corey, a distaff and ironic view of American capitalism's cultural consequences; they were also by nature observers, not actors, upon the scene they viewed as if from a distance.[28]

In the arguments of the time, the view of culture, of the inner human being and of psychological factors had soon taken over large spheres of discussion, putting aside once-familiar arguments about the equations of economics and class in particular. The heavily economic-minded Corey was, of course, the psychic descendent of the Louis Fraina who had delivered perceptive essays on "Socialism and Psychology" in 1913. The same Fraina had foreseen the rise of modernism, observed it closely in the behavior of ordinary jazz dancers, glimpsed the approach of changing gender roles and even the racial dynamics of a changing, more democratized society. A different Corey might have been perfectly placed to reflect upon the cultural experience of the century.

Why did *Crisis,* and Corey's general pronouncements afterward, fail so badly in these various regards? In part, as his friend Louis Hacker observed at the time, Corey tried too hard to drive his data into a narrow interpretive frame. Determined to score the middle class for the historic failings of democracy in order to credit it with democracy's future promise, he demanded an unrealistic political clarity of small property-holders in the English, French and American revolutions.[29] This was due, certainly, to Corey's drive for readable synthesis, but also to an unreflective economism all too common to liberal and radical thought during the depressed 1930s.

One could find similar reasons for his abandonment in *Crisis* of the central racial questions about the nation's past and future and the related questions of empire that Fraina analyzed so precociously. An age whose scholars paid little heed to

xxxiv

W.E.B. DuBois's monumental *Black Reconstruction* (appearing the same year as *The Crisis of the Middle Class*) offered precious little encouragement along these lines. Yet Fraina would surely have done better. Marxian orthodoxy offered little assistance. Perhaps the Beardian view of frontier democracy, offering a shift away from mechanical class theory, proved too strong for a counter critique. Or perhaps, as in Corey of the 1940s and early 1950s, the very notion of an American empire based on race values and economic-military power resonated with too many unwanted implications, past and future alike.[30]

Most likely, and not so different from the various cultural issues, Corey had simply lost Fraina's confidence in the infinite subjectivity of the lower-class subject. He had ceased to expect change from the bottom-up, even if he never ceased to hope that populations guided by sensitive leadership would find their way toward greater social participation. The ideologues of communism and modern liberalism had agreed, after all, about the impossibility of direct democracy by the masses, in the old model of the Industrial Workers of the World or Daniel DeLeon. All this happened long before Corey had declared Marxism wrong-headed, and communism a disaster.

The Crisis of the Middle Class and the life of its author deserve, finally, to be re-evaluated in the light of what they tell us about the damage wrought by the century's disappointments. The missing and forgotten elements once so obvious to Fraina help predict the flare of rebellious political-cultural energy at the end of the 1960s. The suddenness with which this mass bohemian renaissance melted away again, leaving a trail of memories like the 1910s, recalled once more the significance of a utopia dreamed but unrealized. Lewis Corey, without a trace of environmental awareness, predicted in the final paragraph of his most popular book that "a world is dying," but offered the hope that another world might yet be born out of struggle. If no one would now call the communist perspective the "New Enlightenment," as Corey mistakenly did, enlightenment of another kind still surely awaits the searcher. As Fraina might have remarked, the need is more urgent than ever.

[1] Louis Hacker, "Address to the Middle Class," *Nation,* CXLI (November 27, 1935), 625-26. Alan Angoff, "The Past, Present and Future of the Middle Class," *Boston Evening Transcript,* Nov. 30, 1935; John Chamberlain, "Books of the Times," *New York Times,* Dec. 11, 1935; "Corey Says Middle Class has Disappeared," *New York Post,* Nov. 11, 1935.

[2] See Barbara Ehrenreich, *Fear of Falling: The Inner Life of the Middle Class* (New York: Pantheon, 1989), and Loren Baritz, *The Good Life: The Meaning of Success for the American Middle Class* (New York: Alfred Knopf, 1989).

[3] The information and views in the following can be found fully developed in the only biographical volume about Fraina/Corey: Paul Buhle, *A Dreamer's Paradise Lost: Louis C. Fraina/Lewis Corey, 1892-1953* (Atlantic Highlands,

N.J.: Humanities Press, 1994). See this volume also for further references on many points discussed here. I am deeply grateful to a number of Corey's friends, including George Novack and Daniel Bell, the late Sterling Spero and Charles Zimmerman, and to his daughter Olga Corey, for granting me interviews. The kindly Solon DeLeon, Daniel DeLeon's son and the last of Fraina's close friends from pre-1920 days, was also my friend in his final years, a personal living link between Fraina/Corey and myself. These personal sources, plus the Lewis Corey Papers at Columbia University's Special Collections, have been most essential to my study.

[4] Daniel DeLeon's *Preamble to the I.W.W.* (New York: New York Labor News, 1906), reprinted frequently afterward by the S.L.P. as *The Socialist Reconstruction of Society*, offers the clearest expression of this view. Unfortunately, none of the biographical literature on DeLeon has been equal to the task of interpreting his intellectual influence across large sections of the Left. *A Dreamer's Paradise Lost* offers large suggestions.

[5] Regretfully, once more, no historical study has adequately captured the significance of the very important *New Review. Modern Dance* magazine has virtually vanished from examination, even to specialists in that field. My gratitude goes to Lee Baxandall for his studies of Fraina, before mine, and his attention to *Modern Dance*.

[6] For a recent study of this milieu, see Casey M. Blake, *Beloved Community: The Cultural Criticism of Randolph Bourne, Van Wyck Brooks, Waldo Frank & Lewis Mumford* (Chapel Hill: University of North Carolina Press, 1990).

[7] Louis C. Fraina, "Literary Gleanings: The Chasm," *Daily People*, April 9, 1911.

[8] Fraina's link with Reed offered the only moment of

his reappearance from obscurity in recent history: a cameo role of Fraina in 1919 in the 1981 film, *Reds,* by Warren Beatty.

[9] I seek to reformulate this political situation in my volume, *Marxism in the United States: Remapping the American Left* (London: Verso, 1991 edition).

[10] While no adequate account yet exists of this situation in all its complexity, see Theodore Draper's *Roots of American Communism* (New York: Viking Press, 1957), and many relevant entries in the *Encyclopedia of the American Left* (New York: Garland Publishing, 1990), edited by Mari Jo Buhle, Paul Buhle and Dan Georgakas.

[11] Lewis Corey, "How Is Income Distributed?" *New Republic,* XL (May 5, 1927), 323.

[12] This point was made by Theodore Draper, *Roots of American Communism,* 298.

[13] Louis Hacker, on flyleaf of *Decline of American Capitalism* (New York: Covici Friede, 1934); George Soule, "Why Capitalism Is Declining," *New Republic,* XXX (September 19, 1934), 164.

[14] John R. Commons, "Communism and Collective Democracy," *American Economic Review,* XXV (June, 1935), 215.

[15] See the intellectual assessment of Beard's work and influence in Howard Beale, ed., *Charles Beard: An Appraisal* (Louisville: University of Kentucky, 1954); and Bernard C. Borning, *The Political and Social Thought of Charles A. Beard* (Seattle: University of Washington Press, 1962). A standard comment on Parrington is contained in the survey by Henry S. Commager, *The America Mind: An Interpretation of American Thought and Character Since the 1880s* (New Haven: Yale University Press, 1950), 298-303.

[16] See for instance Warren Susman, "The Culture of

the Thirties," in *Culture as History: The Transformation of American Society in the Twentieth Century* (New York: Pantheon, 1983), 150-83.

[17] William Blake, *An American Looks at Karl Marx* (New York: Cordon Company, 1939), 677.

[18] Blake makes this point in ibid., 205.

[19] C.L.R. James (in collaboration with Grace Lee and Raya Dunayevskaya), *State Capitalism and World Revolution* (Chicago: Kerr Company, 1986 edition from 1950 original), 34-35. See also my Introduction to this edition of *State Capitalism and World Revolution,* and the further parallels offered between Fraina/Corey and James in *A Dreamer's Paradise Lost,* Chapter 6.

[20] John Chamberlain, "Books of the Times."

[21] David Ramsey, "The Dilemma of the Middle Classes," *New Masses,* XV (December 1, 1935), 41-42.

[22] Nevertheless, Corey had contributed a thoughtful essay, "Minds of the Middle Classes," *New Masses,* XVI (Apr. 7, 1936). Other contributors included Mike Gold, Granville Hicks, Joseph Freeman and Anna Rochester, but no independent intellectuals except Herbert Agar and union leader Pat Gorman.

[23] I am especially grateful for a 1982 interview with the late Charles S. Zimmerman, retired President of Local 22, for a glimpse of Corey's mentality at this point. I neglect here Corey's prominence as a writer and speaker for the "Lovestone" group of "Right Communists," expelled from the Communist party in 1929 but resolute in their control of Local 22, and intellectually vibrant in their weekly newspaper, *Workers Age.* For my account of Corey's writings for that paper, and the group's high estimation of his work, see *A Dreamer's Paradise Lost,* Chapter 6.

[24] Lewis Corey, "Marxism Reconsidered, III," *Nation,*

CX (March 2, 1940), 307. See Feb. 17 and Feb. 24 issues for the first two parts.

[25] Max Shachtman, "The Marxists Reply to Corey," *ibid.*, (March 9, 1940), 331-32.

[26] See for instance the "official" history, Clifton Brock, *The Americans for Democratic Action: Its Role in National Politics* (Washington: Public Affairs Press, 1962); and the best recent history, Steve Gillen, *Politics and Vision: The ADA and American Liberalism, 1947-1985* (New York: Oxford University Press, 1987).

[27] Corey's insistence, in his unpublished manuscript on Frances Wright, of the ignored importance of women's history remarkably foreshadowed by two decades the rise of the field in U.S. history. The unpublished manuscript, now outdated by several biographies of Wright, is in the Corey Papers.

[28] See, for instance, Alan Wald, *The New York Intellectuals: The Rise and Decline of the Anti-Stalinist Left from the 1930s to the 1980s* (Chapel Hill: University of North Carolina Press, 1987).

[29] Louis Hacker, "Addresses to the Middle Class," 625.

[30] The mainstream historiography of much later decades, accepting the implications full-scale, viewed the settlement of the west as a racially-charged engagement subverting the prospects of democracy at large. But this kind of perspective, implicit though scarcely developed in DuBois, was impossible for even the most determinedly radical observers of the 1930s. See David Noble, *The End of American History: Democracy, capitalism, and the metaphor of two worlds in Anglo-American historical writing, 1880-1980* (Minneapolis: University of Minnesota, 1989) for some interesting observations.

THE CRISIS OF
THE MIDDLE CLASS

Chapter I

PROBLEMS AND APPROACH

THE condition of the world today is truly critical. Never, in modern times, was final disaster more probable. But, as the omens of doom multiply, people still cling to out-worn traditions and futile hopes— they still reject the forces of a new life that might avert a swiftly approaching death. For what threatens is the death of civilization itself.

Underlying the crisis is the economic paralysis which still, after all these agonizing years, holds the world in an iron grasp. Our rulers have shown themselves to be completely incapable of mastering the means for producing and distributing the material things of life on an ascending scale and to wider circles of the people. On the contrary, they now proclaim that incapacity to be the immutable law of life and impose upon the masses of the people the burdens of an artificially created scarcity and increasing misery. The American economic crisis has now become, by and large, a permanent state of affairs, as it has been in Europe, especially in England, Germany and Italy, since the World War. Everywhere the chances of attaining pre-1929 levels of prosperity become still more remote.

The most obvious and demoralizing aspect of the

crisis is afforded by the million-masses of the unemployed. Millions upon millions of manual and mental workers are denied work, although there is an abundance of the means and purposes of working. Millions of *unemployables* in *all* occupations are exiled from the normal pursuits of life and thrust down into the misery and degradation of pauperism because capitalist industry is unable to provide the work they need and want. Large-scale permanent unemployment becomes normal.

This means the creation of a new and wholly unnecessary poverty, as all the means are available for the final abolition of poverty. The dole is now accepted as a permanent institution in England—the dole which condemns millions of men and women, able and willing to work, to subsist on the state's meager and grudging charity. It is becoming permanent in the United States. And what of those who are still fortunate enough to have work? Mussolini tells the Italian people that they must submit to lower standards of living. Hitler tells the German people that their ideal must be one of "heroic poverty." An organ of the bankers tells the American people that the average citizen is "a poor man," who must be satisfied "with the great hope that he will have the same opportunity which our fathers had to better his position." [1] From this "hopeful" poverty it is but a step to the "heroic poverty" of fascism. In either case it is the poverty itself, stripped of its ennobling adjectives, which remains the reality.

Moreover, as the crisis mounts steadily upward

10

into all spheres of life, the future of civilization itself is endangered. Social pressures and dislocations thrust the dispossessed mass of the people on to the struggle for a new social order: a new civilization capable of averting the catastrophe toward which the world is moving. But the entrenched interests redouble their efforts to maintain power, and reaction in all forms is encouraged. Everywhere a desperate capitalism, faced with the threat of a new social order, revolts against its own values and achievements, against its contribution to civilization. Democracy and progress, equality and opportunity, abundance and increasing development of the productive forces of society—all these traditional ideals of the youth of capitalism are being ruthlessly cast aside as they become dangerous to the existing system of property relations. And this sinister reaction becomes a revolt against the future in the fascist repression of *all* progressive forces.

Fascism, the last desperate resort of capitalism to maintain its rule, openly seeks inspiration in the medieval ideals out of the destruction of which modern civilization arose. Already, in Italy and Germany, fascism has erected economic and cultural decline and decay into a system. Fascist ideas, tendencies, movements and leaders are appearing in the United States and England, in all parts of the capitalist world. For there is no immunity to the plague of fascism. It arises out of the needs of capitalism in decay: the need to organize disintegration into a system and to crush the revolt of the progressive forces. Nationalism and imperialism are inflamed. The crisis and capitalist desperation drive relentlessly to new and more destructive wars. A new barbarism threatens to engulf the world.

This nightmare of a new barbarism is not a potential problem of the future. It is an immediate problem which calls upon us, today, for action. The new barbarism would consume our blood and bones, our hopes and ideals, in the onsweep of its destructive fury. The forces of life must rally against an approaching death. . . .

All classes and groups are affected by the crisis of capitalism. But it affects them in different ways, and their reactions are different, for the people are not one homogeneous whole: they are split into a variety of classes and groups, with a consequent variety of immediate economic interests and response to the crisis. Much of this difference in interests is, however, destroyed by the onsweep of the crisis, which consigns people in all walks of life to a common destitution. The difference in response to its effects goes deeper; it is due to a misunderstanding of the nature and significance of the crisis, a misunderstanding which is itself the product of inherited passions and prejudices.

We must learn to appreciate the underlying unity of events, the logic of historical development. The threat of fascism, of new world wars and a new barbarism, arises out of the class necessity of entrenched interests which cling, at all costs, to the old order. This menace to all other classes can be met only by a struggle for a new social order capable of creating a

12

new and higher civilization, for capitalism in decay is now capable only of creating reaction and death.

What of the middle class in this crisis, out of which its own class crisis arises? As the defenses of the middle class are swept away by the whirlwinds of economic disaster, it is driven to action. What shall that action be?

The middle class has played a great part in history, in creating and realizing the values of capitalist civilization. In its creative revolutionary age the middle class fought for the abolition of feudal class and caste barriers, for liberty and democracy, for equality of opportunity. It placed its faith in education, in freedom of discussion and action. It urged the right to free and universal ownership of property (particularly independent small property); which it considered the only assurance of liberty and democracy, and the means for the progressive abolition of poverty and insecurity. It believed in the peaceful development of peoples and of nations.

These ideals were never fully realized, and least of all in the case of the working class. Their realization was limited, however, even for the middle class itself, which was never able to impose its control over the capitalism it did so much to develop. It was increasingly thrust downward in the class-economic scale. Yet, in spite of all limitations, the middle class made a great contribution to progress, particularly in the creation of conditions out of which may arise a new and higher civilization. Now there is a complete reaction against the traditional middle class ideals, for they are incompatible with the needs of a declining capitalism.

Limitation of liberty and democracy and of equality of opportunity (expressed in constantly growing class stratification) becomes complete as fascism consolidates class and caste barriers in the "status" and "hierarchy" of the totalitarian state: *social* serfdom.

Education and freedom of discussion and action are increasingly limited: the one tends to become wholly servile and the other is annihilated under fascism.

The restriction of democratic rights is an expression of the shrinkage of economic opportunity. Free and universal ownership of property becomes still more rare, the progressive abolition of poverty and insecurity is replaced by the multiplication of unemployment and the creation of a new poverty. The final result is complete denial of democratic rights to the industrial and agricultural serfs of fascism.

The peaceful development of peoples and of nations, never very real, it is true, is today made a complete mockery by the flagrant growth of militarism and the cynical preparations for new world wars, while fascism glorifies war *as an ideal and a way of life*.

In terms of the crisis of the middle class the most signficant development has been the constant decrease in the ownership of independent small property, which was its economic basis as a class. For independent property it fought triumphantly against feudalism and unsuccessfully against capitalist big

14

property. In its defense of small property against the big capitalists, the middle class has experienced crisis after crisis. While the crises were apparently overcome, their net final result was to transform the middle class: today most of its constituent elements are propertiless. That transformation is the key to an understanding of the decisive conflict between the past and the future of the middle class.

In the past the middle class was composed overwhelmingly of propertied elements whose interests were identified with the defense of capitalist property. The middle class is now composed overwhelmingly of propertiless elements whose interests are identified with the abolition of capitalist property. It is only by the exploitation of their prejudices and passions, of their inherited allegiance to a system now wholly against their own interests, that the propertiless can still be rallied to a defense of property. Former crises of the middle class moved within the relations of property: the class fought to protect its independent small property against expropriation by big property, against large-scale industry and the concentration of capital. The present crisis moves largely outside those relations. For a majority of the middle class it is a crisis not of property but of *employment:* as in the case of the wage-workers. The propertiless elements in the middle class have no stake in the fight for the rights of ownership; they must fight for the right to work and live. And it is capitalist property which denies them this right, which threatens them with growing oppression, exploitation and new wars, with the slavery and misery of a new barbarism.

Moreover, former crises of the middle class were an aspect of the *upswing* of capitalism. The economic movement was upward and the position of the middle class was still tolerable. The opportunity to own property was increasingly limited, but it was a relative, not an absolute, limitation: independent small ownership was still possible. Even those newer elements in the middle class who were already propertiless were at least assured employment. On the whole, the class maintained a privileged position in society.

The present crisis, however, is an aspect of the *decline* of capitalism. The economic movement is now downward, and the plight of the middle class tends to become desperate. The propertied minority is increasingly deprived of ownership, while independent small property approaches complete extinction. The propertiless majority is sinking into lower and lower standards of living, aggravated by all the degradation of permanent unemployment. Privileges and security are constantly undermined. By far the greater part of the middle class becomes one with the dispossessed workers.

What, then, is to be done?

Action is necessary—it is inescapable. The middle class in America is already in motion, and the demagogues thrown up by the crisis, the paid pipers of reaction, are already making their two-faced appeal to those ingrained habits of mind, those inherited prejudices, passions and allegiances which may serve

16

the interests of a small minority but which are wholly at variance with the interests of the vast propertiless majority and with the existing social and economic reality. Action is necessary. But action must be based on a thorough understanding of the difference between the present and the former crises of the middle class. It must be based on an understanding of the split in the middle class between the propertied and the propertiless elements. It must be based on an understanding of the class-economic forces which are moving toward a new social order. Such understanding of the problem means to discard old allegiances and old illusions. For the plight of the dispossessed, propertiless elements in the middle class is the direct result of the crisis of capitalism; action must be directed against capitalism and for a new social order.

In its youth the middle class glorified Understanding and enthroned Reason as the weapons of revolutionary struggle. The great cultural expression of the bourgeois struggle for power was the Enlightenment, that magnificent defiance of old prejudices and limitations. Man felt himself capable of accomplishing all things. The Enlightenment waged ruthless war on old ideas in economics, politics, religion; it freed the mind of many of its old fetters; it moved toward dethroning the Deity himself.

The spirit of the Enlightenment, according to Immanuel Kant, was "the liberation of man from his state of minority, from the incapacity to use one's understanding."

Its motto was: "Dare to use your own understanding!" [2]

The Enlightenment meant a refusal to accept the traditional merely because it was traditional; it meant a constant struggle to move onward to new and higher forms of man's control over his environment and himself. It meant, in the words of Thomas Jefferson, the most brilliant American exponent of the Enlightenment, *"to go forward, instead of backward"* . . . *to disbelieve "that nothing can ever be devised more perfect than was established by our forefathers."* [3]

Both the achievements and limitations of the Enlightenment arose out of the upthrust of capitalism, whose interests and needs it expressed. To the degree that those interests and needs were progressive— the struggle of a new social order against feudal restrictions, the development of new and higher economic forms, the creation of more rational attitudes toward life—the Enlightenment was an aspect of progress (an idea itself created by the Enlightenment). But the masses and many forms of progress were grossly neglected, for the ideals and practices of the Enlightenment were limited by capitalist necessity.

As capitalism entrenched itself in power and the middle class declined as a force in society, the limitations of the Enlightenment became absolute; its ideals and practices were increasingly whittled down. This reaction was strengthened by the challenge of socialism. It was no longer possible to urge struggle against the traditional in words of flame, for the traditional was now capitalism. Capitalism was based on exploitation and it was dangerous to tell the exploited: "Dare to use your own understanding!" Today the danger is all the greater as capitalism decays and is threatened by a new social order, by an upsurge of those masses whom the Enlightenment neglected and often scorned. Appeals to reason are now replaced by appeals to brute force. Much bedraggled after years of capitalist rule, the Enlightenment becomes a "stinking corpse" (to use Mussolini's elegent words) under fascism.

Yet "what is to be done" is still answerable in the *spirit* of the Enlightenment adapted to the conditions and problems of today.

The struggle is still against the traditional, and courageous, unfettered intelligence is still necessary to understand our world and its problems. The answer to capitalist reaction and barbarism must be a new Enlightenment. For the dispossessed elements of the middle class the immediate task is to explore their own problem: what their class was, what it is, what it may become: its relation—and theirs as the dispossessed—to the other classes, to the general crisis of capitalism and of civilization. The passions and prejudices of outworn traditions and allegiances must be thrown aside. Dare to understand! We must go forward, not backward. Upon that depends the future of the world: *our* future.

Chapter II

STRUGGLE FOR SURVIVAL

AN observer, cut off from all contact with the American scene since the wells of prosperity dried up in 1929, would be bewildered by the present situation. Many questions would press upon him, and among them the suggestive one: Is *this* the middle class?

In the pre-1929 prosperity the goose hung high for the middle class, for all those people who are not big capitalists, wage-workers or farmers. They got an increasingly greater share of prosperity (the big capitalists, as usual, got the greatest share), while the share of farmers and workers, especially the farmers, moved downward. The larger businessmen in the middle class, in spite of severe competition, made substantial profits; opportunities multiplied for the upper layers of professionals, technicians and higher salaried employees. Their incomes, in general, rose steadily, and many of them drank heavily of the heady wine of mounting speculative profits. Standards of living imitated those of the upper crust, even if in most cases it was shoddy make-believe. The goose was not, however, for everyone to feast on. The masses of lower salaried employees were threatened by increasing unemployment. Small businessmen moaned over "profitless prosperity." Many lamented the "plight of the genteel . . . who are passing away before our eyes" [1] (a lament significant of final destruction of the tradition of gentility, formerly always reborn). But they all had dreams of glorious things ahead. The middle class seemed to be thriving as never before.

In Europe the middle class was in the throes of disintegration and crisis, part of the general disintegration and crisis of capitalism. Prosperity after the World War had not surged upward, as in the United States. Economic decline and decay increasingly pauperized the middle class; its different elements were forced, as the workers moved toward the overthrow of capitalism, to choose between communism and fascism. Most of them, in Italy and Germany, chose fascism, which imposed new burdens upon the lower middle class (along with the workers) and prepared the total destruction of civilization. In England the Middle Class Union, potentially fascist, mobilized its forces against the workers in strikes and elections. The crisis of the middle class expressed itself in a constantly more desperate struggle for survival.

But in the United States it seemed as if the middle class had come to a new and enduring power and glory. It was claimed, and this was the faith of the gullibles, that a "new" social order was being created in which prosperity would move everlastingly upward and the whole of society become middle class.

Now an enraged bewilderment and despair torment the American middle class. What, it asks uncomprehendingly, is the black magic which has changed the old dreams to nightmares? For the middle class no longer sits on top of the world: it has been thrown into the depths. Hundreds of thousands of small enterprises are bankrupt; the survivors are threatened by smaller markets and greater competition. Millions of salaried employees and professionals are unemployed; those still at work are oppressed by smaller pay and the terrible fear of losing their jobs.

Out of the economic crisis arises an ideological crisis of the middle class. Its old ideals are crumbling under the impact of stark necessity and hopes destroyed.

Members of the middle class formerly cherished their personal independence and pride; they considered charity the harsh need of the "lower" class of manual workers. Now millions of them, along with still more millions of workers, must eat the salty bread of charity, and eat their pride, too. In New York City, in 1933, one out of five charity patients in the hospitals were salaried employees, *a much greater proportion than in any previous year.*[2] All groups of professionals and technicians formed committees to help their unemployed brethren with cash, old clothes, food, odd jobs; $5 Christmas baskets were accompanied with the consoling thought that one would *maintain a family of four for several days.* Nor was the degradation of the breadline unknown. A government study of urban relief cases (May, 1934) revealed among them 649,000 professionals and clerical and other salaried employees, and 3,134,-000 workers;[3] the proportion of the former becomes

22

constantly greater. Recipients of relief must prove they are stripped of all resources, including insurance: only those who swear the pauper's oath may get the pauper's pittance. Not only do middle class people accept relief, they now *demand* relief as a *right*. They have formed at least one organization to secure for its members "equitable treatment in the allocation of relief funds" [4]—a measure of the great economic and ideological changes in the middle class.

Members of the middle class formerly acclaimed the ideal of rugged individualism. Now they acclaim state capitalism, which means an acceptance of increasing state intervention in economic activity and the suppression of democratic rights. The middle class reacts against individualism and democracy, of which it was the carrier and the builder.

What are the causes of these startling changes, ominous of the future?

The immediate cause of the crisis in the middle class is the ruin wrought by the depression. There was ruin in previous depressions. But never was it on the present gigantic scale; and never, especially, was ruin as widespread in all circles of the middle class. Not only is there a quantitative change in the greater ruin wrought, but a qualitative change in its impact on groups formerly only slightly affected by depression.

Large numbers of small producers, storekeepers and independent professionals are always killed off by depression. But mere assassination now becomes massacre. In only *three* years of the depression, from 1930 to 1932, 578,000 independent enterprisers in industry, trade and the professions, were driven out of business: *one out of six.*[5] The massacre is still on; the survivors tremble.

More significant is the unprecedented unemployment among salaried employees, particularly in the lower salaried groups. They were in the past largely "cushioned" against the shock of depression, because of scarcity value and privileged position; now they suffer almost as much as the wage-workers.

In the spring of 1933, the low point of the depression, when unemployment rose to a staggering total of 17,250,000, nearly 35% of salaried employees were out of work compared with over 45% of the workers. For manufactures alone, in 1933, employment was 41% lower than in 1929 among salaried employees (mainly clerical) and 31% among wage-workers. This is a complete reversal of the experience in former depressions. Nor was it limited to the clerical staffs. Unemployment was greater among technicians than among workers, involving 65% of the chemists, 85% of the engineers, and over 90% of the architects and draftsmen. Incomes dropped disastrously. Public-school and university staffs and salaries were severely cut. By 1934 one out of five school teachers was unemployed. Technicians had to accept drastic pay cuts. The salaries of clerical employees were slashed almost as much as the wages of the average worker and more than the wages of most trade-union workers. Advertisements for "help wanted" offered college graduates weekly wages of $10 for work where their training was useless. In New York City 40% of the needy seeking relief jobs were white collar workers, professionals and intellectuals, including executives, personnel managers, teachers, editors, physicians, dentists, economists and statisticians.[6] Differentials and privileges break down under pressure of the crisis.

More disastrous in the United States because of the former high level of prosperity, the severity of the depression in Europe was aggravated by the prevailing general economic crisis. Revolting against the multiplication of its burdens by the depression, the German middle class rallied to fascism. But Hitler gives little more than promises: he has "organized" the crisis, not solved it. Business income, salaries and employment among the middle class in Italy were mercilessly lowered by the depression, which the fascist dictatorship could neither prevent nor overcome. Unemployment among salaried employees and college graduates in England, an increasingly acute problem since the World War, took on heartbreaking proportions during the depression. The 2,318,000 registered unemployed in 1934 included many lower salaried employees. But it did not include more than 300,000 better-paid technicians, professionals, managerial employees and ruined independent enterprisers, one-third of whom formerly earned from $2,500 a year up.[7] Nor did these unemployed, many of them over forty, receive the dole: they had, cherishing their "British" independence and confident of personal ability to survive, rejected inclusion in unemployment insurance. In addition, salaries were cut, the clerical up to 30%. Competition for jobs destroyed standards and morale. Where small producers and shopkeepers were not wiped out, they must struggle more desperately for survival. . . .

The staggering blows dealt the American middle class are an expression of the unusual severity of the depression, the worst in history. Its costs are greater than those of any previous depression, at least ten times as great as the costs of that of 1921-22. This appears in the tremendous slaughter of the values of capital and other forms of property. More significant is the shrinkage in the potential output of goods and services.

*There was, in the five years of depression 1930-34, a loss of $185,000 million in goods and services which might have been produced if prosperity had not broken down in 1929.**

* According to the Division of Economic Research of the United States Department of Commerce, the shrinkage in the national income during 1930-33 was $93,000 million; an independent estimate makes the shrinkage $33,500 million in 1934. The combined shrinkage at 1929 prices, which allows for the nominal decrease due to lower prices, was probably $94,645 million. Application of the pre-depression rate of increase in the national income (which during the five years 1925-29 was on the average $7,900 million or 11.5% higher than in 1923-24) yields a probable $47,300 million of additional income which might have been produced. Moreover, much of the national income in the depression years was in excess of the income earned by disbursing institutions. Again according to the Department of Commerce, the drain upon corporate surplus and other business savings in 1930-33 was around $27,000 million, or, at 1929 prices, at least $35,000 million, to which must be added another $8,000 million as the loss in potential business savings,

This is stupendous and unparalleled, almost un-graspable in its immensity. The money cost of American participation in the World War, including loans to the Allies and interest and veteran payments to 1930, was $51,500 million.[8] Peace may be economically more destructive than war, and both forms of destruction become increasingly more devastating. . . .

But that is not all. Depression represents, on an enormously larger scale than in prosperity, the capitalist incapacity to use, because it is unprofitable, our economic resources to the utmost. It is always possible to produce more goods and services than capitalism permits us to produce. According to the Brookings Institution, there was in 1929, the peak year of prosperity, an unused productive capacity of 19%.[9] That is a conservative conclusion, an absolute minimum estimate of the capitalist sabotage of the social forces of production. But it amply proves the point, for the mere use of that unused capacity, the unused labor, equipment and materials, might have added $15,000 million to the national income. Hence we may chalk up, for five years of the depression, another $75,000 million of goods and services which might have been produced if capitalism allowed the *utmost use* of *existing* economic resources. *The total losses are $260,000 million, or more than the output of goods and services for the three prosperity years 1927-29.*

which were $2,000 million in 1929. The grand total is $185,000 million.

27

Those are merely the American losses. In Great Britain, with a population one-third that of the United States and an immediate depression not so severe because of the economic crisis already prevailing since the World War, the losses probably exceed $50,000 million. For the world as a whole (excluding the Soviet Union, where economic activity moved steadily upward in all the years of capitalist depression) * the losses were at least $700,000 million. That is roughly equal to four times the combined yearly incomes (in prosperity!) of every family in the world.

There never was economic waste on this gigantic scale. It is a repression of abundance, the creation of an unnecessary and brutalizing scarcity, which damns the social system permitting it. The planned utilization of the wasted resources might easily have meant the final abolition of poverty in the United States, England and other economically highly developed countries, and an approach to its abolition in the rest of the world.

In five years of the American depression the decline in the output of capital goods (equipment and buildings) and durable consumption goods (including automobiles, household appliances and furniture) was, at 1929 prices, $68,500 million.[10] The amount becomes $98,000 million if allowance is made for the pre-depression rate of increase. Most significant is

* During the five years of capitalist depression the planned economy of the Soviet Union, by preventing a cyclical breakdown, produced around $75,000 million of goods and services *which would not have been otherwise produced.*

the loss in capital goods, which approached $70,000 million, for it represents a destruction of potential means for producing goods and services—another indication of our ability to abolish poverty—that persists into the future.

Another significant aspect of the waste was this: Among the goods which might have been produced, but were not, was $22,000 million of construction, nearly three times the 1929 output: $10,000 million was the loss in residential construction. More than half the American people live in unfit homes. Yet the Federal government grudgingly devotes a few score millions for the building of low-cost houses, while the embattled real-estate interests damn even the small appropriations as a "communist" scheme "scaring private enterprise" [11]—the same enterprise which is incapable of providing decent homes for the masses of workers and lower salaried employees. The planned utilization of wasted construction resources might have wiped out slums and taken the first step toward making a nation of gardens. . . .

What was, in terms of income, the distribution of depression losses? They were, as in the case of prosperity gains, unevenly distributed among the different classes and groups of the population.

In four years of the depression, 1930-34, the average yearly decrease in combined wages and salaries was $15,200 million or 29%, while interest and dividends decreased an average of $2,280 million or 20%. Interest and dividend payments are drawn mainly by the big capitalists.

Wages took the worst beating. The average yearly decrease in wages in manufactures, mining, construction, railroads, railway express and water transportation was $8,430 million, or 44%, while salaries in the same industries decreased an average of $1,300 million, or 27%.

The masses of lower salaried employees, however, were almost as severely dealt with as the workers, for their earnings dropped much more than those of the higher salaried employees. Salaries of the officers of corporations, for the three years 1930-32, decreased an average of $680 million or only 20%. Officers are intimately identified with the oligarchy of big capitalists.

The average yearly decrease in the income of farmers was $1,400 million or 30%. This, however, only partly measures the plight of the farmers; the drop in their income came on top of seriously depressed earnings in all the years of the pre-1929 prosperity, in which the farmers had no share.

The average yearly decrease in the income of independent enterprisers in industry, trade and the professions was $5,000 million or 45%.[12]

As usual, the worst burdens of the depression were thrust upon workers and farmers: a small decrease in their income is more serious than a bigger decrease in the income of the upper layers of society. That is an old story. What is new, and of the utmost significance, is the plight of a middle class battered as never before in its history. Millions of salaried employees have been thrown into the depths with the workers.

Independent small enterprisers have been driven out of business on an unparalleled scale. Propertied elements in the middle class have been expropriated of their possessions in an unprecedentedly merciless fashion.

After five years of depression the wealth of the nation depreciated around 40%, a probable decline of $150,000 million. Much of the depreciation was nominal, a slaughter of the values of capital and other forms of property. Much of the depreciation was real, however, while even nominal losses become real as prosperity fails to revive on any considerable scale, for the value of wealth depends upon increasing economic activity and the income it yields. But depreciation involves a gigantic confiscation of wealth—capitalism is a perpetual confiscation—and its redistribution. The result is always greater concentration of ownership. As the workers have hardly any property to lose and the very wealthy are usually able to hold on to property even after considerable depreciation, the burders of confiscation fall primarily upon the farmers and the middle class. One of the objective functions of depression is the expropriation of the owners of small property.

Another aspect of confiscation was the destruction and redistribution of liquid wealth. In the three years 1930-32, the liquid wealth (cash, savings deposits, insurance, stocks, and bonds) of people with yearly incomes below $5,000 fell from $27,000 million in 1929 to $4,000 million, while their relative share fell from 17% of the total to 6%.[13] Most of this wealth was in the hands of the lower middle class: workers and farmers owned very little. The big capitalists now own a larger proportion of a smaller total amount of national wealth.

Pauperization of millions of people is the personal and human meaning of the destruction and redistribution of wealth. The social meaning is an increase in the propertiless and dispossessed elements in the middle class, an expression of the class-economic crisis which is now shaking the foundations of capitalism.

Of the expropriation of wealth one capitalist economist says:

"This is the most rapid, drastic and gigantic dissipation, redistribution and transformation of capital that has, in all probability, ever taken place in so short a period in any individual economy in the history of modern times. . . . That it represents nothing more than a picturesque incident in another of our great 'shifts' of capital is gravely doubtful. It has been far too broad and deep and penetrating this time to allow of easy escape." [14]

No, it is not a "picturesque incident." The unusual destruction and redistribution of wealth is a result of the severity of the depression, which has struck such staggering blows at the middle class. But the severity is neither an accidental nor isolated fact: it is an expression of the crisis of capitalism, of its decline and decay. This results in the inability to restore prosperity on any considerable scale: in *per-*

32

manent depression, in a downward movement of economic activity.

The downward movement of economic activity— its "planned" expression is the organized limitation of output—means that competition for smaller markets becomes more ferocious. As the economic base of society shrinks, the superstructure must shrink correspondingly. Small producers and storekeepers must struggle more desperately for survival, must lower their standards of living, must get out of business. This includes self-employed professionals.

The downward movement of economic activity means that competition for jobs among salaried employees becomes more savage, as permanent unemployment and lower earnings hit steadily increasing numbers. . . . After nearly two years of "recovery," 300,000 out of 700,000 office workers in New York were still unemployed. . . . According to one employment agency there were, in the spring of 1935, 3,833 male applicants and 1,818 female applicants for every 100 office jobs: respectively fifteen times and ten times as many applicants as in 1929. . . . While unemployment and low salaries are the lot of technicians, the President of Stevens Institute of Technology offers optimism: "perhaps" by 1936 "industry will be facing the worst shortage of technically trained men it has ever known." Events belie the optimism. . . . Hospital technicians work free in laboratories under the guise of getting "practical experience," but when they look for jobs they find other laboratories employing "volunteers." . . . Ac-

33

cording to the New York League of Business and Professional Women, "the trend toward male workers first has become a landslide." Mussolini and Hitler must be "emulated," insists one literary reactionary: "Send women back into the home where they belong." . . . Relief is necessary for 500,000 young people, sixteen to twenty-five years of age, out of school and unemployed. . . . The plight of college graduates is tragic. Says one of them: "We are many. Young girls, in our twenties, with a college education done, or half completed for lack of funds —but all of us are searching for some work or interest to claim what little knowledge or experience we have tried so seriously to gain. Yet no matter where we turn the ways are blocked."[15]

These developments are all an expression of the crisis of the middle class. Their manifestation is an embittered struggle for survival which, as in the case of the middle class in Europe, is part of the general crisis of capitalism and of its own struggle for survival.

Struggle for survival: for what and by what means? Most members of the middle class still cling to capitalism, some move toward communism, others flirt with fascism. The confusion is part of the struggle. Out of it emerges clearly, illuminating the whole problem, *the contrast between the present struggle for mere survival and the revolutionary struggle for power which the middle class waged in its youth.* In that contrast is the story of the transformation

34

wrought in the composition, ideology and significance of the middle class: wrought by the development of capitalism, with which it is, *as a class*, inseparably identified.

Chapter III

STRUGGLE FOR POWER

THE middle class first appears on the stage of European history, in the twilight of feudalism, as a class representing the most progressive forces of the age. Its beginnings were petty and it was despised by the privileged circles of the nobility and the church as the offscourings of society. But after consolidating itself as a class, it waged war on all fronts against the old order. Increasingly independent, aggressive and creative, the middle class remade the world: it was the carrier of a new social order and of new ideals of liberty and progress.

If the middle class was progressive and creative, it was because of its identification with the development of capitalism. For capitalism began as a revolutionary force in society.

1

Out of petty trading in the marketplaces of the medieval towns arose a class of men who engaged in trade as an independent occupation. Alongside of them, and stimulated by their activity, arose a class of independent artisans and craftsmen, who bought raw materials and worked them up into goods for sale. Where feudal production was mainly local and isola-

ted, for oneself or for small circles of immediate con-
sumers, it now increasingly became production for
sale and profit, for the marts of trade. These new
forms of economic activity were the beginnings of
capitalism.

At first the middle class moved exclusively within
feudal relations; it was too small to challenge them.
But these relations hampered the growth of capitalist enterprise, since they imposed all sorts of restrictions on economic activity and property rights. With
bound serf labor, trade confined to the nooks and
crannies of society, no free disposal of property, and
dependent personal relations, feudalism was economically a static order in which all the emphasis
was on the customary and the traditional. Capitalism, on the contrary, is essentially dynamic, and constantly revolutionizes old economic and cultural
forms and ideas. The two systems could not live side
by side; one had to give way to the other. Capitalism
moved toward a threefold struggle:

Economic: For the development of trade and industry as a money economy; that is, the transformation of production for local and customary use into
production for profit and the market, including constant expansion of the market and imposition of its
relations on all forms of economic activity.

Political: Against arbitrary domination by the nobility and the church, whose power was based on
economic forms antagonistic to trade and industry;
a major issue in the political struggle was the right
of resistance to tyranny.

37

The economic and political demands of the bourgeois class were both part of the general struggle for new social relations of production, the program of which included freedom of enterprise and the market and freedom of competition; recognition of the liberty and rights of property; abolition of the feudal caste system and its privileges in favor of the legal equality of rights; national economic and political unity. These demands were fiercely resisted by the vested feudal interests; the breakdown of the old order and emergence of the new were marked by wars and revolutions—as in our own age.

Cultural: As the older social relations were supported by the immense traditional weight of feudal culture, the struggle for new relations necessarily gave rise to new cultural ideals. Among them were the new conception of labor,* which now began to be recognized as the source of all wealth, as against the predatory privileges of the lords of church and

* The early bourgeois identified labor and property, a proposition which was measurably true of the self-earned property of small traders, craftsmen and artisans. All the economists, up to and including Adam Smith, considered labor the creator of value. As trade, according to Benjamin Franklin, is "nothing but the exchange of labor for labor, the value of all things is most justly measured by labor." Capitalist economists abandoned the theory after Karl Marx used it to prove that profit is the unpaid labor of wage-workers. Moreover, the cultural emphasis on labor was minor and transitory, for capitalism is based on the subjection and exploitation of labor. The concept of labor was transformed, particularly by the Puritans, into an ideal of work for its own sake which in practice meant capitalist production for the sake of profit and accumulation, not consumption. Much light is thrown on this aspect of capitalist culture by Thorstein Veblen's suggestive analyses of workmanship and the social relations which exploit and degrade it.

38

nobility; individualism, originating in the right freely to own and dispose of property and in opposition to the dependent personal relations of feudal society; rationalism, an expression of the practical, methodical nature of capitalist enterprise and the revolt against submission to authority. All these ideals undermined the values of the old feudal order. They meant rejection of the traditional, or its transformation, in one domain of culture after another. They prepared the way for democracy and enlightenment (within, that is, the limits of bourgeois needs), and they moved toward the new technology and science, the means of man's increasing mastery over the world.

As the middle class, the burghers or bourgeoisie of the towns, became stronger, they secured constantly greater economic and political rights. Some were bought with money, some conquered by arms. The bourgeoisie emerged definitely as a class when it wrested control of the towns from the feudal lords. The free towns (or communes) now became the spearhead of the growing revolt against the old order. Uprisings and wars, in addition to money and diplomacy, were used to secure and maintain independence. For the burghers were not mere moneybags: they were fighters, invigorated by their progressive economic power and cultural ideals which justified their struggle as the means to a new and better way of life.

The Renaissance, the first general expression of the modern age, arose in the free towns of northern

Italy, where capitalism made its earliest conquests. In spite of the admixture of aristocratic dross, the Renaissance was the upthrust of a new civilization. Its spirit was *this-worldliness* as against the *other-worldliness* of the medieval way of life. The new spirit was manifest in the revival of learning, in an art which infused old religious forms with a pagan vitality, in a technology and science animated by the will to *understand* and *do*. The men of the Renaissance were drunk with life and the vision of a new world.

Trade and the spirit of the Renaissance moved northward, undermining feudalism, freeing and broadening markets, strengthening the local forces of economic and cultural change, creating new interests and wants. By the sixteenth century the commercial revolution had overrun Europe and was creating the world market by drawing Asia and the New World within its orbit. While the most important factor was the expansion of trade, there were two other factors which eventually converted commercialism (unlike its ancestors in Asia and the ancient world) into industrial capitalism:

New forms of labor: Another new class was arising, composed of workers who, differing from the slave and the serf, were free to sell their labor for wages anywhere or anyhow. The beginnings of the proletariat were even more petty than those of the middle class, by whom it was despised. Wage-workers were wholly propertiless and enjoyed no rights at

40

all; they secured rights only slowly and through bitter struggle.

New forms of technology: Where formerly technological progress and change had moved almost imperceptibly over the course of centuries, it now acquired a new momentum. Obscure artisans, scorned and disregarded by the masters of society, made one improvement after another in the mechanical equipment of industry; they initiated a series of inventions leading toward a new type of machine and a new type of power which eventually revolutionized the material conditions of production. Progress in technology provided the impulse and the elements for experimental science, the aims of which are practical and concrete. Creative scientists, harried and hampered by the church, explored nature and the means of using its forces to serve man's needs; their work reacted upon and enriched technological progress.

The new forms of labor and technology, and their results in the industrial revolution, created the basis for collective large-scale industry. The proletariat and collective industry moved alongside each other, becoming increasingly ascendant, and with them a new middle class arose: they dominate the world today.

2

As capitalism developed it altered the composition of the middle class, for economic and class rela-

41

tions changed repeatedly and significantly within the general unity of the onsweep of capitalism.

What is the middle class? A British student has correctly defined it as a class "lying between two other classes." He then, however, proceeds to destroy the definition: "The middle class is that portion of the community to which money is the primary condition and the primary instrument of life." [1] But that was true of the middle class only for a time; it is now untrue, for the money "measure" would exclude most elements of the middle class today (salaried employees, professionals) and include the millionaires of the financial oligarchy.

The middle class is an intermediate class. Its social composition and significance vary, however, in different stages of capitalism.

When the middle class first arose in Europe it included the *whole* bourgeoisie, all the new class elements between the peasantry at the bottom and the ruling aristocracy and its auxiliaries at the top. There were no free peasant owners and wage-workers were a rarity. The middle class was composed mainly of independent enterprisers in trade and industry (including craftsmen and artisans), who owned their own means of labor, with a sprinkling of professionals and salaried employees. It was a class of owners of independent small property, self-earned and self-employed.

But the middle class included all the new class elements only in a general sense and for a short time. Factors of differentiation existed from the beginning.

42

Bourgeois development and the struggle against feudalism were accompanied by the transformation and regrouping of the new elements.

An important factor of differentiation was the struggle between masters and journeymen workers in the guilds. Craftsmen and artisans were increasingly thrust downward to the level of the wage-workers, who were now arising out of the dispossessed groups composed of ruined members of the middle class, peasants driven off their lands to make way for capitalist agriculture and to provide the human raw material for industry, and the vagabonds and other outcasts spawned by war and the breakdown of the old feudal order. The dispossessed plebeian masses, in the social struggles of the times, went "in fantasy, at least," beyond feudal and bourgeois property relations to general communist conceptions "afterward found in every great convulsion of the people, until gradually they merged with the modern proletarian movement." [2] Where the dispossessed moved toward independent action, they met savage repression by the middle class and nobility.

Nor did the serfs escape. The breakdown of feudal relations in agriculture (which eventually created a new class of landed proprietors) imposed new burdens upon the peasants. Their revolts, in France, England, Germany, were betrayed by the middle class and mercilessly crushed. Of the peasant rebels in Germany, many of whom invoked his teachings, Martin Luther said, speaking for the middle class, the lower nobility and the great princes in opposition to the Roman church: "They should be knocked to pieces, strangled and stabbed, secretly and openly, by everybody who can do it, just as one must kill a mad dog!" [3]

Other factors of differentiation split the middle class itself asunder. Disintegration of the guilds, the backbone of the earlier middle class, was inevitable because of the restrictions they imposed upon freedom of enterprise; their survivals came under the control of big merchant capitalists, who arose out of the expansion of the market. Large-scale enterprise made rapid strides, especially in mining, overseas trade, and the manufacture of munitions and luxury goods. Elizabethan England was overrun by a horde of capitalist enterprisers and speculators. The Fuggers had interests all over the world and a practical monopoly of mining in the Holy Roman Empire; their profits in 1511-27 (around $5,000,000 gold, not allowing for the higher value of money) averaged 50% yearly on their invested capital.[4] Expropriation of church lands and the spoils of colonial plunder and the slave trade enriched merchants and aristocrats. (Expropriation and downright thievery were most important means of capitalist accumulation of property.) Other aristocrats piled up wealth by the adoption of capitalist methods, argricultural and mining, in the management of their estates. Strategically placed officials in the growing state bureaucracy were enriched by exploitation of power, by extortion and bribery, and they invested much of their shady gains in the enterprises of merchant capitalists. The wealth of the magnates of trade and finance was swollen by profiteering on the needs of the state in the many wars. It was a new bourgeois aristocracy.

The split in the middle class was complete by the sixteenth century. While the big bourgeoisie included the larger landed proprietors and manufacturers and the more wealthy professionals, it was dominated by the big commercial or merchant capitalists. The middle class itself was transformed into a lower or petty bourgeoisie, made up of small traders and producers (including the surviving craftsmen and artisans), independent farmers and an increasing number of salaried employees and professionals. Now, in its new form, the middle class developed one of its major characteristics as an intermediate class: *its upper layers contact the big bourgeoisie and its lower the propertiless workers.*

With its wealth and the admixture of aristocrats within its ranks, the big bourgeoisie was closely identified with the absolute monarchy. Both the bourgeoisie and the royal power had grown strong in alliance and struggle against the turbulent independent nobility, which interfered with trade and flouted the king. The monarchy crushed the independence of the nobility, assured inner order and peace, broke down many of the feudal barriers to trade and industry, and encouraged capitalist economic activity. But it retained many of the old restrictions and created new ones.

Among the new restrictions was the grant, to rich

45

merchants and royal favorites, of monopolies whose exploitation required large amounts of money and yielded large profits. Everywhere the state interfered in economic activity, creating a complex system of restrictions and privileges. The system was summed up in mercantilism, which was, in spite of its varied and often contradictory manifestations, a policy in the interests of the monarchy (including the many surviving feudal elements) and the big bourgeoisie. The petty bourgeoisie, or middle class in the newer and limited meaning, was largely excluded.

Monopoly, and the restrictions and privileges of which it was an expression, naturally met with increasing opposition from the middle class. This class now acquired another major distinguishing characteristic: *as the possessor and defender of small property, the middle class is always waging war upon monopoly, by which it means big property.*

The middle class ideal was one of independent property, assuring independent means of earning one's livelihood, and this ideal was threatened by political privileges and monopoly. Hence, the political and religious spokesmen of the middle class during the seventeenth century (and later) savagely denounced the big merchants and monopolists and the politics which favored them. Where the big bourgeoisie urged the rights of property in general, the middle class emphasized small property and direct ownership, one's own independent enterprise, initiative, thrift and simplicity. While the petty-bourgeois ideals and struggle created and invigorated

46

many elements of the capitalist spirit, they were directed as much against the big bourgeoisie as against the aristocracy. The ideal of the middle class was thus expressed by one Puritan preacher:

"Freeholders [independent farmers] and Tradesmen are the Strength of Religion and Civility in the Land; and Gentlemen and Beggars are the Strength of Iniquity." [5]

There was, however, a fatal contradiction in the ideal. Small property breeds big property. The rights of property include the right to amass property on a large scale. Out of the middle class itself arose enterprisers who, more aggressive or more fortunate, piled up great riches and trampled upon the small property of their former brethren. Capitalist production, moreover, drives as a law of nature toward the concentration of capital and the increasing destruction of independent property. (An aspect of the contradiction was religious. The reform religions after the Reformation, all of them middle class, identified property and godliness, sanctified riches. But great riches undermined godliness, *i. e.*, threatened small property. Some radicals urged the equalitarianism of a mystical communism of property, others the limitation of great riches.) The middle class had begun its long, and hopeless, struggle against monopoly, or big ownership, from the trading companies of the sixteenth century to the trusts of the twentieth: the final result was its transformation into a class composed mainly of propertiless elements. . . .

Although in opposition to many aspects of the

47

monarchical system, the big bourgeoisie was entangled in its relations and had been benefited by
most of its restrictions and privileges. But these
limitations on the freedom of enterprise now hampered the further development of capitalism. Hence
the middle class, in the struggle against monopoly
and for freedom of enterprise, was fighting in the
general interests of capitalism, especially as the class
was increasingly the carrier of the technical-economic forces of the oncoming industrial revolution.

The middle class was now, moreover, the most
militant carrier of liberalism (often cloaked in religious guise, but still liberalism in the concrete historical sense). While the struggle was, economically,
for the rights of independent small property, it
necessarily projected itself in larger cultural and
human terms. A new structure of property relations
creates a new superstructure of cultural relations and
ideals, which react upon their origins. Class struggles are waged on the ideological plane.

Elements of liberalism had developed earlier and
most of them were acceptable to the big bourgeoisie,
but only within strictly defined limits, for this new
class had assimilated many feudal and authoritarian
ideas. Numerous bourgeois bought estates and titles,
many nobles became bourgeois. It was the middle
class that flamingly invoked the right of resistance
to tyranny. It was the middle class intellectuals, often
in bitter polemics with the spokesmen of the big
bourgeoisie, who most fully and aggressively expressed the ideals of liberty and individualism, of

48

equality and democracy. It was the struggles of the middle class, rallying the dispossessed plebeian elements, which enlarged democratic rights in capitalist society (enlarged again, in the nineteenth century, by the emergence and independent struggles of the working class).

There was, thus, a sharp diversity of aims within the general bourgeois unity:

The big bourgeoisie stood "in opposition" to the monarchy. But the opposition was limited to reforms (largely excluding the middle class) in an otherwise acceptable institution. Hence the big bourgeoisie faltered and compromised.

The middle class, against monopoly and for the rights of independent small property, was the most aggressive force in the struggle for democracy, for the overthrow of the monarchical system and its feudal-bourgeois privileges and restrictions. The upthrust of the middle class, in great measure against the big bourgeoisie itself, drove the bourgeois revolutions on to larger issues and achievements.

3

After the Elizabethan Age the big bourgeoisie in England was the most ascendant of any in Europe. The old nobility had been practically wiped out in the Wars of the Roses, the new was measurably bourgeois. Feudalism was almost dead. Two new agrarian classes had emerged: landed proprietors who ran their estates on commercial principles and

49

the yeomanry or independent small farmers. The big bourgeoisie for the most part dominated the policy of the monarchy and was benefited by its privileges and restrictions, but in return it had to put up with the disadvantages of the arbitrary nature of absolute monarchical power. To curb royal prerogatives in the interest of its own limited aims, the big bourgeoisie set in motion the Great Rebellion of the 1640's, but the pressure of the middle class radicals soon carried the struggle far beyond those aims.

These radicals were the Puritans. They were opposed to all monopoly and privilege. They were against the extremes of poverty and riches, urging an approach to equal ownership of small property (including more equality in social and political rights), and stressing individualism, character and integrity. Their theology was a struggle for social ideals built on their class interests, and it invigorated them in the struggle for power. In spite of their crotchety religious manners, the Puritans were rebels whose intolerance expressed a determination to conquer the old world and remake it anew in terms of their petty-bourgeois purposes.

The struggle set in motion by the big bourgeoisie became the Great Rebellion when the middle class seized revolutionary power. It brushed aside the original limited aims and moved ruthlessly against its enemies: aristocrats, big bourgeois, the moderates within the middle class itself. The monarchy was overthrown and the king beheaded. Parliament was purged of its moderate elements, oppositional

50

aristocrats and big bourgeois deprived of their property, monopoly and privileges greatly limited, and many democratic measures enacted.

It was a dictatorship of the middle class, which arbitrarily imposed its rule on society. The dictatorship was in the hands of the army under Cromwell. After throwing out the Presbyterian officers—moderate elements who represented the country gentlemen and a sprinkling of the upper middle class allied with the big bourgeoisie—the army was dominated by the Independents, the left wing of Puritanism. It was composed mainly of shopkeepers and yeomen, of artisans, craftsmen and workers. Called an "organized democracy," the Model army was in fact a revolutionary party; it was knit together, in organization and in spirit, by a system of agitators and councils representing the soldiers [6] (until Cromwell abolished them). Puritan ideals were the inspirational force.

The onsweep of the revolution aroused the masses in the lower middle class and the plebeian elements, who now began to urge more radical action and measures. These masses were represented by the Levellers, the left wing of Independency, who accepted seriously the equalitarian ideals of Puritanism and were the most extreme expression of middle class democracy. The Levellers were especially bitter against the merchants and urged the abolition of *all* privileges. They demanded democratic government and universal manhood suffrage, insisted on realizing in practice the ideal of small property, and were ani-

51

mated with sympathy for the poor [7] (in contrast to traditional Puritanism, which despised the poor). An offshoot, small but significant, were the "true" Levellers, or Diggers, whose ideal was an agrarian communism based on the belief that everyone has a right and property in the earth. The Levellers emphasized *personal* ownership, the Diggers *communal*.

An uprising of the Levellers was brutally crushed by Cromwell. He stigmatized them as persons "differing little from beasts," and added: if society "must needs suffer, it should rather suffer from rich men than from poor men." [8] The "beasts" had spilled their blood fighting the enemies of the middle class (and of capitalism): now they were treated as enemies by the new masters.

The middle class, in the Commonwealth of Cromwell, could not maintain its power. It had to move to the right, toward the big bourgeoisie, after crushing the radicals and weakening its mass support. As a *dictatorship of all property,* which is what the Commonwealth eventually became, it was undermined by big property. The ideal of universal small property was unrealizable; in practice the old "neither rich nor poor" became Cromwell's "rather rich men than poor men." Both the dispossessed masses and the big bourgeoisie were dissatisfied, for the one received no property while the property of the other was limited. The Stuart restoration was acceptable to the big bourgeoisie, which preferred monarchy to the democracy of the middle class.

It was impossible, however, completely to restore

52

the old order. The middle class broom had swept too clean. In the "Glorious" Revolution of 1688 the big bourgeoisie easily stripped the monarchy of absolutism and realized its own limited aims. But the middle class, whose upthrust had cleared the way for the more complete ascendancy of capitalism, was excluded from the circle of political power, its interests and ideals largely rejected and despised.* Except, however, the Puritan sanctification of property and of acquisition for its own sake: they created an ideology which capitalism used against the middle class—and the working class.

In the Puritan revolution appears a third major characteristic of the middle class: *It cannot, as an intermediate class (split, moreover, into antagonistic upper and lower layers), impose its rule upon society.* After rallying the dispossessed masses the middle class, particularly the upper layers, becomes fright-

---

* The middle class radicals kept up their opposition, "dissenting" from dominant practices. But in the eighteenth century many of the old restrictions and privileges still prevailed. Out of a population of 8,000,000 only 180,000 had the right to vote. Adam Smith, whose *Wealth of Nations* appeared in 1776, violently denounced *the mean rapacity and monopolizing spirit of merchants and manufacturers.* He opposed all mercantilist restrictions and privileges and broadened the opposition to include joint-stock companies or corporations, for Adam Smith expressed the middle class ideal of small-scale enterprise in which personal ownership and management are possible. The industrial revolution invigorated the struggle for free trade and against survivals of mercantilism, especially as England was becoming the world's workshop. But farmers were thrown off their lands or impoverished by new enclosures and the subjection of agriculture to industry. And new, more complete and repressive forms of monopoly eventually arose, whose apologists used Adam Smith's ideas to justify practices wholeheartedly condemned by him.

53

ened, abandons them, and accepts subjection, as a propertied class, to the big bourgeoisie. . . .

The middle class struggle flared up again in France, on a higher and more radical level as the delayed bourgeois revolution acquired more momentum. While the results accomplished were larger, the general experience of the English middle class was repeated.

Because of the more intense struggle against feudalism, the crushing of religious reform movements, which forced rebel ideas to assume other and more rational forms, and the emergence of a large class of radical intellectuals, the French expression of the Enlightenment was the most brilliant and revolutionary. Among its carriers were the *Encyclopédistes* or *philosophes,* who developed a magnificent faith in reason, in man's creative powers, and destroyed reactionary ideas in one domain of culture after another. Their rationalism and materialism, in which a significant socialist and communist tendency was apparent,[9] were great driving forces in the onsweep of human understanding. They gave old ideas new and more universal forms, including a new emphasis on progress and the rights of man.

But while the ideas of the *philosophes* soared aloft, their application was limited by the interests of the big bourgeoisie, of whom they were, by and large, the spokesmen. They were, for example, rationalists, but they also considered religion necessary to keep the masses of the people obedient to their masters. (Socially, and in spite of the theology, the middle class

54

religious reform movements were made of more revolutionary stuff than the *philosophes.*) All of them were monarchists, their ideal an "enlightened despotism." Of their politics one recent historian says:

"None of the *philosophes* were republicans. . . . Democracy was undesirable, even unthinkable. For the masses, *la canaille,* they had the most withering scorn and the utmost contempt. According to Voltaire they were cattle, and all that they required were a yoke, a goad and fodder. . . . At best, even the most advanced of the *philosophes,* like Diderot and Condorcet, favored a parliamentary system controlled by property owners, such as prevailed in England." [10]

The despised masses were the middle class, especially its lower layers, and the peasantry. Enlightened despotism meant an oligarchy of big property, including its surviving feudal forms. Even a democracy of all property was rejected!

But neither the social forces nor the ideas set loose by the struggle against the old order could be held within the limits desired by the big bourgeoisie. In spite of the moderate politics the ideas of the Enlightenment were revolutionary. Their revolutionary nature was broadened and deepened by the more radical spokesmen of the middle class and by the struggle of the dispossessed masses which they evoked.

It was Rousseau, against the *philosophes* and against Voltaire most of all, who gave a sharp lower-class slant to the ideas of the Enlightenment. Its upper-class, aristocratic spirit was denounced and rejected. "I complain bitterly of the contempt that

55

Voltaire shows on every occasion for the poor," said Rousseau. He called, against the dominant mood of the times, for a literature of "simple, suffering humanity," of the people and its burghers, peasants and artisans.[11] Equality was meant for the people, not merely for the bourgeois impatient of feudal privileges and restraints. Civilization had destroyed the original equality of men, it would reappear in the higher equality of the Social Contract. The assurance of equality was widespread distribution of property: the right of property became the right of all to property, of all owning their independent means of livelihood. Not all property was just, for labor alone had the right to property. Rousseau's ideal was typically petty-bourgeois radical: *neither opulence nor rags.* * The rights of man became concretely the rights of common folk united in the liberty and equality of independent property ownership. Rousseau's whole emphasis was popular and equalitarian.

Voltaire led to the moderate, or big-bourgeois, stage of the revolution.

Rousseau, whose ideas were seized upon by the

* Rousseau's "neither opulence nor rags" was the same as the Puritan's "neither rich nor poor." The ideal appears again and again, always the same in spite of different forms. The movement created by German Pietism (Koppel S. Pinson, *Pietism as a Factor in the Rise of German Nationalism*, 1934, pp. 36, 106), strengthened and aroused to greater intensity by the influence of Rousseau, made its appeal to "common folk" and "accepted and stressed the idea of equality." But, unable to break through the circle of its lower middle class origins, Pietism agreed with John Calvin that the mass of workers must be kept poor to make them obedient. The equality was, again, one of small property ownership.

56

middle class and the dispossessed masses, led to the Jacobin stage of the revolution.

The moderate revolutionary stage, after the honeymoon of 1789 was over, was dominated by the Girondins. While the most radical of the big-bourgeois factions, they still represented the limited program of the big bourgeoisie and the *philosophes*. The Girondins introduced a constitutional monarchy, excluding the great majority of the people (designated "passive" citizens) from the suffrage: all the bourgeois freedoms in the interest of capitalist enterprise: expropriation of church lands: minor concessions to the middle class and the peasantry.

It was impossible, however, to maintain the moderate policy. The revolution had to go beyond the moderate stage to accomplish even the limited aims of the big bourgeoisie. And an aroused people developed its own program of action.

The middle class was dissatisfied. It wanted to make the bourgeois freedoms more general and concrete in terms of its own interests. Small shopkeepers opposed the big merchants. Artisans, craftsmen and small producers, increasingly thwarted by the policy favoring capitalist enterprise, opposed the big manufacturers. Striking for the rights of small property, for the abolition of all monopoly restrictions and privileges, the middle class moved toward the republic and democracy. It rallied, as usual, the dispossessed masses, who imparted a proletarian color to many aspects of the revolution.

The peasantry, its conditions unchanged by minor

concessions, began its own uprising. Feudal relations, including forced labor, still prevailed. There was no class of small peasant proprietors comparable with the yeomen of England. The new bourgeois nobility had aggravated the exploitation of the peasantry and increasingly deprived it of traditional rights, while conditions were made worse by enclosures which drove peasants off the land. An agrarian uprising was the answer. The peasants began to seize and divide the large landed estates, driving the revolution to a new and higher stage.

Forced to make more and more concessions, in spite of the opposition of wealthy bourgeois and particularly because it was necessary to rally the people for national defense, the Girondins finally became frightened. They had broken with the moderates in the government, whose armed forces massacred the Parisian masses demonstrating for manhood suffrage and other reforms. But the disagreement was largely tactical. The Girondins now began to make common cause with the reactionaries and to sabotage the revolution they could not limit. The Jacobins seized power (after their own moderates had seceded), threw out the Girondins, many of whom were guillotined, and set up a revolutionary dictatorship of the middle class.

The Girondins, comparable to the Presbyterians in England, leaned on the big bourgeoisie and the upper layers of the middle class; they eventually combined with the reactionaries to destroy the revolution.

The Jacobins, comparable to the Independents in England, but on a higher and more radical level, leaned on the middle class (primarily its lower layers), the militant peasantry and the dispossessed plebeians in the towns; they drove the revolution on toward complete destruction of the old order.

It was impossible for the Jacobins to do their work with the support alone of the middle class. They rallied the peasantry against the nobility, encouraged the seizure of estates and urged creation of a class of independent small farmers. They mobilized the workers and other dispossessed elements in the towns, upon whom they increasingly depended as the revolutionary struggle became more acute. Small farmers are petty bourgeois, the lower middle class contacts the workers. The Jacobin appeal was, in the words of Marat, to "the farmers, small merchants, artisans and workers, laborers and proletariat, as the insolent rich call them, to form a free people." [12] Jacobinism was petty-bourgeois democracy engaged in a desperate struggle for power and acquiring, in the struggle, a proletarian color.

Now the revolution became great. The Jacobins rose to heroic heights in the struggle against the inner and outer enemy, including the big bourgeoisie. They had forced the Girondins to make concessions, they now moved to new conquests. Universal manhood suffrage and the republic were proclaimed, social and political distinctions and privileges more fully abolished. Feudalism in agriculture was wiped out, creating an enduring class of small farmers. The property of noble and bourgeois émigrés was confiscated. There were the small beginnings of social legislation for the masses. Revolutionary limitations were imposed on democracy in the struggle for democracy. The more rigorous the Jacobin dictatorship, the more democracy in the concrete terms of limiting the power of big property and permitting small property and the petty-bourgeois masses to participate in deciding their own destiny.

War upon revolutionary France by the royalist powers of Europe encouraged the reaction. The Jacobin answer was swift and ruthless. Invasion was met with a mighty upsurge of the revolutionary people. Reaction was met with the merciless answer of the guillotine, which beheaded nobles and big bourgeois alike. In their epic struggle the Jacobins were invigorated by the action of the plebeian masses, of the *sans-culottes:* the propertiless, for a moment, dominated the revolution. The Jacobin terror was, in the words of Marx, a plebeian effort to dispose of the enemies of the bourgeoisie.

The dictatorship, acting through the Convention and the committees of public safety, was based on the Jacobin clubs. These clubs, whose network covered all France, constituted a petty-bourgeois revolutionary party. The Jacobins were a small minority, but they dominated because they were the *one* organized, disciplined, conscious force. Membership was overwhelmingly middle class, with a predominance of the lower layers. In one group of forty-two clubs, 17% were shopkeepers (including tailors and millers), 18% professionals and 11% peasants, mainly small farmers. Artisans and craftsmen, including small employers of labor, plain soldiers, and workers, constituted 32%.[13] While the number of workers increased as the revolution approached its decisive stage, they were in a small minority. The workers and other dispossessed elements acted in the public sessions of the Jacobin clubs, in the Communes and Sections and on the streets.

As representatives of the middle class, the Jacobins urged universal ownership of independent small property. Their ideal was: "The owners must not be rich and all must be owners." It was an impossible ideal which bred compromise in practice. One Jacobin said:

"A day will come when each individual will possess a certain amount of property and live in comfort from the labor of his hands. But while awaiting that happy epoch, the poor man should respect the rights of the rich." [14]

Again the fatal contradiction, which appears in all the struggles of the middle class. Out of small property arises big property: the right to one includes the other. The Jacobins moved ruthlessly against big feudal property, but not against big bourgeois property.

Reluctant to limit the rights of property, the Jacobins adopted a policy which undermined their power. They were forced to regulate some forms of economic activity, forced, in spite of their principles, to adopt collectivist measures. But the measures were

61

limited and hesitant. The Jacobins refused to nationalize the food supply and the factories (many of them started by the government itself) upon which depended the national defense.

As another result of their property complex and the mixed class interests they represented, the Jacobins rebuffed the plebeian elements in the Sections of Paris who were becoming increasingly vocal and urging more stringent measures against owners of property, speculators and profiteers. (Revolution and war created new elements of the big bourgeoisie, who were antagonistic to their Jacobin protectors.) The workers' demands for nationalization and higher wages were ignored. Strikes were made illegal: the Jacobin clubs almost always sided with employers in labor disputes.[15] They rejected the proposal of Robespierre, who was more radical than most of them, to divide confiscated property among the poor. Jacobinism was marked by a struggle between its petty-bourgeois basis and its proletarian aspects.

As the masses became more insistent the Jacobins were frightened. The representatives of the masses, the Hébertistes (comparable to the Levellers in England, but on a lower moral and intellectual level) wanted rough hands laid on the rights of property. Although more radical than Cromwell, Robespierre imitated him and broke with the left, many of whom were guillotined.*

* In 1796 the Babouvistes, a crude communist offshoot of Jacobinism, comparable to the Diggers in England, prepared an uprising for a dictatorship to realize equalitarian ideals by means of common ownership of property. The conspiracy had considerable

Only a minority of the Jacobins were wholeheartedly with Robespierre, whose power depended on the support of the masses. His break with them encouraged the new Jacobin moderates and they sent Robespierre himself to the guillotine. The radical masses, who had shed their blood for the revolution, were now denounced as scoundrels, cutthroats and beasts.

But the Jacobins had secured and maintained power largely by means of one mass uprising after another. The maintenance of power was possible only by a closer alliance of the lower middle class and the workers, and by constantly greater limitations of the rights of property. The Jacobin class base, always narrow, became narrower after thrusting aside the masses. It narrowed still more after Robespierre's death, which alienated the lower middle class radicals.

The Jacobin moderates represented, by and large, the upper middle class, whose always evident contact with the big bourgeoisie now became more marked. This set the reaction in motion. The masses were disgruntled, the more radical middle class elements crushed, the peasants satisfied with the lands they had secured. The Thermidorian seizure of power meant crushing the revolutionary democracy. Jacobinism was succeeded by Bonapartism, which consolidated the revolution in the conservative terms of the major class interests of capitalism.

support among soldiers and the workers of Paris. It was betrayed, and crushed by Bonaparte.

Beaten down in the struggle for power, the middle class was thrust aside. Its lower layers were deprived of rights almost as completely as the propertiless workers. Economically, however, small property was not completely beaten and was itself an element of the reaction, for Bonapartism was supported by the mass of newly propertied peasants. As in the Puritan revolution, but on a higher level, the chief result was to create more favorable conditions for capitalist enterprise than the original limited aims of the big bourgeoisie: destruction of feudalism, development of the free market and free competition. But the middle class conception of liberty, equality and democracy was rejected.

Chapter IV

THE AMERICAN PHASE

THE American middle class was shaped by conditions peculiar to the New World. Hence its development was in many ways different from that of the European. There were differences in economic and class relations, in the proportion of separate kinds of property, in the ideology of the mass of the people, in the forms of revolutionary struggle because of colonial dependence. But in fundamentals the movement of the American middle class paralleled the European: struggle for independent small property and its ideals, creation of more favorable conditions for the development of capitalism.

1

Colonization arose out of the revolutionary changes in Europe. The onsweep of capitalism created the world market, of which colonial settlement and trade was one aspect. Settlers were mainly drawn from the same elements who drove the bourgeois revolutions on to larger aims and achievements.

Most of the settlers were the lowly and despised of a society based on privilege and exploitation. All of them were oppressed by the old order and the new, by the nobility and the big bourgeoisie. Many of

65

them were conscious rebels. They included small traders and producers, artisans and craftsmen, peasants driven from the soil by the development of capitalist agriculture. Other settlers were dispossessed plebeian elements, among them criminals who were victims of an ugly side of the liberty and rights of property: the ferocious punishments, often death, imposed on men, women and children for petty crimes against property. The settlers either had independent small property or hoped to acquire it in the new world: they were animated by the middle class ideal of owning one's own independent means of livelihood.

Nobles and big bourgeois were scarce among the settlers (except as exiles during Cromwell's dictatorship). But they dominated and exploited the settlements from afar by their control of British policy, privileges and capital: an expression of capitalist enterprise.

The colonial system imposed on the settlements was one of the worst manifestations of mercantilist policy. Colonies were considered only as means of enriching the mother country, which meant primarily the big bourgeoisie and the monarchy. Nor was absolute monarchy the decisive factor, for mercantilism was almost wholly in favor of the triumphant big bourgeoisie after the "glorious" Whig revolution of 1688. The middle class settlers met again in colonial policy, whether of trading companies or of the Crown, the privileges and restrictions of the monopoly they rebelled against in the Old World.

Mercantilism limited the freedom of colonial enterprise. Most raw materials had to be sold to Britain and most manufactured goods had to be imported from the same country. Colonial manufactures were discouraged, where not directly prohibited: they were considered a monopoly of British enterprisers. In some cases the establishment of towns was prevented, so that the region might produce more raw materials for export. British capitalist interests tried to throttle colonial shipbuilding and secure a monopoly of the overseas carrying trade.

As long as a primitive agricultural economy prevailed the mercantilist policy favored colonial development, for Britain assured markets and protection. But as settlements became more numerous and "national," and economic activity more diversified, the system of privileges and restrictions began seriously to limit colonial enterprise. Where colonial assemblies enacted laws endangering British interests, they were "disallowed"—i. e., annulled—by the Crown. Disallowances were mercilessly used to thwart the efforts for economic independence.

The struggle of antagonistic interests moved toward revolution. But within the struggle was another—*an inner class struggle among the colonial settlers*—which drove the revolution on to larger aims and achievements. In this the middle class, making a drive for power as in Europe, was the decisive force.

Colonial class relations inevitably assumed the general forms prevailing under commercial capitalism. Out of economic progress and diversification,

67

and the breakdown of the earlier primitive class relations, arose a big bourgeoisie comparable to the British, although not so big and not so entangled with feudal aristocracy. The colonial scene was increasingly dominated by merchant or commercial capitalists, who acquired great wealth from trade, the traffic in Negro slaves and money-lending. An oligarchy of big merchants ruled ruthlessly in the commercial provinces and shared power—as dominant partners, however—with planters in the South and big landowners in the North. The three groups constituted the colonial ruling class, an aristocracy supported by most of the professionals and the clergy: as in Great Britain, where a handful of big bourgeois and landed proprietors ruled an empire.

The colonial aristocracy secured constantly more local political power, which it used for a twofold purpose: to limit British prerogatives and to maintain the "lower" classes among the settlers in subjection. Colonial aristocracy and royal officials, otherwise suspicious and wrangling, made common cause against the middle class and the dispossessed elements, who answered with a constantly more aggressive struggle for democracy and the rights of small property. This struggle became a major factor in the American Revolution.

Virtually excluded from political power, the middle class—the petty bourgeoisie—was repressed economically by the *inner* system of privileges and restrictions erected by *colonial* big property or "monopoly." Small farmers, the most numerous ele-

68

ment in the middle class, were sharply hostile to the merchants and big landowners: the one oppressed by means of "money power" (sales, loans), the other by means of large landholdings. Most independent and rebellious were the "back country" farmers, the men on the frontier, who engaged in constant warfare with merchant creditors, land speculators and aristocratic planters. Shopkeepers, small manufacturers and artisans and craftsmen—the "mechanics"—depended for a livelihood on the merchants, who used their power mercilessly.

The middle class included, moreover, the small producers whose freedom of enterprise was severely limited by the restrictions on manufactures. Merchants and big landowners were not particularly averse to the restrictions, as they interfered neither with overseas trade nor agriculture. This was another cause of middle class grievance against the big bourgeoisie, which only slowly acquired an interest in colonial industry. Yet the small producers represented the larger interests of developing capitalism in the struggle for industrial freedom of enterprise.

Discontent was abundant among the mechanics and dispossessed masses. Colonial assemblies, with the approval of royal governors, enacted laws to beat down wages and make it difficult for workers to become independent farmers. Tenants on the estates of big landowners, who aped an alien nobility, were restive under semi-feudal relations of tenure and exploitation: an agrarian revolution was in the making. Indentured laborers, who composed nearly one-half

69

of colonial immigrants, were treated almost as badly as Negro slaves. There was no reserve of servile Indian labor to exploit: the redmen were beaten but not enslaved. Imported to overcome scarcity of labor and high wages—due to the ease of acquiring independent small property on the frontier—indentured laborers were means for artificial creation of the propertiless workers upon which capitalist enterprise depends. Many of them fled to the wilderness, rebel outcasts of the existing order.

Armed uprisings (some among Negro slaves) marked the earlier colonial struggle for democracy. The transplanted system of caste could not survive under the social-economic relations of the colonial world: its great spaces and lands and the newly arising, loosely experimental institutions encouraged the sense of democratic individualism and equality. Independent farmers, shopkeepers and mechanics, although low in the social scale, increasingly challenged the superiority of colonial aristocracy and royal officials. An episode of the early 1700's is suggestive:

"As [Royal Governor Dudley] was driving along a country road with high snowdrifts on each side, he met with two loads of wood. The chariot coming to a stop, Dudley thrust his head out of the window and bade the carters turn aside and make way for him, but they were inclined to argue the matter in view of the drifts. Words were multiplied, and one of the carters cried: 'I am as good as you; you may go out of the way.' In a rage the governor drew his

70

sword and struck the fellow, who snatched the sword away and broke it. 'You lie, you dog; you lie, you devil!' cried Dudley. . . . He arrested both carters and threw them into jail. . . . Village New England was becoming surprisingly independent when plain countrymen stood upon their rights against the governor—'nor did they once in the Govrs. sight pull off their hatts,' as Dudley took pains to inform the Queen's justices." [1]

A democratic consciousness was arising—directed against *all* aristocracy—which transformed economic grievances into revolutionary struggle.

Democratic individualism and equality thrived on the possession of independent small property and the ease of acquiring it: these conditions the merchants and big landowners might limit but could not destroy. Independent farmers and mechanics who might become farmers were intolerant of traditional customs and restrictions. This was most marked in the men and women on the frontier, whose individualism was intense and aggressive. Westward moving settlement meant the recurrent rise of new groups of small farmers and democrats. Colonial mobility undermined caste and invigorated the ideals of democratic individualism and equality. While most highly developed in the lower middle class, the ideals spread among the propertiless workers with whom it was in contact.

Underlying the democratic upthrust, whose concrete expression was independent small property, was the petty-bourgeois ideal of universal ownership of

71

property, of independent means of making one's livelihood. This ideal, attractive both to small owners and those aspiring to become owners, was tremendously strengthened by the Puritan revolution and the more radical ideas of the Levellers. Why, where land and opportunity were abundant, should the many be deprived of property or threatened in its possession? Denunciations of the rich multiplied. The dispossessed elements became more discontented. Equalitarian and "levelling" ideas met the increasing resistance of merchants and big landowners, of the rich and well-born, and of their apologists. One New England clergyman argued, in 1732, that poverty is preferable to riches:

"It were better for the most of people to be poor than to be born Rich. For such have in general, really a more comfortable Life here and far less dangerous as to the next Life. . . . A Rich Man has a *miserable* life: for he is always full of Fear and Care. . . . Whereas a man that has but Food and Raiment with honest labour, is free from these Fears and Cares. . . . We *need* to *pity* and *love* Rich Men."

But this was a dangerous argument, as it might discourage the accumulation of riches. So the clerical apologist went on:

"But what am I doing? If this discourage People from seeking after Riches, it would be a great Detriment to the Publick, if not the undoing of the World. . . . A rich Man is a great friend to the Publick, while he aims at nothing but serving himself. . . . Each man coveting to make himself rich, carries on the Publick Good: Thus God in His *Wisdom* and *Mercy* turns our Wickedness to Publick Benefit." [2]

The apologetics of the reverend gentleman (still used to justify the big property of the aristocracy of wealth) were aimed directly at the democratic masses, whose equalitarian ideals of small property threatened the privileges of the rich and well-born.

2

By 1760 the American big bourgeoisie was, by and large, satisfied with the existing situation and confident of the future. It had the monopoly of colonial political power. The royal governors were coming under control and the democratic masses appeared submissive. British restrictive laws (many of which, moreover, favored the colonial merchants and big landowners) were largely unenforced or openly flouted. The big bourgeoise felt that it might be accepted as an equal by its overseas brethren. Loyalism, and its faith in the Empire, was the creed of the colonial aristocracy, of the church, colleges and professions. They yearned for British titles.

Then the storm broke. In the 1760's the British government began a policy of effective enforcement of the laws restricting the freedom of colonial enterprise, a policy approved by Tory landlords and bourgeois Whigs. The answer was a revolutionary upsurge of the colonial Americans, who had outgrown, economically and politically, the hampering "protective" measures of British control.

73

Nearly all classes of the people were trampled upon. Enforcement of the navigation and trade acts threatened many merchants with bankruptcy, as colonial shipping and foreign markets were limited. (Most serious was the blow at the West India trade, from which the colonials got the money to pay their British balances: its destruction meant lowering imports or piling up debts, as restricted and undeveloped colonial industry was unable to absorb British capital in payment.) Merchants who had grown rich out of smuggling were aghast. The export of many products, as other than British markets were closed to them, began to dwindle. Suppression of manufactures, developing in spite of restrictive measures, threatened an important group in the middle class. The livelihood of shopkeepers, artisans and craftsmen was endangered. An attempt was made—partly in the interest of big fur merchants, partly to keep colonies on the seaboard and thus more easily subject to an alien political control—to erect a permanent barrier to Western settlement by prohibiting the sale and occupation of lands: [3] this inflamed the back country farmers (many of them squatters), the land speculators, Southern planters eager for new plantations, and the hard-pressed and dispossessed who hoped to migrate to the West and freedom. Complete denial of the colonial right to issue paper money, to prevent slicing of debts to the British, burdened debtors and threatened a currency crisis. The goods of colonials were made subject to seizure for debts. New and heavier taxation, to relieve British taxpayers

74

and pay the costs of enforcement, imposed burdens on all. A Mutiny Act made the colonials pay for the soldiers sent to subdue them. More pressure was used to limit the political rights of colonial assemblies in favor of the royal governors.

The merchants resisted British aggression. Their protest culminated in the Stamp Act Congress of 1765, which decided to boycott British goods. The boycott was popular and effective.

Backing the protest of the merchants, and encouraged by them, was the action of the masses of the people inflamed by economic distress. It was organized and directed by the Sons of Liberty, a society of mechanics and laborers and of lower middle class radicals in contact with them.

Organized in New York City, the Sons of Liberty quickly spread to most of the towns along the seaboard. One branch of the society was formed in Boston by Samuel Adams, petty-bourgeois democrat and professional agitator identified with the popular party opposed to the colonial aristocracy, who found most of his supporters among the mechanics and sailors. The Sons of Liberty was illegal and conspirative, using an ironclad secrecy to thwart British agents. This plebeian society, bound together by a common policy and an active system of correspondence, became a national organ of revolutionary struggle: it proposed a continental congress in 1767 and suggested the idea of independence.

The Sons of Liberty used mass action in the struggle. They organized demonstrations and riots, inspiring malcontents and intimidating Loyalists. They destroyed the offices of tax collectors, terrorized royal officials and made many of them resign. They enforced the decision to boycott British goods where it was disregarded. In some cases courts of justice and local assemblies were violently set aside. In this usurpation of political power the Sons of Liberty began to create the revolutionary forms of a new government alongside the old.[4]

Although the merchants had encouraged the action of the masses, they now began to fear it. For the action was more than anti-British: it was an elemental democratic and equalitarian outburst of workers and the lower middle class directed as much against the colonial aristocracy as against the English expoiters.

The colonial aristocracy dominated the local government bodies terrorized by the Sons of Liberty. The masses "set upon" other "gentlemen" than royal officials and Loyalists. Action against landowners hostile to the colonial cause began to suggest the threat of an agrarian revolution. The masses might destroy the privileges and political power of the aristocracy! Opposed to "the doubtful experiment of government by the people . . . of the lower classes at that," the merchants, big landowners and upper middle class were "seriously alarmed at the spread of 'levelling principles,' and at the growing sense of importance of the 'lower sort of people,' to such an extent that 'a Gentleman does not meet what used to be called common civility.' "[5] This dread of the masses was

76

shared by those elements in the middle class who employed and exploited labor.

When, in 1770, the British government made concessions, they were eagerly snatched at by the big bourgeoisie and the upper middle class. The radical cause was abandoned by the merchants. In the words of one of them: "All men of property are so sensible of their danger, from riots and tumults, that they will not rashly be induced to enter into combinations, which may prove disastrous for the future." [6]

More important than the violence and its immediate threat to property was the diversity of aims, now sharply apparent, within the general unity of the struggle against British aggression: the same diversity, if different in forms, which appeared in the European revolutions:

The big bourgeoisie wanted freedom of enterprise in terms of independence of the privileges and restrictions imposed by an alien ruling class. Democracy was excluded: the aim was an oligarchy of big property.

The middle class wanted freedom of enterprise in terms of independence of the privileges and restrictions imposed by the colonial ruling class (including break-up of great landholdings in the North). The aim was a democracy of small property: an ideal accepted by mechanics and the laborers and other dispossessed elements who were articulate and active.

When the merchants retired from the struggle, during the conservative reaction of the two years

77

after 1770, it was kept up and dominated by the middle class radicals. British concessions granted practically nothing to the middle class (especially the small industrial producers) and the back country farmers. The democratic mass movement had acquired a momentum of its own. But the independent plebeian phase of the movement was dangerous. So the middle class radicals, among them Samuel Adams, deliberately *excluded mechanics from the revolutionary councils and destroyed the Sons of Liberty.* This was necessary to reassure the more moderate elements in the middle class, whose upper layers contact the big bourgeoisie, and to make it possible to win merchants over to the cause of independence. The Sons of Liberty gave Adams the idea for his Committees of Correspondence, which were practically the Sons of Liberty in a wholly middle class guise, as *mechanics were not permitted to vote freely for members of the committees.* The middle class, as usual, held the workers in check.

But mechanics and laborers were still among the shock troops of the revolutionary struggle. According to one historian, "the most striking development" of 1774 "was the combination of workingmen of two

* There was apparently some slight revival of the Sons of Liberty during the Revolution. Their tradition lived on. It was invoked as late as 1856 in the campaign of the presidential candidate of the Free Soil Party, John C. Frémont. According to a campaign pamphlet, *Sons of Liberty in 1776 and in 1856* (New York, 1856), pp. 7-8: "The mechanic and workingman is degraded by the forced labor of slavery. . . . What is to be done? The Sons of Liberty in 1776 grappled with and overthrew tyranny then. The Sons of Liberty must do it now."

of the chief cities to withhold their labor from the British authorities at Boston," who wanted to strike a blow at the rebels by erecting fortifications to close the port. The royal governor was successful with the merchants but not with the workers, who refused, through their Committee of Mechanics, to provide labor for carrying on the work. Another refusal met the governor when he tried to secure workers in New York City: they had been warned by their Boston brethren.[7] Aggressive and constructive use of labor's power!

In spite of some attempts at independent organization through committees of mechanics, the action of the workers was within the policy and control of the middle class radicals. They had neither the numbers nor the consciousness of independent aims necessary to dominate the revolutionary struggle. Mechanics and laborers (the former largely owning their own means of labor) accepted the petty-bourgeois ideal of a democracy of small property, in which they saw the realization of their own interests.

The merchants again engaged in the struggle when, in 1773, the British government struck at them in an effort to monopolize the tea market for the East India Company. But most of them were lukewarm, in spite of all the efforts of the middle class radicals. The historian who has most fully studied the subject thus describes the attitude of the merchants, the dominant element in the colonial ruling class:

"Threatened with bankruptcy by the parliamentary legislation of 1764-65, the merchants of the com-

79

mercial provinces were the instigators of the first discontents in the colonies. . . . The merchants of the great Northern ports were startled by the mob excesses and destruction of property which their agitation had caused. . . . The developments of the years 1767-70, fomented by the mercantile interests in large part, brought the merchants to a serious realization of the growing power of the irresponsible elements and of the drift of events toward lawlessness. . . . Some merchants did indeed abstain from further activity against parliamentary measures; but a majority joined with the radicals to defeat the dangerous purposes [of the Tea Act of 1773]. The disastrous outcome of this unnatural alliance convinced the merchants as a class that their future welfare rested with the maintenance of British authority. As a matter of tactics, many individuals lingered in the radical movement for the purpose of controlling it. With the advent of the first Continental Congress and its brood of committees, other merchants withdrew from radical affiliations, some of them becoming active Loyalists. . . . Their natural disrelish of the idea of separation was increased by the character of the arguments which the radicals were using to inform and consolidate the mechanic and agrarian classes in support of independence. . . . The radical writers made it clear that merchants were no longer to be regarded as the directors of public policy nor 'a minority of rich men to govern.' " [8]

It was the middle class, rejecting the limited aims

and compromises of the big bourgeoisie, that drove on to revolution and independence.

3

Untiringly and systematically, with a rare under-standing of revolutionary strategy and tactics, the middle class radicals mobilized the forces of the coming struggle for independence. Under the creative leadership of Samuel Adams, organizer of the revolution, they were flexible in immediate tactics and inflexible in final aims. Revolutionary organization and action included:

A network of Committees of Correspondence, clubs of middle class militants which constituted a petty-bourgeois revolutionary party directing and integrating the struggle.

City, county and state conventions which made demands, mobilized protest and action, and challenged the authority of the constituted government bodies.

The Continental Congress, the conventions on a national scale.

After the convening of the Congress and as the struggle moved toward armed insurrection, revolutionary organization and action included:

Committees of Safety to enforce the decisions of the Continental Congress, beginning with enforcement of the new boycott of British goods.

An armed militia to protect the committees and answer force with force.

Forcible purging or complete suppression of legislative bodies and courts of justice hostile to the revolutionary cause.*

Committees and conventions, their revolutionary character assured by a selective choice of members, were dominated by the middle class radicals. Their thrust toward power was marked by violent suppression of opposition and by the mass action of the 1760's on a higher level.

The Continental Congress of 1774, whose most important act was the decision to boycott British goods, was not dominated by the middle class radicals. Its membership was moderate, including Loyalists and merchants who felt it still possible to limit the struggle to mere protest. The second Continental Congress, which met in 1775, after several clashes between colonial militia and British troops, was more determined on decisive action. Yet, in spite of the larger representation of middle class radicals, the Congress was dominated by spokesmen of the merchants and Southern planters, their political sentiments the Whiggery of the aristocracy of big property. It represented the more conscious and militant elements of the ruling class.

---

* American revolutionary organizations and tactics strongly influenced the French Revolution, especially its Jacobin phase: the network of clubs, and committees of correspondence to keep the clubs in touch with one another, the conventions, national guard (armed militia) and committees of all kinds, including the Committee of Public Safety. The Corresponding Society was the form of revolutionary organization in England in the 1790's and 1800's. In 1845 Marx and Engels formed the Communist Correspondence Committee, which two years later became the Communist League.

82

There was nothing flamingly aggressive about the Continental Congress. It was thrown into the revolution largely against the will of most of the members. They were hesitant, moving slowly by means of one compromise after another. But the masses in the lower middle class—farmers, shopkeepers, mechanics —were violently in motion. The action of the revolutionary organizations drove uncompromisingly toward a conclusive struggle. British repressive measures multiplied and inflamed the rebels. Revolutionary war was a fact before it was declared. Thomas Paine thundered for independence and the republic, and met an increasing popular response. In the Congress the middle class radicals and the more far-seeing spokesmen of the merchants, who recognized that the larger interests of their class were identified with independence, united to force a revolutionary decision. Under pressure of events, with some members still doubtful or opposed, the Continental Congress declared the colonies independent of Britain.

In general terms the Declaration of Independence expressed democratic and equalitarian ideals: "All men are created equal . . . inalienable rights of life, liberty and the pursuit of happiness." They were a more radical form of the Whigs' "Liberty and property!" The ideals meant, for the slave-owning planters and the predatory merchants and their spokesmen in the Congress, largely a concession to prevailing revolutionary sentiments. But they were real to the rebel masses in terms of a petty-bourgeois democracy of small property. The Declaration also invoked

83

the right of resistance to tyranny—the right of revolution—most fully and aggressively acted upon by the middle class radicals:

"Whenever any form of government becomes destructive of these ends [life, liberty and the pursuit of happiness] it is the right of the people to alter or abolish it, and to institute new government."

The "new government" was already partly in existence, *for the revolutionary struggle had created the forms of a new government alongside the old.*

Starting as means of agitation and struggle, the revolutionary organizations—committees of correspondence and of safety, county and state conventions, Continental Congress—had increasingly performed government acts. This was forced upon them by the needs of the revolutionary struggle: it arose out of action, not theory. Local legislative bodies, where dominated by Loyalists, were ignored or abolished and their functions performed by extra-legal groups. Called merely to make a protest against British aggression, and directly representing only a handful of people, the Continental Congress declared itself the governing organ of a new nation. Revolution empowered them with the authority of law: the challenge to the old forms of government ended in their replacement by the new.

Loyalists damned the actions as usurpation: they were revolutionary seizure of power.*

* These developments suggest a parallel with the Russian Revolution of 1917. The Soviets of workers and peasants, created as means of revolutionary agitation and struggle, increasingly assumed

The new governments represented a minority of the people in favor of revolution and independence. Probably a third of the people was opposed and another third indifferent. Most of the colonial ruling class in the North, the merchants and big landowners, were actively hostile, and they were supported by most of the office-holders, professionals and clergy. Southern planters, however, accepted independence because, unlike the Northern big landowners, they were unafraid of an agrarian uprising, opposed the restrictions on settlement of Western lands, and were eager to repudiate their British debts, which were later assumed by the new American government. (The Virginia planters, most of them Loyalists at first, were won over to independence when, the royal commander deciding to free and arm the slaves, they were alienated by the "prospect of seeing the Negroes in arms.")[9] The revolution against the British was criss-crossed by civil war among the colonials (and by intensification of the class struggle in England).

Against the formidable Loyalist opposition, almost wholly in the North, the new governments used the merciless measures of dictatorship. The revolutionary army ruled by military law and the Continental Congress repeatedly gave General Washington dictatorial powers. Local assemblies were purged of Loyalists or

government functions, becoming a "dual authority" alongside the bourgeois liberal state. After the Bolshevik seizure of power the Soviets emerged as *the* government. Forms and purposes differed: one was bourgeois and included a minority of the people, the other was proletarian and included the great majority: but the underlying revolutionary similarity is unmistakable.

wiped out and replaced with new ones set up arbitrarily by the revolutionary elements. After 1777 New York was ruled by a small committee of safety. Violence and terror were used to stifle opposition. Small local committees had the power to use imprisonment and harsher penalties: an arbitrary power. Revolutionary limitations were imposed on democracy in the struggle for democracy.

Among the measures of dictatorship was the banishment of Loyalists and confiscation of their property. Confiscations started locally, largely under mass pressure. Later the Continental Congress, partly to raise money for war finances, authorized the seizure and sale of Loyalist property.

After the confiscations were regularized they proceeded methodically and legally. The Convention of the State of New York appointed a Commissioner of Sequestration, who worked through a network of local committees of sequestration. Loyalists declared "attainted" were expropriated of all real and personal property except wearing apparel, necessary furniture and three months' provisions. New York realized over $5,500,000 from the sale of confiscated property. The value of property confiscated by all the revolutionary governments was $35,000,000: "a sum which, considering those times, was really enormous." Commissioners on Conspiracies were empowered to compel the allegiance of Loyalists or banish them. Banishments or voluntary exiles included at least 60,000 persons: 35,000 in New York alone, out of a population of 185,000. Loyalists after the revolution were deprived of political rights.[10]

Confiscation was more than an act of terror directed at the Loyalist enemy. It was part of an agrarian revolution (not, however, in the South) which involved democratic, levelling and equalitarian changes in land tenure.

Much of the confiscated Loyalist property represented great semi-feudal landholdings, many of them truly imperial in size. Four confiscated landed estates, for example, were valued at $1,900,000, the estate of one family at $700,000. They were cut up into small holdings and sold on easy terms, with preference given to the tenants: two estates were sold to as many as 525 different persons.[11] The middle class ideal of independent small property appears again in recovery of their lands by small Loyalist owners who returned after the war. The blows agrarian radicalism struck at big landed property, and expropriation of Crown lands, lifting of restrictions on Western settlement, and abolition of entail and primogeniture were among the most positive democratic achievements of the revolution. It was the agrarian phase of the petty-bourgeois struggle against monopoly.

Within the general unity of the struggle for independence there was, however, a clash of antagonistic class interests and ideals.

Although, as a class, the merchants were hostile to the revolution, they dominated the Continental Congress in agreement with the planters and most of the professionals. Some of the more revolutionary demoₗcratic measures were only grudgingly accepted, others were rejected or sabotaged. Taxation of the wealthy was evaded in favor of paper money and bonds. The Continental Congress interpreted the revolution in terms of the interests of the aristocracy of big property.

This aristocracy was dominant among the officers in the revolutionary army, although many of the lower officers were middle class radicals. The plain soldiers, the farmers and workers, clung to democratic and levelling ideas: many of them fought because the Congress promised free lands for service (which meant the independence of small property ownership).

The Northern revolutionary governments and the committees of correspondence and of safety were under control of the middle class radicals. But in many cases there was a drift to the right as the upper middle class and the big bourgeoisie strengthened their community of interests. Again the middle class was revealing its fundamental inner disunity.

During the revolution the clash of interests was held within the circle of the general struggle against Britain. It broke through the circle after the conclusion of peace.

Inflamed by economic distress and the revolutionary democratic ideals, the petty-bourgeois masses (especially the farmers) struck at the big-bourgeois enemy, who had been strengthened during the war by profiteering, financiering, privateering and speculation in government securities, paper money and public lands. Where the radicals dominated Northern legislatures they issued paper money and adopted other measures against merchants, speculators and money-lenders. Where not in control the radicals set in motion a struggle for political power. Among the most active elements were former soldiers who had not been paid and whose property was being seized for debt. Their mood was thus expressed by one sympathetic observer:

"The applause of the world was fresh on their minds, and they felt a title to retirement and repose. . . . They could not realize that they had shed their blood in the field, to be worn out with burdensome taxes at home; or that they had contended, to secure to their creditors a right to drag them into courts and prisons." [12]

Mass unrest was widespread in most of the Northern states. Rhode Island was thrown into a condition of virtual civil war. Armed insurgents in New Hampshire tried to force the Legislature to issue paper money in accord with the demand of a convention of delegates from thirty towns.[13] Massachusetts was rent asunder with violent demonstrations and riots. The insurgents revived the organizations and tactics used in the struggle against Britain.

Most of the insurgents were farmers, but they included some shopkeepers and many mechanics and laborers who accepted the aims of the agrarian radicals. (The turmoil of the times gave indentured laborers an increasing opportunity to escape from their servitude.) It was a lower middle class protest

89

against immediate grievances, especially of debtors against creditors, and an effort to realize more fully the democratic aims of the revolution: an elemental outburst of populism. The demands included:

More democratic government: abolition of political privileges accorded property, lower salaries for officials, universal suffrage and a free press; relief for debtors, including repudiation, no foreclosures and imprisonment for debt, paper money to help farmers and workers; lower and more equitable taxation; limitation of the powers of the courts, especially in connection with the collection of debts; repudiation of government securities owned by speculators (who had bought them at a fraction of their value) and sale of public lands to pay the balance; destruction of the monopoly of public lands by speculators; free lands for distribution among prospective small farmers.

Underlying the demands was the struggle against monopoly of property, opportunity and political power. It was animated by the democratic equalitarianism which insisted on preserving and extending the independent means of livelihood represented by small property. Contrary to experience in the European bourgeois revolutions, there was no appearance of communist sentiment. Universal ownership of small property seemed wholly possible to the rebels. The ideal of more equal distribution of property and its more equal social and political rights represented an agrarian radicalism which was strongly to color American life.

The struggle was most bitter in Massachusetts. Already during the revolution an oligarchic government of big property had been set up, which levied heavy and unequal taxation (mainly to pay bonds owned by speculators). By 1782, one year before the end of the war, the struggle was on. Bands of armed farmers and workers staged demonstrations and riots, stopped foreclosures, terrorized courts and released prisoners. Committees of correspondence sprang up and several county conventions were held to formulate demands and issue calls to action. In 1786-87 five years of violent struggle ended when the militia defeated nearly 2,000 armed insurgents under Daniel Shays, a captain in the revolutionary army, who, after dispersing a number of courts, marched upon Springfield to capture the arsenal. The insurrection was crushed.[14]

Now farmers and workers, most of whom had been soldiers in the revolution, were denounced as scoundrels and cutthroats by the embattled forces of the aristocracy of property. Their sentiments were expressed by George Washington—military leader of the revolution, but an Olympian aristocrat who never doubted that government was a prerogative of the rich and well-born—when he called the insurgents "desperate characters" and a "scourge" animated by "ignorance and jealousy." [15] The Shaysites were also denounced for advocating "ownership of property in common," but of that there was only a slight trace.

Petty-bourgeois radicals, whom dread of the masses transforms into bourgeois conservatives, joined in the denunciations. Only Thomas Jefferson defended the insurgents: rebellions, he said, were necessary, for "what country can preserve its liberties if its rulers are not warned from time to time that the people preserve their spirit of resistance?" Most of the old middle class radicals, however, agreed with Samuel Adams in his "relentless demands for drastic punishment" of the insurgents, whom he called "enemies to our happy Revolution & the Common liberty." [16] Always the petty-bourgeois democrat and moderate Jacobin, Adams turned against the masses upon whom he had largely depended to make the revolution.

During the post-revolutionary turmoil the big bourgeoisie had been uniting the forces of reaction, whose political expression was Federalism. It included men who had grown rich during the revolution, merchants, landowners and professionals who had been indifferent or hostile to the great struggle, army officers organized in the reactionary Order of the Cincinnati: all who believed in government by the rich and well-born. Federalism was a coalition of the oligarchic interests against whom the democratic upthrust of the revolution had been directed.

Shays' Rebellion precipitated action. It was used to rally the substantial elements in the middle class to "law and order and the defense of property." Conservatives spoke openly of military dictatorship and monarchy to suppress the masses.

Moving conspiratorially, for the democratic opposition was strong, the reactionary forces called a

Constitutional Convention several months after the Shays defeat. The Convention had no popular mandate and all of its sessions were secret. Outside of Benjamin Franklin, the delegates were reactionary merchants, planters, landowners, speculators, and professionals in sympathy with them. None of the old middle class radicals were there: none of the men who had prepared and organized the revolution. Property was the ideal of the delegates, the masses and democracy their dread. "The people!" said Alexander Hamilton. "The people is a great beast."

The Convention, to hide its real aims, was called to revise the Articles of Confederation. Illegally, it prepared a new constitution: to assure a strong national government and limit democracy "to protect the opulent minority," said James Madison, "against the majority." The Constitution set up an oligarchic government, in which big property would dominate over small, machinery to suppress local uprisings (including return to their masters of slaves and indentured laborers who had escaped), and national control of the courts and currency to check the agrarian radicals. The presidency was allowed great powers which, although limited by the system of checks and balances, was capable of being easily converted into a dictatorship. States, moreover, made provisions for a property suffrage.

Its actions illegal, the Constitutional Convention decided on illegal methods of ratification. Afraid that state legislatures would reject the constitution, the conspirators provided for special state conventions

93

which were more likely to be dominated by spokesmen of the reaction. Popular opposition was great. The constitution was ratified by a vote of not more than one-sixth of the adult males. It was opposed by a majority of the social groups which had most actively engaged in the revolution: the lower middle class, small farmers and mechanics.[17] The constitution was inimical to owners of small property as well as to the dispossessed masses.

The victory of the reaction was facilitated by a split in the middle class. Its more substantial elements, particularly the upper layers, were afraid of the masses. Some opposed the constitution, but in a way that weakened the opposition. Said one of them:

"One party is composed of little insurgents, men in debt, who want no law, and who want a share of the property of others; these are called Levellers, Shaysites, &c. The other party is composed of a few, but more dangerous men, with their servile dependents; these avariciously grasp at all power and property; you may discover in all the actions of these men, an evident dislike to free and equal government, and they go systematically to work to change, essentially, the forms of government in this country; these are called aristocrats, &c. Between these two parties is the weight of the community: the men of middling property, men not in debt on the one hand, and men, on the other, content with republican governments, and not aiming at immense fortunes, offices and power." [18]

Again the inner weakness of the middle class. For the "men of middling property," incited against Levellers and Shaysites, rallied to the defense of *all* property, which included big property and its right and power to trample upon the small. Logic, moreover, was with the reaction in the struggle against the loose federation of states desired by the radicals. A strong national government—urged most vigorously by Hamilton, the clearest exponent of the needs of industrial capitalism—was necessary to assure the development of capitalist enterprise, with which the middle class was identified.

Adoption of the constitution consolidated the American Revolution in the conservative terms of the interests of big property and its dominant expression, the big bourgeoisie. Beaten in the struggle for power, and abandoning the agrarian radicals, the middle class was thrust downward. Its democratic ideals were rejected.

Chapter V

JACOBINISM: WORLD REVOLUTION

JACOBINISM, the most creative expression of the middle class struggle for power, had a strong international aspect. It put forth the idea of world revolution.

Capitalism itself was an international development, involving the migration of new economic forces and ideas. They spread from one country to another and returned in new and higher forms. The Enlightenment, the cultural synthesis of many lands and many minds, was cosmopolitan and international: among its hopes (doomed to bitter disappointment) was the end of national prejudices and passions as Reason and trade made peoples one in the fraternity of peace.*

Bourgeois revolutions all had an international influence. Their experience and ideas stimulated new and higher forms of struggle. Colonials in the North American settlements imported European revolu-

* Thomas Paine said: "The world is my country, to do good my religion." Kant wrote a book exploring the idea of perpetual peace. One great exponent of the Enlightenment said (J. Salwyn Schapiro, *Condorcet and the Rise of Liberalism in France*, 1934, p. 145): "Patriotism becomes a source of opposition to useful reforms, hence an instrument in the hands of the secret enemies of the nation. . . . War is a relic of barbarism."

96

tionary ideas, including the doctrines of the Levellers and of Rousseau. The American Revolution sounded the tocsin for the French and its tactics were adopted and improved upon by the Jacobins. Only the ruling class whom they threatened considered objectionable the "alien" character of revolutionary ideas.

The international influence of the French Revolution was tremendous, infinitely more than that of previous revolutionary upheavals. This was mainly the work of the Jacobins. Nor was their influence limited to ideas. They set up Jacobin clubs in the lands occupied by the revolutionary armies, corresponded actively with such clubs throughout the world, sent forth revolutionary agents and literature. "Jacobinism in the 1790's was a genuine international movement; in the various countries it touched it had a roughly similar program, employed a similar technique of political action, attempted through a similar ritual to create a political faith." [1]

Everywhere the Jacobin call to world revolution strengthened the progressive elements. And everywhere Jacobinism was met with denunciation, imprisonment, deportation and war: as was Bolshevism in our own age.

In continental Europe Jacobinism rallied the most aggressive and conscious elements in the struggle against the feudal order. It did as much in Latin America, where it roused to new intensity the movement for independence from the feudal-mercantilist rule of Spain. Plans of the Girondins for revolution

97

in Latin America were more actively carried on by the Jacobins. In 1793 an organization, in which French, Spanish and American radicals participated, was set up in the United States to promote revolution in the North American colonies of Spain. Throughout Latin America, especially in Mexico, the Spanish viceroys bent all efforts to crush the Jacobin menace, imprisoning, shooting, deporting.[2] The Jacobin revolution aroused much more response than the American.

The Jacobin influence was still more significant, however, in England and the United States, where feudalism had been partly or wholly destroyed—another indication of the twofold nature of Jacobinism, whose struggle was as much against the big bourgeoisie as the old nobility.

In England, where Edmund Burke spoke of the masses as "the swinish multitude," Jacobinism was more proletarian than middle class. The French Revolution had aroused ruling class fears but no popular response until the Jacobin phase began. This response was almost negligible in the middle class, for its composition and ideals were being transformed by the industrial revolution. The new factory system created many opportunities for independent enterprisers in the middle class, while the class was being increasingly deprived of its handicraft elements by the new technical-economic forms of production. Practically all other elements in the middle class gained from the industrial revolution. It created an immediate identity of interest, in terms of freedom of enterprise and free trade, between that class and the big bourgeoisie against surviving mercantilist restrictions and the politics of landed property. But the industrial revolution wrought increasing misery among the masses. The factory system needed constantly larger numbers of wage-workers, provided by handicraftsmen, expropriated by the new machines of skill and occupation, and peasants driven off the land by a new enclosure movement. These workers had to endure long working hours, low wages and unemployment. The link between workers and the lower middle class was being broken, for it had been largely forged by handicraftsmen whom the industrial revolution now threw ruthlessly into the depths of wage-slavery. Moreover, the nature of the earlier industrialism allowed the middle class to improve its condition while that of the workers grew worse: one depended on the other. Under these circumstances the revolutionary ideals of Jacobinism, and their emphasis on independent means of livelihood for all, repelled a smugly satisfied middle class "on the make," while they made a strong appeal to the articulate among the dispossessed masses. In imitation of the Jacobin clubs, a shoemaker formed the London Corresponding Society in 1792 with a membership composed almost exclusively of handicraftsmen and laborers: "the very lowest orders." This was true of most of the corresponding societies which sprang up in other towns, although in some cases the middle class radicals dominated. "The strength of the movement lay in the poor; the middle class was

99

on the whole apathetic." [3] Its class composition gave to English Jacobinism a marked proletarian slant. While the movement alarmed the ruling class, which answered with brutal repression, the most significant result was to arouse the beginnings of independent labor action.

The early moderate stage of the French Revolution had no particular influence on the democratic struggle in the United States. It was acclaimed by all, although some of the farseeing conservatives sensed danger. "Too many Frenchmen, like too many Americans," said crusty John Adams, "pant for equality of persons and democracy." Opinion split sharply on class lines as the Jacobins forged to the front in 1792, the republic was proclaimed and the king beheaded. Conservatives savagely denounced Jacobinism. It was greeted with a tremendous outburst of enthusiasm among the middle class radicals. The Jacobin year 1793 was, according to one historian, "utterly without parallel in the history of this country. . . . American citizens gave themselves up to the most extraordinary series of celebrations in honor of the achievements of another country." [4]

American radicals thrilled to the Jacobin seizure of power for two reasons: They saw in it the spread of their own revolution throughout the world and they used Jacobinism in an aggressive renewal of the struggle for democracy.

This struggle had practically ceased after adoption of the constitution. It began to revive as the new government struck again and again at the interests and sentiments of the democratic masses. Tremendous mass resentment was aroused by the government's assumption of $70,000,000 of federal and state debts, whose paper tokens were mainly owned by speculators (including members of the Congress) who had bought them at 10% to 15% of their value. This measure was symptomatic of the general policy. The smoldering resentment burst into flames as the Jacobins swept onward to new conquests. The American Revolution inspired the Jacobins: now Jacobinism inspired the American radicals to rally their forces for a new democratic struggle.

The organizational form of the new struggle was the Democratic Society, modeled on the committees of correspondence and the Jacobin clubs. The Democratic Society of Pennsylvania, formed in 1793, said of the Jacobins: "On the accomplishment of the great objects of their revolution depends not only the future happiness and prosperity of Frenchmen, but in our opinion of the *whole World of Mankind.*" [5] One society in Charleston asked for adoption by the Jacobin Club of Paris: the plea was granted. The identification with Jacobinism was everywhere proudly flaunted to the nation.

Spreading rapidly all over the Union, the democratic societies fought oligarchic government and all social and political distinctions and titles. They proclaimed the levelling principles of petty-bourgeois equalitarianism and democracy. They violently denounced the rich, the bankers, speculators and monopolists. They were blamed for the Whisky Rebellion of 1794, a "back country" agrarian uprising against taxation. The democratic societies had in them much of mock heroics and empty pretense. But their social impulse was sound: they mobilized the middle class democrats and agrarian radicals and drove the struggle against Federalist reaction to new intensity and aims. It was the movement thus set in motion that eventually conquered the traditional democratic rights of the American people.

American Jacobinism seemed the end of all things to the aristocracy of wealth and talents. The challenge was answered furiously and malevolently, with an unbounded hatred and an invective style today reserved for use against communists. All democratic radicals, among them Thomas Jefferson, were knaves, rogues and vipers, the aliens "fugitives from the pillory and the gallows." The democratic societies were "demoniacal clubs" . . . "nurseries of sedition" . . . "hotbeds of atheism" . . . "foes of property and order." Their "mad doctrines of equality of persons and property" threatened "the decay of morality and the family." [6] Jacobinism was denounced as "alien," although the Whiggery of the conservatives was itself an importation.

Dread of the masses and democracy was hysterical, almost pathological. The dread was thus expressed by an apologist of the reaction, a learned physician terrified by the new ideas:

Led by wild demagogues, the factious crowd,
Mean, fierce, imperious, insolent and loud,

Nor fame, nor wealth, nor power, nor system draws—
They see no object, and perceive no cause . . .
See, from the shades, on tiny pinions swell
And rise, the young DEMOCRACY *of hell!*

The petty-bourgeois radicals were animated by popular aspirations and humanitarianism, which were identified with their class purposes. The finer among them expressed glorious if as yet unrealizable ideals. Thus Philip Freneau, soldier and poet of the American Revolution and a Jacobin of the 1790's:

> *How can we call those systems just*
> *Which bid the few, the proud, the first,*
> > *Possess all earthly good;*
> *While millions robbed of all that's dear*
> *In silence shed the ceaseless tear,*
> > *And leeches suck their blood. . . .*

> *And men will rise from what they are,*
> *Sublimer, and superior, far,*
> > *Than Solon guessed, or Plato saw.*
> *All will be just, all will be good—*
> *That harmony, "not understood,"*
> > *Will reign the general law.*[7]

But while the ideals soared aloft, the practical class-economic aims of the democratic movement were a constant brake upon them in reality. Some of the limitations were exposed by one Federalist pamphleteer: "What do those who preach *liberty* and *equality* mean? Do they mean to raise the blacks to

103

equal social rights with the whites? Do they mean to remove the existing discriminations amongst the whites themselves?" [8] It was a good thrust, but it was ignobly used. For the class interests represented by the democratic movement, while they fell considerably short of the ideals so bravely trumpeted, were still more progressive than those of the reaction.

The constitution had imposed the oligarchic rule of big property, of the big bourgeoisie. This was resented by the mass of the people. Small producers were feeling the pressure of manufacturers and the merchants, whose power was being strengthened by the swift development of banking and the credit system. Nor was this offset by new opportunities for independent enterprisers created by the industrial revolution, which had scarcely begun to move. The small farmers, especially the frontiersmen, objected to domination of the government by commercial interests, and to monopoly and speculation in public lands. It was a petty-bourgeois movement for freedom of enterprise in economics and the abolition of Federalist control in politics: another stage of the struggle to complete the democratic revolution.

Middle class radicals dominated the American expression of Jacobinism. Its successor, the larger Jeffersonian movement (which absorbed Jacobinism) was dominated by the agrarian radicals. Both included many workers, who were still involved in the struggle to complete the democratic revolution, although they played no independent part.

It was a carpenter, however, a former soldier in the

104

Revolution, who was the worst sufferer from the Alien and Sedition Acts, those desperate Federalist measures to crush the democratic radicals. The worker was David Brown, whom Fisher Ames described as a "wandering apostle of sedition." With the help of another worker, he erected a liberty pole in a Massachusetts town bearing the inscription: "No Stamp Act, no Sedition, no alien Bills, no Land Tax: downfall to the Tyrants of America; may moral virtue be the basis of civil government." Brown went to another state to work and agitate, but he was arrested, extradited, and sentenced to eighteen months' imprisonment and a fine of $400: the most severe punishment imposed on any violator of the Sedition Act. In spite of many appeals for clemency, the agitator served fully two years and was released only by President Jefferson's amnesty. Brown had a crude idea of class struggle: "There has always been an actual struggle between the laboring part of the community and those lazy rascals that have invented every means that the Devil has put into their heads to destroy the laboring part of society." He was an agrarian-labor radical who denounced the monopoly of public lands and urged their free settlement: "They have sold the lands by fraud and without any power derived from the people to justify them in their conduct. Here is the one thousand out of the five millions that receive all the benefit of public property and all the rest no share in it. Our administration is fast approaching to Lords and Commons as possible—that a few men should possess the whole

Country and the rest be tenants to the others." [9] The workers were already under the influence of the agrarian radicalism that was to shape so much of their future consciousness and action. American Jacobinism developed no proletarian or communist aspect. There were, however, the beginnings of independent labor action in the 1790's: shoemakers and printers organized trade unions, carpenters struck for the 10-hour day and tailors for higher wages.[10] . . .

Jacobinism moved within the circle of bourgeois ideas as a whole. But it gave a lower class slant to those ideas and combined them into the most aggressive expression of the petty-bourgeois struggle for power. The differences in emphasis and aim are clearly suggestive of the differences in class approach:

Liberty: Where liberty of property and enterprise was interpreted by the big bourgeoisie exclusively in its own interests, Jacobinism urged an economic and political liberty which would assure widespread ownership of small property and protect its rights. Liberty included the utmost freedom of speech and action in terms of the interests of the petty-bourgeois masses.

Democracy: Jacobinism, unlike the big bourgeoisie, insisted on universal manhood suffrage as a logical expression of the sovereignty of the people; not merely abolition of the nobility but of all social and political distinctions and privileges. Absolute liberty is impossible. But where the big bourgeoisie limited liberty in the interests of an oligarchy of big property, Jacobinism limited it in the interests of a

106

petty-bourgeois democracy of independent small producers.

Equality: Democracy was inconceivable without equality. The only assurance of equality, according to the Jacobins, was widespread ownership of property in the form of independent means of livelihood. They were not satisfied with mere equality before the law, as was the big bourgeoisie. The Jacobin ideal of equality necessarily excluded the extremes of poverty and riches.

Education: Free universal education to include the poorest child. This was necessary if the competitive struggle was to assure the rough economic and social equality which Jacobinism envisaged: all talents must have the same opportunity for development and expression. Education was to be wholly civil, the function of a state separated from the church and dominated by anti-clerical, if not agnostic, sentiments. Education was, moreover, considered an independent creative force in solving social problems and remaking the world.

Progress: The idea of progress was enriched by the Jacobin emphasis on the perfectibility of man. Underlying the crudity of exposition and proof was a socially sound and progressive concept. Emphasis on the natural goodness of man was directed against the stupefying dogmas of original sin and total depravity. Emphasis on the capacity of all men to move always upward was directed against the "natural aristocracy" with which the big bourgeoisie identified itself. The perfectibility of man was a revolutionary democratic idea which rejected the right of the few to rule because the many were naturally depraved, beastly and swinish. It meant the right of the mass of the people to share in the conquests of progress. It meant the possibility of mankind rising, not to a static perfection, but to continuously higher levels of living: creative realization of conscious social and human values. The essential meaning of "perfectibility" is confirmed by modern anthropology, which clearly reveals that man is "unbelievably malleable."

Jacobinism was strongly national and authoritarian. Nationalism was identified with the realization of the petty-bourgeois democracy of small property. The idea of an authoritarian state (not, however, accepted by the American variant of Jacobinism) originated in the revolutionary "dictatorship of liberty against tyranny." It also involved, however, the need of a strong state to protect the rights of small property, to consolidate a petty-bourgeois democracy unstable in its class-economic basis and threatened from all sides. The nationalism and authoritarianism of Jacobinism were progressive: they became reactionary and brutal as capitalism gave them new forms and meaning.

The ideals of Jacobinism, in spite of a tendency to become general human and democratic rights, were firmly rooted in the concept of a society of small farmers, of a handicraft industry of small masters and workers who might become masters, and of small traders. They were given substance by the "economic equalitarianism" of which "more than a touch" distinguished Jacobinism. Robespierre wanted incomes to be not much higher or lower than 3,000 francs yearly. Marat deplored the tendency of property to accumulate in the hands of a few, leaving the many in poverty and hunger, and advocated "a wage sufficient to enable a workingman, after three years of faithful service, to go into business for himself." Jefferson held the same ideal, a society "of men enjoying in ease and security the fruits of their own industry." [11]

Jeffersonian democracy, which was swept into power largely by the radical movement of the 1790's, accepted the petty-bourgeois ideals of Jacobinism (not, however, universal manhood suffrage) stripped of their revolutionary and proletarian aspects. Jeffersonianism was more definitely agrarian in its slant. The democracy and equality of widespread ownership of independent small property seemed easily realizable in the United States, with its continental areas of new lands, freedom of enterprise and the absence of feudalism (except in the semi-feudal South). Where Jacobinism in France and England contributed to the development of socialism and anarchism, in the United States its elements were absorbed in the wholly petty-bourgeois American Dream.

But while petty-bourgeois democracy, whether Jacobin or Jeffersonian, tried to give a middle class slant to bourgeois ideas, it was imprisoned within the circle of those ideas. And their logic was inescapable. The liberty of property included the liberty to amass big property and deprive others of property. Economic freedom meant the freedom of big enterprise to trample upon the smaller: the freedom to create propertiless workers and exploit them. A democracy which was identified with competition and whose assurance was ownership of small property was limited in itself and limited still more by the emergence of big property. Inequality arose out of equality of opportunity and was justified by it. Progress included the movement of social-economic forces which spelt the doom of middle class ideals.

Petty-bourgeois democracy, moreover, was imprisoned within the circle of capitalist relations of production. It accepted production for profit and the market, with its drive toward larger profits and larger markets and an increasingly larger scale of enterprise. The small producers, whose ideal society is simply a petty capitalism, are doomed. The masses of the people are condemned to become propertiless proletarians, whose subjection and exploitation are justified by the "natural right" to property. This was inevitable, in spite of Jacobin insistence that "all owners must be workers and all workers owners" and Jeffersonian efforts to prevent the appearance of a proletariat.

The ideological and economic imprisonment of petty-bourgeois democracy appeared clearly in Jacobinism, its most revolutionary and aggressive expression. *Jacobinism tried to limit capitalism while retaining all its fundamental relations.* Apparently the middle class waged an independent struggle.

Actually it did not, for it was itself bourgeois and entangled in the network of capitalist relations. Originating in the bourgeois revolution, the "independent" middle class struggle for power was simply the most uncompromising and drastic expression of the revolution in terms of the general needs of capitalist society. In the final result, *Jacobinism was fighting for the larger interests of capitalism and the bourgeoisie as a whole.** It was a progressive struggle, for capitalism was economically still progressive. But the ideals of liberty, equality and democracy were realized only in limited forms, and they were still further limited and degraded by the onsweep of new forms of capitalism.

* Only the extreme left elements, with their crude communism, tried to break through capitalist relations. The efforts were a failure, as they outran material possibilities. They appeared more definitely in the uprising of the workers of Paris in 1848, in which the petty bourgeoisie were first allies and then deserters. Fear of proletarian revolution frightened the middle class in the German Revolution of 1848; capitalism in Germany (and later in Japan) developed without any real bourgeois revolution and its extreme middle class stage. The workers appeared as an independent force in the Mexican Revolution of 1911-20, but they broke apart because of faulty consciousness of aims, and lack of adequate revolutionary leadership and program. In the Russian Revolution of 1917, however, the workers, under Bolshevik leadership, seized political power and broke through capitalist relations.

Chapter VI

MIDDLE CLASS: OLD AND NEW

AFTER its revolutionary struggle for power the middle class was again transformed by capitalist development.

The first transformation, which split off the big bourgeoisie, converted the middle class into a petty bourgeoisie. But it was still a propertied class, composed of small enterprisers who owned independent means of livelihood, including the professionals, most of whom were self-employed. Salaried employees were unimportant, except in the state services. This was the middle class that drove the bourgeois revolutions on to larger aims and achievements in the struggle to make capitalism a democracy of small producers.

Another and more fundamental transformation was wrought by the capitalism of developing large-scale industry. Independent enterprisers became an increasingly smaller proportion of the middle class (and of the people). Salaried employees became an increasingly larger proportion: a "new" middle class deprived, like the workers, of independent means of livelihood. The old middle class of small enterprisers was thrust downward to comparative insignificance by the concentration and trustification of economic activity. Instead of a petty bourgeois democracy of small property, there developed a plutocratic democracy of big property which transformed the mass of the people into propertiless dependents.

1

The middle class ideal of a society of independent small producers was most fully realized in the United States of the 1820's-30's. At least 80% of the people were owners of property, of their own means of livelihood. This was not true, of course, of the slave South. But in the Northern and Western states, a rough economic equality prevailed. Although limited by the polar extremes of riches and poverty and by the increase in wage labor, the limitations were still small and their threat mainly potential. There was a minimum of class stratification and privilege. By the 1820's most states had granted universal manhood suffrage.* Jeffersonian democracy, tainted with the ideas of an aristocratic landed gentry, was recreated in the homespun agrarian democracy of Jackson, who rallied to his colors the frontiersmen, lower middle class elements, and the workers. Democracy, small-scale enterprise, and the frontier apparently offered

* The struggle for universal suffrage met the most bitter opposition in Rhode Island. It flared up in the Dorr Rebellion of 1841, using the tactics of the revolutionary struggle against British rule. An unauthorized convention adopted a constitution which was overwhelmingly ratified by the people in an unauthorized election. As the regular state government resisted, the rebels set up their own, with Thomas Dorr as governor. An armed uprising was crushed, but universal suffrage was granted two years later.

unlimited opportunities for the acquisition of independent small property. "No Americans intended to remain laborers in the sense of living all their lives dependent on wages." [1] Equality was real enough to seem capable of being broadened and deepened, and becoming permanent.

Out of this society of small producers arose the American Dream. It was a dream of liberty and progress moving irresistibly onward to new and higher fulfillments. Most vital was the ideal, determining all the other ideals, of *the liberty and equality of men owning their independent means of livelihood*. The ideal withered, as capitalism made it impossible for the mass of the people to acquire independent property; the American Dream was increasingly separated from the actual trend of social-economic forces and it ended in the nightmare of economic decline and decay. . . .

The society which created the American Dream was dominated by agrarianism. Roughly 75% of the people were independent farmers, whose numbers had been swollen by the break-up of many more great landed estates after the revolution and, particularly, by the settlement of a frontier which moved perpetually beyond the horizon. It was comparatively easy for dissatisfied farmers and workers in the older settlements to pull up stakes and go West, where land was cheap, taxes were low, and needed agricultural equipment a minor item of capital investment. The economy of the frontier regions was still largely self-sufficient, not yet wholly engulfed in the relations of the market. Almost anyone might acquire his own means of livelihood, become an independent farmer or an independent small enterpriser in industry and trade. These conditions invigorated the sense of democracy and equality. "The absence of distinctions among men as property owners tended to make the people disregard wealth as a criterion of fitness and to look upon all men as essentially equal." [2]

The frontier was significant of more than the almost universal ownership of small property. French agriculture was dominated by small farmers, yet they were a conservative force, while the American frontiersmen were radical. The significance of the frontier lay in its many rebirths which invited the migration of the dispossessed, recreated again and again the economic conditions of independent enterprise, and gave great fluidity to class relations. The continual rebirth strengthened the middle class in the older settlements and made the struggle for democratic rights irresistible.

This struggle involved the older mechanics and the newer wage-workers, who had to fight for democratic rights not granted them by the dominant class forces. They secured the right to vote and the right to organize and strike. The workers developed a mighty campaign for universal free education: "until," they argued, "means of equal instruction shall be equally secured to all, liberty is but an unmeaning word and equality an empty shadow." [3] The struggle for democratic rights was inflamed by economic grievances, for capitalist development was depriving mechanics of the use of their skill and multiplying the number of factory workers, whose conditions were miserable. While the workers set up many trade unions, the first form of independent class organization, politically they remained under the influence of the petty-bourgeois radicals, especially the agrarian. (A small agrarian communist movement demanded an equality of land for all the people, or that at least the size of farms should be limited.) There was an increasing demand for free land in the Western regions. The labor radicals believed it wholly possible for workers to become independent farmers or master handicraft producers. The programs of the Workingmen's parties formed in 1828-32 urged the general democratic freedoms: destruction of "invidious and artificial distinctions, unnatural and unjust inequalities," realization of "uniformity of rights and privileges." [4] The Workingmen's parties were not essentially different from Jacksonian democracy, and were absorbed by it.

It was the struggle against "monopoly" which united farmers, small handicraft producers and workers. The factory system and the financial relations of developing capitalism threatened the independence of the small enterpriser and the occupation of the mechanic. Corporations and banks, as an expression of the newer capitalism, were bitterly assailed because they trampled upon small property.

Middle class radicals proposed legislation against corporations. An economist maintained that corporations create artificial power and cause more unequal

116

distribution of wealth; banks are bad, for they aid the corporate enterpriser against the small independent: "A bank is able to put almost any man down, who shall attempt to do business without their agency, and swallow up the proceeds of years of laborious industry." Railroads were denounced because they destroy small enterprise, encourage manufactures and "tend to concentrate the businesss of the country in few hands, to give a monopoly to the capitalist." Organizations of workers, under the influence of petty-bourgeois radicalism, opposed "the legislative aid granted for monopolizing, into a few rich hands, the wealth creating powers of modern mechanism." [5] The struggle against "monopoly" came to a climax when the United States Bank, controlled by three stockholders, was destroyed by President Jackson as a "powerful monopoly."

The anti-monopoly movement was self-destructive, however, for it was entagled in irreconcilable contradictions:

Only by stifling technical-economic progress, which drove on to large-scale production, was it possible to realize the aims of middle class radicals. A society of small producers meant a low level of economic efficiency and low standards of living.

While small producers opposed the new forms of capitalism, they accepted its essential relations: production for profit and the market, freedom of enterprise and competition. Out of these relations arose the big property of the old merchant capitalists and the still bigger property of the new industrial capitalists.

Middle class democracy, identified with freedom of enterprise and competition, created its own doom, as it prepared more favorable conditions for the development of capitalism. The breakdown of old privileges and restrictions permitted freer and more ruthless exploitation of the nation's resources. Destruction of the ideal of "natural" aristocracy was acceptable to the capitalist aristocracy whose one ideal was money, for money is impatient of traditional restraints and prerogatives. A new big bourgeoisie was created, which absorbed the more enterprising elements of the old and thrived on the freedoms for which the embattled middle class radicals fought.

The frontier invigorated the ideal of a society of independent small producers, but it also invigorated capitalist enterprise on an increasingly larger scale (eventually the frontier's greatest influence in American history). Alongside of small property was the speculative fever to amass big property. Many landholdings were wholly speculative, while the chief interest of many small farmers was higher land values rather than bigger crops. Every town was a center of real-estate speculation, into which all elements were drawn, including religion. One minister said: "Religion, when I came here, was considered contemptible. Why did they invite me here? On speculation. A minister—a church—a school—are words to flourish in an advertisement to sell lots." [6] Landholdings

118

in the larger of the frontier's new towns created many millionaires. As farmers got beyond the subsistence level, their surplus products had to be sold in constantly wider markets. Agriculture was becoming more and more dependent on the world market and its complex capitalist relations, and this was also true of the slave South, with its great exports of cotton. While the handicrafts flourished, larger industrial enterprises began to grow slowly but steadily. Speculation, industry and trade made banks indispensable. The new regions demanded railroads and public improvements, which strengthened large-scale capitalist enterprise and the import of foreign capital. A Western big bourgeoisie arose. Agrarianism itself encouraged the capitalism against which the agrarian radicals were rebelling.

Within these developments was another and more decisive one: the industrial revolution which transformed the technical-economic basis of capitalist enterprise. Production under the older commercial capitalism, still largely dependent on handicraft methods, favored the independent small producers of masters and mechanics. The new industrial capitalism, with its more efficient but more costly mechanical equipment, required constantly larger amounts of fixed capital. The handicraftsmen were wiped out. Economic activity became more complex as capital, output and markets became larger and strengthened the need for corporations and banks. The simple society of small producers was doomed to destruction.

Most rebellious against the new developments were the handicraft producers in the lower middle class. As they were destroyed (breaking the link with the workers) the middle class was reconstituted. Its most important element was now the small capitalist producers, many of whom moved upward into the big bourgeoisie. The middle class identified itself with industrial capitalism, thrived on the opportunities it created, and lost interest in the agrarian-labor struggle against "monopoly."

Industrial capitalists and financiers began to dominate the big bourgeoisie, taking power away from the merchants. Unheard-of riches were piled up, a mere foretaste, however, of the fabulous wealth to come. By the 1840's, in New York City alone, seventy-nine persons had fortunes of $500,000 up, nineteen of them millionaires.[7] The polar extremes of poverty and riches moved farther apart.

Industrial capitalism, which constantly enlarged the scale of production, deprived millions of people of independent means of livelihood, converting them into wage-workers who had to sell their labor power to live. By 1859 over 1,000,000 wage-workers were employed in manufactures,[8] and nearly as many in mining, transportation and trade. There were more dependent wage-workers than independent farmers. Almost one-third of all persons gainfully occupied were propertiless wage-workers (not including the increasing numbers of dependent salaried employees). Jeffersonian democracy had dreaded a proletariat and tried to prevent its growth: the proletariat was becoming a majority of the people.

The society of independent small producers was breaking up. The crisis in the middle class—destruction of handicraft industry—was overcome by the multiplication of opportunity and an increase in small enterprise of the newer capitalist type. A new crisis, however, was in the making.

2

In the struggle to wrest control of the national government from the slave South, whose agrarian and free-trade policy blocked the path of industrial development, Northern capitalism rallied the support of the urban middle class and the farmers. The middle class was thriving on the new forms of capitalist enterprise, while its more radical elements set in motion the great Abolitionist movement. Farmers and workers wanted the new Western regions to become free states settled by free labor, not slave. Underlying specific issues was the struggle between two social systems based on the antagonistic relations of slave labor and free labor. Destruction of slavery by the Civil War was a completion of the bourgeois democratic revolution, and it was a cause that aroused the enthusiasm of the middle class radicals.

The Civil War, however, was marked by no middle class struggle for power. Industrial capitalism was strengthened economically and politically. The expansion of industry included an increase in large-scale enterprise. Capitalist interests secured from the government measures they had long desired, among them high tariffs and a national banking system. But the supremacy of industrial capitalism, decided by the War, also decided the final subjection of agriculture to industry and of the middle class to the big industrial capitalists.

Capitalist policy again appeared clearly in the Reconstruction measures. Their purpose was to consolidate the capitalist political control secured during the Civil War. They struck not only at the former slave-owners *but at the Northern middle class radicals and malcontents.* President Johnson, whom the Congress bitterly opposed and tried to impeach, was an old agrarian radical who still clung to anti-monopoly ideas. Abraham Lincoln had told the Congress in 1861 that the republic might be destroyed by the "corporations" and the "money power." In his first presidential message Johnson said:

"Monopolies, perpetuities and class legislation are contrary to the genius of free government. . . . Whenever monopoly attains a foothold, it is sure to be a source of danger, discord and trouble. . . . The government must be held superior to monopolies, which in themselves ought never to be granted, and which where they exist must be subordinate and yield to the government." [9]

This challenge aroused the wrath of a Congress dominated by spokesmen of the big bourgeoisie, intent on consolidating capitalist control of the government and using it to promote capitalist enterprise.

The larger class issues assumed vulgar form in the personal interest of many members of the Congress in government aid to railroads and speculative exploitation of public lands, which Johnson opposed. His policy of conciliating the South was another threat. For it was necessary, to consolidate capitalist control of the national government, that the political rights of the Southern states be severely limited. Otherwise the unity of a freely voting South with the Northern middle class malcontents would have insured a majority to the democratic opposition, prevented the election of Grant, and broken, for the time being, big capitalist control of the government. So the Congress used dictatorship, destruction of property rights, and suppression of the minority to consolidate capitalist political control. Radicals of the Thaddeus Stevens type, who were a driving force against the slave South, proposed an agrarian democratic revolution. They were used, then discarded when their plans became dangerous. Once capitalist control of the national government was consolidated, the Negro, whose rights had been invoked to justify crushing the South, was abandoned to the tender mercy of his former masters.

Industrial capitalism after the Civil War developed at a tremendous rate. It now began to expropriate the new type of small capitalist producers, whom the industrial revolution had encouraged in the earlier stages when capital requirements were still comparatively small. As technology revolutionized old industries and created new ones, the scale of production was steadily enlarged because larger masses of capital equipment were necessary. The accumulation of capital inexorably destroys the conditions of independent enterprise. Either small capitalists became bigger or new capitalists started new and bigger enterprises, or both: but, in either case, it meant the progressive slaughter of small capitalists.

The big producer, moreover, was favored by the freedom of enterprise which capitalism grants alike to all. For the battle of competition was waged by producing goods more cheaply and selling more of them. Cheaper production was secured mainly by using more fixed capital, by means of which relatively fewer workers set in motion greater masses of equipment and raw materials, thereby increasing the productivity of labor. Selling more goods meant securing a larger share of the market. As the scale of production was enlarged, capital requirements moved upward beyond the reach of the small man. Competition encouraged large-scale enterprise, which in turn limited the benefits of free competition to the new gigantic enterprises.

Middle class producers were increasingly harassed and wiped out by the economic effects of the relations and ideals they glorified. An economist, in the 1880's, thus described conditions in Great Britain and the United States:

"Trade after trade is monopolized, not necessarily by large capitalists, but by large capitals. In every trade the standard of necessary size, the minimum establishment that can hold its own in competition, is constantly and rapidly raised. The little men are ground out, and the littleness that dooms men to destruction waxes year by year. Of the [older] cotton mills, a few here and there are standing, saved by local or other accidents, while their rivals have either grown to gigantic size or fallen into ruins. The case of other textile manufacturers is the same or worse still. Steel and iron are yet more completely the monopoly of gigantic plants. The chemical trade was for a long time open to men of very moderate means. Recent inventions threaten . . . utter ruin of the small owners."

Conditions were much more favorable for small storekeepers, as their capital requirements were still small and new opportunities were created by rapid economic growth and the multiplication of distributive services, but large-scale enterprise began to threaten them, too:

"Retail trade, which has been aptly described as, 'until lately, the recourse of men whose character, skill, thrift and ambition won credit, and enabled them to dispense with large capital' . . . in the cities and larger towns [is] being rapidly superseded by vast and skillfully organized establishments." [10]

Economic development was two-faced. It both created and limited opportunities for small enterprisers. A new industry would attract men of small capital, then concentration and competition would destroy most of them. In many fields concentration moved slowly: but it moved. Large-scale industry in its earlier stages multiplied opportunities for small enterprisers, especially in distribution and services, but their position was subservient and precarious. Most favorable were the conditions in the newly developing settlements of the Western regions, where an industrial middle class was reborn as each new area began to move upward economically. But this was increasingly limited by the invasion of large-scale enterprise. Class mobility was still great. But there was more mobility downward than upward, for economic development created more dependent workers than independent enterprisers. It was a mixed situation. The drift, however, was steadily against the independent small enterprisers.

The situation was made worse by the trustification of industry. As concentration enlarged the scale of production, competition became more destructive. Large corporate enterprises combined into trusts to eliminate competition and control production, markets and prices. They were aided by community of interest with the great banks and the railroads (the beginnings of monopoly capitalism) and frequently by legislatures under their corrupt control. The conditions of independent enterprisers became constantly more desperate.

Now the middle class began another great battle against monopoly. In some cases, as in the oil industry, the struggle between the small enterprisers and the big was almost a civil war, in which intimidation and violence were freely used. Beaten on the economic field, the small enterprisers resorted to politics. They tried to break the big capitalist control of legislatures and secure laws in defense of small property.

The farmers, too, joined in the struggle: to oppose, in the words of one of their radical organizations, "the encroachments of concentrated capital and the tyranny of monoply." [11]

Largely because of the settlement of the great Western regions, the number of farmers steadily increased: from 1,449,000 in 1850 to 5,737,000 in 1900.[12] But this multiplication of independent producers (smaller, however, than the increase of propertiless workers) was offset by other factors. There was a distinct tendency toward concentration of landholdings. Hired farm laborers and tenant farmers increased greatly. By the 1890's one-third of the farms were mortgaged and interest rates were usurious. Declining prices and extortionate railroad rates aggravated the burden. The costs of industrialization were largely thrust upon the farmers, whose exports, for example, paid the interest on American imports of foreign capital. Industrial capitalism exploits and degrades agriculture.

The situation was particularly bad in the frontier regions. Where formerly they sustained the society of small producers, they now became a factor in its gradual destruction. The earlier self-sufficient farming was replaced with capitalist farming wholly dependent on far-flung markets. It was increasingly difficult to become an independent farmer, as capital values and equipment mounted upward. Their business largely unprofitable, the farmers hoped for recompense in the speculative rise of values. The frontier regions, moreover, were a vital factor in the development of large capitalist enterprise on a scale undreamt-of in other lands. They were covered by a great network of transcontinental railroads. They provided immense markets for goods and capital, and permitted giant enterprises to enlarge their scale of operations. Where, before the Civil War, agriculture dominated the frontier regions, it was now overpowered by a vast superstructure of manufactures, mining and transportation controlled by the big capitalists. The frontier was swallowed up in the onsweep of industrial and monopoly capitalism which it had itself helped to strengthen.

The labor aspect of these developments was another great increase in propertiless wage-workers (among them many proletarianized small producers), who were rapidly becoming a majority of all persons gainfully occupied. For them, the American dream of the liberty and equality of men owning independent means of livelihood had become the liberty to work for others or starve and the equality of a common dependence on wage servitude. The workers, most of whom now thought simply of improving conditions on the job, organized militant unions in the 1870's-80's and waged great strikes against the capitalist employers. Some workers, however, especially the surviving handicraftsmen, still clung to the ideal of independent small producers: hence the producer's cooperatives advocated by the Knights of Labor. With the formation of the American Federation of Labor the organized workers broke away from the middle class ideal of small producers. If the unions now opposed new types of machinery and concentration, it was in defense of the job, not in defense of the general rights of small property. The Federation was both an advance and a retreat: an advance, as labor separated itself economically from the middle class; a retreat, as exclusive craft unions (ignoring both unskilled labor and the new "white collar" workers) replaced the industrial unions of the Knights of Labor and all independent labor politics was rejected in favor of capitalist "liberal" politics. Yet the unions imposed limitations on the rights of employers in the shops—the initial form of labor's struggle for power. Socialism appeared, proposing to go beyond capitalism to a new social order independent of capitalist control and oppression.

The farmers and small capitalist enterprisers, half-heartedly supported by the workers, set in motion a political struggle against the concentration and trustification of industry. They demanded legislation to avert the doom of small property. The state was to *regulate* the freedom of enterprise and competition *to assure freedom of enterprise and competition:* to limit the rights of property in the interest of small property. This was a formidable shift in the ideas of middle class radicals. *They now urged limitation of the economic freedom which, they formerly believed, was sufficient in itself to realize the economic equality of a society of small producers.* Where

formerly they demanded abolition of all political restrictions and privileges, *they now wanted them
restored in the interest of the independent small
enterpriser.* *

This new "statism" appeared clearly in Populism,
the drag-net of petty-bourgeois discontent and aims.
While Populism urged "cheap money" to ease the
farmers' burdens and prevent foreclosures, its most
important feature was the program of state action
to protect small property. Government ownership
was proposed for "natural" monopolies, such as the
railroads, telephones and telegraph. All other monopolies, primarily the trusts, were to be broken up
to restore conditions of free competition favorable
to small enterprisers. As the exploitation of natural
resources still offered opportunities to the small enterpriser, government was merely to regulate them
in his interest. It was a flexible program, guided
wholly by whether government ownership or regulation or competition would prove most beneficial to
the small enterprisers.

Populism also struck at the concentration of wealth

* Apologists of big capitalist enterprise used Adam Smith's ideas
to argue against state interference with free competition. They conveniently forgot that competition was being destroyed by large-scale
enterprise. Adam Smith himself, moreover, urged some measure of
regulation. While he opposed corporations, favoring small-scale
enterprise, Smith made an exception in the case of banks but
admitted the necessity of regulating them: "Such regulation may,
no doubt, be considered as in some respects a violation of natural
liberty. But those exertions of the natural liberty of a few individuals which might endanger the whole of society are, and ought
to be, restrained by the laws of all governments." (*The Wealth of
Nations*, p. 307.)

and income, which was becoming truly enormous. Millionaires multiplied rapidly and their wealth was beyond the dreams of avarice. Populism proposed by means of inheritance and income taxes, which were violently opposed by the big bourgeoisie, to redistribute wealth and assure more equal incomes. It was a futile effort to revive the old ideal of equality. When, years later and after a great campaign to secure a constitutional amendment, the Populist proposals were enacted into law, the unequal distribution of wealth and income became more unequal. . . .

Populism was rent asunder by inner class weaknesses. It did not stick whole-heartedly to its basic program, but chased after the silver bubble of inflation. Now a minority of the people, the farmers desperately sought the support of the urban middle class, which, however, was itself rent asunder by its antagonistic upper and lower layers. The merger with Bryanism destroyed the class-political integrity of Populism and confused its aims.

While mainly a struggle for survival, the Bryan-Populist revolt had an element of struggle for power: to use the state to restore conditions favoring the small producers. The big bourgeoisie was frightened and massed all its resources against the revolt. Millions were spent to get votes; banks put pressure on small businessmen and farmers; industrial employers threatened to shut down their plants if Bryan was elected; radicals were denounced as criminals, traitors and communists who "should be shot." The coercion made votes for McKinley. Many farmers, moreover, deserted Bryan when the price of wheat began to rise. The revolt was crushed.

With the revival of prosperity in 1897 the concentration and trustification of industry acquired new speed and scope. Anti-trust legislation, adopted earlier under pressure of the middle-class radicals, was unenforced (although used against trade unions!) while the Spanish-American War strengthened the reaction. The multiplication of trusts after 1898 yielded tremendous profits to industrial capitalists, promoters and bankers. By 1904 there were 440 trusts in all fields of economic activity, with a capitalization of $20,000 million: one-third of the capitalization was represented by seven great trusts, over which towered the United States Steel Corporation.[13] Nor was this the only danger to independent enterprise. Underlying the trustification of industry, which was mainly financial in character, was the concentration of industry; technical-economic progress steadily enlarged the size of individual plants, making it still harder for the man of limited capital to become an independent producer.

Large-scale industry, and its expression in trustfication and monopoly, represents a fundamental structural change in capitalism: *the change from personal enterprise to institutional enterprise, to collective forms of economic activity*. In small-scale industry the capitalist producer was personally and directly active in his enterprise: he combined the functions of ownership and management. The functions are completely separated by large-scale industry.

Ownership is vested in a multitude of stockholders who do not manage and management is vested in a multitude of hired managerial and supervisory employees who do not own. Control is usurped by financial oligarchs who operate through the great banks and the great industrial corporations. Industry and the banks merge into a mighty financial mechanism dominated by the oligarchs.

Finance capital, or the "money power" as the middle class radicals called it, made giant strides in the most important fields of industry. By 1912 the dominant financial oligarchy, composed of the House of Morgan, its affiliate the First National Bank and its ally the National City Bank, held 341 interlocking directorships in corporations with total capitalization or resources of $22,245 million.[14] The "money power" represented a tremendous centralization of control over investment capital and credit and their users, over the banks and industry. This overwhelming amalgam was the driving force in the export of capital and imperialism, in the struggle for world markets, now becoming dominant aspects of American capitalist enterprise.

Another battle against monopoly was waged by the middle class in the 1900's. It urged the state to "protect" free competition by means of the intervention and restrictions which once the middle class opposed in the name of free competition. The most decisive of all defeats was the result.

For the battle was now hopeless, as monopoly dominated practically the whole of industry. It was essentially a struggle for mere survival. There was no insistent demand for government ownership (except among the socialists), while the old demand to break up the trusts was modified in favor of "security" for the surviving small producers. Many laws were enacted against "unfair competition." Some trusts were dissolved, only to reappear in new forms. The harassed independent producers now fought only for a "limited" free competition. It was a desperate struggle to regulate monopoly, to permit the man of small capital to survive in fields not yet dominated by the trusts.

Regulation failed to accomplish the middle class aims. The trusts were simply driven to more "legal" and more efficient methods of combination. Although opposed by short-sighted capitalists, some measure of regulation was necessary because of the immensity of monopoly capitalism and the complexity of its relations. Under the prevailing class-economic conditions, regulation meant an increasing merger of monopoly and the state in the interest of the former. This appeared most clearly in the policy of President Theodore Roosevelt, who mobilized popular discontent and action against the trusts while consolidating their power in terms of a stronger unity of state and monopoly.

The final result was another increase of "statism," of the state capitalism with which the middle class replaced its old ideal of "that government is best which governs least." But the monopoly bourgeoisie also resorts to statism, for it increasingly needs the state power to promote its interests, particularly in the imperialist struggle for world markets. The state must perform constantly more economic functions, use the collective resources of society to support capitalist enterprise. State capitalism, monopoly and imperialism become inseparable. By urging state capitalism the middle class called into being new means for its own subjection.

Woodrow Wilson's "new freedom" was the final expression of the middle class revolt. The "new freedom" promised to restore competition and independent small enterprise: "our old variety and freedom and individual energy of development." [15] Great hopes were aroused by the Federal Trade Commission and the Clayton Act, but they were doomed to disappointment. The Federal Reserve System did not destroy control of credit by the "money power," it became more complex, impersonal—and stronger. The "new freedom" ended in more statism, American entry into the imperialist World War, and the final supremacy of monopoly capitalism.

This supremacy was consolidated in the 1920's. Technological changes steadily enlarged the scale of production: mergers and combinations were put through on an unprecedented scale. Monopoly was invigorated by the export of capital and imperialism, which are under control of the great combinations of capital. Never was monopoly as flourishing: never was the government attitude toward it so benevolent.

By 1929 concentration and trustification were overwhelming. In manufactures, 6% of the plants

135

employed 58% of the workers and produced 69% of the output. Concentration was still greater in mining, and greatest of all in railroads and electric power, because of the immense capital requirements. Trustification, which combines scattered plants, outstripped concentration. Thus the 1,349 largest corporations, one-quarter of one per cent of all corporations, received 60% of total corporate net income, as compared with 48% in 1919. Centralization of financial control acquired new magnitude and power. The House of Morgan, its affiliates the Bankers Trust, Guaranty Trust and First National Bank, and its allies the Chase National and National City Banks, held over 2,400 interlocking directorships in corporations with net assets of $74,000 million, 22% of the nation's total corporate assets.[16] This tremendous centralization of financial control, concentrated in the hands of only 167 persons, expressed power over the dominant corporations in all fields of economic activity. The Morgan-Chase-City oligarchy was the most aggressive factor in the American export of capital and imperialism. Monopoly was triumphant and overwhelming.

There was *no* battle against monopoly in the 1920's. The anti-trust laws were practically ignored and only feeble protests were heard. Waged militantly in the 1880's-90's and hopelessly in the 1900's, the battle against monopoly was now abandoned. Yet the economic condition of the two groups which had most aggressively fought monopoly was desperate. Farmers were thrust out of the circle of prosperity, as farm values and prices crashed disastrously. Independent small producers, harried by competition and monopoly, lamented the state of "profitless prosperity." But there was no revolt against monopoly. Its domination was accepted by the middle class.

3

The middle class struggle was hopeless because monopoly arose out of underlying economic conditions. It was not, as in the earlier stages of capitalism, a matter largely of political privilege: monopoly was now rooted in enlargement of the scale of production and mounting capital requirements. To restore the old small-scale industry it would be necessary to break up the great machines, in manufactures, mining, transportation and electric power, created by modern technology. Small producers could survive and multiply only by limiting economic progress and efficiency. The destruction of monopoly, within the relations of capitalism, meant destruction of modern industry itself.

Great structural changes in the middle class, which transformed its composition and significance, made the struggle against monopoly still more futile.

The middle class of the 1820's included a great majority of the American people: small farmers, masters and mechanics in handicraft industry, small traders, all of whom owned independent means of livelihood. Wage-workers, salaried employees and professionals were few and were generally believers in all the middle class ideals. By the 1900's the society of independent producers was almost completely destroyed, while the middle class was a minority of the people and no longer included all its old elements.

Farmers were largely separated from the middle class. Capitalist agriculture destroyed the former unity of the farmers by creating sharply antagonistic class layers among them, with tenants and hired farm laborers becoming the majority. There was no identity of interest between the small farmers, who were still essentially handicraftsmen, and small industrial capitalists, while the upper layer of capitalist farmers accepted the tutelage of the big bourgeoisie. Nor were the farmers now particularly interested in a struggle against monopoly, for they were relatively prosperous because of rising prices. Their "prosperity," however, aggravated the underlying agrarian crisis: it broke in all its fury in the 1920's.

Workers were completely separated economically from the middle class. Many workers approached the lower middle class in their standards of living, but this created no identity of economic interest. The small industrial capitalist was often the worst exploiter of labor and it was difficult to organize workers in small shops. Unions and strikes were opposed by the middle class in the name of liberty, equality and democracy. The virtually final destruction of all handicraftsmen broke completely the old economic link between workers and the lower middle class. Lower salaried employees, especially the clerks, are economically wage-workers, but the trade unions ignored them as they ignored the unskilled workers, because of craft insularity and lack of larger class aims. Only faith in the ideals of the American Dream now linked the workers with the middle class; but socialism was making considerable progress among the workers.

Nor was the middle class any longer composed almost wholly of independent enterprisers. They were now a minority in the class (and a still smaller minority of the people). The slight increase, from 1870 to 1910, in the number of independent enterprisers was accompanied by a large relative decrease. Industrial and monopoly capitalism overwhelmed them.

This increasing destruction of independent enterprisers did not destroy the middle class as a class of intermediate functional groups. For the relations and services created by large-scale industry multiplied the number of salaried employees and professionals. Salaried employees rose from probably 600,000 in 1870 to over 4,500,000 in 1910 or from 5% to 13% of the gainfully occupied; professionals, including teachers and technicians, rose from 414,708 to 2,074,-792, or from 3.3% to 5.4%.[17] These formerly minority elements in the middle class became its majority. *Dependent salaried employees now greatly outnumbered the independent enterprisers*. While most thorough in the United States, changes in the composition of the middle class were almost as great in other highly developed capitalist countries, particularly in Germany and England.

The shrinkage in the old middle class of independent enterprisers and the creation of a "new" middle class of salaried employees was a result of the profound structural changes in capitalism. Economic activity became increasingly collective as large plants, great corporations and far-flung markets replaced small plants, petty personal enterprise and local markets. This complex collective set-up doomed the independent small enterpriser. But it also required increasing numbers of salaried employees to perform his functions and other wholly new functions. As large-scale collective industry separated ownership from management, the directive functions of the former owner-managers were performed by salaried managerial and supervisory employees.* The need of them was augmented by the development of large-scale transportation and distributive services. It was also augmented by the intensive division of labor in modern industry, which created many new supervisory functions. As management became more insti-

* The growing importance of managerial and supervisory employees was foreseen by Karl Marx and Friedrich Engels in *The Communist Manifesto:* "As modern industry develops the petty bourgeoisie sees the moment approaching when it will cease to exist as an independent section of modern society, to be replaced, in manufactures, agriculture and commerce, by managers, superintendents and foremen." While capitalism destroyed one element of the middle class it created another one. The growth of the "new" middle class has been used to prove that Marx was wrong when he prophesied the doom of the middle class. But Marx meant the class of independent small producers, and their economic insignificance today is incontestible. He never prophesied the doom of the elements which compose the "new" middle class. But they are not really a class, merely an aggregation of functional groups wavering between the proletariat and the bourgeoisie of big and small enterprisers, and the overwhelming majority of them are, as we shall see later, economically identified with the working class.

tutional and complex, it increased routine administrative tasks and multiplied the number of clerical
workers. There were scarcely any technicians in
handicraft industry: a whole army of them is necessary in modern industry with its constantly more
complex machines, apparatus and processes. Salaried
employees among professionals increased faster than
the independently self-employed. Finally, the ranks
of salaried employees were swollen by the tremendous growth of government bureaucracy.

As the middle class was no longer composed almost
wholly of independent enterprisers, it was neither
united nor aggressive in the struggle against monopoly. There is no identity of economic interest between independent enterprisers and salaried employees and professionals. Why should the one support
the other? *Most of the salaried employees and professionals were a product of large-scale industry and
directly dependent upon it.* Why should they destroy
their creator in the interest of independent enterprisers? The middle class, in addition to being a
minority of the people, was sharply divided within
itself. The struggle against monopoly resolved itself
into the struggle of a handful of bewildered and dis-
united malcontents against a natural force.

During the 1920's, independent enterprisers became a dwindling percentage of the middle class:
only 30% by 1927. Over two-thirds of the middle
class were dependent salaried employees. The old
middle class of independent small enterprisers was
now too insignificant economically to wage war upon

monopoly, while the "new" middle class was too in-different or too dependent. Salaried employees in the upper middle class were thriving: salaries moved upward, stock bonuses became more generous, and speculative profits were large. Why struggle against monopoly in the best of all possible worlds?

A serious crisis in the middle class was created in the 1870's-90's by the increasing economic weakness of the independent small enterprisers. The severity of the crisis was eased, however, by an absolute increase in their number. This was a result of the great expansion of industry, the lag of concentration in some fields, and the multiplication of distributive services. But the increase came to a standstill in the

Changes in Class Composition, 1909-27

	Independent Enterprisers	Farmers	Salaried Employees	Wage-Workers
1909	3,556,000	6,289,000	4,424,000	19,986,000
1913	3,604,000	6,346,000	5,162,000	21,916,000
1920	3,679,000	6,381,000	6,740,000	23,208,000
1923	3,731,000	6,297,000	7,185,000	24,943,000
1924	3,675,000	6,344,000	7,488,000	25,616,000
1925	3,680,000	6,317,000	7,697,000	26,150,000
1926	3,683,000	6,200,000	7,896,000	26,781,000
1927	3,677,000	6,124,000	8,274,000	27,298,000

Source: Based on W. I. King, *The National Income and Its Purchasing Power*, pp. 56-62.

Independent enterprisers include individual producers, all types of storekeepers and self-employed professionals. Salaried employees include clerical workers and government employees. Wage-workers include hired farm laborers and salespeople in stores.

1900's. *The number of independent enterprisers was practically stationary from 1909 to 1927, while they declined 20% as a proportion of all persons gainfully*

occupied. An upswing of concentration and trustification was the primary cause, aggravated by a down-
swing in the rate of increase in economic activity.

Most significant was *the absolute decrease, for the
first time in American history, in the number of independent producers in manufactures, mining and
construction.* They moved downward from 473,000
in 1909 to 353,000 in 1927,[18] accompanied by a still
greater proportional shrinkage in their output: it
was now insignificant where formerly the output of
small producers was the dominant economic factor.
This sharpened the crisis of the middle class. Nor,
considering the great expansion in trade and services, was there any significant increase in storekeepers and independent professionals.

The economic power of the middle class was
broken, for its former power was based on the small
producers: small enterprisers in trade and the professions have no economic power. The middle class
ideal of a society of small producers, all owning independent means of livelihood, was destroyed: an overwhelming majority of the people were now *dependent*
for their means of livelihood, including most members of the "new" middle class.

Nowhere was the struggle against monopoly waged
as aggressively as in the United States: nowhere was
the middle class as decisively beaten. Yet conditions
were apparently all favorable to the middle class:
no feudalism, vast economic resources, the most complete democracy, competition and freedom of enterprise. They permitted, in the early years of the new

143

American nation, the fullest realization of the ideals of the middle class. Hence its defeat has "an unusual significance," according to one European observer, "because the structure of American economic society offered a unique chance for an attack by the middle class against monopoly capital." [19]

The defeat of the middle class meant the defeat of its ideals of liberty, equality and democracy: they were engulfed in the reactionary onsweep of monopoly capitalism.

It was inevitable that democracy should be undermined. For its form of expression and substantial reality was the *liberty and equality of men owning their independent means of livelihood*. As this condition was destroyed, democracy was limited still more and converted into a fraud and a mockery— as was foreseen by the earlier middle class radicals from Samuel Adams to Jefferson and Jackson, who prophesied that democracy could not survive the appearance of masses of propertiless people.

In addition, monopoly capitalism created a whole series of new and inescapable dependent relations. As the majority of the people are converted into propertiless wage-workers and lower salaried employees, liberty and equality are overwhelmed in the hierarchical organization of corporate industry. Surviving independent enterprisers are practically deprived of all freedom of enterprise. Class stratification becomes final and complete: moving upward from one class to another is wholly exceptional. Authoritarianism increasingly replaces the old liberal ideals. One democratic right after another is limited or destroyed as monopoly tightens its dominion over industry and society.

The reaction is strengthened by imperialism. The subjection of colonial and other economically backward peoples to the ruthless exploitation of monopoly capitalism distorts their economic development and suppresses their progressive democratic forces.* Exploitation and suppression assume the most brutal forms. Nationalism becomes more inflamed and aggressive, militarism mightier and more menacing. The cosmopolitan ideals of free trade and world peace are scrapped in favor of neo-mercantilist restrictions. Monopoly capitalism and imperialism are identified with increasing world reaction. The Ameri-

---

* Monopoly capitalism and imperialism prevent the "normal" development of the middle class in colonial and other economically undeveloped countries. Their industry is discouraged in favor of producing agricultural products and raw materials for export and importing manufactured goods. Monopoly capital develops those industries which dominate an economy and yield super-profits, particularly railroads, electric power and mining. All efforts are used to prevent an agrarian revolution, while agriculture is demoralized by the piecemeal introduction of capitalist farming. Small producers either survive on the old handicraft level or are completely expropriated by the new industrialism. But as this industrialism is now mainly large-scale, requiring great amounts of capital, fewer capitalist small producers appear than was the case in the older countries. Economic development is incomplete and lop-sided. There is no middle class capable of waging a struggle for power and creating democratic traditions. And it may rally to fascism in a futile effort to survive. The struggle for democracy, in colonial and other economically backward countries, becomes involved with the struggle of peasantry and proletariat for the overthrow of capitalism and imperialism. Industrialization, a task fulfilled by capitalism in the older countries, becomes the task of socialism—as in the Soviet Union.

145

can republic in its earlier years pursued a liberal foreign policy, especially in encouraging the Latin-American peoples in their revolt against Spanish rule. Monopoly capitalism and imperialism destroyed that policy. In the 1900's, after the Spanish-American War, a colonial empire was acquired and dominion imposed on the Caribbean republics, while the government's "dollar diplomacy" was wholly imperialist. After the World War, in 1919, American economic power was used to crush the revolts of the masses in Europe. In the 1920's American capital, engaged everywhere in the imperialist struggle for power, aided consolidation of the counter-revolutionary regimes in Mexico, supported brutal dictatorships in Cuba and Venezuela, and provided the money without which Mussolini might have been thrust into oblivion. The outer reaction of imperialism necessarily strengthens the inner reaction.

The reaction against democracy is not limited to the monopolist bourgeoisie. A similar tendency develops in the middle class, formerly the most ardent defender of democracy.

As the old middle class of small producers abandons the struggle against monopoly and strives merely for survival, it increasingly abandons the democratic ideals identified with competition and freedom of enterprise. They are dangerous to survival. Instead of competition and independence and the struggle against monopoly, the small producers (including the more successful self-employed professionals) are now eager for security as a caste within

146

a "controlled" capitalism. Hence the resort to state capitalism and its coercive measures over freedom of enterprise. The class which waged revolutionary war on authoritarianism becomes the defender of a new authoritarianism. This means accepting the dominion of monopoly capitalism and its reaction against democracy. The old liberal ideals are still invoked, but they are infused with a wholly reactionary content.

Because of its indeterminate position, the "new" middle class of salaried employees is divided. It has no single clear-cut attitude. The upper layers of this "new" class, especially the higher managerial, supervisory and technical employees in corporate industry, are wholly identified with monopoly capitalism and its reactionary aims. They, too, want security as a caste. They despise the workers and lower salaried employees. The financial oligarchs depend upon them to manage and exploit industry. These upper layers of salaried employees uphold imperialism: it is an inseparable aspect of monopoly capitalism and it means the export of many employees (and professionals) to colonial and other economically undeveloped countries, where they get privileged positions in the enterprises of their imperialist masters. They assimilate the authoritarianism of the monopolist bourgeoisie.

The masses of lower salaried employees (including the more unsuccessful independent professionals), the great majority in the "new" middle class, waver between democracy and reaction. Forces are set in motion by the big bourgeoisie and the upper middle class to "sell" them security as a minor caste in a new reactionary set-up. The lower salaried employees may respond, for their ideology is still largely middle class. But their concrete economic interests drive them in an opposite direction: toward the working class.

In its revolutionary youth the middle class saw in democracy the means of realizing its interests and ideals. But out of democracy came the liberation of forces which destroyed democracy and the independent small property on which it was based. The middle class moved toward a democratic restoration, whose final American expression was pre-war progressivism. This movement capitalized the discontent aroused by hard times, the increasing stratification of class lines and the declining faith in democracy. Progressivism of all types was futile in its democratic and reformist aims. A democratic restoration was impossible by tinkering with political forms, for the basis of democracy had been destroyed as most people were now propertiless dependents on big property. Many elements in the middle class, especially the independent small enterprisers, were bitterly opposed to reform legislation because it meant an increase in taxation. The most significant aspect of progressivism, particularly as revealed in the ideals and personality of Theodore Roosevelt, was *the identification of democracy and middle class interests with the acceptance of "regulated" monopoly, a state capitalism dependent on bureaucracy and caste, and an*

148

aggressive nationalism and imperialism. Petty-bour-geois democracy was reacting against itself.

The reaction against democracy was invigorated by the upthrust of the labor movement. As they began to coalesce as a class, the workers, brutally exploited by the new capitalism, turned the ideals of liberty, equality and democracy against the bourgeoisie. They fought and secured democratic rights. They used the rights to form trade unions and strike, to limit the employer's power over the job. This partial limitation became absolute in the socialist program, which proposed abolition of the employer; class and socialization of industry. Socialism was in practice, however, primarily a radical democratic movement. Its main source of strength was the struggle for democracy, in which it saw the means for the gradual realization of socialism. Organized labor became the main support of democracy under capitalism. But as labor used democratic rights to struggle for reforms within the general relations of capitalism, the limitation of democracy was urged to curb the "arrogance" of labor. Now, as labor uses democratic rights to organize its forces for the overthrow of capitalism, the fascist destruction of democracy is urged to crush the "pretensions" of labor.

Anti-democratic and authoritarian ideals are used to impose an artificial unity on the middle class and mobilize it against labor. The unity is artificial because merely ideological, and it is merely ideological because there is no underlying unity of economic in-

149

terests. Those interests clash all the more sharply as the crisis of the middle class becomes more acute. The disunity created by diversity of interests is irreconcilable.

Chapter VII

TODAY: A SPLIT PERSONALITY

THE struggle for survival against monopoly capital clearly revealed the growing disunity of the middle class. And the disunity is still growing. The middle class today is wholly a split personality, tormented by the clash of discordant interests.

Never completely a unity, always of mixed intermediate composition, the middle class was most unified when it appeared in the twilight of feudalism. After the first transformation, which converted the middle class into a petty bourgeoisie, the number of antagonistic elements multiplied. But a fundamental identity of interests underlay all the antagonisms:

Economically, the middle class was united as a class of small enterprisers by the ownership of property, of independent means of livelihood.

Politically, the middle class was united by the ideals of liberty, equality and democracy, an expression of the struggle to insure the rights of small property and the conditions of its acquisition.

To these positive factors of unity was added the negative factor of opposition to the big bourgeoisie. The opposition was limited by acceptance of the social relations of capitalist production; it was beset by compromise, often betrayed by the upper middle class, and increasingly abandoned by the class as a whole. But opposition was always at least potential, and a unifying factor, because it met the needs of independent small property.

All the factors of unity were destroyed by the second transformation of the middle class. Large-scale corporate industry doomed the independent small enterprisers, who became relatively scarce, while it multiplied salaried employees and professionals. This transformation deprived the middle class of all class-economic unity. It became completely a mere aggregation of intermediate groups, whose fundamental economic interests are not identical.

Independent enterprises are now a minority of the middle class. Most of its members are propertiless salaried employees who possess no independent means of livelihood. Small property is a rarity. Surviving small enterprisers are split into antagonistic groups. There is no united or aggressive opposition to the big bourgeoisie. Many of the newer elements in the middle class are directly dependent upon monopoly capital and accept its supremacy. The economic interests of small producers and salaried employees clash, for they have nothing in common except the myth of belonging to the same class. As the surviving small producers struggle for "security" within the limits of monopoly capitalism, they become wholly reactionary and mobilize the middle class against the old ideals of liberty, equality and democracy. Yet only the realization of those ideals *in new and higher forms* can promote the interests of the "new" middle class of socially useful salaried and professional groups, most of whom are economically part of the working class.

Ideological lag, the longing for things past but not forgotten, and the anti-democratic reaction may impose an artificial unity. But they cannot make whole the split personality created by the new composition of the middle class, which is significantly different from the old.

No longer can the middle class unreservedly claim the farmers, one of the most important of its former elements. The farmer is a petty bourgeois where he is still an independent enterpriser. But his interests are not identical with those of the industrial small producer, except in the general sense of property ownership. Nor are all farmers owners of independent property: 2,660,000 or 42% of them in 1930 were propertiless tenants.[1] Many other farmers are practically propertiless because of the mortgages that burden their lands. Farm bankruptcies tripled during the 1922-29 prosperity. Absentee ownership grows. Concentration is increasing slowly but steadily, favored by the more intensive mechanization of agriculture. By 1930, 20% of the crop lands were harvested by a handful of big farms of 500 acres up; 50% of the farmers produced only 10% of the cash crops. "If natural forces were permitted to operate— a free market, the growing pressure of fixed charges, foreclosures and bankruptcies—many of the 3,000,-000 small and inefficient farmers would be driven off their holdings and added to the industrial unem-

153

ployed." [2] Capitalism has thrust the majority of farmers down to the level of a pauperized peasantry. Class divisions are becoming constantly sharper. The farmers are divided into an upper capitalist layer of 300,000, an intermediate or middle class layer of 1,600,000 and a lower or semi-proletarian layer of 4,300,000 poorer tenants and owners. The pauperized elements in agriculture become overwhelming if the 2,600,000 hired farm laborers are included. They have nothing in common with the middle class.

All independent small enterprisers in industry, trade and the professions are clearly part of the middle class. They were formerly its dominant elements. But what of salaried employees? Although most of them are economically in the category of wage-workers, they were always part of the middle class and their proletarianization proceeded within its circle. Hence, salaried employees must all be assigned, provisionally, to the middle class, thus including all its former elements except the farmers. The upper income limit of the middle class is set at $10,000 yearly; all independent enterprisers, salaried employees and professionals with higher incomes (a trifling number) are included in the big bourgeoisie.

As broadly defined the American middle class, in 1930, had 12,500,000 members or 25.6% of all persons gainfully occupied, compared with 28,500,000 wage-workers, or 58.5%.[3] While the proportions may differ, the middle class is a minority of the people in all highly developed capitalist countries. In England, in 1924, wage-workers constituted 76% of the gainfully occupied and the middle class 22%, with the farmers a negligible quantity.[4] Proletarianization of the people is overwhelming.

More significant than the minority character of the middle class is the heterogeneity of the elements which compose it. They create the split personality. The 1930 composition of the American middle class clearly reveals the heterogeneity:

Independent small enterprisers in manufactures, mining, construction and transportation, including small corporations owned by one or two persons: 600,000.

Small enterprisers in trade, including all types of storekeepers: 1,500,000.

Small enterprisers in all other fields, including brokers, a variety of other occupations, and 500,000 independently employed professionals: 1,200,000.*

Professionals, independent and salaried, including physicians, dentists, nurses, welfare workers, librarians, photographers, intellectuals and 1,000,000 teachers: 2,500,000.

Managerial and supervisory employees in industry and trade, including minor officers, managers, superintendents, foremen, overseers and inspectors, among them some duplication of professionals and technicians: 1,500,000.

Technicians, including engineers, chemists, architects and draftsmen, 450,000.

* The total of independent enterprisers is 3,300,000. Edwin G. Nourse, *America's Capacity to Consume* (1934),' p. 31, estimates them at 3,200,000 in 1929. The estimate of Simon Kuznets, *The National Income, 1929-32* (1934), p. 33, is 3,268,000 for 1930.

Clerical employees, including clerks, stenographers, typists, bookkeepers and cashiers: 4,000,000.

Public service, including duplication of teachers and some professionals, technicians and clerical employees: 2,500,000.

All other, including salesmen, canvassers, collectors and all types of agents: 1,000,000.[5]

Of the 12,500,000 members of the middle class, only 3,300,000, or 26%, were independent enterprisers. They were a still smaller proportion, only 6.7%, of all persons gainfully occupied. But that was in 1930. They were decimated by the depression, 395,-000 in the two years 1931-32 alone.[6] Today there are probably not more than 2,700,000 independent small enterprisers, not much over 5% of the gainfully occupied.* The vast majority of the people are dependent on jobs for their means of livelihood.

Of the 3,300,000 independent enterprisers, only 2,100,000 were engaged in industry and trade—a strikingly insignificant proportion of the gainfully occupied. Their economic insignificance is still more striking.

Economic activity is dominated by corporations, an expression of the collective forms of modern industry. Many small enterprises are incorporated, but their weight in the economic set-up is inconsiderable.

---

* By adding the 3,500,000 farmers who in 1930 owned their farms, the total of independent enterprisers of all types becomes 6,800,000, or only 14% of all persons gainfully occupied. But that was in 1930, and the total included 300,000 capitalist farmers, 650,000 farmers who were only part owners, and many farmers who, because of heavy mortgages, were merely nominal owners.

In 1929, the smaller corporations with net income below $10,000, roughly 70% of the total, received only 5% of all corporate net income. At the other end of the scale 1,349 giant corporations, 0.26% of the total, received 60% of all corporate net income. The same insignificance appears among non-corporate small enterprisers: only 228,475 of them, three-quarters in trade and services, had average profits as high as $8,000. In manufactures, 144,648 small establishments employed only 10% of the workers and produced only 6% of the total output.[7] A roughly similar situation exists in mining and construction, while concentration in the field of transportation is overwhelming. The small producers in the middle class are economically insignificant crushed by the massed strength of large corporate capital.

Their dependence on big corporations and the banks emphasizes the economic insignificance of the small producers. Most of them must buy raw materials from big corporations whose terms favor other big corporations. The whole output of many small producers is bought by big manufacturing corporations or chain store systems, who often arbitrarily set prices at unprofitable levels. New products constantly encroach on the surviving markets of small producers. They are confined more and more to the nooks and crannies of industry. Banks discriminate against them. Their exploitation is a necessary condition of the monopoly profits of big capital. The independent small producers, deprived of all power, are incapable of economic resistance to monopoly capitalism.

The situation is not much better among independent small enterprisers in retail trade. Storekeepers have been favored by the lag of concentration in their field and by the multiplication of distributive services. Yet, in 1929, 25% of the stores did 75% of the business. Over one-half of the storekeepers did an average yearly business of only $12,000; nearly one-third of all storekeepers did a business of less than $5,000.[8] The profit on even a business of $12,000 could not yield a comfortable living; the plight of the smaller storekeepers drove them to exploit mercilessly all members of the family. Their desperate struggle for survival was made worse by the inexorable growth of chain stores, which in 1929 did 21% of all the retail business:[9] the percentage of the chains is now much higher, for 500,000 independent storekeepers were wiped out by the depression. Concentration once lagged in retail trade; since 1920 it has been making up for lost time.

Concentration becomes greater, too, in the field of general services. Amusements, especially the motion pictures, are dominated by giant corporations. Professional services are being organized by corporate and government enterprises, converting increasingly larger numbers of professionals into salaried employees. In these fields, too, opportunity no longer beckons generously to the man who would be independent.

The middle class of small producers is now merely

a vestigial survival. Small-scale industry is doomed by the inexorable trend toward collective forms of economic activity. Hence the middle class is no longer, as it was in the earlier stages of capitalism, the carrier of progressive economic forces. For the interests of small producers now demand the limitation of technical-economic progress.

Insignificant, therefore, as a class of small producers and other independent enterprisers, the middle class as broadly defined is now overwhelmingly a class of dependent salaried employees. Of the 12,-500,000 members in 1930, 9,200,000, or 75%, were working for salaries. Excluding the farmers, all independent small enterprisers and the big bourgeoisie, there were 37,750,000 men and women, 77% of all persons gainfully occupied, who were dependent on jobs for their means of livelihood: 75% of them were wage-workers and 25% salaried employees. It is a complete reversal of conditions in the early years of the American republic. Wherever capitalism is highly developed it is the same: the middle class is a minority of salaried employees, who are a minority of all dependent workers. The proportions were 84% wage-workers and 16% salaried employees in England (1924) and 77% and 23% in Germany (1925).[10] Capitalism deprives the mass of the people of independent means of livelihood: proletarianization is the accompaniment of economic progress.*

* The proportions vary in different countries according to the stage of economic development. France has a larger middle class of the old type and a smaller proportion of wage-workers and salaried employees. This is still truer in economically backward coun-

Salaried employees and "new" middle class are practically identical, for most of the professionals are becoming salaried dependents. Of the 9,700,000 members of the "new" middle class in 1930 (including self-employed professionals), 95% were salaried employees. The percentage is now higher.

The great increase in salaried employees began after the 1860's with the upswing of concentration and trustification, of collective forms of economic activity. For some time they increased more rapidly than the wage-workers. From 1909 to 1920 the number of salaried employees rose from 4,424,000 to 6,740,000, or 52%, three times the rate of increase in all persons gainfully occupied. That was, however, the crest of the upward movement: it slowed down almost to a standstill in the ensuing years. From 1920 to 1927 the number of salaried employees rose from 6,740,000 to 8,274,000: an increase of only 23%, about the same as the rate of increase in all persons gainfully occupied.[11] But the slowing down was not offset by an increase in independent enterprisers, for they were fewer by 2,000 in 1927 than in 1920. Wage-workers again became the fastest growing group.

This slowing down in the growth of salaried employees was significant for two reasons: it meant a restriction of opportunity for salaried employees, and

tries. But in these countries the middle class of small producers is overwhelmed by an alien monopoly capitalism and imperialism. It is necessary, for tactical purposes, to make a concrete analysis of the composition of the middle class in each separate country.

it created the beginnings of a crisis of employment in the "new" middle class.

Concentration and trustification went on at an unusual rate in 1920-29, while superstructural enterprises in trade and services multiplied rapidly. This, in the past, meant an increase in salaried employees. Now it did not. It did not because scientific management, the most efficient and merciless methods of exploitation formerly reserved almost exclusively for wage-workers, invaded the field of salaried employees. Their displacement in manufactures was larger than the displacement of wage-workers. Increasing efficiency from 1919 to 1929 displaced 2% of the wage-workers and 6% of the salaried employees.[12] That actually meant a displacement of probably 10% of clerical and other lower salaried employees, as the number of officers rose steadily.

A larger reserve of salaried labor was created by this restriction of employment opportunities. Supply outran demand. Students in universities, colleges and professional schools rose from 460,000 in 1920 to 925,000 in 1930; students in high schools, most of them candidates for clerical employment, scored a still greater increase.[13] This meant an overproduction of educated workers and more pressure on the employment, remuneration and working conditions of lower salaried employees. It also meant more intellectual proletarians, larger numbers of men and women who cannot find the work for which they have been educated. The crisis of employment among

161

salaried employees was hidden by the speculative prosperity of the 1920's, and the accompanying bally-hoo. It was blindingly revealed by their plight during the depression and after.

The crisis of the "new" middle class is a wholly new development. All previous crises affected only the small producers, not the salaried employees, who kept on multiplying while assured employment and some hope of higher incomes. Now there are *two* crises: one of property and one of employment. The crisis of the middle class affects all its elements.

And the crisis is now permanent. It is permanent for two reasons: the downward movement of economic activity and employment, because the decline of capitalism results in a sharpening of the class-economic antagonisms which create the split personality of the middle class. No longer are the antagonisms eased by the upward movement of economic activity and employment. The antagonisms are inflamed by the crisis of capitalism and of the middle class.

The old middle class was split by one major antagonism, that between its upper and lower layers. But it was unified by the preponderance of independent enterprisers and their opposition to the big bourgeoisie. Now, however, although there are many independent enterprisers in the upper middle class, *it is dominated by the higher managerial and supervisory employees in large-scale corporate industry, whose interests are opposed to independent enter-*

162

prisers. They support monopoly capitalism.* They are identified with the big bourgeoisie and carry out its policy of crushing the independents. The old antagonism assumes new forms and becomes more acute.

Nor are the middle class enterprisers themselves united. Many of the independent producers, especially those in the upper middle class, are wholly dependent on monopoly capital and are not averse to crushing their brethren to survive. The larger independent storekeepers use the most ruthless competitive measures against the smaller. Both have more in common with monopoly capital than with the small enterprisers.

Formerly the lower middle class was in fundamental accord with the upper layers, for they were all independent enterprisers "on the make." Now, however, the lower middle class is composed overwhelmingly of salaried employees, whose chances of moving upward are slim. That splits the two layers still more sharply. It involves, moreover, a larger and wholly new antagonism in the middle class: *the antagonism between the majority of dependent salaried employees and the minority of independent enterprisers.* The antagonism has two primary forms:

* Another support of monopoly capitalism are the rentiers, an indeterminate number of whom is scattered throughout the middle class. As their livelihood depends exclusively on interest and dividends, the rentiers are a conservative force yearning for social "peace" and "security." Their gentility is scornful of independent small enterpriser and salaried employee alike. They accept all the anti-democratic and authoritarian ideals of the big bourgeoisie. Rentiers are another element in the split personality of the middle class.

163

Salaried employees are exploited almost as mercilessly as wage-workers where they are employed by independent small enterprisers. Nor is their position any longer a transition toward becoming economically independent. Their dependent employment and exploitation are permanent and absolute.

Salaried employees, especially those working for great corporations, have nothing in common with the independent small enterprisers who propose to destroy or limit the collective economic activity of large-scale industry. For, within the limits of capitalist relations, the interests of most of the salaried employees are identical with the corporate industry which created and employs them. Any change, to prove beneficial, must go beyond the relations of capitalist production, whether small scale or large.

The antagonism between salaried employees and enterprisers, which includes the problem of propertiless majority and propertied minority,* is now the major antagonism in the middle class. It destroys all identity of economic interests between old and new elements. The clash of immediate interests is sharp and irreconcilable. The clash of final interests is still sharper and more irreconcilable. *For the old middle class of independent small enterprisers represents the outworn system of economic individualism which cannot be restored: the "new" middle class of salaried employees represents the dominant system of economic collectivism which must decline and*

* This subject is discussed more fully in Chapter X, "Propertiless: Why Defend Property?"

164

decay unless it moves onward to new and higher forms. The clash of interests involves a clash of economic systems. Hence the middle class is not really a class, as its major groups are economically different and antagonistic. The split personality is incurable.

But neither is the "new" middle class of salaried employees a whole personality. It, too, is split by antagonisms.

The conception of the "new" middle class as a "new Third Estate" [14] is unsound. For the Third Estate, in the struggle against feudalism, was a class which represented definite interests and a new economic order *in terms of its own composition and significance.* The Third Estate was the new bourgeois class and it was wholly for the new economic order of capitalism. There might be differences, but the issue was clear: feudalism must be overthrown. That is not true of the "new" middle class of salaried employees. It is, as the creation of economic collectivism, identified with the objective basis of a new social order, but it is irreconcilably split on the issue. The upper layers, especially the higher managerial and supervisory employees, are entangled in all the exploiting relations of monopoly capitalism: they serve the old order as a privileged caste. If and when their economic interests drive the masses of lower salaried employees (and professionals) to struggle for a new social order, they must necessarily unite with the larger class of the proletariat. The struggle for a new social order proceeds outside the circle of the middle class, whether old or new.

165

Upper and lower layers are sharply split, too, on immediate interests and issues. Of the 9,200,000 salaried employees in 1930, not more than 1,500,000 had incomes of $3,000 up. The great majority had incomes below that amount: an average of $1,800 among all of them and a miserable $1,400 among clerical employees.[15] Standards of living differ as sharply, of course, as the incomes; the standards of the masses of lower salaried employees are not much higher than those of wage-workers, while the more skilled workers have higher standards than most of the lower salaried employees. More important than income, however, is the split created by function. For the small upper layer, composed mainly of the higher managerial and supervisory employees, must perform the function of exploiting the lower salaried employees, precisely as the workers are exploited. Office managers must drive the clerical workers and beat down their salaries, as much as plant foremen must drive the manual workers and beat down their wages: and both must prevent or break strikes, if necessary. The upper and lower layers of salaried employees have nothing in common except the term "salaried."

Nor are the professionals united economically. Among them, too, there is a sharp diversity in incomes and standards of living; and, in addition, they are split three ways. Of the 2,500,000 professionals, not more than 500,000 are independently employed in their own personal enterprises. Most of them are dependent salaried employees, often mercilessly ex-

166

ploited by the independent professionals who employ them. And salaried professionals are split into upper and lower layers: a small minority of the better paid, often performing managerial and supervisory functions, and the majority who are economically on the level of wage-workers. There is, of course, a professional identity of interests. But it cannot overcome the economic antagonism of interests, and it is shamelessly used by the independent and higher salaried professionals, who degrade their craft function for purposes of capitalist exploitation, to keep in subjection their lower salaried brethren.

Every profession has its own peculiar antagonisms. Two of them may be cited to illustrate the general situation.

The more prosperous practitioners of medicine, especially those who become fat on the ills of the rich, are bitterly opposed to the cooperative organization of medical services for the mass of the people. Yet this would be of the utmost value to the people and to the physicians with low incomes or no income at all. The more prosperous practitioners disregard the interests of their brethren and the craft function of their profession.

Antagonistic interests split the class-room teachers and the superintendents. Rates of pay are grossly disproportionate. Political favoritism is demoralizing. The superintendents, who usurp the right to speak in the name of the teachers, are creatures of the usually crooked school boards dominated by politicians. Teachers are enmeshed in a network of

167

dependent and humiliating relations and their rights and interests are ignored. Moreover, educational ideals are involved, for superintendents carry out the most reactionary policies and trample upon academic freedom.

Where is the unity in this welter of discordant interests? The unity of upper and lower middle class? Of independent enterprisers and salaried employees? Of independent professionals and dependent salaried professionals? Of upper and lower layers among the salaried? Of propertied minority and propertiless majority? No unity of action is possible where economic interests clash so sharply. To protect property, to save the independent enterprisers, to beat down salaries and maintain profits and the salaries of high officials: all this strikes directly at the interests of the masses in the lower middle class. If this is unity, then there is unity in bedlam.

And there *must* be disunity, for the middle class is not a class. It has no identity of *class* economic interests in terms of a definite mode of production, or economic order. The middle class, it must be emphasized, represents two very different and antagonistic economic systems. Independent enterprisers are identified with the old capitalism of small-scale industry. Salaried employees are identified with the new capitalism of large-scale industry, *whose collective forms of economic activity are the objective basis of a new social order*. The class disunity is sharpened by the caste privileges of the higher salaried employees, who cling tenaciously to monopoly capitalism.

168

They struggle to preserve the old order, and are joined by independent enterprisers hoping to survive. But all the interests of the lower salaried employees are identified with the new social order whose economic forms already exist in collectivism. Thus the clash of immediate interests becomes, particularly as the crisis of the middle class deepens, a clash of final interests: for or against a new social order.

The antagonisms in the middle class make unity impossible. They make it impossible to get up a concrete program of action which represents *all* interests. The antagonisms must be covered up. Hence the "unity" of negation: against democracy, against labor, against a new social order. Hence the "unity" of reactionary ideals: for authoritarianism, for nationalism, for war. The artificial unity serves the barbaric purposes of monopoly capitalism and imperialism.

But there is a factor of unity within the disunity: *the economic collectivism which split the middle class and created the objective forms of a new social order.* The destroyer of the old unity may become the basis of a new unity, *if* the causes and implications of the disunity are recognized.

Collectivism has split the middle class. Collectivism has created the economic forms of a new social order. But part of the middle class, the smaller part, clings to the old capitalist order: independent enterprisers hoping to survive, higher salaried employees who are a caste in the set-up of monopoly capitalism. Their immediate and final interests are opposed to

169

those of the lower salaried employees, who are propertiless, dispossessed and dependent, and whose interests are wholly identified with the transformation of collectivism into a new social order. Instead of an artificial reactionary "unity," more disunity as the means of forging a new unity *outside* the middle class. The lower salaried employees (including professionals) must split off consciously from the middle class, as they are already split off economically; they must accept the social implications of collectivism and unite, with the workers and poorer farmers, in a new struggle for power against the big bourgeoisie: for a new social order.

Chapter VIII

MIDDLE CLASS AND COLLECTIVISM

OUTWORN ideas die hard. They linger as ghosts in the minds of men and seriously affect social action. Thus people still speak of economic individualism and of capitalism as "essentially" middle class.[1] Yet both have been overwhelmed by impersonal and institutional forms of enterprise, by the economic collectivism which gives creative unity and meaning to the changes wrought by industrial and monopoly capitalism, including the transformation of the middle class.

1

Capitalism is today dominated by collectivism. The fact is indisputable, however the interpretations of its significance may vary. Recently a Commission of the American Historical Association reported that "the age of individualism and laissez-faire in economy and government is closing and a new age of collectivism is emerging." The conclusion was amplified by an educational journal:

"New forms of communication, transportation and production have literally destroyed the individualistic economy of the early years of the republic. In place of the relatively independent and self-contained

171

households and rural neighborhoods of the Jeffersonian era, the American people stand today before a vast and complicated economic mechanism embracing the entire country and reaching out increasingly to the far corners of the globe—a *fait accompli* having the most revolutionary consequences." [2]

A liberal member of the fraternity of economists, most of whom still ignore the dominant collectivism of our age, writes:

"Almost unobserved, there has appeared the great collectivism of business. Its technical activities have already been socialized. . . . In the cooperative enterprise each person has his place: to it he brings his mite of service or of property and from it he takes the wealth and the waste which make up his living. Apart from the great industry the individual cannot live his life; from its dominion there is no escape. . . . The commitment to collectivism is beyond recall." [3]

Modern capitalism means more than merely new ways of working and new ways of enterprise. It means more than the great technology, the dominion of large-scale production, industrial concentration and trustification, the complex technical, economic and administrative relations. For all these aspects are unified in collective forms of economic activity: the collectivism of *a new economic set-up* which marks a profound change in the anatomy of capitalism.

Collectivism is sharply opposed to the economic individualism of the earlier stages of capitalism. The old social relations still prevail, but the economic forms underlying them have become significantly different.

Individualism was the motive force of the society of small producers in the America of the 1820's. A largely self-sufficient agriculture, with its masses of independent farmers, was the dominant economic activity. Industry was relatively unimportant; and it was, including the new factory system, still in the small-scale stage. Enterprise, ownership and responsibility were overwhelmingly personal. All these conditions created economic relations of a simple and direct nature. Institutional, or collective, interference of large-scale enterprise scarcely existed. Wageworkers were multiplying rapidly and the big bourgeoisie was acquiring new forms and power, but their threat was still largely in the future. Independent property and small-scale enterprise were the source of economic individualism, personal independence and social mobility.

This society of independent small producers was destroyed by large-scale industry and the collective forms of economic activity which it developed. The struggle for survival of the old society and its individualism was a struggle against the inexorable forces of economic collectivism.

Collectivism is a great inescapable result of the massing of productive equipment and labor in large plants. This industrial concentration is a technological necessity, for the most efficient equipment is unusable in small plants. The logical result is a massing of cooperative labor. In 1929, 200 plants employed 1,000,000 wage-workers, and 2,700 plants employed 3,300,000.[4] They employed, in addition, 150,000 and 500,000 salaried employees, respectively. But the centralization of control over labor was much greater, for many of the plants were part of a larger corporate dominion. Thus, ten giant corporations ruled over 1,000,000 employees, the United States Steel Corporation alone over 250,000. The railroads, dominated by a dozen great systems, employed 1,600,000 workers.[5] This immense massing of equipment and labor, undreamt-of in the earlier capitalism of independent small-scale industry, is almost as great in England and Germany as in the United States, and, to a lesser degree, in other capitalist countries.

There is no individualism in the labor of production: the workers must conform to the rhythm of the machine and the discipline of its organizational relations. The intensive division of labor means the compulsory cooperation of labor in an interconnected series of collective forms of productive activity. Management itself is the collective function of a hierarchy of hired functionaries. Employees are cogs in a wheel; wheels within wheels drive the mechanism of production. The whole is a complex of interdependent relations arising out of the increasingly social character of labor.

A vivid illustration of the great change from individualism to collectivism may be seen in the laboratories of great corporations. Research and invention were once the personal activity of individuals work-

174

ing on their own. Now they are the collective activity of hired employees who work in corporate laboratories, using the most costly equipment. Research and invention are organized and objectives are planned; invention, and the individual and "accidental" activity of thousands of obscure inventors, is today the institutionalized activity of large corporations which appropriate the results. Research and invention have become a part of collective mass production.

Over the massing of equipment and labor towers the structure of impersonal corporate organization. The production of raw materials and the manufacture and distribution of goods involve one series of collective forms of economic activity after another. Plants secure materials and sell their goods in far-flung markets, often in the most remote corners of the world. Production is separated from distribution by a network of intermediate institutions and relations. Organization and planning are required on a large scale, the collective activity of many workers and many minds moving together toward determined ends. Personal enterprise is impossible because it is now economically institutional. It is replaced by the collective enterprise of corporations: they concentrate scattered capital resources and unite labor, talents and wills. The corporation is an impersonal institution whose owners, the multitude of stockholders, are separated from direct economic activity in the enterprise they own but neither manage nor control. Investment itself is now largely institutional, wholly independent of personal initiative: banks and insurance companies invest people's savings, while corporations normally save and re-invest (as surplus) up to one-half of their earnings. Banks and the credit system tie together the innumerable threads of economic activity and mobilize *social* resources for the *private* profit of capitalist enterprise: they are the final expression of the dominant collectivism.*

There are still some survivals of economic individualism. But they exist miserably and precariously in the nooks and crannies of a world of economic collectivism. The personal enterprise of independent small producers is subservient to the larger corporations, from whom materials are bought and to whom goods are often sold. They are all engulfed in the complex relations of the market. Moreover, the survivals of small-scale enterprise today are often large and collective as compared with the earlier stages of capitalism. The survivals of small personal enterprise are mainly in agriculture and trade, but they, too, are dominated by collectivism. Farmers and storekeepers are entangled in all the relations of corporate activity and the market. Farms become

* Industrial concentration and the practical disappearance of independent small enterprise are the solid basis of collectivism in economically highly developed countries. It is somewhat different in economically backward countries, where independent enterprise (much of it handicraft) is still dominant because of the lopsided development fostered by monopoly capitalism and imperialism. But there, too, collectivism is inescapable: the collective enterprise of railroads, public utilities, large plants in basic industries, banks: the dependence on the collective relations of the world market. An extremely unstable situation is created by the relations of monopoly capitalism imposed on an incomplete economic foundation.

larger and capital requirements still larger because of mechanization: one result is the increase of hired farm labor, another the increase in collective agricultural activity, and a third the greater productivity which (under capitalism!) dooms half the farmers to pauperization or displacement from the land. Storekeepers are threatened more and more by the chain stores, whose conquests in a field formerly considered the final bulwark of personal enterprise are the most significant recent expression of collectivism. (Chain store systems are under control of the masters of finance capital, including the House of Morgan.) The surviving independent enterprisers in agriculture and trade are forced to resort to self-defensive collective measures: agricultural cooperatives for mutual selling and the "voluntary chains" of small storekeepers for mutual buying.

Collectivism splits the personality of independent enterprise. It is neither wholly personal nor wholly collective, and it is impaled on both horns of the contradiction. This tragedy of the independent small enterpriser is an expression of the tragedy of a world of economic collectivism which still clings to the social relations of economic individualism. . . .

The immense scope and power of collectivism are strikingly revealed in the resources of the larger American corporations. In 1930, 200 non-banking corporations had assets of $81,000 million, or one-half of all such assets: [6] *nearly four times the total national wealth of Italy and roughly equal to the total national wealth of the United States in 1900.*

177

The handful of giant corporations included the dominant factors in all fields of enterprise: mining, manufactures, public utilities, transportation, amusements and trade. They disposed of immense masses of capital and millions upon millions of workers. Their complex network of cooperative institutional relations represents a vast collectivization of economic activity, the most significant aspect of capitalism in terms of the future.

2

Collectivism is inseparably identified with the transformation of the middle class. For the new capitalist set-up has produced many changes in class composition and relations, among them the emergence of the proletariat as the majority class and the replacement of industrial capitalists by the financial oligarchy as the dominant class. Collectivism and the transformation of the middle class are the joint result of the same economic changes, whose destructive and constructive aspects merge in a contradictory unity.

The destructive *class* aspect of collectivism is the practical extinction of independent small enterprisers: the constructive aspect is the creation of a new "class" of dependent salaried employees who perform economically useful functions.

The destructive *social* aspect of collectivism is the practical abolition of the economic individualism of the earlier capitalism: the constructive aspect is the

178

creation of an economic set-up which represents the objective basis of a new social order.

Thus collectivism and the transformation of the middle class, in their final unity, merge in the movement toward a new social order.

Collectivism is clearly responsible for the practical abolition of the old middle class of independent small enterprisers, for they are wholly identified with the economic individualism of small-scale industry. Their doom is not the result of malevolence, personal incapacity, unfair competition, or misguided legislation. Underlying their doom is the drive of industry toward the more efficient collective forms of economic activity.*

Collectivism is as clearly responsible for the creation of the "new" middle class of salaried employees. Since the 1870's the movement in the numbers of salaried employees and independent enterprisers has been significantly complementary: one up, the other down. A professional economist thus sets forth the relation:

---

* It is often argued that large-scale industry may exceed the optimum size capable of yielding the greatest efficiency. That is very often true, but the optimum is always beyond the limit of small-scale enterprise. Another argument is that electric power permits a decentralization of industry. That is true, but it would not mean a restoration of petty industry. Moreover, decentralization is impossible under capitalism because of its predatory vested interests and its inability planfully to unite industry and agriculture. A new social order would realize a large measure of decentralization, within, however, the flexible and creative collectivism of the unity of all industry and labor. And it would destroy the network of dependent relations which merely serves the exploiting needs of monopoly capitalism.

179

"The shrinkage in the entrepreneurial class is almost exactly balanced by an increase in the salaried class. . . . The true explanation of the relatively rapid increase in the number of salaried employees appears to be that, as industry has been organized into larger and larger entrepreneurial units, those who formerly were independent entrepreneurs have accepted salaried positions, the total office and managerial force of the nation constituting a practically unchanging proportion of the gainfully occupied population." [7]

That is a fundamental aspect of the problem: the conversion of independent enterprisers (or, rather, of their functions) into dependent salaried employees. They are swollen, in addition, by salaried employees who perform wholly new functions, among them the planning of production, and functions several of which were performed by one person but are now split up into specialized routine tasks. But there is another and complementary aspect: the conversion of formerly independent producers, including handicraftsmen and farmers, into dependent proletarians. *Both the proletariat of wage-workers and the "new" middle class of salaried employees are the creation of collective forms of economic activity.*

As the collectivism of "larger and larger entrepreneurial units" destroys the independent owner-managers, their directive functions are taken over by dependent salaried employees. The master in handicraft industry was the personal performer of all directive functions. The owner of independent capitalist enterprises performed the most important functions himself, but more and more of them were delegated to hired employees as the enterprises became larger. In the great corporate enterprises, where ownership and management are completely separated, employees perform *all* the directive functions. It is a collective performance involving division of labor, systematic organization and cooperation. The 1,500,000 managerial and supervisory employees are wholly a product of collectivism. So are, primarily, the millions of clerical employees, whose numbers are multiplied by the multiplication of routine administrative tasks created by the complicated relations of economic collectivism.

These salaried employees, the overwhelming majority of them, are imprisoned within the relations of the collectivism of which they are the product. They must subordinate the systematic organization of work to the systematic organization of exploitation. In the corporate hierarchy managerial and supervisory employees have a measure of independence only in relation to those below them, not to the man higher up. Clerical employees in the larger offices are as disciplined and dependent as wage-workers in the plants, with many managerial and supervisory employees over them. Formerly personal relations become an impersonal system. The impersonality is emphasized by the mechanization of many managerial and supervisory functions.

The growth of professionals is also bound up with collectivism. They were scarce in pre-capitalist forms of society. Capitalism, in addition to multiplying the older types of professionals as the result of higher levels of economic well-being, develops wholly new types. "It is not difficult to account in general for the emergence of new professions. Large-scale organization has favored specialization. Specialized occupations have arisen round the application of new scientific knowledge." [8] While professionals increased rapidly with the upward movement of capitalist industry, their really phenomenal growth came in the second half of the nineteenth century and after, with the immense growth of collective forms of economic activity.

Technicians were scarce in handicraft industry, their functions being performed mainly by artisans. They were more numerous, but still relatively scarce, in the earlier stages of the industrial revolution. But the technology of great industry, inseparably identified with collectivism, requires constantly larger numbers of technicians. The United States in 1870 had only 8,000 technical engineers, chemists and metallurgists: there were 275,000 of them in 1930.[9] This tremendous increase, eleven times as great as the increase in all persons gainfully occupied, took place precisely in the period when industry became more dependent on a complex technology and more overwhelmingly collective in its relations. Many of the technicians, moreover, are essentially managerial and supervisory employees.

The tremendous growth of professional services—health, education, amusements, art—is a direct result

182

of higher standards of living. For professionals, including the intellectuals, increase only as the economic surplus grows: not many of them can be supported in a society with a low economic level. And the higher economic levels, or higher standards of living, are a direct result of the greater productivity with which collectivism is inseparably identified. Moreover, collective forms of economic activity are responsible for the fact that four out of five professionals are salaried employees: as their work becomes institutional, the formerly independent professionals become dependent employees.

Many salaried employees are in trade and other distributive services. They, too, have been multiplied by collectivism. There were few goods in the old days of economic individualism, still fewer were produced for the market, and the market was mainly local. Limited trade and personal enterprise made few demands for employees. Now there is a greater variety of wants and of goods to satisfy them, and more far-flung markets, enlarging the distributive services and making them more dependent on transportation and complex interconnected relations. These developments are another aspect of the higher economic levels and greater productivity of collectivism. Moreover, trade and other distributive services are increasingly organized on a collective basis, replacing the independent enterpriser with salaried employees who are as dependent as those engaged in production.

The employees in government service fall into two

183

categories. One of them is an old one: performance of the repressive functions of the state. Their numbers vary in different countries, according to the stage of capitalist development. They are greatest where the workers are most rebellious, and where imperialism, colonialism and militarism are most highly developed. All these activities, and this is one of their charms for the "new" middle class, absorb many well-paid functionaries and minor employees. The repressive bureaucracy was always large in the older states of Europe. It was small in the United States of the 1820's: today it is almost as monstrous as in England, France and Japan. The decline of capitalism, which multiplies the need for repression and for state activities to prop up the tottering economic system, swells the number of parasitic government employees.* The parasitic bureaucracy becomes all-devouring under fascism, with its immensely greater forces of repression and militarism and its imperative need for more government jobs to take care of petty fascist leaders.

But the second category of government employees is not parasitic. The state has always had to perform

* Of the 2,500,000 employees in the American government service, probably 1,000,000 are wholly parasitic. Parasitic employees are not, however, confined to government service; there are large numbers of them in industry. Many managerial and supervisory employees are necessary only because they aid in the more intensive exploitation of labor, while some of them are engaged in direct repression (*e. g.,* directors of spy systems and of company unions). Salesmen, advertising men, canvassers, agents and most financial employees are parasitic. The parasitic employees in industry, numbering at least 1,500,000, are products of *capitalist* collectivism, not of collectivism itself.

184

some constructive functions along with its general business of repression. These functions have been greatly amplified by collectivism, which has forced more and more social services upon the state. Public education alone absorbs 1,000,000 teachers. Probably another 500,000 government employees are engaged in research, useful work for agriculture and industry, the maintenance of public health. The significant thing about the social services is that most of them were formerly performed by private enterprise or not at all. They are now made possible by the higher economic levels created by collectivism. Moreover, most of the services are overwhelmingly collective and must become social functions. Their scope is immensely enlarged in the new social order toward which collectivism moves, but their performance would be stripped of all bureaucratic evils.

3

Collectivism, wrecker of the old and creator of the "new" middle class, has destroyed the economic basis of the old democratic ideals. For those ideals, it must be repeated, were firmly rooted in the concept of *the liberty and equality of men owning their independent means of livelihood.* But today, of the 51,-000,000 persons gainfully occupied (only figuratively so in the case of 12,000,000 unemployed wage-workers and salaried employees), over 42,000,000 are hired men and women dependent on jobs for their livelihood. And, in addition, nearly 3,000,000 farmers are dependent on others for the right to till the soil.

The ideal of economic independence was always incompletely realized; it was bound up with inequality and oppression, and it generated the seeds of self-destruction. It was a hope more than a reality. Now, in the world of collectivism, the ideal is gone beyond recall, and "rugged individualism" becomes a ghost used by the oligarchs to scare people into not-thinking.

There is a group, the Agrarians, who wish to restore the old society of independent small producers. The Agrarians realize that the basis of such a society is independent small-scale agriculture. Hence they propose to multiply the number of small tillers of the soil. But the agricultural crisis, a cause of which are the higher levels of efficiency, makes it necessary that one-half the farmers leave the land and go into industry; the Agrarian ideal in practice becomes the subsistence farm. Industry, moreover, is now the dominant economic activity, and its forms are overwhelmingly collective. The Agrarians propose to break up as much of modern industry as possible; but they are forced, by the logic of economic facts, to exclude so many large-scale industries that the majority of the people would still be dependent wage-workers and salaried employees. And, in addition, the proposals would mean lower economic levels and lower standards of living. This is frankly admitted by one Agrarian: "An agrarian economy has a different method of dealing with the problem of scarcity. It devotes some effort to the matter of increasing the amount of goods available, but comparatively little.

Chiefly it meets the problem by reducing the number and the variety of material wants." [10]

It is neither possible nor socially useful to destroy collectivism. For it offers the objective means of creating a new society in which standards of living and liberty and equality would move onward to new fulfillments undreamt-of in the old order.

But collectivism today, under capitalist control, negates both the past and the future. Where, in this nation of hired men and women, are liberty, equality and opportunity? Ownership is a small vested interest. The great majority of men and women must work for a handful of great corporations. They are imprisoned within an institutional set-up beyond their control. And newer forms of liberty, equality and opportunity are prevented from emerging by the relations of capitalist collectivism.

For collectivism, capable of liberating mankind, becomes the basis of predatory monopoly capitalism, under the control of a small oligarchy of great capitalists. In 1929, the 167 directors in the financial oligarchy dominated by the House of Morgan held directorships in corporations with assets of $74,000 million, or 22% of all such assets.[11] The 200 giant corporations, which in 1930 owned one-half of all non-banking assets, had 2,000 directors, but their "ultimate control was in the hands of a few hundred men." [12] Capitalist collectivism, because of its corporate forms and the separation of ownership and management, makes possible a concentration of economic power unparalleled in the earlier stages of

187

capitalism. Capital increasingly assumes the form of finance capital—the unity of industrial and financial capital under control of the great banks which dominate monopoly capitalism and impose a dictatorship over economic activity.

Individualism and freedom of enterprise? They now exist only as outworn ideals used to justify the predatory power of the oligarchs, who crush all individualism and freedom of enterprise. They simply do not exist for the millions of wage-workers and salaried employers. And they have little meaning for the hard-pressed independent small enterprisers and the millions of pauperized farmers.

All these structural changes in capitalism have produced a tremendous shrinkage in its class basis. Fewer people are involved in the capitalist relations of ownership and personal enterprise. Yet bourgeois apologists argue the contrary, on the basis of the multiplication of stockholders, and the argument is accepted in some labor circles. A British Laborite, G. D. H. Cole, admits that Marx was right about concentration, but: "The diffusion of the ownership of large-scale business enterprises over the whole of the classes above the wage-earning level—and even to a small extent over a section of the wage-earners, especially in the United States—is a highly significant and important social phenomenon. For this broadening of the basis of capitalism prevents effectively the complete polarisation of classes which would result from a concentration of ownership as well as control in the hands of a shrinking class of great capitalist magnates." [13]

This argument is totally false. It accepts exaggerated estimates of the number of stockholders, and it forgets that *the increase in stockholders has been accompanied by a still larger decrease in the number of independent owners and enterprisers.*

The United States, used most often to prove the "broadening of the basis of capitalism," offers a convincing refutation of the argument. Stockholders in 1928 numbered 3,750,000 (of whom 325,000 owned 80% of the stock) ; [14] today there are probably not more than 3,000,000. Independent enterprisers number 2,700,000, and probably 500,000 of them are stockholders. That makes 5,200,000 persons who are directly involved in the ownership of capitalist industry. But independent enterprisers have shrunk from 15% of the gainfully occupied in 1870 to 5%; if the former proportion now prevailed, independent enterprisers would number 7,600,000. Hence there are roughly *2,400,000 fewer independent enterprisers and stockholders than if the 1870 proportion had been maintained.** The class basis of capitalism has narrowed, not broadened.

It has, moreover, narrowed still more than appears in the statistics. For independent enterprisers get their income, wholly or mainly, from their property. That is true of only a minority of stockholders. In

* The decrease is actually larger. No allowance is made for stockholders in 1870, as figures are not available. While most stockholders then were also enterprisers, there must have been many thousands who were not.

1928-29, the 2,600,000 stockholders in the income groups below $3,000 received average dividends of only $100. Among them, of course, were some petty rentiers, but to the great majority their dividends were merely a small additional income. Only an insignificant proportion of the people depend upon property for their income. As property income has grown the number of its recipients has diminished, while most of it flows into the hands of a shrinking class of great capitalist magnates.*

The basis of capitalism has become narrower in another sense: the creation by collectivism of the economic forms of a new social order. This represents the historical limits of capitalism. The economic forms of socialism press against the fetters of capitalist relations. *It is an objective clash of new and old social orders.* The clash becomes subjective on the ideological plane of class interests, consciousness and struggle. Collectivism is transformed into socialism when stripped of its capitalist social relations.

Collective forms of economic activity are not in accord with the relations of private ownership and appropriation. Enterprise is now institutional, not personal: one overwhelming proof is the separation of ownership, management and control. Capitalist ownership and profit are wholly parasitic. Owners as stockholders perform no function except that of

* The picture is not changed by inclusion of the farmers. They were 24% of all persons gainfully occupied in 1870; if the same proportion prevailed today, the farmers would number 12,000,000, but actually there are only 6,000,000, of whom nearly one-half are propertiless.

190

ownership, and the passive nature of this ownership strips it of all social value. Profit was considered necessary to reward personal initiative and management in economic activity; but that theory is another ghost of yesterday, for they are now, in their constructive economic aspects, impersonal, cooperative and institutional, while the initiative and management of the financial oligarchs are simply the exaction of tribute. Collectivism, as an integrated economic mechanism, destroys the old relations and motives.

Corporations clearly reveal the limitations of personal enterprise. But the limitations of corporate enterprise are as clearly revealed in its own shortcomings and its increasing dependence on the state. Corporate activity is collective, but incompletely, for it is distorted by capitalist ownership, vested interests and competition. Corporations are marvels of technical-economic planning, but their social relations are anarchic and destructive. They are incapable of controlling the tremendous productive forces and complex institutional set-up of collectivism; the relations move in direct ratio: the greater the inner corporate organization, the greater the outer social disorganization. Hence the state is constantly called upon to perform economic functions, to make good the shortcomings of corporate enterprise. It was the state which, in 1933, saved the American economic structure from complete breakdown. Everywhere capitalist society resorts increasingly to state capitalism. It does so all the more desperately and on a larger scale as the decline and decay of capitalism become worse and depression and the economic crisis become permanent.

State capitalism is an aspect of the clash between new and old social orders. For it uses the collective resources and action of society to aid capitalist enterprise and its private owners, and is itself, in a negative sense, an expression of the movement toward a new social order. But, in a positive sense, state capitalism is an expression of the old order: it retains all the predatory relations of capitalism, and its "planning," imprisoned within the necessity of recognizing vested interests and profit, is merely an effort to make the old order more workable and prevent the emergence of the new.

That new order is socialism, arising out of the objective socialization of industry which collectivism represents. Ownership is now vested in a small class and stripped of all constructive functions: why not ownership by society? The majority of the people are wage-and-salary dependents on the oligarchy of monopoly capitalism: why can they not work for the community of labor? Industry is collective but appropriation is individual: why not collective appropriation of the fruits of industry? A change is needed simply in the *capitalist relations* of collectivism to transform it into socialism.

Socialism breaks the capitalist fetters now imposed upon collectivism and liberates the forces of economic progress. The dependent relations of collectivism are converted into the independent relations of socialism, creating new and higher forms of liberty, equality and democracy. Capitalism is mastered by its productive forces: socialism masters the productive forces and planfully uses them for determined ends. The interests of the masses of lower salaried employees and professionals, as much as those of the wageworkers, are identified with the great task of realizing the new order potential in economic collectivism. That is socialism. Socialism is the creative unity and meaning of the changes wrought by collectivism in forms of economic activity and class relations, including the transformation of the middle class.

Chapter IX

THE DECLINE OF CAPITALISM

A TRAGIC contrast dominates the world today, the contrast between capitalist decline and decay and the economic and cultural possibilities of a liberated collectivism.

All the economic elements of a new social order are already in existence: immensely efficient forces of production, an abundance of skilled labor and of raw materials (including the increasing creation of synthetic materials), and a constantly larger mass of scientific knowledge capable of technological application—all united in the collective forms of production which are the objective basis of socialism. It is wholly possible today not only to abolish poverty but to make plenty available to all; and it is wholly possible to multiply almost indefinitely the professional and cultural services which it is the function of many groups in the middle class to provide.

Why, instead of forging ahead to the liberation of man's creative powers, are we oppressed with economic breakdown? Why the deliberate sabotage of production while millions of manual and mental workers are permanently unemployed: the growing curtailment of the means of education: a decreasing application of science to technology, save in the production of more efficient engines of destruction in preparation for new and more devastating wars? *Because too much productivity is a threat to capitalist prices and profits.* Instead of the fuller life of a new social order: lower living standards and creation of the new and wholly unnecessary poverty represented by want in the midst of plenty.

This tragic contrast is the clash between old and new social orders made visible. Dominant capitalist interests resist the transformation which collectivism now imperiously demands. They mobilize all their forces to prevent the emergence of the new order, which means strangling technical-economic progress. That is the general crisis of capitalism, of which the middle class crisis is a part. The limited aims of capitalism are insufficient to control the great productive forces brought into being by collectivism. Plenty cannot be made available to all because its distribution is incompatible with capitalist profit. A new social order is now necessary. The clash of old and new orders is the underlying factor in capitalist decline and decay. For collectivism, unless it is wrenched from the control of a desperate and declining capitalism and transformed into socialism, may become the destroyer of mankind instead of its liberator.

1

The decline of capitalism, in its historical aspects, is the negative expression of the law of social progress: no society based upon class rule and exploita-

195

tion is eternal. One social order succeeds another in the upward and onward march of humanity. The moment comes when revolutionary overthrow and creative transformation of an outworn social order are necessary to fulfill the promise of existing economic and cultural possibilities.

Arising out of the revolutionary bourgeois struggle against feudalism, the creative idea of progress was a concept of prime value to civilization. It revealed the transitory character of the old order and the necessity for the new, and by its moral sanction invigorated the bourgeois struggle for power. The inspiring ideals of a liberated humanity created by the Enlightenment were an expression of the idea of progress, of mankind moving always onward and upward to new and higher fulfillments.

But after their conquest of power, in which the middle class was the driving force, the bourgeoisie reacted against the larger implications of the idea of progress, since capitalist society was necessarily considered eternal by the dominant class. Progress was now severely limited to mere reform within the limits of the existing order, where it was not indeed wholly rejected by the more reactionary bourgeois apologists. But socialism arose to challenge capitalism and to impart new meaning to the idea of progress. Capitalism, performing the great historic task of multiplying the productive forces of society, was at the same time creating its own antagonists: the collectivism of large-scale industry, which is the objective basis of socialism, and the carrier of socialism, the

196

working class, including, in the final constructive sense, the useful functional groups of salaried employees and professionals in the "new" middle class.

As capitalism originated in the slowly changing economic forms of feudal society, so socialism originates within the shell of capitalist society, in the collectivism created by capitalist production. Where capitalist production was once personal and individualistic, now it is impersonal and collective. The individual appropriation of private ownership clashes with the necessity for collective appropriation of the products of industry. Capitalist property relations become fetters upon the productive forces, and economic activity moves downward. The conflict between the old order based on capitalist profit and exploitation and the new based on the liberation of the collective forms of production develops the conscious struggle for socialism. This struggle is threefold, as was the bourgeois struggle against feudalism: economic, political and cultural.

Economic: For the transformation of collectivism into socialism by the destruction of capitalist property relations, which now strangle the development of the productive forces of society.

Political: Against capitalist control of the state and to establish the new revolutionary state which will destroy capitalist property relations and begin the building of socialism. Abolition of both the state and class rule is the final objective.

The struggle is for new social relations of production. It demands the conversion of productive property, whose ownership is now virtually the monopoly of a handful of big capitalists, into the social property of the community, the replacement of production for profit by production for use, and the abolition of all class privileges and restrictions. Out of these new social relations arise new and higher forms of liberty, equality and democracy.

Cultural: As capitalist social relations of production are supported by the dominant culture, the struggle for socialism necessarily expresses itself in new cultural ideals. In its negative aspects it is a struggle against the capitalist limitation of culture, clearly evident in the enslavement of education to capitalist needs, which now include the increasing restriction of education, the degradation of personality by means of the subjection of labor to capitalist oppression, and the distortion of all cultural values to serve the ends of the old, dying order. In its positive aspects it is a struggle for the abolition of all relations and values which degrade functional labor, for the creation of a revolutionary culture of the working class. That includes, in the struggle for a new social order, the salvage of all that is progressive in bourgeois culture. It means the liberation of science and education and their rebirth as the creators of a new civilization moving within the realm of freedom and not, as now, within the realm of necessity.

The historical advance of the new social order meets capitalist resistance. There is capitalist encirclement of the Soviet Union, which is building the new socialist order. There is, in every nation, the repression of trade unionism, socialism and communism, which assumes its most brutal forms under fascism. This resistance to progress is identified with the threat of a new barbarism. Socialism, and the communist struggle for its realization, becomes the positive expression of the law of social progress.

The decline of capitalism, in its economic aspects, is an expression of the objective limits set upon capitalism by its own law of motion. One manifestation of this limitation may be seen in the periodical crises and depressions which have always afflicted capitalism. These cyclical breakdowns, the temporary inability of production to develop further on a capitalist basis, were a *relative* form of expression of the antagonism between the material forces of production and their social relations. Only relative, for crises and depressions were completely overcome and succeeded by higher levels of prosperity; they were temporary set-backs to the upswing of capitalism, but the general movement was upward.

Now, however, the antagonism assumes an *absolute* form. Absolute, for crises and depressions are only incompletely overcome and are succeeded by lower, not higher, levels of prosperity. *The formerly temporary inability of production to develop further on a capitalist basis becomes permanent.* This sharpens the clash of new and old social orders, which in final analysis arises out of the antagonism between the material forces of production and the capitalist social relations which hamper their development.

199

The economic forms of socialism, represented by collectivism, are more fully developed and press more insistently for release, while the capitalist relations of ownership and appropriation become more repressive and reactionary. This, and it is the doom of the existing order, means an *absolute limitation of capitalist production and accumulation in terms of increasing profits and their conversion into capital.* Capitalism is strangled by its objective economic limits and must decline and decay. It is the crisis and breakdown of the system.

The crisis and breakdown were foreseen by Karl Marx. His foresight was dismissed as the mere wish-fulfillment of his revolutionary purposes. Now it has been verified by life itself. Capitalist economics is unable to explain, in all its fundamental aspects, the inability of capitalism to solve the economic crisis and continue functioning progressively on a world scale. Some recognition of this helplessness is appearing among the professional economists. One of them admits that "there is a growing feeling that orthodox economic science has failed miserably to account for the predicament in which we find ourselves," and concludes that Marx, in his "difficult aim" to offer "a theoretical explanation and deduce a certain necessary line of development for the future" of capitalism, "was actually successful to a large degree [as] is evidenced by the cold facts of economic life since his day." [1]

Capitalist economics offers neither an explanation of the crisis of capitalism nor a guide to action in terms of the future, and clings to the apologetics of the old order. The older type of surviving classical economists, who want to move backward, argue that there would be no crisis "if only" monopoly were not so rigid in its control of prices and output, "if only" national economic barriers were not so great, "if only" competition were more free: they argue against the inevitable accompaniments of highly developed capitalism. They want to restore a "middle class capitalism" which created its own doom and is gone beyond recall, and which, moreover, was rent asunder by recurrent crises and depressions. They still speak of freedom of enterprise, although it is almost destroyed by monopoly and state controls and offers freedom only to the oligarchy of big capitalists.

The newer institutional economists, who want to stand still (or, rather, take one step forward in a direction that compels taking two steps backward), aim merely to save capitalism by a patch here and a control there: to prevent emergence of the new social order. Institutional economics claims Thorstein Veblen as a guiding spirit, conveniently forgetting that he damned it as "a science of business traffic . . . imbued with a spirit of devotion to things as they are shaping themselves under the paramount exigencies of absentee ownership as a working system." [2] Institutional economists are organizing and justifying the planned limitation of production, a monstrous expression of the "conscientious withdrawal of efficiency" and the "business sabotage" so

201

bitterly and repeatedly denounced by Veblen. They offer salvation to the capitalism which Veblen prophesied must inevitably decline and decay. They desecrate the spirit of the man who, six months before his death in 1929, said: "Just now communism offers the best course that I can see." [3]

Not the least significant cultural expression of the decline of capitalism is the final exposure of capitalist economics' total inability to understand the working of the existing order. The inability is inescapable, for it arises out of the necessity of offering explanations and prescriptions to make capitalism workable and prevent the emergence of socialism. Marxism, on the contrary, offers an explanation and a guide to action in terms of the objective limits of capitalism, its creation of the economic forms of a new social order, and the necessity of class action to strip those forms of their capitalist fetters.

2

The decline of capitalism is economically inevitable. It is inherent in the underlying forces and movement of capitalist production itself.

Profit is the driving force of capitalist production. That conclusion is accepted on all sides, both by the apologists and the critics of the existing order. Profit must become accumulation of capital. Accumulation comprises the production of surplus value by the workers (production of a surplus product over and above the value of the product represented by wages), the appropriation and realization of surplus value as profit by the capitalists, and the conversion of profit into capital. The strategic factor in this process of accumulation is an *increasing* output and absorption of capital goods, for two reasons:

1. Capital goods represent the concrete form of capital, whose ownership provides means for the exploitation of the workers, a claim upon labor, production and income. Assume that there is no output of capital goods, or that they are limited to replacements: profits must be consumed, as they cannot be productively invested, and there is no accumulation of capital,* which depends upon an increasing output of capital goods, involving the employment of an increasing proportion of the workers and an increasing capitalization of surplus value.

2. Accumulation creates, for a time, the conditions of its own upward movement. The production of capital goods sustains the industries producing consumption goods, with a consequent expansion of industry, markets and consumption. For not one penny of the consumer purchasing power (wages, most of salaries, and part of profits) distributed in the capital goods industries is spent on their own output. All of it, except minor savings and expenditures on services, is spent on consumption goods, whose output accordingly mounts. As decisive, moreover, is another aspect of the situation: No final

---

* Under this condition, unconsumed profits could be invested only in the form of debt claims, which would lower the rate of profit and become a burden upon productive accumulation.

accumulation of capital is represented by the consumption goods consumed by the workers engaged in their production (nor consumption by capitalists and other non-productive elements); final accumulation is represented only by that part of consumption goods which is consumed by capital goods workers, all of whose output becomes productive capital.

Thus the expansion of capitalist industry depends on an increasing accumulation of capital. When the self-expansion of capital meets limits and begins to contract, capitalist production must break down. The breakdowns are periodical, for accumulation eventually results in an overproduction of capital which fetters its self-expansion.

Capitalist enterprise is perpetually engaged in enlarging the scale of production and, simultaneously, in raising the productivity of labor to increase the yield of surplus value, or profit. This means the relative displacement of labor (including, in recent years, lower salaried labor) and smaller relative wages, because fewer workers set in motion a larger mass of equipment and raw materials and produce a larger output. Prosperity mounts upward as accumulation mounts. Always the output of capital goods rises more than that of consumption goods, and relative wages shrink. Capital goods output was 52% higher in 1928-29 than in 1921-22, consumption goods only 32% higher, while the proportion of the former to total industrial output was larger.[4] Relative wages, the share of wages in value added by manufacture, fell from 42.7% in 1923 to 36% in 1929.[5] Combined

204

wages and salaries (minus officers' salaries) fell from
49.8% of value added to 44.9%. The final result
is a development of the productive forces of society
beyond its consuming powers in terms of available
markets and sales. Accumulation creates an antagonism between production and consumption.

A symptom of this antagonism is excess capacity,
used and unused. In 1929, the great prosperity year,
unused capacity was conservatively estimated by one
authority at 19%,[6] and was probably nearer 30%.
Over one-quarter of industry was unused, although
2,500,000 workers were unemployed and most of the
American people had standards of living below the
minimum comfort level. Now that is clearly a bad
thing from a social angle: it represents an unused
capacity to produce goods which could easily abolish
poverty. But it is still worse from a capitalist angle:
the overproduction of capital expressed in excess
capacity exerts a terrific downward pressure on the
rate of profit (although the mass of profit may rise).
If an excess capacity is used it may throw goods upon
saturated markets and break prices and lower profits.
If an excess capacity is unused it employs no labor
and yields no surplus value, or profit, while its overhead costs, particularly the fixed portion, eat into
the profits realized on the active capacity. The rate
of profit moves downward.

Capitalist enterprise tries to overcome the fall in
the rate of profit. It tries by installing more efficient equipment to lower labor costs and raise profit
margins, and by stronger competition to capture a

larger share of the market. These measures promote an activity in the capital goods industries which reacts favorably on general industrial expansion and sustains the upward movement of prosperity. But they also involve an increasing overproduction of capital, and the rate of profit begins to fall again. Eventually the overproduction of capital becomes an absolute barrier to further expansion and accumulation. The constantly mounting productive capacity presses upon limited markets, for the accumulating potential deficiency in consumption, a result of industry distributing more investment than consuming income, now becomes an actual deficiency, *the inescapable condition of previous accumulation.* Overproduction prevents an increasing sale of commodities and the realization of their values as profit. A crisis appears in the capital goods industries. The demand for new capital goods begins to fall, creating unemployment and lower purchasing power among the workers (and lower salaried employees) producing them. This reacts unfavorably on the consumption goods industries, creating more unemployment and lower consumer purchasing power. As the production and realization of surplus value are limited the rate of profit begins to fall disastrously. Industry moves downward into depression.

Underlying all the manifestations of the cyclical crisis is the crisis in accumulation represented by a decreasing output and absorption of capital goods, a result of the overproduction of capital.

Economic disproportions are created or sharpened,

and they contribute to the drive toward cyclical breakdown. But they are effects, not the cause. The cause is accumulation itself, which *must* result in an overproduction of capital. For accumulation must go on at constantly faster speed to overcome the downward movement in the rate of profit. And it ends in creating the conditions of a disastrous fall in the rate of profit. Accumulation breaks down as the result of its own momentum. Profit-making ends in making production unprofitable.

Depression prevails as long as there is no renewal of activity in the capital goods industries, whose output falls more than that of consumption goods. Industry is made unprofitable by two conditions: the low level of general economic activity, and, within that low level, an increase in the proportion of consumption goods to total industrial output. Depression is overcome by a contradictory movement: an "easing" of the overproduction of capital and renewal of the production of capital on an ascending scale.

The overproduction of capital is "eased" by scaling down values through liquidation and bankruptcy, the depreciation of existing equipment and the postponement of replacements. This process is accompanied by readjustment in other element (*e.g.,* wages, prices, capital claims). Eventually an equilibrium is restored on a lower level. The demand for capital goods revives as replacements become no longer postponable, as industry orders more efficient equipment to increase the productivity of labor and make low prices more profitable, as some particular industry begins an unusual expansion. Renewal of activity in the capital goods industries makes possible the renewal of accumulation on an ascending scale: production and consumption mount, more surplus value is produced and realized as profit, and more profit is converted into capital.

If, however, the revival of demand for capital goods is based wholly or mainly on replacements, recovery is incomplete and prosperity depressed, for the stimulus to production and prosperity is limited by three factors:

1. The replacement of capital goods means merely a replacement of existing equipment; productive efficiency mounts, but not capital accumulation.

2. The limited re-employment in the capital goods industries (limited still more by higher productive efficiency) creates only a small increase in consumer purchasing power, and results in a limited stimulus to the consumption goods industries.

3. Replacements are always more efficient than the old equipment. There is consequently a displacement of labor: fewer workers set in motion a larger mass of capital equipment and raw materials. Relative displacement becomes absolute. Unemployment must increase even if production rises to pre-depression levels, as the higher productivity of labor is not compensated by an industrial expansion capable of absorbing all the displaced workers and the new workers coming into the labor market.

To move on to higher levels of prosperity, recovery must be invigorated by non-cyclical long-time factors of expansion: the development of new and old industries, particularly the former, capable of creating a steadily increasing demand for capital goods. Industrialization of new regions, which may become an aspect of imperialism, is another long-time factor; it was particularly important in the United States, whose undeveloped inner continental areas absorbed constantly larger masses of capital goods and provided great markets for consumption goods. In the earlier stages of capitalism the element of expansion was primarily the mechanization of old industries; in the later stages it was primarily the creation of gigantic, wholly new industries, such as railroads, electric power and the automobile. Both meant an increasing output and absorption of capital goods and more accumulation of capital. American recovery in 1921-22 and prosperity in 1923-29 were invigorated by expansion in electric power, automobiles, motion pictures (especially theatres), rayon, radio and airplanes, in addition to the upsurge in construction because of the war-time shortage in building and the demands of economic expansion. Activity in the production of capital goods sustained the upward movement in the consumption goods industries, permitting an increasing production of surplus value, its realization as profit, and the conversion of profit into capital. Accumulation, moreover, was invigorated by a great increase in the export of capital as American imperialism enlarged its scope and power.

The primary factor in the depth and duration of

the depression of the 1930's, the slow revival and incomplete recovery is the development of absolute barriers to an ascending accumulation of capital. All the efforts of state capitalism to overcome the barriers have miserably failed. The Roosevelt Administration by means of a multitude of state capitalist agencies, including the NRA, poured billions of public money into private industry, a huge subsidy to promote revival and recovery. The results were slight (except in organizing the new major industry of relief). They were slight because, while government aid may stimulate the bare beginnings of revival, a revival must seize upon more substantial underlying economic forces to move on to recovery and prosperity. These forces comprise the possibility for an ascending accumulation of capital, expressed in an increasing output and absorption of capital goods. But, and this convincingly reveals the limitations of state capitalism, there was no real upward movement in capital goods: even the demand for replacements appeared on a small scale.

One reason for the lack of effective demand for capital goods is the overequipment of industry in terms of markets, prices and profits, a result of the unusually great production of capital goods which sustained the pre-1929 prosperity.

Another reason, and the most important one, is the measurable exhaustion of the non-cyclical long-time factors of expansion: the failure of new and old industries to develop and the stagnant condition of the export of capital. The older industries are overequipped. Newer industries are not in sight. There is no prospect of great technological changes which would revolutionize the material structure of old industries or create gigantic new industries, with large and mounting demands for new capital goods stimulating an upsurge of prosperity. Technology offers merely minor gadgets and refinements on existing equipment. Mere improvement in the efficiency of existing equipment tends to make the situation worse, for it creates permanent unemployment because displacement of labor is not compensated by renewed industrial expansion. Nor are these developments offset by the industrialization of new regions, and its absorption of capital goods, as the world crisis severely limits the export of capital.

The absolute barriers to an ascending accumulation necessarily create a crisis of the capitalist system, whose dynamic law of motion is the accumulation of capital. What are the social-economic results?

One result is an incomplete revival of prosperity, for the depression, if on higher levels, moves toward permanence. There may be some sharp upward spurts of economic activity, but they relapse quickly into nervous exhaustion. Prosperity is lower, fitful and shorter, cyclical breakdown more frequent, depressions deeper, more grinding and longer.

Another result is permanent unemployment. Assume 2,000,000 workers formerly employed in the capital goods industries are now unemployable by them: that means, roughly, 4,000,000 unemployable workers in the consumption goods industries, with repercussions in trade and professional services. To employ these workers in the production of consumption goods is, from a capitalist angle, disastrous. For it would mean that 6,000,000 workers, whose end product formerly was accumulation in the form of new capital goods, now produce merely to consume: and consumption under capitalism is possible only within the limits of profit and accumulation. It means, moreover, a deduction from profits, for the additional consumption goods, since they represent no final accumulation of capital, are consumable only if the workers receive a larger share of the product of industry in the form of higher wages or lower hours, or both. But, under these conditions, the rate of profit must fall disastrously and threaten capitalism itself.

Capitalism, to protect the rate of profit, limits production, throws millions of workers and salaried employees into permanent unemployment, and lowers mass standards of living. Planned limitation of output becomes necessary if capitalism is to survive.* Of the restrictive provisions in the old NRA codes, a committee of the American Society of Mechanical Engineers said:

* The limitation of production, always an aspect of capitalism, becomes increasingly necessary under the conditions of monopoly and decline. According to H. G. Moulton, of the Brookings Institution, in *Income and Economic Progress* (1935), protection of existing business enterprises, *rather than the distribution of goods and services*, has come to be the watchword of business and government. "For more than fifty years this process has been developing through devices of corporate consolidation, pools, trusts, cartels, trade associations and Code Authorities. Particularly since

"If restrictions like those presented had prevailed in American industry during the first quarter of this century, much of the industrial progress, and the rise in standards of living, would never have been enjoyed." [7]

That is true, but it misses the whole point. Capitalist production was only beginning to slow down twenty-five years ago, now it is definitely moving downward. If capitalism cannot expand, it must contract. Hence the limitation of production to maintain profits: better restriction than abolition. But now new antagonisms are created: the limitation of production, in addition to considerable destruction of capital and an increase in excess capacity, means that millions of unemployable workers produce no surplus value and limit the accumulation of capital, while their unemployment means a further decrease of the social forces of consumption. Production, profits and accumulation are increasingly restricted,

the World War, and often with the active assistance of governments, efforts have been going forward to 'stabilize' existing business situations and to underwrite the prosperity of individuals, corporations or large business groups by attempting to stabilize prices. . . . They result inevitably in 'freezing' situations which, in the interest of economic progress, must be left as fluid as it is possible to make them." But restoration of the old fluidity is impossible, for it now threatens capitalist enterprise and profit. Capitalist "stabilization" means "freezing" economic forces and stifling economic progress, but that is the necessity of declining capitalism. Monopoly and state "controls" over industry destroy the old economic freedom without introducing a complete creative control of economic forces. The answer is not restoration of the old competitive capitalism: that is inimical both to vested capitalist interests and to economic progress. The answer is the transformation of collectivism into socialism: the liberation of abundance and the planfully creative control of economic forces.

while the objective limits of capitalism become clearly visible. This is the crisis of the system.

Underlying the crisis of the system is the drive of capitalist enterprise for an increasing production of surplus value and its realization as profit and capital, which results in developing the productive forces of society beyond its forces of consumption. An increase in surplus value means a decrease in relative wages (even when, as in the past, real wages rise) and an increase in capital claims and investment income, limiting the conditions of mass consumption in relation to production. The contradiction was overcome as long as industry absorbed an increasing proportion of the workers in the production of capital goods, thus creating a strategic addition to consumer purchasing power and converting an increasing surplus value into profit and capital. But with a decreasing proportion of the workers engaged in the production of capital goods, production and consumption must be arbitrarily controlled, that is, limited, for the meaning of a "controlled" capitalism is limitation of output to save the profit system, if on a lower level of economic activity.

The price of saving the profit system is economic decline and decay, whose most dramatic expression is permanent unemployment. Nearly 40,000,000 persons are unemployed throughout the capitalist world, including the fascist nations. Only in the Soviet Union is there *no* unemployment, for there can be none when industry is run to serve the needs of man and not the needs of capitalist profit. In the

United States, in 1935, unemployment ranged from 12,000,000 to 14,000,000—*one out of every four persons gainfully occupied.* Among the unemployed are over 3,000,000 salaried employees and professionals. Relief, and all its degradation of the will to work and the human spirit, becomes an institution.

And the prospects of prosperity and re-employment are bleak. Even a substantial recovery would not help much. A return of American economic activity to the levels of 1929 would still leave up to 9,000,000 unemployed wage-workers and lower salaried employees, because of the increase in productive efficiency and in new employables. Economic activity, to absorb all the unemployed, must go around 35% beyond the 1929 levels and 100% beyond existing levels: a remote possibility. For prosperity must be limited, and it must again break down.

The problem of permanent unemployment, or *dis*employment, is recognized by the spokesmen of capitalism in England, where government commissions speak of a surplus population. It is being recognized, too, in the United States and accepted as a fact of nature. Speaking of the planning of cities, whose "blind growth" has "scarred them with slums and blighted areas, poverty, ugliness, squalor and disease," one authority warns that *preparation must be made for long-time unemployment at levels considerably higher than they were prior to 1929.*[8] A professor of educational psychology observes that this country is rapidly accumulating *"a surplus population that is both unneeded and unwanted."*[9] And

215

spokesmen of the Agricultural Adjustment Administration argue that half the farmers (3,000,000) are unnecessary in American agriculture. The *unneeded and unwanted* surplus population includes wage-workers, salaried employees, professionals and farmers. One of its most tragic aspects are the young people who may never know work. Our children may yet sing, as they sang in Germany:

> *One, two, three, four,*
> *Only fools work any more.*[10]

Yet there is an abundance of the means and purposes of working. Capitalism cannot solve the problem. The great productive forces of society are utilizable only by a great increase of the forces of consumption, but capitalism can find no way of increasing consumption without threatening profits. The antagonism between the material forces of production and their social relations now assumes an absolute form. Capitalism must decline and decay.

The liberal economists argue that the crisis of the system is "merely" a "crisis of abundance," which can be solved "if only" capitalism increases mass purchasing power and consumption. That is the solution, from a strictly economic angle; but the liberals forget that capitalist economics cannot be divorced from capitalist social relations. To increase mass consumption, under the condition of a descending accumulation of capital and a descending output of capital goods, means to abolish profit itself. Capitalism accepts the liberal prescription, but in the form

216

of limitation of production in order to "balance" lower output with lower consumption on a level which insures *some* profit.

The liberal economists forget, moreover, that the "crisis of abundance" is bound up with the economic forms of a new social order, for our capacity to produce abundance is an aspect of collectivism. They ignore the implications of collectivism, which is *a practical abolition of capitalism within the relations of capitalist production itself.* They offer a "controlled" capitalism, or the organization of decline and decay, when the problem is to release the economic forms of the new order from their capitalist fetters.

Under capitalist social relations collectivism becomes the basis of monopoly capitalism and imperialism. Monopoly limits production, hampers technological progress, and prevents the free play of economic forces. It is wholly predatory, and makes industry increasingly the object of speculation and plunder. In 1923-29, the profits of financial corporations rose 177% and speculative profits 300%, while the profits of non-financial corporations rose only 14%.[11] Monopoly prevents the full development of productive forces during prosperity and hampers recovery after depression because of the controls it imposes on production and prices. It is the expression of capitalist decline and decay. Imperialism exploits economically backward peoples, aggravates international antagonisms, and prepares new and more destructive wars. Under the title, "War—Not Imminent, but Inevitable," an American business journal cynically observes that the peace of 1919 "was only a military truce; economic warfare has been uninterrupted since 1914, really began before that." [12] Monopoly and imperialism are the final stage of capitalism, that stage where economic activity is under control of a wholly predatory finance capital and capitalism is rotten-ripe for change, when its survival may destroy civilization itself. For in the effort to prevent the emergence of the new social order, to strangle the oncoming socialism, monopoly and imperialism throw the world into the convulsions of death.

The convulsions of dying capitalism may assume forms that are often hailed as a new social order. They are merely the old capitalism using new means to maintain its power.

Is state capitalism a new social order? No. It is merely capitalism using the state power to make good the shortcomings of capitalist enterprise and prevent an economic collapse. The "national planning" which accompanies state capitalism is not planning in any real sense, for planning depends upon abolition of the anarchy of private profit relations; it is merely piecemeal aid to capitalist industry and planned limitation of output to prevent complete breakdown and a revolt of the workers. State capitalism is an unworkable compromise between the old and the new (a negative expression of the need for a new social order) and aggravates the antagonisms of declining capitalism. It is an expression of the mercantilism of monopoly capitalism and imperialism, and, like its ancestor, is primarily in the interests of the big bourgeoisie.

Is fascism a new social order? No. Fascism, using the discontent of the middle class (which is later betrayed, as in Italy and Germany), is the final desperate resort of capitalism to preserve the old social relations of production. Capitalism still prevails under fascism, but it is a capitalism become putrid, in complete revolt against its own achievements, organizing economic decay and mass misery into a system, rejecting the ideals of liberty, equality and democracy, fighting against civilization itself. The historical meaning of fascism is the effort forcibly, at all costs, to prevent the transformation of collectivism into socialism, to prevent emergence of the new social order. Hence the suppression of all democratic rights and of all forms of labor organization (including independent liberal middle class organizations) as means of stifling progress. Fascism is the final expression of the new barbarism.

American capitalism is now definitely in the stage of decline. It is organizing economic destruction and disemployment into a system. It strangles the social forces of production, the most highly developed productive forces in the world, capable of realizing socialism with the speed of a locomotive. Driven by exhaustion of the inner continental areas, which once provided increasingly larger markets for capital and goods, by the pressure of the productive forces for release, and by the imperative need of invigorat-

219

ing the accumulation of capital, American capitalism prepares to struggle more savagely for world markets by means of more aggressive imperialism and mightier armaments. This is the twilight of American capitalism: it may become the dread night of fascism.

And the ideals of the American Dream, and their resplendent hopes? They are thrust into the mire after being increasingly degraded. Even their former incomplete realization is no longer possible, and they move toward final destruction. The ideals of liberty, equality and democracy are no longer upheld by the society of independent small producers and by perpetual renewal of the frontier. They now become the liberty and equality of starving or going on relief, the democracy of common servitude to an oligarchy of wholly predatory capitalists. Opportunity? Its limitation is now complete; for the great masses it is merely the opportunity of suffering a little less than one's neighbor: the opportunity, at best, to survive. Increasing mass well-being? It now becomes the reverse: the workers' hope of improving their conditions (labor's variant of opportunity) is shattered by disemployment and lower standards of living. Absence of class stratification? The stratification of classes is now complete and prepares the "ideal" stratification of the fascist totalitarian state; class mobility becomes a *mobility downward* into the social depths. Education? This, the most noble ideal of the American Dream, is shorn of its aspirations; education is constantly limited economically and degraded intellectually, its task now wholly the systematization of passions and prejudices in the capitalist struggle against the forces of the new social order. Peace? The dangers and horrors of war multiply, while fascism rejects peace and offers war as an ideal and a way of life. Progress? It is repressed as dangerous; retrogression to barbarism replaces progress toward a new civilization. Thus are the ideals of the American Dream trampled upon by capitalist decline and decay. But more: the ideals themselves must be destroyed *as ideals,* for the faith of the million-masses may urge action to fulfill them in new and higher forms. Their destruction is the task of fascism.

The crisis of the American Dream is an ideological expression of the class-economic crisis of the middle class. The dream was its creation, and the dream is now a nightmare. Nightmares of capitalist decline: the alternative to socialism.

3

The decline of capitalism means increasing misery for the workers and farmers. It is a repetition, on a larger scale, of the increasing misery of the industrial revolution, when peasants were expropriated from the soil and skilled artisans deprived of their occupation, women and children were thrust into the mills while the men were unemployed, and hours became higher and wages lower. But there are differences of the utmost class-economic importance.

Economic progress accompanied the increasing misery of the industrial revolution, which liberated and multiplied the productive forces of society and prepared the upswing of capitalism. It was, moreover, succeeded by some improvements in the condition of labor. Now the increasing misery of the masses is accompanied by the stifling of economic progress and the decline of capitalism.

The middle class was not affected by the increasing misery of the industrial revolution: only the workers and peasants. Not all independent handicraft producers were expropriated, and many of them became small industrial capitalists. Opportunities were multiplied for middle class enterprisers, and they thrived on the exploitation of the workers. Salaried employees began to grow more rapidly, and their status was definitely lower middle class. The new technological basis of industry needed the services of many technicians. Professionals were encouraged by rising standards of living in the middle and upper classes. All this was possible because the economic movement was upward. Now the economic movement is downward, and increasing misery affects large groups of the middle class.

Identified with the beginnings and the upswing of capitalism, the old middle class of independent enterprisers was increasingly limited by the development of large-scale industry, but it managed to survive and even to increase in numbers because of general economic expansion. Now economic contraction makes their situation constantly more hopeless.

Independent small producers in manufactures, construction and mining began to decrease in the

1910's, *when the rate of economic expansion was slowing down.* As the rate comes to a standstill, and begins to be minus, the decrease in small producers must necessarily become greater. One of the conditions of capitalist decline is the destruction of capital to maintain the rate of profit on the surviving capitals. The dominant corporate giants will evade destruction of *their* capital. This must mean the doom of many small producers, and a more desperate struggle among the survivors. Moreover, monopoly profits depend on the exploitation of independent enterprisers, and this is still truer under the conditions of capitalist decline and its limitation of profits. What is offered the small producers? The demagogues say: "We must encourage the growth of small business units." At the same time they urge "securing cheaper and better methods of production by the ruthless scrapping of plant and machinery." [13] But that necessarily helps the big producers, encourages industrial concentration, and makes the lot of small producers worse.

Storekeepers are in as bad a state. One-third of them were thrown out of business by the depression, and the massacre is still on. For competition becomes more savage as consumption and sales are limited. The chain stores struggle more aggressively for a larger share of the business, and their share mounts. Moreover, the smaller storekeepers are dependent for their trade on wage-workers and lower salaried employees, whose disemployment and depressed standards of living are a direct threat to sales. The

223

fate of most of them is interlocked with that of the working class.

Nor can the small enterprisers escape. They rallied to the NRA, yet of it one of their spokesmen said: "Small business suffered terribly under the NRA. It would have suffered without the NRA, but not to so great an extent." [14] That is an admission that small businessmen must suffer anyway: their prospects become increasingly bleak.

Still more bleak are the prospects of the "new" middle class of lower salaried employees and professionals. Employment among them must contract with the contraction of economic activity. The "labor reserve" of salaried employees and professionals, already apparent in 1929 and enlarged by the depression, must become permanent and, in addition to the misery it directly creates, it must threaten the salaries and privileges of the employed. It is an inescapable aspect of capitalist decline that dooms the performers of salaried and professional services to an inescapable servitude and degradation.

Clerical employees are hit hard. Their economic condition becomes wholly that of the wage-worker, as was clearly revealed by the depression. They, too, are ruthlessly thrown out of their jobs by lower levels of economic activity. But that is not all. As profits fall, so must costs, and clerical work is "rationalized" more and more. The office staffs must work harder: speed-up and mechanization are increasingly introduced, adding more clerical workers to the unemployed, and salaries are cut. Discipline and exploitation are strengthened as privileges are lessened. By and large, the situation is the same among the lower managerial and supervisory employees.

Technicians, too, are thrown out of work by lower levels of economic activity and their working conditions are worsened by the decrease in their scarcity value. This is accompanied by a greater degradation of their craft function. For technicians, in whom the pride of workmanship is strong, must see equipment unused and technological progress sabotaged. They must resort to means of limiting production, become destroyers instead of creators, when their sense of workmanship calls them to release the enslaved productive forces. They must knuckle under to the predatory masters of industry, whose interests are promoted by limitation of production and not by the liberation of its powers. This tragedy of the technician involves the deliberate limitation of man's control of the world and of himself: the *rejection* of *greater* control.

Professionals share in the tragedy of the technician. Lower standards of living must severely limit the demand for professional services. This was clearly revealed by the depression: it becomes permanent under the conditions of capitalist decline. The tragedy of the professionals, moreover, is intimately connected with the tragedy of the masses. Professionals were not affected by the increasing misery of the industrial revolution, for scarcely any of them served the masses of the people. But the major cause of the multiplication of professional services, in the epoch of the upswing of capitalism, was the rising standards of living of wage-workers and lower salaried employees. Now the professionals are directly affected by the disemployment and smaller incomes of the masses. The numbers of independent professionals shrink, and employed salaried professionals become fewer. Their craft function is increasingly degraded: the demand for services grows as their performance declines. It is a crisis of the professions.

The crisis appears, too, in the teaching profession, for as the burdens of taxation increase the state cuts down on the social services. Educational facilities were sadly neglected during the depression. Unemployment among teachers rose while salaries fell, school budgets were pared and overcrowding of pupils became worse. Nor did the colleges escape. Teaching offers another example of degradation of craft function. The degradation appears again in the lower quality of education and in the training of students for work they may never do.

Intellectuals? Their struggle to survive becomes harder. And they must witness the degradation of the human mind, the degradation of culture to preserve the old capitalist order. The decline of capitalism breeds a crisis of culture. As the old order decays it threatens all the progressive elements of culture, elements capable of creating, if liberated, a new and finer culture. Fascism offers the final expression of the crisis: it deliberately revolts against the human mind and progressive cultural manifestations in order to create the new barbarism. . . .

226

The farmers are irresistibly drawn into the whirlpool of disaster. After being crushed by post-war deflation, they were practically excluded from the ensuing prosperity. In 1929, 84% of the farmers had incomes below $1,500; 48% of them, or 2,880,000, had incomes below $600.[15] In addition to lower living standards, a surplus population has appeared in farming. In 1930 there were 1,000,000 fewer persons working on the farms than in 1910.[16] The surplus must grow as agricultural markets contract and efficiency mounts. That great agrarian philosopher, R. G. Tugwell, says: "When lands now unfit to till are removed from cultivation, something around 2,000,000 persons who now farm will have to be absorbed by other occupations." [17] Where and how? The other occupations are unable to absorb their own claimants as disemployment grows. In addition, mounting efficiency and limitation of production will displace more farmers. Already the government's "acreage control" has deprived scores of thousands of their means of livelihood, particularly Negro share-croppers in the South. Nor is this merely a result of the depression, for depression, if on higher levels, becomes permanent under the conditions of decline. Imperialism is another threat to agriculture: the restriction of foreign markets for American foodstuffs is accompanied by pressure on this country to import more foodstuffs to permit payments on American foreign investments. Commercial agriculture is doomed.

All these developments sharpen the crisis of the

227

middle class. The sharpening reveals clearly and acutely that this crisis differs from all former crises of the class.

The crisis of the middle class after the industrial revolution, expressed in destruction of independent handicraft producers, was easily overcome by the multiplication of small capitalist producers; it meant some changes in the middle class, but the class as a whole was temporarily strengthened by the new composition. The crisis of the middle class after the 1860's, when independent small producers were being overwhelmed by industrial concentration and trustification, was partly overcome by the increase in their numbers and in distributive services and by the multiplication of salaried employees and professionals; while the middle class was weakened and split asunder, the transformation was not yet disastrous. Both crises were overcome because of the upswing of capitalism, of the upward movement in economic activity. But the new crisis of the middle class is involved with the decline of capitalism. This changes the whole character of the problem, for it means that the crisis cannot be overcome within the relations of capitalist production. The problem is twofold, moreover, as there are now *two* crises in the middle class.

One is another crisis of the old middle class of independent small enterprisers, which moves within the relations of property. They fight the old battle to survive and protect the property which they may still own. But it is a hopeless struggle: all the conditions that doomed the old middle class during the years of capitalist upswing work with greater fury now that capitalism is declining.

The other crisis is one of employment among the masses of lower salaried employees and professionals in the "new" middle class. As they are propertiless, their crisis moves *outside* the relations of property. *This is something totally new, and none of the old middle class ideals and forms of action meets the problem.* It cannot be met by defense of independent enterprise and property, for they offer nothing to the dependent and propertiless unemployed in the "new" middle class nor to the employed whose salaries, working conditions and standards of living are mercilessly thrust downward. It cannot be met by common action with the old middle class, for its issues and aims do not affect the problem of unemployment, nor can they restore prosperity or prevent the decline of capitalism. The crisis of the lower salaried employees and professionals in the "new" middle class, in all its fundamentals, is identical with the crisis of the workers.

Hence the decline of capitalism aggravates the split personality of the middle class. Antagonistic interests are sharpened on immediate issues. They are sharpened still more on final issues. It becomes clear that economic and cultural decline and decay can be averted only by the transformation of collectivism into socialism, the socialization of productive property—and the masses of lower salaried employees and professionals are identified with collectivism.

Chapter X

PROPERTILESS: WHY DEFEND PROPERTY?

THE middle class is property conscious. Its ideals of liberty, equality and democracy are shaped by the ownership of property, which it identifies with the "good life." Even the propertiless elements in the "new" middle class, whose ideology developed within the circle of the old class, are dominated by property consciousness.

Hence the demagogues, now exploiting the discontent aroused by the crisis of capitalist decline, all cling to the rights of private property. Defense of property is always basic in their programs, no matter how "radical" they may appear. The words of an American demagogue are typical: "Civilization cannot prosper unless the natural right to property is protected." [1] The appeal is made to "the people," but the demagogues have in mind the middle class, which makes an almost mechanical response when the defense of property is urged. The appeal becomes emotional and is used to arouse the worst passions and prejudices: and it must, because the masses of the people, including dispossessed groups in the middle class, are propertiless. Only the most contemptible demagogy and distortion of the truth can make dispossessed, propertiless people rally to the defense of property—the property of which they are deprived and which oppresses and degrades them.

Nor is it only the "radical" demagogue who urges defense of the rights of property. Thus the openly reactionary Ogden L. Mills pleads for the "widest possible distribution of ownership" on which to base his argument that civilization "cannot survive destruction of the substance of ownership." [2] This union of middle class radical and capitalist reactionary, in spite of minor differences, is inescapable: for both accept capitalism, and the defense of property must include defense of the property of the big bourgeoisie. It is the fatal, traditional contradiction which has always bedeviled the struggles of the middle class.

While thus exploiting the middle class ideal of property, the demagogues also exploit the old ideal of equalitarianism: they issue meaningless calls to "share the wealth" . . . "tax the rich" . . . "redistribute wealth"—meaningless because these slogans are hoary with age, and their past invocations always ended in an increasing concentration of wealth. The traditional middle class struggle for the defense of small property always met defeat and was inevitably accompanied by the increasing dominion of big property: it must again. The demagogues, moreover, speak as if great numbers of the people still owned property and the chances of its acquisition were still plentiful. But that is no longer true. Capitalist development steadily diminished the opportunities for the free acquisition of property, and small, independent property owners are almost wiped out under the conditions of capitalist decline. Nor is this a limitation only on the masses of wage-workers; it includes farmers and the middle class as well. One bourgeois liberal observes:

"There is a steady shrinkage in the possibility of moderate wealth . . . of the farming group and still more of the middle class group which we are content to believe, or have always believed, was the fundamental necessity of a democratic civilization." [3]

Civilization and democracy are already doomed if it is true that they "cannot survive destruction of the substance of ownership." Not only is there a steady shrinkage in the possibility of acquiring moderate wealth: nearly 90% of the American people are today deprived of ownership in productive property and of independent means of livelihood.

The propertiless condition is most general among wage-workers and clerical employees: in 1928, 32,-500,000 of them, constituting 68% of all persons gainfully occupied, owned only 4.7% of all income-yielding wealth. Most of that insignificant share consisted of small savings deposits and insurance: it was not real property ownership. At the other extreme were 382,200 persons with yearly incomes of $10,000 up, or less than 1% of all persons gainfully occupied, who owned 46% of income-yielding wealth.[4] The concentration of liquid wealth (cash, savings deposits, insurance, stocks and bonds) was still greater: in 1929, 1% of the American people owned 83% of the nation's liquid wealth.[5] The "substance of ownership" is the monopoly of a small class. The same conditions exist in all capitalist nations. Thus in England, in 1924, 77% of the people owned only 6% of all wealth, while 1.6% owned 66%: [6] yet there, too, the demagogues are invoking the natural right to property.

It is a favorite argument of conservatives and even of liberals that the destruction of independent small property by corporate enterprise is offset by the multiplication of stockholders. But an examination of the statistical facts quickly reveals the falseness of this claim. In 1928 there was a total of only 3,-750,000 stockholders, 325,000 of whom owned 80% of all corporate stock, while the holdings of 2,600,000 small stockholders yielded average yearly dividends of only $100. [7] Today, there are probably not more than 3,000,000 stockholders, out of 51,000,000 persons gainfully occupied. In that small number of stockholders it is impossible to find many of those poor, poor widows and orphans whose interests are tearfully invoked by capitalist magnates. These legendary widows and orphans induced the financial overlord of the Associated Gas and Electric Company, according to his own claim, to lobby righteously against utility-control legislation; yet his company, in 1929-33, *paid not one cent in dividends,* while the overlord, his partner and members of his family, in the same period, received $28,260,000 in salaries and profits.[8] The poor widows and orphans!

233

Much of the small amount of wealth owned by the masses of the people was wiped out by the depression. Savings were drained by unemployment. The assets of building and loan associations declined by $111,000,000 in four years, while nearly 2,000,000 small homeowners were foreclosed: [9] purchase of a home by better-paid workers and salaried employees offers no security, as unemployment and shrinkage in value destroy the owner's small equity. Destruction of savings becomes worse under the conditions of capitalist decline, which multiplies insecurity.*

The proletariat was always propertiless. Hence its condition is nothing new. The significant new aspect lies in the fact that today the proletariat is a majority of the people, where formerly it was a small minority. Still more significant is the fact that farmers and the middle class, whose distinguishing mark was ownership of independent property, are now mainly propertiless. And yet the "people" are still called upon to defend property!

Practically all farmers were independent property-owners a century ago, and 80% of them were still independent in 1870: propertiless tenants and farm laborers were still a minority. But the independence of agriculture was undermined by its increasing subjection to industry and by the adoption of capitalist methods of farming. In 1930 not much more than

* Savings, moreover, are limited to a minority of the people, and the minority now becomes smaller. Security is realizable only as a social, not as an individual, measure: not by capitalist social-insurance schemes, which offer pitifully small doles, but by the all-inclusive and adequate social insurance of socialism.

50% of the farmers were independent owners, and many of these were crushed by oppressive mortgages and debts.[10] Including hired farm laborers, nearly 60% of the persons engaged in agriculture are wholly propertiless: twice the percentage of sixty years ago. Farmers were formerly a majority of the people, and made possible a majority of small property owners; they are now only 12% of the gainfully occupied, and half of them are propertiless.*

The middle class in the 1920's still had a substantial property stake, considerably larger than that of the farmers. But its ownership was highly concentrated: 20% of the members in the upper middle class owned 60% of the class wealth.[11] Much of that wealth was wiped out by the depression; the 20% shrinkage in class numbers was accompanied by a still larger shrinkage in the ownership of wealth and an increase in its concentration.

A large part of the middle class wealth, moreover, represents merely savings deposits and insurance. Ownership of productive property is limited. The middle class has probably 3,700,000 owners of productive property—2,700,000 independent enterprisers and 1,000,000 stockholders among salaried employees and professionals—or only 28% of the members of the class. But the old ideal of the class was *property in the form of ownership of independent means of livelihood.* Dividends received by

* The situation is still worse in England, where imperialist capitalism practically destroyed agriculture to promote foreign investments and trade, and the independent propertied farmer is a rarity.

235

most of the stockholders are merely a small addition to salary income, not a source of livelihood. If we assume that there are 300,000 officers of corporations and rentiers whose stock yields a substantial income, and add them to the 2,700,000 independent enterprises, we get a total of 3,000,000 persons, or only 23% of the middle class, whose livelihood depends on the ownership of property. In other words, and stressing property as a means of livelihood, 77% of the middle class are propertiless.

Most of the members of the "new" middle class, over 95% of them, are wholly propertiless. Yet they, too, are being called upon to defend property—these masses of lower salaried employees and professionals who are as propertiless as the proletariat. Why should the propertiless defend property?

Ownership of all forms of productive property is extraordinarily limited. It is distributed among 2,700,000 independent enterprisers, 2,500,000 stockholders (excluding 500,000 who are enterprisers), and 3,000,000 propertied farmers: a total of 8,200,-000. But at least 2,000,000 stockholders receive dividends which are merely a small addition to income. Hence there are only 6,200,000 persons, out of 51,000,000 gainfully occupied, whose livelihood is wholly or mainly dependent on the ownership of property: 12% compared with 80% a century ago. That means that 88% of the American people, *seven out of every eight,* are dependent on the property of others for the chance to earn a livelihood; and among them are 77% of the members of the middle class.

A nation of owners of small property and of independent means of livelihood? That middle class ideal is gone beyond recall. The United States today is a nation of employees and of propertiless dependents. But as ownership of property was always the distinguishing mark of the old middle class, *the propertiless masses of lower salaried employees and professional workers in the "new" middle class are thrust, economically, into the working class.*

This conversion of the mass of the people into propertiless dependents on the property of others is the final result of the social relations of capitalist production.

Early capitalism enlarged the basis of property ownership, which was very narrow under feudalism. Capitalist enterprise created new forms of property, particularly by the multiplication of small producers. The slogan of the bourgeois struggle against feudalism was: "Liberty and property!" It expressed the constant increase of property ownership among larger circles of the people, in spite of the growth of propertiless proletarians and the great riches amassed by the big bourgeoisie. The greatest diffusion of property was achieved where the revolutionary bourgeoisie expropriated the great feudal landholdings and divided them among the peasants. Property ownership was most widely diffused, however, in the early years of the American republic, because of the great numbers of free farmers made possible by the new lands of the frontier regions and the absence of feudalism.

237

But capitalism after the industrial revolution, although it favored some new forms of small property, reacted against the earlier widespread distribution of property. Industrial capitalism and corporate enterprise drove irresistibly toward large-scale production and concentration of ownership, accompanied by expropriation of the small property of independent enterprisers. The middle class was increasingly deprived of property and transformed into functional groups of salaried employees. But small property was still acquirable, although its relative importance decreased. Under monopoly capitalism, however, and particularly under the conditions of capitalist decline, the number of small property owners decreases absolutely as well as relatively. Expropriation of property becomes constantly more active as a source of wealth when the springs of new wealth begin to dry up.

The middle class, as owners of independent property, was always the great bulwark of capitalism. Now that bulwark is economically undermined, for the propertied middle class is a small and shrinking minority of the people. But the minority clings desperately to property, and it uses the most desperate measures to rally the propertiless elements in the "new" middle class to the defense of property. It is, however, a hopeless struggle. The interests of lower salaried employees and professionals are not in that struggle, and the struggle is, for them, a form of class-economic suicide.

Yet there are liberals who urge the "restoration"

of private property and an increase of the middle class. They completely ignore the experience of history. If it was impossible to prevent the annihilation of independent small property, why should restoration be easier? Small property and the middle class shrank constantly in the upswing of capitalism, when new wealth was being abundantly created: must they not shrink still more as economic activity moves downward? The middle class is doomed.*

Underlying the tremendous concentration of property ownership is the dominion of corporate enterprise over economic activity. In the earlier stages of capitalism, especially in the United States, ownership was largely limited to property that the owner might directly and personally manage. Ownership was identified with responsibility, with management and control. All that was changed by the corporation, which made possible a concentration of property ownership undreamt of in the old society of small producers. Great masses of productive property are concentrated in giant corporations, and management is converted into a hired function; property becomes a mass of paper tokens, ownership of which by one individual may represent scores of different corporate enter-

---

* This is still truer of the Negro. The theory that the Negro can emancipate himself by acquiring property and creating a middle class was always limited, because of his social-economic subjection. It is now more limited. For, under the conditions of capitalist decline, property and the middle class must shrink in Negro circles more than the general shrinkage. Moreover, what middle class there is among the Negroes is almost exclusively composed of salaried employees and professionals, whose economic interests are identified with the great propertiless masses: with socialism.

prises. Finance capital, stript of the constructive functions of the older industrial capital, imposes a dictatorship over economic activity and limits economic progress.

Separation of ownership from management means separation of ownership from responsibility. Stockholders have no responsibility for the enterprises they own, and are simply interested in dividends. The hired managers do not own, while the financial oligarchy converts the paper tokens which represent ownership into an object of speculation and plunder. Marx thus pictured the significance of these developments:

"This is the abolition of the capitalist mode of production within capitalist production itself, a self-destructive contradiction, which represents on its face a mere phase of transition to a new form of production. . . . It is private production without the control of private propetry." [12]

Corporate enterprise is the capitalist form of social property, "the abolition of capital as private property within the boundaries of capitalist production itself." [13] But it is social property with private ownership: it is economic collectivism with individual appropriation of the fruits of collective economic activity. The propertiless condition of the masses of the people, including three-quarters of the members of the middle class, is inseparably identified with capitalist collectivism, whose relations of private ownership sabotage the forces of production and create economic decline and decay. Collectivism is the basis of socialism: the interests of the propertiless dependents of capitalism, including the proletariat and the masses of lower salaried employees and professionals, are bound up with the conversion of social property now privately owned into social property owned by the community of labor. Socialization of productive property, by liberating economic forces, means a multiplication of personal property for the exclusive use of the individual.

Many liberals still urge the restoration of independent small property to insure freedom and democracy, "as private property was the original source of freedom" and "it is still its main bulwark." [14] That statement is false as an historical generalization, for private property is identified with all systems of despotism, including the Cæsarian and the feudal. The liberal means that the development of *bourgeois* private property was the source of *bourgeois* freedom. But that was true only against feudal restrictions and oppression, and the new forms of property were a source of oppression of the propertiless masses. The bourgeois slogan, "Liberty and property," was limited because it necessarily excluded liberty for the propertiless, offered more liberty to the big property owners than to the small, and promoted an overwhelming concentration of property. Middle class radicals tried to overcome the limitation by the ideal of equality of property ownership as the only sanction for liberty and democracy. The ideal was futile and is now dead. Yet they attempt to revive it, when independent small property is vanishing and fascism

241

annihilates liberty, equality and democracy to preserve the "rights" of property! The "main bulwark of freedom" becomes the bulwark of fascist barbarism.

Liberals still think of Thomas Jefferson's prophecy that the rise of a propertiless proletariat would mean the doom of democracy. Jefferson was right. But he was wrong in thinking the doom could be averted, for multiplication of the proletariat is inherent in capitalism, whose whole development is an inescapable process of proletarianization. And proletarianization includes the great functional groups in the middle class. Jefferson was wrong, moreover, in thinking of the proletariat in terms of old Rome: as a disinherited rabble incapable of creative class action. *For the modern proletariat, as the product of that economic collectivism which is the basis of socialism, is the carrier of a new social order.* Everywhere the proletariat, the propertiless masses of the people, challenge capitalism: now partly, now wholly, always acquiring constantly new vigor. The challenge is being fulfilled by the building of socialism in the Soviet Union. . . .

The property "rights" of a small capitalist minority bar the road to progress; they cry to the progressive forces: "You shall not pass!" The rights of property are interlocked with the crisis of capitalism, and with the crises of property and employment in the middle class. It is capitalist property that prevents liberation of the abundance industry is now capable of producing. It is capitalist property that throws millions of workers and lower salaried employees and professionals into the degradation and misery of permanent unemployment. It is capitalist property that drives toward imperialism and war. The product of man's labor becomes his enslaver, degrading social intelligence and stifling creative social action. Civilization and progress are endangered, a new barbarism is threatened: all to protect the property of a small capitalist minority. That: while abolition of capitalist property, the conversion of social property now privately owned into the social property of the community of labor, means a new upsurge of progress. Yet liberals still wander in the mazes of a dream now become nightmare; unable to think clearly and act decisively, they mouth the mumbo-jumbo of a past that was never very real and whose recapture is now impossible. Let the dead past bury its dead! The forces of a new social life are stirring, stirring, and they call insistently for release.

Society must go forward, not backward. New and higher forms of liberty, equality and democracy are necessary, and new sanctions for their being. Liberty of property must become the liberty of labor. An unrealizable equality of ownership must become the equal right to share in the social property of the community. The democracy of independent small producers must become the socialist democracy of free, creative workers: including the workers in the useful functional groups of the middle class.

Chapter XI

MIDDLE CLASS AND THE WORKERS

IN addition to being property conscious the middle class is animated by an antagonism to the workers. Defend property! Against labor! They are manifestations of a rallying call which is in complete disaccord with the existing conditions and needs of the masses of lower salaried employees and professionals, who are propertiless and dependent on jobs for a livelihood. For these groups property consciousness and antagonism to labor are an ideological inheritance completely at variance with the realities of their existing situation. This is the most significant aspect of the split personality of the middle class and its incapacity to formulate a class program expressing the concrete economic interests of all groups.

1

The old middle class of independent enterprisers was antagonistic to the workers. Even in the guild system, where workers and small producers were closely united, the masters exploited the journeymen and gradually converted them into proletarians. In the bourgeois revolutions, particularly the Jacobin, the lower middle class rallied the propertiless workers to the struggle; their support was necessary, and the workers responded because they had no independent program and identified their interests with petty-bourgeois democracy. But the workers were betrayed and abandoned by the middle class. The small producers who arose after the industrial revolution were necessarily and more completely antagonistic to the workers, for handicraftsmen constantly decreased and the capitalist, whether big or small, must get his profits by appropriating an increasing yield of surplus value from the workers. As the middle class waged its struggle against concentration and trustification, in defense of independent small enterprise, it sought the support of the wage-workers—but on a middle class program which generalized its interests as the people's interests, and always strictly within the limits of the capitalist order. That was the essential character of American populism and progressivism. The underlying tendency was to discourage and repress the independent action of labor.

As they grew in numbers and emerged as an industrial proletariat, organized by the collective mechanism of capitalist production itself, the wage-workers moved increasingly toward action independent of the middle class. The ugly reality of capitalism made a mockery of the ideals of the bourgeois revolution. Workers were denied democratic rights and secured them only after bitter struggles, particularly in Europe. Increasing misery marked the earlier stages of industrial capitalism; the betterment of conditions was agonizingly slow and incomplete, while the rate of exploitation mounted. Trade unions arose and

245

socialism issued its challenge to capitalism. The challenge emphasized the temporary historical nature of capitalism, which was itself creating the conditions of a new social order: economic collectivism, the objective basis of socialism, and the proletariat, the class carrier of socialism.

Trade unionism and socialism, by and large, strengthened the middle class antagonism to labor. The class was rarely neutral in strikes. It created the myth of "the public" whose interests transcended the struggle between labor and capital; in practice the myth favored the capitalist exploiter. And propertied enterprisers were frightened by the socialist proposal for the socialization of productive property.

But the middle class was still in the radical stage. Its lower layers were in contact with the propertiless workers and it was still engaged in the struggle against monopoly. Many small producers, especially the surviving handicraftsmen, were being thrust downward into the proletariat. Hence a radicalism, mainly in the lower middle class, which often assumed the form of petty-bourgeois socialism. The mixed elements of this "socialism" included defense of handicraft labor and other forms of small industry, cooperative workshops as the basis of a new social order, nationalization of big enterprises and the broadening of democracy. This petty-bourgeois socialism, most clearly developed in Europe, was doomed to disaster, for it represented the disappearing pre-industrial small producers and accepted the relations of capitalist production. In many struggles,

246

especially for democratic rights, the lower middle class and the workers united their forces. But the radical middle class was constantly vacillating between capitalism and socialism, between the bourgeoisie and the proletariat.

Antagonism to the workers was necessary to the small industrial capitalists in the middle class. It still is today. They are employers and exploiters of labor; although increasingly crushed by capitalism, they are inseparably entangled in capitalist relations. The antagonism to labor, in varying degrees, dominates other types of enterprisers, among them small shopkeepers and independent professionals. But the economic interests of these groups are not antagonistic to labor, for the masses of small storekeepers and professionals must depend for their livelihood on labor's patronage; they quickly feel the effects of lower standards of living, of unemployment and wage cuts, among the workers, and may combine with them in the struggle against capitalist exploitation. On the whole, however, the antagonism to labor conforms to the interests of the old middle class of independent small enterprisers.*

* The antagonism to labor conforms only to the interests of the small upper layers of capitalist farmers and of the type of tenants who rent farms to exploit migratory labor. Propertiless farm laborers and the mass of tenants and poorer farmers have nothing to gain from antagonism to the workers. They are beginning to appreciate the identity of interests; unions are being formed of farm laborers, share-croppers and other types of tenants, and industrial workers in the small towns in contact with agriculture. In a number of recent strikes farmers and workers have demonstrated their solidarity in action.

247

But antagonism to labor is wholly opposed to the interests of the masses of lower salaried employees and professionals. Capitalism has proletarianized them, and it increasingly thrusts them downward to the economic level of wage-workers. That produces a substantial identity of interests that *must* break through inherited antagonisms and ideological differences.

2

Salaried employees and professionals were clearly members of the middle class in the earlier stages of capitalism. A gulf separated them from the wage-workers. Professionals were practically all self-employed; a profession was measurably a form of independent property. Salaried employees were scarce (wage-workers developed much more rapidly); they became a big group only after collective large-scale industry assigned to them the tasks of management, administration and supervision. Their scarcity value and highly skilled functions, in spite of the proletarian relation involved in the sale of their skill to an employer, assured salaried employees security, good incomes and social standing; they were "on the make," salaried dependence being largely a mere transition to the independence of one's own enterprise. But economic collectivism proletarianized their functions while multiplying their numbers. Most salaried employees were converted economically into wage-workers and most professionals into salaried employees by corporate enterprise and its specializa-

248

tion and simplification of tasks formerly performed by highly skilled persons.

One group, however, retained and strengthened its privileges. The small upper layer of higher salaried employees became more closely identified with capitalism as corporate enterprise increased its importance, income and power; the members of this group may be called institutional capitalists, for they perform the more decisive functions of the older independent enterprisers. But the great masses of lower salaried employees moved downward. Their scarcity value, privileges and income were increasingly impaired as collective activity transformed their work into mechanical routine and the multiplication of their numbers created a labor reserve among them. These occupational changes depressed the social standing of lower salaried employees, but they clung pathetically to middle class ideals and, especially in the United States, scorned strikes, unionism and identification with labor.

As the masses of lower salaried employees moved downward the wage-workers moved upward, after the increasing misery of the industrial revolution. Their standards of living rose, especially among the skilled industrial workers, and their personal and class independence was invigorated by unionism and socialism. The economic differences separating the masses of lower salaried employees and the wage-workers are small and becoming constantly smaller.

Occupational changes are most striking among clerical employees. The clerk was an honored employee 150 years ago, and still more so in earlier times. His position was a confidential one, the employer discussed affairs with him and relied on his judgment; he might, and often did, become a partner and marry the employer's daughter. The clerk was measurably a professional and undeniably a member of the middle class. But all this was changed by the collectivism of large-scale industry. Specialization and division of labor, and mass education, increasingly deprived clerks of their old skills and scarcity value, particularly after office appliances began to mechanize not only skill but intelligence itself. The mechanization of clerical labor becomes constantly greater; a typical large office is now nothing but a white-collar factory. Real clerical earnings were practically stationary in 1914-26, but real wages rose.[1] In 1929 the average clerical salary was $1,400 yearly, not much more than the wage-worker's $1,200, while many organized skilled workers earned more than the great majority of clerical employees.

Managerial and supervisory employees are comparatively well paid and secure, and they include the "institutional capitalists" in the upper layers. But here, too, there is a proletarianizing tendency; where management was the personal function of independent enterprisers, it is now the impersonal, dependent function of hired employees. Moreover, management and supervision are increasingly becoming mere routine tasks, simplified, specialized and mechanized, and displacement is a growing danger because of mechanization: as in other phases of economic activity, mechanism replaces the person. Large numbers of managerial and supervisory employees earn below $3,000 yearly and are threatened by insecurity. But the great majority is still a privileged caste.

Technicians were almost independent professionals in the earlier stages of industrial capitalism. But large-scale capitalist enterprise, while multiplying their numbers, degraded the economic condition of most of them. A few may earn big incomes by exceptional ability or, more often, by lowering their craft function to the basest needs of capitalist exploitation: the wealthy technician is usually an enterpriser, not a craftsman. But most of the technicians earn below $3,000 yearly, many of them less than organized skilled workers. Modern industry, moreover, becomes constantly more automatic, and technicians, in spite of their knowledge and training, are increasingly limited to the performance of routine functions, while many workers become junior technicians: one moves downward, the other upward. The proletarianization of technicians is marked and inescapable.

Professionals were formerly scarce and practically all of them were independently self-employed. Now there is an overproduction of professionals (only, however, in relation to the ability of capitalist society to use their services) and not more than 500,000 are independent: *four out of five professionals are salaried employees*. Even physicians are constantly becoming salaried dependents: in 1929 there were 21,000 American physicians, or one out of seven, working for salaries, while the proportion was larger and growing more rapidly in England.[2] This is a significant proletarianization of professional functions. The majority of professional employees earned below $2,500 yearly, great numbers of them below $1,500, and they usually perform the most routine tasks. Elementary and secondary school teachers, the largest single group of professional employees, earned an average of only $1,365, in the prosperous year 1928;[3] nor was the average much higher among college teachers. The increase in the real earnings of teachers in 1914-26 was smaller than the increase in real wages,[4] and this was true of other professional employees.

The situation was not much better among independent professionals. It *was* among a small upper layer, usually the more unscrupulous practitioners of business methods and degraders of their craft function. Nevertheless, the income of more than half the dentists was below $3,000 in 1929, and of 24% of the physicians below $2,000.[5] The most significant aspect of proletarianization, however, is the conversion of professionals into dependent salaried employees as the performance of professional services becomes increasingly a function of corporate enterprise and the state.

Of the 9,200,000 salaried employees in 1930, not more than 1,250,000 had incomes of $3,000 up: the incomes of over 85% were below $3,000. *Millions of organized skilled workers earned more than the majority of lower salaried employees.* Nor did this mean, as capitalist apologists claim, that wage-workers were moving upward into the middle class, for their standards of living were even then nothing to brag about; *it meant that the masses of lower salaried employees were economically moving downward into the proletariat,* and the process has accelerated since 1930. However stubbornly they still maintain the middle class antagonism to labor, capitalism makes them one with the dispossessed workers.*

* A summary sketch of proletarianization, on the basis of the German experience, is given by Hans Speier, "The Salaried Employee in Modern Society," *Social Research,* February, 1934, pp. 116-18: "The quantitative changes have been accompanied by qualitative ones. *The social level of the salaried employees sinks with the increasing extent of the group.* This qualitative change, which has been termed the 'proletarization of the white collar worker,' shows itself in a number of ways. It is most evident, perhaps, in the especially great increase in the women salaried workers, who mostly perform subordinate work. . . . It is the man who typically has the principal authority, the girl who is typically the subordinate. . . . The great increase in salaried employees is especially traceable to a demand for subordinates, not for fully qualified responsible persons. As a result the average chance of advancing has declined. The majority of the subordinate employees in the large offices perform duties which are specialized and schematized down to the minutest detail. They no longer require general training; in part only a very limited and brief training is necessary, in part previous training has become quite unnecessary. The process in the course of which the body of salaried employees became a mass group rests on the successful attempt to replace the personal experience of the individual by a rational scientific business administration, so that an increasing proportion of the workers can be changed without danger to the efficiency of the enterprise. One social result of this development is the rise of the unskilled and semi-skilled salaried workers, whose designation already indicates the assimilation of the processes of work in the office to that in the factory. In the case of the salaried workers who serve as subordinates on one of the many modern office machines, or, for example, who sell in a one-price store, the difference in the nature of the

There is still a differential between the earnings of wage-workers and lower salaried employees. But it is significant of the proletarianizing tendency of capitalism that the differential has steadily decreased. While the average earnings of clerical employees on the railways in 1890 were 13% higher than the wage-worker's average, they were only 0.6% (or $10 yearly) higher in 1924; in New York the differential in favor of clerical earnings decreased from 74% in 1914 to 34% in 1923.[6] The breakdown of differentials, which affected the majority of lower salaried employees, was accompanied by another development: small as was the increase in real wages the increase in real salaries was still smaller. Proletarianization included a breakdown in the differentials of security and privileges, of confidential relations with the employer, and of the opportunity to move upward into higher jobs.

Middle class demagogues use the breakdown of differentials to incite the lower salaried employees against the workers, particularly against union workers. It is an effort to becloud the issue. For the masses of lower salaried employees moved downward more than the workers moved upward. And, in the 1920's,

duties between such workers and the manual workers is completely wiped out. . . . Especially revealing with regard to the sinking of the social level of the white collar workers is, finally, the change in the social antecedents. The growing tendency to employ salaried workers of 'proletarian origin' indicates that the number of untrained and poorly paid positions is increasing faster than the number of middle and principal positions. In other words, the salaried employees as a whole are being subjected to a process of decreasing social esteem."

differentials in the earnings of lower and higher salaried employees became greater; the most flagrant expression was the constantly mounting salaries of corporation officers. Profits, moreover, greatly increased, partly because of the depressed earnings of lower salaried employees. It was possible to pamper salaried employees when they were few; but as they became numerous and enlarged the salary bills, aggravating the problem of overhead costs, capitalist enterprise began to apply scientific management and rationalization. Salaries as fixed costs had to become variable costs and smaller in amount. Lower salaried labor and wage labor, approaching one another in economic condition, are equal objects of capitalist exploitation. It is significant of proletarianization, and of the split in the "new" middle class, that lower salaried employees increased much more rapidly than higher salaried and the differentials in their earnings became greater.

Another, and strikingly significant, aspect of proletarianization is the exposure now of lower salaried employees to all the rigors of depression. They were formerly protected by their security and privileges. Few salaried employees were discharged and salaried earnings were largely maintained, while the wage-workers bore the brunt of depression. Of clerical salaries, symptomatic of salaried earnings in general, one professional economist says:

"The assertion that the salaries of clerks are not reduced as much in times of depression as are the wages and earnings of manual workers is abundantly confirmed. During the depressions of 1908 and 1914 the average salary, instead of decreasing, actually increased, both on the railways and in the factories. The same was certainly true of railways during the depression of 1894. In the great recession of 1921, the average reduction in manufacturing establishments was less than 1% and only 5% in the case of the railway clerks." [7]

That security was destroyed in the depression of the 1930's, and it is gone forever. The earnings, employment and privileges of lower salaried employees (*not* the higher) were mercilessly slashed, almost as mercilessly as among the workers. . . . While the proportion of lower salaried employees thrown out of work was slightly smaller than that of wage-workers, it was larger by 25% in manufactures. . . . Unemployment among technicians was catastrophic; it included 50% of the pharmacists, 65% of the engineers, especially civil engineers, because of the almost complete stoppage of construction, and 90% of the architects and draftsmen. . . . By 1934, over 200,000 teachers were unemployed; 5,680 college teachers were dismissed in 1933-34. . . . At least two-thirds of the 15,000 members of the American Federation of Musicians were unemployed. . . . Clerical salaries were cut as savagely as wages; by 1935, office workers in New York City were earning as little as $12 weekly. . . . The earnings of nurses, which before the depression were not much over $1,200 yearly, dropped to $478 in 1932. . . . Pharmacists and drug clerks had their salaries cut up to 50% or more, with

NRA codes establishing minimums of $13 to $16 weekly. . . . School appropriations were severely reduced while the number of pupils rose, and there was one cut after another in salaries; by 1933-34, the average teacher's salary was only $1,050 yearly, a decline of 20%, with many salaries as low as $450 and still lower among Negro teachers. . . . The extent to which the salaries of technicians were cut appears clearly in the minimum of $14 weekly established for qualified chemists by one NRA code; in another code technical employees got 35¢ to 45¢ an hour. One commentator observed: "The technicians now find themselves in many cases receiving about *half* the wages of skilled labor under the NRA codes. No provisions have been made for them, the technicians being conveniently regarded as 'superintendents' or 'executives.' In many cases the men are receiving only the minimum wage provided for unskilled labor." . . . Earnings declined seriously among independent professionals. The net income of a group of more successful physicians was 40% lower in 1932 than in 1929, and the decline was greater among the lower groups, many physicians being forced out of practice. This condition was general among other types of independent professionals. . . . Thousands of trained men desperately accepted the jobs of skilled and unskilled workers; millions of lower salaried employees and professionals were forced on relief.[8]

Nor was the breakdown of security, privileges and earnings merely a result of the unusual severity of the depression of the 1930's, for the depression of 1894 was almost as severe. It was the result of occupational changes that broke down the differentials favoring the lower salaried employees, an expression of their practical proletarianization.

It is not a temporary breakdown. The condition is permanent and must become worse as prosperity fails to revive on any considerable scale. One significant proof is that, during the slight economic revival after 1933, *more wage-workers were re-employed than lower salaried employees*. Not that the workers are favored, but they are directly productive and salaried labor is part of the overhead costs which must be cut ruthlessly as industry goes on iron rations and profits become lower. Hence rationalization and scientific management are applied more completely, lessening security, privileges and earnings. Many salaried employees work in superstructural enterprises which flourish only when there is a high level of prosperity. There is, moreover, a definite ratio between the number of employed wage-workers and of lower salaried employees and professionals; as one moves downward the other must also move downward. The prospect is one of permanent unemployment, more insecurity and impoverishment. For the increasing misery of capitalist decline engulfs millions of lower salaried employees and professionals. They may think they are "different" and "better," that as members of the middle class, even if only of the "new" middle class, they are deserving of special

258

treatment, but the capitalist employers treat them as they do the workers.

3

It is clear that the masses of lower salaried employees (including salaried professionals) are *not* members of the middle class, which was always a class of independent propertied enterprisers. Propertiless salaried dependents cannot, economically, be included in that class.

Neither can they be logically included in the "new" middle class. This class must bear some definite economic resemblance to the old middle class of independent enterprisers. *It can include only the higher salaried employees, the managerial and supervisory, who perform the capitalist functions of exploiting the workers, receive incomes substantially above the proletarian level and are owners of property.* Only these groups (including, of course, petty rentiers) are unquestionably new middle class, for while they are not independent enterprisers they are capitalists in the institutional sense and their relation to production is clearly bourgeois. It is otherwise with the masses of lower salaried employees with incomes below the overwhelmingly proletarian level of $2,500 yearly—at least 8,500,000 of them out of a total of 10,300,000 salaried employees—who are not "new" middle class in their relation to production and income: *they are economically and functionally a part of the working class: a "new" proletariat.*

Lower salaried employees, as much as the workers,

are separated from ownership of the means of production and are propertiless dependents on the social property owned by a small capitalist minority.

Lower salaried employees, as much as the workers, must sell their labor power to earn a livelihood. Their labor is not always superior to that performed by millions of skilled workers, and is often of lower grade. Skilled labor, according to Marx, "is multiplied simple labor," [9] and if salaried labor is superior it may be called multiplied skilled labor. But it is still labor power which must be sold to an employer if its owner is to earn a livelihood. That is a proletarian relation. It is emphasized by the increasing breakdown of differentials in security, privileges and earnings.

Lower salaried employees, as much as the workers, are the product of economic collectivism and the proletarian conditions its capitalist forms impose on the majority of the people. This is the basis of an historical unity that must eventually overcome differences in development and ideology. United by their economic origins and by their propertiless, dependent condition, the interests of workers and salaried employees acquire a final unity in socialism, which arises out of the transformation of collectivism. Both are necessary in the new social order.

The "new" proletariat, however, has its peculiar traits. It developed later than the proletariat and much more slowly in the earlier stages. Proletarianization of lower salaried employees proceeded within the circle of the middle class, to which, by and large, they clung desperately. They developed no ideology and forms of action expressing their own class-economic interests. The workers, on the contrary, created unionism and socialism, moving toward independent class objectives and action.* While this was truer of Europe than of the United States, the American tendency was the same. Workers almost as much as the middle class were under the influence of the ideals of the American Dream arising out of petty-bourgeois democracy, but they formed unions, they went on strike, they waged aggressive struggles against the employers. And this included the "aristocracy" of better-paid skilled workers, who did not become middle class but were among the most militant organizers of unions and strikes. Organized workers had a *labor* policy, if restricted and reform-

---

* The problem of the middle class, and particularly of salaried labor, was neglected by orthodox socialism. It was not aware that a new type of worker had arisen and was satisfied with mechanical repetition of the prophecy of Marx that the middle class was doomed. But Marx meant the middle class of independent small enterprisers, and his prophecy is amply fulfilled under monopoly capitalism. Marx analyzed the relation of the proletarian struggle to the middle class on the verge of the bourgeois revolution or still engaged in the revolutionary democratic struggle, and his general strategy and tactics were brilliantly and successfully realized by Lenin. But there was no real understanding of the middle class in economically highly developed nations, and of the "new" middle class out of which the "new" proletariat emerged. There were two equally wrong policies: sectarian neglect of the middle class and opportunist adaptation to its demands. Liberals and revisionist socialists used the "new" middle class to prove that Marx was wrong and that the middle class was growing. But the "new" middle class is not the old and lower salaried employees are neither old nor new middle class. The new type of salaried worker was also neglected, especially in the United States, by the trade unions, but they are now beginning to overcome the error.

ist in scope. When, moreover, the unions imposed limitations on the employers in the shops, it was the initial form of the struggle for power by the working class. But unions and strikes and all forms of independent labor action were largely rejected by the lower salaried employees, whose middle class gentility and prejudices they outraged. The rejection of an identification with labor was strengthened by another condition: the salaried employee (and professional) may earn from $1,000 to $10,000 yearly without going outside his group, while the worker must cease being a worker to go beyond an upper income limit. This condition was always the means of creating the illusion that the interests of all salaried employees are the same, and one result was the ideological identification of lower salaried with the higher, and with the middle class and monopoly capitalism. This tendency is strengthened by the salaried employees who are engaged in purely parasitic and predatory enterprises, including those performing the repressive services of the state. Moreover, while differentials favoring lower salaried employees are breaking down more rapidly, their average earnings are still higher than those of the workers (although not among all groups). And for years becoming a salaried employee, if only a clerk, represented opportunity and advancement to the children of wage-workers. Hence the "new" proletariat may absorb, against its own economic interests, the middle class sense of superiority and caste.

The sense of being "different" from the workers,

262

of being "better" than them, is deliberately and brutally exploited by fascism. But only the forms of exploitation are new. It was always exploited by employers to prevent lower salaried employees from organizing unions and striking, and to mobilize them against the workers, while salaried labor steadily approached more closely to the economic condition of the workers. An American writer, John Corbin, anticipated much of the fascist appeal in 1922 by drawing the logic of the sense of superiority and caste. He said:

"The white collar workers have stood neutral. Being more highly educated and thus less easily replaceable, they were less often turned off their jobs; or, when they were, their larger pay and their habits of thrift tided them over the rainy day. They looked on the struggle between labor and capital as a thing apart. . . . But eventually they learned, or are learning, that there are conflicts in which it is dishonor and death to remain neutral."

It *is* dishonor and death to remain neutral in the struggle between labor and capital. But what did Corbin suggest—that salaried groups in the middle class unite with labor in the struggle against capital, that they fight for progress and a new social order? No; he argued that labor, not capital, is responsible for their plight and urged them to act as agents of the employers to break strikes, which might include strikes of lower salaried employees. Deliberate incitement of one type of workers against another! Clearly and bluntly Corbin offered the masses of

263

lower salaried employees and professionals, whom he identified with the upper middle class, for sale to the capitalist exploiters:

"Today, with class warfare threatening, the blindest employer can see in the middle class a powerful and indispensable ally."

An ally of the employers! But it is the employers, not the workers, who exploit the dispossessed salaried masses, who degraded their economic condition and impaired their security, privileges and earnings. Yet Corbin calculatingly and ruthlessly inflamed the inherited and now wholly disastrous antagonism to the workers:

"If the forgotten folk, who are remembering themselves as the middle class, are to feed their minds with the knowledge of books, their lives with human contacts; if they are to have children and hand on the education and the larger tradition which they received—if, in short, they are to fill the position and do the work which is owing to themselves and the nation, it can only be by a frank recognition of inequalities and distinctions. They must have a life scaled in higher opportunity, and in expense, than the life of the man whose capacity is for merely manual labor." [10]

Observe the contempt for manual workers, millions of whom are more skilled than the majority of lower salaried employees. Are machinists, electricians, locomotive engineers and printers inferior to the clerk, the stenographer and typist, the canvasser and agent who walks from door to door? *Manual*

264

workers must have a life scaled in lower opportunity while a few multiply their enjoyments. Observe the repudiation of the ideal of equality and democracy for which the old middle class radicals fought. *There must be frank recognition of inequalities and distinctions.* It means a new system of caste. Instead of urging a fuller life for all, the insistence that a small minority must have more than the masses of the people. Corbin's ideology is that of the petty rentier, of the man who lives on an income without working. To assure his privileges he must rally the dispossessed masses of lower salaried employees and professionals to the defense of the capitalist, against their own interests, damning their own future in a fratricidal struggle with the workers. The final result is fascist annihilation of all labor rights, including the rights of salaried and professional labor.*

* The higher salaried employees play the same game to maintain their own privileges against the lower salaried. A highly conscious expression of this tendency was revealed by the Deutschnationaler Handlungsgehilfen Verband, which was always aggressively nationalist, imperialist, anti-socialist and anti-Semitic, and in the 1920's rallied to Hitler. "According to [the superiority theory of the D. H. V.] the position of the salaried worker differs fundamentally from that of the manual worker because of the special functions which the former performs in the modern enterprise. His functions are to be conceived as delegated entrepreneurial functions. From the subordinate bookkeeper to the official empowered to act for the entrepreneur the salaried employee takes part in the guidance of the enterprise. In contrast to the manual worker he has a profession, and in 'normal times' advancement is typical for him. Finally, responsibility and a greater or less degree of independence are the signs of his superiority over the manual worker. [This pseudo-aristocratic theory] is not based on an analysis of the economic situation of the average salaried employee today but rather upon that of the past, which still holds true only for a minority of principal salaried employees.

And the intellectuals? They are to forget their own oppressive conditions while multiplying the security and enjoyments of the few; to use their minds and culture to inflame the antagonism against labor and misrepresent the struggle for a new social order; to degrade their craft function, the liberation of understanding, in the cause of reaction; to war on enlightenment and progress.

For whose benefit? Not the masses of lower salaried employees and professionals: they are delivered to the mercy of their employers, and their standards of living must decline as capitalist reaction strangles the productive forces and progress. The beneficiary of the new caste system would be a small minority in the upper middle class—and monopoly capitalism.

No: the masses of lower salaried employees and professionals, including the intellectuals, must break away from the middle class that excludes them because of their propertiless, dependent condition. They must recognize their identity with labor. That

In questions of education the D. H. V. teaches its members to despise the 'street cleaners' ideal' held by millions, 'who will not or cannot raise themselves above a purely instinctive life.' In politics it struggles with all its power against the manual workers, in order to maintain the social distance between them and the white collar workers. The salaried employees who live in its spirit do so with the consciousness of the nationalist who, according to the famous formula of Möller van den Bruck's *Drittes Reich,* is not a member of the proletariat because he does not wish to be one. In a word, in this theory the salaried workers appear not as a 'new proletariat' but as a 'new middle class,' which, being a nationalist middle class, is a guaranty of the continuation of the ruling social order." Hans Speier, "The Salaried Employee in Modern Society," *Social Research*, February, 1934, pp. 125-26.

means growing an economic backbone by the organization of unions, acquiring a sense of independence and power, making collective demands on the employer, instead of pleading or being silent, imposing on him a recognition of collective rights. It means *becoming a part* of the labor movement and *taking part* in joint action with the unions of wage-workers. The labor movement has neglected the salaried workers? But it neglected the unskilled workers, too, and both errors are being overcome: the unions are coming to realize that they must broaden their scope or perish. There is no group of lower salaried employees and professionals that cannot form unions, to whom unions are unnecessary or alien. Many of them have already formed unions: clerks and technicians, teachers and other professional groups. Only a beginning, but they are increasing under the influence of depression and capitalist decline, with their devastating impact on employment, earnings and general working conditions. The new unions and the old are learning to work together, to develop a creative spirit of solidarity in action. Unions are opposed by the upper layers of salaried employees and professonals; but the lower layers must consider their own interests and take the action that flows inevitably from those interests. They must, in organizing unions, resist control by higher salaried employees and the efforts to separate from the working class: they must resist the transformation of their unions into means of struggle against labor, for capitalist reaction and fascism.

267

As organized workers the masses of lower salaried employees and professionals belong in a labor party arising out of the unions and other organizations of labor.* The unions must broaden their struggles to include political issues. While the program of a labor party is limited, it sets the working class in motion *as a class,* including the unorganized workers, and challenges capitalist control of the state. It is a means for uniting all the workers, of all types of labor politics, on transitional issues and forms of action against capitalist reaction. But as the crisis of capitalism sharpens it appears clearly that limited reformist action is not enough. For under the conditions of economic decline and decay reformism drives the two groups of the working class apart and replaces united struggle with a cat-and-dog fight for "salvation" against one another. That creates the

* Including organizations of the farmers. It is necessary, however, that farmers should not be represented by organizations of the upper layers of farmers, whose interests are opposed to their own poorer brethren and to labor. These organizations are prone to speak in general terms and adopt a policy in their own exclusive interests. How a program "for all the farmers" may prove disastrous to the lower layers is proven by many of the measures of the Agricultural Adjustment Administration; its most brutal results are produced by the acreage reduction program, particularly in cotton, where the big planters get all the benefits while scores of thousands of tenants, share-croppers and laborers have been deprived of their means of livelihood. The diversity of class interests among the farmers makes imperative the formation, and their representation in a labor party, of unions of farm laborers, tenants and poorer independent farmers, including industrial workers in the small towns who are in a strategic position in relation to industry and agriculture. The interests of all these groups are identified with those of the wage-workers and lower salaried employees and professionals.

opportunity for fascism. It becomes clear that the only answer to the increasing misery of capitalist decline and the menace of fascism is the communist struggle for the overthrow of capitalism and the transformation of collectivism into socialism.

The economic forms of socialism are fully developed in collectivism. Its transformation into socialism needs simply the appropriate class action. Whose class action?

Not the action of the middle class, as usually and broadly defined. For it is split by discordant interests and by the clash of new and old social orders within itself. It is not, as a class, the carrier of a new social order, and it is incapable of dominating and reconstructing society.

Not the old middle class of independent small enterprisers, who are a dying class struggling for survival within the relations of monopoly capitalism. They are not identified with the new social order potential in collectivism; on the contrary, they are opposed to collectivism. Independent enterprisers represent reactionary class interests, for they can survive only by limiting collectivism and become strong only by destroying it: an impossibility which denies all social progress. They are, however, terribly exploited by monopoly capitalism, and it is possible—more, necessary—to rally small storekeepers and petty producers to socialism and the communist struggle for its realization. But the *class* is opposed to socialism.

Nor is the "new" middle class of salaried and professional groups capable of transforming collectivism into socialism. While identified with collectivism, it, too, is split by discordant interests and the clash of new and old social orders within itself.

The higher salaried employees and professionals, the "new" middle class in the strict sense, are a privileged caste whose relation to production and income assures their support of capitalism. They are identified with collectivism, but still more they are identified with the exploiting relations of its capitalist forms, for collectivism is now both a systematic organization of economic activity and a systematic organization of exploitation. This is particularly true of the managerial and supervisory employees. Some liberals argue that these groups, since they are independent of ownership and develop "professional" standards of their own, may become a force moving toward a new social order. But one of the liberals answers his own argument: "They [managerial and supervisory employees] are not free men. They are not neutral, hired to serve all interests alike. They are employed by stockholders to promote the interests of stockholders." [11] It is the managerial and supervisory employees, moreover, who carry on the exploitation of labor, including salaried labor, and crush unions and strikes. Management as a hired function, which makes the capitalist superfluous, is an aspect of the new social order, but it is now limited and degraded to serve capital: socialism would liberate its potentialities. The prospect of liberation may rally to socialism many of the managerial and supervisory employees, particularly in the lower groups, as their incomes are slashed and they are thrown into unemployment. This is still truer of independent professionals, for declining capitalism increasingly limits and degrades their craft function. But the "new" middle class, as a whole, struggles to become a caste in a new reactionary set-up—against labor and socialism.

The masses of lower salaried employees and professionals, the "new" proletariat, are identified with collectivism, but not with its capitalist exploiting relations. Hence they are identified with the new social order. But that new order is socialism. The struggle for socialism proceeds outside the circle of the middle class, old and new. It proceeds within the circle of the working class, and the lower salaried employees and professionals can struggle for socialism only as they recognize that they are part of the working class.*

Socialism originated as the policy of the proletariat, when salaried and professional groups were not numerous and were definitely middle class. It is the policy of the working class, which now includes the dispossessed salaried and professional workers.

---

* There are engineers who imagine they can, as a group "above the classes," manage and control industry to prevent cyclical breakdown and limitation of production. But that is impossible because capitalist relations of production cause all the trouble. Engineers may play, as part of the working class, a creative part in the struggle for socialism. The idea of a "revolution by engineers" is, however, fantastic. Thorstein Veblen, who originated the idea, made it conditional on *the support of the workers:* not "the public" or "all the classes."

271

The proletariat is the dominant element in the working class. It is massed in the decisive industrial enterprises, in objective control of them, and has an unusual homogeneity, collective consciousness and discipline. It is not a split personality: the minor antagonisms between skilled and unskilled, the organized and unorganized, are resolvable within the relations of the class. The proletariat is wholly identified with collectivism and the new social order; it is the carrier of socialism, as the bourgeoisie was the carrier of capitalism. Salaried employers and professionals are not as homogeneous, collective and disciplined as the proletariat; they are still, in many respects, intermediate elements, their proletarianization within the middle class has left its imprint, and they are apt to be unstable in the class struggle. But that excludes them neither from the working class nor the labor movement and its potential revolutionary struggle, for it merely offers a problem in understanding and control:* offered, in other forms, by other groups of the working class.

The relation of class forces is decisive in the struggle for a new social order. One of the most important developments in that relation is the proletarianization of large groups in the middle class and the in-

* The problem is mainly ideological. What makes the problem more acute is that one of its aspects, especially in the United States, includes millions of workers still under the influence of middle class ideals and illusions. A concrete approach is necessary, ideological and occupational, to the different groups of lower salaried employees and professionals; it must stress the craft functions of technicians, professionals and intellectuals, who may be inspired by the prospect of their liberation.

crease of the working class. But this is denied by many. The British economist, G. D. H. Cole, says:

"The proletariat of wage-workers came to form a smaller proportion of the total population in the most advanced industrial countries. . . . The basis of capitalism grew broader with concentration, and the absolute and relative numbers of intermediate groups increased. There was no polarization of classes, but rather a growing difficulty in marking off one class clearly from another—blurring of the lines of division, even if the essential characters of the outstanding classes remained plain and distinct." [12]

That theory is offered in a much cruder and more fantastic form by the American liberal-radical, Stuart Chase:

"Already the middle class in America, not including the farmers, outnumbers the working class. . . . Adding farmers to the middle class, the majority in sheer numbers is large. . . . America still has a proletariat, but every automatic process, every battery of photoelectric cells, diminishes its numbers and its political importance." [13]

The middle class, as usually and broadly defined, including all lower salaried employees and professionals, is a small minority: it is 25.5% of all persons gainfully occupied, the wage-workers 59.3%. Where is the "outnumbering" of the working class? Adding farmers to the middle class (and it must be remembered that nearly half the farmers are propertiless) gives no "large majority in sheer numbers,"

273

CRISIS OF THE MIDDLE CLASS

Class Divisions in the United States, 1870-1935

	1870		1935	
Class	Number	Per-cent	Number	Per-cent
Wage-workers *	5,600,000	44.8	30,250,000	59.3
Farmers †	4,500,000	36.0	7,400,000	14.5
Middle Class ‡	2,300,000	18.4	13,000,000	25.5
Salaried	*600,000*	*4.8*	*10,300,000*	*20.2*
Enterprisers	*1,700,000*	*13.6*	*2,700,000*	*5.3*
Big Bourgeoise	100,000	0.8	350,000	0.7

* Including hired farm laborers and salespeople in stores.
† Including laborers working on home farms.
‡ Middle class as usually and broadly defined, including all lower salaried employees and professionals.
Source: Computed from material in the Census reports of 1870 and 1930; A. M. Edwards, "A Social-Economic Grouping of the Gainful Workers of the United States," *Journal of the American Statistical Association,* December, 1933, pp. 1-11; United States, Bureau of Internal Revenue, *Statistics of Income, 1929.* The 1935 estimates are approximations based on a projection of the 1930 distribution.

for both are only 40% of the gainfully occupied compared with 54.4% in 1870: they are now a minority. Wage-workers, on the contrary, moved up from 44.8% to 59.3%: they are now a majority.

The middle class, again as usually and broadly defined, grew only slightly more than wage-workers in 1870-1935 as a proportion of the gainfully occupied: 39% compared with 32%. They both gained at the expense of the farmers. And the liberals ignore the great change in the composition of the middle class. It is historically wrong and tactically misleading to ignore that change. *Independent enterprisers fell from 74% of the class in 1870 to only 21% in 1935, while salaried employees rose from 26% to 79%.* The change is all the more significant as salaried employees were clearly members of the middle class in

1870, while only a minority are now. Add that minority—the 1,800,000 higher salaried employees and professionals—to the surviving independent enterprisers, and the middle class becomes 4,500,000, *or only 9% of the gainfully occupied compared with 18% in 1870, a decrease of 50%*. Include the masses of lower salaried employees and professionals, who are *not* middle class economically, and the working class becomes an overwhelming majority: 38,750,000 persons, or 75% of the gainfully occupied.

Economic development, including every automatic process and every photoelectric cell, has not destroyed the proletariat, although it has practically destroyed the old middle class of independent enterprisers. There has been much ado about the slight decrease of industrial workers in the 1920's; but it was slight, the industrial workers are still a majority of all wage-workers, and they are a larger proportion than in 1870—55% compared with 46%.[14]

Salaried employees have not displaced the wage-workers, and they cannot. They grew faster than the workers in the earlier stages of large-scale industry, but their rate of growth was almost at a standstill in the 1920's. Salaried employees increased 52% in 1909-20 compared with 16% among the wage-workers; but their increase fell to 23% in 1920-27, while that of the wage-workers rose to 18%.[15] Capitalist industry must reduce its overhead costs, which include the costs of salaried labor. This becomes all the more imperative under the conditions of capitalist decline and lower profits. The prophecy that the proletariat will disappear is based on the suppo-sition that technology *under capitalism* moves on toward universal automatic production. But that is fantastic, for it would mean a multiplication of the productive forces and an abundance that would strangle capitalism. Already capitalism depends on the planned limitation of production to survive, which means the limitation of technological progress. Instead of salaried employees displacing the wage-workers, both are being increasingly displaced by the crisis of capitalism and thrown into permanent unemployment.

The changes in class relations have not broadened but narrowed the basis of capitalism. Intermediate groups have increased only because of the great changes in the middle class and the emergence of the "new" proletariat. But this has strengthened the working class and weakened the middle class, for the intermediate functional groups are overwhelmingly proletarian in their economic conditions. A middle class, as usually and broadly defined, that consists of 65% of proletarian salaried employees and profes-sionals is not as much of a barrier to socialism as a middle class composed almost exclusively of inde-pendent propertied enterprisers. There is still an ideological barrier, but the economic barrier exists no longer. It is much easier to win a propertiless salaried employee to socialism and the communist struggle for its realization than the propertied enter-priser whom he has replaced. All the more as col-lectivism is now dominant and the decline of capitalism sharpens the crisis of the system, of which the crisis of the middle class is an aspect.

Moreover, social transformation and revolutionary struggle are not an arithmetical problem. Numbers are important, but more important is the relation of a class to production and to the emerging new social order. The bourgeoisie was a minority of the people, yet it was the rallying force in the struggle for the new capitalist order. The working class is a majority, and depends on its numbers; but the working class depends still more on its control of industry, its historical significance as the carrier of socialism, its revolutionary initiative and action. That is the might of the working class, which includes the interests and struggles of all the oppressed, as socialism includes all humanity.

Chapter XII

MIDDLE CLASS AND FASCISM

CAPITALISM moves toward socialism. That is the historical meaning of the great class-economic changes in the structure of capitalism. It is the meaning of collectivism and the decay of the old middle class of independent enterprisers; of the conversion of the majority of the people, including the masses of lower salaried employees and professionals in the "new" middle class, into propertiless, proletarian dependents on the property of a capitalist oligarchy.

But the emergence of a new social order is not automatic: the masters of the old do not easily yield to the new. They resist, as in the past the lords of other outworn systems have always resisted, as the masters of capitalism now resist the transformation of collectivism into socialism. Progress is remorselessly strangled in order that a social order may live on beyond its useful historical period; economic and cultural decline and decay set in. Capitalism, to survive, must "plan" to limit abundance, to limit and sabotage and destroy the technical-economic resources of society, for they are now a threat to capitalist profit. It does all that to survive, instead of increasing general well-being and raising the level of civilization. The forms of the new social order strain more

278

insistently against their capitalist fetters, and capitalism mobilizes all its vast repressive forces against the threat. But this action in itself aggravates and emphasizes the crisis of the system: the crisis becomes general and permanent.

All social classes are set in motion by the persistence and deepening of the crisis created by capitalist decline. As the crises of property and employment are sharpened, the middle class, too, is set in motion. It calls upon traditional ideals and forms of action to defend its interests: democracy, more reforms, more intervention by the state in economic activity. But these measures, which in the past provided some degree of temporary relief, now prove wholly ineffective and break down. For the new, and final, crisis of the middle class is a product of the *decline* of capitalism, which permits no "easing" of the crisis. Now, while the social forces of production and consumption are being stifled to save capitalist profit from the threat of abundance, the old middle class of independent small enterprisers is not only limited more severely, it must move toward final destruction. And millions of lower salaried employees and professionals are thrown into permanent unemployment: their fate is economically one with that of labor and they share in labor's increasing misery under the impact of capitalist decline.

As the old ideals and forms of action collapse, and the pressure of the crisis becomes unendurable, the middle class begins to move toward new ideas and new forms of action. What shall they be? If they are still conditioned by the illusion that the class crisis can be solved within the relations of capitalist property, the middle class completely abandons its old democratic ideals and mobilizes against labor, whose struggle for the new socialist order becomes ever more conscious and aggressive. By that act the middle class throws itself into the consuming fires of fascism.

1

The middle class, as we have seen, has no independent class interests sufficiently all-embracing to unite its economically antagonistic groups. Whose interests, therefore, are served in mobilizing middle class sentiment against labor and against the transformation of collectivism into socialism? Only the interests of the surviving independent enterprisers and of the higher salaried employees, particularly the managerial and supervisory hirelings of the great corporations, who are identified with the needs of monopoly capitalism.

Independent enterprisers want to save their property. Higher salaried employees want to save their privileges as a dominant caste in the set-up of monopoly capitalism. They are all in agreement on the fundamental proposition of rallying to the defense of capitalism. But there is an underlying antagonism, for small enterprise must find the means of limiting monopoly in order to survive, and monopoly must more intensely exploit small enterprise as economic activity moves downward. A compromise, or the appearance of one, becomes necessary, for the privileged

280

and well-paid managerial and supervisory employees of large-scale industry and finance cannot permit limitation of the monopoly capital which sustains them in their favored position. The demagogic outbursts of their political spokesmen to the contrary, independent enterprisers gradually abandon the struggle against monopoly, their resistance being all the weaker because the upper layers of the old middle class contact the big bourgeoisie and are involved in all the coercive relations of finance capital. The struggle against monopoly must be abandoned for another weighty reason: it is a dangerous struggle which may aggravate the existing instability and provide an opportunity for the revolutionary upthrust of labor. Hence security and the crushing of labor become the new ideals. The old middle class of independent enterprisers gives up its fight against monopoly, limiting itself to a struggle for mere survival within the relations of monopoly capitalism, in a new set-up of caste and rigid class stratification enforced by the repressive might of the state. This meets the approval of the higher salaried employees, who are accustomed to the hierarchical relations of corporate industry and are not averse to imposing them on the whole social and political life of the nation.

This new course of action compels the old middle class to abandon its ideals of individualism and freedom of enterprise, and the democratic ideals built on them. For survival as a caste means limitation of economic freedom and the denial of democratic rights to the workers. Formerly the middle class struggle for independent small property involved a struggle for liberty, individualism and democracy; now the struggle to save such property as still survives from the all-consuming maw of monopoly capitalism drives the class to reaction, to negation of the ideals for which it fought in its youth.

The elements of this reaction are not altogether new. They began to arise as monopoly capitalism enlarged its dominion over industry and the state. Small enterprisers began to desire mere survival and security within monopoly capitalism as it grew more and more evident that the struggle to overthrow or limit monopoly was hopeless. Their resort to the coercive measures of state capitalism meant an increasing loss of faith in the democratic ideals identified with individualism and free enterprise. The reaction was strengthened by three other factors: the growing power of trade unionism and socialism, the authoritarian ideas of higher managerial and supervisory employees in the hierarchy of corporate industry, and the emergence of a more aggressive nationalism resulting from the imperialist enslavement of colonial peoples. These developments were most notable in Europe, where the class struggle and imperialism were both more highly developed; but they were clearly evident in the United States as well. They appeared in the emphasis of pre-war progressivism on the "new nationalism" (justifying barbarous imperialist repression in the Philippines and the Caribbeans), on state capitalism, bureaucracy and caste, on the necessity of the middle class accepting monopoly capitalism and reaction.

This earlier *tendency* to reaction is strengthened as the middle class clings desperately to the idea of achieving security and a caste position in a declining capitalism, under which the class crisis is sharpened and all social relations are increasingly unstable. The old middle class, to survive, must crush the labor movement and the new order toward which society moves. More, it must crush *all* progressive forces, for capitalism in decay revolts against all forms of progress. Out of the middle class leaps the monster of fascism: the class that once waged revolutionary war on authoritarianism now provides, in a final desperate struggle for survival, the ideology and mass support for a new authoritarianism determined to destroy all the remnants, and the very concepts, of liberty, equality and democracy.

The reaction of the middle class becomes fascism when it merges with the reaction of the big bourgeoisie, of the magnates of finance capital. A part, even if only a minor part, of all the capitalist relations of production, the middle class is incapable of independent class action: its apparently independent struggle for survival and caste privileges becomes an expression of the needs of dominant capitalism.

Monopoly capitalism and imperialism represent a natural reaction in the direction of a new authoritarianism, against the democratic and progressive ideals. Monopoly and the hierarchical relations of corporate industry are by their very nature intolerant of democracy; and monopoly measurably limits technical-economic progress in order to insure monopoly profits. Imperialism must necessarily crush democratic rights among enslaved colonial peoples, and it stifles many forms of progress because they are dangerous to imperialist domination. Monopoly and imperialism, in all their terrific power, challenge the state and manipulate the state, moving toward an all-inclusive economic and political dictatorship: a concentration of political power to match the concentration of economic power. The reactionary tendency, always in action, is now strengthened by the decline of capitalism. Economic breakdown and falling profits, the need for increasing state financial aid, the burden of the social services, and the growing revolt against capitalism drive the big bourgeoisie to action. It must more completely merge monopoly and the state, use state aid more generously to promote its own economic policy, make impossible the opportunity to articulate inimical class interests provided by the democratic system, limit the social services, unify all the national forces for imperialism and war, and mercilessly crush all opposition: *all* opposition, and particularly that of labor, including salaried labor. Monopoly capitalism needs a new despotism.

But that cannot be done arbitrarily or by the old methods. Moreover, as repression is multiplied, monopoly capitalism forfeits the confidence of the masses, including the petty-bourgeois masses. The discontent of the people assumes dangerous forms.

Labor's demands become more pressing and the threat of proletarian revolution appears, while the middle class opposition is inflamed. The old democratic methods of rule break down: new methods are necessary. *Out of breakdown, popular discontent and revolt the big bourgeoisie must create new sanctions for itself and its rule.* Normal sanctions and methods are impossible under the abnormal conditions of capitalist decline. So the reaction of the middle class is used to set up a new dictatorship of capital: open, terrorist, brutal, stripped of all limitations. *Fascism, using radical phrases and middle class action, provides the ideological justification, the "popular" sanctions and the mass support to suppress violently all progressive forces and prevent the transformation of collectivism into socialism.* To call anything else fascism is to misunderstand its nature and bedevil the struggle against its menace. Fascism is the absolute dictatorship and reaction of finance capital *masked in popular forms:* it destroys *all* democratic rights and *all* organizations of labor, including those of salaried labor, in an effort to prevent *any* action against the dominant capitalist order, and provides a mass basis for those actions that no "reaction from on top" is capable of providing.

But where, in all this, are the interests of the "new" proletariat, the masses of lower salaried employees and professionals? Their interests are ignored and excluded. As propertiless workers they belong with the struggle against capital and for the transformation of collectivism into socialism, which alone can solve their crisis of employment and liberate them from the dependent relations of capitalism. But if they do not recognize the identity, if they are not drawn into the unions and the struggle for socialism, salaried and professional employees become the shock troops of fascism. How? By the exploitation of traditional passions and prejudices, particularly the traditional antagonism to labor, and by the promise of a minor caste status in the fascist set-up.*

Fascism must exploit passions and prejudices, it must offer "ideals" in place of a concrete program, for the groups it mobilizes are antagonistic in their economic interests. It is the only way that dispossessed, propertiless masses can be rallied to the defense of property. It is the only way an artificial unity can be created in the middle class. All the most reactionary ideals of capitalism, and many that capitalism itself has rejected, are erected into a system by fascism; even when it uses progressive national traditions it twists them into reactionary forms. The petty-bourgeois masses are imprisoned within the

* The basis of the fascist appeal to the farmers is the protection of property, and it is directly aimed at the upper layer of capitalist farmers. But the majority of farmers are propertiless, hence all sorts of lavish promises of high prices and larger incomes, and flattery of the farmers as the "backbone" of the nation. At the same time, fascism mobilizes its hordes against the militant farmers who may act militantly or express radical ideas. In agriculture, too, the concept of caste appears: the big farmers—the exploiters of hired labor and the poorer farmers—are to become a privileged caste. But fascism offers nothing that may solve the agrarian crisis, because that solution depends on multiplying the forces of production and consumption, and they are strangled by fascism as the final brutal expression of capitalist decline and decay.

circle of the new reaction, its ideals fetters upon their self-action.

Fascism, moreover, exploits the social pathology of declining capitalism. Foul passions are created or unloosed by the barbarous rigors of permanent unemployment, the tortured pride of declassed elements, the degradation of men and women on relief, the fear of insecurity among those still employed, the frightful hatreds of the property owner whose possessions are threatened, and, above all, the furies of the rulers of finance capital at the prospect of dethronement. Fascism in Italy and Germany has shown what use can be made of this social degeneration and the scum it throws up out of the depths. No means are too vile for capitalism to employ in the effort to maintain its power. But it must not be forgotten that fascism creates nothing new, theoretically or ideologically, that it merely fuses into a system the existing reactionary elements of capitalism and the reactionary ideals of many scholars and philosophers: they provide the opportunity and the justification for the social scum of fascism.

Underlying the growth of fascism is the declining faith in capitalism of the petty-bourgeois masses and the revolt against their misery. It is the task of fascism to recreate the faith and transform the revolt into a support of monopoly capitalism. Hence fascism must use radical phrases, it must clothe itself in plebeian garb to gain popular following. Fascism exploits traditional radicalism and the strength of the rebellious mood of the people. Syndicalism was bastardized by Mussolini, socialism by Hitler. They rant against the slavery to debt and interest, against speculators and bankers (especially if they are Jews or aliens), against the wicked rich. They may even proclaim that "capitalism is doomed." An American fascism may exploit the older populism and progressivism, invoke the democratic traditions of the early years of the republic, use again the old battle cries against "monopoly" and the "money power." But it is all demagogy to snare the gullible. The concrete purposes of fascism are all *acceptable and necessary* to monopoly capitalism:

1. Defense of property. Fascism always stresses this point. As the great majority of the people are propertiless and most of the nation's property is owned by a very small minority, there is nothing here to which the capitalists can object.

2. State capitalism, often euphemistically called "controlled capitalism." This, imagines the old middle class of independent enterprisers, will protect small property, while the liberals imagine that it will "regulate" and "plan" capitalism. State capitalism does nothing of the sort, for it is merely a more complete merger of state and industry under control of dominant finance capital. A "controlled" capitalism is an impossibility, a contradiction in terms, for all the vested interests of capitalist ownership and profit are retained, with their anarchic effect on economic relations. Neither planning nor control are possible where the social forces of production are disorganized by the antagonistic relations of capitalist profit.

288

What is really accomplished by state capitalism is the subjection of both capitalism and the state to more effective control by monopoly capital, which requires that control to prevent a catastrophic economic breakdown, to plan the limitation of production to maintain profits, and to increase the systematic organization of industry for the purposes of imperialism and war. State capitalism is not fascism, but fascism necessarily includes state capitalism.*

3. The antagonism to labor. All organizations of labor, not merely the communist, must be destroyed by fascism, for the independence of labor is dangerous to the authority of the totalitarian state. But antagonism to labor and the destruction of its organizations are also necessary to monopoly capitalism; under the conditions of capitalist decline labor must be sweated more mercilessly to insure profits, expenditures on social services must be cut to the bone, and labor unions must be smashed to prevent strikes for higher wages and to mobilize the masses for the struggle to overthrow capitalism. Hence fascism, by inflaming middle class antagonism to labor and inciting its hordes to smash unions and break strikes, is directly serving the interests of monopoly

* It is suggestive that Dr. Hjalmar Schacht, the economic "dictator" of fascist Germany, was in 1920, when capitalism was in danger of overthrow, an advocate of "modified" or "controlled" capitalism as the alternative to socialism. After the Nazis became a great party in 1930, Schacht leaped onto the bandwagon, urging the capitalist necessity of destroying the labor unions. There was logic in the transition, and a ministerial portfolio. The honest, if gullible, liberals who sincerely believed in a "controlled" capitalism are either dead, being tortured in jails and concentration camps, or degraded into silence.

289

capital. Moreover, the fascist destruction of labor unions works against the interests of small enterprisers, particularly storekeepers and independent professionals, who depend on the patronage of the working class: the defeat of labor is the beginning of still lower standards of living. And it is contrary to the interests of the masses of lower salaried employees and professionals, who are deprived of the right to organize and strike for improved conditions.*

4. The reaction against democracy. Fascism urges, as an ideal, the destruction of all democratic rights. There is nothing in this unacceptable to monopoly capitalism, for it means depriving both the workers *and the middle class* of democratic rights. Parliamentarism, too, must be destroyed. It was useful in the struggle against feudalism; later it served as a forum for the adjustment of clashing capitalist interests without disturbing the dominion of a capitalism that was still progressive. Now, when the dominion of capitalism is crumbling, parliamentarism is dangerous because it provides a forum for the expression of class interests which are increasingly unadjustable. More important, the democratic rights of the workers must be destroyed, for they permit unions and strikes and the struggle for a new social

* An American fascism may attempt to inflame the great masses of unorganized workers, hitherto neglected by the American Federation of Labor, against the trade unions and even to organize fascist "unions," as one demagogue has already tried. Obviously the organization of the unorganized unskilled and salaried and professional workers into labor unions is the only defense against such an attempt.

order. There must be no interference with the dictatorship of capital if it is to save a declining social order that multiplies the burdens of the people.

5. Nationalism, imperialism and war. Nationalism is inflamed to obscure class lines and interests, to make the masses of the people forget their concrete economic needs, and to replace the class struggle with the struggle for national aggrandizement. The exploitation of sentimental patriotic traditions, and the prejudices based on them, is a means of disguising the dominion of monopoly capitalism, and of justifying that dominion in terms of national power. An inflamed nationalism, moreover, is necessary to promote more aggressive imperialism and war preparations.

6. An authoritarian state and the caste system. All capitalist states are authoritarian, but they are limited by traditional democracy; the new authoritarianism of the totalitarian state is necessary to crush *all* opposition and *all* progressive forces. A new caste system means the stratification of class lines and inequality under the iron control of the state and its masters, the capitalist oligarchy. The new authoritarianism and caste are the final expression of the reaction against progress created by the decline of capitalism.

All these fascist purposes are offered as classless "ideals," but their reactionary capitalist character is plain. The "independent" action of the middle class, its final struggle for survival, moves toward fascism and fascism becomes the final desperate effort of declining capitalism to survive.

Capitalism resorts to fascism only in the most desperate situation. The capitalists despise and mistrust the fascist upstarts. They prefer an all-inclusive economic and political dictatorship within the old forms of rule. They realize that the totalitarian state of fascism, by abolishing parliament and all parties, makes political power a monopoly of the fascist party and measurably frees the state and its bureaucracy from direct control of the capitalists. The absolute terrorist dictatorship of finance capital is possible only by granting fascism the monopoly of political power. But the price must be paid, as desperate measures are necessary in the desperate situation created by declining capitalism.

Hence, from the beginning, the more far-seeing capitalists support fascist movements. (One group of big capitalists, moreover, may use fascism against another group in the inner conflicts of the class: that was particularly true in Germany.) Mussolini was financed by the Union of Industrialists, Hitler by the Krupps, Thyssen and the bankers: dominant interests urged the government to make premiers of the adventurers. Mussolini, "without saying much about it . . . and while emphasizing the fascist appeal to the sentimental attachments sanctified by Italian history . . . was careful to serve the material interests of the Italian employing class." [1] Behind the anti-capitalist demagogy lies the reality of capitalist objectives and control.

Fascism has conspiratorial elements, but it is more than a conspiracy of finance capital, which seizes on forces in the middle class already moving toward fascism. An "independent" revolt of the middle class, determined to save private property and a dying capitalism and to crush labor, must necessarily accept the reactionary relations of the dominant monopoly capitalism. The middle class, which contacts both the big bourgeoisie and the working class, must accept the program of one or the other: capitalism or socialism. Small enterprisers cannot hope to destroy the great corporate combinations of capital, and the attempt to do so would be resisted by the higher managerial and supervisory employees (the driving force of an American fascism). Not only would an attack on monopoly capitalism meet with the resistance of decisive elements in the middle class itself, but it might create disastrous economic and class disturbances and encourage the revolutionary action of the masses. The rallying of all reactionary forces and ideals, moreover, must necessarily serve the reaction. By its defense of capitalist property and its rejection of democracy, by its acceptance of the totalitarian ideals of fascist dictatorship, the middle class offers itself up to the mercy of monopoly capitalism.

2

Fascism comes to power with the consent of the bureaucratic capitalist state, which surrenders as it did to Mussolini and Hitler, who represented only

293

a minority of the people. The state surrenders to avert a civil war that might aid the revolutionary struggle of the working class. Now fascism combines with all the openly reactionary forces, while imposing the new party control over them and retaining all the old demagogy. It proceeds to destroy the communist, socialist and trade union organizations: Mussolini destroyed them one after another, Hitler all together in one annihilating swoop.

All the idependent organizations of labor, *including the unions of salaried and professional workers*, are destroyed: labor is now the lowest caste in society. New fascist organizations of "labor" are set up, but they are merely means to control the workers. An economic enterprise becomes a feudal barony: workers are serfs and the employers are masters. Industrial relations in the German system are at the mercy of the employer and "trustees of labor" *not* elected by the workers. No expression of opinion is allowed: no opposition to *any* managerial measures.

The destruction of independent organizations *includes the organizations of the middle class*. Most dramatic was the suppression by the Nazis, shortly after coming to power, of the militant League of the Middle Class, composed mainly of small shopkeepers.[2] When the fascist party becomes the state it purges itself of all "radical" elements, of those who took seriously the old anti-capitalist demagogy and might incite the middle class masses, especially the lower salaried employees and professionals, to defend their interests against the new regime. Fascism deprives the middle class of all independence: it must, like the workers, submit silently to the new authoritarianism of the totalitarian state, for freedom of action is now a monopoly of the state and its big-capitalist masters.

Liberalism is as thoroughly suppressed as communism. The political system of liberalism is incompatible with the needs of declining capitalism and fascism. The intellectual aspects of liberalism must be suppressed because all oppositional ideas are dangerous to the new reactionary set-up. Fascism feeds on the corpse of intellectual death.

The crises of the middle class—of property and of employment—are aggravated by fascism. It neither solves the crisis of capitalism nor prevents the inner class changes which increasingly convert the middle class into propertiless (and largely unemployed) salaried dependents. Nothing is changed except for the worse. For fascism is not a new social order: what is new is the fascist technique of creating "popular" sanctions for ruthless suppression of the forces moving toward a new social order. Fascism saves capitalism, for the time being, from overthrow, but not from decline, disintegration and decay: it merely organizes them, and their mass misery, into an oppressive, barbarous system.

Fascism offers nothing new economically. Its policy is merely the old state capitalism, only more of it: the old policy of piecemeal aid to industry to prevent total collapse, of state financial aid to private capitalist enterprise, of the planned limitation of production. But state capitalism in the non-fascist nations neither prevented depression nor revived prosperity, and the results of its fascist variants are still worse. The levels of pre-depression prosperity were lower in fascist Italy than in other nations and the depression was much more severe. Fascism in Germany did not end the depression; instead it prepared an economic catastrophe. In two years the Hitler regime spent 18,000 million marks on armaments and "creation" of labor: mainly the former, with nearly 60% of industrial output being absorbed in feverish war preparations.[3] In Italy, too, where the state spends billions in assuming the losses of private enterprises and insuring their profits, economic activity is sustained by the expenditure of public money, especially for armaments. That means eventual collapse, for no national economy can indefinitely exist on such a program. Economic activity is depressed, unemployment high, and standards of living sinking among the workers, lower salaried employees and professionals, and the peasants.

While fascism bluffs about "controlled capitalism" and the "corporate state," these offer no control over fundamental economic forces because they represent the repressive merger of monopoly capitalism and the state, and accept the vested interests of capitalist property and profit. There is simply more control by the dominant capitalist interests: where limitations are imposed on capitalist enterprises the purpose is to promote the interests of capitalism in general, particularly of the masters of monopoly. The corporate state assures absolute control of the workers, including salaried workers, by the employers, and control of the small enterprisers by the big capitalists. Planning is impossible, as all the anarchic, disorganizing relations of capitalist production still prevail. What fascism plans is reaction and war.

This planning for war is interlocked with the efforts to create national economic self-sufficiency, or *Autarkie*. There are people who spoke, and still speak, of economic self-sufficiency as a means of averting crises and war. It is the opposite in fascist practice. It is an aspect of inflammatory nationalism and reaction. No nation is economically self-sufficient; both Italy and Germany lack essential raw materials (coal, metals, petroleum), which they must import. Moreover, as national markets are increasingly limited by fascism, a more imperative need arises for foreign markets. Mussolini and Hitler spend billions to stimulate foreign trade, and pin their hopes on territorial expansion. The only thing left of *Autarkie* is the effort to become independent of other nations in essential war materials, one means being the creation of synthetic raw materials whose costliness is a burden on industry. Efforts to create national economic self-sufficiency disorganize the world markets and drive toward war.*

---

* The United States is economically the most self-sufficient of the capitalist nations, but it, too, must import many raw materials. It would be driven toward foreign expansion under a fascist regime because of the tremendous productive forces and the absolute necessity of exporting surplus goods and capital. Fascism anywhere is necessarily imperialistic.

Economic forces are not liberated by fascism, they are more tightly repressed. The freedom of enterprise of the older capitalism is completely destroyed: monopoly and bureaucracy increasingly fetter the forces of production. This means the final destruction of the progressive economic aspects of capitalism. The crisis of capitalism originates in the crisis of an abundance that now threatens capitalist profit. Fascism strangles the forces of production and consumption to maintain high prices and profits, but economic activity moves downward. The state imposes new collective relations and strengthens economic collectivism, within which, however, the proletarianization of the middle class proceeds more rapidly. Using collectivist measures to prevent the transformation of collectivism into socialism, fascism (more than the older state capitalism) is a negative, destructive expression of the onward thrust of a new social order. Neither the old capitalist individualism nor the new socialist collectivism, fascism must imprison the productive forces and bring about economic disaster and increasing misery.

And as the misery of the people grows, fascism answers by making misery itself an ideal. Hitler talks of "heroic poverty," and Dr. Hjalmar Schacht adds: "We must renounce the comforts of life." [4] Mussolini asserts: "I know you are not looking for a comfortable life. Therefore I announce to you the approach of a hard period." [5] Renunciation is all the more necessary because of the limitation of social services, one of the main capitalist objectives. Fascism reverts to medieval glorification of poverty.

The heaviest burdens of the new misery are thrust upon the workers. They are sweated more severely, must work longer hours for lower wages, are deprived of all rights. The workers under fascism are a caste of helots. Fascism considers them only as material for national glory and war: for death, not life.

But the majority of the middle class, too, is engulfed in the economic disaster: it may try, but it cannot separate itself from the increasing misery of labor. Its numbers shrink as economic expansion shrinks and opportunity is more and more limited. In Italy and Germany, under fascism, the middle class has decreased probably 25% to 35% as a proportion of all persons gainfully occupied. And its burdens have multiplied.* Fascism benefits only the

* This is as true of the peasantry. Neither German nor Italian fascism kept its promises to break up the great landed estates. Fascism encourages agriculture to promote national economic self-sufficiency (for war purposes) and to consolidate the peasantry as a reactionary force. But this is accomplished by means of higher prices, which lower standards of living among the workers and the middle class masses, and by favoring the big landowners over the poorer farmers and tenants. The Italian peasantry has been burdened with debt to pay for land improvement schemes out of which speculators reaped great profits, and for great arterial highways which the peasants never use. In Germany the earlier financial aid of the state and larger incomes from higher prices were used mainly to pay old debts. Unemployed workers are forced to work on the great landed estates at practically no pay: a new form of serf labor. In addition, fascism has multiplied the burdens of taxation oppressing the peasantry. Fascism has "stabilized" but not solved the agrarian crisis. In Europe, where production is low, fascism may encourage agriculture. But not in the United States,

small minority in the upper middle class, which be comes a dominant caste within monopoly capitalism: either in industry or in the swollen fascist bureaucracy. The security and privileges of a small group are assured by degradation of the great masses of the people, including the lower middle class.

The middle class rallies to fascism to defend the "natural right" to property and is then increasingly deprived of that right. Again the fatal contradiction: the rights of property include the right of big property to trample upon the smaller. Concentration of property ownership under the fascist regimes of Italy and Germany has moved upward probably 30% to 40%. Big property mercilessly expropriates the smaller, for expropriation is multiplied as capitalist decline limits the creation of new property. Fascist chieftains, moreover, acquire wealth by the simple method of throwing into prisons and concentration camps the persons whose property they covet. Hitler is majority stockholder in a publishing house that issues 318 daily, weekly and monthly publications; the manager of the house is president of the Reich Press Chamber, with dictatorial powers which he uses to destroy competitors and force reluctant advertisers to buy space. That is not exceptional, it is a system. Göring "muscled in" as a stockholder be-

where the agrarian crisis is largely one of overproduction. What can fascism offer the 3,000,000 American farmers who, the experts agree, are unnecessary in an efficient agriculture? In the United States, even more than elsewhere, the agrarian crisis can be solved only by releasing the forces of production and consumption: by stripping industry and agriculture of their capitalist fetters.

fore granting a larger order to an airplane concern. Streicher was "permitted to annex" several industrial enterprises. Göbbels threw the wife of a capitalist into prison and released her only on payment of 4,000,000 marks.[6] It is no longer the mere bribery and graft characteristic of capitalist states; it is organized *private* expropriation, the merciless use of state power, imprisonment and death to secure property, including dwellings, to enrich the fascist chieftains and their favorites. Fascism defends the rights of property and multiplies the propertiless.

Independent small enterprisers rally to fascism for "security," but it makes them still more insecure. As economic activity moves downward the small enterprisers are more rapidly thrown out of business. Profits are lower and the competition of the big corporations is more severe. Small enterprisers thought that fascism meant security, but the dominion of monopoly is now more mercilessly repressive.

Independent small producers are desperately hard-pressed under fascism. The state encourages rationalization and trustification, but by slashing wages and lowering mass consumption, the antagonism between production and consumption is sharpened. Independent producers are hit from two sides: the increased efficiency of corporate enterprise and the smaller markets. In Italy, after fascism came to power, small enterprisers in industry disappeared by the scores of thousands, more rapidly and in greater numbers than in any other nation. The state pursued, and still pursues, a policy of encouraging industrial concentration and trustification, often by force, but usually by means of lower taxes, loans, subsidies and government assumption of losses. An Italian fascist journal, *Economia,* says: "One must eliminate less perfect enterprises which produce at higher prices." [7] Concentration and monopoly, which had lagged in Italy, have made enormous strides under fascism: at the cost of the small producer. Hitler's Germany made promises to aid the small producers, but actually cartel combinations were favored, even enforced, and large-scale industry and monopoly have tightened their grasp on economic activity.[8] One reason for the fascist policy is the greater control of the state by monopoly capitalism; another is the desire to strengthen big industry for purposes of militarism and war. Fascism massacres the independent small producers.

Small storekeepers, too, are massacred. They rallied to fascism to destroy consumer's cooperatives and big department stores; the cooperatives were practically destroyed, in Italy and Germany, but not the big stores, which absorbed most of the business of the old cooperatives. One German observer has thus described the situation:

"Small tradespeople went about in 1932 in the big department stores looking at the places where they proposed to set up their businesses under the Third Reich in accordance with the point in the party program which demands the 'immediate communalization of the department stores and their lease at low rentals to small tradespeople.' [But the

302

pledge was completely forgotten after fascism came to power.] While the middle class leaders wanted to destroy the department stores, and ignorant local governments, regarding only popularity, were supporting them, the Reich government was trying to preserve the posts of the employees, and gave the department stores credits from government money to the total of many millions of marks." [9]

One of the reasons for not breaking up the department stores is very significant. It meant throwing the employees out of work—an expression of the antagonism of interests between the old middle class of small enterprisers and the "new" middle class of salaried employees. . . .

Moreover, survival is more difficult for the small storekeepers as mass standards of living are lowered. Wages in Italy were severely cut after fascism came to power, as much as 40% during the depression: *wages are now at the level of a century ago.*[10] They were cut 50% in the two Hitler years 1933-34.[11] The earnings of lower salaried employees were cut almost as much: the Italian government recently made a cut of 20% in both wages and salaries (while prices rose some 15%).[12] In both fascist nations unemployment is "reduced" by lowering wages and salaries to permit the hiring of more persons. Empty ideals replace economic issues.* Declining mass consumption,

---

* "The main issue with the workman is not his ridiculous wage-pennies but the dignity of his position; and ultimately wage questions settle themselves if the worker respects himself. In the last resort the mine worker cannot be paid with money at all; what he receives is only a petty remuneration for his unremitting labor.

a result of lower earnings and higher prices, means fewer sales for the small storekeepers. And whom does fascism blame for this and the consequent mass discontent? The small storekeepers! An illustration of that occurred in Germany during the summer of 1935:

"Numerous butcher and food shop proprietors have been arrested. One Nazi leader has advised the police to 'use harsher means than protective custody for those trying to plunder the people.' The middle class shopkeepers have been among the most enthusiastic supporters of the National Socialist movement. . . . The measures and denunciations now levelled at them, therefore, taste all the bitterer because they come from men they helped to put in power. As a matter of fact they are more the victims of Nazi economy than profiteers, for wholesale prices have gone up even more rapidly than retail prices. . . . But it is part of the Nazi plans that the hapless middle class traders are supposed to absorb the larger share of price increases." [13]

Fascism sharply aggravates the crisis of property in the old middle class of small enterprisers. What of the crisis of employment in the "new" middle class of salaried employees and professionals? The upper layers are measurably protected by their caste privileges and the multiplication of employment in the

It is therefore all the more ridiculous for people to begin to haggle about such little things." Dr. Robert Ley, chief of the German Labor Front, in an address to Neukirchen miners; reported by the Berlin correspondent of the London *Economist*, September 14, 1935.

government bureaucracy, but millions of lower salaried employees and professionals are permanently
unemployed, while the earnings of the employed
move steadily downward.

The crisis of employment can be solved only by
liberating the forces of production and consumption.
But fascism strangles them. As among the wage-workers, the unemployment of lower salaried employees is
"reduced" by cutting salaries and instituting forced
labor. German fascism boasts of having "liquidated"
unemployment, although the government still admits
there are millions out of work. But the figures omit
"invisible" unemployment (which includes mainly
salaried and professional labor); thus for October-
December 1934 the official estimate was an increase
of 705,000 unemployed, where the actual increase
was 1,500,000. Fascism, moreover, gets rid of the unemployed by other means than giving them work.
These are some of the "reductions" in German unemployment: 1,500,000 struck off the unemployed
registers, 900,000 women ousted from their jobs,*
600,000 men conscripted into the new army, and
300,000 workers sent to do forced labor, at practically
no pay, into the country: a total of 3,300,000.[14] What
slight relief in unemployment there has been is the
result of expansion in the armaments industry, not of
the normal and socially useful upswing of industry.

Lower levels of economic activity mean the dis-

---

* This is an aspect of the reaction against equal rights for
women, against the rights secured after years of struggle. Fascism
reverts to the medieval ideal of woman—the pleasure mate of
man and the breeder of soldiers.

placement of large numbers of technicians and the greater degradation of their craft function as more of them are forced to plan the limitation of production: to create artificial want in the midst of potential plenty. A German professor of engineering in 1930, after pointing out that only 20% of technical graduates got jobs for which they were trained and another 20% any kind of job, asked: "Is it not time to put a stop to this mass striving for higher learning?" Fascism, as in Italy, made the situation worse: Hitler's Germany cut yearly admissions to the universities from 40,000 to 16,000. But that is not all. Students in the summer semester of German universities and technical schools dropped from 130,000 in 1932 to 77,000 in 1935, the new students from 20,000 to 7,000. Lower schools, moreover, are being reorganized to cut two years from the total study period. All that, according to Nazi commentators, is only a beginning: more reductions are expected. The reductions are hailed as "recovery from inflation in higher education" and a victory in the campaign "against intellectualism in favor of brawn." [15]

Fascist limitation of education throws tens of thousands of teachers into permanent unemployment. Other professional workers are affected by the decline in living standards: the degradation of their craft function is tragic, as the people's need for professional services mounts while their performers cannot find employment. According to one report on conditions in fascist Germany: "The professional classes are poorer now than before." [16]

Taxation multiplies the burdens of the middle class. The costs of state financial aid to big industry, of make-work schemes and greater armaments, and of the all-devouring bureaucracy must be met by taxation. Wages are taxed, but there is a limit and blood cannot be drawn from a stone. Great corporations and the rich are able to evade taxes, but who is left? Fascist taxation presses most brutally on the smaller enterprises and the middle class, which pays and pays. Fascism increased Italy's national debt to $11,000 million, or approximately 60% of the national wealth. Germany's national debt, increased by 20,000 million marks in two years of fascism, represents over 50% of the national wealth while debt services absorb 15% of the national income. The German government, in its desperation, virtually stole the savings deposits and insurance of the middle class to meet the state's money needs.[17] Taxation becomes expropriation.

What happens under fascism is this: the middle class, determined to save itself, against labor, is engulfed in the economic catastrophe produced by fascism. That comes from the retention of capitalist relations of production which, under the conditions of declining capitalism, means strangling production and consumption. For as fascism brutally prevents the logical working out of economic forces, the transformation of collectivism into socialism, it must become merely the organization of economic disintegration and decay.

As it fails to solve the economic problem, fascism

must increasingly resort to suppression and ideology to maintain power. Its ideology is increasingly irrational, the most bestial inflaming of all the worst passions, prejudices and hatreds,* the inculcation of pre-capitalist ideals of "destructive exploit and status." The intellectuals are imprisoned in the circle of an increasingly reactionary ideology, miserable dependents of the totalitarian state, forced to enslave intelligence and reason instead of liberating them. The social pathology of declining capitalism assumes more revolting forms. Out of the intensification of reaction and suppression arises the greater threat of war, for to the imperialist drive toward war is added the drive of the fascist dictatorship intent on using nationalism and war in a desperate struggle for survival: against its own people.

Fascism sets in motion no forces for the replacement of its dictatorship. It can set no such forces in motion: dictatorship is considered an ideal and eternal. As its task is to "organize" the disintegration and

* Consider these utterances of Herr Darre, Hitler's minister of agriculture: "The Semites reject everything that pertains to the pig. The Nordic peoples, on the contrary, accord the pig the highest possible honor . . . in the cult of the Germans the pig occupies the first place, and is the first among the domestic animals. This predominance of the pig, the sacred animal destined to sacrifices among the Nordic peoples, makes it right to conclude that the religion of these peoples has drawn its originality from the great trees of the Germanic forest. . . . Thus out of the darkness of earliest history arise two human races whose attitude in respect of pigs presents an absolute contrast. The Semites do not understand the pig, they do not accept the pig, they reject the pig, where this animal occupies the first place in the cult of the Nordic peoples." "A London Diary," *New Statesman and Nation,* February 3, 1934, p. 148.

decay of capitalist decline, the dictatorship must be "eternal" to crush opposition and must "forever" suppress liberty, equality and democracy. Under those conditions the fascist dictatorship and its bureaucracy increasingly determine policy in their own interests and become independent of all responsibility to other social factors. Fascism drives toward constantly more disintegration, suppression, reaction and war. It is capitalism become the new barbarism.

What happens under fascism to the middle class, and to the workers and farmers, is a continuation of what happens in democratic nations under the conditions of capitalist decline: only worse. For fascism is simply a stage of declining capitalism, arising out of the sharpening of its crisis and its needs. No nation is immune. The scornful cry was thrown at Hitler: "Germany is not Italy!" But it was. The forces of fascism exist in all capitalist nations. There exist, too, the forces capable of preventing the victory of fascism.

Chapter XIII

FASCISM: WORLD REACTION

FASCISM rallies the middle class masses to the defense of an endangered capitalism: it develops the ideals and the new forms of action necessary to set those masses in motion as the militant factor in the capitalist struggle to retain power. Hence fascism resembles Jacobinism in the use of petty-bourgeois masses to fight for the interests of the whole bourgeoisie and of capitalism. But there are class-historical differences of the utmost significance: differences more significant than the resemblance. One meant progress; the other means reaction.

1

In all stages of capitalism the big bourgeoisie is a small minority of the people, and under the conditions of democracy it must have the support of the petty-bourgeois masses. This is all the more important since the lower middle class contacts the workers, and may influence them. The forms of middle class support have varied in accordance with three different stages of capitalism:

1. The stage of revolutionary struggle. In the struggle against feudalism the big bourgeoisie had to rally the middle class. But the big bourgeoisie faltered

and compromised when it became necessary to strike the most violent blows at the reaction, to adopt new, more aggressive and more revolutionary forms of action. It was the middle class, whose lower layers rallied the workers to the struggle, that made a clean sweep of feudal reaction by means of revolutionary dictatorship; and it was forced to act against the opposition of the big bourgeoisie itself. This was the Jacobin phase of the bourgeois struggle for power.

2. The stage of upswing and ascendancy. Capitalism was dominant and the middle class acquiescent, if critical and often in opposition. The institutional relations of capitalism were, by and large, accepted by the people, especially the middle class, which moved from revolutionary struggle for power to reformist struggle for survival. The majority of workers accepted reformism, influenced largely by the upper layers in contact with the lower middle class. Capitalism was still on the upswing and economically progressive, the revolutionary threat still only potential. Ideas and social action were dominated by the philosophy of progress: the belief in an everlasting, if slow, upward movement to higher things by means of democracy and reformism. Petty-bourgeois democracy was the support of capitalism. Force underlay that democracy, but the resort to force was not always necessary and it was compatible with democracy—force is an aspect of democracy.

3. The stage of decline and approaching downfall. Capitalism is now in a condition of decline and decay, reacting against progress. As the productive

forces are strangled capitalism creates an economic crisis which oppresses all layers of the people. They move toward revolt. The old institutional relations become insecure and are no longer blindly accepted. Not only is the proletariat in revolt, but petty-bourgeois elements in contact with the workers incline toward the proletariat. Reformism reveals its limitations, for the costs of reform weigh heavily on a declining capitalism. The danger of democracy is that it permits within itself opposition and the organization of revolutionary struggle for a new social order. Again the petty-bourgeois masses must be rallied to wage violent war on the enemies of the bourgeoisie. Violent blows must be struck: democracy must be destroyed and all opposition crushed: the use of force must become overwhelming, permanent, normal. Fascism recreates the confidence of the petty-bourgeois masses in capitalism, seriously shaken by the crisis, and throws them into the fight to defend the interests of the whole bourgeoisie and of monopoly capitalism.*

Now, as in the earlier stage, capitalism again needs the violence of the petty-bourgeois masses: against progress, however, not reaction: against the working class, not the feudal nobility. The aims are now counter-revolutionary, not revolutionary. Hence, while fascism performs the same task as Jacobinism —mobilizing the petty-bourgeois masses to fight the

* It is hoped, moreover, that the lower middle class may rally the workers whom it contacts. But neither in Italy nor Germany was fascism able to rally the workers: the proletariat was overwhelmingly against fascism.

battles of the bourgeoisie—the significance of the task is totally different.

Jacobinism represented all the creative elements of the youth of capitalism: it gave the most *progressive* expression to the *progressive* ideals of bourgeois society.

Fascism represents all the destructive elements of the old age of capitalism: it gives the most *reactionary* expression to the *reactionary* ideals of bourgeois society.

Jacobinism fought for a new social order, fascism fights against the new social order emerging out of capitalist collectivism. One was the "dictatorship of liberty against tyranny," the other is the dictatorship of tyranny against liberty. Although the fight is still for the cause of capitalism, the social character of the objectives is completely reversed. Within these differences is involved another: Jacobinism was, for a time, the dictatorship of the petty bourgeoisie; fascism is always *from the beginning* the dictatorship of the big bourgeoisie, in its modern variant of finance capitalists. There was a measure of middle class independence in the Jacobin struggle; while it expressed bourgeois ideals, it gave them a lower-class slant and made efforts to realize them in new and higher forms.* Fascism does nothing of the sort: it,

* The great Jacobin radicals influenced communism and socialism: they occupy a crucial place in the continuity of social progress. To break that continuity is the task of fascism. Its "radicals" are more reactionary than the conservatives; they are intent merely on more complete and barbarous domination by the fascist bureaucratic caste. The "radical" fascist emphasis is still on capitalism, on reaction, nationalism and war. They still wage war on progress

too, expresses bourgeois ideals, but in a form wholly acceptable to the dominant capitalism. The only independence manifested by fascism is in its defense of the interests of the "totalitarian" bureaucracy.

Fascism marks a complete reaction against the old democratic ideals of the middle class, particularly in the Jacobin forms which strongly colored the American democracy of the 1790's. The ideals are now dangerous and must be destroyed. They are dangerous to the old middle class of independent enterprisers and the new middle class of higher salaried employees and professionals, who aim to "freeze" class-economic relations in order to insure their own survival as a caste. They are dangerous to capitalism, for the masses have seized upon the ideals and strive to realize them in new and higher forms; democratic rights were tolerable when the working class used them merely to struggle for reforms within the relations of capitalism, they are dangerous when the working class uses them to organize its forces for the overthrow of capitalism. The final reaction appears in the fascist reversion to the medieval concept of *estates:* of caste and hierarchy and the rigid stratification of *legally enforced inequality*. Where Robespierre and Jefferson urged an equality of income, property and rights, Mussolini and Hitler, and the American fascist playboys, urge inequality as an unbreakable law of nature.

and the new social order. The great Jacobin radicals tried to break through capitalist relations; the fascist "radicals" accept those relations and try to twist them in the interests of a bureaucracy and caste become measurably independent of their masters.

314

Fascism accepts some of the old Jacobin ideals, such as nationalism and obligation to serve the state, but degrades them into the most reactionary forms. They were means of struggle against the big bourgeoisie for the realization of middle class ideals; they become means of serving the big bourgeoisie of monopoly capitalism against the middle class, against civilization. Fascism is degenerate Jacobinism.

Fascism strengthens reaction throughout the world. The ideals and agents of Jacobinism everywhere aided the most progressive forces. The ideals and agents of fascism everywhere aid the most reactionary forces. Agents of the German and Italian fascist government in other countries terrorize their own nationals, kidnap their opponents and give aid and comfort to the local reaction. Italian fascism inspired the German; French fascists urge an "understanding" with Hitler against the Soviet Union; the British Union of Fascists flaunts the plumage of Mussolini's approval. The incipient forces of an American fascism borrow ideas from the European brethren: communism is condemned as alien, but fascism is not. Imperialism and war are pursued more aggressively as the mere extortion of tribute. Fascism, moreover, provides ideas and inspiration for the most sinister reaction in economically backward countries, which adopt a sort of feudal fascism that prevents emergence of the middle class as a revolutionary class and stifles the progressive economic forces of capitalism, resulting in the monstrosity of a "stabilized" feudal-capitalism. The world revolution of Jacobinism becomes the world reaction of fascism.

The reaction of fascism is the most brutal, systematic and institutional reaction of declining capitalism. For the middle class *as a class* is interlocked with capitalism. It was progressive when capitalism was progressive, it is reactionary now that capitalism is wholly reactionary. The middle class has no independent class policy. But fascism is more than capitalism: it is the expression of capitalism become putrescent in the final stage of decay, multiplying capitalist reaction against progress, threatening a relapse into barbarism.

2

Civilizations do decay; they may relapse into barbarism. There is no automatic upward movement of progress, for progress may alternate with retrogression. One great illustration of that was the decline of Roman civilization and its aftermath in the Dark Ages. In spite of all the differences between our own and the ancient world, the Roman catastrophe throws light on the capitalist threat to civilization.

The fundamental cause of the decay of Roman civilization was class-economic (remembering, however, that the class-economic is always interwoven with the cultural). Roman society gradually stifled the forces of economic progress; the old ruling class became wholly reactionary and parasitic and incapable of ruling by the old methods, while savage civil wars flared up again and again. Cæsarism was the answer: new methods of rule and the organization of decline and decay into a system. The Roman Empire plundered the world of its wealth, expropriation of property was the primary source of enrichment, and intolerable burdens were imposed on man and industry. Desperation among the dispossessed masses of the people was converted into an engine for waging perpetual wars of conquest and rapine. Economically unproductive classes became legion, luxury an abomination in the eyes of man. No new forms of economic activity arose (except the small beginnings of serfdom), no new class representing those forms and capable of making them the basis of a new social order. War and expropriation were an ideal and a way of life. The rulers became increasingly predatory, economic and cultural decay more putrescent, the condition of the masses more hopeless as they turned to the other-worldly consolations of Christianity. The shell of the empire broke easily under the impact of the barbarian invaders; economic and cultural resources were drained of all vigor, while the masses, steeped in the most abject misery, were either indifferent to the invaders or gave them welcome. Society relapsed into a village and agrarian economy, into the barbarism of the Dark Ages; new forces of progress emerged slowly and agonizingly.

Can civilization again break down? All the reactionary forces of declining capitalism work in that direction. Society is now dominated by capitalism and its civilization is capitalist. That civilization must decay as capitalism itself decays, for the decline of capitalism means a reaction against its contribution to civilization, against its own values and achievements *and the possibility of a new social order involved in them.* These values and achievements, which distinguish capitalism from its predecessors, may be conveniently expressed in summary form:

1. Reconstruction of the technical-economic basis of society.

a. Capitalist civilization developed the forces of production to unheard-of heights; it increasingly limited scarcity and made potential abundance possible for all.

b. Capitalist civilization greatly increased man's mastery of the world and of himself, as growth of the productive forces was conditioned by the development of technology and science: the purposive utilization of natural forces to serve man's objectives.

c. Capitalist civilization, after the increasing misery of the industrial revolution, developed an increasing mass well-being, a larger participation of the masses (formerly almost wholly excluded) in the conquests of civilization.

2. Reconstruction of the cultural basis of society.

a. Capitalist civilization stressed the rational and the scientific, the appeal to reason; it emphasized this-worldliness as against the other-worldliness of medieval culture.

b. Capitalist civilization, particularly its American expression, set forth the ideals and the practice of liberty, equality and democracy: the right of the people to share in economic and cultural progress and to participate freely and fully in all forms of social activity.

c. Capitalist civilization, as an aspect of its emphasis on science and technology and on the rational, enlarged the ideal and the practice of education: it developed an increasing participation of the masses in education and a creative concept of education as the means of mastering society and solving all social problems.

d. Capitalist civilization, at least in its earlier more progressive and revolutionary stages, set forth the great ideal of world peace: of a world peacefully and cooperatively moving onward to international unity.

3. The creative idea of progress was forged by capitalist civilization: the concept of an onward and upward movement to new and higher things, which stripped man of intellectual limitations and slavery to the traditional. Moreover, and this is the decisive element, capitalist civilization developed the economic forms, the intellectual concepts and the class forces of a new social order and a new civilization: its greatest achievement and proof of progress.*

* It must be emphasized that the achievements and values of capitalist civilization are largely limited to a handful of economically highly developed countries, particularly those where the middle class waged its revolutionary struggle most aggressively and the labor movement was most active. But the achievements and values scarcely appear in economically backward countries, which combine the worst elements of feudalism and capitalism. Nor in Japan, where a mighty capitalism has grown almost exclusively as a system of exploitation.

Now all the ideals (most aspiringly expressed in the ideals of the American Dream) and the achievements of capitalism were limited. They expressed the class-economic interests of the capitalist class and were definitely limited by those interests: many of the ideals and achievements appeared in spite of capitalist opposition. The development of capitalism was accompanied by oppression and injustice, by brutal exploitation of workers and farmers: for capitalism was a system of class exploitation. While production moved upward, it always lagged behind technical-economic possibilities and deliberately limited abundance, because the profit system made necessary what Veblen called "business sabotage" and the "conscientious withdrawal of efficiency." Liberty meant primarily the liberty freely to own and dispose of property. Equality was more an ideal than a practice; it was largely limited to an unsatisfactory and hypocritical equality of rights before the law and to an ideal of equality of property ownership whose "realization" was a constantly more unequal distribution of ownership. Democracy was bourgeois democracy, the form of expression of capitalist class rule: the workers had to struggle desperately for their limited share of democratic rights. Man's mastery of the world and of himself was stultified by the class limitations imposed on technology and science, and was mocked by the recurrent cyclical breakdowns of the economic order (the American experience includes thirty-three major and minor breakdowns in the years 1796-1923, and now the worst breakdown of

320

all) .[1] Mass well-being was never willed by capitalist civilization. It was merely a by-product, and at best it was accompanied by grinding poverty in the most prosperous nations and increasing misery among colonial and other economically backward peoples exploited by capitalism. The share of the workers in the conquests of capitalist civilization was always smaller, much smaller, than the share of the masters of capitalism. The magnificent rationalism of the Enlightenment was largely degraded into the "practicality" of business enterprise, while capitalism, for its own purposes of dominion, tolerated and encouraged the most abject types of old and new superstitions. Education for the masses was limited by its enslavement to capitalist necessity, and never realized the ideal of acting as the solver of social problems. The ideal of universal peace was quickly rejected by capitalism, which multiplied the instruments of death and the destructive character of war. After its consolidation of power capitalism restricted progress to routine reform within the limits of the existing order, which was considered eternal, while a whole philosophy arose directed against progress. The idea of progress was deprived of its creative aspects and degraded into the belief that progress was automatic and irresistible; it became a means of reconciling the oppressed masses of the people to their subjection by offering them hopes.

The limitations of the values and achievements of capitalist civilization clearly indicate its transitional character. It is a preparation for the future,

321

and its real contribution to progress is the development of economic and cultural conditions out of which a new social order may arise.* But there *was* progress, for the limitations were still only relative. Now, however, the limitations are absolute. Capitalism reacts against its own values and achievements, which are increasingly limited as they turn into their opposites and threaten the dominion of capitalism. For those values and achievements strain more vigorously against their capitalist forms: they must move onward to new and freer forms, or they must decay. Hence capitalism reacts particularly against the progressive forces of the oncoming socialist order, strengthening world reaction and endangering civilization itself.

Underlying capitalist progress, its values and achievements, was multiplication of the productive forces. That is the law of motion of capitalist production, for it means constantly larger profits and their

* One may divide the development of civilization into two great stages: the agrarian and the industrial. All pre-capitalist civilizations were dominantly agrarian, almost wholly dependent on agriculture and a primitive technology. Some of them, especially the Chinese, developed all the possibilities of an agrarian civilization, including stability and an integrated culture. Capitalist civilization is dominantly industrial, almost a complete departure from the agrarian in its dependence on a highly developed technology, the supremacy of industry—which includes the increasing industrialization of agriculture—and the instability of social-economic relations. But capitalism has fully developed neither the economic nor the cultural possibilities of an industrial civilization, and its economic instability is matched by the lack of integration and "wholeness" in its culture. Capitalism is the most transitional of all social systems, the anticipation of a new and higher social order capable of fulfilling the promise of industrial civilization: the fulfillment of socialism.

conversion into capital. But now its own law of motion reacts against capitalism. Industry is so highly developed, the productive forces so gigantic, that profits and the accumulation of capital must move downward. To overcome the crisis of the system which now rends it asunder, capitalism deliberately limits the productive forces, organizing the planned limitation of production. Our industry is capable of producing all the goods and services needed by the people: capable of providing the means for the creation of higher cultural levels. Capitalist limitation of production means the deliberate destruction of that promise.

Limitation of production increasingly represses economic progress. It becomes disjointed, piecemeal, retrogressive. Instead of limiting scarcity, capitalism now makes the production of scarcity its major industry. No longer can capitalism plead justification by multiplication of the productive forces: it now reacts against its greatest achievement.

Limitation of production represses the growth of technology and science, for their growth under capitalism is conditional on the upward movement and profitability of production. Never fully utilized even during the upswing of capitalism, the utilization of technology and science must steadily decrease under the conditions of capitalist decline. That means the erection of mounting barriers to man's mastery of the world and of himself. It is ominous that technology and science are already most actively engaged in perfecting the instruments of war: the forces capable of liberating mankind may become its destroyer.

Limitation of production reverses the onward movement of mass well-being. A new and unnecessary poverty arises, including the permanent unemployment of millions of workers, lower salaried employees and professionals. It means the creation of a new class of outcasts.

Limitation of production is the most acute expression of the decline of capitalism. For capitalism, whose motive force is economic expansion, must decline and decay where there is no continuous upward movement of the productive forces. That necessarily means cultural decline and decay. The lowering of economic output limits cultural development: the scope of culture, in final analysis, depends on the economic resources of society. More important, however, is the disastrous impact on the spirit of culture. For the desperation of declining capitalism engenders a revolt against all the progressive aspects of culture. The limited forms of liberty, equality and democracy are limited still more, and move toward destruction. That is an aspect of the new reaction whose stupefying fumes deaden the spirit of culture, for the freedom of cultural creation is dangerous and *all its vital urge is toward the new social order*. Education is increasingly restricted: its costs are irksome to declining capitalism and unemployed intellectual proletarians are a menace. Educational values are degraded to the level of black magic to meet the needs of a social order now violently reactionary;

instead of the solver of social problems, education must become the means of *preventing* creative social action. The final result is the revolt against rationalism: the irrational, and its motivation in prejudices, passions and hatreds, is the ideology of declining capitalism. Reaction completes itself in new, more frequent and bloodier wars.

Capitalism now revolts against its own creation, the idea of progress. The liberals meant by progress a steady upward movement, uninterrupted and irresistible, and insisted that capitalism was moving of its own momentum to higher things. But capitalism itself destroyed that illusion. The early socialist, Fourier, argued that every social order moves downward as well as upward; Marxism, moreover, made progress conditional on *the purposive revolutionary action of the class in society embodying the forms of a new social order: the proletariat.* Liberals rejected the arguments, but they are now proven by the decline of capitalism and the dependence of progress on class action to transform capitalist collectivism into socialism. Hence capitalism must revolt against progress to survive. Reactionary intellectuals justify that revolt by damning progress as "wishful thinking" and the romantic legacy of Rousseau. American sociologists reject the term progress and prefer "social change" because it is "free from dogmatic or moral implications." [2] But there *is* progress in social change: not mechanical, but an expression of the dialectic movement of social forces. The decline of capitalism is not a disproval of progress: it merely

325

means that capitalism has exhausted its progressive drive. Within capitalism are all the elements of progress, created by capitalism itself: collectivism and its class-cultural accompaniments. Progress is now dependent on the struggle for a new social order. The rejection of progress is the necessity of declining capitalism and the justification of a new barbarism.

All the symptoms of declining capitalism offer a striking parallel to the decline of Roman civilization. A group of American scientists, in a report on economic conditions, particularly agricultural, recently said: "The comparison of such a situation with the final days of the Roman Empire is not too far-fetched." [3] The parallel is complete in fascism. For, in words and in action, fascism makes it clear that it is the new Cæsarism. Oswald Spengler speaks of "the Cæsarism that approaches." [4] The philosopher of fascism, Vilfredo Pareto, speaks more clearly:

"When the higher classes are averse to the use of force, which ordinarily happens because the majority in those classes come to rely wholly on their skill at chicanery . . . it becomes necessary, if society is to subsist and prosper, that the governing class be replaced by another which is willing and able to use force. Roman society was saved from ruin by the legions of Cæsar and Octavius." [5]

The meaning is clear, although Pareto, as usual, evades the fundamentals of the problem: *A moment comes when the old ruling class is decaying and cannot rely simply on the old institutional relations and sanctions, or on its own inner capacity; it is not "averse to the use of force,"* but must incorporate in the governing system new social elements and new sanctions to make use of new and more overwhelming force if the ruling class (not society) *"is to prosper and subsist."* It is a revolution in reverse: for reaction. That was Cæsarism, and it is fascism.

Fascism, as much as Cæsarism, is the resort to new forms of dictatorship by a class become wholly reactionary and decadent and a festering fetter on social progress, incapable of ruling except by means of the most sinister elements in society.

Fascism, as much as Cæsarism, stifles economic progress. The social crime of fascism is greater, for Roman civilization, unlike the capitalist, had not developed the economic forms of a new social order. Not economic activity but expropriation of property —downright theft—is the source of enrichment. Cæsarism defended the rights of property, but owners were repeatedly expropriated in favor of new owners who possessed political and military power. That is already a marked feature of fascism in Italy and Germany, where the adventurers exact their price in property and money. The defenders of property are its devourers.

Fascism, as much as Cæsarism, means complete suppression, the enslavement of the people to an all-inclusive despotism. That appears in the fascist concepts of "hierarchy" and the "totalitarian" state. As the carrier of a new social order the proletariat must be annihilated politically and morally: including the masses of lower salaried employees and professionals.

But there are no rights that fascism recognizes, and the omnipotent bureaucracy may suppress *any* person, including the individual capitalist. All are in subjection. The Roman god-emperors are revived in the godly persons of *il Duce* and *der Führer,* and, in his own petty fashion, of the British mountebank Mosley. Responsible Nazi leaders, among them Göring, clearly express the god-emperor idea: "The way to God is the way our Führer has shown us." . . . "Let no one object if we prefer to lift up our hearts to the idea of our Führer rather than listen to the chatter of quarreling clerics." . . . "The person of the Führer is sacred." [6] Underlying deification is the conception of a state religion to buttress the totalitarian state and reaction. The revolutionary bourgeois ideals, rationalism and the separation of church and state, are rejected. Mussolini makes peace with the Papacy, using it for his own reactionary purposes—Hitler tries to make the church a state institution and to create a "national" religion out of old German paganism. It is the irrational erected into a new system of obscurantism.

Fascism, as much as Cæsarism, thrusts the masses of the people into the utmost degradation and misery, and makes them the sport of adventurers and madmen.

Fascism, as much as Cæsarism, means cultural decline and decay. The spirit of fascist culture is expressed in the Nazi ideal of education "based on brawn, instinct, tribal customs and morals." [7] According to one observer of the new Germany, in an

328

address to an American council of teachers: "The natural sciences have fallen to a lower rank [than racialism, personal heroism, especially military, physical culture and ardent nationalism] and the scientific method has been abolished as a product of 'Jewish intellectualism.' . . . After the present generation of German young people grows up there may be very few traces of the era of enlightenment that began with the Renaissance." [8] Education is submissive and irrational, deprived of all independence and creative force. Culture is perverted and made the plaything of mountebanks and degenerates as parasitic social groups and luxuries are multiplied. Monuments are built, but the people perish.

Fascism, as much as Cæsarism, makes war an ideal and a way of life. Hitler foresees the subjugation and occupation of Europe by "250,000,000 Germans in less than a hundred years from now," and invokes the Deity: "We want arms again! [Everything must] be put into the service of this great mission till the smallest boy is repeating: 'Almighty God, bless our arms; Lord, bless our fight!' " War, according to Mussolini, is the supreme creative force: "War is to man what maternity is to woman. Only a sanguinary effort can reveal the great qualities of people and the qualities of the human soul." [9] Those ideals have been expressed before, but never by people possessing the power of fascist dictatorships, which make war a normal explosive expression of the creeping paralysis of economic and cultural decay. Fascist nations must devour one another and civilization itself.

329

Fascism, as much as Cæsarism, is the organization of social disintegration and decay: it makes them permanent, institutional, normal. Fascism is the systematic suppression of progress, its whole philosophy a denial of progress.

That is the spirit of fascism, the complete opposite of the spirit of the great men of the Enlightenment, who "recognized no external authority of any kind; religion, conceptions of nature, society, political systems, everything was subjected to the most merciless criticism, everything had to justify its existence at the bar of reason or renounce all claims to existence." [10] But fascism rejects reason in favor of the irrational, of brute instinct and force. The rejection is necessary: only a progressive social order has no fear of reason, only a revolutionary class dares appeal to reason. Fascism, moreover, rejects the perfectibility of man; this ideal of the old middle class radicals, especially the Jacobins and the American democratic radicals they inspired, is replaced by fascist contempt of man and his personality. Man is not man if he is deprived of the rational and the right to understand, of the urge to struggle for perfection. Fascism is a nightmare whose final results might justify the mournful prophecy:

> *Here lies, and none to mourn him but the sea*
> *That falls incessant on the empty shore,*
> *Most various Man, cut down to spring no more.*
> *Cut down, and all the clamor that was he,*
> *Silenced.**

* From a poem by Edna St. Vincent Millay.

It *is* a nightmare. The death of civilization is threatened by declining capitalism and its final expression in fascism. It is not, however, an inevitable morphological doom that must be met with the meretriciously magnificent resignation of Spenglerism. The decline of capitalism is a dialectic process; within capitalism are all the elements of a new social order capable of creating a new upsurge of civilization. It is because that new order is increasingly emergent that capitalism resorts to fascism. But life revolts against death. The forces of life rally to the revolutionary struggle for the new order: life is already triumphant over death in the developing socialism of the Soviet Union. Man, the worker, wills progress and fights for it.

Chapter XIV

MIDDLE CLASS AND SOCIALISM

CAPITALISM moves toward socialism. That is the meaning of the capitalist reaction against progress. It is the meaning of fascist barbarism, whose particular aim it is, savagely using the most repulsive and violent means, to prevent the emergence of socialism by annihilating the independence and struggle of the working class: including the masses of lower salaried employees and professionals. That involves strangling the productive forces, and their capacity to produce abundance, where socialism means their liberation.

Abundance is a fact. It was possible, in 1929, by the mere use of the unused capacity of American industry and without depriving the upper layers of their swollen incomes, to raise to $2,500 yearly the income of every one of the 19,400,000 families whose earnings were below that amount; [1] more equal distribution of income would have meant still more for the poorer families. But that was not all. It was possible, in 1929, to increase industrial output by 30%, and to increase it nearly 75%, within eighteen months, by raising all of industry to the level of the most efficient existing practices.[2] Capitalist industry strangled abundance.

By freely and fully using all our economic resources, and limiting incomes to $10,000 yearly, a
limitation that would affect fewer than 300,000 persons out of 51,000,000 gainfully occupied, every
American family can be assured a minimum income
of $4,000. Yet, in the most prosperous year 1929, the
great majority of wage-workers had incomes below
$2,000; while 80% of the middle class, which, in the
futile hope of saving itself by mobilizing against
labor, may rally to the capitalist program of strangling the productive forces and to the barbarism of
fascist reaction, had incomes below $3,000—below
$2,500 in the case of the majority of lower salaried
employees and professionals.

Nor is that all. Even the most efficient existing
industrial enterprises might become still more efficient if capitalism did not limit the technological
application of science to "save" the profitability of
industry by strangling abundance. According to one
scientific observer:

"There can be no doubt that it lies within the
immediate capacity of physical science to solve completely the material problems of human existence.
In an organized world it should be possible for every
present need of man to be satisfied with something
between one and three hours work a day, and beyond that lie possibilities for extending the capacity
of enjoyment and activity indefinitely." [3]

The existing capacity to produce abundance is one
of the economic elements of socialism, and is inseparably identified with the other element: collec-

333

tivism. Socialism, in its simplest terms, is the liberation of the capacity to produce abundance by transforming *capitalist* collectivism into *socialist* collectivism. That means the liberation of science and of all the other creative forces of society. It means the end of the tragedy of a world moving backward to reaction and barbarism in the midst of all the elements of a new civilization.

That tragedy is the crisis of capitalism, of which the crises of the middle class are an aspect, and capitalist efforts to overcome the crisis merely make the tragedy all the greater. For the efforts are limited by capitalist relations and profit. Governments usurp more and more economic functions, but the major results are larger tax burdens and an increase in the economic rigidity introduced by monopoly. Production is limited, increasing scarcity and unemployment. Billions for unemployment doles are spent by governments, but they are unable to provide work by the revival of economic activity. Agricultural "controls" limit output and multiply the number of unemployed farm workers. Governments control the output and price of international commodities; the controls break down and whole nations are plunged into unparalleled misery. As markets shrink, governments protect them with mounting tariff barriers, lowering living standards and sharpening the antagonisms among nations. All the capitalist efforts to overcome the crisis of capitalism result in strangling the productive forces and their capacity to

334

produce abundance. The alternative is to liberate them, and that means socialism.

1

Collectivism and the capacity to produce abundance are two elements, the economic elements, of socialism. The third is a class element: the class forces capable of action to transform the objective economic elements into socialism.

Capitalism moves toward socialism, but the coming of socialism is not automatic: it meets unrelenting resistance. The development of collectivism was an almost mechanical series of economic changes; its transformation into socialism is a dynamic process of purposive class action. Collectivism, as it transformed economic individualism, met middle class resistance, but not that of the big bourgeoisie; the change was not revolutionary, for capitalist relations still prevailed and the middle class managed to survive under their new forms. But the transformation of collectivism into socialism is a revolutionary social change which destroys capitalist relations of production. Hence it meets the resistance of the big bourgeoisie, including groups under its influence; the resistance is uncompromisable, for the big bourgeoisie cannot survive under socialism. Social changes accumulate slowly and gradually, until the moment comes when a decisive change is necessary—a sharp break with the past in order to begin creating the future. Society moves toward revolution: the conquest of polit-

335

ical power by the class capable of destroying the old order and constructing the new.

The class forces of socialism already exist within collectivism, created by its proletarianization of the masses of the people. These forces must be set in motion to transform quantitative economic changes into qualitative social change.

The class changes produced by the onsweep of capitalist collectivism are a preparation for socialism. Independent small enterprisers become increasingly insignificant economically, crushed by the collective activity of large-scale industry: wholly superfluous and predatory financial capitalists replace the industrial capitalists, whose managerial functions are now a collective task, while the multitudes of stockholders are socially useless: the industrialization of agriculture, which constantly proletarianizes the farmers and lessens their relative numbers in the new collective set-up, points to the day when the farmer, as farmer, will disappear in the collective unity of industry and agriculture. But the working class grows as collectivism grows, becoming a majority of the people, the typical class product of capitalism—and the carrier of socialism. The class includes the useful functional groups among the lower salaried employees and professionals. Within the working class is the industrial proletariat, massed in the strategic enterprises of the nation; its upthrust and action, rallying the other elements in the class and all the dispossessed in society, are the decisive factor in the struggle for socialism.

336

That struggle is not new, but it is invigorated by the decline of capitalism, which sharpens class antagonisms and sets all classes in motion. It sets in motion the 38,750,000 propertiless wage-and-salary dependents, 75% of all Americans gainfully occupied, whose interests are identified with the transformation of collectivism into socialism. Within this great group, however, are important differences in historical development, relation to production and ideology. These differences do not cancel the fundamental unity of interests arising out of their propertiless, dependent condition and their constructive identification with collectivism. But the differences do produce variations in the response to the conditions that set the classes in motion, for the initial response is largely determined by traditional forms of action. It is fatal to ignore these differences or to blur them in a vague appeal to "the people." The struggle against capitalism demands a creative understanding of the concrete relations and peculiarities of class forces.

Labor's traditional forms of action are the strike and unionism. The strike is the self-action of labor, the union its self-organization. They mean that the proletariat recognizes and asserts its independence as a class, issuing its challenge to the employers and their state. Strikes and unionism were totally new forms of class action, separating the workers from the middle class and the whole of bourgeois society, which was thrown into the air by labor's elemental upthrust. However conservative and limited the im-

337

mediate aims, the mere organization of workers *as workers* was potential of revolution. The strike is a primitive form of their struggle for power which assumes higher forms as the workers grow more conscious of their final interests and aims. The imposition of union controls and limitations over the employer's rights in industry is potential of the abolition of those rights in a socialist society. Socialism is the logic of the proletariat's relation to production and the action and aims arising out of that relation. That logic drives the proletariat to act as an independent political force to secure control of the state and use its power for the socialist transformation of society.

Labor's traditional forms of action are strengthened, broadened and deepened by the sharpening crisis of capitalist decline. The multiplication of economic pressure forces unorganized workers to form unions and drives the unions to more militant action. Unions realize that it is necessary to organize more workers and that the old craft insularity is dangerous. As wages are slashed and working conditions impaired, and the employers oppose strikes and unions more vigorously because they now threaten profits more directly, the organized workers are thrown into more united and aggressive struggles. An aroused and mightier labor movement meets the increasingly savage resistance of the employers, who use all means, including control of the state, to limit the right to organize and strike.

Political action now becomes more conscious and militant. Unemployment, the struggle over social

338

services and the constantly greater use of state power against the workers impresses upon them the prime necessity of the struggle for political power. That is necessary because all issues in the class struggle are political issues, the final issue being: what class shall control the state power and to what ends? Reformist political action—the politics of reform, of piecemeal change and gradual "working into" socialism—must break down, for the decline of capitalism eventually makes reforms too costly and capitalist interests revolt against them, the institutional weight of capitalism acts against the workers unless its political power is destroyed, and capitalist violence is used to prevent the gradual construction of socialism (*cf.* the resort to fascism). As the limitations of reformism appear, and the class struggle sharpens, communism becomes increasingly ascendant. Communism drives toward the conquest of political power, using transitional issues and forms of struggle, yet planfully and purposively directing them toward the final issue: control of the state and the destruction of capitalist property and power. This is the indispensable beginning of the construction of socialism.

All issues and all social action are increasingly embodied in the struggle of the two great antagonists: the proletariat and big bourgeoisie, who typically represent the clashing new and old social orders. As industrialism now dominates all economic relations, so the struggle of the proletariat and big bourgeoisie dominates all class relations. Intermediate or minor classes and groups must move and act within the circle of that struggle. For it represents the issue of socialism or capitalism: there is no alternative, the issue is inescapable, and it involves the future of civilization.

As the middle class, too, is set in motion by the sharpening crisis of capitalist decline, it cannot escape the issue of socialism or capitalism, which includes all other issues thrown up by the crisis.* The middle class, incapable of an independent class policy, must align itself with one or the other of the great antagonists: they express the class-economic relations of the new socialist and the old capitalist social orders, where the middle class is split by an inner clash of those orders and must move toward the struggle of one or the other. But neither struggle represents, nor can represent, the interests of the *whole* middle class.

The struggle of the proletariat—in the immediate form of organizing unions and a labor party, in the

* The class-economic development of capitalism is uneven. Hence one may distinguish three "types" of the middle class in the capitalist world today. The middle class in economically backward countries, which have had no bourgeois democratic revolution, is dominated by independent small enterprisers, mainly handicraftsmen closely akin to the workers. Then there is the middle class in countries which have had their bourgeois democratic revolutions but where capitalism has not fully developed industrial concentration; the middle class is still largely a class of independent enterprisers, including handicraftsmen and petty capitalist producers. The third "type" exists in the United States and England, particularly the former; the middle class is overwhelmingly a "class" of salaried employees and professionals, with small enterprisers (few of them handicraftsmen) a comparatively unimportant minority. The approach to the middle class, in concrete tactical terms, must vary in accordance with the different "types."

final form of the communist struggle for power—*includes* the interests of every useful functional group in the middle class: only those of the upper middle class are excluded.

The struggle of the big bourgeoisie—in the immediate form of political and economic action against labor, in the final form of fascism—*excludes* the interests of every useful functional group in the middle class: only those of the upper middle class are included.

Two struggles, irreconcilable and overwhelming! The struggle of the big bourgeoisie rallies all forces to the defense of capitalism. That means economic decline and decay; it means thrusting the burdens of the crisis onto the masses of the people, including the lower middle class; it means driving down the standards of living of lower salaried employees and professionals by unemployment and the slashing of salaries. The struggle of the proletariat rallies all forces whose interests are identified with socialism. That means, in its immediate aspects, the struggle against unemployment, falling wages and salaries and increasing speed-up, against reduction of unemployment relief and other social services, against throwing the burdens of the crisis onto the masses of the people. That struggle clearly includes the "new" proletariat of lower salaried employees and professionals, the useful functional groups in the middle class. It includes, too, the interests of the smaller independent enterprisers whose markets are com-

341

posed mainly of members of the working class.* In its final aspect as socialism, the struggle of the proletariat includes the interests and the liberation of all the oppressed elements in the middle class.

Hence the appearance of an inner struggle in the middle class, including the lower salaried employees and professionals still under its ideological influence. The old middle class of independent small enterprisers resorts to its traditional issues and forms of action to "solve" the crisis of property: more democracy, more reforms and more state intervention in economic activity. It is a struggle that, moving within capitalist relations, comes increasingly under control of the new middle class of managerial and supervisory employees identified with monopoly capitalism. While the appeal is to "the people," the interests and issues are those of the upper middle class, which aims to become a dominant caste in a new reactionary set-up. But that excludes the interests of the

* Including the interests of the great majority of farmers. Agriculture must decline as capitalism decays and mass standards of living are lowered while monopoly (aided by the capitalist state) maintains artificially high prices for industrial products. The issues and forms of action of hired farm laborers are proletarian: wages, hours, unions and strikes to enforce their demands. The interests of the poorer farmers, independents and tenants, are sacrificed as consumer purchasing power falls in the working class because of unemployment and lower wages and salaries. But the upper layers of farmers are agrarian capitalists; they exploit hired labor and the poorer farmers. The farmers, no more than the middle class, are capable of an independent class policy. They are split, and the split involves an agrarian class war in which the dispossessed majority is thrown into action against the capitalist minority and, forging the unity of agrarian and industrial labor, into action against capitalism: on immediate issues (e.g., cancellation of mortgages and other debts) and on the final issue of socialism.

smaller enterprisers and, particularly, of the lower salaried employees and professionals tormented by the crisis of employment. The petty-bourgeois masses are drawn toward the struggle of the working class, which exerts a powerful attraction because of its onsweep and the underlying community of interests. The struggle between the proletariat and the big bourgeoisie, involving the clash of new and old social orders, becomes a struggle *within the middle class* for the support of its lower layers.

As capitalist decline sets the middle class in motion, its confidence in capitalism is shaken. That is a significant ideological expression of the crisis of capitalism, for it undermines support of capitalism by the petty-bourgeois masses and the workers under their influence.

The smaller independent enterprisers, especially the petty storekeepers, are oppressed more mercilessly by big capital and the chain stores, the burden of taxation becomes unendurable, and their sales and earnings are depressed by lower standards of living among the wage-and-salaried workers. They begin to sympathize with the workers' struggle for higher wages and more purchasing power, they rebel against capitalist oppression, they are violently against higher taxation and want to throw its burdens on the wealthy. It is a mood that, under appropriate conditions and by means of transitional issues and forms of struggle, may rally smaller enterprisers to the working class and the struggle for socialism.

The "new" proletariat of lower salaried employees

and professionals—the useful functional groups in the middle class—have no traditional issues and forms of action expressing their own class position and interests. They rally, at first, to those of the old middle class. But they are drawn to the issues and forms of action of the working class under the pressure of unemployment, lower salaries and speed-up. As differentials break down the old "gentility" breaks down. Lower salaried employees and professionals begin to think as workers, to use organized action on the job for higher salaries, shorter hours and control over working conditions. They demand unemployment relief and social insurance. The more militant organize unions and strikes, join in mass demonstrations. *Lower salaried employees and professionals, as they break loose from the ideological influence of the middle class, are forced to adopt proletarian forms of action:* unions, strikes, mass demonstrations, labor party, all moving toward the communist struggle for power and socialism—the final logic of their proletarianization and identification with collectivism.*

The struggle in the middle class is sharpened by the radicalization of intellectuals. They increasingly

* The masses of lower salaried employees and professionals are not "allies" of the working class, they are part of the working class and its struggle for socialism because of their economically proletarian condition, their identification with collectivism, and the necessity of their labor under socialism. (Only a minority of salaried employees and professionals are socially useless and parasitic.) The allies of the working class are petty enterprisers and independent small farmers, whose condition is not economically proletarian and who are not wholly identified with collectivism, but whose oppression identifies their immediate and final interests with the struggle of the working class and socialism.

344

desert capitalism and the middle class as the economic pressure becomes unbearable and the crisis of the capitalist system mounts upward into all spheres of social life. Economic decline and decay means cultural decline and decay. The more progressive and farseeing intellectuals realize the threat to culture of a dying social order; they reject the revolt against progress, the constantly mounting reaction and the resort to fascist barbarism. These intellectuals are invigorated by the upthrust of creative life within the proletariat and inspired by the cultural vistas of a new social order. They rally to the revolutionary struggle, carry on the class war on the cultural field, undermine the ideological supports of capitalism. They demonstrate in their own creative activity that all the progressive forces of existing culture are doomed unless they are recreated in the higher fulfillments of socialism.

Capitalism must restore faith in itself among the petty-bourgeois masses, particularly as they influence the more backward workers. That is the task of fascism. It is the task of *turning the revolt of the petty-bourgeois masses against their own interests* by mobilizing it against labor, against democracy, progress and socialism.

The struggle against fascism includes defense of the concrete democratic rights of the workers: the right to organize unions and carry on strikes, the right to struggle for a new social order. But the defense of democratic rights is not enough, it is a transitional form of struggle to rally forces for a higher form.

Fascism arises out of bourgeois democracy itself, under the conditions of rapidly declining capitalism, unbearable economic pressure and increasing instability of class relations; the middle class loses its faith in democratic government while monopoly capitalism finds it more necessary to crush ruthlessly the constantly more militant struggle of the workers. That means fascist destruction of democratic rights unless the defensive struggle becomes an offensive against capitalism. For, as the crisis of capitalism sharpens, the struggle against fascism must break apart, and the petty-bourgeois masses move toward fascism, unless the revolutionary proletariat rallies its forces, the forces of the working class and of all the oppressed, in the struggle for power: destruction of the power of capitalism to control social action.

For socialism is the only alternative to declining capitalism and fascism. The policy of moving "gradually" toward socialism by means of democracy and reforms is disastrous, as democracy and reformism must both be destroyed under the conditions of capitalist decline. Power was thrust upon the Social Democratic Party of Germany in 1918, but it refused to use that power to introduce socialism and crushed the revolutionary forces of the communist proletariat. The Party had at least the negative support of the petty-bourgeois masses, but that support was destroyed by a policy of "correcting" the mistakes of capitalism and making it "workable." But capitalism was declining and its burdens were thrust primarily upon the middle class and the peasantry, *who made*

346

the Social Democratic Party and the trade-union workers responsible for all the misery of capitalist decline. Reformism defeated one of its avowed purposes, not to drive away the support of the petty-bourgeois masses: it drove away that support by a policy which, since it did not prevent capitalist decline and its oppression of the petty-bourgeois masses, made them turn away from the working class in the hope of relief through fascism.

Slowly or swiftly, according to the movement of class-economic forces, the final uncompromisable issue looms up clearly: fascism or communism, the fascist dictatorship of monopoly capitalism or the communist dictatorship of the proletariat.* Fascism rallies all reactionary elements to sustain the old social order and crush the new: it accepts and consolidates the relations of decaying capitalism and stifles progress. Communism rallies all progressive forces to destroy the old social order and build the new: it rejects capitalist relations and destroys them and liberates progress. The transfer of political power from the capitalist class to the working class, a sharp revolutionary break, is the culmination of

* The basis of the dictatorship of the proletariat is soviet power, a form of government whose representation is occupational; representatives are chosen directly in the places where men and women work. That occupational representation includes the masses of lower salaried employees and professionals: only those elements are excluded which are not working class. Bourgeois democracy is formal, largely excludes the masses who have not the leisure or the money, and makes impossible the creative democracy of the producers. Soviet democracy is concrete, its ideal is mass participation in government, and its whole objective is the creative self-government of the community of labor.

347

previously gradual class-economic changes and makes possible the gradual building of socialism.

2

Socialism abolishes production for profit and introduces production for use. Economic activity is determined by social needs, not the profit of the capitalist. That means liberation of the forces of production and consumption: the abundance industry is capable of producing is made available to all.

The planned economy of socialism, unfettered by the vested interests of capitalist property and profit, imposes an unbreakable control over economic activity. That the control works is amply proved by the Soviet Union. The technical-economic level of the United States and England is much higher than that of the Soviet Union, but the Union, unlike the capitalist nations, is able to control its economic activity. It alone escaped the catastrophic depression of the 1930's. The United States, it may be repeated, suffered losses of $260,000 million during five years of the depression, while the planned economy of the Soviet Union, by preventing a cyclical breakdown, produced around $75,000 million of goods and services that would not have been otherwise produced. The index of industrial production in the Union *rose* from 100 in 1929 to 201 in 1933; it *fell* in the United States to 64, in Germany to 66, in France to 77 and in England to 86.[4] While employment, the national income and wages decreased disastrously in

348

all capitalist nations in 1928-32, in the Soviet Union there was:

An increase of 100% in the employment of workers and office workers.

An increase of 85% in the national income.

An increase of 67% in the average yearly wages of workers and office workers.[5]

Nor was the reason the active industrialization of the Soviet Union, for all capitalist nations on the same technical-economic level as the Union experienced depression. The reason is a fundamental difference in social organization. Planful control of economic activity in the Soviet Union is one of the momentous facts of history, a great divide in the development of industrial civilization. Man is master of economic forces, they are no longer his master.

Control is merely one aspect of creative socialist planning. Another aspect is the unfettered development of the productive forces and their multiplication by the constantly more purposive technological application of science. Socialism not only liberates the abundance that capitalist industry is capable of producing, it makes a still greater abundance possible by freely and fully utilizing all the most efficient means of production offered by technology and science. Economic activity is no longer fettered by capitalist property and profit. Socialism makes creative use of all its productive forces, of all the skill, talent and capacity of its people: an increasing mastery of man's world.

It used to be argued, and still is, that socialism

349

would stifle economic progress. But while all capitalist nations are in the midst of an inescapable economic retrogression, the socialist Soviet Union makes steady and irresistible economic progress. An American "agrarian" shifts the argument against socialism from the problem of progress to that of freedom:

"While socialism would give to the people in general more material goods and greater economic security . . . it appears equally probable that socialism would involve even a greater loss of economic freedom on the part of the mass of the people than capitalism has inflicted upon them. The essence of socialist production is a carefully worked-out plan with little or no regard for individual preferences, vagaries, whims, dislikes, prejudices or traditions." [6]

Socialism, on the contrary, greatly enlarges the scope of *real* economic freedom. That freedom under capitalism was limited to the freedom of the enterpriser, his right to control production and make profits. Today economic freedom is increasingly restricted by capitalist decline. Where is the freedom to work, to build homes, to utilize our tremendous productive resources? The worker never had any real freedom; his lot was always insecurity and dependence. Socialism liberates him by making him the master of industry and by multiplying the leisure which alone can insure individual freedom in a complex industrial world. Socialism, moreover, means *freedom of consumption*. That is insured, for one thing, by the increase of consumption under socialism, which greatly increases the output of goods and services and the purchasing power to absorb them. And since production is for use, not profit, it means that production increasingly and consciously adapts itself to the needs of the individual. Freedom of consumption is not excluded by socialist planning, it is one of the aims of planning. . . .

What becomes of the middle class under socialism?

The middle class has already gone through two transformations. By the sixteenth century it had become a petty bourgeoisie and begun its unsuccessful war in defense of independent small property against the big bourgeoisie. After the industrial revolution, with the onsweep of economic collectivism, the middle class became decreasingly a class of propertied independent enterprisers and increasingly a "class" of propertiless, dependent salaried employees and professionals. The *third and final transformation* appears under socialism: the old middle class of surviving independent enterprisers completely disappears, their functions absorbed in the fuller collectivization and socialization of industry, while the useful functional groups in the "new" middle class —economically and socially the "new" proletariat— are absorbed in the community of labor. Socialism completes the process, already almost completed under capitalism, of converting independent owner-managers into employees,* while employees are lib-

* Independent small enterprises that employ no workers are not immediately socialized; this is particularly true of small store-keepers, who are formed into cooperatives (they now form "voluntary" chains to compete against the chain stores) as a step toward final socialization. The socialization of American large-

351

erated from their dependence on monopoly capitalism.

Employees are liberated by the right to work and to an income, by occupational liberty and destruction of the dependent relations of capitalist industry. They are liberated by the security of all-inclusive social insurance and by the multiplication of leisure and the independence and individualism that leisure makes possible. Employees become free, creative workers in the community of labor. Instead of their standards of living being lowered by declining capitalism and fascism, they are raised—along with the

scale enterprises (including large farms) would include roughly 80% of all economic activity, where in Russia it included only 20%. That dominant 80% gradually, by force of example, draws the other 20% within its circle. Socialization of large enterprises is immediate, and it means this: their salaried managers work for the community instead of for a handful of parasitic stockholders and financial capitalists. Nor is it necessary, in the United States, to proceed rapidly with the collectivization of agriculture. That was necessary in the Soviet Union because of the preponderance of an individualistic peasantry and the backward state of agriculture. The larger American farms—roughly 30% of the total with 70% of the output—are socialized and the smaller farms formed into co-operatives (already used by the farmers). Experience would prove the necessity of socialization, as only that can solve the problem of farmers being displaced by more efficient agriculture, for whose products there is a limit. In final analysis, however, socialization of agriculture might become complete most rapidly in the United States, because of the larger size of farms and their greater mechanization. Nowhere, moreover, is there a threat of 50% of the farmers being displaced by the more efficient utilization of agricultural resources. Socialization involves more than mere collectivization: it involves the problem of agricultural displacement, of integrating varied forms of farming, of absorbing the displaced farmers in industry, of decentralizing industry and planfully uniting it with agriculture. Socialism destroys the antagonism between industry and agriculture and between town and country.

352

standards of the workers—by the liberation of the productive forces.

The upward movement of economic activity under socialism means a constantly greater need for the functions now performed by salaried employees. For socialism needs increasingly larger numbers of clerical and managerial and supervisory workers. As economic activity more fully realizes the promise of technology, completely automatic production, it becomes more and more an activity of organization, management and supervision. But when managerial and supervisory functions are stripped of their exploiting capitalist relations, their performance becomes wholly a form of productive social labor.

The number of technicians must grow as automatic production grows and more of the work is performed by technicians. Their craft function is liberated from capitalist limitations, while manual workers are increasingly converted into technicians. Already, in modern industry, technicians are becoming workers and workers "junior" technicians. This is of the utmost cultural significance, for it breaks down the distinction between manual and mental labor, a tendency clearly apparent in the most modern plants. The worker's new requirements of "mental alertness, general intelligence, 'polytechnic literacy' and loyal dependability" make him, according to one management engineer, "more and more an intelligent human being, an all-around educated man, defining 'educated men' as 'those who can do everything that others do.' This transition in the

353

functional characteristics of workers is slowly but surely obliterating not only the 'division of labor' . . . but it is also steadily abolishing the distinction between the 'man in overalls' and the 'white collar man.' " [7] Thus technology itself confirms one of the most derided "utopian" ideas of Karl Marx, who fifty years ago wrote of the "higher phase of communist society, after the enslaving subordination of individuals to the division of labor and with it also the antagonism between manual and mental labor have disappeared, after labor has become not merely a means to live but is itself the first necessity of living." [8] Friedrich Engels elaborated the point:

"When the whole of society shall carry on industry, communally and purposively, then workers will be needed whose capacities have been developed from every point of view, workers capable of taking charge of the entire system of production. The division of labor already undermined by the machine system, the division of labor which compels one man to be a peasant, another a shoemaker, another a factory hand, another a broker on the stock exchange, will completely disappear. The young folk as they pass through the schools will be taught the whole system of production as part of their education, they will be in a position to pass from one branch of industry to another according as social needs shall require or their own inclinations impel. They will no longer, as today, be one-sided in their development. Thus a communistically organized society will be

354

able to provide opportunities for the cultivation of all-around capacities." [9]

Already this condition is developing under capitalism, limited, however, by its exploiting relations. Fulfillment depends on socialism, with its unrestricted technological application of science, its emphasis on the human values of machinery and industry,* its reconstruction of education, and its mass participation in higher learning. That means a cultural revolution whose creative value is incalculable: a liberation of human personality and individuality beside which the capitalist individualism of the market place is a monstrosity.

Architects, as much as the technicians, are liberated from the limitations now imposed on their craft function. They are needed in constantly larger numbers and their work assumes unusual scope and social significance under socialism. For capitalism has

---

* "Machinery and human beings are now looked upon simply as different sides of production costs. . . . The machine is designed to employ the cheapest and, consequently, the most monotonous labor. This is completely contrary to the spirit of mechanical inventions. Those operations which are repetitive and monotonous are just those that could be done best by machines themselves. What people speak of as the slavery of man to the machine is really slavery of manufacturers to profits. If machines had been designed from the point of view of the worker rather than that of minimum cost of operation, they would be as interesting to work and far less laborious than farming or hunting. . . . The massive parts of machinery can now be controlled by very small forces. The modern factory need only be operated through a distant control room with mechanics to deal with unforseen breakdowns. On a large scale this is the human equivalent of what has been built up through millions of years of evolution in animal organs." J. D. Bernal, "If Industry Gave Science a Chance," *Harpers*, February, 1935, pp. 259-60.

miserably neglected the application of architecture while multiplying its technical possibilities. The masses of the people live in unfit homes, including the homes of workers, lower salaried employees and poorer farmers, cities are monstrously congested and scarred with filthy slums, while factories are prisons. Socialism offers the architect a tremendous opportunity for creative work. There must be homes fit for the new age and the new man, factories must become inspiring places in which to work, whole cities must be rebuilt to combine the values of town-and-country life. Architecture already provides all the means for making a thing of beauty of the place in which people live: socialism converts the means into action.

Science, too, is liberated as technology, architecture and all social forces are planfully directed to serve the growing needs of man. The dependence of science on profit is broken and its scope enlarged by the greater technological application of scientific discovery. Socialism must necessarily encourage science, for its aim is mastery of the world. The values of science are wholly realizable only under social relations that permit their fullest and freest technological and cultural use.

As the economic surplus and standards of living rise under socialism, there is a constantly greater demand for professional services. Unlike the tragic situation now prevailing in the capitalist world—millions of people denied professional services while the performers of these services are degraded by unemployment—socialism liberates the professional

356

workers by providing conditions for the free and un-limited performance of their craft functions. That is made possible by multiplication of the productive forces and releasing more people for professional services, and by the planful organization of those services. The tendency is already clearly apparent in the Soviet Union. Two non-communists report that socialization of medicine in the Union, which they consider a "great achievement" and a "challenge" to the capitalist world, has "removed the doctor almost completely from the field of monetary competition and has thus abolished a chief source of inadequate medical care." They are moving toward the *free* provision of *all* medical services. All salaried work-ers are included in health insurance and other forms of social insurance. The ideal is preventive medi-cine. Another non-communist reports that the basis of mental hygiene in the Soviet Union is security and opportunity for self-expression yet oneness with others in the community. The socialization of pro-fessional services offers their performers more leisure and more satisfactory compensation, more personal integrity and more opportunity for creative labor.[10]

Socialism opens up immense opportunities for edu-cational workers. The mere introduction of smaller classes would be a great achievement, multiplying the number of teachers, easing their burdens and making educational work more productive. But that is simply a beginning. The Soviet Union was "catch-ing up" when it increased intermediate school stu-dents from 2,415,000 in 1928 to 6,991,000 in 1934 and

357

university students from 180,000 to 471,000. It was an extremely significant act of pioneering, however, when the Five Year Plan for 1932-37 called for *universal, compulsory high school education—the first time a nation has set itself that aim.* This, according to Valerian V. Ossinsky, of the Soviet State Planning Commission, is a "decisive step toward the abolition of all distinction between the manual and the mental worker. . . . The new, growing generation will consist of men and women who have all had an equal mental training and who will have an open sesame to all the resources of modern culture." [11] The final aim is universal college education, not only for occupational purposes but for its cultural value, for purposes of *living.* The mechanic, the cook, the miner, the clerk: higher learning is for them, for everyone, not for a small elite. Socialism and the later stage of communism are inconceivable without a mass participation in higher learning. For socialism can accomplish its great purpose—the creation of a new man, master of the world and of himself—only by a cultural upsurge which involves the multiplication and transformation of education. Socialism realizes the ideal of the great radical bourgeois educators: education becomes Enlightenment, the means of solving social problems and of creating and realizing new and finer ways of life.

Socialist education and culture are animated by the integrity and creative force of labor. Man became man by labor and labor sustains society. Yet labor has always occupied an inferior social-economic position, enslaved to exploitation and conquest, to luxury and the aristocratic ideals of a leisure class. The inferiority of labor was always a corrupting element in civilization. Socialism annihilates the social relations that degrade all forms of labor, wage and salaried, that make workmanship irksome and disreputable while the social ideal is the exploiter, the aristocratic idlers and wastrels.

As the servitude *of* labor is broken man is released from servitude *to* labor. For socialism, by freely and fully utilizing all technical-economic and scientific resources, may easily lower to fifteen hours weekly the amount of labor necessary to produce the collective goods and services of society. Leisure under socialism is neither exceptional nor limited to a few. Within that leisure there is ample scope for labor of a purely personal, cultural character. One may anticipate a revival of handicrafts, by which men and women produce things for themselves: not out of economic necessity, but out of the urge to express one's individuality and personality. The bourgeois ideal of property as an expression of personality is replaced by the socialist ideal of creative cultural labor.

Socialism transforms culture while universalizing it. Not culture as the ornamental gilt of a leisure class, but as a vital aspect of life, of all life and all people. We want no lilies, often poisonous, that must flower out of social swamps. We want a culture liberated from an emphasis on the exclusive that justifies the aristocratic pretensions of the ruling class:

359

a culture liberated from the snobbery of invidious distinctions and class privileges. The early bourgeois, in the revolutionary struggle against feudalism, revolted against the culture of aristocracy; the triumphant bourgeois created their own aristocracy and its meretricious cultural trappings. There are intellectuals who want to retain the old culture in spite of its evils and, if necessary, with all its evils. They forget, although some glory in the fact, that the culture is limited, a culture of the few while the many are degraded. They forget that the culture is corrupted by a non-social individualism that is the sanctification of exploitation, that its values flourish in the midst of superstitions and bestial prejudices, that it harbors dread forces of ferocity now mobilizing against civilization. The progressive values of culture are, moreover, threatened by declining capitalism and fascism. Socialism, on the contrary, retains all that is worth while in bourgeois culture: there is a dialectic continuity in history, and socialism builds upon the past to create the future.

Leisure, the expansion and recreation of education, and the new socialist culture offer unlimited possibilities to the intellectuals—the writer, musician, artist. They are freed from the fetters of profit, from the sterile estheticism of the "elite," from the ingrown individualism that bourgeois society has cultivated in them. They gather new strength from the upsurge of labor and the new social order, from the destruction of class barriers and the liberation of man. They become one with the masses of the people. The intellectuals come into their own as one of the great creative forces in shaping the new world and the new man. It is their fulfillment.

Thus socialism offers the useful functional groups in the middle class—from which they are economically thrown out by their proletarianization and propertiless, dependent condition—the liberation of their craft function and multiplication of the opportunity for its performance, while declining capitalism and fascism offer them the direct opposite. They must choose!

The choice is inescapable. It means, simply, whether they choose to liberate or strangle the productive forces of society. All the decline and reaction of capitalism and fascism result from the necessity of strangling the productive forces to save profit, which makes inexorably necessary the limitation of technology, education and science, the degradation of culture, and the denial of all democratic rights to wage-workers, lower salaried employees and professionals. All the fulfillments of socialism arise out of liberating the productive forces, out of permitting the logical working out of collectivism into socialism. For socialism is no aspiration after the impossible: the conditions already exist for its realization. Liberation of the productive forces means the creation of a new world: the multiplication of plenty and leisure, the resurgence of education and culture.

Unlike fascism, which makes an ideal of dictatorship, authoritarianism and caste, socialism includes liberty, equality and democracy in new and higher forms.

Communist dictatorship is wholly functional and temporary. It is the political power of the working class used, as the bourgeoisie used dictatorship in its revolutions, to destroy the power of the old ruling class and create the relations of a new social order. But within this new order there is no class below the working class to exploit and oppress. Where fascism urges dictatorship as an ideal and eternal, *there is not one word in communist literature which conceives dictatorship as other than a temporary, transitional measure.* Still more important, *socialism sets in motion the forces that steadily lessen the necessity of dictatorship:* the abolition of classes, the merging of the workers and the useful functional groups in the middle class in the unity of higher and freer forms of labor, the multiplication of abundance, leisure and education.* The dictatorship is brief, it is modified and disappears. Eventually the state

* This includes the bureaucracy, which is a problem in the earlier stages of socialism and tends to acquire vested interests. The problem is most acute in economically backward countries, because of the lower economic and cultural heritage: it is not much of a problem in the more developed countries. Being an aspect of socialist construction, the bureaucracy must develop the economic and cultural conditions that eventually make bureaucracy unnecessary and impossible. That tendency is strengthened by the decentralization of industry (within the limits of socialist planning). There are, incidentally, two other aspects of the problem: bureaucracy is largely a hangover from capitalism, among other hangovers, and the bureaucracy is composed of groups who now perform salaried functions in the middle class. That makes the struggle against bureaucracy all the more necessary.

itself is replaced by the self-governing community of labor.

Socialism repudiates only the limited bourgeois forms of liberty, equality and democracy: they are realized in new and higher forms in the socialist order. The old middle class forms and sanctions of the ideals were incomplete: they are limited still more by monopoly capitalism and destroyed by fascism. But socialism makes liberty real by destroying class and caste privileges, by assuring security of employment and income, by multiplying leisure and education and their cultural individualism. Socialism assures equality by its classless condition and the access of all to the social property of the community that makes abundance available to all. Socialism means the democratic self-government of the community of labor, within which there are no vested interests to trample upon democracy. Where is the class under socialism whose interests are promoted by the limitation or suppression of liberty, equality and democracy? Socialism moves from the realm of necessity into the realm of freedom and a larger and more purposive mastery of the world. That is possible only by the liberty and democracy of a society of the free and equal, the freedom of ideas and action.

There are problems under socialism, for it is not utopia; there are beginnings that move onward slowly, but steadily, to greater fulfillments. But the abolition of capitalism and the construction of a new social order are achievements of the first magnitude and they force new achievements. They create the conditions for the increasing mastery of problems and of solving them by the creative free play of social forces, initiative and ideas.

That socialism moves in that direction is amply proved by the tendency in the Soviet Union. But an American socialism would realize itself much more easily and rapidly, as the objective basis of socialism —collectivism and the capacity to produce abundance—is most highly developed in the United States. The tasks of socialist construction were enormously complicated in the Soviet Union by its low economic and cultural heritage * (including a scarcity of the useful functional groups in the middle class, particularly technicians and professionals). The Bolsheviks were forced to devote the major part of their great work to industrialization, the construction of a modern industrial plant. That is a task already accomplished by capitalism in our country. More: there was no experience for the Bolsheviks to draw upon, for theirs was wholly pioneer work. Yet they moved toward socialism, imposing a creative control over economic forces. We can learn from their experience and their trials. The construction of socialism in the Soviet Union is not a pattern for blind imitation, as much of it was conditioned by Russia being an economically backward country; but

* "If the Party had come into the possession of power within a machine technology environment comparable with that, say, of the United States, in which there were a disciplined industrial proletariat and sufficient resources at hand, the problem of effective application would have been relatively simple." Gustavus Tuckerman, Jr., "Applied Marxism in Soviet Russia," *American Economic Review*, December, 1933, p. 638.

the *general* features of socialist construction there are applicable in any highly developed country. With that experience, and our higher social heritage, an American socialism would avoid most of the problems, difficulties and mistakes of the Bolsheviks. Our task would be the comparatively simple one of introducing the relations of a socialism whose economic forms are already fully in existence.

A world is dying. It is dying as the old feudal world died, accompanied by revolutions and wars. Capitalism emerged slowly, agonizingly, almost blindly, for there was no real understanding and control of the drift of social forces. It took 500 years of struggle to create the new world of capitalism. But the struggle for socialism, in the midst of the dying world of capitalism, is more purposive, easier, more capable of speedy realization. For our struggle is animated by the purposive understanding and control of Marxism, which is communism: the perceiver of a new world and its creator. It is the new Enlightenment, and it calls to struggle for a new world that is already appearing on the horizon. The Marxist Enlightenment, too, urges the challenge of the old: Dare to understand—forward, not backward!

NOTES

CHAPTER I

[1] Editorial, "American Family Incomes," *American Banker*, March 2, 1935, p. 4.

[2] Ernst Cassirer, "Enlightenment," *Encyclopedia of the Social Sciences*, v. V (1931), p. 547.

[3] Harry Elmer Barnes, *History and Social Intelligence* (1926), p. 316.

CHAPTER II

[1] Katharine Fullerton Gerould, "The Plight of the Genteel," *Harpers*, February, 1926, p. 310.

[2] New York *Times*, November 6, 1933.

[3] New York *Times*, February 17, 1935.

[4] New York *Times*, May 5, 1934.

[5] Simon Kuznets, *National Income, 1929-32* (1934), p. 33.

[6] Lewis Corey, *The Decline of American Capitalism* (1934), p. 248; editorial, "Unions for Technicians," *New Republic*, January 24, 1934, p. 295; United States, Department of Commerce, *Census of Manufactures, 1933,* Preliminary Report; T. F. Hamlin, "The Architect and the Depression," *Nation*, August 9, 1933, p. 152; New York *World-Telegram*, November 14, 1932.

[7] Editorial, "The Middle Class Unemployed," *Spectator*, March 9, 1934, p. 361.

[8] United States, Department of Commerce, *Statistical Abstract of the United States, 1931*, p. 220.

[9] Edwin G. Nourse and Associates, *America's Capacity to Produce* (1934), p. 416.

[10] Simon Kuznets, "Gross Capital Formation, 1919-33," *Bulletin 52*, National Bureau of Economic Research (1934), p. 6.

[11] New York *Times*, November 24, 1934.

[12] United States, Department of Commerce, *The National Income, 1933* (1935), p. 6; Bureau of Internal Revenue, *Statistics of Income, 1929-32*.

[13] Robert R. Doane, *The Measurement of American Wealth* (1933), p. 32.

[14] Doane, *American Wealth*, p. 28.

[15] New York *World-Telegram*, March 22, 1935; New York *Times*, December 2, 1934; *Bulletin of Federation of Architects, Engineers, Chemists and Technicians*, January 1, 1935, p. 13; Irene Kuhn, "Women Struggle to Keep Jobs," New York *World-Telegram*, November 6, 1934; New York *Times*, November 24, 1934; New York *World-Telegram*, October 19, 1933.

CHAPTER III

[1] R. H. Gretton, *The English Middle Class* (1917), pp. 1, 8.

[2] Friedrich Engels, *The Peasant War in Germany*, pp. 42-45, 56.

[3] Engels, *Peasant War*, p. 61.

[4] Jacob Strieder, *Jacob Fugger the Rich* (1931), pp. 86-89.

[5] M. James, "Puritanism," *Encyclopedia of the Social Sciences*, v. XIII (1934), p. 4.

[6] Eduard Bernstein, *Cromwell and Communism* (1930), pp. 61-62.

[7] Margaret James, *Social Problems and Policy During the Puritan Revolution* (1931), p. 69.

[8] Bernstein, *Cromwell*, p. 164.

[9] Karl Marx, "French Materialism," *Selected Essays* (1926), pp. 193-94.

[10] J. Salwyn Schapiro, *Condorcet and the Rise of Liberalism in France* (1934), p. 60.

[11] Matthew Josephson, *Jean-Jacques Rousseau* (1931), pp. 267, 276.

[12] Louis Gottschalk, *Jean Paul Marat* (1927), p. 106.

[13] Crane Brinton, *The Jacobins* (1930), p. 51.

[14] Brinton, *Jacobins*, p. 171.

[15] Brinton, *Jacobins*, p. 163.

CHAPTER IV

[1] Vernon L. Parrington, *The Colonial Mind* (1927), p. 126.

[2] Rev. Joseph Morgan, *The Nature of Riches* (1732), pp. 3-6, 14, 19; Lewis Corey, *The House of Morgan*, pp. 20, 80, 241.

[3] S. M. Morison, *Sources and Documents Illustrating the American Revolution* (1923), pp. 1, 70.

[4] Ralph Volney Harlow, *Samuel Adams, Promoter of the American Revolution* (1923), pp. 79-82; S. G. Fisher, *True History of the American Revolution* (1910), p. 191.

[5] Harlow, *Samuel Adams*, p. 159.

[6] A. M. Schlesinger, *Colonial Merchants and the American Revolution* (1917), p. 240.

[7] Schlesinger, *Colonial Merchants*, pp. 386-87.

[8] Schlesinger, *Colonial Merchants*, pp. 591-93.

[9] W. H. Siebert, "General Washington and the Loyalists," *Proceedings of the American Antiquarian Society* (1933), pp. 35-36.

[10] A. C. Flick, *Loyalism in New York During the American Revolution* (1901), pp. 139, 150, 179-80; L. P. Edwards, *The Natural History of Revolution* (1927), p. 187.

[11] A. G. Bradley, *Colonial Americans in Exile* (1930), pp. 113-14; Flick, *Loyalism*, p. 160.

[12] George Richards Minot, *The History of the Insurrections in Massachusetts* (1788), pp. 16-17.

[13] Minot, *Insurrections*, p. 47.

[14] Minot, *Insurrections*, pp. 26, 45, 86, 146.

[15] Morison, *Sources and Documents*, p. 218.

[16] Harlow, *Samuel Adams*, p. 316.

[17] Charles A. Beard, *An Economic Interpretation of the Constitution of the United States* (1913), pp. 324-25.

[18] Parrington, *Colonial Mind*, p. 291.

CHAPTER V

[1] Crane Brinton, "Jacobinism," *Encyclopedia of the Social Sciences* v. VIII (1932), p. 362.

[2] John Rydjord, "The French Revolution and Mexico," *Hispanic American Historical Review*, February, 1929, pp. 68, 73-74, 82, 96.

[3] P. A. Brown, *The French Revolution in English History* (1918), pp. 69-72; R. Birley, *The English Jacobins from 1789 to 1802* (1924), p. 9.

[4] C. D. Hazen, *Contemporary American Opinion of the French Revolution* (1897), pp. 153, 164.

[5] Hazen, *French Revolution*, pp. 189-94.

[6] Vernon L. Parrington, *The Colonial Mind* (1927), pp. 323, 360; Hazen, *French Revolution*, p. 204.

[7] Parrington, *Colonial Mind*, pp. 366, 376-77.

[8] Charles A. Beard, *Economic Origins of Jeffersonian Democracy* (1915), p. 236.

[9] F. M. Anderson, "The Enforcement of the Alien and Sedition Laws," *Annual Report of the American Historical Association,* 1912, pp. 119-25.

[10] John R. Commons and Associates, *A History of Labour in the United States* (1918), v. I, pp. 69, 109-10.

[11] Crane Brinton, *The Jacobins* (1930), p. 169; Louis Gottschalk, *Jean Paul Marat* (1927), pp. 23, 102; Beard, *Jeffersonian Democracy,* p. 420.

CHAPTER VI

[1] Carl Russell Fish, *The Rise of the Common Man* (1927), p. 88.

[2] A. M. Schlesinger, *Political and Social History of the United States* (1927), p. 4.

[3] Fish, *Common Man,* p. 212.

[4] John R. Commons and Associates, *A History of Labour in the United States* (1918), v. I, p. 193.

[5] Guy Stevens, *Selections from the Economic History of the United States* (1909), p. 736; C. B. Haddock, *An Address Delivered Before the Railroad Convention at Montpelier, Vt.* (1844), pp. 8-10; Commons, *History of Labour,* p. 216.

[6] Vernon L. Parrington, *The Romantic Revolution in America* (1927), p. 140.

[7] M. Y. Beach, *The Wealth and Biography of the Wealthy Citizens of the City of New York* (1855), pp. 10-19.

[8] United States, Department of Commerce, *Statistical Abstract of the United States, 1931,* p. 813.

[9] Louis M. Hacker and Benjamin B. Kendrick, *The United States Since 1865* (1932), p. 34.

[10] David A. Wells, *Recent Economic Changes* (1889), pp. 97, 109.

[11] Hacker and Kendrick, *United States,* p. 299.

[12] *Statistical Abstract, 1931,* p. 637.

[13] John Moody, *The Truth About the Trusts* (1905), p. xi.

[14] Lewis Corey, *The House of Morgan* (1930), pp. 354-56.

[15] Louis D. Brandeis, *Other People's Money* (1914), p. 1.

[16] Lewis Corey, *The Decline of American Capitalism* (1934), pp. 383-84, 403.

[17] T. M. Sogge, "Industrial Classes in the United States," *Journal of the American Statistical Association,* June, 1933, p. 199.

[18] W. I. King, *The National Income and Its Purchasing Power* (1930), p. 62.

[19] Alfred Meusel, "Middle Class," *Encyclopedia of the Social Sciences,* v. XI (1933), p. 410.

CHAPTER VII

[1] United States, Department of Agriculture, *Yearbook of Agriculture, 1932,* p. 42.

[2] *Yearbook of Agriculture, 1932* p. 491; Louis M. Hacker, *A Short History of the New Deal* (1934), p. 100.

[3] Computed from United States, Department of Commerce, *Census of Occupations, 1930.*

[4] A. L. Bowley and Josiah C. Stamp, *The National Income, 1924* (1927), pp. 61-63.

[5] Computed from *Census of Occupations, 1930;* Alba M. Edwards, "A Social Economic Grouping of the Gainful Workers of the United States," *Journal of the American Statistical Association,* December, 1933, pp. 379-82.

[6] Simon Kuznets, *National Income, 1929-32* (1934), p. 33.

[7] Computed from United States, Bureau of Internal Revenue, *Statistics of Income, 1929,* pp. 15, 234; Department of Commerce, *Census of Manufactures, 1929,* v. I, pp. 61-63.

[8] Computed from United States, Department of Commerce, *Census of Distribution, 1929.*

[9] New York *Times,* November 14, 1931.

[10] Bowley and Stamp, *National Income,* pp. 61-63; William T. Ham, "Salaried Men's Organizations in Germany," *Journal of Political Economy,* December, 1929, p. 663.

[11] W. I. King, *The National Income and Its Purchasing Power* (1930), p. 60.

[12] *Census of Manufactures, 1929,* v. I, p. 16.

[13] United States, Department of Commerce, *Statistical Abstract of the United States, 1934,* p. 107.

[14] John Corbin, *The Return of the Middle Class* (1922), p. 10.

[15] Computed from Statistics of Income, 1931, p. 39; Lewis Corey, *The Decline of American Capitalism* (1934), p. 312.

CHAPTER VIII

[1] Walter B. Pitkin, *Capitalism Carries On* (1935), p. 223.

[2] Editorial, "Collectivism and Collectivism," *Social Frontier,* November, 1934, p. 3.

[3] Walton H. Hamilton, "Collectivism," *Encyclopedia of the Social Sciences,* v. III (1930), pp. 635-36.

[4] United States, Department of Commerce, *Census of Manufactures, 1929,* v. I (1934), p. 62.

[5] United States, Department of Commerce, *Statistical Abstract of United States, 1931,* p. 417.

[6] A. A. Berle and Gardiner C. Means, *The Modern Corporation and Private Property* (1933), pp. 19-28.

[7] W. I. King, *The National Income and Its Purchasing Power* (1930), pp. 52, 58.

[8] A. M. Carr-Saunders, *Professions and Their Place in Society* (1928), p. 6.

[9] President's Committee on Recent Social Trends, *Recent Social Trends in the United States* (1933), v. I, p. 282.

[10] Troy J. Cauley, *Agrarianism* (1935), p. 112.

[11] Lewis Corey, *The House of Morgan* (1930), p. 448.

[12] Berle and Means, *Modern Corporation,* p. 46.

[13] G. D. H. Cole, *What Marx Really Meant* (1934), p. 119.

[14] Lewis Corey, *The Decline of American Capitalism* (1934), p. 329.

CHAPTER IX

[1] Paul M. Sweezy, "Economics and the Crisis of Capitalism," *Economic Forum,* Spring, 1935, pp. 71, 73.

[2] Thorstein Veblen, *Essays in Our Changing Order* (1934), p. 12.

[3] Joseph Dorfman, *Thorstein Veblen and His America* (1934), p. 500.

[4] Computed from Simon Kuznets, "Gross Capital Formation, 1919-33," *Bulletin 52,* National Bureau of Economic Research (1934), p. 8.

[5] Computed from United States, Department of Commerce, *Census of Manufactures* for the respective years.

[6] Edwin G. Nourse and Associates, *America's Capacity to Produce* (1934), p. 439.

[7] New York *Times,* December 2, 1934.

[8] William Haber, Relief Administrator of the State of Michigan, New York *Times,* July 21, 1935.

[9] Prof. Mark A. May, of Yale, New York *Times,* November 24, 1934.

[10] Frieda Wunderlich, "New Aspects of Unemployment in Germany," *Social Research,* February, 1934, p. 105.

[11] Lewis Corey, *The Decline of American Capitalism* (1934), p. 412.

[12] Editorial, "War—Not Imminent, but Inevitable," *Business Week,* April 6, 1935, p. 48.

[13] New York *Times,* April 19, 1935.

[14] New York *Times,* March 21, 1935.

[15] Nourse, *America's Capacity,* p. 199.

[16] United States, Department of Agriculture, *Yearbook of Agriculture, 1932,* p. 498.

[17] Webster Powell and A. T. Cutler, "Tightening the Cotton Belt," *Harpers,* February, 1934, p. 308.

CHAPTER X

[1] Father Charles E. Coughlin, New York *Times,* May 23, 1935.

[2] New York *Times,* April 19, 1935.

[8] A. A. Berle, "The New Deal and Economic Security," *The Annals of the American Academy of Political and Social Sciences,* March, 1935, p. 43.

[4] Lewis Corey, *The Decline of American Capitalism* (1934), p. 350.

[5] Robert R. Doane, *The Measurement of American Wealth* (1933), p. 28.

[6] Josiah Wedgwood, *The Economics of Inheritance* (1929), p. 47.

[7] Corey, *American Capitalism,* p. 329.

[8] New York *Times,* August 21, 1935.

[9] United States, Department of Commerce, *Statistical Abstract of the United States*, 1933, p. 425; New York *Times*, July 2, 1935.

[10] United States, Department of Agriculture, *Yearbook of Agriculture, 1932*, pp. 910-11.

[11] Corey, *American Capitalism*, p. 350.

[12] Karl Marx, *Capital*, v. III, p. 519.

[13] Marx, *Capital*, v. III, p. 516.

[14] Walter Lippmann, *The Method of Freedom* (1934), p. 101.

CHAPTER XI

[1] Paul H. Douglas, *Real Wages in the United States* (1930), p. 364.

[2] Maurice Leven, *The Income of Physicians* (1932), p. 94; A. M. Carr-Saunders, *Professions and Their Place in Society* (1928), p. 5.

[3] United States, Department of Commerce, *Statistical Abstract of the United States, 1931*, p. 109.

[4] Douglas, *Real Wages*, p. 202.

[5] Leven, *Physicians*, p. 81.

[6] Douglas, *Real Wages*, p. 367.

[7] Douglas, *Real Wages*, p. 363.

[8] United States, Department of the Interior, Office of Education, *The Deepening Crisis in Education* (Leaflet No. 44, 1933); E. C. Lindeman, "The Future of the Professional," *Social Work Today*, July-August, 1934, p. 261; E. Sydenstricker, "Sickness and the New Poor," *Survey Graphic*, April, 1934, p. 161; New York *Post*, July 25, 1935; Editorial, Unions for Technicians," *New Republic*, January 24, 1934, p. 296; Simon Kuznets, *National Income, 1929-32* (1934), p. 246.

[9] Karl Marx, *Capital*, v. I, p. 13.

[10] John Corbin, *The Return of the Middle Class* (1922), pp. 36, 47, 98.

[11] Sumner H. Slichter, *Modern Economic Society* (1931), p. 887.

[12] G. D. H. Cole, *What Marx Really Meant* (1934), pp. 112, 121.

[13] Stuart Chase, *The Economy of Abundance* (1934), p. 257.

[14] Lewis Corey, *The Decline of American Capitalism* (1934), p. 560.

[15] W. I. King, *The National Income and Its Purchasing Power* (1930), pp. 56, 60.

CHAPTER XII

[1] A. N. Holcombe, *The New Party Politics* (1933), p. 75.

[2] New York *Times*, March 1, 1934.

[3] New York *Times*, July 26, 1935.

[4] New York *Times*, February 10, 1935.

[5] New York *Post*, May 7, 1935.

[6] Ludwig Lore, "Behind the Cables," New York *Post*, April 27, 1935.

[7] Ellen Wilkinson and Edward Conze, *Why Fascism?* (1934), p. 134.

[8] New York *Times*, December 24, 1933.

[9] Konrad Heiden, *A History of National Socialism* (1934), pp. 272, 287.

[10] Editorial, "The Bluff of the Corporate State," *New Statesman and Nation*, March 17, 1934, p. 402.

[11] Ludwig Lore, "Behind the Cables," New York *Post*, July 3, 1935.

[12] New York *Times*, July 24, 1935.

[13] New York *Times*, July 29, 1935.

[14] New York *Times*, February 9, 1935; *Nation*, August 21, 1935, p. 197.

[15] M. Rubinstein, "Relations of Science, Technology and Economics Under Capitalism and the Soviet Union," *Science at the Crossroads* (1931), p. 9; New York *Times*, June 17, 1934; September 22, 1935.

[16] New York *Times*, April 11, 1934.

[17] New York *Times*, August 25, 1935; Ludwig Lore, "Behind the Cables," New York *Post*, July 26, 1935; New York *Times*, July 30, 1935.

CHAPTER XIII

[1] W. L. Thorp and Wesley C. Mitchell, *Business Annals* (1926), p. 42.

[2] William F. Ogburn, "Change, Social," *Encyclopedia of the Social Sciences*, v. III (1930), p. 330.

[3] Charles A. Beard, "The Educator in the Quest for National Security," *Social Frontier*, April, 1935, p. 15.

[4] Oswald Spengler, *The Decline of the West* (1928), v. II, p. 507.

[5] Vilfredo Pareto, *Mind and Society* (1935), v. III, p. 1293.

[6] New York *Times*, June 30, 1935; July 7, 1935; July 15, 1935.

[7] New York *Times*, June 17, 1934.

[8] Dr. Esther C. Brunauer, New York *Times*, December 2, 1934.

[9] Celia Strachey and J. G. Werner, *Fascist Germany Explains* (1934), pp. 18, 27; New York *Herald Tribune*, May 27, 1934.

[10] Friedrich Engels, *Anti-Dühring*, p. 23.

CHAPTER XIV

[1] Edwin G. Nourse and Associates, *America's Capacity to Produce* (1934), p. 429.

[2] Report of the Columbia University Commission, *Economic Reconstruction* (1934), pp. 90, 92.

[3] J. D. Bernal, "If Industry Gave Science a Chance," *Harpers,* February, 1935, p. 265.

[4] Harry Elmer Barnes, *The History of Western Civilization* (1935), v. II, p. 1014.

[5] Joseph Stalin and Others, *From the First to the Second Five Year Plan* (1934), p. 42.

[6] Troy J. Cauley, *Agrarianism* (1935), p. 92.

[7] Walter N. Polakov, *The Power Age* (1934), p. 119.

[8] Karl Marx, *The Gotha Program,* p. 31.

[9] Friedrich Engels, "Principles of Communism," in the Ryzanov edition of *The Communist Manifesto,* p. 335.

[10] A. Newsholme and J. A. Kingsbury, *Red Medicine* (1933), pp. 309-11; A. J. Haines, *Health Work in Soviet Russia* (1932), p. 19.

[11] Valerian V. Ossinsky, "The Second Five Year Plan in Action," Mary L. Fleddérus and Mary van Kleeck (editors), *On Economic Planning* (1935), p. 106.